*Kitty had never
had trouble with men...*

Even when little more than a girl, Kitty had made handsome, reckless Tyrone Duncannon do what she wanted before she gave him what he desired.

She made spoiled weakling Johnny Stokes act like a man and defy his robber-baron father in order to make her his wife.

She made brilliant Dr. Howard Bergman her virtual servant and then her lover as she helped him turn his medical dreams into reality.

But now as Kitty tried to rule her sons—wild, irresistibly charming Jay, and darkly brooding, determined Bart—she felt the reins being torn from her hands by furies bred in the blood and raging in the heart...

*Berkley books by Edward Stewart*

**BALLERINA**
**FOR RICHER, FOR POORER**

# For Richer, For Poorer

## EDWARD STEWART

BERKLEY BOOKS, NEW YORK

This Berkley book contains the complete text of the
original hardcover edition.
It has been completely reset in a type face designed for easy reading,
and was printed from new film.

FOR RICHER, FOR POORER

A Berkley Book / published by arrangement with Doubleday
& Company, Inc.

Printing History
Doubleday edition published 1981
Berkley edition / February 1983

ISBN: 0-425-05397-0

A BERKLEY BOOK ® TM 757,375
Berkley Books are published by Berkley Publishing Corporation,
200 Madison Avenue, New York, New York 10016.
The name "BERKLEY" and the stylized "B" with design are trademarks
belonging to Berkley Publishing Corporation.
Printed in the United States of America

*for mothers—*
*Helen and Wilma and Loris*

# *Chapter 1*

*"HER."*

The finger pointed—not at the Chief Justice of the Supreme Court administering the oath, not at the man taking it, but at a gray-haired woman watching the ceremony from the grandstand on the north side of Pennsylvania Avenue.

She sat straight-backed and tall, commanding the space around her with iron pride and dignity. She did not blink away from the ruthless January sunlight or attempt to hide her age-lined face behind dark glasses or a veil. She wore her years exactly as she wore her black Siberian sable, her platinum-set diamond necklace: as an acquisition—defiantly and without apology.

She was seventy-nine, almost as old as the century, and in a frightening way she was beautiful.

*"She's* my story," Deborah Thomas said. "Sixty-two years ago government soldiers tried to gun her down in Bartonville, Pennsylvania. Today she's watching her son take the inaugural oath."

Deborah Thomas' escort, who happened to be Secretary of State, crinkled a skeptical eyebrow. "You'll never get Kitty Stokes to talk to you."

Dictators and murderers and movie stars routinely jumped through hoops to be interviewed by Deborah Thomas; cardinals on their deathbeds had received her and spilled the goods. "She'll talk—they always talk on the Big Day."

After the ceremony Deborah Thomas slipped a virgin cartridge into her Sony cassette recorder. With a quick apology to the Secretary of State, a promise to meet him back at the reception she plunged into the human maelstrom. Ahead of her she could see Kitty Stokes shoving aside reporters.

The man from UPI thrust out a mike: "Mrs. Stokes—"

"I don't give interviews."

The woman from the Washington *Post:* "Mrs. Stokes—"

*"I don't give interviews."*

Slicing and separating with the flat edge of her well-practiced hand, Deborah Thomas caught up with her quarry. "Mrs. Stokes, we sat next to one another at the Martin Luther King Memorial dinner? I'm Deborah Thomas of NBC Special Projects?"

For one instant their gazes locked together. The old woman radiated stubbornness. Deborah Thomas knew she would have only one question to get her hook in. She raised her voice, shouting over the racket.

"Today, on your own son's inaugural, you were sitting alone. Whose idea was that? Yours? His?"

"Mine," Kitty Stokes said. "Sitting alone at my age helps keep things in historical perspective. Now if you'll excuse me, I don't give interviews." She raised her silver-tipped walking stick and with the threat of a smart slap forced Deborah Thomas aside.

The head of NBC Special Projects lost her balance, stumbled in front of UPI and AP and the Washington *Post*. "I'll sue that bitch!" she cried.

But there was no need to bluster or try to save face. UPI and AP and the *Post* were no longer watching Deborah Thomas: their eyes were nailed to the dirty-faced little boy in a floppy checkered hat who had darted around the startled chauffeur and was holding the door of Kitty Stokes's limousine.

"Mrs. Stokes," the boy said in a voice that was barely past piping, "I represent the student newspaper of Thomas Jefferson grade school in Wilmington, Delaware. I've been assigned to interview you."

Kitty Stokes looked at him—a child. She looked back at

the circle of reporters—hungering animals. She softened.

"Get into the car. You have three minutes."

The old woman and the little boy got into the car, and after the driver had closed the door the boy opened a small, spiral-bound notepad. His hands were shaking and Kitty Stokes could see he had prepared his questions in a careful looping scrawl.

"The students of Thomas Jefferson congratulate you on the occasion of your son's inauguration." The awkward formality was touching in one so young.

"Thank you," Kitty Stokes said.

"The students of Thomas Jefferson would like to know the single most important thing you've ever done in your life."

After a lifetime a person aches to tell the truth to someone. "Did you ever hear of a place called Bartonville?" she asked.

He shook his head. "No ma'am. I never heard of it."

*They don't teach it nowadays,* she realized. *It may not even be in the history books anymore. No wonder. I paid to have it taken out.*

"When I was a young girl in Bartonville, long before you were born . . ." She looked at him. "Long before your parents were born . . . I made a promise."

There was silence and Pennsylvania Avenue and its crowds and police slid past the sealed windows of the black Lincoln Continental. The boy was obviously disappointed.

"That was the most important thing?"

"Promises can be important," she said, and she thought: *Mine was.*

The boy shook his head dubiously. "I need specifics—who what why when where and how. What was the promise?"

She was not sure she could bring herself to utter the words of that promise again, not even in memory. She drew in a deep, fortifying breath.

It was not Kitty Stokes's habit to leave a question unanswered any more than it was to leave a job undone. She reached toward the boy and he let her put her hand over his.

"Don't write for a minute," she said.

Mentally, Kitty Kellogg Stokes began to frame her reply; and the boy waited.

# *Chapter 2*

SEPTEMBER OF 1922 was a dry month in northwestern Pennsylvania, and the afternoon of the Bartonville massacre was a scorcher.

Kitty Kellogg kept the door and the one window wide open. Still the air in the shack would not stir. Because her dad was there, with his Bible—watching her but pretending not to—she had to invent activities.

She swept the shack twice. The floor was bare earth. A two-foot-square hole had been dug in it and covered with boards. Kitty and her dad stored potatoes beneath the boards, when they had potatoes. They hadn't had any since the strike began. She made the bunks extra-carefully. She dusted the shelves. Finally she sat and pretended to read an old magazine. From the corner of her eye she watched her dad pretending not to watch her.

Annoyance filled her, rising like water in a glass.

She knew why he watched. She was a girl. She was seventeen. If he'd been on the job, if she'd been on hers, there'd have been no need or chance to watch her. But the men were on strike. The company had closed the store where she worked. So he watched. There was love in his watching, and pride. But she sensed something else too: a fear that if he looked the other

4

way, let her out of his sight even an instant, he'd lose her. Maybe not quite the way he'd lost her mother, but lose her just as bad.

Now that her mother was dead he'd become, too late, a good husband: no more drinking, no more women. He spent his free time sitting near the window with his Bible—watching.

Something rumbled far away. Kitty's dad shut the Bible. His hand made a rough red scar against the leather cover.

"Thunder," he said hopefully.

Kitty stared out the window. She could remember the day her dad had broken the glass in a fit of anger. Now the window had cardboard from a Del Monte bean carton. Nails held it in place. They stuck out like thorns. If you wanted the view you had to take the weather too, full in your face.

Today the weather was not a hot autumn stillness. Hundreds of concrete shacks with tarpaper roofs stretched shadows across the dry, bulldozed land. A silence flowed over the earth. It filled the shack and it bothered Kitty. A single thin cloud was beginning to catch the pink of the late-afternoon sun. She thought how clean the colors were up there, as if they'd just been washed.

She thought how she was going to miss her date if she couldn't think up an excuse to get out of the shack.

"Couldn't be thunder," she said. "The sky's clear."

"Couldn't be anything else." Her dad's eyes had kept their child's blue. They made the rest of him gray and weary by contrast.

"Then I'm going to take a walk. Stretch my legs before it rains."

Her dad looked hurt. Better hurt, she thought, than angry. She could handle him hurt. Angry, there was no holding him.

"Seems you've always got somewhere to run off to."

"I ain't been out all day."

He tugged at a damp fold of undershirt. There was black beneath his fingernails, oil crescents that never scrubbed out. "You won't be long now, will you?"

"Ten minutes. Maybe fifteen." She knew it would be twenty-five at the soonest. She knew he knew it too.

Her dad's questioning eyes made her feel mean and deceitful. She hurried outdoors, quick while luck was with her.

There was nobody in the lanes between shacks. Not even children; not even dogs. It was the fault of the heat. A day like today, if you could find shade you clung to it, pulled it over you like a tent and went to sleep. Today there wasn't even a horse or wagon down in the road. No need since the company store had put the green shutters up over its windows. There was nothing to buy, nothing to haul.

The only thing the company hadn't managed to shut down was the pump in the dusty town square. It was fed by an underground spring. For the employees of Stokes Petroleum and their families, it was the only water. If you lived in one of the outlying shacks you had to trudge a half mile to the pump and back, and there were times when you'd just as soon do without the washing.

Kitty bent down to the pump. Its curved handle was shiny from a hundred thousand handshakes. She pumped till the water flowed cold. She had herself a long swallow. And then she ran, the only moving thing in the street or fields.

To the west of town, the company geologists had found there was no oil, and trees still grew in a four-acre crescent, a scar of green on the bald, torn earth. The trees looked out of place, idle and graceful among the oil rigs, a last tiny remnant of what had once been a forested plain.

The underbrush in the crescent had grown thick and forbidding, but Kitty could see a pathway recently beaten down. She knew the workmen took turns bringing their girls here. And she knew her sweetheart had other girls besides her. It did not bother her. She knew she was different from the others.

On the day of the massacre Kitty Kellogg crept through the shield of greenbrier. She blinked her eyes and had to stand still a moment. After the burning sunlight of the oil fields the little forest seemed a cave of cool darkness.

At the center of the forest was a spring. Kitty's sweetheart had shown her the spot and they had met here, secretly, through spring and summer.

Tyrone Duncannon was sitting on the far bank. He had propped his feet comfortably against a tree trunk. He was musing as she had seen him do for half hours at a time.

"Sorry I'm late," she said. "Couldn't get away from Dad."

A sunbeam glinted on the spots of gold that flecked his hair. Two dark curves marked the ridges of strength in his shoulders. He was a handsome fellow, Kitty thought, and the miracle was that he was hers in a way he was no other girl's.

He sat there watching while Kitty took off her shoes and

waded across the cold spring water to him. He smiled his green
eyes at her. She settled herself down beside him. They rested
a long moment side by side, barely touching, which made Kitty
all the more aware of the faint faraway pressure of his knee.

"You're thinkin' too hard," she said.

"I'm thinkin' we've got to win or we're dead," he said.
"There's a rumor Stokes has called for state troops."

"To break the strike?"

"To arrest us. The Governor signed an emergency procla-
mation. They've built compounds. They're goin' to haul us in
trucks to the penitentiary—every damned man, woman and
child of us."

"But what have we done wrong? Does it say in the law
books you've got to work for Stokes or go to jail?"

"We're on his property."

Kitty looked about her at this airy space, friendly and shel-
tering and cool and private. And she thought how strange it
could be owned by anyone but God.

"All because you want to organize," she marveled. "Well,
your union friends'll look out for you. Haven't they given you
food and tents, just in case?"

He looked at her. "Food and tents ain't the answer." He
began explaining about the crisis of class struggle, instructing
her again, just like a priest.

Kitty listened, letting him think it interested her. He had
often told her his dreams, and they were different from hers.
He dreamed of changing the world, and she dreamed of living
in it. He dreamed union dreams: higher wages, better job conditions. She dreamed of him beside her in a brass bed; of a
house with a wood floor and running water and, in time, electric
lights; of children, lots of children.

He talked a long time and Kitty nodded yes, yes, yes and
began to feel ignored. She thought what a waste it was to talk
politics in a sanctuary like this. She wondered whether he would
try to kiss her. He always tried, and she always liked his trying,
but today felt different. She felt an odd disappointment stirring
in her belly. She sneaked a teasing finger beneath the neck of
his work shirt. His skin felt cool and soft to her touch.

He stopped talking. His eyes were on her blouse, on the
white freckled triangle where she had undone two buttons because of the heat. Time and silence enclosed them, swelling,
drifting, passing in great waves.

"You've got beautiful breasts, Kitty. You know you're beautiful."

She pulled away from him. She pretended to be annoyed. She always pretended. Secretly she felt pleasure that he wanted her as much as he wanted those other girls. "You'd think you'd never seen female flesh," she said, "the way you carry on."

His hands went around her neck. His lips came down onto hers. Her blood began galloping. She tasted his tongue in her mouth. Her head went dizzy. He rolled halfway on top of her. Through the thin cotton dress she could feel the hard strength of his penis.

For an unresisting moment she pressed back against him. And then she realized how badly she wanted him, not just his arms and mouth, but all of him, everything, now please God now. She yanked free.

"No."

"Oh, Kitty, why the hell not?"

Sparks of sunlight flew across his face like fragments of broken glass.

"You know why not," she said.

"We'll marry, I've told you that. Just wait for this strike to be settled."

"Sure. One day the strike'll be settled and Jesus Christ'll come back to earth and ice cream'll be free and we'll get married. In the meantime you want me to wallow with you like Teresa McCoy and that fat Costello girl. Well, I'm not a whore and you wouldn't want me if I was, so don't ask me to."

He was gawking at her, white-faced. "Who told you about Edie Costello?"

'Everyone knows about you and her. The whole town's laughin'. I got problems enough, thank you." She had to feel sorry for the swift, guilty look on him, so like a boy's. "Oh, Tyrone, I love you and I want you, but I can't."

He was silent a moment. "What if somethin' happens today?"

She sensed slyness: a bargaining. "What's goin' to happen today?"

"What if somethin' happens to me?"

"Don't you try to frighten me, Tyrone Duncannon. If anythin' happens to you I'll—I'll kill myself."

"I'd rather have you alive in my arms," he sighed, "then both of us dead."

"No one's goin' to die."

"You don't know that, Kitty. What if this is the only chance for us ever? Right here, right now?"

She gazed into his eyes, groping for the truth of him. He was different from the Tyrone she'd seen face down bullies and armed police and hold off three drunken thugs with a broken beer bottle. There were tears in the corners of his eyes and when she touched his forehead the skin was cold and studded with sweat.

"Why are you scared, Tyrone?"

His face opened to her. "I'm only scared of losin' you."

He wasn't lying, she could see that. But he was bargaining. Well, she could bargain just as tough.

"You'll marry me?" she said. "Not after some strike is settled, but tonight? We'll go to the church and tell Father Jack what we've done and you'll marry me?"

"I feel married to you already."

"That's not enough. You'll come to the church with me tonight—yes or no?"

He nodded. "I'll come to the church with you tonight."

"Swear—as God is your witness."

"I swear."

She believed him and belief carried her over the threshold of decision. She took one deep breath and braced herself and pressed her mouth against his. It was a kiss with no turning back after it.

He lifted her blouse and kissed her breasts. He unhooked her skirt and she helped him get it off her. She reached between his legs and guided him into her. There was a tearing and a splitting and her lungs gasped. Pain came in a rush. She held to him and did not scream and it passed, leaving only warmth and a completeness stranger and realer than anything she had ever felt or imagined.

Without ever pulling away from one another they made love three times, each act flowing into the next. *This is eternity,* she thought, and there was a moment where she almost glimpsed the smile on the face of the universe.

"I conceived," she said dreamily afterward.

He laughed. "You what?"

"Your child is inside me now. I could feel the life begin."

He stared at her wonderingly and then pulled her toward him. "Might as well be hanged for a horse as a sheep," he said.

He began to make love to her again, but she suddenly realized what time it must be. She leaped up and dressed quickly.

"Where are you rushin'?" he asked, trying to hold her back.

"I've been in your arms enough for one day. Come on. I should be fixin' my dad's supper."

"Oh Kitty, you can stay another ten minutes, he won't starve."

"You don't need me another ten minutes, Tyrone Duncannon. You've got me for your whole life now. And don't forget—we have a date tonight, in church."

Kitty took a tin box from the shelf. Before the workers had gone on strike there had been three dozen cans. Now there were only five. It was so hot in the shack her hand broke into a sweat just working a rusty can opener around the rim. She emptied the beans into a pot and lit the tiny paraffin burner.

It took an eternity for the beans to come to a bubble. Her stomach gritted against the stink of them. Her dad kept rattling onionskin pages: Old Testament. She blew out the burner and went to the plank table and dolloped supper onto chipped plates.

Her dad bowed his head. The skin at the back of his neck still showed pitted where he'd been burned fourteen years ago in an oil well explosion.

"Bless this food to our use," he prayed, "and us to Thy service. In Jesus' name. Amen." He looked up. "Kitty, I didn't hear your amen."

She looked at her dad. Joe Kellogg was enormous, huge in the arms and thighs and chest. The beer belly from his drinking days had become an age belly, veined and swollen like a workhorse's. She saw the silent strength of his shoulders and wondered what had gone wrong: him or life, which was to blame? There were plenty of poor micks who'd made good, and it baffled her that Joe Kellogg with his strength and kindness had not been one of them.

He'd failed at everything he'd attempted—he'd come from Ireland a starving, broke kid, worked farms and fishing boats, timberland and salt furnace and coal mine, got drafted into the Great War and come back to find his savings and his three acres gone and his wife and kids scattered in the Chicago piece-work shops. There'd been nothing for Joe Kellogg then but the oil rigs: the company rented you a house and a family could be together if they didn't mind the squeezing. So he'd gathered his family into this shack, just in time for the diptheria outbreak that had swept the town. There'd been no doctor, no medicine, no money. His wife and the two younger kids had died, leaving him and Kitty silent in their company shack while the debts mounted up and walled them in.

Why her dad had to say thanks to the God who had kicked him in the teeth time and time again, Kitty couldn't for the life of her fathom. "I'm not thankin' anyone for beans," she said. "I'm sick of the taste of 'em."

"Sicker than me, are you?"

Since her mother's death, Kitty's dad had had no one to argue with. He'd taken to permitting Kitty a pinch of sass. She never knew just how big a pinch.

"Then why don't you hop down to the company store, Miss Kitty Kellogg. See if they'll open up and let you have a nice sirloin of beef. Ask if you can pay for it next year." He thumped a fist on the Bible. "Damn it, child, you'll eat beans, 'cause beans is all we got!"

"I'd sooner starve."

"Then starve you will. But you'll not insult the Lord in your mother's house."

"This place was never hers. It belongs to Stokes Petroleum. And it's not even a house. No water. No lights. No floor. If you're a rat you can come and go as you please. If you're a tenant you're stuck with the back rent."

"It's kept the rain off your head a good long time."

"So would a jail cell."

"Which is where you'll end up with talk like that. I'm waitin' to hear you thank the Lord."

"A plate of beans can't be that important to Him."

"You'll not defy me, child." Her dad gave her a look and raised the back of his hand to her. She braced, knowing she was going to get it.

A foot scraped at the open door. A young man stood silhouetted and tall against the last of the daylight.

"As for you, Tyrone Duncannon," Kitty's dad shouted, "when I want a Communist in the house I'll send for one! Till then you're welcome to stay out!"

For a moment, catching his breath, Tyrone Duncannon did not speak. He held one hand pressed to a stain in his denim shirt and his chest rose and fell rapidly.

"It's happened." His words came hoarse and breath-starved. "Stokes has called in the state militia." His glance took in the shack with a dark sweep that lingered on Kitty. "They're down in the road, truckloads of 'em and more comin'."

"We've nothin' to fear," Kitty's dad said. "No one in this house is a lawbreaker."

"You're a trespasser, Kellogg, same as all of us. No one's paid rent since the strike began."

From down on the dirt road Kitty could hear a rising murmur of motors. A tinny crash punctured the air. Gunfire.

Joe Kellogg muttered and pushed up from the table. Kitty wrapped a kitchen knife in a rag and slid it into her skirt pocket.

"Come on, now." Tyrone Duncannon hurried Kitty and her dad through the door.

Kitty stared down past the rows of huts. Trucks were piling up along the road. Soldiers jumped down, noiseless and swift as butterflies. The spiked tips of their rifles glinted in the late sun. She felt she must be dreaming them.

"Keep the huts between you and them," Tyrone Duncannon said. "Head for the graveyard, quick now."

"What the hell are we goin' to do in the graveyard?" Joe Kellogg said.

"The union'll give you a tent. Now get goin'."

"I ain't pitchin' no tent on someone else's grave!" The veins in Joe Kellogg's face stood out red. Kitty was amazed at her dad: soldiers were pouring up the hill and he wanted to stand squabbling with Tyrone Duncannon. She knew it wasn't the communism her dad hated: it was Tyrone's youth, his drinking, the whispers of his whoring. He had all the freedom that time and fear had stolen from Joe Kellogg.

"You'd rather it was your own grave?" Tyrone Duncannon shouted.

The soldiers were zigzagging up through the company huts. They butted rifles through doors and windows. The hillside was shaking with cries and gunfire and a dim, growing thunder of running feet. Families came scattering out into the open, hands in the air. Kitty could not believe it was happening.

"This is Stokes's land," Tyrone Duncannon said. "Stay here

and he'll have you in prison. The graveyard is a church land. He can't touch you there."

"None of this would have happened," Kitty's dad shouted, "if you and your damned union hadn't stirred things up!"

Tyrone Duncannon stared at the older man a moment, jaws working. "Get your tent set up and wait for me in the church. We'll need all the hands we can get bringin' supplies through."

A finger of ice brushed Kitty. "Tyrone, ain't you comin' with us?"

Tyrone Duncannon's gaze locked with hers and went soft. "You just take care of your dad, Kitty. I'll be along." He gave her a push and without a word of goodby set off at a run, hair and shirttails flapping.

By now the soldiers had swept like a tide halfway up the hill. The explosions came closer together, tinny and vicious. They triggered cries that blurred into one high whine. Joe Kellogg gripped his daughter's hand. He led her at a running crouch, a hut at a time.

Three huts ahead, soldiers blocked the path. Kitty's heart contracted.

Her dad thrust a hand over her mouth. His thumb tasted of beans. He pulled her with him up around the back of the hut, then gestured her back, out of sight. He leaned forward, his eyes fumbling to pierce the confusion. He listened, squinting, then motioned.

He pulled her forward into the cloud of dust and screams, through the rattle of bullets. Women were screaming like dogs caught on barbed wire.

Kitty ran, lungs exploding inside her. Gunfire came in splintering crashes. Her dad paid no attention: the sounds did not slow him. He kept tugging her forward.

All down the hillside there were bodies and broken glass and blood and mud flowing into one another. Shacks were burning, hissing. Roofs flew up and walls tumbled out. *Dynamite*, Kitty thought. It was happening too quickly. Everything was smoke and flames and screaming, tumbling shadows. Concrete and glass gashed the air. The earth and the sky were coming apart.

They broke into a flat-out run. Something zinged in the air like a snapped string. In front of them a handful of sod jumped kneehigh. Kitty's dad shouted, "Down!"

They threw themselves down in the dust on their bellies. They scampered crawling to the next hut. Kitty risked raising her head. A bullet bit into the tarpaper roof, screeching like a tiny murdered animal. She ducked again.

Her dad motioned her to stay low, stay tight against the concrete wall. Her blood pounded in her ears. Her lungs were on fire.

A dead woman lay across their path, blocking the way. Window glass had sprinkled across her hair. Who was she? Kitty wondered. Whose mother, whose wife? And the answer came pounding in her blood: *she is no one, she is dead, keep going!*

They crawled around her and came to the last row of company huts. From here the ground dipped steep and unprotected to the cemetery. The wood church had weathered to the color of earth. Kitty had heard that the whole town had once been wood, before Stokes Petroleum, and the steeple had been the tallest thing for miles, before the oil rigs. Her eyes traveled the hundred yards that stretched from where she stood to the church a hundred yards of no shelter at all.

Army trucks crowded the edge of the graveyard that bordered the road. They were beginning to fan out across the field, motors howling.

"In two minutes they'll have us cut off," Kitty's dad said.

There were shouts. Kitty looked back. A tidal wave of men and women came ripping out between the huts, screaming, stumbling, the wave poured over itself like gushing blood, poured toward Kitty and her dad.

He gestured her up. "Make a run for it. Don't stop for anything."

Kitty ran. Her heart was pounding like a jackhammer at her ribs Volleys of gunfire rolled together into one air-shattering thunder. Her foot caught on rock. She went down on her knees. She heard herself cry out. The human wave came crushing down on top of her.

'Dad!" she screamed.

Her dad stopped and saw and dove back after her into the sea of legs. For one too long instant he vanished, and then she felt a hand dragging her up from the whirlpool.

She staggered to her feet, breath fierce and hoarse and sharp as blades in her lungs. Her eyes had seen death. Her dad put an arm under her shoulder and lifted her. They went at a rushing stumble through the human forest. Her dad chopped with his free hand, clearing a channel, pulling her through with him. She heard his voice telling her to keep going, keep going, don't stop.

The mob surged around them now, a torn and sweating human armor that crushed them and carried them lurching and spinning forward with no will of their own. There was still one last opening between the trucks' closing claws. Motors howled and wheels spat dust and rifle cracks came in dots and dashes. But the wave kept going and it swept Kitty and her dad across the last yard, off of Stokes's land and onto God's.

Kitty sobbed a long time after the bullets had stopped.

Her dad hugged her. "It's okay, child. We're safe."

Kitty blotted her eyes dry on her fists. She stared around her. A hundred or more people had managed to flee to the little graveyard. They thronged the path to the church door, clinging to the shelter of the yew trees. They glanced anxiously beyond the gravestones, past the frail line of law, to where soldiers waited and gears screeched and wheels skinned the earth.

The trucks, unhurried now, lumbered to close their circle. They belched sour white clouds. Soldiers crouched behind the trucks. They kept their rifles aimed at the graves and didn't move. They were square and blunt in their bulletproof helmets and they did not have the shape of men. In the deepening dark their bayonets gave the trucks the jagged outline of prehistoric skeletons.

On the church steps two bearded union organizers handed out canvas tents and wooden pegs, one set to a family. The patched canvas looked like Great War surplus.

Kitty's dad said, "I slept in one of these in France."

He led his daughter through the sweltering twilight. By now the graveyard was dense with tents. Screaming children, worried men and women crowded the lanes between tombstones. The sun had set. A tiny star, just visible, touched the tops of the yew trees.

An explosion stuttered through the graveyard.

There was a panic of voices. Kitty whirled just in time to see a wounded man being carried into the church. One of his boots dangled as though there was no foot at all in it. Even at this distance she could see strips of blood ribboning his shirt and trousers. Even in this light she could see the man was Tyrone Duncannon.

She clenched her fists to keep from screaming.

"I'll be back, Dad." She ran before he could stop her.

They had laid Tyrone Duncannon on the floor of the little sanctuary. The statue of Saint Veronica gazed down smiling at him. Reflections of her candles glistened in the wet red on his shirt. The dark stain reached down to his belt.

Kitty forced her way between two men. She knelt and touched a hand to Tyrone Duncannon's face. His eyes opened, green and deep and baffled. His head struggled to free itself from the stillness that had begun to grip his body.

"Is that you, Kitty?" he said.

"It's me, Tyrone."

A stranger pushed Kitty aside. "Give me some light." His voice was sharp, used to being obeyed. He had the hard, intelligent profile of a Jew. Wire-rimmed glasses gave his eyes a grim sparkle.

He lifted the flap of Tyrone Duncannon's shirt. There was no skin, only a mass of raw flesh dotted with flecks of bone.

Kitty covered her mouth.

The stranger shook his head. He set down his leather satchel. It was as worn as the cover of Joe Kellogg's Bible. His fingers slipped a syringe together. He pressed a needle deep into Tyrone Duncannon's shoulder. Then he snapped the satchel shut and got back to his feet.

"That's all you're going to do?" Kitty cried.

"It's all I can do. He'll die comfortably now."

Kitty pressed her teeth together. She bit down on the scream inside her.

"Will you step aside, please." The stranger's touch was firm. It hinted at the power to flatten her if she stood in the way of his work. He pushed past her.

Outside, the sky crackled with rifle fire. Kitty knelt again beside Tyrone Duncannon. A vein shivered in his neck.

"Are you holdin' my hand, Kitty?" There was no voice to his asking, only hoarse, labored air. "I can't feel you."

"Tyrone," she pleaded, "don't go! Don't leave me!"

She clung to his hand. Her heart darted from hope to denial to prayer. But reason told her that in minutes there would be no Tyrone Duncannon. She had carried a dream in her heart and the dream was ending in this church, in this moment.

She breathed deep and drew herself up. She said to the men

who stood there, "Find the priest. Bring Father Jack. Quick."

Kitty stayed crouched beside her dying sweetheart. Gunfire raked the lengthening minutes. The smell of blood filled the sanctuary. It was a metal smell, rust smell—not human, not even animal. Tyrone Duncannon was going back to his elements.

She placed a hand on his stomach, slowing the outrush of life. Her heart pounded in her, but with an even beat now. Shock gradually passed. It left no feeling in her except the certainty of what she must do.

She tore a piece of cloth from her skirt. She wiped a trickle of blood from Tyrone Duncannon's mouth.

The breath whimpered in his throat. "Still holdin' my hand, Kitty?"

The gate squeaked as the priest stepped through. There were only three of them in the sanctuary now: Kitty, the priest, the dying man.

Father Jack's gaunt, unshaved face held no greeting for Kitty. He knelt beside Tyrone Duncannon.

"Father Jack?" Tyrone Duncannon said. "Damn, then I know I'm goin'."

"You'd best make your peace with the Almighty." Father Jack adjusted a thin purple stole around his neck. Levi's showed beneath his patched cassock. "When was the last time you made your confession?"

"Can't remember."

"Mass?"

"Don't know. Christ, it's been years."

Father Jack's lips pressed tight on a frown. "Let's hear your sins."

"Oh, God. I've failed in my duties to Holy Mother Church. I've been impure in thought and deed—"

Father Jack placed his fingertips across Tyrone Duncannon's mouth, cutting short the labored whisper. Latin came in a mumbled rush. *"Te absolvo ab omni vinculo excommunicationes, suspensiones et interdicti in quantum possum et tu indiges. In nomine Patris, Filii, et Spiritus Sancti. Amen."*

Father Jack carved a sign of the cross out of the dust that floated above Tyrone Duncannon's head. A burst of gunfire shook the church walls. Father Jack took a phial from the pocket of his cassock. He twisted the lid loose and dipped his right thumb into the saturated wad of cotton within.

*"Per istam sanctam unctionem indulgeat tibi Dominus quid-quid deliquisti. Amen."*

Father Jack traced a cross on Tyrone Duncannon's brow. The oil smeared the grime on the young man's face and left a greasy track.

Kitty took the priest by the elbow. "Father Jack."

"Yes, Kitty?"

"Marry Tyrone and me."

Amazement splashed the priest's face. "I'll do nothing of the sort." He pushed her hand off his arm. "The boy's halfway to heaven, please Christ."

Kitty drew the kitchen knife from her skirt. "Marry us, Father."

Father Jack opened his mouth in a long moment's silence, then bellowed. "Do you know what you're doing, Kitty Kellogg? You damn your soul when you lay violent hands on a priest. Now put that knife away and I'll forget this foolishness!"

She pressed the tip of the blade against the priest's rib. "I ain't foolin', Father."

His eyes pinched. "Does Tyrone want to marry you? Did he ever say so?"

"Indeed he did. Only today he asked me."

"And you want him for a husband? Like *this?*"

"That I do, Father."

Something fierce rushed across Father Jack's face. "Then consider it done in the sight of heaven. *Benedicat vos, Omnipotens Deus. In nomine Patris, Filii, et Spiritus Sancti. Amen.* And God forgive us all."

Father Jack pushed the knife aside. There was contempt in his eyes. He stuffed the purple stole into his pocket. "Excuse me. I'm needed out there."

He hurried from the sanctuary. Kitty closed the gate behind him.

She knelt. Tyrone Duncannon's face was sad and still now, folded in on the death that was devouring him. His eyes searched hers from far away.

'Oh Kitty, they've killed me."

"You're alive. You're my husband."

"I wanted to be. I wanted it so much."

"You will have a son, Tyrone. Your son will live. I swear it.'

He strained. His hands urged her face down to his. They kissed. They kissed. She would always remember this. They kissed.

And then he sank back onto the stone floor.

"Tyrone!" She gripped and shook him, but he lay still. His eyes stared unmoving. She pressed an ear to his chest. The utter silence of his body bewildered her and then it frightened her and then, gradually, it filled her with rage.

She stood up slowly and gazed at her husband. Rigid and still and streaked with dirt, Tyrone Duncannon had already become part of the earth. She would have liked to cry. Tears would have been a relief. But the blood in her howled for something else.

She went to where her father had pitched the little tent. "Tyrone Duncannon's dead," she said.

Her father sighed. "God rest him."

Kitty's eyes traced a line from the tents to the idling trucks. The smell of fire singed her nostrils. Her body ached with hate. "They'll pay," she said.

Her dad's eyes peered up at her, unspoiled blue in the wreck of his face. "Who'll pay—the soldiers?"

She nodded. "The soldiers."

"Ain't their fault," Joe Kellogg said. "The politicians sent 'em."

"The politicians'll pay too. And Stokes'll pay, because he owns the politicians. Stokes'll pay most of all."

Joe Kellogg shook his head. "Those people never pay."

"This time, by God, I'll make them pay."

Her dad reached a hand and drew her gently beside him. "My poor sweet Kitty," he said. "You don't even have a gun."

"It's them that need guns. Not me."

# *Chapter 3*

THE STRIKE did not last.

Officials of Stokes Petroleum said it had cost the company five and a half million dollars in property damage and lost contracts. They offered employees their old jobs and the shacks that were still standing—provided the men ceased all union agitation and worked at reduced wages till the loss was paid back.

The governor of the state promised amnesty to men accepting the offer.

In barbed-wire compounds outside the state prison, the workers by show of hands voted *yes*. In the graveyard of the little Catholic church, cut off from food and water, the workers voted *yes*.

State troopers returned their prisoners to the shacks of Bartonville. The soldiers who had encircled the graveyard for two days turned their trucks around and drove peaceably back to the armory. Behind them they left nine dead: six men and two women shot, an infant burned; fifty-eight wounded; and a thousand exhausted and beaten human beings.

The day after the workers gave up, Tyrone Duncannon was buried.

The company would not give time off, so he was laid to earth during the lunch break. The graveyard was humped and bald and rutted where trucks and feet and pegs had chewed it. The pallbearers wore work clothes. The bell tolled from the wood steeple, tinny and out of tune with itself.

There were two dozen mourners. Father Jack performed the service. Teresa McCoy and the Costello girl wore black. Kitty Kellogg did not.

Her mourning was a lifelong thing, not a dress to be put on and taken off. More than that, it was a private thing. She realized, if she was to succeed in what she intended, she must be private now as never before.

She stood separate from the others, in gray. Grief was still in her, but shorn of its numbing softness. Purpose had hardened it into something cold and sharp which fitted exactly into the secret hollow where love had once been.

The mourners were clustered around the fresh-dug grave. Their faces were empty, quiet, jumbles of wrecked condolence. Overhead, the sky was a pale burning blue, stretched so high and thin it looked as though it might come apart. Sally Duncannon, the dead man's sister, stood beside the priest.

Kitty watched Sally Duncannon, gauging her.

Sally had put on a black tent of a dress. She had put on a black hat with a pinned-on veil that did not quite come down to the lump of her nose. She wobbled on her feet as though she were more than a little drunk.

Kitty's eyes went to Father Jack. His mouth made an angry dark rip in his beard. Sunlight showed up the patches in his cassock. His arms swept the air like the wings of an undernourished eagle.

"Earth to earth," he intoned, "ashes to ashes, dust to dust. In sure and certain hope of the resurrection unto eternal life . . ."

Kitty had taken the precaution of making her confession to Father Jack two days earlier. Among her sins she had confessed to marrying Tyrone Duncannon—not because she felt the marriage to be sinful, but to keep Father Jack from ever revealing it.

The priest's thumb fumbled through the tattered pages of his missal. "Let us pray for our brother Tyrone Duncannon to our Lord Jesus Christ, who told us: I am the resurrection and the life . . ."

The red bones of the priest's face seemed to scream out

against the injustice that had brought this boy to the grave at his feet. *That's what priests are for,* Kitty thought; *screaming*. The roof of her mouth tasted of bitterness and resolve.

"The man who believes in me will live even though he dies, and every living person who puts faith in me will never suffer eternal death. Lord, you wept at the death of Lazarus, your friend: comfort us in our sorrow."

The dead man's sister stood motionless as an animal in a field, silent, head lowered, barely shifting weight as the minutes and prayers flowed past. Father Jack thrust out a reddened hand and gave three shakes to his holy water sprinkler. Tiny drops splattered the casket and the grave, and Sally Duncannon stared at a splash on her skirt and moved back a step.

One of the women mourners made a choking sound. Way back in the fields an oil rig throbbed.

The priest closed his prayer book. The covers slapped like a bullet. The mourners remained in place, not moving, letting the stillness wash across them, a stillness thick with hate and impotence.

"Let us pray as our Lord taught us," Father Jack sobbed: "Our Father, who art in heaven . . ."

The mourners' voices could not keep up with Father Jack's. They were lame voices, stumbling and stunned. When the prayer was done Sally Duncannon stepped forward. She cast a sprinkle of earth on the casket. Her shoulders were huge and stooped beneath her black shawl. She held a checkered handkerchief bunched to her mouth. She stared down at the open wound in the earth and broke into screams.

Teresa McCoy and the Costello girl were instantly at her side, murmuring and soothing, passing white hankies over her as though to clean dribble from a helpless baby. Sally Duncannon clawed them away. Kitty understood: they had had their moment. They were wearing their black to prove it. This was Sally Duncannon's moment, and she wasn't about to share it. She stumbled away from the grave on her own. All her fat seemed to have spilled onto one hip. People parted for her, frightened. In their eyes Kitty could see the embarrassed apology that they should be alive and Tyrone Duncannon dead.

At the edge of the graveyard, Sally Duncannon stood alone and stiff in her grief. The others approached her hesitantly. The men stooped close to her, whispered, pressed her black-gloved hands between their naked red palms. The women kissed

her. Kitty could see them offering condolences inaudible and
helplessly bent, condolences dropped and stuttering and lost.
Sally Duncannon accepted it all, nodding.

Kitty stood at a distance, awaiting the moment when Sally
would be alone. She felt herself slipping into a pool of indecision. Half of her wanted to turn, flee, abandon the whole
scheme. But the other half told her she had promised: she could
not take back a promise to the dead.

Kitty went to the dead man's sister. Determination drummed
in her like a second heartbeat. "Oh Sally, Sally—I'm so sorry."

Sally Duncannon's eyes came up, sad and soft.

Kitty fell into step with Sally's limp. "Well, at least there's
one mercy," Kitty said.

Sally gave her a look that seemed to wonder if there could
be mercy for any of them in this time or place. "And what
mercy would you be meanin'?"

"He got the last rites."

Kitty could understand the change that came over Sally
Duncannon's face: hadn't Tyrone shouted slogans against the
Pope and the opium of the people?

"Did he *ask* for the last rites?"

"I was there, Sally. I saw it with my own eyes."

Sally Duncannon took Kitty Duncannon's hand, gravely,
miserably, gratefully. *She doesn't know about Tyrone and me,*
Kitty realized: *she'd hate me if she knew, just like she hates
Teresa McCoy and the Costello girl and any other woman
wearing black today.* Kitty could feel something sway between
them, a crime hovering in the air.

"He asked for you," Kitty said. "Just before he went."

"Tyrone asked for me?"

"You were the last name on his lips. He was worried, would
you keep workin' for the Stokeses, doin' their laundry?"

Sally Duncannon's stomach seemed to draw itself up into
her bosom. "What else am I goin' to do—starve?"

"You'd touch their clothes, then—them that murdered your
only brother?"

"Did he say that, Kitty? Did he really say that?"

Kitty nodded. "Could you bear it, Sally? To go back to
them? There must be rich folks in other towns that need their
washin' done."

"And how would I get to another town to find out? Do you
know what a coffin costs, plain pine? I ain't got a penny left."

"I got nine dollars saved." Kitty drew a purse of dollar bills and nickels and dimes from her pocket. "Would it help tide you over?"

"Oh Kitty, I couldn't. From what I hear, we're all goin' to be a lot poorer with this strike settled. You'd best hang on to your savin's."

"You'll pay me back when you find a new job." Kitty pressed the nine dollars into Sally Duncannon's hand. The coins made a friendly, tinkling sound. "Take the money, Sally—please."

Sally Duncannon's fingers half-surrendered. "You're doin' this for Him, ain't you. I suppose you loved him too, then?" The ghost of childhood envy flickered in her eyes.

"Didn't all the girls?" Kitty said. "But he never even knew I was alive, not him."

The money slid silently into Sally Duncannon's pocket. "Thanks, Kitty. You're as good as a sister."

And Sally Duncannon pressed a sad damp kiss against Kitty's cheek.

Kitty Kellogg sat at the window of the shack that night. She stared out at the sliver of view of the street. A little before ten, she saw Sally Duncannon with two old hatboxes trudging in the direction of the state highway.

It was a half hour's trudge to the bus stop, and there was a ten-thirty to Cleveland.

Kitty blew out the kerosene lamp. She kissed her dad in his bunk. He did not stir. She drew the sheet across the shack, making the little privacy that was her bedroom.

She lay down but she did not sleep. She planned. Planning was good.

It eased the hate.

She did not go to her job at the company store the next day. After her dad had left for the fields, she took the enameled wash bucket down to the pump. The splashes came hot from the spout. She carried a pail of lukewarm water back indoors.

She undressed and sponged herself, erasing all the dirt from her body. When she was dry she laid a newspaper where she had clipped out the notice of Tyrone Duncannon's funeral Mass. She drew a cardboard carton out from under the bunk. The carton was marked DEL MONTE BAKED BEANS. She had not opened it in four years. It contained a violet print dress, a lady's comb of genuine tortoiseshell, some costume jewelry, all cocooned in layers of yellowed tissue paper.

She put on the dress. She perched her dad's shaving mirror on a shelf. By stooping and then getting up on a chair she was able to see herself in sections. The dress had been her mother's. She experimented with different ways of bunching the extra cloth. Finally she let it hang in back in two pleats, safety-pinned from the inside so the pins didn't show.

When she had finished dressing, she passed a damp sponge over her shoes. The moisture helped hide the cracks in the leather.

From the bottom of the Del Monte carton she took a tiny bottle, an inch cube of cut glass with the label rubbed beyond readability. There was very little liquid left in it. She uncapped the bottle and tipped an amber drop onto her finger. A needle of regret pierced her. She touched her ears, her throat, the skin between her breasts. That was all she could afford.

She locked the shack. The padlock on the door was burning hot from the sun. She put her fingertips to her lips. She walked quickly, taking the road west out of town. She walked on the grass, so the dirt would have a harder time smudging her shoes. The land was low and dusty, stretching away to horizons that had been stripped of trees, where oil rigs grew instead.

She turned north at the state highway. Her shadow stayed one step ahead of her, a small wobbling pool at her feet. The sun seemed to have stuck at a midpoint in the sky. Far ahead of her, where the highway's white line wavered in the rising heat, a rapidly moving car caught sun and sparkled. As it approached, the white pinwheel flicker of its tires slowed. The driver turned his head to look at her. She could see a smile beneath the shadow of a straw boater.

She recognized the son of John Stokes Sr. She had seen him in magazine photos and once in the company store when he had bought a Coca-Cola. For one instant he was no more than an arm's length from her, close enough—if she'd had a weapon—to kill.

John Stokes, Junior's eyes rested on her for a blank smiling moment, his forehead high and vulnerable as an eggshell. Then the spinning white tires swept him past, and he and his car shrank with a motor-scream into the dry asphalt distance.

Kitty stood a moment and stared after him. Hatred swelled

within her, lifted her like a balloon. When she began walking again, it was without weight or fatigue, her legs quick and accurate like shears snipping off the distance between her and her purpose.

It was afternoon by the time Kitty reached the gates of the Stokes estate. Dampness had begun to rise on her shoulder blades and the cotton dress was sticking to her. High elms stretched waves of leaves against the sun, screening off its heat. She stopped in their shade, out of sight of the gatehouse. She stepped out of her shoes and blew the dust off them.

She approached the gatehouse smiling. Her heart thumped tightly against her chest. "Who do I see about a job?"

The guard sat drumming his knuckles on the ledge of the open window. He was a heavyset man. His ruddy face was bored and beginning to need a shave. "That depends who sent for you."

He had the accent of County Kerry, same as her dad. Kitty laid on the brogue.

"No one sent for me, exactly."

"Then no one's exactly who you'll see."

She came close to him. She laid her fingers on the window strip near the naked skin of his arm. "I hear Mr. Stokes's girls all quit."

A frown blunted his forehead. "Some did."

"I hear they're scared they'll get beat up if they keep workin' for him."

"Some are."

"Well, *I* ain't scared. And I can cook. And scrub. And do laundry."

"Mr. Stokes hires from an agency in Chicago."

"Then he'll be grateful that you saved him the bother."

"He's got a fence and a gate to save him bother."

"The poor man's got no help. He needs a girl here and now. So why can't you do him a favor and tell him about your friend Kitty Kellogg?"

"So we're friends, are we?"

She lifted her head, showing the white of her throat, and gave him a wheedling downward eye along the arc of her cheek. "And why shouldn't we be?"

"Because I don't know you, Kitty Kellogg."

"And what would you like to know? I live in town. My dad

works in the oil fields. I sing in the church choir." She made
her voice and eyes coaxing, like summer rain. "You can vouch
for me, can't you?"

"I can vouch for your red hair. And your freckles. And your
cheek."

"And what else does a girl need for cookin' and scrubbin'
and laundry?"

His face gleamed with a sudden burst of smile. "What the
hell." He stood and swung one arm into a jacket. "It's a fact
they're short a laundress. Come on." He put his hand through
the leafy pattern of the iron gate and swung it open.

Kitty followed him along the white-pebbled drive. They
passed banks of rhododendron and pruned evergreen. Suddenly
she could see the Stokes mansion. She had to stop a moment
and gape.

It was a huge three-story house built of pale-brown stone.
Kitty wondered how they'd made such a variety of rocks all
fit together. There were windows of every kind, all shining
like dark pools: flat windows and bay windows and fan-shaped
windows, and way up high there were circular windows, all
of them edged in white, clean as cake frosting. There were
white shutters, and at the front door a flight of white steps led
up to a porch with white pillars. High rippling oaks and elms
bushed about the house, cooling it.

*So that's how murderers live,* Kitty thought: *safe behind
stone and dark glass. Maybe I should be a murderer too.*

Two men stood on the porch. Kitty did not recognize the
dark-haired man, stubby and plump in a business suit, gesturing
to the other's back. She did recognize John Stokes Sr. from
the face on the company scrip. He seemed even taller and
thinner than she would have supposed: skeleton, and no flesh.
He wore a dark three-piece suit, and a gold chain dangled
between his vest pockets, and he was pacing.

"You keep saying, 'Damn the public,'" the short man
shouted, "and sooner or later the public will say, 'Stokes be
damned!'"

John Stokes Sr. said, "Let them." He saw the guard. "Where
are you going, Harry?"

"Beggin' your pardon, Mr. Stokes—around to the back."

"And who's that you've got with you?"

"This is my cousin Kitty Kellogg, from the village. She's
come to fill in for Sally."

The guard gave Kitty a push that sent her stumbling up the steps. She d never stood on the front steps of a house before; never been in a house that had had any. She fixed a smile in place.

"Sally who?" Stokes snapped.

Kitty had never seen a murderer so close. Stokes's face was the color of bone. It seemed to have shrunk too small for his wedge-shaped skull. He smelled faintly of bay rum, as though he'd measured a teaspoon of it into his bath.

"The laundress that quit, sir."

"The laundress too, eh?" John Stokes Sr. squinted at Kitty. It was a long, unhurried squint. "I don't know who's doing the hiring—the whole place is in an uproar." He tossed a nod toward the house. "Go talk to Mrs. Stokes."

"Thank you, sir." Kitty slipped past him and stepped across the threshold of the Stokes mansion. The house smelled clean and cool and large. Potted palms lined the wall. She went forward slowly. No one came to meet her.

*Are there no murderers at home?* she wondered.

Her eye took in the curved staircase, the balcony, the row of crystal chandeliers. She felt something final, something permanent reach down through her cracked leather shoes. It pushed out and it took root.

She had brought Tyrone Duncannon's son home.

She came to an open door. The room within was dim. Squinting, she picked out the mahogany curve of a grand piano; a tasseled shawl was flung across it, anchored with gold-framed photographs. In the distance, on the far side of two sofas that faced one another like opposing armies, a small-boned woman sat in an armchair. She was biting her lips, stitching a linen cloth.

Kitty raised her hand and knocked on the oak doorframe.

Melissa Stokes's eyes narrowed. She made out a shadow, black against the gray, hovering in the doorframe. "Who is that?"

"Beggin' your pardon, ma'am . . ."

Melissa Stokes slid her needle neatly to rest in the linen. She laid the altar cloth on the table beside her. "Would you come into the light, young lady? My eyes are tired."

Kitty moved forward. Beige carpet silenced her feet. The room smelled of roses and floor wax, of largeness and of air that moved.

What struck Melissa Stokes was the girl's posture, her skin.

Melissa Stokes had once had posture and skin like that.

The stranger was smiling at her. Melissa Stokes had not seen a smile in days, not since the shootings. She rose from the armchair and held out a hand. There was a brushing of fingertips.

"If you're from the church . . ." She threw a nod, an apology, toward the unfinished stitching. "I'm behind schedule, I'm afraid."

"No, ma'am. I'm not from the church. I'm from town. My name is Kitty Kellogg."

"Yes, Miss Kellogg?"

"It's about the laundry, ma'am."

"The laundry?" In view of recent events, Melissa Stokes could imagine strangers wishing to discuss many things with her, but laundry was not one of them.

"I thought you might need a laundress, ma'am—with Sally gone."

"Sally—poor Sally—she's gone, then? They frightened her too?" Melissa Stokes's eyes blinked, flicking away confusion. Her feet took a backward step, knowing exactly the position of the chair. She sat. Her fingers touched the armrest, tracing a familiar thread of gold brocade. "They frightened all our girls. It's not right to frighten girls."

Kitty realized Mrs. Stokes did not know why Sally Duncannon had quit. *You don't just live on a hill,* she thought: *you live in the clouds, clouds with money linings.* "No, ma'am," she agreed. "It's not right."

"You're a laundress, you say?" Melissa Stokes stared at Kitty as though it were a sad and unimaginable thing to be a laundress.

"And a good one, ma'am. I'm strong and hard-workin'."

"And you wouldn't be frightened to work for us? You wouldn't be like Sally?"

At that instant Melissa Stokes's life lay in ruins. She had believed in certain things—comfortable things—and now, in the exploding light of an armed attack on a graveyard, she saw she had been wrong. If it had been simply the tragedy, Melissa Stokes might have borne it. Tragedy called up all one's strength. But disorder was another matter. Disorder called up nothing. Half the staff had quit without notice, leaving her three frightened girls to run a thirty-room house. She did not know if she could survive it.

"Sally wasn't frightened, ma'am," the unknown young lady

was saying. "But her brother..." The serene half-smile left something unsaid.

"Her brother, what about him?"

"He was killed, ma'am. In the graveyard."

Melissa Stokes seized her altar cloth. The needle swooped into the stem of a new rose, no matter that the thread was the wrong color.

"We didn't know," Melissa Stokes said after a very long silence. "When my husband asked the governor to help, we had no idea..."

She meant: *It was I who had no idea*. She meant: *I had no idea who or what my husband was; I have an idea now*.

"How could you have known, ma'am? It's not as though you or Mr. Stokes had been there holdin' the rifles, is it?"

Melissa Stokes's fingers slowed their labor. Eagerness carried her forward on her velvet cushion, almost unbalancing her. "I've never touched a gun. I couldn't even shoot a rabbit."

"Me neither, ma'am. I'm scared stiff of guns."

It was a relief, after four days, to have something in common with another human being. Melissa Stokes wanted to ring for tea, for cucumber sandwiches delicious and cool beneath a damp cotton towel; she wanted to sit and chat and find out more about this stranger with the lovely posture and calm green eyes and smooth white skin.

"About the laundry, ma'am. I could start in right away. Today, if you like."

Melissa Stokes looked down at the girl's hands. "But your hands."

The girl's hands offered themselves. "They're experienced, ma'am."

"But you'll ruin them."

"Ruin them?" The girl smiled. "Hands are for workin', ma'am. At least *these* hands are."

"And your family..." Melissa Stokes could not quite order her thoughts. "Do you have a family?"

"There's only my dad, ma'am."

"And is he...was he...in the strike?"

"He wasn't hurt, ma'am."

Gratitude rushed out of Melissa Stokes in a sigh. She hurried to the bell cord. She gave two tugs. "We paid Sally four dollars a week."

"Very kind of you, ma'am."

A silence passed. Melissa Stokes was able to draw breath. A woman in dark gray appeared in the doorway.

"Miss Hagstron," Melissa Stokes said, "this is Kitty Kellogg, from the village. She'll be taking over for Sally."

"But, ma'am, I've already sent to the agency." Miss Hagstrom turned tight-lipped toward the newcomer. For an instant window light flashed like storm lightning in her spectacles. "The new girl will be here tomorrow."

"Then you'll have to telephone the agency and cancel."

Miss Hagstrom sighed. "Very well, ma'am. Come with me, Kitty."


Miss Hagstrom led with a quick step that snapped her skirt behind her, keys jangling at her hip. Kitty followed her through a vaulted dark dining room into a pantry. Miss Hagstrom thrust out an empty hand.

"I'll see your references, please."

"I haven't any," Kitty said.

Miss Hagstrom's eyebrows rippled. "How do I know you're reliable? How do I know you can even do laundry?"

Kitty laid on the meekness. "Please give me a chance, ma'am. You'll see I can do it."

"We're not a charity," Miss Hagstrom said. "And we're not a training school."

A flight of creaking plank steps took them to the cellar. Kitty felt concrete through the soles of her shoes. Feet never touched earth in this house.

They came to a room that smelled of ammonia. There was more space in it than in three company shacks. Miss Hagstrom ran a tapping finger along the washtubs and shelves, explaining. Laundry had to be separated by color and type of clothing. Maids' uniforms were never to be washed with any of the Stokeses' clothes. She explained which loads took bleach, which took none, which had to be scrubbed and which had to soak and which had to be scrubbed and soaked. Mistakes would not be tolerated.

Kitty followed Miss Hagstrom into the drying room, which had a drain in the floor and a dozen clotheslines running wall to wall. When it was raining, Miss Hagstrom said, the wet laundry would be hung here.

She took Kitty upstairs and outside to the servants' garden, which wasn't a garden at all but more clotheslines hidden behind tall hedges. "On sunny days you'll hang laundry here. The sun is strongest between ten and two. So you'll be sure to have the wash hung by ten."

Miss Hagstrom wore a steel pocket watch pinned wrong-side-up to her bosom. She flicked it out with one finger and made a quick face at the time. Kitty hurried behind her into the house again.

"This is the servants' stairway." Miss Hagstrom's gray mesh stocking flashed sinew. "You will never use the front stairs—unless you are cleaning them."

"Beggin' your pardon, Miss Hagstrom: I thought I was hired to do laundry."

Miss Hagstrom wheeled to a stop. "Does the job sound too hard for you, Kitty? The girl from the agency doesn't mind doing a little extra."

They came to the upstairs hallway. Miss Hagstrom placed a hand on a brass doorknob. "You will never enter a room without knocking." Miss Hagstrom knocked and swung the door open.

There was no one in the room, which seemed to Kitty a terrible waste. A bowl of fresh-cut flowers sat on the table. There was a carved mahogany fourposter that a family could have slept in, and a chest of drawers with a mirror you could angle any way you pleased. And if that wasn't mirror enough for you, there was a silver-backed hand mirror lying on a lace doily on the bureau top, next to a silver brush and comb. There were paintings and standing lamps and a marble fireplace with an easy chair drawn up beside it.

"Guest rooms will be made daily when in use. Otherwise, the linen will be changed weekly. You will make the beds with hospital corners. Do you know what a hospital corner is, Kitty?"

"I'll know if you show me, ma'am."

Miss Hagstrom took hold of the bedspread. She yanked it up and exposed a smooth white thigh of sheet. "That is a hospital corner."

Kitty hardly had time to look before Miss Hagstrom ripped the bedding loose.

"Let me see you do one."

Kitty remade the bed. Miss Hagstrom stood frowning.

The floors, Miss Hagstrom said in a sudden rush, were to be waxed once weekly. "And, of course, the bathrooms." Miss

Hagstrom led Kitty through another door. "You will scour the porcelain daily—all the porcelain. The floor as well."

Kitty had never seen such a glorious room for brushing your teeth in. The tub on its lion's claw feet of bronze was large enough for Tyrone Duncannon himself to have stretched out in, and his toes wouldn't near have grazed the end of it. *And it should have been his,* she thought. The sink was so deep and wide you could have waded in it. There were bronze faucets marked "hot" and "cold" and "ice." The mirror took up half a wall. There were so many black and white tiles on the floor you could have had friends in and played twenty games of checkers all at once. There was a flush toilet too, with a brass chain and a polished wood seat that lifted.

*Murder must pay,* Kitty thought. *Lord, it must pay good.*

"Bath linen will be changed and hampers will be emptied daily." Miss Hagstrom's finger searched and flicked an invisible dust ball from the lid of a wicker basket. "Never let dirty clothes pile up."

They returned to the hallway. Miss Hagstrom knocked and opened the shut doors. This was Mrs. Stokes's room; that was Mr. Stokes's room; this was young Mr. Stokes's room. All of them with their own bathrooms. Kitty's knees ached at the thought of all that scrubbing. Around the bend there were three more guest rooms—each one with bath.

"Do I do all them rooms, ma'am?"

"Till we have a full staff."

Kitty wondered why Miss Hagstrom had not thought of sending to the agency for an upstairs maid, or better yet, two dozen of them.

When Miss Hagstrom came to the end of the corridor she stopped and stood silent in the half-light. She looked a long moment at a door no different from any of the others, but she looked at it in a way that suggested it was very different. Kitty wondered uncomfortably what task lay behind the carved oak panels with their gleaming brass knob and hinges.

Finally Miss Hagstrom raised a finger and pointed. "You will have no need to go into this room—ever."

It seemed odd to Kitty that there should be a room that required no cleaning. "Is it a bedroom, ma'am?"

"That is none of your concern."

A last door opened onto a narrow stairway leading to the attic. Miss Hagstrom led. The uneven steps buckled beneath her flat heels. She threw open a door without knocking.

"Servants' bath."

Kitty glimpsed a dim unwindowed closet with a tub no larger than a suitcase.

"You're allowed one bath a week. Don't hog the tub when another girl's waiting."

Miss Hagstrom strode down a dark corridor. The air was stifling. Her shoes clicked hollowly.

"This will be your room."

The tiny room was folded in under the bare beams of the roof. It smelled of camphor, which suggested that if your nose was a detective it smelled of something worse. There was a thin mattress on a low board; a three-legged stool; a window just large enough for a cat to crawl through; an overhead electric bulb with a string dangling from it.

*I've lived through worse,* Kitty thought; *and I've got an indoor light at last.*

"You're not to bring food or drink here, ever. Do you smoke?"

"No, ma'am."

Disappointment flickered in Miss Hagstrom's spectacles, as though she'd have liked to lay down one last rule. "Did Mrs. Stokes tell you your wage?"

"She said I'd get four dollars a week."

"You'll get four dollars a week, and if you want to stay employed, you'll give fifty cents of it to me."

Kitty's dad was waiting up for her when she got home to the shack that night. "And what are you doin' in your mother's dress?" he said. The day's growth of beard stubbled his face like a snow on a meadow.

"She left it to me, didn't she?" Kitty said.

"She never wore that dress except to church."

"Where I been's just as important as church."

"And where was that?"

"I been to get me a new job."

He studied her, eyes lidded with concentration. "What kind of work do you have to look that pretty for?"

"I couldn't go lookin' like I was fresh from the pigsty, could I?"

"You'll take off your mother's dress."

He reached as though to rip it off her. She stepped clear.

"You and your oily hands. You'll get me as black as that Bible of yours."

"A little black wouldn't hurt. The whole town's in mournin', child."

"I'm grievin' just as bitter as you ever did for Mama. Only I haven't the time to sit and wail."

"Kitty, where the hell have you been? Have you forgot your mother and your church?"

"I ain't forgot nothin'. And the church don't tell me what I can wear, not till I'm a nun, which, please God, I'll never be."

"Have you been drinkin', child?"

"Hell, no."

"The way you talk back. The way you look at me. Somethin's changed you."

"And don't we all change? You sit there with your Bible—too scared to touch liquor, too scared to look at a woman, too scared to stand up and ask for a decent wage. Don't tell me you haven't changed plenty. I got a right to change just as much as you."

Kitty slid her suitcase out from under the bunk. She snapped it open and began laying her clothes into it.

"And what do you think you're doin' now?" her dad said.

"Packin' my things."

"Movin' out, are you?"

"You'll be glad for the extra space."

"Not so quick, child. Where are you goin'?"

"I told you. I've got a new job."

His eyes jabbed, sharp and sudden. "Do you sleep over on this job?"

"It ain't a whorehouse, if that's what you're wonderin'."

"There's a lot worse places than a whorehouse. And I *am* wonderin'."

"I'm going to work at the Stokes place. Doin' laundry and such."

Her dad's face gaped in slow astonishment. "The devil you will."

"The devil I won't. What's the difference workin' in their store or in their cellar? *You* work for them, don't you?"

Anger rose in her dad's face, a scarlet tide inching up from his undershirt. "You won't sleep under their roof. I'll not permit it."

"I ain't walkin' eight miles a day just so's you can watch me sleep."

"Damned right you ain't. You'll stay right here where you belong."

Kitty looked at her dad. The distance between them was only a few feet, but she knew at that instant it would last forever. She said, "I'm takin' this job."

Red rage bloated her dad's eyes. "I forbid you!"

"Take it easy," she said. "I'll be back. They're givin' me Thursday afternoons. And Sunday mornin' for Mass."

Her dad spat on the dirt that had been the floor of their home. "Go to them and you don't need to come back to this house, Kitty Kellogg."

At that moment she saw him differently, with a sadness that surprised her: He was an old man, tired and dirty. He was a failure. He had no money, no possessions, no friends. Over the years he'd squandered them all. As for kin, they were dead or back in Ireland; there'd never even been a letter. He had no one but her, and she was leaving. She tried to imagine him, alone with his Bible, saying grace over a can of beans.

*This can't be me,* she thought, *doing this, letting it happen.*

And yet she'd never felt more real or solid or certain of herself.

"All right," she said. "I won't come back."

She had taken two steps into the night when she heard the door slam shut behind her.

# Chapter 4

AND SO KITTY DUNCANNON went to the Stokeses.

The Stokes mansion was a house of corridors and stairways and endless darknesses; of murmurs and whispers and silence. For all its electric light and bustle of servants, it did not strike Kitty as a happy house. It stood exiled on its hill, lonely and brooding behind its guarded fence. At its heart, beneath the gleam of polished wood and the ringing of crystal and the soft touch of Persian carpet, lay something dangerous and silent as a grudge.

Tempers were heard to flare in the dining room. Doors were often slammed. A mysterious dissatisfaction seemed to drive the Stokeses. *Murderers are never satisfied,* Kitty thought. And the justice of that thought sustained her through all the exhaustion of her work.

For exhausting it was. If she had not been young and strong, Kitty did not know how she could have managed it all.

She had to begin the wash at five in the morning, an hour before the servants' breakfast, to get through all the clothes and linen that had piled up. The soaking and scrubbing took most of the morning and sometimes the afternoon too. Ironing could go on well into evening.

Between the scrubbing and the ironing, she had to take care
of her upstairs duties, and she had to be sure she didn't disturb
the Stokeses. They slept till different hours and napped at
different times and shut themselves into their rooms unpre-
dictably. She found herself running up and down the servants'
stairs two dozen times a day, knocking on Melissa Stokes's
door to determine if her mistress was still asleep, rushing back
to the cellar for some piece of lace-frilled lingerie that was in
danger of soaking too long.

At the end of the day she would fling herself down on her
attic bed, aching in every nerve and fiber. There were nights
when her body despaired and she would wonder if there was
any sense or hope to the course she had set herself.

She would pray for strength. She did not know if it was
God or the devil who answered, but every morning she awoke
and found she had the strength for just one more day.

Once, hurrying past the locked door on the second story,
Kitty heard a sound. She had a load of fresh sheets in her arms.
She stopped, held her breath, and listened.

The sound came again, a heavy shuffle like a sick dog
knocking against furniture. It came from behind the door.

Kitty set her sheets on the table. She put her ear against the
carved oak panel. Very faintly, she could make out sobbing.
She cupped a hand around her ear, pressed hard against the
wood. She was able to make out a woman's voice, so bent and
pitiable as to be almost unrecognizable. There was a spill of
shattering glass, a carpet-deadened thump.

Kitty held herself rigid against the door. She tested the
doorknob. It would not turn. She listened again, but there was
no sound, no movement, only silence.

When she asked the other girls about the forbidden door,
they shrugged. Trina thought it was a storage room for family
mementos. Elsie said it had been the nursery of the daughter
who had died. In any case, the girls agreed, Kitty ought to be
grateful that there was one less room to dust and scrub.

In great houses servants always gossip about masters. Stories are passed down in whispers. They become legends, and
it isn't always easy to tell how much truth there is in any of
them. But Kitty saw things and heard things and this is the
story she was later able to piece together:

In the last century, at the time of the oil strikes in northern Pennsylvania, John Stokes Sr. was a young man with no more than a hundred dollars to his name. But he had a sort of cleverness different from other people's. He bought the cheap, barren land near the oil fields and he mortgaged it to build storage tanks.

Pennsylvania gushed forth oil, too much to be hauled by horse and barrel. John Stokes stored the surplus in his tanks. The more the surplus, the more tanks he built and the more he charged for storage. The land kept gushing forth oil that no one could haul, and John Stokes foreclosed his customers. He took their land and their oil at a tenth of their value, as he took all things.

In those days Pennsylvania was the only oil anyone knew of in America, and John Stokes possessed what was later called a monopoly. When people began running out of oil for their lamps and stoves, John Stokes raised the price sky high. He went to the banks and borrowed on his tanks and bought more oil land and raised the price even higher.

He offered the railroads four times their going rates to build lines to his tanks and ship his oil to market. In their haste for his money, the railroads duplicated one another's routes. John Stokes then said he would ship by the cheapest carrier. The railroads had to cut their rates to the bone just to get their investment back. Why, John Stokes even had to lend them money, taking bonds for collateral, and eventually, of course, he had to foreclose—which was how he got into railroads.

When there were oil strikes in Texas, John Stokes again bought worthless land and built tanks. Oil men were smarter now. Some held on and waited for the railroads. But John Stokes was the railroads' biggest customer. If they shipped a rival's oil he made them pay him a whopping commission. The railroads had to raise their price to the rival, and when the rival could not pay and went bankrupt, John Stokes bought him out.

Eventually, John Stokes owned Texas oil lands too.

He bought these lands in a hundred different company names. By the time people realized one man owned all the oil in North America, Henry Ford had invented the motorcar and John Stokes was buying up all the oil in South America and Asia. He was many times a millionaire—some said billionaire—by the time he was forty, and he was hated.

It was around this time that Melissa Barton entered the

story. The Bartons were gentlefolk whose money came from grain and dairy. They'd had their land for three generations, and the town of Bartonville was named for them.

One day a little black puddle was noticed in one of the cow pastures. Like the rest of the country, the Bartons went crazy for oil. It turned out they were floating on a lake of it. They borrowed. They put up 50 oil rigs, and 48 of those came in gushers.

But for some reason, though oil was fetching a good price elsewhere, the market turned suddenly bad in their own part of the country. Worse yet, the railroads quadrupled their rates, and the Bartons couldn't afford to ship to where the price was good. Overnight they were cleaned out, broke.

Within the month a middle-aged man in a plain black suit— so plain it was almost shabby—came to the door of the Bartons' mansion hat in hand. Since they'd had to let go their help, it was Mrs. Barton herself who admitted the stranger. He had the bright eyes of a vulture, and Mrs. Barton in later years said she'd taken him for a preacher of some fierce Puritan sect.

He came straight to the point. He had bought up the Bartons' land and their oil and their debts, and he wished to marry their daughter Melissa.

The Barton girl was, at that time, a beauty. She knew music and flowers and French, and she was engaged to a handsome Army general. The engagement had to be broken off. After a suitable period, Melissa Barton married John Stokes Sr.

He built a mansion bigger than her parents', and she rarely went out of it. A daughter was born, and died. A son was born, and he did not die. They named him Johnny.

John Stokes Jr. had the best governesses and the best clothes and the best schools. He inherited from his mother a tendency toward the arts, especially drawing. This did not please his father, but it was tolerated. Johnny was allowed to study art in the university, and he was even sent to Paris for a year to the school of fine arts there.

It was understood that art was to be no more than a hobby, and Johnny eventually came home and studied business administration. He became engaged to the daughter of a New York banking family. It was understood, too, that he would one day take over the management of the family enterprises.

But one day the Bartonville workers went on strike and there was a massacre in the graveyard. Only a handful dead, but to the papers it was a massacre. The banker's daughter broke the engagement and Johnny Stokes began changing—changing, the servants said, in odd and mysterious ways.

The end result of all this Kitty could see with her own eyes. The Stokeses were not a family.

When he wasn't in one of his offices in Bartonville or Youngstown or Cleveland or New York, John Stokes Sr. shut himself up in his office in the ground floor of his home, a great dark room of oak filing cabinets and bookshelves. The never-ending ringing of his telephones could be heard throughout the house. He had girls to take the phone calls, girls to take dictation, girls to receive visitors. Kitty often saw men in dark suits balancing briefcases on their laps, waiting on the hallway sofa for an audience with the man who owned all the oil in America.

Every day but Sunday, the mailman without fail brought two full sacks of mail to the house, one in the morning, one in the afternoon. John Stokes Sr. didn't smile and, except for the odd hello, he didn't bother talking with the servants. He walked with a quick step for an old man. He read his mail at the table. He was a very, very busy person.

From what Kitty observed, Melissa Stokes was not a busy person at all. She drifted from room to room, parlor in the morning, library in the afternoon, music room after dinner. Sometimes she shut the door and sometimes she did not, but whether the door was open or shut she was always pale and silent and alone.

She wore lovely clothes, as though she might possibly go out on a visit. But the only visit she ever made was on sunny days, when she would put on a sunbonnet and overalls and work bare-handed in her three favorite rosebeds, which the gardeners were forbidden to touch. Rainy days she might take breakfast in bed and not appear dressed till lunchtime or even dinner.

And then there were peculiar days when she would vanish into the locked room at the rear of the second story and miss meals entirely. Mornings after these days, Kitty found that Melissa Stokes's bed had not even been slept in.

Johnny Stokes was the closest thing there was to a cheerful Stokes.

From what Kitty could see, he didn't spend any time at home at all. He was always putting on striped blazers and colored shirts and roaring off in his sports car. He made a habit of missing dinner, and he'd sit in the kitchen eating warmed leftovers, trying to joke with the servants, who always laughed politely. He'd smell of peppermint mouthwash, and Kitty wondered if it was to keep his parents from sniffing bootleg liquor on his breath.

It took Kitty longer than she'd planned to catch Johnny Stokes's eye. In fact, he didn't seem to notice her at all until her second week on the job.

She knocked on his bedroom door, balancing a bundle of fresh sheets and towels on one arm. There was no answer. She opened the door. The room was dark. She crossed to a window and raised the shade. She turned and then she saw the bed and stopped.

The blanket lay in a heap on the floor. A gold wristwatch and a ring sparkled in the ashtray on the bedside table. She could see the long curve of a body beneath the bedsheet, a thick spill of hair on the pillow.

She stepped closer, stealing a glance at Johnny Stokes. His lips were parted in a smile that was not quite happy. She thought, *so that's what a murderer's son looks like.*

Suddenly one of his eyes was open. It had the sly glint of a new coin. "What are you staring at?"

Kitty jumped. "I'm sorry, sir. I thought the room was empty. Seein' as you're usually up and about by now."

Johnny Stokes propped himself up on one elbow. The sheet fell away. His chest was pale and slender. "You've memorized my habits, have you?"

"No, sir," she stammered. "But I knocked, and I didn't hear any sound. I didn't mean to disturb you, sir. Beggin' your pardon, I'll come back and make your bed later."

Johnny Stokes shook blond hair away from his eyes. "Wait a minute. What's your name?"

"Kitty, sir. Kitty Kellogg."

He gave her a long squint, as though his eye had picked out something remarkable just below her nose. "You're new, aren't you?"

"Yes, sir. I've been here a week."

"What happened to the other girl, what's her name—the chubby one?" He swung his legs out of bed. He was wearing silk pajama bottoms. His feet fumbled into their patent-leather slippers. "Did Hagstrom finally give her the sack?"

"I don't know, sir." Kitty edged toward the door. "I'm sorry to interrupt your sleep, sir. It won't happen again."

"Kitty."

"Yes, sir?"

"Come here."

Kitty approached the bed. Johnny Stokes sat looking at her. At first Kitty felt an uneasiness at standing in front of a half-naked stranger. His gaze was pale and blue and it did not leave her face. Gradually the uneasiness left her as she realized he must like her looks. She was used to men liking her looks, though she was not used to waiting while they fiddled with their watch straps.

Johnny Stokes moved the ashtray, making space. "You can put your sheets there on the table."

"Thank you, sir." Kitty set down the linen.

"Give me ten minutes." Johnny Stokes stood. A heartbeat flexed the narrow ridges of his chest. He seemed very tall to her, standing so close. He smelled overpoweringly of cleanness. "I'll be dressed and out of your way."

"I didn't mean to rush you, sir."

"It's a lucky thing somebody rushes me. I'd sleep my life away otherwise."

"Please take you time, sir." Kitty moved to the door. "I got plenty else to do."

"Kitty."

"Yes, sir?"

"It's nice to see a smile around the house."

Kitty had seen enough of Johnny Stokes's comings and goings to know that he got home around twelve-thirty every night. There was only one road that passed the house, Route 12. The way he drove that sports car, she could figure he passed the Bartonville intersection a little after twelve-fifteen.

Her second afternoon off work, Kitty stayed out late. At midnight she was walking along the highway. The night was cold. A few solitary cars swept by, flashing their headlights. Two of them slowed but Kitty smiled and shook her head, *No, thanks*.

She must have walked a mile or so when from far in the distance a moving fan of light scooped her out. The trim shadow of a sports car neared. One of its headlights was busted. It slowed to keep pace with her and the horn tooted.

Kitty shaded her eyes. She could see a profile behind the windshield: a flat-brimmed hat, a chin half-angled in her direction.

The white wheels came crunching to a stop. The driver leaned across the seat and flipped the passenger door open.

"Hello, Kitty." Johnny Stokes lifted his hat in salutation. His eyes rested on her. They were puffy and bloodshot. "Heading back to the house?"

"If my legs'll hold out."

"Save your legs and hop in." His voice was faintly slurred.

Kitty slid into the car. It smelled of leather upholstery and of Johnny Stokes's shaving lotion. There was another smell too, something faint and sour that came in waves when he turned to look at her. He was smiling, his mouth a gash of boldness against the delicacy of his face.

The unexpected forward leap of the car flattened Kitty against the seat. Trees blurred past in a scream of wrong gears. Johnny Stokes's hand stabbed at the gearshift knob.

"What are you doing out so late?" he said. "Or doesn't a gentleman ask?"

"I was visitin' a friend in Bartonville. We got to talkin' and I lost track of the time."

He tilted his head, appraising her. "A boyfriend?"

Kitty's eye skimmed pine trees leaning into the night, slanting their branches into the window of the car's passing. "My girlfriend."

The road was unsteady in the windshield. Johnny Stokes held a pickling jar between his knees. He worked the top off one-handed. He offered the jar to her.

"What's that?" she said warily.

"They say it's whiskey, but if you believe that you believe in Santa Claus."

The night surged toward them, a black river dotted with sparse headlights. Kitty took the jar and pretended to sip. She handed it back.

Johnny Stokes put the rim of the jar to his smile and poured. A clear yellow liquid ran down the corners of his mouth. The sour smell came again. Kitty rolled down the window. The breeze spooned her hair toward him. He put the jar back between his legs. He did not screw the top back on.

"Pretty horrible stuff, isn't it?" he said.

"I've tasted worse," Kitty said, smiling at him.

"You're a game girl, Kitty."

The road began a curving ascent. Johnny Stokes's toe danced on the gas pedal. The tires hummed, taking nibbles of the white dividing line. At seventy miles an hour the highway became a tangle of ridges and turns.

"Curious what I'm doing out so late?" he asked.

"None of my business."

"I've been to Medford."

Kitty had heard of Medford. It was a college town forty miles away. Rich kids went there, stupid rich kids who couldn't get into the colleges back East.

"A fellow called Howie runs a speakeasy there," Johnny Stokes said. "I got looped."

Cool blasts rippled the shoulder of Kitty's dress. "You don't look looped to me."

"That's because I'm a good driver," Johnny Stokes said. "I take that back. Tonight I'm a lousy driver. I ran the car into a fence post back there. Busted one of the lights. My father will murder me."

Kitty flung her mind into a calculation. "Your father doesn't need to know," she said.

"Are you kidding? This car was a graduation present. Cost him a packet. He'll know. And he'll know I was drunk."

"I can get the light fixed for you," Kitty said.

Johnny Stokes laughed. "Kitty, I almost believe you could do it. You're a really game girl, aren't you."

He put his hand on Kitty's knee, but he had no time to squeeze or pat. They were at a railroad crossing and he had not bothered to slow. The car took the ties in two wild slaps. The steering wheel spun free and he had to seize it in both hands to bring it back under control.

A lightness bubbled up in Kitty's lungs and she wondered if Johnny Stokes was going to kill them, him and his stupid drunk driving. She pushed her feet against the angled felt on the floor. She braced her mouth in a smile.

"Kitty," Johnny Stokes said, and he sounded serious now, "is it true you're from Bartonville?"

"I sure am."

"Do you have family there?"

"Only my dad. He works on the oil rigs."

Johnny Stokes shook his head. "I'm sorry about the way Dad handled the strike."

"I'm sorry too."

"I wish I could apologize, but I don't suppose it would make any difference, would it?"

She looked into his face with the pale-blond hair swept back from the forehead, the eyes blue and beseeching. She saw it wasn't just Kitty Kellogg he wanted in his drunkenness, it was forgiveness as well, and if he could get them both in one package, so much the better.

"We're havin' such a nice drive," she said softly. "Let's not talk about it."

He nodded, humbled, and they did not talk for the rest of the drive. She could feel his mind thrashing, and she was almost certain she'd gotten her hook into him.

A night guard in a gray Pinkerton uniform opened the estate gates to them. The gravel drive was bone-white in the moonlight. The mansion towered against the sky. Shadows played over the pillared facade.

Johnny Stokes swung the car into the garage. He cut the motor and sat very straight. He belched and then he opened the door and stuck a foot out. He lurched badly, and she walked behind him.

A flagstone path led across the slope of lawn up to the front porch. Johnny Stokes bent sideways at the steps. He leaned against a pillar and vomited into the flowerbed, staining his lapels and shirt front.

Kitty stood ready to catch him, but he did not fall. When he stopped retching she stooped and found a rock. She stirred the vomit into the earth until it was invisible.

"Why don't you take off your jacket and shirt?" she said. She took his clothes and rolled them into a lump, clean side out. She steered him up the porch steps.

He stood at the door, trying to blunder his key into the lock. She took over and opened the door for him. She pushed him up the stairs. His torso was white and racked like a medieval saint's, icy beneath her hands. Little spasms kept shadowing the hollows between his ribs.

She got him to his room and sat him on the edge of the bed. He stared at some phantom four feet in front of his eyes. She dropped his clothes into the bathroom hamper.

"You'd better lie down," she said.

Gripping her hand in his, he obeyed. "Kitty, you're a game girl."

"Sure I'm a game girl, and these pants'll be ruined if you

don't let go of me so I can hang them up."

She hung up his pants. When she looked at him again he was asleep and he was smiling.

Kitty set her alarm clock an hour early. She got up at four the next morning. She quickly washed and dressed and crept down the servants' stairs. She borrowed the bicycle that Tony, the yard man, had left in the toolshed. She waved good morning to the Pinkerton man at the gatehouse and bicycled into Bartonville.

Dawn was coming and the oil rigs stood out black as gallows against the blood-washed sky. It was practically day by the time she reached Sam the blacksmith's place on the far side of town. Though she had politely told Sam Anderson "no" on two occasions, she suspected he still had an eye for her.

Sam slept in a back room at his shop. It was a tumbledown place where he put shoes on horses and hammered dents out of fenders and sharpened plows for farmers who hadn't been pushed out of the country by oil. Kitty rapped on the window. Sam came to the door rubbing his eyes, one hand holding up his long johns.

"Sam, you have to help me," Kitty pleaded. "We've had an emergency out at the Stokes place. Can you come right now?" She put a hand on his arm, clinging, and she could feel the muscle in him turn to butter.

"Sure, Kitty." The blacksmith got into his dungarees. He put some tools into his pickup truck along with the bicycle. He was still rubbing his eyes when Kitty showed him the broken headlight in the Stokeses' garage. She promised he'd get his money next payday. She closed the doors so the hammering wouldn't carry to the big house and she hurried back to the kitchen.

Emma, the cook, was stirring the servants' oatmeal. She asked where Kitty had been, so red-cheeked and breathless at this hour.

"I don't know why," Kitty said, "but this mornin' I just had to see the sunrise."

Emma grunted, as though one sunrise was pretty much the same as another.

Johnny Stokes came swaying down to the cellar that morning while Kitty was measuring bleach into the laundry. "I'm sorry about last night," he said. His eyes were feverish with hangover and she could see him wince at the clang of a washtub lid. "I made a damned fool of myself."

"You did no such thing, sir," Kitty said.

"Please don't call me 'sir.'"

"Well, Mr. Stokes, what'll I call you then?"

"Anything but 'sir.' I don't feel like a sir. I feel like an idiot."

"Doesn't make a man an idiot to take a drink now and then."

"I was an idiot to wreck that car."

"You didn't wreck anythin'. You bent one of the headlights a little and I've taken care of that."

A questioning squint came into his eye. "You took care of it, Kitty?"

She gave a little half-laugh. "I'm no good with headlights, but I got a friend who is, and he was glad to help."

Johnny Stokes tilted his head as though to see her at a clearer angle. "A boyfriend?"

"If you mean, is he my fiancé, I ain't got a fiancé yet and it ain't likely I ever will."

"Why do you say that, Kitty?"

"Well, a girl ain't had a proposal by the time she's twenty-one, she gets to wonderin' if she ever will."

"I can't believe you're twenty-one."

"Indeed I am," she lied. "Three years past consent and a full-fledged votin' citizen, that's me."

"And no man's ever asked you to marry him?"

"Marriage ain't everythin', is it?" She gave him a long, smiling glance. "There's plenty you can enjoy in life without a priest sayin' 'I now pronounce you.'"

Johnny Stokes stared at her and she could see his tongue probing his cheek out like a tiny mouse in his mouth. She began washboarding her towels.

"Would you mind if I sketched you, Kitty?"

"Sketch me?"

"Sometimes I do little charcoals and pastels." He spoke in a tight, quick rush. "I don't know if I could get you down, but I'd like to try."

"You can do what you want with me," Kitty laughed. "So long as it don't get in the way of my work."

"It won't get in the way at all. I want to sketch you at the washtub. The way you are now."

"Fine by me," Kitty said. "You know where to find me. And when."

\*   \*   \*

The next morning Johnny Stokes awoke with only half a hangover. He took his sketch pad and his box of colored chalks out of the closet. They were childish things and he knew he should be reading his business texts, but he craved one morning of childish freedom.

He went down to the cellar.

Kitty was already at her tub, sleeves rolled up, arms sudsy to the elbow. She smiled when she saw him. "Well, Mr. Stokes, you weren't kiddin' me, were you."

His eye flicked over her smooth cheeks and the curve of her hips and her long arched calves. His heart banged shut in him like a slammed door and for an instant he could not get his breath.

"Keep moving," he said in the formal voice artists use to distance themselves from a model's nakedness. "Just act naturally."

He pulled a chair into the light. He propped the pad on his crossed knees. He took a piece of dark chalk and began rounding the tip, drawing back-and-forth lines, and slowly his breath came back to him.

"Pretend I'm not here," he said.

"And why should I pretend that? You don't think I get company down here every day, do you?"

So they talked.

She told him about her family, all of them dead now but her father in the village. She told him about her friends and the company store and Saturday nights when the boys would get a jar of moonshine and a couple of bottles of Coca-Cola and take the girls to the church social and Father Jack would have no idea they were all drunk. The life she described was a sad, monotonous thing, yet she spoke of it with such humor and color that Johnny Stokes found himself smiling and telling her about his own family—oddities like his mother's prize rosebeds that no gardener was allowed to touch; or his father's eight telephones in the Youngstown office, all ringing at once and his father so old-fashioned he didn't dare answer any of them himself but had to hire eight secretaries. He talked about college. He talked about art, which he loved, and fraternities, which he could take or leave, and when he mentioned girls he found himself hinting that they'd all in their different ways disappointed him.

He did not tell her he had been engaged and the girl had dropped him. That slap still stung, and it had changed his standards in women in a way that he was only dimly beginning to grasp.

He knew he liked Kitty and he knew it was odd that he should. After all, she was one of what history professors and union leaders called "the people," and he was not. But he was content to sit in the cellar with his chalks and sketch pad, trying to get her down on paper, talking, and he was not about to question contentment. There was little enough of it in his days.

Three mornings in a row he covered page after page with chalk. And there were partial successes. He found he could get the red hair curling in little tongues at her shoulders. He could get the wide-set green eyes, cat-like and alert even when the eyelids seemed drowsy. He could capture the instant of her body bent over the tub in the long curve of a dancer, suggest the swaying line of her hips when she lifted the basket of damp linen.

But none of the sketches satisfied him. He could not express, he could not find the essence of her. Something about her gave him a tiny thrill in the rib cage, and it escaped his understanding just as it escaped his colored chalks.

He thought perhaps the light was to blame. "I'd like to sketch you in the sun," he said. "Do you ever go outside?"

"Of course I go outside," she laughed. "You don't think I dry these sheets by blowin' on 'em, do you?"

The next day he sketched her outside, behind the hedges where webs of clotheslines stretched. The wind flung her hair out, making dark-red stripes on the sheets. It molded her skirt to her body.

"Do you know what I wish, Kitty?" he said. "I wish you'd stop calling me Mr. Stokes and call me Johnny. Mr. Stokes sounds like my father, and I'm not like him at all. Couldn't you call me Johnny, the way I call you Kitty?"

She smoothed a sheet out on the line and clamped it down with clothespins, anchoring it against the wind. "You call me Kitty because I'm a servant."

"I call you Kitty because I like you."

She looked at him sharply, and then she bent quickly to scoop another armful of dripping sheet from the basket. She did not answer.

"Does it embarrass you?" he asked.

She spoke through a mouthful of clothespins. "How can you like me? You don't know me."

"I know every curve and color in you," Johnny Stokes said. "I've got a good eye. Trained in France."

She stood tapping a clothespin against a thoughtful frown. She was almost certain she had hooked him now and she knew better than to risk losing the catch by reeling him in too quickly. "Sometimes, Mr. Stokes, I'm not a hundred percent sure what you're talkin' about. And neither are you."

"We both know exactly what I'm talking about."

He looked straight at her, not even blinking or blushing. *Give him one thing*, she thought: *he's got nerve*.

She stood shaking her head. "What if your dad's watchin' us this very minute?"

"Father wouldn't waste the time. Time is money."

"Well, your dad wouldn't want you flirtin' with a servant girl, I'll tell you that."

Johnny Stokes frowned. "Is that all it is to you, flirting?"

"Flirtin's a good word. And as good a way to pass a mornin' as any."

A terrible longing melancholy descended on Johnny Stokes. "I'm sorry you feel that way," he said. He shut his sketch pad. He put his chalks back in their box. His mouth was dry and there was a sudden ache in the bottom of his stomach. She had hurt him.

When Kitty went to Johnny Stokes's room the following morning, she found a portrait propped against the dresser mirror. She laid down her linens and broom and dustpan. She stepped back and she stood a long, staring moment.

In a way, the face in the portrait was hers.

The chin held high, the arched nostrils, the hair swept back from the forehead—these matched the features she saw in the mirror. But the expression puzzled her. The lips smiled in a way that suggested not so much humor as tolerance. The eyes, alert behind narrowed lids, stared out with a pride that verged on haughtiness. She had never, in any mirror or photograph, seen that expression on her face. But she had to admit that she had felt it inside her, wanting to come out, once or twice. And she was astonished that Johnny Stokes's eye had detected it.

Strangest of all, he had not dressed her in her uniform. Instead, he had given her a gown that was totally make-believe—emerald green with a texture like velvet, off-the-shoulders with puffed sleeves. It was almost a costume. A great ruby brooch, crusted with tiny diamonds, dangled at her breasts.

She bent near the portrait. This was no sketch, but a finished drawing, every detail sharp and real as a snapshot. He must have put hours into it. Did he see her that way, she wondered, a lord's lady from some other century?

There was a sudden movement behind her and Johnny Stokes's voice said, "What's the verdict?" He was standing, dressed, in the bathroom doorway. He was smiling. "If you like it you can have it."

"It's—strange," Kitty said. "It doesn't seem real."

"But it's all real." Johnny Stokes came forward and his finger touched the green dress. "The gown is my grandmother's. On the Barton side. She's wearing it in a portrait we keep in the attic. The brooch is my mother's. She never wears it. But it goes with the gown. And they go with you, don't you think?"

Kitty felt a flush inching up from her maid's collar. "I think maybe you're pokin' fun at me."

"You can only poke fun at people who aren't aware. But you're aware, Kitty. Look at the portrait. Look at those eyes. They see everything. And look at the mouth. It tells nothing. It just smiles ever so slightly."

"I suppose it's a good picture," Kitty said uneasily. "But I don't care for it."

"Why not?"

"It's me in a way, but it's not the me I want people to see."

"That's a high compliment. It means I've stumbled on a piece of the truth. You stumbled on a truth about me yesterday. And it hurt me very much."

"I never meant to hurt you, Mr. Stokes."

"You told me I was flirting with you."

Anger flared in her. "Well, weren't you?" She was fed up with him and his grinning college-boy games, his lying pictures and sly smiles.

"Yes, I was flirting. And it was wrong of me. Because you're better than that, Kitty. You're more than just a servant girl—if there is such a thing as 'just a servant girl.'"

*Now he's going to tell me all men are created equal*, she thought. *Thanks a million, Johnny Stokes.*

"And I'm more than just a rich man's son," he said. "At least I hope so. I'm your friend. And I want you to be mine. I want you to call me Johnny. Not Mr. Stokes, not sir. Johnny. Can't you do that one little thing for me?"

She was calm now, but she was worried. He'd gotten her angry and she didn't like that. Anger meant loss of control. Anger meant you cared. She didn't want to care about him, not in any way, good or bad.

"If I called you Johnny, they'd sack me in a minute."

"You don't have to call me by my first name in front of other people. But when we're alone, like this, can't I be Johnny to you?"

"And when are we goin' to be alone like this? I got no business in your bedroom, not with you standin' here!"

He put on a soothing tone, but she sensed it was meant to tease. "Come on, Kitty—do I make you that uncomfortable?"

"That's what you're wantin' to do, ain't it?"

Johnny Stokes's mouth smiled at one corner. "Don't you like me at all?"

"Mr. Stokes, I *need* this job." She knew she was handling it wrong but she couldn't help herself. "If you get me fired, I'll—"

He gripped her wrist. "Then call me Johnny, damn it!"

She tried to jerk free. But for all the skinny look of him he was strong. His fingers dug in tight. She did not know at that instant if she was still playing a role or if she truly feared for her job. Real tears came to her eyes and her voice was tight with begging.

"Please let me go—*please, Johnny.*"

He did not let her go. He pulled her toward him. His lips touched her forehead. It was a solemn kiss, like a token between adult and child. And she realized, suddenly, that they had crossed the first boundary.

"There," he whispered. "Was that so bad?"

"No, Johnny. That wasn't so bad."

She pulled back, smiling. And then she froze. In the mirror she saw Miss Hagstrom, scowling in the open doorway.

"I beg your pardon, sir." Miss Hagstrom took two swift steps into the room. "But it looks like a storm coming up, and Kitty's left the wash hanging outdoors."

"I'll see to it, ma'am," Kitty said quickly.

Miss Hagstrom's jaw was set like a hatchet in a log. She did not step aside. Kitty had to make herself small and duck around her.

Miss Hagstrom tipped a nod toward the picture on the dresser. "I see you're drawing again, sir."

"Pastels." Johnny Stokes said. "It's Kitty. I hope you don't mind my borrowing her."

"Kitty, is it?" Miss Hagstrom said. "Yes, I suppose it could be. Lovely green, sir. Flatters her."

"I think she flatters it."

"That could be too. If you'll excuse me, sir, I have to be seeing to lunch."

Miss Hagstrom saw to lunch. She saw to the afternoon housework. She saw to dinner. All the while rage was building a wall at the edges of her mind. By evening the wall was so high her thoughts could not get past it. She remembered the other times, the other girls, and her stomach turned over.

She went to her room and she lit a candle. She placed her grandfather's Swedish Lutheran Bible on her lap. Her thoughts battered the wall that rage had built but they could not breach a hole in it. She opened the Bible but her eyes could not see the print.

She lay down and in her mind she went over what she had seen and pieced together: the meetings in the cellar, the laughing in the back yard, the kiss in the bedroom. And she was certain of what she had sensed from the first: Kitty Kellogg had aims.

Hedda Hagstrom had been with the Stokeses two decades, and she had seen Master Johnny grow from a laughing tot into a tall strong man almost worthy of his parents. She had seen worthless girls throw themselves at Johnny Stokes. When it had happened under this roof she had dealt with it as ruthlessly as she would a blot on a carpet. She knew, in this case, exactly what had to be done.

When her watch hands pointed to two in the morning, she tiptoed down to the pantry. She unlocked the silver cupboard and she found the serving platter that had been Mrs. Stokes's tenth anniversary present from a chairman of the board of the Erie-Lackawanna Railway. It was a fine piece of work, solid silver and almost flat.

She took the platter upstairs. The next day, while the girls were working, she slid it under the mattress of Kitty Kellogg's bed.

At three in the afternoon she summoned the girls into the pantry. She lined them up against one wall. She strode in front of them like a general. She pointed to a cabinet door.

"Which of you," she asked, and her voice crackled with righteousness, "stole Mrs. Stokes's Thanksgiving turkey platter from that cabinet?"

One by one, the girls each denied having done it. Their voices were shaky, their denials weak. Miss Hagstrom looked them in the eye, Emma and Lucy and Kitty and Connie, a hard accusing stab of a glance for each of them. One by one they recoiled, like the culprits they were.

"Well, since you're all so innocent," Miss Hagstrom said, "you'll have no objections if I search your bedrooms."

The girls gave one another trapped looks and shook their heads. Miss Hagstrom saw that Kitty Kellogg was just as white-faced as the others and she was pleased.

She went to the music room and explained the situation to Melissa Stokes, who was seated at the piano. Melissa Stokes's eyes pinched with sudden pain. The two women climbed the stairs to the attic. Miss Hagstrom searched the girls' rooms. She discovered the missing platter in the fourth room, beneath Kitty Kellogg's mattress. She held it up. Silver flashed.

Melissa Stokes watched from the musty corridor. She did not want to see. Her hand was at her throat, fidgeting for pearls that were not there. She stared at the slanting wall with its naked beams.

"There's no insulation," she said, surprised.

Kitty Kellogg was summoned to the drawing room. Melissa Stokes stood before the window. Her hands were a nervous tangle behind her back.

"Do you deny you stole this platter?" Miss Hagstrom cried. "Do you deny you hid it under your mattress and intended to sell it?"

"I deny that."

"I'm sorry, Kitty." Melissa Stokes's voice was weary with the resignation of the betrayed. "But I saw it with my own eyes."

"I have never stolen anything." Kitty stared straight at Miss Hagstrom.

"I've no choice," Melissa Stokes sighed. "Pack your bags.

Miss Hagstrom will give you your wages. You may have dinner but you may not spend another night in this house."

Rage ripped at Kitty's insides. She unhooked her two dresses from the clothesline she had strung beneath the rafters of her tiny room. One she put on. The other she placed with her few possessions in her cardboard suitcase. It was a shabby old case, thin and worn as though mice had been nibbling at the corners. It had belonged to her mother. She lashed it with a length of thick cord, but she feared it would not survive another change of address.

Out of a sense of order she stripped the narrow bed. She folded the coarse linen with her uniform in a neat pile to be handed back to Miss Hagstrom. She sat down on the hard naked mattress. Her shoulders ached in their sockets from all the scrubbing and lifting. She wanted to cry.

She was not angry at the old Swedish woman, who could not help the way she was bent. Kitty was angry at herself. She'd had her chance and she'd wasted it. She sat a long while watching the sunlight slant through the tiny window.

She didn't cry. She took stock.

The only thing she had coming to her now was Tyrone Duncannon's son in eight months and God only knew how many days. That and a free dinner in two hours. She had half a mind to chuck the dinner. Who needed their food?

But she thought about it and saw that the dinner gave her two more hours in the Stokes house.

Two hours would have to do. That was all there was to it.

# Chapter 5

FOR TWO WEEKS, since the breaking of his engagement, Johnny Stokes had not varied his afternoons. He napped at four to prepare himself for the evening's debauch. At five he bathed and shaved to make himself attractive for the girls. At five-thirty he apologized to his mother that he would not be home for dinner. He would then drive to Medford, where he would spend the hours from seven till ten getting drunk at Howie's Speakeasy, and ten to midnight getting laid upstairs by one of the whores.

That afternoon, when he came downstairs to look for his mother, a strange woman was standing in the pantry.

"Kitty," he said, surprised. He had never seen her in ordinary clothes before. She was wearing a dress of violet cotton and it was too big for her. There was a suitcase at her feet, and when her eyes met his they were red. "What's happened?"

"Hagstrom gave me the sack."

Johnny Stokes felt as though a fist had punched him in the stomach. "Why? What have you done?"

"Kissed you, that's what." She fumbled a handkerchief to her nose and ran to the back door.

Johnny Stokes ran after her. "Kitty, don't go. I'll fix it up,
I promise."

"There's nothing to fix up. Hagstrom wants me out and
she's turned your mother against me."

"I'll talk to Mother. Wait here. Just give me two minutes."

Johnny Stokes flung open the drawing-room door. Melissa
Stokes looked up from her needlepoint.

"What's this about Kitty being sacked?"

"She stole some silver," Melissa Stokes said quietly.

"I don't believe it."

"Miss Hagstrom found it in her room."

"Miss Hagstrom's lying."

"I saw it with my own eyes, Johnny."

He found Miss Hagstrom in the servants' dining room, sitting down to a cup of tea with a piece of angel food cake. She
listened to his shouts. She looked at him forgivingly.

"You can't treat people like cattle!" Johnny Stokes cried.
"She has no money, nothing—she'll starve without work!"

"Girls like her," Miss Hagstrom said, "don't starve."

"You'll hire her back—and that's an order."

Miss Hagstrom's eyebrows rippled thinly. "Perhaps we
should discuss that with your mother."

Melissa Stokes was waiting for them in the hallway. A deep
crease darkened her forehead. Her raised hands begged for
silence. "Please, Johnny. You'll disturb your father."

"Jesus Christ!" Johnny Stokes's face was red and the veins
stood out in his neck. "Do you think that's the worst thing that
can happen in this house?"

"Johnny, Johnny," his mother implored. "How has this girl
managed to work you up so? What can she possibly mean to
you?"

"She's a human being, the same as any of us. That's what
she means to me."

Melissa Stokes shook her head. In one hand she held a
crumpled sheet of sketch paper that Miss Hagstrom had re-
trieved from a trash barrel. "And what's this drawing?"

"All right—I was sketching her. Is that a crime?"

"Oh Johnny, you're so young," Melissa Stokes sighed. "You
think you understand everything but you have no idea. The girl
was after you."

"And the girl last summer?" Johnny Stokes said. "And the
girl before her?"

Miss Hagstrom crossed her arms. "Thieves—every one of them."

Johnny Stokes wheeled on her. "And how did they get to the silver when you keep the key on your belt?"

Melissa Stokes stepped between them. "I won't have you insulting Miss Hagstrom. Please apologize, Johnny."

"Please, ma'am." Miss Hagstrom's slate-colored eyes brimmed with tolerance. "There's no need."

"*You'll* apologize," Johnny Stokes said. "You'll both apologize to Kitty."

The sketch fluttered in Melissa Stokes's fingers. "Now, Johnny, you're not going after her!"

Johnny Stokes strode to the doorway. He stared at his mother, eyes pale and narrow. "Forget dinner."

He turned and vanished. The door slammed behind him. Reflections trembled in the hallway mirrors. Melissa Stokes winced at the five stomps of English boots on the porch steps.

John Stokes Sr. stepped into the hallway scowling. "How the hell do you expect me to talk to San Francisco with all this ruckus?"

Melissa Stokes listened for the sound of a car motor. "Go back to your phone, John. There won't be any more ruckus. Not for a little while at least."

By the time Johnny Stokes caught up with her, Kitty had walked almost a third of the way to the Bartonville turnoff. The cord handle was beginning to cut into her flesh and she had to stop every ten steps and shift the suitcase from one hand to the other.

She heard the tooting of a horn, and the brown-and-yellow Stutz Bearcat swung in front of her and pulled off to the shoulder of the road. Johnny Stokes jumped out.

"Come on home, Kitty. Everything's going to be all right."

He took the suitcase from her and she let him help her into the front seat.

"I can't go back there, Johnny. Anywhere but there."

He gave her a bright, anxious look. His fingers rippled around her hand.

"It's good to sit," Kitty sighed. She went limp against the leather backrest. "It's good to do nothin'. I wish I could sit here all day."

Johnny Stokes slipped the car into gear and pulled back onto the highway. Kitty gazed wordlessly out the window. Horizons of oil fields flowed past. The workmen on the rigs seemed tiny. They could have been insects caught on strips of steel flypaper.

They drove smoothly through checkerboards of cornfields and forests and unplowed meadow. They drove through a college town and red brick buildings and white frame homes. They came to a stop at a half-timbered inn on the edge of a wood.

A man in a dark suit came bustling and smiling to escort them in through the kitchen and into a tiny dining room out back. There were three tables set with linen and sparkling glass. Kitty and Johnny were the only diners. The man offered them cocktails.

"I'd say you've earned one," Johnny Stokes said.

Kitty smiled, her lips parted ever so slightly. Her mouth reminded Johnny Stokes of a sleeping child's. It seemed so trusting. He ordered two martinis and said they'd be having the veal scallops and plenty of white wine.

Kitty looked around the dining room with its dark wood and potted palms. The windows were mirrored over. Her dress looked plain and out of place to her. "Bootleggers," she said.

Johnny Stokes smiled. "And damned good cooks."

He had very white teeth, perfect in their smallness. Kitty wondered how many girls he'd kissed, how many he'd been to bed with. She'd heard that rich college boys had their pick of girls. His knee brushed hers now and then, light and accidental beneath the table.

The waiter brought a liver pâté with a clear aspic crust, set on a bed of lettuce. Kitty had seen Emma, the cook, devise such things for Melissa Stokes's solitary lunches.

"Something wrong?" Johnny Stokes said.

"All these knives and forks. Which one do you start with?"

"Kitty, you're priceless."

"Don't make fun of me. I didn't ask to come to a fancy place."

"I'm not making fun. And it's not a fancy place. If you want to see a really fancy place, I'll show you one some evening."

"I better learn about forks before I get any fancier."

"You start at the outside—the little fork."

Kitty knew pâté was not the sort of food you wolfed down, so she tried to nibble. She tried to chat too, but she was so busy nibbling that she mostly listened.

Johnny Stokes talked about the girl he had almost married. "It would have been the worst mistake of my life. I know that now."

Kitty nodded. She sensed she had him now. She felt sorry for him but she did not feel guilty. He was scheming just as hard as she was. The only difference between them was he wanted her for the night and she wanted him for a little longer than that. It was going to be a good close contest.

"You're straightforward, Kitty. It's a rare quality and I like it."

She threw him a hinting glance across the rim of her wineglass. "You're pretty straightforward yourself."

Their knees touched and stayed touching.

The waiter brought the main course, filets of veal in sweet wine sauce. He poured them more wine. For the next hour Kitty matched Johnny Stokes swallow for swallow. When her head began to spin she slowed down. Either Johnny did not notice or he did not care. She let her glass sit on the table, half full, and watched his get empty, over and over.

"Humor's a nice quality," Johnny Stokes was saying. "Do all the Irish have it?"

"Not so's you'd notice," Kitty said.

"*You* certainly do. You could make a man smile his whole life long."

"I can't promise," Kitty said. "But I sure could try."

"Please come back." Liquor was slurring Johnny Stokes's voice now. "Please, Kitty. Come home."

"I can't, Johnny. I've explained. Please don't ask me again."

"I wish you liked me. It's unfair how much I like you, and you don't even like me a little."

A well-dressed young man and woman had taken the next table. They were glancing at Kitty and Johnny.

"We're shouting." Kitty touched Johnny's hand. "Maybe we should pay up and go somewhere else."

"Damn it, Kitty. Give me some kind of answer."

"Not here, Johnny. Come on."

Kitty tried to help Johnny Stokes out of his chair. He stumbled and fell and pulled the cloth halfway off the table. A wineglass shattered on the floor. The girl at the next table laughed. The waiter lifted Johnny by the shoulders and propped him on his feet.

"He'd better lie down," Kitty said. "Have you got a bed?"

They walked Johnny through the kitchen and up a flight of stairs. Kitty could hear voices and music. The waiter guided them down a hallway and unlocked a door. There was a tarnished brass bedstead, an old chest of drawers, two wicker chairs.

"Maybe one more bottle of that wine," Kitty said. She sat Johnny Stokes on the bed.

The waiter brought two glasses and a bottle in an ice bucket. Kitty felt through Johnny Stokes's pockets and found a dollar tip. The waiter wished them a goodnight.

Kitty undressed Johnny down to his underpants and stretched him out. She had herself a glass of wine and then another. She stood at the window and looked down at the parking lot. Young people stumbled laughing out of bright new cars. A drunk tenor was strumming a ukulele and singing "Bye Bye Blackbird."

Kitty closed the window and lowered the shade. She undressed. She stared at the stranger sleeping on the bed. His skin was paperwhite from neck down. She thought of Tyrone Duncannon's suntanned body. She was afraid she was going to cry.

*Jesus,* she prayed, *don't let me cry. Not yet. I've got to get through this.*

She approached the bed. Her eyes examined Johnny Stokes. The sinews of shoulder and thigh stood out, rigid as the bands of a wire trap. She gripped the bedpost, steadying herself against the sudden betrayal of her legs. She eased herself down onto the mattress.

Johnny Stokes was breathing hoarsely. Music and voices pushed up in waves through the floor. They seemed to come from another universe. Thoughts rushed in on her. So this was to be her second time: no husband, no priest . . . It seemed to her the saddest moment of her life, sadder even than her widowing. There had at least been honor in that. But in this there was only calculation, a tossing of dice. Her blood whispered in her that nothing could come of it but loss.

She pushed the thought back. She bent down and kissed

Johnny Stokes hard on the mouth. His eyes flicked open. He came swiftly to life. He pulled her down to him, rolled over on top of her. She cried out. She had to make him believe she had never done this.

"Go slow," she whispered. "I've never . . ."

She saw shock flicker in his eyes and prayed it was only surprise, not suspicion or, God forbid, disbelief. She'd counted on his being drunk enough and infatuated enough to believe whatever she claimed.

A frown crossed his face and his eyes clouded. She saw he'd lost hold of his doubt and didn't even remember what he'd been thinking. It had been the instant's cold sobriety that sometimes flashes through drunkenness, and it had gone.

She dug her fingernails into his nakedness. Little welts of blood rose on the white of his shoulders. His mouth took starved gulps of her. She raked her nails up and down his back. She bit. She scratched. She wanted to make him suffer and bleed as his people had made her suffer and bleed. He lunged and thrashed like a goaded horse, and the wine and the lunging and the thrashing made her dizzy and sick.

Her eye picked a spot on the wallpaper, a black dot on the petal of a rose. She tried to anchor herself to it. But the rose could not blot out the smell of the sweet soap in Johnny Stokes's hair or the salt sweat of his body or the chemical thing that surged up from his lungs with each breath. She tried to imagine that the black dot was a beetle and then a bullet hole. She closed one eye and then the other and the dot hopped back and forth. She told herself the dot was real, the dot and nothing else.

But this was real now: Johnny Stokes, the sex they were doing together, the honor going out of her with each thrust. The mattress twisted and screamed beneath her. There was no pain. If at least there had been pain! But there was only a warmth that melted her and made her yield like candle wax.

She tried to fight the yielding and she lost. She heard herself cry out at the same moment as Johnny Stokes.

And then he lay leaden on her, still.

A cold dread descended on her. She did not know if it was regret or guilt or if she had probed some new pocket of her conscience. But she knew there was no turning back ever again for Kitty Kellogg Duncannon.

* * *

Johnny Stokes awoke and did not recognize the room. The window faced an unfamiliar direction. He could see the dawn in it. He sighed and his breath felt full and sweet in his lungs. His hearing was uncannily clear. He could pick out the tiny chirping of a bird, a scurrying in some bush not far away. A rooster crowed somewhere and the sound was bright and hard as a tiny jewel.

There was a stirring in the bed beside him. He looked down at the girl cuddled small in his arms. Kitty gazed up sleepily at him. He thought, *what a young thing she is—what a dear helpless young thing*. A deep rush of love lifted him. He squeezed her tight against him.

"You're mine now," he said. "You know that, don't you?"

"I'm no one else's," she murmured. "You're all I've got now."

"Oh, Kitty, you don't know how I've dreamed of hearing you say that."

"Well, Johnny, you've got your dream. But what do *I* get? One night a week in a room at an inn?"

"What do you want, Kitty?"

She looked tiny and wounded and frightened. "Are you givin' me any choice, Johnny?"

He drew her face up to his. He kissed her nose, her eyelids, her lips. "I'll give you anything you want," Johnny Stokes said. "Anything at all."


It was two o'clock when Kitty and Johnny got back to the house. The white shutters and window trim blinked in the bright blue afternoon. Johnny let them in with his key.

"Mother!" he called. "Father!"

Melissa Stokes came running out of the drawing room. Her skirt was a flutter of lavender at her knees. "Johnny!" she cried.

Johnny bent and kissed her.

"Your father and I were sick with worry. You could have phoned."

"I've been with Kitty," Johnny said.

Melissa Stokes's gaze took hold of Kitty. "I'm sorry, but Kitty's not welcome in this house."

"Now, Mother, just relax, will you?" Johnny put an arm around Kitty.

Melissa Stokes's eye rested uneasily on the hand that touched Kitty's shoulder. She moved backward, one step nearer the bench. She swayed, but she did not sit.

"Mother, are you calm?" Johnny's voice had the brightness of a little boy's knife. "I've got news for you. Kitty and I are married."

A dreadful dullness came into Melissa Stokes's eyes. They glided across Johnny, fixed on Kitty.

"Let's go tell Father," Johnny said.

"No. I'll handle your father." Melissa Stokes moved quickly to the door of John Stokes, Senior's office. She rapped twice and entered. She glanced at the girl at the desk and crossed to the inner office. "John," she said. "They've married."

John Stokes was writing with one hand and phoning with the other.

"I said they've married, if it's of any concern to you."

John Stokes finished his phone call. He gave his wife an annoyed look. "Don't mumble, Melissa. Who's married?"

Melissa Stokes shut the door so the secretary could not hear. "Johnny and the girl—Kitty."

John Stokes stabbed his pen into its marble holder. "The hell, you say."

"They went off somewhere last night and got married."

John Stokes kicked his swivel chair back and stood. "Well, you hired her because she was clever, didn't you? And now you're surprised?"

"Don't you try to blame this on me, John Stokes. He would have married Edie Fairchild if it hadn't been for that strike."

"Spilled milk." John Stokes stared out the window at the landscaped hill. "Spilled milk and sour to begin with. How much money does this Kitty say she wants?"

"She didn't say." Melissa Stokes came forward and placed a hand firmly on her husband's desk. "She may not want money."

"Oh, I suppose she married Johnny for Johnny, did she?"

"What's so improbable about that?"

John Stokes studied his wife, a gray shape barely daring to detach itself from the shadow. "Melissa, don't you have any grasp of human nature?"

"A little, I think."

"Well, just stop fretting. I dislike it when you fret."

"John Stokes, we've got an Irish servant girl for a daughter-in-law and you tell me not to fret?"

"She's not going to be anyone's daughter-in-law for long. How's Johnny taking it?"

"How do you expect him to take it?"

"He's scared I'll lash the hell out of him, I suppose."

"He doesn't look scared at all. If you ask me, he looks happy. And proud."

"Proud of marrying an Irish tramp? Give the boy a little credit."

"We don't know for a fact she's a tramp. Only a thief."

"And how else do you think she trapped him? She wasn't darning altar cloths, I can tell you that."

Melissa Stokes stepped into the window light. "She may surprise you; Johnny may surprise you too."

John Stokes chuckled. "And next thing I know you'll be surprising me too, eh, Melissa? Now, fetch them in here and let's untangle this. I've got work to see to."

With a briskness he would never have suspected her capable of, Melissa Stokes was gone from the room. John Stokes told his secretary he would take no phone calls for the next ten minutes. His wife returned with Johnny. The boy looked calm and possessed, although his white suit was rumpled. He had his arm around a girl in an ill-fitting cotton frock.

John Stokes smiled as he would have at the beginning of any business conference. "I understand we've had a slight change of status here."

"We're married, Father," Johnny Stokes said. "Kitty's a member of the family now."

"So I hear, so I hear." John Stokes glanced at the girl. Her eyes met his straight on, unafraid. He was not pleased. He preferred strangers to be afraid. He expected little Irish nobodies to be scared stiff. "Why don't we all sit down?" he said. "Would anyone care for coffee?"

The Irish girl said, "I'll have some brandy, thanks."

John Stokes frowned. He told the secretary to bring some brandy and one snifter.

"Mr. Stokes," the Irish girl said. "I think we could get down to brass tacks faster, just you and me alone."

"I have nothing to say that my wife and son can't hear."

The Irish girl said, "But *I* do."

"Now, Kitty," Johnny said, "let's not complicate this."

She turned and touched the palm of her hand to Johnny's cheek. "Don't you trust me, Johnny?"

"Of course I trust you."

The secretary brought the brandy decanter and one large snifter.

"Come on, Mother." Johnny led Melissa Stokes from the room, and John Stokes Sr. was alone with the Irish girl.

"What's your price?" he said.

"You couldn't meet it."

"See here, miss. I don't know what kind of man you take me for. But I'm ready to cut that boy off without a cent or a regret. So you'd better name a realistic price, or you'll get no price at all."

The Irish girl tipped the decanter at the snifter. She poured herself a half inch of brandy. "It's you that's not realistic, Mr. Stokes."

John Stokes unhooked his pocket watch from its gold chain. He thumped it down on the desk. "You will swear that this marriage has not been consummated. You will swear it in writing. You will renounce all claim to my son and his fortune. You will renounce it in writing. You have thirty seconds to name your price. Dollars and cents, girl."

The Irish girl raised her snifter. Her eyes were serious, unhurried. "To your very good health, Mr. Stokes."

The watch ticked off ten seconds and another ten and then five. Neither John Stokes nor the Irish girl moved. On the tick of the thirtieth second she set down her brandy.

"To meet my price, you'd have to breathe life back into every man, woman and child your soldiers murdered in the Catholic cemetery. And until you can do that, John Stokes, don't you high-hat me with your dollars and cents."

Rage struck John Stokes in a slap. He could not speak.

The Irish girl reached a hand and flipped the watch face-down. "If you want insults," she said, "I'll give you ten for one. If you want to talk business, I'm willin'."

John Stokes took a deep calming breath. "What kind of business could we talk? Reasonable money doesn't interest you, and I can't raise the dead. That seems to narrow our options."

"We can discuss plenty. For a start, you can accept that Johnny and me are married and no one's goin' to unmarry us."

"Under no circumstances shall I accept that."

"Mr. Stokes, I'm makin' you an offer. I'm willin' to join your family and I'm willin' to pressure Johnny into stayin' in your family. Say what you want, he's your son and I don't think you want to lose him."

"You're overlooking one thing, girl. With all the goodwill

in the world, there's no way you can join this family. You're not one of our kind."

"And whose kind were you when you married Mrs. Stokes?"

"See here." John Stokes slapped both fists on the desk. He stood.

"All I'm sayin' is the truth," the girl went on pleasantly. "You married Mrs. Stokes because she was fine people and that's what you thought you wanted to be. So now you're fine and it ain't worth it, is it? And you've got a son and he's fine, and he ain't worth it either."

"You'll not insult my family, Kitty whatever-your-name-is." John Stokes took two steps toward the Irish girl. "Get out of this office. Get out of this house. My lawyers will deal with you."

But she didn't budge. "I'm the same as you, John Stokes, and I'm talkin' the language you understand. I can give your son backbone and you know it. I may not have proper speech and manners—yet—but I do know life and I do know how to fight, and I'm goin' to teach your boy everythin' I know. You have a choice, John Stokes. You can keep us in the family and I'll turn him into a man. Or you can throw us out and I'll turn him into a man just the same and Johnny will learn he doesn't need or want a blessed thing you've got."

John Stokes felt as if the wind had been kicked out of his lungs. He sank back into his chair. Johnny could have done worse, he had to admit. Johnny could have married a Melissa.

"Keep us," the Irish girl said, "and I guarantee—I'll give you a son who can step into your boots."

John Stokes swiveled in his chair and stared out the window. He thought. All his life he'd built. He was too old now to know how to stop building. He was stuck with an empire that he loved and a wife that he didn't and a son he couldn't respect. He knew Johnny could never manage the company after his death. Stokes Petroleum, his pyramid, his immortality, would pass out of family hands, dissolve under the assaults of government, competitors, mismanagement. Unless . . .

Unless there was something to what the girl said.

"I'll admit," John Stokes said, "you're a very interesting girl, Miss—what did you say your name was?"

"Stokes," she smiled. "Mrs. John Stokes Jr."

*  *  *

John Stokes Sr. locked himself in his study. He smoked three pipes of Virginia tobacco and he thought the matter out.

The Irish girl was young and pretty. She knew how to look pitiable. If he went to court, and that was the only choice she was giving him, the newspapers would take her side; and so might the judge and jury. John Stokes Sr. prided himself on being a practical man. Better to have a powerful ally, he reasoned, than a victorious enemy. Besides, since the girl was sure to get a favorable press, he might as well reap some of the benefit himself.

After a half hour's deliberation, he gave his consent. He embraced his son. He kissed the Irish girl on both cheeks. He called her "Kitty, my child." Hell, she was no different from what he'd been at her age. He told his wife to be a realist about this thing, goddammit: go to her room if she needed to cry.

Then he placed a long-distance phone call to the man who managed publicity for Stokes Petroleum.

Justin Lasting arrived by car that evening. He was a short man and he wore dark suits that tended to hide his powerful arms and chest. They also hid the fact that he was running to fat on the good salary he earned.

They were five at the dining table that evening: the Stokeses, Justin Lasting, and the Irish girl. John Stokes's publicist got a good look at the problem. He had a feeling he'd seen the girl before, but he didn't know where.

Kitty knew where: on the porch the day she'd first come to the house.

After dinner, John Stokes took his publicist into the study. They lit up Havana cigars. Justin Lasting blew a smoke ring. "We won't announce that they've married," he said. "Instead, we'll say they've been secretly engaged for some time. Folks always love a Cinderella. We'll give them a bang-up formal wedding in, oh—a couple of months."

John Stokes shook his head. "Can't wait that long. We don't know how long they've been screwing. Could turn out bad for us."

Justin Lasting took a long draw on his cigar. "Then we make it a bang-up wedding in a couple of weeks or so. It'll be a rush, but the office can handle it. We invite newspapermen. Politicians." Justin Lasting paused. "And we invite your workmen. We invite all of Bartonville, even the wives and kids."

"I doubt they'd come," John Stokes said.

"Give them a day off. Pay them a bonus. You could repair a lot of damage, John. If a little Irish girl your soldiers almost murdered is willing to marry the son of a Stokes—why, who's the rest of the world to say he's an enemy of the poor?"

"I wish you wouldn't call them my soldiers. They were state militia."

"And the biggest mistake you've ever made. Here's a God-sent chance to correct it. This will turn your reputation one hundred eighty degrees around."

John Stokes was thoughtful. "I suppose the children will be raised as Papists. Don't the Irish always insist on that?"

"Forget the children. That's a detail."

"A Catholic church wedding?"

Justin Lasting closed his eyes. He visualized. "Hell, your dining room's bigger than most churches. We'll have the wedding here and a tent reception. A Barnum and Bailey three-ring tent reception. It'll make every newspaper in the country."

Kitty was a good winner. She knew when to stop winning. She raised no objection when the Stokeses wanted a second ceremony. She let them give her clothes and money and a chaperone too. She let them book her into a suite in the best hotel in Youngstown, Ohio, the nearest city large enough to have a hotel. She was to stay there till the wedding—for propriety's sake; and for fittings; and for an interview with newspaper reporters that Justin Lasting had set up.

The interview went well. The reporter stuck to Lasting's questions and Kitty stuck to Lasting's answers.

In all matters relating to her marriage and new family, she was as helpful as she could possibly be. When John Stokes Sr. summoned her to the Cleveland office for a conference with Justin Lasting, she listened closely to the discussion. The problem, Mr. Lasting said, was her father. She was not surprised.

"What's Dad done now?" she asked pleasantly.

"He won't come to the wedding and give you away," Lasting said. "He says, 'How can I give away what I already threw out?'"

Kitty smiled. She was aware that Lasting had insulted her. With his heavy face and small sharp features he reminded her of a fox who had put on weight. She understood his thinking and she was cautious because she sensed he understood hers.

"Your father's got to come," John Stokes said. "We've

absolutely got to have him at the ceremony."

"He'll come," Kitty said. "Give me a couple of hundred dollars cash and I'll handle it."

Sunday after Mass, Father Jack was in his sacristy counting the scrip in the collection plate. There was a rap at the door. He looked up.

"Kitty Kellogg—you dare to set foot in this church!"

She gave him a look of innocent perplexity. "Ain't I still a Christian, Father Jack? Even if you've put an end to my bein' Catholic?"

"It was you that put an end to it."

She was wearing a clean dark dress, cut to her figure, and a hat with a little veil. A hint of perfume hovered about her. "I see you still got rainwater runnin' down Saint Veronica. You should put some new shingles on that roof."

"And where would we get the shingles? We'll be lucky if we can get tarpaper."

"Fancy that—the Lord's house a tarpaper shack, same as all the others."

"Our Lord was born in a manger," Father Jack said.

"And died without a roof over his head."

"You'll not blaspheme."

"I'm sorry, Father. I'm just makin' talk, tryin' to soften you up for a favor."

"Come to the point, then. What do you want?"

She eyed the rolltop desk. A plate of beans weighted down a stack of bills. Father Jack was suddenly ashamed of his lunch. He slid the beans into a pigeonhole, out of sight.

"Could you give me the name of the doctor that tended Tyrone at the end?"

Father Jack's anger faltered. He found the doctor's address in his desk. "Yes, here we are." He copied it for her.

"What was it you taught us in Sunday school, Father Jack? God works in mysterious ways, didn't you say that?"

"It's the hymn that says it: God moves in a mysterious way."

Kitty's handbag snapped open. She tucked the address into it. "I wonder if He's movin' right now."

"If you've come to make your act of contrition—"

"Oh no, Father. I wouldn't trouble you."

"I couldn't help you anyway. It's a matter for the bishop now."

"No sense botherin' His Eminence. Besides, it's easier, me not bein' a Catholic anymore. Did you hear, Father Jack—I'm goin' to marry Johnny Stokes."

"I did hear." The news had not surprised Father Jack. He'd heard of many a poor Irish girl forsaking her church to marry a rich Protestant. In his heart he couldn't condemn them: everlasting life was distant and scant compensation for never-ending poverty here and now.

"You're not pleased, Father Jack? But what could it matter to you, what two heathen do?"

"Your soul matters to me, Kitty. And your estrangement from God matters to me."

"You're good to worry about my soul, Father. You with so many to look after. Tell me—do you see my dad?"

"Every Sunday at Communion."

"Then he's been makin' his confession?"

"Now, Kitty, you'll not pry into matters that don't concern you."

"But how can he make confession without repentin' his hatred of me?"

"Your father doesn't hate you."

"Oh, indeed he does—hates me somethin' terrible lately. Why, he won't even come to my weddin'. Can you imagine that, a man hatin' his own daughter so bad he won't even come to her weddin' and give her away?"

"Did it occur to you that maybe your dad doesn't approve of this wedding?"

"But you could set him straight, Father. Your word is law to him. He'd never go against you."

Kitty reached into her purse. She placed a bundle of green paper on the desk. Father Jack's heart gave a knock against his ribs: the top bill was a twenty, and there looked to be ten or more of them.

"For the poor box, Father—or any other needs the church might have. I was goin' to give you a hundred fifty now and a hundred fifty after the weddin'. But I believe in you, Father Jack. I believe you want my dad to be right with the church. I'm givin' you the whole three hundred now, so you can get started on those shingles before the next rain."

Shortly after her return to Youngstown, Kitty went to the ad department of the Youngstown *Tribune* and placed a three-line "position available." For the next two days she conducted interviews in her hotel suite.

Seventeen young ladies presented themselves. She found none of them suitable.

Miss Victoria Jennings, the eighteenth applicant, was a little older than Kitty. She had bobbed blond hair and an arrogant blue dress that exactly matched her eyes. Kitty told her to take a seat on the sofa. Miss Victoria Jennings sat and her back did not come within eight inches of brushing the backrest.

Kitty examined the references, which came in their own soft-leather folder. There were copies of scholastic degrees from a young ladies' seminary in Evanston, Illinois, and from an *institut* in Lauṣanne, Switzerland. There were letters on crested, heavy cream paper from a Mrs. Armour and a Mrs. Dupont; they praised Miss Jennings' character and her skill with children.

"With your background," Kitty said, "I can't understand why you're hirin' out as a governess."

There was intentional malice to the question. The others had blushed and blurted tales of family fortunes lost, mortgages, invalid mothers. Kitty wanted to see what sort of liar Miss Jennings was.

"I need the money," Miss Jennings said. "I'd hoped to be a concert pianist. My father sent me to Switzerland to study. He was not a rich man. He died. I've had to support myself for three years."

"Oh, so it isn't at all what you want to do."

"But as you can see from my references, I do it well."

"It's a tough job," Kitty said. "You'll have to teach table manners, proper speech, proper dress, the works. And you'll have to teach 'em fast."

"That depends how fast a learner the child is."

Kitty rose and paced. Miss Jennings rose and waited.

"Tell me the truth, Miss Jennings. You look down your nose at me, ain't that so? I talk like a mick. I'm wearin' expensive clothes and I'm wearin' 'em wrong. I stepped out of a shanty into a twenty-dollar-a-day hotel suite and I stick out like my dad's thumb. I'm gold leaf on a tin can, and you can see right through me, can't you, Miss Jennings."

Miss Jennings hesitated. "I apologize. I didn't intend to give that impression."

"Didn't you? Then why do you talk that way—or walk

without ever lookin' down, like you expect the ground to be ready and waitin' for you? And look at your clothes—that dress didn't cost you more than two bucks, and it's better on you than two hundred on me. It seems to me givin' impressions is your specialty."

Miss Jennings' face flushed. She gathered up her references. "I'm sorry I've wasted your time."

"Not so fast." Kitty's voice was lower now. "If you want it, the job's yours."

Miss Jennings, halfway to the door, stopped in her tracks.

"Fifty dollars a month," Kitty said. It was twice the going rate in the Chicago ads. "If you're any good, the pay goes to sixty in two months."

Miss Jennings swayed slightly on her heels. "When may I meet the child?"

"You've met her, Miss Jennings." Kitty went to her, hand extended. "*I'm* the child."

One day after Victoria Jennings agreed to remake Kitty Kellogg into Kitty Stokes, a doctor by the name of Howard Bergman was entering a free clinic in a slum on the other side of Youngstown.

The clinic was below street level. It had once been a storage cellar. A strip of overhead fluorescent tubes lit the patients. Their faces stared up at Dr. Bergman—silent faces, gray faces, feverish faces. There was no beginning to them, no end: just old men and women, dusty and wrinkled and soaked through with pain, jammed along benches, backed up to the door.

Dr. Howard Bergman was twenty-six years old, young for a doctor, but he felt old, as good as used up. He knew no matter how long he lived and how hard he worked they would still be there on the benches, the hopeless infinity of the sick.

A woman was sitting in the second row. She looked young and clean. The doctor noticed the cream color of her suit and the silken salmon of her blouse. There was no hint of pain or hurry about her. She did not belong there.

In a whisper he asked the nurse about her.

"Her name's Kellogg and she won't tell me what the problem is. She insists on seeing you, not Dr. Chrysler."

Dr. Bergman took the patients in order. He probed eyelids. He pressed down tongues. He swabbed throats. He listened to lungs and hearts. He put thirty-eight stitches into a stevedore's head. After three and a half hours Miss Kellogg's turn came. When she sat down in the circle of desk light he saw she was far younger than he had supposed.

"We haven't seen you here before," he said.

"I got your name from Father Jack in Bartonville." She told him in her alert green gaze.

"How is Father Jack?" he asked.

"Just fine, thanks."

"Miss Kellogg, this is a free clinic. We're here to serve poor people."

"I know that, Doctor. And I can see you got your hands full."

Dr. Bergman gave her a long look, thinking now that there was something half familiar about her. The skin of her throat was smooth and pale. Nets of blue veins pulsed there. "You'll excuse my saying it, but—you're not poor."

"And I'm not sick either. I came to talk business with you. Can you give me one minute of your time?"

"Miss Kellogg, I've patients waiting."

"I'll pay you good money. Two hundred fifty down, seventeen hundred fifty to come." The clasp on Miss Kellogg's purse made a bright snap. She placed a bundle of bank notes on the desk.

"What are you asking me to do?"

"You most likely don't remember me, Doctor, but we've met once before. I know a little about you. I know you're straight. You're not afraid to take a risk. You can face facts without flinchin'. And I know you can use this money for your clinic, so I'm givin' you first crack at it."

Dr. Bergman knew that nothing in this world except disease and death came free. "What are you asking, Miss Kellogg?"

"I'm speakin' to you in confidence, right? Like I would to a priest?"

"Naturally."

"I'm to be married in two weeks. My fiancé and me . . . well, to make a long story short, I'm pregnant. My husband's family don't know. I don't want 'em to know."

Dr. Bergman wondered now if he had seen her face in newspaper photographs. She looked a little like that oil-town girl who had snagged the son of the oil baron. "It's a hard thing to keep secret," he said.

"Not with medical help it ain't."

The bank notes were bound in a band of clean white paper. They exuded promise. "I won't do that, Miss Kellogg."

"Now, how do you know what I'm askin'? You ain't even heard me out. I don't want to murder the baby. All I want is to postdate the birth, so it comes nine months and a week or so after the weddin'."

"There's no way to delay birth."

"I ain't talkin' delay. I'm talkin' fraud. I want to pull the wool over my in-laws' eyes and I need you to help me do it. And believe me, Doctor, if I told you their name, you'd know you're on my side and not theirs."

Dr. Bergman thought of two thousand dollars. He thought of Dr. Dessauer in Germany, who only last year had published results on X-ray therapy. Two thousand could mean equipment, medicine, another nurse. He could go on with his cancer research.

"And just how do you think I could help you pull the wool over John Stokes's eyes?"

Miss Kellogg's eyes dipped. Her lips parted in a catlike suggestion of a smile. "Nothin' could be easier, Doctor. I got it all figured out."

Kitty dressed for the wedding in the music room. Two minutes before the service the modiste and her assistants were still fitting the gown to her. They babbled French and rushed around the hem with needles. Through the closed doors Kitty could hear the deafening murmur of hundreds of guests. It was a hungry sound and it frightened her.

She peeked through the curtained window. There were Rolls-Royces and limousines parked in the drive and overflowing onto the lawn, buses that had been hired to truck the workmen and their families to the service. Gardeners in shirtsleeves had been struggling for two days with canvas and colored lights. A huge striped tent had arisen by the fountain. Kitty watched waiters in cutaways scurrying through the flaps with trays of glasses.

She had known the day would come. She had wanted it to come and now that it was here she felt afraid.

The door opened a crack and Justin Lasting slipped through. He wore a white carnation in his lapel. "All set, my dear?" he asked.

A dead silence fell on the house. Kitty could hear her heart thumping. The palms of her hands felt dry, electric. She forced a smile to her lips. She nodded. "All set."

"Come along, then."

Kitty's dad was waiting in the empty hall. She had known he would be there. She had wanted him there. And yet he too frightened her. He was wearing white tie and tails. They made him different, grand. He gave her a terrible accusation of a frown. From three feet she could smell whiskey on his breath, heavy as autumn fog.

"Wait till the music starts," Justin Lasting said. He went on tiptoes to the closed dining-room doors.

"Well, well, well," Joe Kellogg said hoarsely. "You look like a million, Kitty."

"You're lookin' pretty handsome yourself, Dad."

"First suit I ever had that fit. Stokes paid."

The rented organ began "Here Comes the Bride." Justin Lasting swung the doors open. He beckoned to Kitty and her dad.

The sight of the dining hall startled her. The caterer had supplied folding chairs. It was as full as a church at Sunday High Mass. Kitty's heart fluttered like a burst balloon. Her cheeks were burning. She hung back at the rear of the hall. She tightened her grip on her dad's arm.

"C'mon," her dad whispered. "It's what you wanted, ain't it?"

One side of the aisle glittered with colorful dresses, jewels, starched white collars. The other side was calico, jackets that were patched and shiny. Women's heads turned. Kitty's dad tugged her forward. She had no more will to move than a stone. They advanced slowly up the aisle. She could feel the music dragging.

The looks on the poor people's faces froze her: they didn't want her anymore. The rich people had cold faces too: they didn't want her either. Teresa McCoy and fat Edie Costello were there in the eighth row, poking one another. Sam Anderson, the blacksmith, was there in the third row. He wore a bright-blue suit and he looked serious and sad.

At the end of the aisle Melissa Stokes's altar cloth had been laid on a cherrywood chest. There were lit candles and a solid gold cross. The minister from the Methodist church waited, huge and unsmiling as Jehovah.

Johnny Stokes stood to the side with his best man, his

Princeton roommate. They wore morning clothes and Johnny looked elegant and nervous. He threw Kitty a smile. The organ hit a final chord.

Joe Kellogg's voice was low in Kitty's ear. "I'll ask you one last favor, Kitty Kellogg. Get the hell out of my life and keep out of it!"

He gave her a push so strong she almost stumbled. She caught herself, dazed, not believing he had done it.

Johnny came forward and took her hand. He guided her to the two green velvet cushions. They knelt side by side. She could feel him glancing at her, smiling encouragement, but her mind was still locked on the hatred in her father's voice.

"Dearly beloved," the minister read from his prayer book, "we are gathered here today . . ."

As the deep monotone droned on, panic gripped Kitty. Sweat rose on her shoulder blades. She had an impulse to turn and run to the poor people, her people, to shout that it was all a mistake, to beg them to take her back. Her hand tensed in Johnny's. His fingers stroked hers till they relaxed.

"If there is any man here who knows any reason why these two may not be lawfully wed, let him speak now or forever hold his peace."

The minister looked up.

Kitty held her breath. The silence went on forever. She wished someone would scream. She thought of screaming herself.

"Who gives this woman to be wed?"

"I do!" Kitty's dad shouted, laying on the Irish. Kitty could feel shock pass in a wave through the hall. A woman tittered behind her, on the rich side.

The minister asked for the ring and the best man stepped forward. The minister asked if Johnny took this woman to be his wedded wife.

Johnny said, "I do."

"Do you, Kitty, take this man to be your wedded husband, for richer for poorer, in sickness and in health, to love, cherish, and obey, till death do you part?"

She had heard the words at a dozen marriages, at rehearsal only yesterday. Only now did she hear them as a question demanding an answer. The reply stuck in her throat. How could she promise God to love Johnny rich or poor, sick or healthy, to love him till death? How could she promise to love him at all?

Her heart was thumping beneath the Flemish lace, and the blood in her ears whispered that it was not too late, she still had one last chance to turn back. There was a growing stir in the hall behind her. Johnny squeezed her hand. His eyes had a drowning look.

Kitty heard herself whisper "I do" so softly it was a wonder anyone else heard it.

The minister pronounced them man and wife. Johnny kissed her, and the wedding march burst from the organ pipes like the breaking of a dam.

At the reception afterward over six hundred guests crowded the house and lawns. Justin Lasting introduced Kitty to E. W. Scripps and William Randolph Hearst, who owned the two biggest newspaper chains in the country. Scripps had white hair and had come with his wife. Hearst had gray hair and had brought his mistress, a Hollywood bit-player who waved an incredibly large diamond ring and told Kitty she should be in movies.

"Sweetheart, she's in movies already," said Joseph P. Kennedy, a handsome thirty-five-year-old millionaire who owned controlling interest in a movie studio and, apparently, in the ermine-wrapped star clinging to his arm. "And what's more, fellas—" He laughed and bit into a cigar. "She's working for me."

Two newsreel photographers from Kennedy's studio asked Bernard Baruch and Billy Sunday to stand a little to the right, please. They photographed Kitty smiling between Gloria Swanson and an oil-rigger's wife.

"You're doing just fine, Kitty kiddo," Justin Lasting whispered, and afterward he told her the wedding had been a great success. "Mission accomplished," he said.

# Chapter 6

THE HONEYMOON took eight days.

Kitty and Johnny went by train, in one of the company's private cars, to Lake Louise in Canada. They stayed at a rambling Victorian hotel with tennis courts, a golf course, trails for horseback riding. Johnny scooped Kitty up in his arms and carried her over the threshold of their suite. The bellboy who held the door got a twenty-dollar tip.

Johnny made love to her two times, three times a day. Kitty tried to dislike the sex, but sometimes in spite of herself she gripped him and cried out. Afterward, she felt she had betrayed Tyrone Duncannon.

On the morning of the ninth day Kitty and Johnny boarded the train for home. Home, for the time being, was John Stokes, Senior's house. The old man had made his son a wedding gift of twenty-two of his own acres. A house was to be built on the land, but the contractor estimated it would take a year to realize the architect's plans. In the meantime doors had been cut between three of John Stokes's guest rooms. They would serve as a temporary apartment for the newlyweds.

Her first day home Kitty put the next step of her plan into action. She spoke privately with John Stokes Sr. "What would you think if Johnny worked by your side for a while, here in your office?"

"Johnny's never asked to work by my side," John Stokes said a little sadly.

"He could see how you manage things. It would be a lot better trainin' than anythin' he could learn in that business school."

"I'd like that very much," John Stokes said.

Kitty went to Johnny and she said, "Isn't it amazin' how that old man loves you. Why, all his life he's been wishin' you'd work with him in his office. And I'll bet he never mentioned it to you."

"He certainly didn't," Johnny said.

"I guess he's really a softie and never had the nerve to ask you."

"Never had the nerve?" Johnny marveled. It didn't sound like his father.

Johnny gave it a try and went to work with his father. He managed the office when John Stokes Sr. went on business trips, and he managed it well. He made a trip to Cleveland on his own to look over a refinery. His recommendations struck John Stokes Sr. as sound, and the next month his father sent him to Tulsa and Dallas.

In the meantime, every day from nine till noon, Kitty shut herself in the music room with Miss Jennings. She read aloud from the plays of John Galsworthy. Miss Jennings corrected her pronunciation. They took lunch alone at a dropleaf table in the morning room. The maid was instructed to lay elaborate settings. A breast of chicken became a five-course meal, with empty soup bowls and sherbet glasses and fingerbowls. Kitty devoured phantom banquets, and Miss Jennings pointed out her every false move.

There were many.

"Always tip the soup bowl away from yourself," Miss Jennings said. And, "Never cut fish with a knife." And, "Don't ever use your fork to anchor your meat."

"Then how the hell do you hold the meat still?"

"Never say 'hell.' Drop that word from your vocabulary. You put the fork in the piece that you're cutting off. And don't hold the knife in your fist. A meal is not a battle."

Once a week they would go into Youngstown and shop for

clothes. "Stop calling the saleswoman 'ma'am,'" Miss Jennings whispered.

"But she's older than me."

"It doesn't matter. You've got to be ever so slightly rude to salespeople. And to servants. Otherwise, they'll never respect you"

"Do I have to be ever so slightly rude to you?"

"To me especially."

They studied fashion magazines. Miss Jennings pointed out which clothes were vulgar and which were not. It astonished Kitty that expense was no guide: a thousand-dollar original from Benwit's in New York could be just as vulgar as a three-dollar frock from Sears.

"Never take anything on authority," Miss Jennings said, "except what I'm telling you. *Harper's* is good and *Vogue* is better but they're catalogues, nothing more. Never base your ensemble on a photograph in a magazine, and never ever wear anything you see on the cover. People read these magazines and the important people look down on them and they'll look down on you."

"Then how the dickens do I learn how to dress?"

"Never say 'dickens' unless you mean Charles. For the moment you'll dress as I tell you. You'll learn to judge fashion, not to follow it. In time you may learn to set fashion."

Kitty laughed. *"Me set fashion?"*

"There are women who do," Miss Jennings said, "and you've got the looks and the figure."

There remained the matter of Miss Hagstrom to be dealt with. Kitty now possessed the power to have her fired. But Johnny's mother had relied on the woman for twenty years and had come to rely on her totally. Melissa Stokes seemed vaguer and idler than ever, drifting from room to room alone and never seeing anyone, varying the routine of her days only to vanish into her private locked room. Kitty hadn't the heart to knock one of her last props out from under her. So, instead, she took Miss Hagstrom aside and said, "You've been skimming money from all the girls' salaries."

Miss Hagstrom's eyes had a trapped, hating look, like slits of raw liver. Her throat made a denying sound but no clear word came out.

"You'll pay back every cent to every girl and you'll do it this week. Or I'll have you sacked, Hagstrom."

When she went to Medford that Thursday to pick up the week's groceries, Miss Hagstrom stopped at the savings window of the First Pennsylvania National Bank. She withdrew four hundred sixteen dollars cash from her personal account. It was a tenth of her life savings, and it hurt.

That night in her room she divided the cash into eight plain white envelopes. The following day envelopes of over a hundred and thirty dollars went to Emma and Lucy and Connie. Four envelopes containing fifty cents each went to the four new girls. Miss Hagstrom informed the servants that until further notice they would receive and keep their full salaries.

Without a word, she handed Kitty an envelope containing a two-dollar bill.

Miss Hagstrom then retired with dignity to her room. She stuffed a rag into her mouth. She lay down on her narrow bed, jaws clenched so tight her teeth ached. For exactly one half hour she beat and kicked the mattress. She then placed her bruised feet on the floor and her bruised hands on her Swedish Lutheran Bible.

In the language of her fathers, poor farmers who had traded a rocky acre of Sweden for a rocky acre of Minnesota, she beseeched God, who had once said vengeance was His, to prove it and strike Kitty Stokes dead.

Six weeks after the wedding, Kitty went to Youngstown to confer with Dr. Howard Bergman. At dinner that evening she told the family she was just over a month pregnant.

Johnny jumped up from his chair to embrace her. John Stokes Sr. said, "This is an occasion." He called for brandy. They toasted the unborn child.

Melissa Stokes kissed Kitty on both cheeks. "You will be careful now, my dear," she said. "First pregnancies are the most dangerous."

John Stokes gave his wife a look, and Kitty remembered that the Stokes's first baby had died.

The months that followed brought changes in Kitty's body. She gained weight. Her breasts swelled and became tender to the touch. She had to wear special brassieres day and night.

There was a burning in the pit of her stomach. Dr. Bergman prescribed belladonna.

When she developed leg cramps, Dr. Bergman prescribed hot towels and plenty of milk.

Her nipples became darker. Tiny red marks appeared on her stomach and breasts. She felt a fluttering in her belly. Dr. Bergman put the stethoscope to her stomach and let her listen to the baby's heartbeat.

The baby began kicking at night. Kitty's gasps would wake Johnny up. He would press his head against her stomach and listen. "I can hear it, Kitty—I can hear our child!"

She felt sorry for him, but she felt no guilt—only joy at the process irreversibly taking place within her. By the middle of the sixth month her stomach was so rounded none of her dresses fit. She was twelve pounds above her normal weight. She looked six months pregnant, not five, and she knew she could delay no longer.

She went into the bathroom She stirred two teaspoons of mustard into a glass of warm water. She drank the concoction. She held onto the edge of the sink and she strained and threw up. Her heart was banging against her ribs and her skin was running cold sweat. She stumbled back to the bed and collapsed. The light went on.

"Kitty—darling!" Johnny cried. "What's the matter?"

"Something's wrong—oh God, something's wrong inside me!"

Johnny's face was a pale moon of terror. "I'll get the doctor."

Her hand touched him. "No. It's passed now. Just let me rest."

"Poor Kitty. Dear Kitty. You rest."

Johnny got a sponge from the bathroom and all night long he stroked her forehead and her neck and swollen breasts. In the morning Kitty said she felt worse. Johnny phoned for the doctor.

Howard Bergman arrived at the Stokeses' just before noon. Johnny took him upstairs. The doctor moved quickly, as though it was not a house he chose to linger in.

Kitty opened her eyes weakly and stretched out a hand from her bed. "I'm sorry to be such a nuisance, Doctor."

"You're no nuisance at all, Mrs. Stokes."

Howard Bergman took Kitty's blood pressure. He examined her mouth and her eyes and ears. He looked at the skin along the inside of her arms. He listened to her lungs and her heart. He listened to the baby's heart. For half an hour he probed and squinted. His face became more and more serious.

"Mrs. Stokes," he said, "how's your appetite?"

"Oh, I manage to eat." She smiled weakly. "Plenty of milk and lean meat. For the baby's sake."

"You should be hungry as a starved cow." Dr. Bergman motioned Johnny to come with him into the hall. "Has anyone in her family had tuberculosis?"

The blood drained from Johnny's face.

"We'd better get some X-rays," the doctor said. "I don't like the look of it."

Two days later, Dr. Bergman phoned and told Johnny there were spots on the X-rays, possible lesions of the right lung. Mrs. Stokes's weight gain was not at all satisfactory. She had a low fever, cough, sleeplessness, lethargy, all the signs of general weakness that pointed to imminent physical breakdown. The doctor urged immediate and drastic preventive measures.

"There's a clinic near Aspen, Colorado. They've had excellent results with these cases. I recommend she stay there till after the baby's born."

Melissa Stokes was skeptical. "I've never heard of such a thing. Who *is* this man Bergman? You say he treats poor people in Youngstown?"

"She seems to trust him," Johnny said.

"Aspen, Colorado, is a very strange idea," Melissa Stokes said. "Kitty should see a good doctor."

Kitty went to Melissa Stokes's doctor. He found the baby's weight, its position, its heartbeat all to be normal. He suggested puncturing the membrane and examining the fluids around the embryo. It would be possible to test for hereditary disease.

Dr. Bergman flatly refused. The procedure was too risky. TB could not be transmitted to an embryo anyway, and four months of good mountain air would clear up Kitty's problem.

Melissa Stokes's doctor, who was an old society man used to high-strung ladies, worried about the mother's emotional state. She appeared to be nearing some sort of breakdown. He agreed with Dr. Bergman that Aspen might be a good idea.

"What the hell, let her go," John Stokes said. "Doctors are all fools, but Aspen's a nice place to rest. She's been through a lot."

Arrangements were made for Kitty to wait out her confinement in the Colorado mountains. At the last moment Dr. Bergman imposed a surprising condition. "There's been a lot of publicity and she's under a strain no expectant mother should be asked to bear. I want her to register in the clinic under a false name."

After a moment's reflection, John Stokes agreed that this was a sensible idea. It would keep reporters away.

"To protect her identity," Dr. Bergman said, "there will be no visitors—no phone calls. The family must make no effort to contact her directly."

"Seems a little extreme," John Stokes remarked, but he could see no overriding grounds for objection.

"What about letters?" Johnny asked.

"Letters will be forwarded through my office," Dr. Bergman said.

"It'll be four months," Johnny said. He squeezed Kitty's hand. "I won't be there when the baby's born."

"Dear Johnny." Kitty kissed him weakly on the lips. "I'm such a nuisance and you're so patient. How I'm going to miss you, Johnny. You'll write to me, won't you?"

"Every day," Johnny promised.

Early spring was a time of promise in the mountains. It seemed to Kitty that Tyrone Duncannon was with her, that these were the first days of their marriage. She sat like a contented cat beneath the clear skies. She watched the ice melt. She watched the earth come to life. The nurses brought her letters from Johnny, in envelopes forwarded from Youngstown. She answered every week, sending her replies through Dr. Bergman.

By mid-May the trees were in leaf. The poplars fluttered, announcing every breeze. Kitty did not think she would ever forget the sound of those overexcited leaves.

Week by week she had to change to larger-waisted dresses. The doctors examined her daily. By June she was eighteen pounds over her normal weight, but she felt inexplicably lighter. The doctors explained that the baby's head had dropped into the pelvis. Her waistline seemed lower and a little less enormous, but she walked with a terrible, comic waddle. She could not take three steps without feeling winded. She had to be carted in a wheelchair to her favorite aspen tree beside the spring.

The evening of June eighteenth she felt pain low in her stomach. It lasted thirty seconds. It came back in a half hour. The nurse told her she could have no more to eat or drink. During the night the pains came at shorter and shorter intervals. Kitty gripped the steel bedposts and tried to cry out. She did not want to have to take drugs. She wanted to be there when Tyrone Duncannon's son came.

At four in the morning the nurse said the baby's head was visible. Kitty was wheeled into the delivery room. The doctor was smiling as though it were the middle of the afternoon.

"I'm going to give you a needle, Mrs. Evans," he said.

The contractions were almost unbearable, but Kitty said, "I don't want to go to sleep."

"It's only twilight sleep," the doctor said. "You'll be much more comfortable."

The nurse gave her the needle. An echoing voice told her to push down, push down. She kept sliding from pain to sleep, back and forth. She heard someone screaming. She dreamt the nurse was holding a wriggling red doll.

When she awoke it was day and she was in her own private room. The nurse handed her a very clean, very noisy baby wrapped in a white blanket. The face was wrinkled and the skull was astonishingly soft, and the minute Kitty touched it the child stopped screaming.

*He knows me!* Kitty thought.

"You've got a wonderful, healthy boy, Mrs. Evans," the nurse said. "You must be very proud."

Kitty held the baby up. He was smooth and red and shiny. It seemed a miracle. He was here. He was safe. He was born and breathing at last. He was so small he fitted in her two hands, and one day he would be a man as big as his dad.

The little baby made faces and fists and sprayed her with spit. *Such a devil*, she thought; *such an angel*. He had his dad's temper, she could see that already. He had his dad's dimples. He had Tyrone Duncannon's lips and Tyrone Duncannon's eyes.

"Little Tyrone," she whispered. "My own little Tyrone."

Of course she could never call him Tyrone. What did it matter? He was Tyrone Duncannon Jr., no matter what name they gave him. And she would see to it he had everything his dad ought to have had: that and more, much, much more.

She held the baby in her arms and gazed down on it and in

her heart she swore a solemn oath: just as the Stokeses had
taken life from Tyrone Duncannon, his son would take from
them all that they had wrested from the world. Kitty Duncannon
would see to it.

Four weeks and two days later, Dr. Howard Bergman telephoned the Stokeses. He informed them that Kitty had given
birth the night before to a healthy nine-pound male. Her tu-
bercular condition had improved astonishingly, as often happened in cases of pregnancy. He saw no reason that she could
not be home in five weeks.

Kitty was much too nervous. An almost physical dread tore
at her stomach. The plan that had seemed so easy while it was
only a dream was now fact, real as the infant asleep on the
cushioned seat beside her, real as the train hurtling her past
cornfields and factories and into Youngstown.

She stared out the window. Houses blurred past, piled on
top of one another, spotted with billboards. A whistle shrieked.
The train slowed. Momentum tugged her forward in the seat.
She gazed out at the train station, no longer blurred but clear
now. Johnny was there somewhere, waiting in the crowd.

Her heart stammered in her. She reached to lift a suitcase
down from the baggage rack.

The nurse reached faster. "Don't tire yourself, Mrs. Evans.
You just go on ahead and find your husband. I'll take care of
the bags and I'll be right along with the baby."

Kitty saw Johnny on the platform, looking for her, looking
just as panicked as she felt. The act of putting on her hat and
white gloves calmed her. The train came groaning to a stop.
She took a deep breath and stepped down onto the platform.

"Johnny!" she cried.

He turned. His face broke into a lopsided grin. He came
running and caught her in his arms and spun her around. His
mouth was on her lips and her cheeks and her throat.

"You're crushing me," she laughed, pulling back.

He held her at arm's length, studying her. Tears gave his
eyes a blue sparkle. "Four damned months, Kitty! I was beginning to wonder if you were real, if the baby was real . . ."

The nurse came briskly along the platform. She had a porter
in tow and she carried a bonneted bundle wrapped neatly in a
blue blanket. She handed it carefully to Kitty.

"Hi there, fella," Johnny said. He diddled a finger in the baby's face.

The baby stirred in its blanket. A tiny fist worked loose and pawed at Kitty's dress. The nurse stepped close and whispered, "He's hungry."

"I'll feed him in the car," Kitty said. "Is it parked far?" she asked Johnny.

"Just outside," Johnny said. And then, "May I hold him?" There was a happy sort of terror on his face. "I've never held a child."

"Well, you'd better get used to it. Just put out your arms and take him."

Johnny held out his arms and Kitty laid the boy in them. "Am I holding him too tight?" Johnny asked.

"You're doing just fine."

The child gazed up at Johnny with cool blue eyes. There was neither fear nor excitement in them, only curiosity.

"Does he like me?"

"Of course he likes you. You're his dad, aren't you?"

"Does he know that?"

"All children know their dads. It's an instinct."

The nurse cleared her throat. "If that will be all, Mrs. Evans?"

"Of course." Kitty reached into her purse. She took out a white envelope and handed it to the nurse. "Thank you for all your help."

"You're quite welcome. Good luck with the boy." The nurse pocketed her pay and hurried away, angry—Kitty suspected— that she had not been hired for at least the first year. She was an older woman, with a modern disapproval of breast-feeding that she had not attempted to hide in all the two thousand miles they had shared a Pullman compartment. Kitty was not sorry to see the last of her.

' Johnny gave Kitty a teasing glance. "'Mrs. Evans,' eh?"

Confusion flashed through Kitty. She had not wanted anything to link her to that clinic. And now the foolish old nurse had blurted out the most important link of all. Kitty's mind raced through possible replies.

"Everyone has to have a name," she said lightly. "And mine was too well known."

Johnny arched his head down to kiss the baby on the forehead. "Hello there, Son. How would you like to be called Charles?"

They began walking toward the car. The porter pulled the creaking cart of luggage behind them.

"My favorite uncle was called Charles." Johnny tickled the child's nose. "Hi there, Charley."

"I don't know about Charley," Kitty said. She had already made up her mind. It was essential that John Stokes Sr. love the child with the blindest, fiercest devotion that could possibly be inflamed in him. The child would therefore bear the name John Stokes III.

"I had an uncle called Charley too," Kitty said. "I didn't like him."

Johnny gave her a quick, searching look. "I didn't know you had any uncles."

"We didn't get along."

"Then we'll just have to think of another name." Johnny tweaked the baby's cheek and the baby giggled. "His skin is so soft." There was amazement in Johnny's voice. "It's like your skin, Kitty."

"It's our skin, Johnny. My skin and yours both."

The liveried chauffeur was waiting for them beside the Rolls. "Welcome home, Mrs. Stokes," he said, holding the door for her.

Kitty settled herself and the child in the passenger seat. Johnny tipped the porter and slid in beside her. His leg touched hers softly, reestablishing intimacy. The baggage thumped into the trunk behind them. The car eased slowly into the teeming Youngstown street.

Kitty looked at Johnny. Tiny lines crinkled the corners of his eyes and mouth. It was incredible, but he had aged in four months.

"How have you been, Johnny?" She slid one hand out from under the baby and rested it on Johnny's thigh.

"Oh, I've been okay."

"You don't look okay. What's the matter?"

"A little too much excitement, I guess." He threw her a little sideways glance of a smile. She could see it was a brave smile; and a lying one.

"What kind of excitement, Johnny?"

"Suddenly I'm a father. And after four months I'm a husband again. Wouldn't you be nervous?"

"No, Johnny. I'd be happy, not nervous."

"I'm happy too. I couldn't be happier. I'm with my family now. My real family."

A warning bell jingled faintly in the back of Kitty's head. She understood Johnny Stokes. She understood the things he said and, more importantly, she understood the things he did not. She had gone to Colorado knowing she risked losing some of her grip on people and events in Bartonville. Now that she was home she would have to determine how far things had slid and how best to get them back in line.

"How about your mother and father? Are you getting along?"

"I didn't say we weren't, did I?"

"What's the trouble, Johnny?"

Johnny shrugged. "It's not them, exactly. It's the job."

She waited for some further sound to come out of him. "Are you having trouble with the job, Johnny?" She laid her hand, cool and forgiving and firm, on his cheek.

He gave her a smile. It was the handsome self-mocking smile he was so good at, the smile women liked. "Oh, Kitty— sometimes I wonder if I've got what it takes."

"Of course you've got what it takes. That and more."

"I had to go to New Mexico last month—straightening out one of Father's usual messes."

"You're good at that. People hate him, but they like you. You're an asset to him, Johnny. And he knows it."

"I stood there under that incredible sky wishing I had my paints and my brushes and wishing I had the skill to get it down."

Kitty sighed. "What about the job, Johnny? Were you able to do it?"

"I did it in two days. I had four days left over to stare at sunsets and deserts."

"There's nothing wrong with sunsets and deserts once you've done your work."

"Oh, Kitty." He shook his head. "You're the practical one and I'm the dreamer. No wonder Father likes you. Now you've got two little boys. Think you'll have time for us both?"

"Sure. One hand for each of you."

"I'm glad you're back, Kitty. You can't imagine how glad. Now that you're here, I think I might be able to bear it."

\* \* \*

The evening of her first night home, Kitty could see that the months had changed John Stokes Sr. He smiled at dinner. There was affection in his glance and there was interest in his questions. How much had the boy weighed at birth? Had it been a hard delivery? Had Kitty and Johnny thought of baptism?

"Of course we want the child baptized," Kitty said. "Don't we, Johnny?"

Johnny nodded and the nod seemed to come from far away, as though he weren't even at the table with them.

"Could I ask . . . what religion?" John Stokes asked.

Kitty thought it odd. Four months ago John Stokes would have ordered the child's religion, just as he ordered a new telephone for the office or eight-inch pipe for the oil rigs. And here he was asking. *Could it be he's gotten kind?* she wondered; *or just clever?*

In any case, she had researched the religion question and had already made up her mind. The child was to be given every earthly advantage possible. Since the socially important Protestant sects recognized one another's baptism and since John Stokes was a Methodist, the child would be baptized in that church. Later, of course, he would have to be confirmed in the Episcopal Church, and John Stokes—if he were still alive to object—would have to be brought around somehow.

"The child's a Stokes." Kitty smiled. "He'll be baptized in the Stokes church—won't he, Johnny?"

Johnny nodded again and Kitty thought how pale he had become.

"Have you decided on a name?" John Stokes asked.

Kitty glanced at Johnny before answering. "John Stokes the Third might be a good name. And since John and Johnny have already been spoken for, we could call him Jay for short. Do you like that idea, Johnny?"

"It's a good idea," Johnny said. There was not enough caring in his voice and Kitty wondered where his thoughts were.

John Stokes Sr. sat back in his chair. He had no belly at all, but he unbuttoned his jacket like a contented fat man. His eyes danced. "It's good to have you back, Kitty. We've missed you."

"It's good to be back, Mr. Stokes. I've missed all of you too."

"Kitty, I want you to call me Father. And I want you to

call my wife Mother. After all, we're all one family now, living under one roof."

For one instant Kitty could have sworn she saw something scream in Johnny Stokes's eyes. "I'd like that very much," she said. "Thank you—Father."

Five days later, John Stokes III was taken to be baptized in the Methodist church, a sparkling building with new stained glass and fresh paint and shingles that didn't leak. A boy was standing at the bushes beside the steps. He wore a patched shirt and dungarees and Kitty at first thought he must be the gardener's helper. But he was not working. He was staring at her. His eyes were strange.

As she mounted the steps with the child in her arms, the boy turned and ran. Kitty wondered if it could have been litle Timmy Dwyer, who used to buy licorice from her at the company store.

She felt Johnny's hand on her elbow. "What are you dreaming of, Kitty?" And she saw that the others had already gone inside.

The minister was waiting at the rear of the church, the same man who had married her. Beside him stood Justin Lasting, who had come from Youngstown to act as godfather, and Mrs. Lasting, who had agreed to be godmother. She had steel eyes and a slow, measuring glance. John Stokes Sr. and Melissa Stokes were there as witnesses.

They stood in a circle around the stone font: seven people reading from prayer books and one screaming baby. It seemed to Kitty there was more of God in those screams than in all the tiny print of the book in her hand.

The rest of the church was emptiness and silence: polished pews and brilliant colored windows and no one at all. Kitty had heard that John Stokes had built the church years ago, when the Baptists had refused his tithes.

The minister spoke of Noah, of the children of Israel and the Red Sea, of Jesus and the River Jordan. He spoke of the Holy Ghost. Mrs. Lasting shifted weight and Kitty could see the woman's fingers dig into the baptismal gown like chicken claws. No wonder the child was screaming. Kitty felt an impulse to snatch him back.

"I demand therefore," the minister intoned, "dost thou, in

the name of his child, renounce the devil and all his works, the vain pomp and glory of the world, with all the covetous desires of the same, and the sinful desires of the flesh, so that thou wilt not follow, nor be let by them?"

The words were like pins. They stuck. They had meanings that Kitty could not brush aside.

Her voice joined in with the others: "I renounce them all; and by God's help will endeavor not to follow, nor be led by them."

"Dost thou believe all the articles of the Christian faith, as contained in the Apostles' Creed?"

There was a trembling of Melissa Stokes's veil. No voice came through it. John Stokes spoke his "I do" in a loud, clear croak.

*He believes in all this,* Kitty realized: *he believes in his new stained glass and his pews that are never full and his payrolled minister. He believes God is here.*

The minister emptied a pitcher of water into the font. Kitty hoped the water had been warmed. With the edge of his hand the minister cut a sign of the cross over the font. "Sanctify this water to the mystical washing away of sin; and grant that this child, now to be baptized therein, may receive the fullness of thy grace and ever remain in the number of thy children. Through Jesus Christ our Lord."

Kitty joined in the "Amen."

The minister took the child from Mrs. Lasting. His hands were large and thick-veined, and the child stopped screaming. The minister said, "Name this child."

"John," Kitty said, and she heard the others like an echo, and Johnny was the weakest echo of all.

The minister dipped the baby in the font. Kitty's heart stopped. Terrible, stupid ideas rushed through her mind: the child would catch cold, drown, never come up again. But the minister brought little John up from the water and the child was alive and wide-eyed.

"John, I baptize thee in the name of the Father and of the Son and of the Holy Ghost. Amen."

The child began laughing.

The minister made a cross upon little John's forehead, and Kitty remembered Father Jack drawing the same cross on Tyrone Duncannon. After lecturing the godparents on their duties, the minister closed his prayer book. Kitty took little John back from his godmother and pressed him against her heart. She thanked the minister and she thanked the Lastings and then she hurried into the sunlight on the church steps.

With a flap of the white cotton blanket she wiped the residual dampness from little Jay's forehead. She pressed her lips to his cheek. His blue eyes shut and he was asleep in her arms.

*It is done*, she thought, and her lungs exhaled a sigh. *Tyrone Duncannon's son is a Stokes. He shall have all the Stokeses have, all and more.*

The minister and John Stokes Sr. came onto the steps, talking pleasantly of money for new organ pipes.

"May I hold him?" Johnny asked.

"He's asleep," Kitty said. "Let's let him rest." And she hugged little Jay tighter to her.

What happened next came swift and unexpected as a bullet.

Something struck Kitty on the arm. There was blood on the baby's face. A voice shouted, "You're a whore, Kitty Kellogg, and your little boy's a bastard!"

The daylight shattered into a flurry of hands and shrieks and someone pushed her back into the church. Her blood screamed *No, not this, not again, dear God!*

There were shouts outside. A car engine roared into life. John Stokes was yelling, "Catch him!"

It came to her, slowly, that the child in her arms was kicking and shrieking, not dead. She drew back the muddied blanket. Little Jay was not dead, not even wounded. He was kicking, he was spitting, he was grabbing. The wound was hers. Something had cut her arm. She had bled on him.

*Forgive me, Jay. I bled on you on your baptismal day.*

But the wound didn't matter. She couldn't even feel pain. Little Jay was alive, shouting and kicking and alive. That was all that mattered.

She slumped back against Johnny, grateful for his arms. But she would not let him take the child from her.

That afternoon John Stokes Sr. summoned his foreman into the inner office. "A boy threw mud at my grandson," John Stokes said. Rage stuck in his throat like a lump of potato. "He insulted my daughter-in-law. He looked like one of those Irish kids from town."

The foreman stood cap in hand, face grim, knowing what was going to be asked of him.

"I want the boy's name," John Stokes said.

"I'll ask around, sir."

"Matt, you have seven days to find out that little bastard's name."

# *Chapter 7*

TWO PEOPLE CAN sometimes inhabit the same house and sleep in the same bed and think they are living in agreement; yet, in their hearts, they are leading completely different lives. It was that way with Kitty and Johnny Stokes.

For a long time Johnny Stokes had not been happy. For a long time he had supposed he could live with unhappiness. The people around him managed, so why shouldn't he? He had felt disgust with his father before; the disgust had passed. He had felt fear for his safety before; the fear had passed. But when a little urchin hurled a lump of mud at his wife and son, Johnny Stokes felt something else and he knew it would not pass.

He felt shame.

He saw that he had two choices. One choice was to act on his shame: to cut himself off from his family; to stop taking their money and food and shelter and stop doing their work for them. He would then have to make his own life, one that did not violate the lives of others.

The second choice was to ignore the shame and the warning that came with it. He could remain a Stokes, stay rich and well-fed and secure, and try not to hate himself.

For a while he chose the second course. After all, he had

a wife and child to think of. There was a great deal of work to be done in Stokes Petroleum, and he threw himself into it like an alcoholic into liquor.

State legislatures had begun attacking Stokes Petroleum. Many had passed laws limiting single owners to no more than 40 percent of a state's oil resources. Some had even begun to forbid common control of intrastate drilling, refining, and retailing. To get around these laws, which John Stokes Sr. decried as the death knell of free enterprise, Johnny set up dummy corporations outside of the problem states. The contested holdings were divided up among these dummies. As a further defense, ownership of the dummies was divided and assigned to charitable foundations in third states.

Theoretically, the foundations were autonomous; in fact, Stokes Industries appointed and controlled the boards. As a result of Johnny's ingenuity, a state like Louisiana—in order to get its oil back—would have to go after eighteen corporations in as many different states and forty-three charitable foundations in thirty-nine.

It was a clever instance of using the law to evade the law; yet Johnny could not feel proud of his accomplishment. He kept wondering what a pint of kerosene for a workman's stove or a gallon of gas for his car cost down in Louisiana. He wondered what a loaf of bread cost in the company store that was no longer Stokes Petroleum's but a charitable foundation's. He knew that the better he made things in one sense, the worse he was making them in another. He felt he was being torn in two.

For Kitty Stokes it was different. There was no agony of choice. She had made her decision long ago—a lifetime ago, it seemed. Hers was the satisfaction of seeing that decision realize itself step by step, day by day.

She told her in-laws that she would do everything for little Jay herself. They made startled protests, but she would not yield. She permitted no nanny, no wet nurse, no bottle feeding. She gave the child suck herself. She bathed him. She took care of his diapers. She put his cradle in her bedroom, and when he cried in the night she took him to her breast.

This meant that Johnny could not often have sex with her. She recognized that this was a problem and she intended, in time, to cope with it.

She recognized also that, though the Stokeses had built

themselves a fine position, it was in a corner of the world. It was not central enough for Tyrone Duncannon's son. This too was a problem, and eventually she would cope with it as well. But for the moment life was good: the baby was healthy; the family was together; the fortune was solid. She was even managing to acquire a little polish from Miss Jennings, so that Tyrone Duncannon's son would never need to be ashamed of her.

So it was more than a surprise for her, it was a shock, when Kitty opened the bedroom door and saw that Johnny Stokes was packing the bags. The closet doors had been thrown open. There were bureau drawers on the floor. Suitcases covered the bed. Johnny held an armload of suits.

"What in the world are you doing?" she cried.

"We're moving."

"Now, Johnny, we can't move till the house is finished, and that won't be for three months."

"Then we'll rent a place. We'll go to a hotel if we have to." His words and movements were sharp and quick as knife thrusts. "We can't stay here."

"Why not? Who's throwing us out?"

"*I'm* throwing us out."

"Did you argue with someone?"

"I wish I had."

"Johnny. Darling. Leave those clothes alone. You're spoiling the press." Kitty lifted the suits from his arms. She placed them on a chair. "Sit down a minute and just tell me what's the matter."

"Damn it, Kitty." Johnny sank down onto the edge of the bed. Something dull and beaten showed in his eyes. "Maybe I haven't got a head for business."

"Sure you have a head for business."

"Then I haven't got a heart for it."

Kitty sat beside him. She stroked his forehead. She took a light, smiling tone. "And what would you prefer? Sitting around painting pictures all day?"

"Why not, if that's what I love?" Johnny said, and she saw it was wrong to treat the subject lightly.

"But, Johnny, you've got responsibilities. You've got a son now."

"Don't you have any confidence in me at all, Kitty?"

"Johnny Stokes, I have more confidence in you than I have

in anyone else in this world. It's you that don't have confidence. It's you that wants to cut and run when the going gets tough."

"The going isn't tough," he said. "The going couldn't be easier. I'm better than nine tenths of the lawyers on Father's payroll. In two years I could be better than all of them. There isn't an antitrust law in the country that I couldn't find a loophole to get around. Father knows it and he pays me damned well for it. That has nothing to do with why I'm getting out."

She had sensed a restlessness in him from the start, but she'd never supposed it would go this far. She felt helpless and stupid. Instinct told her to keep talking, keep him from shutting those suitcases. He was a child, it was a mood, the mood would pass.

"Getting out, are you Johnny, before you've given it a fair try?"

"I've put in the better part of a year. I've worked ten to sixteen hours a day. I haven't had a minute to see you or my son. And I've hated every degrading moment of it."

"Hush, Johnny. Be reasonable now. Your dad has stuck with you twenty-five years. You could stick with him a little longer than a few months."

"I've done more in those months than all his lawyers in thirty years." Words came spewing out of him, cold with pent-up disgust. He said he'd traveled ninety thousand miles, set up companies in two thirds of the states of the Union. Instead of breaking the law illegally, as it had done for its entire history, Stokes Petroleum, thanks to Johnny, was now breaking the law legally.

Kitty listened and she nodded but all the time her mind was racing. She was thinking of the danger to Tyrone Duncannon's son if Johnny were allowed to do this crazy thing. "Johnny, you're not being fair to yourself. You're a good lawyer and you've a head for business and there's nothing illegal about that. Your dad may not show it all the time, but he's proud of you. And he needs you."

"Why me? Harvard University turns out sixty men a year good enough and greedy enough to do what I've been doing."

"You're his only son, Johnny. He's an old man. Walk out on him now, and you may never get another chance to make things right between you."

"How can I stay? The more I see what he's doing the more I hate myself for being part of it. You don't *know*, Kitty."

"Johnny, I know. I lived down there in Bartonville. I lived on the receiving end. But like it or not, we're part of it now. We have to make the best of it."

He gave her a long, sad look. He got up and snapped one of the suitcases shut. "We're getting out while we still have a chance."

"It'll kill your dad."

Johnny turned. His eyes appraised her. "Will it kill *you*, Kitty?"

"Oh, Johnny, be reasonable. You're in a temper."

But she could see he was not in a temper, and that was what worried her. He was cool, he was certain of himself, he was dangerous.

"You don't know me, Kitty. You don't know me at all."

"I love you, Johnny, and I only want what's best for you."

"I'm tired of being rotten."

"You don't know what you're saying. You're in a state."

"Listen to me, Kitty. When I married you I was using you. All my life I've been trying to break from my family. I never had the courage to do it on my own." Johnny paced to the window. He stared down a moment at the green policed privacy of John Stokes, Senior's two hundred acres. "I was hoping they'd throw me out when I married you. But it didn't happen."

Kitty knew that now was her chance: she must laugh, cry, do something to break the irreversible flow of confession. But he didn't give her an opening.

"I seem to be more of a Stokes than ever. We've got to get out, Kitty, before I turn into *him*. We've got to take our own stand, and to hell with Father. We've got to live free even if we live poor."

"Johnny, Johnny, you're a dreamer. A lot of people live poor, but no one lives free."

Johnny gazed at her. He looked hurt, but more than that, he looked surprised. "Aren't you on my side, Kitty?"

Kitty was in movement again. She was at his side, close and smiling. "Sure I'm on your side, and I want you to stick with your dad. If there are things you don't like in the company, you'll be running it soon enough and you'll change them. You've got to work from the inside, Johnny. That's the only way anything ever gets done. Walk out now, and you'll never have a chance to accomplish anything at all."

He turned his back on her. It was a movement like the

slamming of a door. She could not keep her voice from rising. Her only thought was that Johnny was endangering her son. The words were out before she'd even considered them.

"Walk out of this house, Johnny, and you'll walk out alone. You're not taking me and you're not taking little Jay."

"You mean that, don't you?"

"I mean it, Johnny."

He stared at her with a child's amazement. "I've never seen you so cold."

"There's a lot you've never seen."

"And a lot I never want to."

He snapped a suitcase shut. He walked straight to the door without even looking back. She saw she had made a terrible miscalculation. She had meant to frighten him: fear would make him soft. But she had angered him, and anger made him hard.

He strode into the hallway. She couldn't believe it was happening. She waited, willing him to come back. But there was only the vanishing sound of his footsteps. She rushed from the room screaming "Johnny! Johnny!"

But there was no answer, no sign of him.

*He's only playing a game,* she told herself. *He'll be back.*

Johnny did not come back that day. She felt growing uncertainty, a dread that through some stupidity, some blindness, she had caused or allowed this thing to happen.

Johnny was not back that night. She had to make excuses to John Stokes Sr., saying that Johnny had gone to check out the distribution of stock in one of the Arkansas dummy corporations.

"Good for him," John Stokes said. "He's showing initiative. This is your doing, Kitty. And I'm grateful to you."

Kitty covered her fear, swallowed all pride. She went to the servants. She asked the chauffeurs where in the past they had driven Johnny. She asked the girls where in the past, if anywhere, they'd gone with him. They admitted to certain vague, secondhand knowledge. She investigated the places they hinted at: speakeasies, parks, lake shores, hills with sunset views. He was not at any of them.

She sat adrift in her chauffeured car. She reasoned with herself. She knew her husband a little, didn't she? She knew when he was upset he drank; he found cronies. From a pay phone she called Johnny's Princeton roommate long-distance. Was Johnny there? she asked.

No.

Where might Johnny be?

How could she expect him to know that, the roommate said.

Kitty expected he knew a great deal, but she had to plead and lay on the emergency before the roommate told her, very hesitantly, a phony name Johnny had once used and a hotel he'd once gone to.

Kitty suspected he'd used the name more than once and gone to more than one hotel. She had a crying fit into the receiver. The roommate asked her please to get a grip on herself. She said how could she when her life and marriage were coming apart and Johnny was out there on a drunk but, pray God, not doing any of the foolish things he'd threatened?

An alarmed pinch came into the roommate's voice. He admitted to vaguely remembering certain other hotels and rooming houses.

Kitty thanked him for saving her marriage and her life and Johnny's. The blood slammed in her ears. She rushed through Youngstown hotels. Porters and desk clerks and switchboard girls took her money and shook their heads.

"Sorry, ma'am."

"Not here."

"Never heard of him."

She had the chauffeur take her through back street after back street. She spent the day walking, driving, searching, begging. No use. No Johnny. She returned home late that evening, deadened from running, from not eating, from fear.

Miss Jennings was waiting for her on the stairs. She was holding little Jay. The baby was screaming. "He hasn't been fed all day," she said.

Kitty was shocked to think how many hours little Jay had gone without feeding. "Oh, Jay, I didn't forget you, I promise I didn't."

She took the baby to her bedroom. She loosened her breasts from her clothing. The child gazed up at her, blue-eyed and calm now.

"I'll never forget you, Jay," she promised. "Never ever."


Toward sunset the next day the foreman presented himself in John Stokes's inner office. "The boy's name is Timmy, sir."

"What's his last name?"

The foreman sighed. "Dwyer, sir."

The name meant nothing in particular to John Stokes. He needed something particular, something he could get his hand around or break. "Who is he?"

"Just one of the town kids, sir. A high-spirited lad. Always foolin' aroun. Playin' pranks and such."

"Does his father work for the company?"

"I'm sure the lad didn't mean any harm, sir."

"Does this Timmy Dwyer's father work for us?"

"The boy's got two younger sisters and a brother, sir."

"I'm not asking about his brothers and sisters. Is his father on our payroll?"

"Yes, sir. Tom Dwyer works the oil rigs."

"Fire him."

There was red disbelief in the foreman's eyes. "The lad was jokin', sir."

"It's no joke to have mud slung at my grandchild. Any father who could raise such a son does not belong with Stokes Petroleum."

"I'm sure Tom Dwyer regrets it, sir, sincerely regrets it." The foreman's hands worked rapidly at the brim of his cap, kneading it like a lump of raw bread. "Couldn't you talk to him, sir? He'd apologize. And he'd whip the boy."

"I have no interest in talking to the man. He is fired as of today. He has five days to remove himself, his belongings, and his family from company property."

"But Mr. Stokes—sir—"

John Stokes had no use for pleading, no time for defiance. "Matt: so long as you are my employee you will carry out my orders."

"Yes, sir." The foreman turned, slump-shouldered, toward the door.

"I did not dismiss you, Matt."

A dark foreknowledge came over the foreman's face. "Is there something else, sir?"

"I want this Tom Dwyer blacklisted."

"But, sir—" the foreman's voice broke. "The man has to work!"

"Not for any company that expects to do business with Stokes Petroleum. I want him blacklisted the same as any common agitator. And I want his family blacklisted. That's all, Matt. You may go now."

* * *

Tom Dwyer had spent forty-one of his forty-seven years working with his hands. His hands had worked the soil in County Derry in Ireland. They had worked the coal in the hills of Kentucky. They had worked the iron ore in the steaming cauldrons of Pittsburgh, and they had worked the oil drills in eight states of America.

In his quiet way he was a proud man. His hands were his and he owed no man money. He was good to his wife and his four children. He went to Mass faithfully and always had a quarter for the collection plate. He believed God loved him.

The dismissal and eviction notice in his pay envelope gave him a moment's unbelieving terror. After a drink the terror subsided. He had coped before and he knew he could cope again.

What he did not understand was why God had done this thing to him.

He spoke to Father Jack, who assured him he had in no way offended God. Father Jack gave him ten dollars. Tom Dwyer took the ten and the fourteen he had saved. He did not tell his wife about the notice in the pay envelope. He said he'd heard of opportunities out of state, good jobs, better pay.

He got on a bus and he spent four days going from company to company asking for work. He traveled over three hundred miles. He went to the oil companies. He went to the railroads. He went to the mines and he went to the steel mills. He went to the automobile factories. He even went to the dairies and the farms.

The little men couldn't afford to hire him. The big men seemed to have some secret shared knowledge about him. He saw them hiring other men, but for some reason Tom Dwyer wasn't good enough for them.

A terrible realization came to Tom Dwyer. He saw that for his entire life he had been wrong in his deepest belief. He saw now it was not enough to own your own two hands. You had to own a piece of the earth, an oil well or a lump of ore or coal. He looked at his two hands. He saw they were useless. They could not feed his family or make a roof for their heads.

He counted the money in his pocket. He had four dollars. He counted the days before the company threw his family out of their shack. He had one day.

He could not bear to tell his wife and children that Tom Dwyer's hands were useless. He could not bear it. His mind tugged and tore at the problem, but the problem was like rock and it tugged and tore right back at his mind.

Finally, his torn, tired mind could devise only one solution.

He spent eighty cents on a pint jug of red-eye. He spent thirty cents on six cartridges for his shotgun. He took the bus home and had a last supper with his wife and four kids. He got roaring drunk and told them he was celebrating a new job he'd found.

After they were asleep he shot them dead and then he put a bullet through his own head.

It was evening when the Pinkerton men drove up to the Stokes estate and fanned out at twenty-yard intervals along the fences. The sun had almost set when the company foreman strode nervously to the house and, hat in hand, gave the doorbell three sharp rings.

The maid told him the Stokeses were at dinner, he would have to be so kind as to wait. He said it could not wait. She saw the terror that wrinkled his eyes. She did not understand it but it infected her. She hurried to the great oak doors of the dining room.

The Stokeses had sat down to an uneasy dinner. There had been sounds that evening and they had reached even to the dining room: traffic on the road, dogs barking, voices beyond the fences that walled off the estate, distant thunder that contradicted the clear amethyst sky. None of these sounds was in itself extraordinary, but for all of them to happen in the space of one sunset was unsettling.

Melissa Stokes stared at the parsley flakes floating in her consommé. John Stokes remarked it was odd Johnny had not phoned or written or sent a wire. He kept glancing toward the windows. Kitty said she was certain there would be word in a day or two.

The maid came on tiptoe across the room. John Stokes bent an ear to her whisper. He nodded and excused himself from the table.

He was gone a little over a minute. He returned white-faced. In an unsteady voice, he told the others to finish their meal without him.

Melissa Stokes rose. "Who is in the hall with you, John?" she said.

"It doesn't matter. Sit down and finish your dinner."

Melissa Stokes did not obey. She went to the carved oak

door. She pushed past her husband. She saw Matt the foreman standing in the hallway with his wrinkled hat in his hands. "What has happened?" she said.

The foreman shot John Stokes a look of utter helplessness.

"It doesn't concern you, my dear," John Stokes said.

Melissa Stokes looked at her husband. She looked at the foreman, bent as a question mark. She sniffed sharply and with quick, long steps she went to the front door. She swung it open and stared down the lawn into the twilight.

Men in uniforms clustered at the gates. Through the trees, gray shapes of armored trucks moved dimly against the road. Far away there were cries. To Melissa Stokes they were the most terrifying cries of all, the animal shouts of human beings.

John Stokes was beside her. He eased the brass doorhandle from her grip. He placed a soothing arm around her waist. Melissa Stokes could feel that the arm was lying.

"Matt here tells me there's been a little accident," John Stokes said.

Melissa Stokes understood certain things about her husband. She knew he drew a tricky line between truth and falsehood, and she knew he was doing it now. She knew the distance from falsehood to murder could be short as an inch. "What kind of little accident?" she said.

Drops of sweat were forming in the wrinkles of her husband's brow. "A man died this evening. One of the workmen."

Melissa Stokes winnowed the scream from her voice. "How did he die?"

"He was shot," John Stokes said.

Melissa Stokes felt the mirrored hallway go liquid. It began to ripple and flow past her. A current tugged her down. She clutched a hand to the wooden banister. "Who shot him?"

John Stokes hesitated.

The foreman stepped forward. "He shot himself, ma'am."

Melissa Stokes saw white masks, the ignorant faces of women and the knowing faces of men. She knew this was only a fragment of the truth. She felt a rush of hatred for all the bent fragments of truth that littered her life. *I would rather be killed by the truth,* she realized, *than live one moment longer on deception.*

She made a sword of the question and drove it at her husband: "What happened, John? Don't lie to me!"

The foreman's eyes flashed apology to John Stokes.

"Apparently the man was despondent," John Stokes said. "He was drunk, wasn't he, Matt?"

The foreman nodded. "He was a terrible drinker, ma'am."

"Men don't kill themselves because they're drunk." Melissa Stokes advanced one step on her husband. His feet edged back an inch. "There are soldiers at our gates. There are armed trucks at our walls. There's a village out there screaming for our blood. What did we do to that man, John? For once in your life will you tell me the truth?"

The answer came lashing out of John Stokes like a whip. "The man was a weakling and a criminal. He shot his family and he killed himself."

Melissa Stokes's teeth bit into her fist.

"He was a coward and a murderer, and if you wish to weep for such a man, then you're as big a fool as he."

Melissa Stokes made a hard-cutting edge of her hand. She wheeled with her whole weight and slapped her husband's face once, twice, forehand, backhand. John Stokes recoiled.

"It was the father of that boy!" Melissa Stokes shrieked. "You fired him and had him blacklisted!" She whirled on the foreman. Words kept spitting out of her. "And you helped! You went to the refineries—the railroads—the factories. You told them not to hire that man. For all you cared, he and his family could starve—just because a little boy made you angry! What kind of men are you?"

No one spoke.

Melissa Stokes cried, "How many are dead? Someone tell me how many!"

The foreman stood twisting his hatband. His voice was hardly more than a whisper. "Six, ma'am."

"Six!" Melissa Stokes held tight to the banister post. Her eyes went screaming from face to face. No face, no scream answered.

Gradually the rage in her fell back like a defeated army. She put a foot on the first step of the stairway. She moved one step at a time, balancing carefully.

"I am going upstairs," she said, her voice suddenly serene. "I do not wish to be disturbed."


Five minutes later, Kitty went to Melissa Stokes's bedroom. It was empty.

She went to the locked door at the back of the second floor.

She pressed her ear to the panel. Beneath the whisper of her blood she heard another sound, a rustling that came and went as though a rag mop were being dragged back and forth across a floor.

Kitty rapped softly. "Mother, are you all right?"

The rustling stopped. But there was no answer. She rapped again, sharper.

"Mother. It's Kitty."

She tried the door handle. It would not turn.

"Please let me in."

"I'm busy," a voice said. In a way it was Melissa Stokes's voice, but in another way it was someone else's, someone that Kitty had once heard sobbing behind this very door.

"Mother, we've got to talk. It's not good for you to be alone."

"I'm busy," the voice said, slurred and deformed. "Let me be."

Kitty waited by the door, hoping Melissa Stokes might change her mind. A silence seeped through the crack above the lintel. It rose around Kitty like iced water. She shivered and hurried down the stairs.

John Stokes sat alone in the dining room, calmly finishing his dinner.

"Mother's locked herself in that room," Kitty said. "May I have the key?"

John Stokes looked up at her as though she had said something quite stupid. "That's Melissa's room," he said. "For her moods."

Kitty wanted to knock the fork from his hand, slap the righteousness from his smug old face. But she had come to know him and she knew that no word, no blow could pierce the ignorance that armored him. He had driven his son from the house and his wife into a locked room; he had ripped the lives off men like wings from flies; and he did not see it. He sat peacefully chewing roast beef, and he thought these things happened through the weakness and wrongness of others.

She forced her voice down to a coaxing softness. "Mother might hurt herself. She's very upset. We mustn't leave her alone."

John Stokes shrugged. "I doubt she could do herself much harm up there. No more than she's done already."

But Kitty sensed infinite harm behind that locked door. Her

son was asleep and defenseless upstairs, and she knew that harm not caught early could spread like disease or fire. "Father, give me the key. Let me go talk to her."

John Stokes finished chewing. "I don't have the key."

Kitty stared at the placid old man. She felt hatred rip through her like a scream. She went quickly through the pantry door and found Miss Hagstrom in the servant's dining room. "Give me the key to Mrs. Stokes's room."

Miss Hagstrom's lips took on a thin, satisfied curve. "No one has the key but Mrs. Stokes. No one's to go into that room but her. Those are my orders." Miss Hagstrom dipped a piece of angel cake into the tea in her saucer. She sucked it dry and then chewed it.

"What goes on in that room?" Kitty said.

"I couldn't say, ma'am. I've never put my eye to the keyhole or listened at the door. It's a private room, for her moods. That's all I've been told."

Kitty searched Miss Hagstrom's eyes. They were colorless and clever and they did not evade. She saw Miss Hagstrom was telling the truth. She saw it was a truth Miss Hagstrom liked telling.

"Fix Mrs. Stokes some food," Kitty said. "Leave it on a tray outside the door."

Miss Hagstrom smiled tolerantly. "It won't do any good, ma'am. Mrs. Stokes never eats during her moods."

"You will fix her a nourishing meal," Kitty said, "and you will leave it outside the door."

Miss Hagstrom left a tray of roast beef outside the door.

When Kitty looked in the morning, it was still there, untouched. When she put her ear to the door there was only the rustling and the silence and once, dimly, a sound that might have been a voice.

She ordered a tray of chicken salad and crackers. It remained till evening, untouched. She ordered fresh trays twice a day, and for four days they went back to the kitchen untouched.

Because of the shootings, the Stokeses had to live like prisoners. There were four Pinkerton men at the gate now, night and day. They wore ugly black revolvers on their hips. Armed guards patrolled the miles of fence that enclosed John Stokes's acres. A team of electricians went to work running two hundred volts of electricity into the steel mesh and barbed wire. Signs were nailed to trees: TRESPASSERS MAY BE ELECTROCUTED. TRESPASSERS WILL BE SHOT.

For four days Kitty went outside to look up at Melissa Stokes's window. For four days the shade was drawn. On the fifth day, the shade was raised. That afternoon, as Kitty sat with Miss Jennings in the living room, a crash splintered the silence overhead.

Kitty rushed upstairs. The door at the end of the hallway had been thrown open. The tray of food had been kicked aside. Shads of translucent china dotted the carpet. Melissa Stokes stood in the open doorway, dressed from head to toe in widow's black.

"I've called for a car," she said. "I'm going out for a drive."

A cold sanity gleamed in the pupils of her eyes and it baffled Kitty. "That's a good idea, Mother. The air will do you good. You've been cooped up too long."

Melissa Stokes moved stiffly. She placed a gloved hand on the banister rail. "I think I'll go to church. I think I'll pray a little."

Something frightened Kitty. Melissa Stokes was all neatness and balance and calm, and yet she had kicked a tray of food down the hallway. She had left the door to her private room open, the room that had always been shut and secret. Kitty's eye scanned quickly, searching for the secret. There was a dark upholstered sofa, two chairs, a standing lamp with lion's feet, a radio.

"The furniture came from my room in my old home. I brought it with me when I came to live with John Stokes. Do you like it?"

"It's very pretty, Mother."

"Sometimes I have moods. It calms me to sit in familiar surroundings. It's not very good furniture but I'm fond of it. Perhaps it should be dusted more often." Melissa Stokes shook her head. "Perhaps we'll give it away. I won't be using the room anymore."

Her hand gripped the wood railing cautiously, as though she were letting herself down a rope.

"You don't need to tell my husband I'm going out."

A bulge of certainty rose in Kitty's mind. There was something wrong here. "Mother," she said. She hurried down the stairs after Melissa Stokes. "I'll come with you. We'll go to church together."

Melissa Stokes turned in a tight and noiseless movement. Her eyes studied Kitty and she held out a hand. "Yes. You're right. They'll hate me less if you come along."

The two women hurried down the trimmed slope of lawn. Kitty's mind was racing. She saw that Melissa Stokes had a purpose, a plan, but she could not understand it. She only sensed a danger that might in some way brush her son.

The Stutz Bearcat waited in the driveway, motor idling. The liveried chauffeur held the door. "Good afternoon, ma'am," he said to Melissa Stokes. In a subtly different voice he said the same words to Kitty.

The women settled themselves in the back seat. Melissa Stokes played with the little finger of her black glove. "We'll be going to church," she instructed the chauffeur.

"The Methodist church, ma'am?"

Kitty watched an odd half-smile touch Melissa Stokes's mouth.

"Today," Melissa Stokes said, "I'd like to go to the Catholic church. You used to go there Kitty, didn't you?" The pupils of Melissa Stokes's eyes had taken on a deadly laughing shine. "Wouldn't it be nice to see your old church?"

The breath stuck in Kitty's throat. She recalled John Stokes and his talk of Papists; John Stokes's building his own church and hiring a Methodist minister. She did not know if John Stokes believed in the devil, but if he did, that devil was surely a Catholic.

"Mother," she said, "Father wouldn't want you going there."

"John Stokes be damned," Melissa Stokes said; and then, thoughtfully, "John Stokes *is* damned. But there may still be hope for me."


John Stokes completed his phone call to Saint Louis. Pleasure expanded in him like a budding flower. He had set in motion papers and judges and lawyers. Out of their labor would issue General Petroleum of Missouri. He had saved the filling stations which that socialist and foolish state had tried to wrest from his empire.

He hooked the receiver back onto the phone. He strolled to the window. In a moment he would talk to San Francisco, but just now he wanted to stare at his lawns and sculpted hedges.

He saw two women in a moving car. The pleasure in him shriveled to a tiny stabbing pin.

He strode into the hallway. He glanced up the stairs at the open door. He shouted for Miss Hagstrom. She glided out of the dining room with a bowl of cut roses.

"Where is Mrs. Stokes going?" he demanded.

Miss Hagstrom paused long enough for the echo of his question to die. "The men at the garage say she's gone to church, sir."

"Church? It's not Sunday. Why the hell is she going to church?"

A thin smile slit the line of Miss Hagstrom's lips. "I don't know, sir. But they say young Mrs. Stokes is taking her to some kind of Mass."

"Mass?" John Stokes's voice rose. "Which church are they going to?"

"I couldn't say for sure, sir. But I do believe one of the men mentioned the Catholic church in Bartonville."

# Chapter 8

THE CHAUFFEUR STOPPED the car at the entrance to the church-yard. The women got out. Melissa Stokes stood adjusting a finger of her glove. Kitty stared at the little path winding through the tombstones to the church steps. It was overgrown with weeds and it seemed to her as dangerous as a trail in an unknown forest.

"But Mother," Kitty said, "you can pray in the other church."

Melissa Stokes's jaw was set. "It has to be here." Satisfied now with her glove, she did not wait for Kitty. She took the path in long, quick steps. She pulled the church door open. It made a deep squeak. A smell of cheap incense and human flesh packed tight came wooshing from inside.

Kitty caught up. The two women stood at the back of the church. The pews of the little building were almost full. The men in the congregation wore oil-stained work clothes. The women wore patched and shiny black dresses.

The closing door made a slam. A dozen heads turned at the sound. Questioning eyes lingered on the newcomers.

From the pulpit where he stood, tears streaking his face, Father Jack's eyes met Kitty's. A deep breath swelled his cas-sock. His glance brushed her aside. "Oh Lord, who giveth and taketh away," he read in slow, aching cadences, "we pray thee be merciful to thy servants Thomas and Amanda and Mary and James and Martha and Timothy."

Six coffins of plain pine filled the space before the altar rail. Four were adult-sized, two very small. They were covered with ragged bouquets of wild flowers that looked as though they had been picked from the fields.

Understanding slammed through Kitty's mind. Melissa Stokes had brought them to the funeral Mass for Tom Dwyer's family. The men wore work clothes because the company had not given them time off. This was their lunch hour. *I'm dressed wrong,* Kitty realized in panic: *I'm wearing a turquoise dress and jewelry, and they think I'm mocking them.*

A whisper ran through the church. More heads turned. More eyes stared, brimming with hate and anger.

"Mother," Kitty whispered, "we shouldn't be here. We have to go. Right now."

Melissa Stokes brushed Kitty's hand aside. She moved slowly up the aisle. At first, perhaps, some of the villagers took her for a mourner, a latecomer searching for a seat. But she walked past the empty seats. Questioning voices buzzed. Recognition spread. Father Jack stopped in mid-sentence.

Melissa Stokes clutched at the hand of a man in the congregation. "Forgive me," she pleaded. The man pulled back and she grabbed another hand. "Forgive me!"

The hands kept pulling back and Melissa Stokes kept grabbing, begging the shocked faces for forgiveness. They were familiar faces and Kitty knew every one of them: Mary McGrory, Jack Feeny, Edie Costello, dozens more. She watched as they twisted and recoiled in amazement.

Melissa Stokes stared wildly across the congregation. She lunged at the priest. "Forgive me!" she screamed.

Father Jack, helpless and stunned, stepped back. Melissa Stokes was on her knees now, whining pathetically, crawling like a dog. She reached for the nearest coffin. Her hand skidded the flowers off it into the aisle.

A dismayed whisper surged through the church.

Melissa Stokes pulled herself up across the coffin. Her fists hammered the wood. "Forgive me!" she howled. She might have gone on howling and hammering forever if the church doors had not flung themselves open with a crash.

John Stokes stood in the doorway. He stared one icy moment

and then he moved swiftly. His eyes bulged, red and huge. He went straight to the coffin where his wife had thrown herself. He pulled her up by her hair and slapped her. The blow caught her on the side of the face with a cracking sound like the snap of celery.

She hung on to the coffin and he swung at her again. She screamed in his face: "Murderer!"

She kicked and scratched and spat at him. He grabbed at her. She broke free and staggered to the altar rail. John Stokes came after her. He slapped her again and this time the blow knocked her down. For a moment she seemed stunned, unable to move, and then she pulled herself up by the littlest coffin. Blood was running from her nose down over her lip. Her hands gripped the pine. Her fingernails dug into the soft wood.

John Stokes seized her by the waist and pulled. She struggled for breath. Slowly she lost her grip. Her fingernails dug tracks in the unvarnished pine. He dragged her up the church aisle. She was screaming and begging for help. Tears streaked her face. Blood caked her mouth.

Not a hand in the church raised itself in her defense. Faces swiveled. Eyes stared—blank, not even horrified. Women crossed themselves. So this, the unspoken whisper rushed through the church, so this was God's justice.

Kitty saw it but she did not believe it was happening: the old man, tough and scarlet with anger, the old woman screeching for help. She did not believe the army of faces, surrendered to disbelief. *I am dreaming this,* she thought; *we are all dreaming this.*

It was the thud of the slammed door, the murdered-dog howl of a car engine, that brought her bolting up out of the dream. She ran to the church door and swung it open. The car was still waiting at the end of the path. The chauffeur was stubbing out a half-smoked cigarette.

"Where's Mrs. Stokes?" she cried.

She sensed a strange satisfaction in the chauffeur's eyes. "Mr. Stokes took her in the other car, ma'am."

Kitty slipped quickly into the back seat. "Follow them."

John Stokes dragged his wife into the house and up the stairs. She fought him, kicking and scratching. But his old man's rage was stronger than her old woman's panic and he had the strength to pull her up to the landing. By the time the servants had come running into the hallway, he had thrown open her bedroom door and pushed her inside.

"How dare you set foot in that church!" John Stokes's heart was pounding. He did not care if it were counting out its last strokes. "How dare you abase yourself in front of those people! How dare you make a fool of me!"

"Yes—I dared." Melissa Stokes's eyes met his, not afraid. "How you must hate me for that, John. I dared. At long last."

John Stokes kicked the door shut. "You'll never leave this house again."

"Oh no, John. I'll leave again and again and again, and one day I won't come back."

"You'll never show your stupid drugged face in public again. You will never humiliate me ever again!"

She placed a hand against his cheek. There was laughter in her face. If it had been crazy laughter he could have borne it. But it was the laughter of angels he had seen in paintings, easy and kind and forgiving.

"You're afraid of me," she said. "I can see it in your eyes. Why are you afraid of me, John?"

John Stokes felt a softness spreading from the touch of that hand through his entire body. He could not endure it. He summoned every ounce of denial in his being. He pushed her from him.

"Oh, my poor poor John. How lonely, how unloved you must be!"

His hand found an ashtray of cut glass. Though anger blinded him and his eyes were clenched shut, still he saw that terrible, kind smile. He struck one swift blow at it.

"Where are they?" Kitty demanded.

"Upstairs," Miss Jennings stammered. "Her room."

Kitty ran. She flung open the bedroom door. She found John Stokes huddled over his wife's body, gasping and choking.

"I've killed her," he said.

Kitty looked down at the silent, still woman. There was a bruise on her forehead, puffy and purple and glistening as a burst plum.

"Father," she said. "Help me. Take her feet."

Kitty took Melissa Stokes by the shoulders and John Stokes took her by the feet. It took all their combined strength to lift the dead weight. Together they pulled her across the floor and managed to get her onto the bed. Kitty loosened the buttons of the dress. She leaned an ear to Melissa Stokes's breast. She could hear the faint retreating drum of a heartbeat.

Melissa Stokes's hand slipped over the side of the bed. It dangled at a terribly wrong angle. Kitty realized that the arm was broken. If there had been any consciousness at all in the woman she would surely have been screaming from the pain of that wound. Kitty lifted the hand gently, as she had seen doctors do in the oil fields, and laid it across the stomach.

She went into the bathroom. She ran warm water in the sink basin, dipped a towel in it, and returned to the bedroom. With slow, careful strokes she cleansed the blood from the forehead, the eye, the scalp. There was a deep tear beneath the hair. By pressing the towel down on it she was able to slow the flow of blood.

Melissa Stokes's lips trembled. Kitty bent close to hear what she was whispering. There was no whisper, only a tiny bubble of red at the corner of the mouth. Kitty wiped it with the tip of the towel. She could hear John Stokes behind her, pacing the room like a crazed dog.

"Father," she said without turning from her work, "dip another towel in warm water and bring it to me quickly."

John Stokes brought the towel. He stared down at the old woman on the bloodied bed. His eyes were narrow and terrified. "I've killed her."

"She isn't dead," Kitty said. "Dead people don't bleed."

John Stokes gripped his hands together. "I'll call the doctor," he said. "That man Jones in Medford. He stitched her up when she cut her wrists."

"No one in the world would believe she did this to herself," Kitty said. She looked up at John Stokes and could see the panic gathering in his eyes.

"What are you saying, Kitty? Should we let her die?"

"I'm saying we must be very careful."

The bleeding from the scalp had almost stopped. Kitty reached down a thumb and peeled back one of the eyelids. The eye did not move. The pupil was as tiny as a black pinprick. The pupil of the other eye was larger.

"I've always taken responsibility for my actions," John Stokes said in a pale pinched voice.

"You struck her in anger," Kitty said automatically. "You weren't responsible."

"I've always paid my debts."

Kitty was not thinking of John Stokes and his debts. She was thinking of John Stokes III. She was thinking of Tyrone Duncannon's son. "Father," she said firmly, "come here and press this towel down tight. Wait for me."

She heard the old man sobbing quietly behind her as she left the room and shut the door. She went downstairs to Victoria Jennings' room and rapped sharply.

"Miss Jennings, I need your help. Can you come with me?"

Miss Jennings went with her. Kitty led with quick strides and thrust open the door of Melissa Stokes's bedroom. Miss Jennings' mouth froze open at the sight of the old wrecked woman on the bed and the old man pressing a bloody towel to her head.

"Stay with him," Kitty commanded her.

Miss Jennings' eyes shrank back only an instant, and then in a voice that barely trembled she said, "Yes, Mrs. Stokes," and went past Kitty into the room, taking charge.

Kitty hurried downstairs to John Stokes's inner office. She placed a call to Dr. Howard Bergman's free clinic in Youngstown.

"Doctor, this is Kitty Stokes. I'm calling for my father-in-law. He needs your help immediately and he'll pay whatever you ask."

"What happened to that woman?" Dr. Bergman asked.

"You know as much as I do," Kitty said.

Dr. Bergman fixed her with his cold brown gaze. "Someone tried to murder her."

"I didn't see it happen," Kitty said.

"But you know who did it."

Kitty did not answer. They were sitting in her bedroom, the two of them alone. Their coffee was turning cold. Dr. Bergman had examined Melissa Stokes and an ambulance was on its way.

"I'll have to tell the police," he said.

"Why?"

"Because even John Stokes hasn't the right to take a human life."

"No one's taken her life."

"She has a double cranial fracture. God knows how many blood vessels in the brain have burst. She may never regain muscular control or consciousness."

"But she's not dead."

"It's still attempted murder."

Kitty needed Dr. Bergman, which gave him an advantage over her. She recognized that he was in the right and she in the wrong, which made his advantage dangerous. He had let her tempt him once, but she knew she could not tempt him further in his present state of judging calm. She had to anger him or humble him or inflame some appetite in him. She had to get him off-balance and she had to do it fast, before the ambulance arrived.

"You hate John Stokes, Doctor. You hate him because you envy the strong."

Dr. Bergman shook his head in disgust. "I hate him because of his contempt for human life. He killed nine people last summer; he got away with it. He killed a family of six last week; he'll get away with that. Today he tried to kill that woman. And I'm not going to let him get away with it."

"You can't prove he even touched her."

"The police will prove it."

"And if they prove it and lock him up, what good will that do?"

"It's time justice was done."

"Justice," Kitty echoed. She thought of Tyrone Duncannon and his communism. She thought of men and all their bright useless banners. "Put him away and you may have justice, but you'll have nothing else."

"Justice," said the doctor, "is enough."

"Will it build hospitals? Will it buy bandages and medicines? Will it mend broken bones or put vision back in blind eyes or cure the dying? Is justice worth more than that to you?"

The doctor was silent.

"You have John Stokes in a position where you could get anything you want from him. Anything at all. And if all you want is justice, then you, Doctor, are a fool."

"And I'd be less of a fool if I blackmailed him into putting up a hospital?"

"It's not blackmail." She explained that Stokes Petroleum was reorganizing into small corporations. The stock in those corporations was being assigned to charitable foundations. "John Stokes could easily set up a medical foundation and appoint you director. You'd have money for your work. You wouldn't have to operate from under a Youngstown sidewalk. Think what you could do, Doctor, if John Stokes gave you a foundation."

Suddenly Dr. Bergman's eyes were caves of thoughtfulness.

"The lawyers can have preliminary papers drawn up in two days," Kitty said.

"Cancer research," Dr. Bergman said. "I could do cancer research."

"You could have the finest cancer research center in America. In the world. The resources of Stokes Petroleum would be at your disposal. You could save lives, Doctor. Hundreds. Thousands. More lives than John Stokes has ever taken or ever will. Now, isn't that worth a little more than—justice?"

After the ambulance had taken Melissa Stokes and her doctor, Kitty went to John Stokes's room. Victoria Jennings was sitting with the old man. "Now, Father," Kitty said, "there's absolutely nothing to worry about. Mother had an aneurysm in the brain. It burst. It could have happened to anyone her age. The aneurysm burst and she fell and hurt herself, but her condition is stable."

"I wanted to kill her," John Stokes said dully.

Miss Jennings looked up. Her eyes caught Kitty's and Kitty shook her head sharply. "Father, you don't know what you're saying. Miss Jennings, could I have a word with you?"

Victoria Jennings looked quickly at John Stokes. In a different way from the old man she seemed dazed herself. She rose from her chair and followed Kitty into the hallway.

Kitty spoke in a lowered voice. "You understand he doesn't know what he's saying."

Miss Jennings nodded. Her lips tightened till they were almost thin. "I understand," she said.

A chilly draft was blowing in the hallway and Kitty led Miss Jennings farther away from the old man's door.

"He didn't lay a hand on her," Kitty said. "He wanted to, but wanting and doing are two different things. You understand."

Miss Jennings did not answer. A cold dignity rippled out from her.

"Did he talk while you were alone?" Kitty asked.

Miss Jennings nodded.

"The things he said weren't true. He believes them, but they're not true. You do understand, don't you?"

A great deal depended on Miss Jennings' reply, and no reply came. It was as though she weren't there at all. Kitty saw a look on her face she had never seen before. She realized Miss Jennings was judging her.

"Mrs. Stokes, I haven't lied since I was a child. Please don't ask me to now."

Kitty controlled her voice and her face. "I'm not asking anything of the sort. All I want is your understanding."

"I've told you I understand."

Kitty was alarmed at the young woman's complete control of herself, because it meant she might be beyond Kitty's control.

"I can only promise you I won't repeat a thing I've seen or heard here today."

"I've no choice," Kitty said. "I'll have to believe you." It was not what she wanted: she would have preferred being believed to having to believe.

"I've made you a promise and I'll keep it. I don't lie, Mrs. Stokes. That's all you need to know about me."

Kitty stared. She had taken Miss Jennings at face value as a walking book of etiquette. It occurred to her now that there might be more to the straightness of that spine than simple finishing-school deportment.

It had been many years since Kitty had trusted another human being. The caution in her struggled with the courage and the courage won, barely, because she had no choice. She held out her hand and Miss Jennings took it.

"I'm going to have to rely on you," Kitty said.

"You can."

"It would be easier if you'd call me Kitty."

"I will if you like."

"And may I call you Victoria?"

"Friends call me Victoria. Family call me Vicky."

"I think we're family now," Kitty said. "I hope we'll be friends some day."

"Perhaps I'd better talk to the other servants," Vicky Jennings said. "They've heard enough to be wondering."

Kitty could see it was a good idea. The servants would trust

Vicky Jennings as one of themselves. "Thank you," she said. "Thank you, Vicky."

She stood alone in the hallway a moment, organizing her thoughts and her strategy. When she had decided on the best approach she returned to John Stokes. He was talking as though she had never left the room.

"I wanted to kill her but I never had the courage to try. I gave her that room and all the morphine she needed to do the job herself. But she never did. She always came out again."

Kitty gripped the old man's hand. "Now put those thoughts out of your head, Father. We have other matters to think about."

He tilted his head up at her. There was wonder in his eyes, a sort of childish contrition that Kitty had never seen in him before.

"Now you've had a shock, Father, but try and follow what I'm saying. Our futures depend on it. What have you done with Stokes Petroleum of New Jersey?"

John Stokes blinked.

"Who controls the stock?" Kitty prodded.

John Stokes flexed his mind and squeezed out the answer. "General Tri-State Petro."

"Have you assigned the stock in General Tri-State Petro?"

John Stokes squinted. His eyes fixed inward on figures filed in his head. "The papers haven't gone through," he said.

Kitty pressed his hand hard. She spoke very clearly and very slowly. "Tri-State Petro will be assigned to the Howard Bergman Cancer Research Foundation. Are you following me, Father? Dr. Bergman is with Mother. He's taking care of her. Dr. Bergman diagnosed Mother's aneurysm. We are going to charter a cancer research foundation for Dr. Bergman. Can you hear me, Father?"

John Stokes nodded. "Yes. I hear you."

"There is very important work to be done in cancer research. It will be a magnificent gesture. Dr. Bergman deserves a magnificent gesture."

John Stokes looked up at Kitty. His face slumped.

"He deserves our gratitude, Father."

"Yes." John Stokes nodded. "He deserves our gratitude."

That Sunday, for the first time since Kitty had known him, John Stokes did not go to church but sat in the study with a Bible shut on the table before him.

"Aren't you coming to church, Father?" she said.

"How can I?" he asked.

Two hours later, when she looked in again, he was still in the study, and the Bible was still shut.

In six days Kitty went to check on Melissa Stokes's condition.

"She'll have to stay in the hospital," Dr. Bergman said.

"How long?" Kitty asked.

They sat in Dr. Bergman's office, beneath the Youngstown sidewalk. The door was shut. The sick and the dying on the other side could not hear them.

"Till she dies."

Kitty took a deep breath. "How long will that be?"

"Days . . . years . . . there's no telling."

Kitty had seen Melissa Stokes, a gasping mummy of tubes and bandages. She weighed days and years. "No. We won't abandon her. She comes with us."

"She'll never move a limb. She'll never talk again. She can't feed herself or control her bodily functions. She'll live the rest of her life in utter helplessness."

Kitty's mind winced. It was grim, but it had to be faced. "All right. We'll get her a nurse. The nurse will feed her and diaper her and do whatever else needs doing." A terrible question occurred to Kitty. "Tell me, Doctor: can she see or hear? Is she at all conscious?"

"There are signs of vision and hearing. We can't be sure."

A dull sadness throbbed in Kitty. "The nurse will read to her," she said. "The nurse will keep her company."

Dr. Bergman looked at Kitty long and fixedly. "Mrs. Stokes, did you know that your mother-in-law has been taking morphine?"

Kitty thought of the locked room and the trays of uneaten food. Her gaze met the cool brown disgust of Dr. Bergman's eyes and did not flinch. "Is she addicted?"

"Yes."

"Then we'll give her morphine."

"It's not legal," Dr. Bergman said. "And it's not right."

Kitty rose and paced and whirled on him. "The woman's a vegetable, Doctor. What difference can it possibly make now? I'm not saying you have to push the needle into her arm. The nurse can do that. All you have to do is put your name on the prescription."

Silence came tumbling out of Dr. Bergman. He was staring at her with a strange mixed look. It could have been disgust, it could have been fear. Kitty didn't care. She thumped a bloated legal document down onto Dr. Bergman's desk, two hundred thirty-eight pages of single-spaced type with little red lines drawn at the borders, all bound with a pretty blue ribbon.

"There's your foundation, Doctor. Now you can damned well start earning it."

Johnny Stokes cursed his hands. They were shaking, over-worked. There was a fever in his fingers. His eyes ached from staring into the slanting light on the windowsill. He frowned at the porcelain jug balanced there. For the hundredth time he tried to see into its enigma.

Its flowered pattern had faded almost to the color of the gray background. But there was a deeper mystery. The jug was somehow alive on the windowsill; present; solid, with an ac-tuality that rippled out into space. Why, then, couldn't he make it real on paper?

Seven days ago he had arrived in the little town thirty-two miles west of Medford. He had holed up in a rooming house with eighty dollars cash and three quart jars of corn liquor. With chalks and watercolors, brushes and paper, he had sketched flowers, weeds, the landlady's tabby cat.

They had all escaped him.

His thoughts kept running in the same tight circle: *Am I running away? Am I an artist or is this just junk?* His eye went to the wastebasket overflowing with aborted beginnings. Sud-denly he hated the gray jug and its almost gray flowers. He hated the sunlight and the window and the dingy room. He ripped the sheet off his sketch pad and crumpled it and dropped it on the floor.

A knock came on the door and a voice cried, "Lunch!"

The landlady stepped in with a tray. Lunch was included in the rent. Today it was an exploded sausage in a gravy lake on a mound of mashed potato. The plate sat on a newspaper that had been folded open to an inner page. The landlady was a fat, good-natured woman, and she was talking in her rambling way.

"Society beauty, she was . . . It's a shame, why did she have to go marry that horrible old man? Just because he was rich as Croesus, I suppose. I don't wonder it gave her a stroke."

Johnny Stokes frowned and took the newspaper. The landlady caught the plate before it could spill and dirty her nice clean rug. She watched her tenant's eyes devour the news story.

"Something the matter, sir?"

Sweat poured down the young man's forehead. His shirt was stuck to him, wet through and clear as cellophane. She wondered if he was sick, if she would have to boil his sheets.

He crunched up the paper and let it fall into the wastebasket along with those crazy drawings of his. The landlady sniffed. Poor old Esther Peabody down the hall was counting on reading that paper.

"How much do I owe you for the rent?" the young man said sharply. "I'll be leaving right away."

Kitty saw that, for all its uncertainty, the present held the seeds of opportunity: Johnny was absent; Melissa Stokes need never again be reckoned with; John Stokes, though he would mend in time, was for the moment a broken man. Now was the moment to move.

She put on a navy-blue dress with two strands of matched pearls. They made her look older. She had the chauffeur drive her to the Empson Building in Youngstown, where Justin Lasting had his office.

"Justin, I need your advice."

"Yes, my dear?"

He waved her to a leather chair. He sat at his desk, making this a business conference, billable to the company.

"Justin, do you really think Stokes Petroleum should be run from a telephone in a hamlet eighty miles from nowhere? Besides the people in Bartonville hate us. Do you suppose we should move?"

This was only a tiny portion of Kitty's thinking. She recognized that Bartonville was a small, unimportant village. People who lived in small, unimportant villages led small, unimportant lives. Even the Stokeses. They had lackeys galore, but no friends of any worth. No politicians, no financiers, no artists or social leaders came to share their meals. The Stokeses had power of a raw sort, but they had not used it to attain position. Without position, life might as well be lived in a workman's shack. Tyrone Duncannon's son, Kitty had decided, would not grow up in Bartonville.

But the push could not come from her.

"There's something to be said for relocating the family . . ." Justin Lasting hooked his thumbs into his vest pockets. "As for relocating the business . . ."

"That's an idea," Kitty said, as though it had been his. "Do you think we might move everything?"

"I could see transferring some of the operation. In Cleveland we'd have a direct link to the stock exchange."

"You have a head for details, Justin. I can see why Father has such respect for you."

"The secret, my dear, always lies in the details."

"Cleveland would be easier for the family too. Mother could get good care there. Father wouldn't have to be reminded of . . . what happened in Bartonville. I think it depresses him. Have you noticed he's been depressed lately?"

"A little depressed, but understandably."

"Of course, there is one drawback to Cleveland . . ." Kitty paused, drawing out the silence. "It *is* awfully close to Youngstown, and the doctor who treated Mother knows . . . everything."

Justin Lasting's eyebrows pinched up alertly. "What do you mean, 'everything'?"

Kitty leaned forward in her chair. She spoke in a rapid nearwhisper. "Justin, they could send Father to jail."

He drew back. "I hardly think jail is a probability."

"People are so envious and cruel. They'll use any pretext to destroy him . . . and the company." Kitty stood. She paced to the window and stared down at the seventh-story view of the financial district. She turned. "We've got to get him as far away from here as we can, Justin. We've got to discharge the servants. We've got to sever completely with anyone who could link him to . . ." She said no more.

Justin Lasting's eyes narrowed. "To what, Kitty?"

"If I told you, wouldn't that make you an accomplice?"

"Not unless we're discussing some sort of felony."

Kitty scooped up her purse. She moved, fleet as an apology, to the door. "Forget we've had this conversation. I've said too much."

Justin Lasting bounded up from his chair. "My dear, you've said nothing at all. But you've managed to worry me deeply."

She took his hand. "Then you agree. We ought to get away,

go someplace where we could start over." She stared into Justin Lasting's skittering gray eyes as though she were dredging inspiration from their depths. "What would you think of New York?"

"New York?" he repeated.

"After all, it is the center of banking and stock markets, and radio and press . . ." She let the words *radio* and *press* linger and drift into silence. What, after all, was Justin Lasting's work except the bribing of the press and—with the growing rage of radio—of the broadcasters? What greater opportunity could there be for the man who had practically invented the profession of public relations than a move to New York, one of the capital cities of the world? She knew he must often have dreamt of such a chance. The only thing holding him back would have been the fear of losing the Stokes account. She could see the dream sparkle now, hungrily, in his eyes. "Don't you think we belong at the center, Justin?"

"But now?" he stammered. "Right away?"

"I knew you'd understand, Justin. Can you come to dinner tonight and make Father understand? He so respects your judgment. And you could see your godson too."

Justin Lasting joined Kitty and John Stokes that evening for a dinner of roast stuffed veal. After soup, Kitty prodded the conversation ever so slightly. Justin Lasting brought up the move to New York.

John Stokes at first resisted the suggestion. He reminded Kitty of a tree refusing to be transplanted even though the earth at its roots had totally eroded. She said little, allowing the two men to joust around the real issue. After the plates had been cleared and the fingerbowls brought, after the men had worn one another down sufficiently, she spoke.

"It seems to me Mother would be far happier in New York."

John Stokes's eyes were running one way and another like trapped animals.

"Bartonville has so many associations for her," Kitty went on smoothly, taking the pulse of his alarm. "There are so many bad memories here. And medically speaking, this is an outpost. Mother would have much better care in New York."

"And privacy," Justin Lasting added.

"There's no privacy in Bartonville." Kitty stared straight at her father-in-law, making sure her meaning sank in.

John Stokes was silent. A tic pulled at his jaw. When he finally spoke, his voice was sad. "It makes sense, I suppose. All the same . . . No, it makes sense."

"A great deal of sense, Father."

And so, with Johnny gone and his mother speechless, with no one to oppose her, Kitty settled the matter. She hired extra servants and movers and threw herself into a round-the-clock battle plan of packing and crating and shipping.

When Johnny returned home two days later, looking haggard and unfed, she did not skip a beat or waste a minute. She kissed him and asked him when he had last eaten. It was her experience that men argued less when their mouths were full, so she had the cook fix him a large roast beef sandwich.

"Johnny, we're moving to New York. The company's leased two floors at 15 Broad Street. That'll be your office. We've taken eight rooms at the Plaza Hotel. We'll live there till we find a house."

Johnny squinted at her, as though squinting made her less unreal. Perhaps he was drunk. She couldn't tell; he wasn't swaying. "Why are you doing this, Kitty?"

"It's Justin's idea. It's for the good of the company. And for our good too. People hate us here. You hate it here. Why else would you have run away? It's not a place for little Jay to grow up."

"But Mother—"

"Mother's coming with us. That's the whole point. We've got a wonderful nurse for her. Don't you worry about any of that."

"I want to see her."

"Of course you can see her." Kitty went upstairs with him.

Half of Melissa Stokes's face had twisted in on itself like a crumpled photograph. She sat propped up on pillows like a Raggedy Ann doll grown ancient. She did not speak. Her eyes were fixed in a dead-ahead stare. There was not so much as a twitch of recognition.

"Mother," Johnny pleaded. "Mother!"

Luckily, the nurse was there. Miss Carlin was twenty years old, fresh from nursing school. Kitty had hired her because she did not need Melissa Stokes's nurse dying before the patient. Miss Carlin smelled clean and competent, like peppermint, and she knew her stuff. She gave Johnny sixty seconds and then bustled him right out of the sickroom.

He started down the stairs very slowly. His eyes were beginning to glaze as though he had taken a slow-acting drug. "She didn't even know me."

"Of course she knew you," Kitty said.

Johnny was staring beyond her, beyond words. "I looked into her eyes and they were empty. There's no one there."

"She *is* there, Johnny. And she knows you're her boy. And we're going to take care of her. The very best care in the world."

He took her hand and his fingers dug into hers. He had none of the gentleness of the strong man, only the fierce tearing grip of the weak man cornered. She could see he was in shock. She could see he would accept any command.

"Come on, Johnny," she cajoled. "These things happen. There's nothing we can do but keep going." She slipped her arm into his. "Wouldn't you like to see your son? He's missed you."

Kitty saw no choice. There was no telling which of the servants might have heard a shouted word or blow. There was no telling how, left together, they might assemble their scraps of hearsay and evidence. They had to be dispersed—all except Miss Jennings, who in eight months had become one of Kitty's necessities.

Kitty wrote the servants fine references. She rewarded them with two months' severance pay each. Some of the men sniffled and some of the girls cried, but only Miss Hagstrom asked permission to say goodby to her mistress.

There was no decent way to refuse.

Miss Hagstrom was let into the sickroom dressed in black from head to toe. She wore a low-hemmed skirt and a wide-brimmed hat twenty years out of date. A red smell of scouring soap hovered about her, like the scathing sanctity of a Puritan saint.

She approached the bed. She stared a stiff, silent moment at the figure buttressed with pillows. "I've come to say goodbye, Mrs. Stokes."

Melissa Stokes's hands, quietly folded, rested on the quilted spread on her lap. The nails were clipped and clean. A hem of percale bedsheet stretched across her bosom like a bandage. Its lace edge rose and fell with each faint sigh of breath. There was no other movement.

Miss Hagstrom's two hands gripped Melissa Stokes's. "I'm being tossed out, ma'am, like a bag of picked-over soup bones. But don't you think for a minute your Hedda is abandoning you. I've cared for you twenty-five years, and I'll never stop caring for you."

Miss Hagstrom turned for one instant. She aimed a glance over her shoulder that nailed Kitty to the door. "Oh, Mrs. Stokes, I don't know who's done this to you or why. But I know someone's lying. This house was right so long as Hedda ·Hagstrom was here to keep it right. Everything was right till that woman came. And I know why she's sending me away. So you'll have no friend, no one to protect you. But I make you this promise."

Miss Hagstrom went down on her knees beside the bed. Her arms encircled the paralyzed woman.

"For the harm she's brought you and your family, I'll see that she pays."

Miss Hagstrom covered both hands in kisses. Revulsion coiled in Kitty's stomach. She was powerless to move. She felt she was watching a snake caress a rabbit.

"I'll make things even. Oh, my poor sweet missus! You can count on your Hedda!"

The nurse moved forward. "I'm sorry, you'll have to go now."

Miss Hagstrom was babbling Swedish. The nurse struck her calmly and accurately across the cheek, the standard nursing-school slap for hysterics.

Miss Hagstrom got to her feet. Silence came ripping from her. She moved to the door. She took the reference Kitty had written her and tore it to bits. She threw the flakes of paper at Kitty's face.

Kitty did not budge or blink.

Miss Hagstrom went down the back stairs for the last time. Her luggage, two meager black suitcases and a hatbox, was waiting in the kitchen. A taxi was ready for her at the back door. There were tears of righteous rage in her eyes and she did not even see the Pinkerton man at the gate wave goodby.

"Take me to the bus stop," Miss Hagstrom instructed the driver.

As the taxi lurched along the dusty highway she perched on the forward edge of the passenger seat. Her hands gripped the armrest so tightly that her knuckles showed white and jutting as bleached bone. Her gaze dug into the rearview mirror above the driver's head, where the gates of the Stokes mansion receded into a distant and irreversible infinity.

She saw that she had reached the most important crossroad of her life. She must decide what her beliefs and her honor were worth and whether she was willing to pay the price. For that there was a price, she now had no doubt.

She made a brief and bitter inventory of her assets. True, she had no friends, no family, and, for the moment at least, no prospects of employment. But she had a bankbook with current deposits totaling almost thirty-six hundred dollars. In her heart she had a well of hatred that would never run dry. She calculated the price of honor. It seemed to her that with luck and planning and the help of the Almighty, she could meet it; certainly she could afford to make an immediate down payment.

She snapped open the catch of her purse. She took out a small notebook bound in imitation leather. She turned to the page where she had written the address of Dr. Bergman's clinic. She had copied it from mail entering the house.

She could not help suspecting Dr. Bergman, suspecting his diagnoses, his prescriptions, the dark glint of his eyes. She suspected his hand in the ruin of her hopes, and though she knew Kitty Kellogg was too clever not to cover her tracks, she suspected that the doctor was too inexperienced in intrigue to cover them thoroughly.

"How much to take me to Youngstown?" she asked the driver suddenly. She told him the street name but not the number.

"That'll be fifteen dollars," he said.

"Ten," she snapped back.

They settled for twelve dollars and fifty cents. She gave no tip. She carried her two black bags and hatbox three blocks and she found a rooming house. She was able to knock the landlady down to six dollars a week.

Steeling herself against honking horns and filthy gutters, she explored her new neighborhood. She found Dr. Bergman's clinic, and not far from it she found a hardware store and a pharmacy. She bought a penknife and a bottle of rubbing alcohol. It was cheaper than disinfectant.

The following day in the privacy of her rented room she disinfected the knife blade, rolled up her skirt, and plunged the blade into the fatty tissue of her thigh. She bandaged the wound and gave the pain fifteen minutes to subside. It did not, but she had no more time to waste. She presented herself at the Bergman Clinic precisely five minutes after the doors had opened for the day.

It was Dr. Bergman's associate who treated the wound. He asked how she had gotten it.

"A quarrel," she said. "Nothing important." She had never seen a pauper's clinic so clean or with so much chrome-plated equipment. She smelled Stokes money.

The nurse helped Miss Hagstrom back into her skirt. The doctor told her to return in two days.

"How much do I owe you?" she said.

"This is a free clinic," he said.

"I don't take charity," Miss Hagstrom said. "I haven't any money, but I'm an experienced housekeeper. A good waxing on that floor out front would help keep it clean."

The doctor tried to refuse. Miss Hagstrom, with a near-hysterical imitation of gratitude, refused the refusal. That evening after office hours she waxed the floor in the front room. Two days later when she returned for a fresh dressing she waxed the floor in the doctor's office and polished the wooden cabinet where patients' records were kept.

A week and a half later, Miss Hagstrom returned to the clinic with a badly bruised hip. Two weeks after that she was waxing and dusting the clinic on a regular basis. Dr. Bergman's associate felt sorry for her. She had no money and it was clear that the poor soul's husband beat her sadistically.

The doctor gave her seven dollars a week and a key to the front door.

# Chapter 9

THE STOKESES CLOSED their mansion and traveled to New York by private Pullman car. They moved into two connecting suites of the Plaza Hotel. From the window of the sitting room Kitty and little Jay could look down at Fifth Avenue and the statue of General Sherman. Horses and carriages queued along Central Park, awaiting tourists and honeymooners. Double-decker buses with open tops towered above the never-ceasing traffic. Even from the twelfth floor you could hear the cacophony of car horns and Irish cops blowing their whistles. Kitty had never seen so many cars or people or pigeons gathered at one crossroad.

She had the manager install a small kitchen in one of the walk-in closets so that she could warm little Jay's food herself. He had progressed to strained meats and vegetables. Though she still gave him her nipple, there was very little milk left in her breasts. On the advice of the pediatrician, she diluted and sweetened commercial milk, warmed it, and fed it to Jay in a bottle with a rubber nipple. She felt, obscurely, that she was deceiving the child, letting him down. But facts were facts: her breasts were like John Stokes's oil wells—you couldn't get more out of them than God had put in.

The service and food at the hotel were excellent—and they cost an excellent price, too; but a hotel was not the same as a home of one's own.

The lobby was as public as the street and sometimes just as dangerous. One afternoon Kitty got pushed to the wall by a mob of autograph hunters and newsmen descending on Fannie Brice, the Ziegfeld Follies star, who was trying to have tea in the Palm Court with a man said to be a gangster. A week later, pickets surrounded the hotel, protesting Isadora Duncan. It was unclear to Kitty whether they objected to Miss Duncan's baring her breasts onstage or to her Bolshevik poet husband. But they did keep Kitty from crossing Fifty-ninth Street, and little Jay had to forego a sunny afternoon in Central Park.

There were disturbances even on the twelfth floor, where the Stokeses had their suite. One morning when the noise from a wild party had kept little Jay awake and screaming till 3 A.M., Kitty dressed and went next door to ask for quiet, please.

A man who said his name was Scottie Fitzgerald listened to her problem and then insisted on escorting her around the room. He introduced her to Edith Rockefeller, the divorced daughter of John D., who was dancing a drunken Charleston with Gene Tunney, the prizefighter.

"This is Kitty Stokes, and she wishes you'd be quiet," Scottie Fitzgerald said. He took her to the piano and introduced her to Cole Porter. "She wishes you'd stop playing, Cole."

Kitty tried to apologize. "It's just that my child can't sleep," she said.

"You see, Cole?" Scottie's wife Zelda roared. "Your music is unsuitable for children!" She thrust a bottle of champagne at Kitty. "This should keep the brat quiet."

Kitty left the bottle by the door and went back to her suite. She complained to the management, but the party went on till six.

That afternoon Cole Porter sent a dozen American Beauty roses and a handwritten apology. It was the first note Kitty had ever had from a celebrity, and she kept it; but she began spending little Jay's naptime searching for a more suitable place to live.

She wanted two townhouses, preferably side by side: one for herself and Johnny and little Jay; the other for John Stokes and Melissa and the nurse. She found attractive possibilities on Sutton Place and on a tree-lined street in the East 60's and on a street of brownstones just off Madison in the 50's. In each instance the discussion with the real estate agent went well; the price was agreeable, and naturally there was no need for a mortgage. Yet, within a day, each agent called back and said he was sorry, but the house was no longer for sale. Kitty had Vicky Jennings phone, inquiring about the properties, and all three were still available.

"Why aren't they selling to us?" she asked Vicky. "Would it do any good to offer them more money than they're asking?"

"No," said Vicky. "They'll only sell to one another."

"Who is 'one another'?"

Miss Jennings left the room for a moment. She returned and handed Kitty a small, thick book, almost square, with a cover of black-papered pasteboard that felt curiously cheap in her fingers. It was entitled New York Social Register. Vicky explained that every leading city in the United States had a similar book.

Kitty flipped through the pages. They were thin, like the onionskin of a Bible, but of a slickness that suggested poorer quality. They were not bound, but glued to an inner paper spine. She saw that the book was essentially a telephone directory. Many of the families listed had phones not only in Manhattan but on Long Island and in Westchester and Duchess counties, some as far away as Arizona and Palm Springs. Daughters who had married were asterisked, their new names indicated.

At a glance, Kitty caught six dozen names identical to those of directors of corporations doing business with Stokes Petroleum. She noticed gaps too. No Italians. No Jews. No Spanish. Only a few French and German, mostly of the "de" and "von" variety. There were Protestant Irish, like Dufferin and Macadam, but no Costellos or obvious Catholics.

"Is it because I'm Irish?" Kitty asked. "Is that why they won't let me buy?"

"It's because of the way Mr. Stokes made his money."

"He made it exactly the same way as anyone else in this book—they're all thieves, and the only difference is that John Stokes is a bigger one."

"And a newer one... These are old families."

"I see. It's a club. Well, we've got to get into it." It was clear to Kitty that little Jay had to go to school with the children of these people; he had to marry one of the daughters of these people; he had to *be* one of these people. "I want my son to be listed in this book by the time he's able to walk. How much will it cost?"

"You can't buy your way in."

"There's nothing in this world that isn't for sale at some price. Who do I see, who do I go to? Miss Jennings, I hired you because you know these things."

Vicky sighed. "Mrs. Stokes, I'm a poor woman. I've no wealth, no husband, no standing. Yet I'm listed in the Detroit Social Register; and I'll be listed till I'm married, and, depending whom I marry, I may remain listed. I'm listed because my father was listed and his father before him and they married women who were listed. Even though my father lost his money, he didn't lose his listing. So you see, it doesn't have to do with money—not exactly."

"But your grandfather was rich."

"Very rich."

"So the money gets you in, and once you're in you stay."

"In general, yes. But if you divorce, you're dropped. If you commit a crime, you're dropped."

"Crime?" Kitty cried incredulously. "There are Astors and Vanderbilts in here—robbers and fur traders and rum runners! Rockefellers and Morgans—hell, the federal government indicted them! And Tiffanys—tradesmen!"

"But all that fur trading and rum running was a long time ago."

"Well, I'll be damned if I'm going to wait *that* long. I'll think of a way."

"You're wasting your time, Mrs. Stokes."

Kitty remained convinced that, no matter what Miss Jennings said or believed, money was power. It was money that commanded troops; it was money that had aimed a rifle at Tyrone Duncannon and put a bullet through him. Yet the fact that Miss Jennings and her kind were embarrassed, if not silent, about money suggested that the power of wealth was as disturbing to those who wielded it as that of religion or sex.

It came to her that the Stokeses, with a fortune so great that the interest on it could not even be totaled from one day to the next, much less the principal, were excluded from society not because they lacked wealth, but because that wealth was naked. It had no clothes.

She saw that much was required: right address, right possessions, right habits, right friends. Of all these, the real estate problem—once Kitty had grasped the nature of the difficulty—was the easiest solved.

Two townhouses faced in marble, just off Fifth Avenue in the 60's, exactly fitted her requirements. They bore discreet FOR SALE signs, discreet flaking paint. Instead of phoning the real estate agents, Kitty phoned the man from the United States Trust Company who handled several of John Stokes's portfolios. She had him make inquiries. She learned that the houses were mortgaged, as she had suspected, and that the mortgages were held by commercial banks.

She went to confer with John Stokes. He had a visitor, a hard-eyed Yale graduate named Henry Luce, who was trying to raise money to start a weekly news magazine to be called *Time*.

"And how is this magazine going to treat big business?" John Stokes wanted to know.

"Fairly and honestly," Henry Luce said.

"That's not good enough," John Stokes said. "Sorry."

"I think you may have made a mistake," Kitty said after the young man had gone.

"I can afford mistakes," John Stokes said.

"Well, Father, I've a proposal for you that's not a mistake. I've found two lovely townhouses on East Sixty-second Street. They're next to each other and they'd be perfect for us. Mother could have a roof garden for her roses."

John Stokes nodded an old man's nod.

"We could save a great deal of time," Kitty said, "if we bought the mortgages. One is held by the Bank of New York and the other by the Chase."

"But if we bought the houses we'd automatically assume the mortgages."

"That would take time; Father, we've already been eight months without a roof of our own. I think we should make deposits—large cash deposits—at the Bank of New York and the Chase. They'd be happy to sell us the mortgages."

John Stokes looked at her strangely. "You want to foreclose on the owners?"

It seemed odd for John Stokes, of all people, to hesitate at foreclosure. "No one's foreclosing, Father. The property is for sale. I just want to be sure we get it, and get it quickly."

John Stokes waved a hand weakly. "Speak to the trust company. I'll sign whatever needs signing."

It was strange, Kitty thought, and in a way sad. *He's changed. He didn't even ask what the houses cost.*

Three days later, two grim-faced men—a Devereux and a Washburn, both listed in the Social Register—signed the transfer papers in the boardroom of the United States Trust Company. For three hundred eighty thousand dollars, the Stokeses became owners of two Stanford Whites. They traded the suites at the Plaza for their own tall windows, marble fireplaces, dark wood paneling and swooping staircases. Kitty engaged servants: a staff of four to look after John and Melissa Stokes; and a staff of six to look after her own household.

Social acceptance proved a more difficult question. For the next several months, alone with their servants in the two marble palaces, Kitty feared that she had traded a Bartonville of open skies and green lawns for one of skyscrapers and pavement. Nevertheless, she religiously studied the society notes in the newspapers, noting who was marrying whom and in what church, who was making her debut and by whom escorted. These names were invariably drawn from the Social Register: even a girl in Greenwich, Connecticut, marrying the son of a naval captain from Annapolis, was somehow worthy of a mention with photograph in the New York *Times*—always because of that square black book.

But there was one social area where Kitty noticed the occasional Irishman, the odd Jew or Italian. These were the charitable and cultural events. Here the Social Register and outsiders appeared to mix, if not as equals, at least as convenient necessities to one another. These parties were reported as "fundraisers" and they were said to benefit museums, symphony orchestras, the Metropolitan Opera, orphans, polio victims, survivors of shipwrecks and burned-out tenements. It was as though New York would swoop on any disaster as an excuse for dancing.

At these events one name led the others, often as chairman: Cornelia Barnes Whitney. The Social Register listed her in a townhouse on Park Avenue and Seventy-fourth Street and a string of "dilatory domiciles" from Nova Scotia to Palm Beach.

"What do you know about this Whitney woman?" Kitty asked Miss Jennings.

"I believe she's a widow and rather old."

"She seems to head a lot of things. Have you ever met her?"

"Once, when I was a child. It was at my aunt's in Grosse Pointe. We had money then."

"Can you introduce us?"

"She wouldn't remember me. And besides, I'm a servant now."

"What's her favorite charity? Orphans? The blind?"

"There's cancer in her family. Her mother and grandmother both died of it."

Kitty had seen no cancer balls announced in the New York papers. "What are her cultural interests?"

"Only one—opera."

From what Kitty had read in the papers, the Metropolitan Opera was always on the brink of more lavish productions—and greater bankruptcy. "We'll buy a box at the opera. Next to hers. We'll give money. We'll underwrite one of their galas. We'll get our names in the program. Patrons. At the top of the list. She'll have to acknowledge us."

Miss Jennings made a slightly disapproving face. "Mrs. Stokes, things don't work that way."

But Kitty was thinking of little Jay. "Things can be made to work that way."

Kitty decided on a direct line of attack. The Wall Street firm of Kuhn, Loeb was handling issues of stock in the reorganized Stokes companies. They were making 12 percent clear profit and they owed the Stokeses a favor or two. The principal partner in the firm, Otto Kahn, was known to be an art fanatic; and he was the chief financial backer of the Metropolitan Opera. Kitty made an appointment to call on him at his office.

He was a small, bald man with a probing squint to his eye. His clothes were tailored in immaculate taste that stopped just short of being dandified. His handshake was firm and quick and Kitty saw no point in wasting the time of either of them.

"I believe you've handled some transactions for us."

A smile took shape, unsymmetrically, on Otto Kahn's lips. "I believe we have. And do you have some further transactions in mind?" The man had a curious accent, slightly British, slightly Prussian, like plum pudding on pumpernickel.

"I want a subscription to the Metropolitan Opera."

"You hardly need to come to me for that."

"I want the same series as Cornelia Whitney, and I want a parterre box next to hers."

Otto Kahn's smile vanished. "Don't you realize, Mrs. Stokes, that those boxes are subscribed years in advance?"

"There must be vacancies now and then. People die, don't they?"

Otto Kahn seemed to have lost the power of speech.

"My family," Kitty said, "wishes to make a contribution to this year's opening gala. We wish to contribute whatever it takes to get that box."

It took eighty thousand dollars to get the box: three thousand dollars for a season subscription of sixteen performances, seventy-seven thousand as a tax-deductible contribution to the new production of *Der Rosenkavalier*.

Kitty forced her husband and father-in-law to come to the opening night. With mounting excitement, she recognized faces from newspaper photographs: Whitneys, Devereux, Chases, Vanderbilts, Morgans, Fords, presidents of banks and corporations and brokerage houses, the interlocking directorates of America's top industries, all of them there in that horseshoe of parterre boxes. The men sat like stuffed penguins in their white ties and dark tails, the women like enamel birds in their tiaras and gowns. Kitty marveled at the furs that the husbands hung in the anterooms to the boxes, at the wives' necklaces and glowing skins.

Cornelia Barnes Whitney sat in the next box. Turning slightly to the left, pretending to angle her program for better light, Kitty could study the ruler of New York society. She had never before realized that, with money, age could be made beautiful.

From neck down, Mrs. Whitney was green silk and diamonds. Hair of perfect snowy whiteness crested her head. Her face was narrow, heart-shaped, with pale eyes that played like iridescent sapphires. The skin was smooth, curiously unwrinkled; the lips smiled even in repose. Mrs. Whitney nodded with great animation, agreeing with her companions in the box. Among them Kitty recognized Mr. and Mrs. J. Harrison Prewitt, who owned the townhouse just east of hers. She had never spoken to them. She also recognized, from newspaper photographs, the very young Vanderbilt girl. Two men, shadowy but for their white shirt fronts, sat back from the light.

The houselights dimmed. There was applause for the conductor, a Czech. Beneath Kitty, in the dark, the audience glistened like freshly plowed earth.

She gave all her attention to the crashing orchestra, the soaring voices. Opera was new to her. She wanted to understand it as those around her did. From time to time she could feel curious eyes from neighboring boxes turned on her, inspecting her. She sat absolutely straight, shoulders not even touching the back of the chair, as Miss Jennings had taught her.

She thought, *If only you knew, Jay, what your mother was doing for you, you'd be proud of her.*

In intermission Kitty pulled Johnny into the bar reserved for patrons who had contributed two thousand dollars or more to the opera. John Stokes Sr. doddered behind them. Vicky Jennings brought up the rear. Kitty had commanded her attendance, hoping to exploit her connections—however tenuous—to New York society.

"Johnny," Kitty said, "you know these people—introduce me."

"I don't know them. I do business with them."

"Honestly, Johnny. We're as good as anyone here."

"Kitty, please . . ."

Kitty made a beeline for Mrs. J. Harrison Prewitt, head of fund-raising for the New York Foundling Infirmary, whose daughter had married a Ford last summer in Saint Thomas' Church or Fifth Avenue. Mrs. Prewitt was standing alone while her husband worked his way through the crowd at the bar.

"How do you do, Mrs. Prewitt," Kitty said. "I'm Kitty Stokes. We're neighbors on Sixty-second Street."

Astonishment seeped like a stain across Mrs. Prewitt's face. "How do you do," she said, and not a word more. Her eyes gazed past Kitty, denying her very existence. When J. Harrison Prewitt arrived with two champagne glasses there was no further introduction. The Prewitts plunged deep into the chattering, glittering crowd and were gone.

Johnny and his father and Vicky Jennings huddled in a deserted corner. They looked like sheep in a storm. "Kitty," Johnny said, "I think this was a mistake."

"You'll never win a fight in your life," she said, "if you start with that attitude."

Still, she had to admit there was a definite ribbon of emptiness enclosing them, cutting them off from the other patrons, from the laughter, the voices, the clinking glasses. Kitty caught glances in their direction, hands lifted to mouths like shields cupping whispers. A unanimity rippled through the room, and somehow the Stokeses were not part of it.

When they returned to the box, Kitty saw that Johnny had been right. Every other box in the parterre was empty. There were not even fur coats in the anterooms. The golden horseshoe was wiped out, as though a plague had hit.

*And the plague,* Kitty realized, *is us.*

Well, she decided, New York was just going to have to get used to the plague.


Kitty spoke to her lawyers the next morning and arranged a Pullman car to Youngstown for the afternoon. When she went to Howard Bergman's clinic the following day she found Dr. Bergman between appointments, sitting in his office frowning over lab reports. His head jerked up when she came in.

"How would you and your clinic like to move to New York City?" she said.

Howard Bergman remained motionless a moment, staring at her out of fixed, measuring eyes. "That's complicated," he said.

"Complications can be handled," she said.

"Why do you want me to move?"

"My reasons don't concern you, Doctor. All you need to know is I want a clinic in New York and I'm willing for it to be yours."

The office was unpleasantly warm. Its cleanliness smelled chokingly of ammonia and rubbing alcohol and formaldehyde. In the dispensary beyond the shut door children were screaming at the prospect of inoculations.

Kitty spelled out the amount of capital that she would make available to a New York clinic. Without answering, Dr. Bergman lit a cigarette. She saw that his hand was trembling.

"You'd have space, Doctor. You wouldn't have to have your office in the dispensary." She pointed to the steaming pan against the wall. "And you wouldn't have to boil hypodermics in your office. You'd have a lab for that."

The cigarette steadied in Dr. Bergman's hand. She saw he was not a man who allowed others to know what he felt or how he reached a decision. He was a hard man to move, and not simply because there was five foot eleven and a hundred seventy-five pounds of him.

"In New York you'd matter," she said. "Your work would matter."

"My work and I matter here."

"Not enough."

His wide-set eyes took their time studying her. "Why do you feel you have to keep bribing me?"

"Who's saying 'bribe'?"

"If you offer a clinic in New York," he said, "it's a bribe. If I ask for one it's blackmail. That's our working relationship, Mrs. Stokes. We have the goods on one another. It's a nasty way to do business and a lousy way to practice medicine. I'm in pretty deep with you already, but at least we're even. You can expose me with a word and send me to jail, and I can expose you with a word and send you to jail. Now you're raising stakes. Since we can already destroy one another, I'm very tempted to say enough is enough."

"You're not that big a fool, Doctor."

He looked at her without giving the slightest hint what he was thinking. It occurred to her he might be appraising her sexually. She found herself imagining what it would be like to be naked and touching him.

The phone on his desk rang. He lifted the receiver and began arguing with a plumber about a clogged sink in the nurses' lavatory.

"In New York," she said when he hung up, "you wouldn't have to fight with plumbers."

"Why not, don't they have plumbing?"

"You'd have professionals to do your arguing for you."

Cornelia Barnes Whitney was furious. She was always furious when she did not know what to expect.

At ten on a Thursday morning her man from United States Trust telephoned and suggested it would be advisable—his very word, "advisable"—to see the Stokes woman; after all, the Stokes-controlled holdings in Whitney Aluminum were not inconsiderable.

At ten-thirty the phone rang again. A woman claiming to be Mrs. Stokes's social secretary—her very words, "social secretary"—asked when and where it might be convenient for Mrs. Whitney and Mrs. Stokes to meet. Cornelia Whitney quickly calculated what would be least convenient for Mrs. Stokes.

"Here," she said, "in half an hour." She did not quite slam the receiver onto its hook so much as replace it very firmly.

She spent the next half hour in her morning room, stabbing open letters with her ivory letter knife. She wondered why in the world Mrs. Stokes was risking a second humiliation. She sensed that the woman was going to attempt to extort forgiveness; or worse yet, to ingratiate herself. She shuddered.

At eleven o'clock precisely she heard the distant ring of a doorbell. The butler announced that a Mrs. John Stokes Jr. had called and was waiting.

"You may show her in," Cornelia Whitney said icily.

The morning room faced south. Perhaps it was the fault of the direct sunlight, dazzling at that hour, but the woman who stood in the doorway had green eyes of astonishing boldness and waves of soft red hair, and her gray dress shimmered like mother-of-pearl.

"You're very kind to see me," the visitor said.

"Not at all." Cornelia Whitney intended to get the interview over with as quickly as possible. In her least hospitable tone she inquired if the woman would care for tea.

"No, thank you. I'll only stay five minutes. I don't want to impose on you."

*Then why,* Cornelia Whitney wondered, *has your broker threatened to dump ten thousand shares of Whitney Aluminum on the stock exchange?*

"Why are you here, Mrs. Stokes?"

"I'm here to ask for your help."

With a nod, Cornelia Whitney indicated a chair. It was Limoges silk and it faced the sunny window. Mrs. Stokes would have to squint.

Cornelia Whitney was silent. She sensed she was in the presence of either great stupidity or great courage. She had seen enough of both in her lifetime to know they could work equal damage.

"I thought money could accomplish anything," the woman said. "I see now that it can accomplish very little by itself."

In a flash, Cornelia Whitney understood. The pretty little

*nouveau riche* had come to wedge her clan of robber barons into the Social Register. Mrs. Whitney could not but be impressed by the scale of such audacity.

"You want *my* help, Mrs. Stokes?"

"My family has set up a cancer foundation in Youngstown. I want to move it to New York and make it the best in the world."

The conversation had taken an unexpected turn. This little social climber did not matter, but cancer did. Cornelia Whitney paid attention.

"Why New York?" she said.

"Because New York is the center. Everything starts here—your art, your money, your politics, your medicine. The best men are always going to be in this city. Sure, we could pay more and bribe them into coming to Youngstown. But we'd only get the second-raters. The foundation has got to be here—at the center."

"What do you mean, *here?* You want to build a clinic on Park Avenue?"

"We've got an option on twelve acres over on the East River."

"And how in the world do you think *I* can help you?"

"The head of our foundation is a doctor called Howard Bergman. He's a genius. But he's a Jew. And I'm sure you know, Mrs. Whitney, the higher ranks of the medical profession are not exactly—open to outsiders. Dr. Bergman can't fight cancer if he's spending half his time fighting the Jew-haters."

"I still don't see how I can help."

"I want to give a fund-raising ball for the foundation. Fund-raising isn't the point—we've got the money. The point is, I'd like you to serve on the committee—as president. If people see that you put first things first, they'll fall into line behind you. You're a leader."

It was a great deal to absorb at once—cancer, committees, Jews. Cornelia Whitney had known several Jews—Germans, mostly; musicians. Only eighteen years ago she had led the cabal that had persuaded the board of the New York Philharmonic to hire Gustav Mahler. He had been a very bad-tempered man with no manners, but he had certainly improved the orchestra. And Otto Kahn had single-handedly bailed out the Metropolitan Opera for almost twenty years. They weren't all bad people, Jews.

"Tell me about this doctor," Cornelia Whitney said, "this Bergman."

"He's young—thirty. But he'll need all the years he's got, because it's an uncharted field. He's working on a new system of killing the cancer cells. It's an alternative to surgery."

"I didn't know there was any alternative."

"There is. It's X-ray radiation. They're developing it in Germany. They're only at the beginning, but it looks promising. It'll take work and research and money. It'll take machines people haven't even designed yet. All that's easy. The hard part is, it'll take the cooperation of the entire medical profession."

"Why the *entire* profession?"

"Because cancer can hit any organ, any tissue. It's no good having your ophthalmologists over there and your bone men there and your neurosurgeons somewhere else. You've got to bring them all together, like an army. You'll never win the battle if all your soldiers are running off in different directions. We can't have bone men and blood men and lung men and brain men treating cancer. We've got to have cancer men treating bone and blood and lungs and brains."

It was a far better answer than Cornelia Whitney had expected. It disturbed her—perhaps because there was a hint of brogue to it; or a hint of sense.

"I see what you're saying. It's a question of changing the approach." But something nagged at Cornelia Whitney. The girl was young, she was healthy, she was rich. What could she want? What was her motive? "But tell me, Mrs. Stokes: why are you so interested in cancer?"

"My mother might be alive today if the right specialist had existed to treat her."

Cornelia Whitney thought of her own mother, of her grandmother. She thought of the fear that lurked inside her and of her daily attempt to deny it. "Of course I don't know this man, this Bergman. But I don't think that's necessary. I'd like my lawyers to look into your foundation before I give my answer."

"Your lawyers can talk to mine anytime they like."

Cornelia Whitney's lawyers looked at the Foundation. They recommended not only that she preside over the committee, but that she immediately reassign a tenth of her aluminum holdings to the Clinic. There were many advantages to the arrangement, two of them enormous: it would minimize any danger of the Stokeses' dumping, and—while Mrs. Whitney would naturally retain voting control—she would escape the nuisance of the new graduated income taxes.

The following Tuesday, Cornelia Whitney called at the Stokes townhouse. Over tea, she and Kitty mapped plans for the fund-raising gala. Mrs. Whitney proposed other committee members: Mrs. Plimpton, Mrs. Gaddis, Mrs. Mansfield. "They run the Junior League," she explained. "They've had experience in this sort of thing. I think you'd get along with Sally Gaddis."

And so it was that Cornelia Whitney's friends began calling at the house on East Sixty-second Street. They were stiff, well-dressed women. They balanced on the edge of their chairs. They were always looking to Mrs. Whitney for their cues. Their eyes never quite trusted Kitty. She coaxed them into accepting tea and lunch and then, quite brazenly, dinner. Return invitations began arriving in the morning mail.

In the second month after Cornelia Whitney's decision to serve as president of the committee, Kitty and Johnny dined at home only twelve times. Johnny's face would be tired and drawn when he got back from the Broad Street office and saw Kitty in her evening gown.

"Kitty, why the hell are we doing this? Can't we just sit home and have some cold roast beef?"

"We're doing this for little Jay. There'll be plenty of time for cold roast beef afterward. Get a move on now; they're expecting us at seven-thirty."

The Committee for the Bergman Clinic Ball—C. Whitney, president, K. Stokes, vice president—voted to hold the gala in the St. Regis Hotel ballroom during the spring debutante season. The committee set the price of tickets at an unheard-of five hundred dollars the pair.

Within two weeks of the mailing, the gala was fully subscribed.

By ten o'clock, Kitty knew that the Clinic Ball—"little Jay's party," as she thought of it—was a success. The top tenth of the Social Register were there, and they were just as rowdy as a bunch of drunk micks—only they dressed neater and drank better rotgut.

Kitty and Johnny shared a table with Cornelia Whitney and

her escort, a curator of the Metropolitan Museum of Art. He wore a goatee and told jokes.

Howard Bergman, naturally, was at the table too, and since he was still unmarried he was seated next to Mrs. Whitney's niece, Phoebe Huntington, a pale blond girl in a greenish gown. Howard Bergman's behavior toward the girl struck Kitty as the absolutely perfect balance of interest and respect. Even though Phoebe didn't seem at all Dr. Bergman's type—she was much too pale and unsure of herself, and of course he was not at all, socially speaking, hers—still he did a marvelous job of seeming interested; and Mrs. Whitney was plainly delighted to see her niece making such a success with a handsome bachelor.

A director of Kuhn, Loeb and the president of the Chase Bank had bought the other places at the table. Their wives spoke of Hobe Sound, a resort in Florida. They said Kitty and Johnny absolutely must come down next winter. "You can take Harry McCann's place: he's never there in March."

Johnny sipped at his champagne. He ignored the blur of dresses and starched shirts spinning by. With his fork he made lines on the tablecloth. Kitty wondered how on earth he could be bored so early in the evening. The ballroom had been decorated with trellises wound with real gardenias. On tables circling the dance floor were cut-glass bowls of orchids floating in water. Debutantes fluttered past, lovely and slim-hipped and flat-chested in the style of the day. Waiters, skillful as tightrope walkers, dashed through the crowd with trays of bootleg champagne balanced on upraised hands. Resting dancers recovered their strength on velvet divans that lined the curve of the ballroom.

There were three bars, serving scotch from Scotland and rum from Cuba and gin from England—only the best contraband at little Jay's party! The four buffets served turkeys and hams and jellied pheasants, salads of lobster and out-of-season avocados, teasing infinities of hors d'oeuvres and canapés. Kitty could not help thinking how odd the economics of life was: you could have fed all the shanties of Bartonville for six months on that pile of food—and it was all going to be eaten or thrown away in a single night.

A twenty-piece orchestra never stopped playing: they blared out tangos and show tunes and foxtrots and Viennese waltzes that kept the dancers in a swirl. There was a new craze, the

Charleston, and Cornelia Whitney kept making faces at the acrobatics of young girls in beaded skirts.

Kitty danced: first with Johnny, then with the other men at the table, and then with men she had never met before, lawyers and financiers and senators, whose names she made sure she caught. Some of them danced well: they took her in their arms and whirled her around with cool arrogance, as Tyrone Duncannon had done at Saturday night socials. Others were drunk and fumbled and tripped. Kitty kept her talk to "yes" and "no," laughter and a listening smile, and she could tell she was charming them all.

The whole world seemed to be enjoying itself. All around her voices grew louder and merrier, the laughter more abandoned, with each passing minute. The ballroom was an endless explosion of music and giddy shouts and clinking glasses.

As the chairman of the board of Corning Glass escorted Kitty back to her table, a waiter whispered that she had a phone call. She excused herself and followed the waiter to a phone booth off the ballroom. As she slipped into it and slid the door shut, a little fan began whirring overhead, stirring up eddies of Chanel perfume. The receiver crackled in her hand like a radio.

"Mrs. John Stokes Jr.?" a voice asked, faraway, female, officious.

"Speaking."

"Go ahead, Bartonville."

Kitty's heart clenched in her. She wondered why in the world anyone in Bartonville would be phoning, and why tonight of all nights.

"Kitty?" a man's voice shouted above the crackling. "I've had a devil of a time tracking you down."

A premonition gripped her. "Father Jack," she said, "is that you?" She pictured him calling from the crank phone in the company store, standing among the burlap bags of dried beans and flour, his cassock hem uneven and dragging on the dirty floor.

"There's been an accident," he was saying. "Your father—"

The music was so loud that even the closed glass door could not blot it out. The orchestra was playing "Bye Bye Blackbird," and voices struggled along with it. Father Jack's voice came in uneven waves, but Kitty could piece together bits of what he was saying.

Joe Kellogg had taken a fall from one of the rigs.

"How serious?" she cut in.

"He's dying, Kitty."

She felt a rising, panicky confusion. She was certain she hadn't heard him right, that something was wrong with the telephone connection, all the crackling noise was twisting Father Jack's words around.

"He's asking for you, Kitty. If you want to see him, you'd better get out here fast."

Kitty gazed through the glass door at waiters scurrying past with trays of filled glasses; tipsy debutantes on high heels; young men in white tie and tails.

"Tell him I'm coming," Kitty said. "Tell him I'm coming right now."

She made one phone call, then hurried back to the table and whispered to Johnny. She made her excuses to the guests. Cornelia Whitney, who must have had three glasses of champagne by now, kissed her on the cheek. "Lovely party, Kitty my dear, simply lovely."

Kitty had the chauffeur stop at the house. The maid handed her a suitcase through the front door. The chauffeur sped on to Pennsylvania Station. An employee of Stokes Petroleum took Kitty's suitcase and led her through thickets of rumpled travelers to Track 46, where a locomotive and a private Pullman car were waiting.

The company limousine could take her no farther than the Bartonville town pump. Kitty had to walk the hill herself. The soil was treacherous with pebbles and rocks. Her high heels kept slipping. The path was narrow, the spring night damp. She hugged her sable tight around her.

The shacks were dark except for one halfway up the steep slope. In Joe Kellogg's window a kerosene lamp flickered. Kitty knocked. Father Jack opened the door.

She had forgotten the smell: the sweetness of canned beans warmed on a paraffin flame night after night; the sourness of clothing thrown unwashed into a corner. The shack was a mess. Empty bottles and tin cans overflowed cardboard cartons. Dust balls coated the shelves and floor and window ledge.

Father Jack was silent and grim. There were new lines in his face. He nodded toward the cot where Joe Kellogg lay.

Kitty sat on the edge of the mattress. Her father's eyes were shut. His cheeks were stubbled gray and his skin had the brittle dry feel of old newspaper. His face seemed centuries old and at the same time it seemed very young, wrinkled yet innocent as a day-old baby's. His fingers gripped the hem of the torn sheet. They were fleshless as chicken bones that had been boiled for soup.

"Oh, Dad," Kitty sighed.

She did not know what to think, but she knew if she did not think she would panic. This was not possible. He could not be dying. He was her father: she could not imagine a life where he was not there. She did not care whether he loved her or hated her so long as he was there. She touched his hand and it twitched in answer. *He's only asleep,* she thought, *not dying.*

"How did he fall?" she asked Father Jack.

"Drinking again," the priest said. "Ever since you married."

"You're telling me it's *my* fault?" Kitty shot back.

"I'm telling you the facts."

They must have raised their voices without realizing it, for Joe Kellogg opened his eyes. They were a dimmer blue than she remembered, peaceful and wondering, like the eyes of a child coming out of a dream. His lips shaped a smile.

"Ah, it's you, Kitty. Just in time to see me off, are you?"

"Don't say that, Dad. We'll make you well. We'll get you to a hospital."

"God bless you, child." The old man spoke in a croak of a voice. "But I'm afraid there's not much hope for Joe Kellogg, not this time."

"Save your strength, Dad. Don't talk." *This is the first man I ever loved. This is the first man I ever hated.*

"You're lookin' pretty, child. Pretty as your mom. Stand up and turn around and let me look at you."

Kitty stood up and turned around and let him look at her. She could feel the priest's eyes taking her in: the sable coat, the tailored green silk dress, the pearls. She wished now she had not bothered with pearls.

"God forgive me for sayin' it, but you're prettier than your mom. And it ain't just those clothes. You'd be pretty in calico or dungarees."

She buried her face in his blanket. His fingers combed her hair weakly.

"I'm proud of you, child. I always meant to tell you, but I

never got around to it. You don't need the Stokeses' clothes. You don't need their money. You're better than them, Kitty, and don't you ever forget it."

Panic filled her. It was clear, bright, like a light turned into herself. For one instant there were no shadows, no secret places. "What'll I do without you, Dad?"

"You'll manage, Kitty. You're not like the others. You've always managed. Your brothers went and your mother went and now I'm goin', but you'll survive. You're strong. Stronger than sickness and stronger than most men. You don't need me, Kitty."

*This man is my roots. If he goes, how will I stand?* "I do need you, Dad. I was only strong because there was no other way."

*I should have stayed,* she thought. *I should have looked after him.* But how could she have? She'd made a promise.

"Stop worryin' yourself, child. I done okay. I had my life. It wasn't a bad life."

Kitty thought of her dad's life. It seemed to her a narrow path leading nowhere, walled in by famine and debt and sickness; a path that her son, please God, would never set foot on.

"Do one thing for me. I want your word."

"Anything, Dad. Anything I can."

"You're not a Stokes and I don't want you turnin' into one. Take your little boy and get out of there. Promise me that much."

She drew in her breath. "Divorce Johnny?"

"I don't care how you do it." Joe Kellogg's voice was barely audible now. She understood. He had no strength. Weakness was the one weapon left him. "I don't care what the law says. I don't care what the Church says. Get as far away from them as you can. They're rotten, child. I don't want my little girl and my grandson turnin' rotten like them."

"You can't mean that, Dad."

"It's the last thing I'll ever ask of you. Promise you'll leave them. Promise here and now, in front of Father Jack."

"And have little Jay growing up in a dirt shack? Is that what you want?"

"You grew up in a dirt shack, didn't you? I grew up in one, didn't I?"

"But not little Jay. He's not growing up in any dirt shack." *And he's sure as hell not going to die in one,* she thought.

"I know you love the child. I know you want to spare him
sufferin'. But sufferin's part of life. If you wrap that kid in
money and cut him off from sufferin' he won't grow up to be
a man. He'll be a freak. He'll be a Stokes. And what's more,
the day will come when he curses you for it. For your own
good, Kitty, for his—leave those people."

Kitty shook her head, clenching back tears. "I'll not have
my son working oil rigs for five cents an hour. He'll not have
to live on flour with rat dung in it. I've worked, Dad—you
don't know how hard I've worked to get little Jay where he is
now. And by God he's staying there—and I'm staying right
behind him, backing him up every step of the way. Your grandson's going to the top, Dad. You'll be proud of him. He's
going to be someone!"

"I don't care if he winds up President of the United States.
I don't want you or him in that house!"

"You're telling me it's him or you. But he's my son—he's
got his whole life ahead of him!"

"Not if he stays in that house."

"Jesus help me, what can I say?" She remembered another,
earlier oath. "I won't swear it. I can't."

Joe Kellogg sighed and turned his head away from her.

"Can't you see it my way, Dad? Can't you try to understand?"

He did not answer. His eyes were fixed stubbornly on a
plank in the ceiling. She shook him by the shoulders. The
thinness of them astonished her. There was no movement beneath the sheet, not the slightest ebb or swell. It came to her
that there was no hearing or seeing left in him.

"Dad!" she screamed.

She felt Father Jack lift her gently.

"Why are you looking at me?" she cried. "I didn't kill him,
did I?"

The priest did not answer, but there was accusation in his
eyes.

"What was I supposed to do? Lie to him? Is that what you
wanted, Father?"

"I didn't say anything, Kitty."

"It's easy to stand there and judge and not say anything."

"I'm not judging you, Kitty. It's you judging yourself."

"Okay, it's me judging myself. Why not? I'm as fair a judge
as you—or him. And I've done the right thing!"

"Whatever you say, Kitty."

She felt tears coming. She did not want to cry in front of this priest, not ever again. "If you'd be so kind, Father Jack, I'd like to sit with him alone."

Father Jack's eyes measured her. He nodded and went.

She sat on the cot and stared at the body, small and twisted and helpless beneath the skimpy blanket. Memories surged up in her: arguments, kisses, piggyback rides.

"Oh Dad, you stubborn, stupid old . . ."

The tears broke through. She held her dad's hand. She could feel the warmth creeping out of it.

She wept till dawn.

# *Chapter 10*

A SECOND SON, Barton Harkness, was born eighteen months later. They called him Bart for short.

It was not the same as it had been with little Jay. Kitty now had a clinic to look after, a new foundation for the encouragement of the arts; there were three houses, dinners, dances, social contacts to be maintained. She had very little free time.

She hired a wet nurse to breast-feed the baby and a nanny to look after Bart.

The years of the boys' growing up brought a whirlwind of change. Women wore their hair short and then they wore it long. Hems rose and fell and so did kings and emperors. Stock markets crashed and fools who had put their trust in paper were wiped out. Armed farmers attacked milk trucks. Former millionaires lined up in the street for free soup. Prohibition was repealed and men could forget again.

America was broke. Socialists swarmed the White House. Machinery, companies, land, even men could be had for pennies.

The Stokeses were in oil and oil had not crashed. They bought America and bought it cheap.

* * *

There was no question but that little Jay must attend the very best private school in New York. Kitty researched the *Who's Who*'s of finance and law and government. She discovered that the Buckminster grade school, located on a tree-lined street in Manhattan's East 70's, had graduated four dozen bank directors, three members of the Federal Reserve Board, two senators, two Supreme Court justices, and a President of the United States.

"That will do nicely," Kitty decided.

She visited the school. The faculty numbered fourteen and enrollment was limited to one hundred twenty sons of the rich. It was the perfect place for little Jay's education. Kitty was shocked when the headmaster said applications were generally made at birth and the school had an eight-year waiting list.

"Are you telling me you won't take my sons?" Kitty said.

The headmaster was a small, gray man. He wore an expensive dark suit from Brooks Brothers that did not quite fit the stoop of his shoulders. "I'm terribly sorry, Mrs. Stokes," he said, "but there's simply no way."

Kitty was determined that little Jay would play in the kindergarten sandbox with sons of bank presidents and Wall Street lawyers. She discussed the matter with Johnny, who asked if there weren't other schools just as good. She discussed the matter with John Stokes Sr., who went stomping into the Bank of New York and bought the mortgage on the building at twice its value.

Jay was enrolled in Buckminster in the fall, Bart the following year.

At the same time, Kitty entered both boys in the Sunday school at Saint Thomas' Episcopal Church on Fifth Avenue.

"Isn't it a long way to walk?" John Stokes said. "There's a Methodist church around the corner."

He had not been to any church, Methodist or otherwise, since his wife's stroke, and Kitty saw no reason not to confront the religious question head-on.

"The Episcopal church will be better for them, Father. All their classmates go there. You wouldn't want them to feel different, would you?"

John Stokes sighed. "No, I don't suppose I'd want that."

"Then it's settled."

* * *

The boys were as different from one another as their fathers. Jay was blond and athletic and laughing. Bart was dark. He read books and made few friends. He had no skill at catching a ball and his brother was always defending him from the teasing of schoolmates.

In the fifth form, Jay caught whooping cough. His grades suffered badly and he had to be sent back a level. That spring, at the commencement exercises in the school auditorium, Bart won a prize for scholastic achievement. Jay won none.

Kitty was shocked. After the ceremony, she sent the boys out of the auditorium—Bart clutching his little plaque, Jay empty-handed—and told them to wait in the limousine. She went up to the stage, where the headmaster was talking to a group of mothers. Anger hammered in the pit of her stomach.

"Mr. Henderson," she interrupted, "may I have a word with you?"

The headmaster stammered an excuse to the startled mothers. Kitty took him aside.

"Didn't we agree," she said, "that my two boys were to be treated exactly the same?"

"And they have been, Mrs. Stokes."

"Then how do you explain that Bart has a prize and Jay does not?"

"Bart's grades have been better than Jay's."

"That's a problem I've been meaning to discuss with you."

"You might do better to discuss it with Jay."

"The fault is not Jay's, Mr. Henderson. I'm the first to admit he can be high-spirited. Handled wrong, he can be difficult to control. That's no excuse for your teachers' slighting him in favor of Bart."

The headmaster flinched as though he had been slapped. "Buckminster teachers do not slight their duty. They're the finest professionals in the state of New York."

"Not fine enough, Mr. Henderson."

Incredulity splashed the headmaster's face. He drew himself up. "If you're dissatisfied with our work, perhaps you'd care to place Jay at another school."

"With the grades your teachers have been giving him? No, Mr. Henderson. Jay will complete his elementary education at

Buckminster, the same as his brother. And he will graduate with honors—the same as his brother."

Kitty offered her hand, terminating the discussion. The headmaster fumbled with it.

"Have a pleasant summer, Mr. Henderson. We'll see you in the fall."

The following afternoon a caravan of two chauffeured limousines and three station wagons began the day-and-a-half journey from New York to John Stokes, Senior's country estate on the Maine coast, carrying Kitty, Melissa Stokes, and the boys—with requisite servants—to their summer home. The Stokes men generally came up later in the season, when work slowed.

After dinner the first night, Jay went upstairs to his room to listen to his radio, a crystal set that he had put together himself the year before. He gazed at his comic books, but he was restless and hurt and he did not want to be alone. He prowled into the hall. There was a light under Bart's door. He tapped and his brother called, "Come in."

Jay sat on the edge of the rocking chair. Leather albums were spread on Bart's bed. One was open, showing stamps that glistened in their cellophane windows. "Would you like to listen to my crystal set?" Jay asked. "I'm picking up Bangor."

"No, thanks," Bart said. "I've got a whole packet of commemoratives to mount."

Jay's eyes searched about the room. There were shelves of books. The lid of the Victrola was raised and RCA Red Seal classical records filled its pouch. Jay knew the honor plaque had to be somewhere, and suddenly he saw it. Bart had taken a photograph from its silver frame. He had placed the honor plaque within the frame and put it on the bureau.

The plaque did not fill the frame and Bart had slid a piece of cardboard behind it to hold it in place. Jay had never known his brother to be any good with his hands. The plaque looked off-center and clumsy.

Jay peered down at his hands. He wondered at the strength that writhed in them. His hands made him afraid. He did not know if he could control them. He locked them between his knees. He knew the pains that came from outside, the fistfights and touch football skirmishes, the burn of daring to hold a lighted match too long. He had faced these and they held no strangeness, no terror. But he knew nothing of the pain that came from within, and it terrified him.

He tried to understand why he felt as he did. Dimly, he sensed that Bart had taken from him something that was rightfully his. He had always been the older brother, the stronger; he had always protected his little brother. But now Bart had an honor plaque and he had none. It wasn't fair: it wasn't even possible.

Yet the plaque was there. It screamed and filled the room.

"Want me to help you with your stamps?" Jay said.

"You hate stamps," Bart said.

"But I can paste them straight. You always paste them crooked."

"Thanks, but I want to learn to do it myself."

Jay watched his brother, bent over the album with fierce concentration. *Maybe he'll learn to paste them straight*, Jay thought; *maybe he'll learn to do all kinds of things. Maybe he won't ever need me again.*

He wished his brother would just reach a hand to him. "Bart," he said, "can't we do something together? Why can't we wrestle or read comic books or listen to the radio?"

"Because I don't want to."

Bart had never been independent before. It stung Jay.

"Can't we at least talk?"

"What do you want to talk about?"

Jay rocked back and forth in the chair. After a while he said, "I don't know. I guess there's nothing to talk about."

Jay went back to his room and lay down. He felt he was crashing into some deep pit within himself. He did not know how to haul himself out. He buried his face in the pillow, but still he saw the honor plaque.

Suddenly he sat bolt upright, rigid in cold, sweating certainty. He knew that the thing consuming him was hatred. It seemed that for all his eleven years some part of him had known he would one day hate his brother, some part of him had prepared for this moment. The hate was like the current in a river. He had no choice but to float with it or drown. It took him soundlessly down the stairs.

He moved through the house on tiptoe. He took a steak knife from the dining-room sideboard, a flashlight from the pantry. He crept into the woods. He came to a clearing. A rope swing hung in a deep well of moonlight. Bart had built the swing by himself last summer; he had not even asked for his brother's help. Jay had been too proud and hurt to ask if he might use the swing.

He stared at the swing now, taking it apart in his mind. The rope dangled, U-shaped, from the low bough of an elm. A two-foot plank, notched at each end, formed the seat. It was a clumsy contraption, the work of soft hands that knew nothing physical. He circled it as though it were a caged animal. He smiled.

He gripped the rope and pulled to test each of the two knots that held it to the bough. He did not want the knots to give way. He had something more intricate in mind. He decided the knots would do.

He gave the wooden seat a push. He observed the arc. The calculating part of his mind estimated weights and strains. He pressed the edge of the steak knife to the rope at a point midway up. The serrated blade drew crumbs of hemp that fell to his feet in a golden stream, like the pollen of flowers.

With patient strokes he sawed through hemp fibers in a dozen invisible places. He weakened the wound strands but he did not sever them. The ropes that held the swing still looked strong and trustworthy, and no one but he knew their secret.

When he had done, he backed off and breathed deeply and studied the deception. The swing hung motionless, innocent. He was pleased with his hidden labor. It seemed perfect to him.

He returned to the edge of the forest. He could see the warm lights of his grandfather's mansion. Crickets chirped. Dimly, he could hear the laughter and music of a radio in the servants' wing.

He crept back into the house and he slept.

In the morning Jay went into the woods with his binoculars. All morning he waited, hidden in the trees. He propped his arms on a branch. The binoculars never left his eyes and his eyes never left the house. His thighs ached from waiting.

Just before noon his brother wheeled their grandmother onto the terrace. He sat and read to her. Jay could not help wondering at the sadness of it. His grandmother had never spoken a word or moved a muscle in his lifetime. Food had to be put between her teeth with a steel spoon. Yet Bart spent two hours a day reading words she could not hear, and when the wind blew her shawl loose he adjusted it, as though she could feel the wind.

Today, for the first time, he suspected why Bart did all this. It was a performance to make his mother notice him, to make the servants whisper, "Isn't he good, isn't he kind!"

A maid appeared on the terrace. Lunchtime.

Jay returned to the house. Throughout the meal he made himself calm and still. His blood was drumming so loud in him he wondered that his mother and brother could not hear it.

After lunch he took up his hidden watch again. He was ready and he did not mind waiting.

Before sunset Bart came out of the house. He stood looking toward the ocean. He crossed the lawn toward the woods. His walk was loose, unathletic; he carried one shoulder lower than the other. He vanished into the trees.

Jay moved silently, guided by his brother's clumsy crashing through brush and branch. The binoculars picked out the flicker of cotton shirt, its bright-red stripes spanning the undeveloped chest.

Bart moved at a stumble. He had no skill in the woods. He walked into vines and brambles, heading straight toward the trap.

Jay's blood was screaming. He crouched behind a bush and soundlessly lifted a branch aside.

Bart took hold of the swing. He steadied the seat. He lowered himself onto it. There was a sissy sort of caution to his movements. His feet were still on the ground. The ropes were not yet taking his full weight. With his legs he gave a long, slow push backward.

He arced forward. His feet lost contact with the ground. The swing carried him forward and up. He was smiling like a six-year-old in a playground.

A snap echoed through the forest, clear and musical as a harp note. Bart looked round him wildly. The rope came apart like hands unclasping. The seat tilted and pitched him sideways.

Jay adjusted the binoculars. He wanted to see the scream in his brother's eyes.

Bart's hands clawed at empty air. His legs shot out straight, braced against nothingness. For one instant he was flying like a storm-ripped kite, and then he crashed to earth.

Jay stepped out from behind the bush. He moved forward, not hurrying. He watched his brother's twisted attempts at movement. He watched until the movements stopped and his brother was a silent, motionless heap. And then, removing the evidence of what he had done, he took down the remnants of the swing.

Kitty knew she ought to have been calm. She was sitting on the terrace, listening to Jay talk about raccoons. The day's letters, the long-distance phone calls were all behind her. She had her old-fashioned and dinner to look forward to, then a warm bath and bed.

Yet something prompted her again and again to glance over her shoulder toward the edge of the lawn. Why did the woods make her uneasy tonight? She put it down to imagination.

It was almost seven o'clock. The nurse wheeled Melissa Stokes, as usual, onto the terrace. John Stokes Sr. had had the notion that Melissa Stokes enjoyed the sunset. Weather permitting, the nurse always wheeled the old woman out for her evening feeding.

Kitty said to Jay suddenly, "Where's your brother?"

Jay reached into a potted begonia. He picked up a handful of earth and let it run through his fingers. He said, "How should I know? It's not my job to watch him."

That was all he said. But Kitty sensed some secret, some boyish thing he had done and did not want to tell her. She wondered if this was the first seed of distance between them.

"Bart ought to be here." She angled her wrist to make sure of the time on her watch. "It's almost dinnertime."

"You're always worrying about him," Jay said. "He's not a baby."

Kitty glanced at the boy. It seemed to her he was looking pale. "Bart might have gotten lost in the woods," she said. "It's dark and he has no sense of direction."

"Why would he be in the woods?" Jay said, his voice flat and unconcerned.

"Maybe he went reading. You know how he loves to take books into the woods. He almost ruined your grandfather's set of Thackeray."

"He'll be back," Jay said. "He can't read in the dark."

The sun was going down rapidly. The ocean had no color.

Kitty could hear it slam into the rocky shore. It made a noise like the crying of a mob. Shadows crept across the lawn. Night began staining the earth.

Kitty drew her cardigan around her. She looked at Jay. He had turned to stare at the ocean. His face was hidden from her. He stood strangely stiff and silent.

"I wish your brother would hurry," Kitty said.

At seven forty-five she told the maid to serve dinner: Bart would simply have to eat his meal cold. At eight o'clock she heard thunder, and by eight-thirty she was worried. She called the groundsman and Vicky Jennings. They put on their canvas coats and went searching.

They searched for over an hour. The hard, steady drizzle of rain turned icy on Kitty's naked face and hands. They called Bart's name till their throats were tight and hoarse. There was no answer.

Water pelted the trees and bushes with an angry slapping sound. Dead leaves made squelching noises beneath their feet. The woods had a rotted smell.

The groundsman's flashlight probed thickets and underbrush. He thrust a clutch of brier aside and peered down. His face washed white with shock.

"Over here, ma'am."

Kitty stumbled to his side. His flashlight played across the ground. A puddle of light slipped over a mound of clothing and flesh with leaves clinging to it like baggage stickers.

"Bart!" Kitty cried.

The body lay on its stomach. The face was turned to the side, gasping on a mouthful of earth. One eye was swollen shut and looked more like a slit in a purple grape than an eye. He had left a track through the wet leaves. His arms were stretched ahead of him and his fingers were clenched into the dirt as though he had tried to drag himself to shelter.

"Dear God." Vicky Jennings pressed a fist to her mouth, and her head was shaking "no."

Kitty knelt beside her son. She turned him gently onto his back. His lips were crusted with blood but she thought they moved a little. She pressed an ear to his chest. Beneath the damp cotton shirt and the thin ribs she heard the slow, faint knocking of a heart.

"Help me lift him," she said. "Be careful. He may have broken something."

The groundsman took Bart's shoulders and Kitty took his legs and Vicky Jennings walked beside them, aiming the flashlight along the path. They carried Bart back to the house and laid him on the living-room sofa. Kitty fought down the terror in her and examined the boy's bruises and lacerations. She told the groundsman to bring one of Melissa Stokes's wheelchairs. They wheeled Bart unconscious out to the car.

It was a ninety-minute drive, through pounding rain, to the hospital in Hanover, Maine. Kitty and Vicky Jennings sat in the waiting room and sipped cold coffee. Kitty kept glancing at the wall clock and wondering why the doctors were taking so long with the boy.

Finally a doctor took her aside and said Bart had been very badly hurt. Two ribs were fractured. The jaw would have to be wired. Blood pressure was low. Vital processes were dangerously depressed. The boy was in shock.

"Doctor," Kitty said, "what happened to him?"

"He had a fall," the doctor said. "Damned near killed him."

When she got home at four in the morning, Kitty went straight to Jay's bedroom. A question was gnawing at her and it could not wait. She rapped on the door and switched on the light. Jay lay in bed hugging a pillow. His eyes were closed and he seemed to be sleeping.

Kitty went and sat on the edge of the bed. She shook him. "Jay. Wake up."

He opened his eyes and stared at her. A lock of blond hair had fallen across his forehead. He looked sleepy and confused and younger than his eleven years.

"Your brother's been hurt," Kitty said. She was watching her son very closely.

Jay pushed himself up quickly on his elbows.

"Jay," she said, "what happened in the woods? Were you and Bart jumping from trees?"

Jay's face made an effort. It was as though he couldn't remember anything at all about the woods.

"Did you tease your brother this afternoon? Did you dare him to climb a tree and jump?" For she knew as certainly as she knew her right hand from her left that Bart would never have done such a thing on his own.

Jay was staring at the mantelpiece, at the stainless-steel softball trophy he had won in third form at Buckminster. His eyes were pale blue and steady. She waited for him to say something but he kept staring at the trophy.

"Jay," she said. "Answer me."

He shook his head and his bangs tumbled down over his eyes. It was difficult for her to know if he was looking at her or not.

"I didn't dare him," he said quietly.

"You promise you didn't?"

"Promise."

"Look at me, Jay."

Suddenly Jay's arms went around her. He pressed his face against her bosom. She could feel stifled sobs. Without thinking she put her hand to his head, combed the hair away from his eyes.

"Bart's not badly hurt, is he, Mummy?"

"There's no need to cry," she comforted.

"Will he be all right?"

"It will take a little time. He'll be all right in a few weeks."

"I'm glad, Mummy." Tears glistened on Jay's cheeks. "I don't want anything to happen to any of us, ever."

When Bart was well enough to have visitors at the hospital, Kitty took him a box of candies. They were his favorites, an assortment of chocolate-coated caramels and nougats and nuts. There was a diagram inside the lid explaining which candy was where, and Bart studied it a long while before choosing a caramel.

"You're looking better," Kitty said, more relieved than she dared admit. The swelling in his face had gone down and his eye was less purple. He was able to sit up in bed and he could move his right arm.

"I'm feeling better," Bart said, but his glance was dark and wounded and it avoided hers.

Kitty sat straight in the steel hospital chair. "Bart," she said, "I want you to tell me the truth."

He turned to look at her.

"How did you hurt yourself? Did you fall?"

Bart didn't answer. His thoughts seemed far away.

"Were you in a tree? Did you slip?" *Dear God,* she prayed, *let him have slipped.* "Did you jump?" She bit down on her lip. "Were you—pushed?"

"No one pushed me."

"Then how did it happen? Was Jay with you?"

He shook his head. She sensed a cunning in him and it baffled her. It was not a sly or evil cunning: she could have dealt with that, slapped it aside with a single word. But Bart's cunning smelled of loneliness and hurt and she didn't know how to deal with it.

"Did Jay dare you to go out to the end of a branch? *Did he?*"

Bart's eyes seemed very tired, very old for so young a boy. There was a yearning in them that she could not fathom.

"Was your brother with you?" she blurted. "Don't protect him, Bart. If he was with you I want to know."

Bart gazed at his mother. His mind worked cautiously, like a wounded hand unsure of its ability to grasp. He knew his swing had been sabotaged and he knew, because at the moment of free fall he'd seen his brother step out from the bush, that Jay had been responsible. Whether Jay had wanted to harm or merely to frighten him he didn't know, but he had had time to think in the hospital, and he had decided that it was a more terrible thing to want to hurt another person than to be hurt, that it was worse to hate than be hated.

He felt sorry for his brother, sorrier than for himself; and he felt sorry for his mother, because there was no place in her picture of Jay for the hatred and hurt in him. She loved a falsehood, and he could not bear to tell her a truth that would only wound her. So he played the lawyer's game and gave her the little truth that was a lie.

"No, Jay wasn't with me. He was somewhere else."

"Thank God," Kitty sighed. Relief flooded through her. She rose and bent over him, covered his bruised face with kisses. "Oh Bart, I was so worried—you don't know."

"You don't have to worry, Mom," he said in that odd grown-up way of his. "I know."

The incident in the woods frightened Kitty and frightened her badly. She could not understand what had happened or why or how. When her mind had worn itself out twisting the riddle this way and that and still not breaking it open, she finally spoke of it to Vicky Jennings one night after the boys had gone to bed.

They were alone before the log fire and Vicky seemed to catch exactly what was on Kitty's mind. "I have a theory," Vicky said. "Do you want me to bore you with it?"

Kitty had a feeling Vicky's theory would help her see into the problem. "I wish you would."

"Lives remind me of lines. Up close they look straight, but if you can get far enough away to really see them, they're curving. Sometimes the curve is so slight you can hardly measure it. Sometimes two lives when they're very close look like two straight lines running parallel. But each is following its own curve and sooner or later the distance between them changes. I think that's what's happening with Jay and Bart. They looked parallel when they were children and now they're coming out of childhood and the distance between them is beginning."

Kitty was comfortable with Vicky Jennings. She liked the intelligence of her face and the calm of her voice. She liked to sit by a fire and hear Vicky Jennings change lives into lines and produce geometric solutions. It gave her hope that there was some way of understanding the world after all.

"What's to be done?" Kitty said.

"Each boy has to go his own way, free of the other. Have you thought of sending them to boarding school? They're the right age now."

Kitty mulled the suggestion silently.

"You don't like the idea," Vicky said.

"No."

"But you don't like what's happening to them either."

"No, not at all."

"Then send them to separate schools. I know it hurts to see them leave the nest, but sooner or later they have to learn independence—especially from one another."

Kitty sighed. "Their father made most of his business contacts in school; most of his friends too. Johnny's always saying that the right boarding school is far more important than the right college. Of course they'll go to college too."

"Of course," Vicky said. "After they've gone to separate boarding schools."

Kitty started into her scotch. "I'll be sad to see them go. It will feel like the end of an era."

"The era ended two weeks ago out there in the woods," Vicky said.

Kitty's gaze flicked up. "Vicky, what happened in the woods?"

"Do you really want to know?"

"No," said Kitty. "I don't."

"But I think you do know, deep down. And I think you know what to do about it."

In the twelve years they'd known each other Kitty had come to respect Vicky Jennings' advice. It echoed and focused her own intuitions. She discussed the matter with Johnny, and he agreed it was time to send the boys away. After a month's hesitating and agonizing Kitty drew the knife across the umbilical cord. The boys were sent away that fall.

Jay went to Johnny's alma mater. Bart went to an experimental place that was well spoken of in the New York *Times*.

Kitty missed her sons and she tried to miss them equally. She wrote them letters weekly. Bart answered weekly, but it was Jay's letters—short, scribbled notes that came once every three months or so—that she saved in a notebook.

During the boys' second year in boarding school a package wrapped in brown paper arrived at the Sixty-second Street house. Kitty tore open the wrapping and sat down and stared at the new edition of the New York Social Register. She turned to the S's and saw the listing halfway down a left-hand page.

"Look, Vicky," she called, and her voice shook. "They included us this year."

Vicky smiled. "It's almost noon. Don't you think this calls for a drink?"

"A light scotch for me," Kitty agreed. "Very light."

She tried to feel excited, but instead she felt surprisingly let down. Now that she and Johnny and Jay and Bart and all their domiciles and clubs and schools were there in print, the whole thing seemed strangely unimportant, a little ink on cheap paper, nothing more. The fight had meant far more than the victory.

She found herself wondering about the other goals she had set herself, about the promise she still steered her life by. After all, the world was changing and she was changing with it. She was not the same ignorant, lost girl who had shaken her fist in that graveyard. She was a young Park Avenue matron—

well, if not Park Avenue, Sixty-second Street. She was a cultural and philanthropic leader; her vote counted at the Cosmopolitan and Colony clubs. The New York *Times* asked to print her menus and guest lists and people recognized her when she went shopping at Saks.

Sometimes she had trouble making her old dreams fit her new life. Sometimes when they came true they didn't seem to matter at all. She phoned Johnny and told him the news.

"That's wonderful, Kitty," he said. "Are you happy?"

She'd hoped *he* would be happy. "Of course I'm happy. Vicky and I are about to get drunk."

Johnny laughed and said he had to take a call on another line.

Vicky came back with a little silver tray of drinks. Kitty put on her best smiling face and they toasted success. "You look odd," Vicky said.

"I thought I'd feel something, but all I feel is numb."

"Feel happy," Vicky said. "You've made it—despite my direst predictions. You ought to fire me."

"No, I ought to give you a raise."

"I'm game."

Kitty frowned at the book. It was a little too ugly to put in a bookcase.

"What's the trouble?" Vicky said.

"I wish I could believe ink on cheap paper really mattered."

"There's some ink on cheap paper that men kill for."

Kitty held up the book. "Do you think anyone's killed for this?"

Vicky smiled wryly. "In its long distinguished history I'll bet someone has, somewhere."

"Thank God. Then it matters."

As the thirties drew to a close, it seemed to Kitty that the tempo of events was speeding up like a silent film run too fast.

Amelia Earhart tried to fly around the world and couldn't.

The next year, Howard Hughes tried and did.

Breadlines seemed to be here to stay, and so was Bingo. Bart showed a surprising gift for math; at age fifteen, Kitty learned from his headmaster, he had mastered differential and integral calculus. Jay failed Latin, and Kitty couldn't see why living boys were required to learn dead languages. A tutor got him through his exams.

Hitler declared war on Poland and invaded; Britain and France declared war on Germany and didn't. Roosevelt had the King and Queen of England to his Long Island estate for hotdogs. They left with lend-lease in their pockets, and American neutrality was out the window. Stock in Stokes-controlled companies rose spectacularly on the market.

Roosevelt began an unheard-of third term by prodding Congress into an unheard-of peacetime draft. The country was mobilizing for war and Stokes profits were at an all-time high. Work kept Johnny so busy that by 1940 he was falling asleep in the study with company contracts he'd brought home; Kitty stopped waiting up for him, and by the time the Japanese attacked Pearl Harbor their hours were so different she'd stopped expecting him to come to bed at all. He took over the guest room, and in a way she was relieved.

Neither of them suggested the arrangement be made permanent, but neither of them objected when that was what it became.

Soon the news was full of names like Corregidor and Bataan and Guadalcanal, and Stokes Petroleum was pumping three hundred million gallons of crude per month and selling it all to the government at 270 percent profit. The Germans turned on their allies, the Russians, and the Italians turned on their allies, the Germans, and like a tide that had silently crept out under cover of dark, Kitty and Johnny's sex life was gone.

Unlike the tide, it never came back.

# Chapter 11

KITTY HAD NEVER thought of herself as a romantic woman, yet in small ways she regretted the dying of romance in her life. She was subject to vague and sometimes panicky feelings of pointlessness. Food had less taste. Sunsets had less color. When she looked back over datebooks and calendars bristling with engagements she could not see that much had been accomplished.

In idle moments, of which she seemed to find more and more, she discovered herself thinking about reincarnation and wanting to come back not as a wife but as someone's other woman.

If she were the other woman, her lover would remember her birthday and their anniversary. Johnny did not. His secretary picked the presents and sometimes they arrived by office messenger.

Her lover would notice her appearance and compliment her taste. Johnny did not—even though she weighed exactly what she had when they'd married and she never wore the same gown twice in a season.

With a lover she would have a sex life. With Johnny sex had been a game of wait and rush, waiting for weeks for him to get into the mood and rushing through the act in two minutes while he satisfied himself. And now even that unsatisfying game seemed to be over for good.

A lover might even tell her that he loved her. Johnny rarely said anything of the sort. Their conversations would have made a very long anthology of extremely short stories.

She realized that in blaming Johnny for her boredom she was also blaming him for her life. It was a trite and dishonest thing to do, though not as trite and dishonest as taking a lover. She made a point of keeping busy, taking on more boards and committees and charity balls. She reminded herself that she possessed what few women had: a name, a fortune, a dream achieved.

And still—quietly, tritely—she yearned.

Kitty was intrigued and pleased when Dr. Howard Bergman phoned and invited her to lunch at the University Club. Dr. Bergman had never invited her anywhere, and there were few firsts in her life anymore. Even though it meant postponing the board meeting of the Metropolitan Opera, she accepted.

The University Club, she discovered, had not only a women's day but a women's dining room. It reminded her of what she had read of ancient churches, when women had not been allowed to mix with the men.

Dr. Bergman was sitting at a corner table near the window. He was staring at a martini as though it interested him to see it evaporate. Kitty hurried to him.

"Sorry to be late, Howard."

As he rose to take her hand she was struck by his dark pinstriped suit, not by the neatness of the tailoring but by the way it revealed the strong, exercised curve of his back. She remembered hearing he'd been a runner-up in the Racquet and Tennis squash finals.

"Not late at all, Kitty," he said. "You're right on the button, as usual."

Which of course she was. It was one of the advantages of having one's own chauffeur.

Howard Bergman pulled out a chair for her. She sat with her hands resting neatly in her lap. She glanced at his drink. "Is there time for me to have one of those, or are you rushing off to an operation?"

"You're the busy one, Kitty, not me. I feel damned lucky to have snagged you on seven days' notice."

"I'm not that busy, Howard." She shook her head. "Not importantly busy."

He smiled. "What's 'importantly busy'?"

"I don't know. I was hoping lunch with you would be."

He caught a waiter's attention and ordered Kitty's martini. She was pleased that it turned out to be a double. She sipped and studied Howard Bergman's taut, silent profile. She could feel his mind working.

"Kitty, I need your help."

She was disappointed. "How much do you need?"

"Not your money, Kitty. I need you."

Like a child guessing a surprise, she tried to imagine what Dr. Howard Bergman could want of Kitty Stokes.

"I've no right to ask you this, Kitty. I realize how full your schedule is."

"Let me tell you exactly how full my schedule is," she said. "The most exciting thing that happened to me last week was that you invited me to lunch this week, and the most exciting thing that's happened to me this week is finding out you want something from me. I'm intrigued. I'm not a trained nurse, you're not after more money, and I don't think you invited me to your club to ask me to be your mistress."

His face flushed slightly. "Don't be too sure," he said.

She felt a burning in her cheeks.

"Kitty, I want you to join the board of directors of the Clinic. Can you?"

The request was surprising in its illogic. "But why, Howard? I'm a founder, I'm a patron, I'm a supporter. What can I do on-stage that I'm not already doing much more effectively behind the scenes?"

"I need a hostess," he said.

"Then put your wife on the board."

"In a way, she already is—and that's the problem. Now don't laugh at me, Kitty. This sounds pretty melodramatic, I know. But my wife doesn't understand my work."

Mentally, Kitty summoned up her most recent impression of Mrs. Howard Bergman, nee Phoebe Huntington, a pretty enough blonde five years or so younger than her husband who spoke with a Philadelphia Main Line accent and got giddy on half a glass of wine and had a habit of laughing uproariously at men's jokes before they reached the punch line.

Kitty lit a cigarette and stared at the Inness painting above the mantelpiece. It looked too undistinguished to be a reproduction. It occurred to her that what Howard Bergman was asking was much more subtle but no less damaging to a marriage than taking a mistress.

"Won't Phoebe mind?" she said.

"Phoebe would be relieved. She hates meeting strangers."

There were not many strangers Kitty liked either. But the offer was a fresh breeze in a musty room. "All right, Howard. I'll try it—on a test basis."

Kitty threw herself into her new duties with all the enthusiasm of a beginner. She knew after the very first fund-raising party that she would like standing beside Howard Bergman in the reception line. Five weeks into her new job she was having difficulty making time for her other activities. Eight months into it she was barely aware of mailing lists and caterers and rented ballrooms. Accomplishment carried her along in an unexpected and delicious rush of eagerness and energy.

She put her reaction down to novelty, but novelty was not at all what she felt when she worked with Howard Bergman. She found herself recalling things which must have lain in the back of her mind since childhood, details of Bartonville and the First World War, of names and faces and a feeling of life beginning that she had almost forgotten. She recalled her father and the way she had seen him as a young girl, strong and alone and unafraid of the world.

Now she saw Howard Bergman with a bit of the same impossible magical glamour. He was a man who knew what he wanted to do and who did it. He got hospital wings built. He rammed experimental drugs down the FDA's throat. He got risky procedures past the AMA. He saved lives, and Kitty Stokes helped him. Helping Johnny had never seemed important, but helping Dr. Howard Bergman did. Suddenly one small pocket of her life was meaningful and rewarding in a way she had never imagined possible.

She supposed she was developing a crush on Howard Bergman. She refused to feel guilty about it. He was the right crush at the right time. It was trite as all hell, but it kept her out of trouble and she loved it.

\* \* \*

In April of 1940, three days after Germany had occupied Denmark, Kitty was in her study going through the mail. There were a dozen invitations that had arrived that morning alone, to be sorted into "accept" and "refuse." There were three letters from doctors asking about positions at the Clinic; a letter from a midwestern newspaper, requesting an interview; letters from student artists and composers, crude pitches for handouts that ought to have gone direct to the Stokes Foundation for the Arts.

Sometimes it tired her just to look at the stack of unopened envelopes with postmarks from all over the world: they were a chorus of voices, begging, whining, shouting, demanding. Sometimes she wondered if she shouldn't have an office, like Johnny's, outside of the house. It would be a moat protecting the castle.

A soft knock at the door made her turn. Vicky Jennings was standing there, smiling mysteriously. "You have a visitor."

"I'll be right down." Kitty made a mental note: she must answer the letter from the hospital in Palestine personally. Someone from the Clinic could handle the letter from Hong Kong. She glanced at Vicky's typed list of today's engagements. There was no visitor scheduled for eleven-fifteen.

Omissions annoyed her. So did mysteries.

She took the elevator down to the ground floor. A man stood in the entrance hall, his back toward her. A tweed topcoat hung carelessly over one arm, dripping snow onto the rug. It had taken the dealer four months to locate a Persian rug narrow enough to fit the hallway. She wondered, irritably, what composer or inventor Vicky had taken pity on today.

"May I help you?" Kitty said.

The man turned and a shock of joy went through her.

"Jay!" she cried.

He came to her, tall and broad-shouldered. He bent down and kissed her on both cheeks and then he hugged her to him. He smelled of fresh snow and his cheek was smooth and cool. She held him at arm's length. He had grown in the months since she'd last seen him.

"Come into the living room. Sit down. You must have had a long trip. Are you hungry? Have you eaten?"

Kitty rang for the maid. Cold turkey sandwiches were produced, and a tall glass of milk. She watched Jay's jaw strain. He gobbled as though he hadn't eaten in weeks. He kept smiling at her between mouthfuls.

"Is it vacation time already?" she asked.

"They let me come home early."

*He's only a boy,* Kitty thought. *How did he manage the trip by himself?* And then she thought: *he's sixteen. Of course he managed.*

"I'm glad," she said, and then she thought to ask, "Why did they do that?"

"I've taken my midterms. There was no point hanging around." He took a long swallow of milk and with the back of his hand wiped the white mustache from his upper lip. "How are you, Mom?"

"Busy," she laughed. "We're adding a wing to the Clinic and all sorts of people are asking the Foundation for grants. Cornelia Whitney says she's too old to chair the Clinic Ball, so I'll be doing that myself this year. It's a lot of nonsense, really, but it keeps me out of trouble. But I want to hear about you, Jay. How are your marks? How are you doing in basketball?"

Jay stretched out his long legs and made himself comfortable in the armchair. He said trigonometry was murder, a mess of secants and cotangents. Basketball was fine—he was still the best dribbler on the varsity.

"You want to concentrate on trigonometry then," Kitty said. "Till you've got it down pat."

"I'll manage," Jay said.

"Of course you'll manage."

It seemed there were a hundred topics to discuss: his roommate, the fat boy whose father owned Pittsburgh Steel—were they getting along any better? How were his French marks? And was the snow in New Hampshire as bad as last year?

They chatted and laughed. Kitty felt warm and alive and reckless. She adored her older son. She drew courage from the strength of his young face and the straight set of his body. She drew peace from the smiling calm of his blue Irish eyes. The happiest moments of her life were when they were together, alone like this. There weren't many such times now that he was in boarding school. The separations made her acutely aware of the changes that time was working in him. He already had a man's voice, deep for his years. Sometimes, listening to him, she could hear his dad, and there was an ache in her.

She knew that one day Jay, too, would leave her. But that was a long way away. He was here and they were laughing and that was all that mattered.

A distant bell rang with tiny shrillness. A maid came into

the living room. "Telephone, Mrs. Stokes."

"Take the message, Millie. I'll call back."

"It's Mr. Stokes's office; urgent."

Jay shifted in his seat. Kitty apologized. She went to the phone.

"It came special delivery." Johnny's secretary sounded embarrassed and uncertain. "Mr. Stokes is in conference, and since it's addressed to both of you . . ."

"Who's it from?" Kitty asked.

"Saint Justin's Academy, Willettston, New Hampshire—office of the headmaster."

An absurd and troubling notion flashed through Kitty's head. There couldn't possibly be a connection between Jay's arriving unexpectedly and a special delivery letter from his school, could there?

She turned and watched the boy, sprawled long and supple in the leather chair. His face had a dreaming look. She had never seen anything purer or lovelier.

"Send it up by messenger," she said.

The office boy arrived in a taxi twenty minutes later, just as Jay was telling his mother about the new indoor swimming pool at Saint Justin's, bought with Stokes money. Kitty listened and smiled, but a shadow hovered over her thoughts. The maid brought the letter on a small silver serving tray, as though it were a canapé at a cocktail party.

Jay's eyes flashed up. "What's that, Mom?"

"Just something from your father's office," Kitty murmured. She took the letter from its envelope. She read it once, quickly, and again, very slowly, to be sure she understood. She felt as though she'd been sandbagged. It was a moment before she could move.

She handed Jay the letter. She watched his eyes. They scanned the page without flinching. His gaze turned sad.

"I didn't know how to tell you, Mom."

"What happened—what did you do?"

"It was a group of us. We teased one of the boys."

It didn't make sense to Kitty. She'd heard about boys' schools. There was teasing all the time. It couldn't be serious enough to merit dismissal. "They've expelled a group of you for *teasing?*"

"Not the whole group. Just me." Jay pushed himself up from the chair, swift and impatient. "It didn't make sense, throwing everyone out for something so dumb. The other fellows were scared. So I volunteered."

Kitty tried to put the pieces together. Jay's schoolmates were scared and he had protected them. It was a brave thing to do—brave and foolish. Like his dad. At that moment Kitty loved him more than she had ever imagined she could love anyone. She would have done anything in the world for him.

"Oh Mom, what does it matter? Saint Justin's is a stuffy place and stuffed shirts run it and I'd just as soon go somewhere else."

"It's not fair, Jay, and it matters."

His eyebrows flexed oddly and she realized he was studying her, taking the measure of her determination.

"You relax, Jay. You must have been through an ordeal. Have another sandwich."

Kitty took the elevator up to her study. She shut the door. She stood at the window and stared down at the garden. A light snow was beginning to blank out the gravel path and the burlapped flowerbeds. Without leaves, the hedges separating the property from John Stokes, Senior's seemed skimpy and precarious.

After a moment's reflection she placed a telephone call to the headmaster of Saint Justin's. It took an eternity for the call to go through. She identified herself to a secretary, and after a slightly shorter eternity the headmaster came gruffly onto the line.

"Mr. Austin, this is Kitty Stokes—Jay's mother. Thank you for your letter."

There was a silence that seemed icy and astonished at the same time. After a skipped beat, Mr. Austin said, "You're quite welcome."

"Your letter is a little vague on certain points."

"I trust not on the essential point. Your son is no longer welcome at Saint Justin's."

"I understand that, Mr. Austin. But I do feel Mr. Stokes and I are entitled to the courtesy of a more detailed explanation."

"If you wish."

"Frankly, Mr. Austin, we do wish. When may Johnny and I talk to you? The day after tomorrow?"

"Mrs. Stokes, the academy's position is final. It's hardly worth your troubling to make an eight-hour journey—"

"That's no trouble at all, Mr. Austin. Shall we say three o'clock, in your office?"

Mr. Austin's inhalation was sharp and audible. "Four-thirty."

"You're very kind, Mr. Austin. We'll be looking forward to meeting you." Kitty dialed Johnny's direct line at the Broad Street office. "There's been a misunderstanding," she said. "Jay's school has sent him home."

"What the devil has he done now?" Johnny sounded a little cranky. He was often cranky these days.

"They won't say. So I've arranged to meet with the headmaster the day after tomorrow. We'll drive up and take Jay back with us."

"I can't do that. I've got appointments."

"But Johnny, you're so good at handling these things in person. I'm sure if we go there and sit down with Mr. Austin we can clear it up in fifteen minutes."

"Hell of a long way to go for a fifteen-minute talk."

"Oh Johnny, that's so good of you. Now, just in case Mr. Austin's unreasonable, could you look into the mortgage situation?"

"What mortgage situation?"

"There's bound to be some kind of mortgage on the school. Why else would they badger us with those fund-raising drives? You could have your lawyers phone their affiliates in New Hampshire and find out just how deeply mortgaged Saint Justin's is. Find out which bank is holding the mortgage and how much business we do with them."

"Now, Kitty, Saint Justin's is a fine old school and it so happens I spent six very happy years there. I don't want to push them around."

"But if it's our money they're spending, we're entitled to some say in how they run things, aren't we? I doubt we'll even have to mention the mortgage, but why not be prepared?"

Kitty and Johnny and Jay drove to New Hampshire the next day. Mr. Austin greeted them in his office at exactly four-thirty.

"How do you do, Mrs. Stokes?" he said stiffly. "And you, Johnny—how have you been?" He shook Johnny's hand and held on to it with a sort of remembered affection.

"Pretty well, sir," Johnny said, and Kitty wished he wouldn't "sir" the old man.

The headmaster's eyes went to Jay and steel came into them. "I'm afraid," he said, "Jay is not welcome on the grounds of this school. I'm sorry if my letter did not make that clear."

Jay's face was as blank as a window with the shade pulled down. Johnny blushed and looked terribly embarrassed. Kitty realized she had vastly underestimated the headmaster's power over her husband.

"Johnny," she said, "why don't you and Jay go for a ride in the car? Mr. Austin and I can have a little talk. And you might as well leave those papers."

Johnny unzipped his leather portfolio. Misgiving flickered in his eyes. "Look," he said. "Maybe I should handle this. Mr. Austin and I are old friends, after all."

"I can manage," Kitty said pleasantly, and she took the thick manila envelope from his hand.

"Goodby, sir," Johnny said.

"Goodby, Johnny. Come see us sometime." There was no goodby for Jay. It was as though, in the world of Saint Justin's, he no longer existed.

When Johnny and the boy had gone, the headmaster strolled to the window. He stood staring out at the iced-over athletic fields. He lit his pipe and took several reflective puffs and then turned and offered Kitty sherry.

She accepted half a glass of amontillado. It was sweet, not at all to her taste. They sat on two facing armchairs. There was a coffee table with copies of *Fortune* and the alumni magazine laid out in a neat fan.

The headmaster sipped and puffed and Kitty studied him. He looked close to seventy. He had a fringe of white hair and his face had crinkles within crinkles. Beneath his Harris tweed jacket he wore an Anglican collar.

"It's a disagreeable business," Mr. Austin said, "but Johnny seems to be taking it well. He always did take things well."

Kitty watched the headmaster. He was staring at a ray of sunlight in his sherry. "Mr. Austin," she said, "can you tell me what it is exactly that you claim my son has done?"

"I'll do better than that." The headmaster was suddenly on his feet. He went to the door and said something to his secretary in the other room. In a moment a short, fat boy stepped through the door. "Shapiro," the headmaster said, "tell Mrs. Stokes what her son did to you."

The boy's glance brushed Kitty's and skittered away. "He

wrecked my room." His voice was barely audible.

"Shapiro," the headmaster said, "speak up. Start at the beginning, with the fountain pen."

The boy looked again at Kitty, and she wondered why he was frightened of her. "Jay borrowed my fountain pen for a history exam. He lost it." The boy's jacket cuff was frayed and his trousers had no press. He did not look or sound at all like a Saint Justin's student. "I asked him for a dollar fifty to buy a new pen. He said my pen had been a used pen, not worth more than fifty cents. I complained to Mr. Austin."

"I told Jay he had to pay the price of a new pen," the headmaster said, "the same as any gentleman. Tell Mrs. Stokes what happened then, Shapiro."

Shapiro swallowed. "He came to my room with two friends. He had a hundred fifty pennies in an athletic sock. His friends held me down on the bed and he whipped me with the sock."

"Shapiro," the headmaster said, "show Mrs. Stokes your stitches."

The boy approached Kitty. He bowed stiffly, like a waiter new at the job. Between the bristles of coarse hair Kitty could see an ugly pink line with three fresh cross-stitches.

"And what did Jay call you, Shapiro?" the headmaster said.

"He called me a dirty kike bastard."

Kitty felt rage flush across her face. She wanted to jump to her feet and scream denials. But she looked at this child who was fat and wore thick glasses and moved awkwardly and she knew he was not lying. She imagined his mother, a nervous immigrant like her own people, who fed him too much and nagged him to study and warned him against playing with other boys. She understood Mrs. Shapiro, who in hope and terror had somehow managed to send her son into a foreign land called Saint Justin's.

"I apologize for my son," Kitty said.

The boy gave her a blinking stare and the headmaster said he could go.

Kitty was silent a moment, assembling her strategy. "Are there witnesses to what that boy claims?" she asked.

The headmaster's face puckered in on itself like a fist. "Naturally there are witnesses. I've made a most thorough investigation."

"All the same, hazing couldn't be that rare—even at Saint

Justin's." Kitty toyed with the corner of the envelope that held the mortgage papers.

"This was not simple hazing, Mrs. Stokes. It was anti-Semitic brutality. Such behavior is intolerable at Saint Justin's. This school is not Nazi Germany; and, God granting, it never will be."

Kitty assayed her adversary. His throat was a half inch too thick for his Anglican collar. He had devoted his life to the patronizing of little boys who grew up to become bank presidents and Supreme Court justices. A vein of smugness ran through this old man, secret and treacherous as a fault, and instinct told her that a correctly aimed blow could shatter him.

"My son did not learn the word 'kike' in Nazi Germany, Mr. Austin. And it wasn't Adolf Hitler who taught him to strike a helpless boy. Whatever it was that Jay said or did, he learned it here, at your academy."

"Mrs. Stokes, we do not teach young Christians to despise the religion of others."

"And what else are you doing when you admit to your school one frightened, fat, nearsighted Shapiro? I'll lay you twenty to one he's smarter than the ten top Christians here and he can't even hold a baseball bat—and if you don't think he's hated for that, you don't understand boys. You set him up for that beating, Mr. Austin—you and your enlightened policies."

The color of Mr. Austin's face darkened. Something began to nibble at the complacency of his jowls. "Are you saying, Mrs. Stokes, that we should admit no Jews?"

"I'm saying better none than one."

Mr. Austin's throat flexed against his Anglican collar. "And what makes you think we've only one Jewish student at Saint Justin's?"

The headmaster's eyes were sly with the foretaste of victory. Kitty saw that she must bluff him and bluff him colossally. Nothing less would save her son.

"I know for a fact you've only one Jew in this school, and so do you. I saw it looking in his face and I can see it looking in yours. That's the reason we're sitting here having this talk. And frankly, Mr. Austin, if you're half the Christian that collar claims you are, I think it's a matter we ought to clear up."

\* \* \*

Afterward, Kitty went on foot across the icy pavements back to the inn. Her mind was spinning like the wheel of a stuck car. Jay was not evil: with all the certainty of her heart she knew he was not. How, then, had this thing come about?

Snow lay in high, smooth drifts at the sides of the streets. The sun was blinding. The wind stabbed at her face. A trickle of eyewater froze to her cheek.

At the door of the inn the answer came to her, swift and clear. Jay had been influenced. He had picked up ideas from the other boys—horrible, stupid, false ideas. The contempt she felt for the sons of the rich was exceeded only by the fear she felt for Jay. He must not be allowed to turn into one of them.

She found Johnny and the boy seated in the lounge before the crackling log fire. "You look like an icicle," Johnny said. "Have a whiskey."

"Order me one, would you?" she said, and then to Jay, with the same forced brightness, "Come upstairs with me for a moment."

Mother and son did not speak in the elevator. When she had closed and chain-locked the bedroom door, Jay stood fidgeting with his wristwatch. He had the scared, guilty look of a six-year-old waiting to be spanked.

Kitty fought down a rush of tenderness. She steeled her voice. "What you said and did to that boy breaks my heart. And it would break your dad's too, if he knew."

Jay was silent a moment. "Everybody hates Shapiro," he said finally.

She heard no guilt, no regret in his voice; not even the ghost of a denial. "All the less reason for you to."

Jay's eyes were deep and blue and baffled. "You don't understand, Mom. He's a greedy little Jew. His father drives a cab in New York."

Kitty's mouth fell open. "And who are your people that you're any better than a cab driver's son?"

"At least I don't have to go to school on a scholarship."

"Now, you listen to me, Jay Stokes. You've no right to look down on a boy who's smart enough to win a scholarship. You should admire him."

Jay's brow rippled as though he were trying very hard to understand her. "Admire *Shapiro?*"

"And why not? Are Stokeses so much better? You never

heard of any Shapiros gunning down unarmed families, did you?"

"Oh, *that*," Jay said contemptuously. He shrugged and turned away.

Kitty advanced two steps and spun him around by the shoulder. "Yes, that!" She slapped him across the cheek. Rage came spitting out of her. "You just remember what you came from! It's in the newspapers. It's in the history books. Johnny Stokes's people are killers and Kitty Kellogg's were County Kerry dirt!"

Jay's eyes were huge and unbelieving. His body made tiny, helpless movements, like a rabbit caught in a bear trap. There was the dark blush of a bruise on his cheek. He did not lift a hand to it. He stood staring at her. A reply stuttered on his lips and she read terror in his eyes.

"I swore I'd lift you out of the dirt and the murder," she cried. She shook him with both hands. "And by God I will, if it kills the both of us!"

She sensed something go limp in him, some barrier give way. Sobs came welling up from inside him and he threw himself into her arms. She found herself comforting him, stroking him as though he were a babe.

"I'm sorry, Mom."

He was tall and strong as a grown man, but he was her boy and she pressed him against her and let him spill his repentance onto her shoulder.

"I know you're sorry," she soothed. "You'll apologize to the Shapiro boy now, won't you?"

He lifted his eyes and nodded. "Does Dad know?" he asked.

"Your dad will never know," Kitty said. "I promise you that."

It was a long drive home through snow-snarled streets of small towns and along icy country roads. Kitty and Johnny rode in the back seat of the Rolls with the heater turned high and the windows rolled up except for one tiny crack. The glass partition had been raised, and the chauffeur could not have heard them even if they had talked.

But they did not talk.

Kitty did not know how to begin. She could see that Johnny was very tired. It would be best for Jay's sake, she reasoned, to wait till his father was in a good mood.

The Rolls-Royce glided through a landscape without visible

human or beast. Sunlight soaked the bright subfreezing air. Snow chains made a crunching rhythmic sound. Johnny dozed and Kitty brooded how best to tell him of the accommodation she had reached with Mr. Austin.

As with so many of the great and small tribulations of her life, Kitty took her uncertainty to Vicky Jennings. They sat in Kitty's workroom and Vicky listened as Kitty tried to put her feelings into clear and logical form.

She couldn't. Her logic kept breaking down. "I can't understand how he could deliberately want to hurt another human being. It seems so stupid, so sadistic."

"Maybe he was experimenting," Vicky said. "Maybe he wanted to know what it was like to act stupidly and sadistically."

"But why?"

"Because he's a boy."

"But what kind of boy could be such an animal?"

"Listen to me, Kitty. No boy or man or human being could be as perfect as the picture of Jay you've built up in your head."

Kitty's eyes fixed on Vicky Jennings.

"There were other boys involved," Vicky said. "He could be shielding his friends."

"Why do you think that?"

"I know Jay and so do you."

"Maybe I'm the one who's doing the shielding," Kitty said. "I've always shielded him and maybe it's a mistake."

"And what's wrong with that?" Vicky said. "Do you want it on his record that he was expelled from prep school?"

Kitty gazed out the window. Snow lay in patchy splotches in the garden like half-nibbled pie crust. "If he deserves punishment, maybe he should face up to it the same as anyone else."

"It's for others to have that attitude—and believe me, they do. You're his mother. He needs you."

Viewed from that angle, any possible question vanished. Kitty saw exactly what she must do.

"Isn't Harry Nesbitt still with the State Department?" she asked Johnny that evening at dinner.

"He was still there the last I heard," Johnny said.

"He must owe you a favor or two."

"Most people owe us a favor or two," Johnny said.

"Would it be difficult for him to arrange an immigrant visa?"

"Who's immigrating?"

"Mr. Austin wants to bring a talented German-Jewish boy to Saint Justin's."

Johnny's gaze, colorless behind bifocal lenses, lingered on her curiously. "Why the dickens does Austin want a German-Jewish boy at Saint Justin's?"

"Mr. Austin says it isn't fair," Kitty said. "Hitler has stripped the Jews of citizenship but Roosevelt won't let them into the United States, even though the German quota isn't full. Roosevelt says the Jews are stateless and can't come in as Germans. Congress won't set up a Jewish quota. So there you are. If you took the train down to Washington you could talk to Harry Nesbitt. He could arrange a special visa. I told Mr. Austin we'd be glad to pay for the scholarship."

"Why are you doing this, Kitty? One visa and one scholarship aren't going to help German Jews."

"One visa and one scholarship will help Jay," she said.

Johnny looked up at her sharply. "I see. You've cooked all this up to keep him in school."

Kitty didn't deny it.

"What exactly did Jay do?" Johnny said. "You've never told me the details."

"There aren't any details. He was part of a group that hazed another boy. It happens all the time. He was caught. He's shielding his friends."

Johnny lifted a water glass and sipped slowly. "Why don't we let Austin handle this the way he thinks best? There are plenty of other schools."

"Mr. Austin wants to bring a talented German-Jewish boy to Saint Justin's. That's how he wants to handle it."

"If you ask me, Kitty, in the long run this isn't going to help Jay one bit. Sooner or later he has to take responsibility for his actions."

The years had changed Johnny in more ways than one. Kitty had begun to sense a stubborn streak in him. It was not his most attractive quality. "It's Mr. Austin's school, Johnny—not ours. Let him handle discipline his own way." Kitty smiled and leaned across the table to touch Johnny's hand. "And promise me you'll talk to Harry Nesbitt tomorrow. Promise me, Johnny?"

\* \* \*

That was the time in her life when Kitty—except on those occasions when she needed his help—thought very little about Johnny. At first she was grateful that he didn't question her about her work with Dr. Bergman or complain about her unpredictable hours.

But then it came to her that something was wrong. She was used to Johnny's showing less and less curiosity about her, but it occurred to her that lately he hadn't even been showing awareness of her. They slept in separate beds, bathed in separate tubs, and, for all they said to one another at the breakfast table, might have been living in separate houses.

It was a dinner party at Mrs. Whitney's that brought home to her how alarmingly little companionship was left between her and Johnny. Cornelia Whitney was fond of mixing what she called interesting guests, and on this occasion she had mixed perhaps a little too interestingly.

Bertrand Russell had asked Charles Lindbergh why he lent his good name to an organization like America First. "Because I happen to share their aims," Charles Lindbergh said, "and so do a great many other people—like Henry Ford and Norman Thomas."

"And Lillian Gish," Mrs. Whitney put in.

Bertrand Russell looked politely amazed. "The actress?"

"The actress," Cornelia Whitney said.

"Good God, don't tell me she's helping the fascists too."

"There's nothing fascist about America First," Charles Lindbergh said.

"Their anti-Semitic stuff sounds like straight *Mein Kampf*," Bertrand Russell said.

"Why is it anti-Semitic to point out the truth?" Charles Lindbergh said. "Jews control radio and movies in this country and they could easily drag us into another world war."

"I should think they'd have to control something more important than movies," Kitty said.

Bertrand Russell gazed at her. "Like oil, Mrs. Stokes?"

Kitty took a very deep breath. "And what are you doing in our country, if I may ask, while the fascists are blitzing yours?"

"I'm teaching philosophy at City University."

"I hear the courses are crowded," Cornelia Whitney said.

"Mine are," Bertrand Russell said. "But that's because the Catholics think I'm wicked."

"I hope they don't burn you," Kitty said pleasantly, and then—wondering why Johnny had been gone from the table for so long—she excused herself and went looking for him. She found him in one of the bedrooms, alone.

He was sitting in the easy chair, head hung forward and eyes shut as though he were trying to relax the muscles of the back of his neck. He looked tired. Kitty had noticed he hadn't touched his squab at dinner and she remembered he'd barely taken a mouthful of grapefruit at breakfast.

"Johnny," she said. "Is something the matter?"

He glanced up at her quickly. "Oh, I don't know. I guess I've had enough Hitler talk for one evening."

She tried to identify the tone in his voice and realized he must have been arguing with someone. "You're acting strangely," she said. "Why did you sneak off from dinner like that?"

"Sometimes I like to be by myself and think things out. That's all right, isn't it?"

"Do you really think dinner is the time or Cornelia's guest room the place?"

"I'm sorry, Kitty, but sometimes all that chatter drives me crazy and I need a little privacy. It's just the way I am."

"But it's *not* the way you are," she said. "You've never done a thing like that before."

"Well, now I've done it. Maybe I'm changing. We all have a right to change from time to time, haven't we?"

She didn't know which made her more uneasy, that they seemed to be picking a fight with one another over absolutely nothing at all, or that they were doing it in someone else's bedroom where anyone could pop through the door. "Johnny," she said, "what were you doing in here?"

"I just had to get away for a minute."

"You mean you just had to get away for a minute and phone someone," she said, for the telephone was right there on the table by his elbow where she would have expected to see a drink.

Johnny looked at her, eyes bright with a willed hardness. "Not that it's any of your business," he said, "but I wasn't phoning anyone."

If he hadn't denied it, the phone call wouldn't have mattered. But he had denied it, and denied it rudely, and therefore it mattered very much. There was a space in his life now and she knew nothing about it. She closed her eyes and could see a woman—faceless, nicely dressed—hanging up a telephone. She could feel Johnny leaving, slipping away from her. She had supposed that they would always be friends, together in one way or another, and now she saw herself alone in a townhouse with Persian rugs and a top floor full of Matisses.

"Don't ever lie to me, Johnny."

"Let's neither of us lie," he said. "Let's not discuss the things we'd have to lie about."

"Then you're not going to tell me."

"What's there to tell you?"

"Who you were talking to?"

He had rarely taken a firm tone with her, and when he did it always surprised her, as though a trusted dog had turned. "You enjoy a great deal of privacy, Kitty. I should think you'd allow me a little."

"I'm sorry," she said helplessly, admitting a wrong but not sure what it was.

"Facts are facts," he said. "Sometimes they just can't be helped."

"I don't have any idea what you're talking about, Johnny. Do you?"

"Yes, and I think we should stop the conversation right now before we both say things we regret." He crossed the room and held the door for her. "Come on, Cornelia must think we're boycotting America First."

# Chapter 12

FOR FOUR YEARS Jay stayed out of trouble. He didn't do so well the fifth year, when the Harvard dean of undergraduates sent Kitty and Johnny a letter very like Mr. Austin's. The letter came to the house, and Kitty did not bother showing it to Johnny. The world was still at war, and he had other matters to attend to. She phoned the dean herself and made an appointment to see him.

She arrived a quarter hour ahead of time. The administration building, a Greek Revival block of pillars and brick and fresh white trim, was set just inside the walls of Harvard Yard. She announced herself to the secretary and sat down on the sofa with a copy of *Life* magazine. She leafed through photographs of the American Fifth Army taking Naples. Some of the soldiers looked even younger than Jay.

"Mr. Sloane will see you," the secretary said, and Kitty rose, exchanging nods with the man in the doorway. He let her go first into the office.

Jay stood there, pulling at the cuff of a dark suit. His eyes met Kitty's sheepishly, and his fingers went to the club emblem on his green silk necktie.

She kissed him on the cheek. He had the clean masculine smell of scented shaving soap.

"Hello, Mom," he said. "Sorry about all this."

There was a third man in the office, Jay's age. The dean introduced him as Willi Strauss. Kitty said, "I take it you're a party to this dispute, Mr. Strauss?"

The stranger smiled. He wore his blond hair slicked straight back from his forehead. His clothes were of an immaculate shabbiness that suggested he might be attending Harvard on scholarship.

"As far as I'm concerned, Mrs. Stokes, there is no dispute." His voice was deep and confident and it bore a faint trace of accent, like a scar almost perfectly healed. Kitty liked him.

Without waiting to be invited, she sat. She lit a Camel cigarette and laid it smoking in a glass ashtray with a Harvard shield cut into it. She shot the dean of freshmen her most lethally calm stare. "Mr. Sloane," she said, "I'm listening."

H. Avery Sloane cleared his throat. It seemed to take him a good deal of time to clear it to his satisfaction. *Good,* Kitty thought. *He's nervous, on the defensive.*

"The charge against your son," Mr. Sloane said, "is that he hired Mr. Strauss to take a history examination in his place."

Kitty drew in a deep breath, creating the sort of silence the occasion demanded, then broke it sharply and clearly. "I take it you have proof that Jay gave Mr. Strauss money. May I see it?"

"We've no canceled check," Mr. Sloane said, "if that's the sort of proof you mean."

"I mean simple physical proof, Mr. Sloane. Either you have it or you don't." Kitty glanced at Jay, sitting tall and thin-lipped in his straight-backed wood chair; and at Willi Strauss, whose eyes met hers without sham or apology. "Has either my son or Mr. Strauss corroborated this allegation?"

The dean of freshmen gave an exasperated sigh. "You must understand, Mrs. Stokes, that the expellable offense is not that your son gave Mr. Strauss money, but that Mr. Strauss took the examination in your son's place."

"Have you witnesses who can place Mr. Strauss at the examination? And more importantly, have you witnesses who can place my son elsewhere?"

"No, Mrs. Stokes, we haven't witnesses. Over six hundred

students took the examination in the auditorium at Memorial Hall. But we do have these."

Mr. Sloane dealt documents across his desktop like playing cards. Kitty craned forward. There were blue examination booklets, photocopied transcripts of grades. Mr. Sloane's eraser tip tapped each item of alleged evidence.

"Mr. Strauss took the same course last semester. He got a top grade on his examination. Your son, as you can see, has barely managed to pass the course; yet the booklet bearing his name also received a top grade—precisely the same grade as Mr. Strauss's. Finally, the handwriting in your son's English examination in no way resembles the handwriting in his supposed history examination."

Kitty opened the blue examination booklets. Her eye compared looping *l*'s and swooping capital *s*'s, tight little *e*'s and roundly dotted *i*'s. "And it in no way resembles the handwriting in Mr. Strauss's examination," she said.

"If necessary," Mr. Sloane said, "an expert could determine that."

Kitty dismissed the alleged evidence with a wave of her Camel. "But no expert could give you a case, Mr. Sloane. Why in the world would Mr. Strauss take Jay's examination for him—out of sheer love of my son? You admit you have no proof of money changing hands."

"It's perfectly obvious," Mr. Sloane said, "why Mr. Strauss helped your son. He's deeply indebted to your family."

"Mom," Jay said, "Willi won the scholarship at Saint Justin's—the scholarship we set up."

Kitty looked again at Willi Strauss. There was a quiet, almost smiling arrogance to the way he carried himself. He did not at all resemble the pictures of German-Jewish refugees she had seen in *Life* magazine. And he certainly did not resemble the Shapiro boy. His trousers were pressed.

Kitty inhaled on her cigarette, giving herself time to reorganize her strategy. "Mr. Sloane, you've given me surmise and conjecture but not a jot of evidence that would hold up in a court of law. Is it a crime that my son writes a good examination?"

"It's an anomaly when he's been failing the course."

"In other words, you're penalizing the boy for pulling himself up by his bootstraps?"

It was Willi Strauss who spoke. "Mrs. Stokes, if the university expels us on this charge, we have grounds for a libel action. I recommend that Jay discuss the matter no further with anyone without the advice of a lawyer."

Kitty stubbed out her Camel and sat back in her chair. She admired Willi Strauss's approach. He had shifted the burden of proof back to the accusers, and he had raised the stakes prohibitively.

Mr. Sloane laid his pencil parallel to the examination booklets. His voice was tight, like a coiled spring. "The university finds Mr. Strauss's attitude—and your son's—tantamount to a confession of guilt."

"We're not yet living in fascist Europe," Kitty said. "The Gestapo may take attitudes for confessions, but American juries don't."

"These young men have not even denied the charges."

"Nor have they admitted them, Mr. Sloane. Now, are you so reckless you'd take this matter to court, which is where I intend to see it goes if you press it, or do you have the courage to settle it here and now?"

"We could settle it here and now if your son and his friend had the courage to tell the truth instead of hiding behind evasions."

Kitty studied the dean of freshmen. He had narrow slits of eyes, the unsteady color of tea with milk. His nose had a delicate patrician arch. She sensed she was staring at a last remnant of an ancient and dying race. Law offices and banks and Roosevelt's Washington were crawling with his kind. They had murdered the Indian and built America out of the sweat of immigrants and blacks, and now they were exhausted, fast passing out of history. The Catholics and the Jews and the foreigners were already within the gates, and H. Avery Sloane had crawled into a corner and swaddled himself in a blanket of snobbery and petty authority.

"Whether or not this matter goes to court," Kitty said, "no matter who wins the libel action, with one phone call I can cut this university's endowment in half. Now, is that what you want?"

Dying embers seemed to flare up in Mr. Sloane's eyes. "If you think you can threaten me—"

'I wouldn't waste time threatening you, Mr. Sloane. I'm

threatening the university. They'll sack you, of course, when they learn how you've handled this."

Mr. Sloane looked amazed and fascinated and very frightened, like a child staring at a cobra in a zoo.

"Now, what was this history course," Kitty said. "European history? Is that what all this trouble's about?"

"Modern European history," Mr. Sloane answered.

"Very well. I'll give you a choice. I'll endow a chair in modern European history—"

"The course is modern *Eastern* European history," Willi Strauss said.

Kitty glanced at him. He knew how and when to make use of small points. She liked him even more. "I'll endow a chair in modern Eastern European history—or I'll sink this university's portfolio so quickly and so thoroughly you'll think a U-boat torpedoed it."

"You're asking me to drop this inquiry?"

"I'm *telling* you to drop it, Mr. Sloane."

Kitty snapped her cigarette case shut. It was gold, from Van Cleef and Arpels, and it made the sound of a small-caliber bullet ripping through paper. She stood and smoothed her skirt. It was aquamarine, Chanel, and it matched her sapphire brooch.

Mr. Sloane was staring at her. There were three parallel creases across his forehead now, as though a toy tricycle had zigzagged over his face.

"The trains are just impossible with this war," Kitty said. "I couldn't get a seat back to New York till tomorrow. I'll be spending the night at the Ritz. You can reach me anytime before noon, Mr. Sloane, and let me know your decision."

She bent to kiss Jay and then she took Willi Strauss's hand. "I'm so glad to meet you at last, Mr. Strauss."

Willi Strauss lifted her hand to his lips. His eyes met hers. "It is I who am glad, Mrs. Stokes—and honored."

Kitty was in her hotel room that evening reviewing a foundation report when the front desk rang to announce her son. She took off her reading glasses and hid them in their leather case.

A moment later Jay knocked and she opened the door. He placed a kiss on her cheek. His lips were ice and his breath was minty. She sensed something askew in him. He went to the window and stared down at the streetlights on the edge of the Boston Common. He toyed with the lace curtain hem and then he went to the dressing table and toyed with her silver brushes.

Finally he faced her. He was twenty years old. His eyes were a deep blue and they seemed to be staring past her at something very sad. "You'd better sit down, Mom."

Kitty sensed a tightness in the voice. She sat down in one of the Ritz's purple brocade armchairs. Jay sat in front of her. He looked at her a long while. His face went through a great effort and finally the words heaved out of him.

"It's true, Mom."

Kitty could not imagine what in the world he was talking about. The curls of his hair were light red, almost blond: he was broad and strong and his shoulders filled his jacket so full there was not a ripple in the seersucker. Built like his dad, he was.

"Are you listening to me, Mom?"

Kitty positioned herself in the security of the chair. "I'm listening."

"I paid Willi. I paid him to take that exam for me."

Kitty shut her eyes, instinctively blotting out pain. *Tyrone Duncannon's son has lied,* she thought; *he has cheated, he has as good as stolen another man's work. This can't be real.*

After a moment she opened her eyes. Jay was still there, erect and real in his armchair, watching her, waiting. Something flickered in his face: guilt perhaps, or concern. She nodded and rose. She went into the bathroom and fumbled for a long while with the cold-water faucet and a tumbler and a bottle of Bayer aspirin.

And then a thought occurred to her: her son had had the guts to tell the truth. He'd made a terrible mistake and he'd admitted it. Surely that took courage—the courage of Tyrone Duncannon.

She splashed cold water in her eyes and returned to the bedroom. "Why?" she asked.

Her son stood. He was a foot taller than she. He laid his hands on her shoulders. They were powerful hands but their touch was considerate. "The election next week," he said. "That's why."

"What election are you talking about?"

"I'm running for president of the club."

She remembered: they had clubs at Harvard, not fraternities. Jay had joined one of the best.

"Damn it, Mom, I know it's silly of me. When I should have been taking that exam I was out lining up votes. But it's going to be a damned close election and somehow the votes seemed more important. In the long run, I mean."

For an instant Kitty was shocked. She wondered if her son was lazy or stupid or lying. And then she thought of Tyrone Duncannon with all his union talk. He'd had to round up votes too, and it had been hard work. She remembered that last afternoon by the brook, the bright dream in his eyes.

"No," she said. "It's not silly of you, not silly at all. Tell me again now—who's in this club of yours?"

Jay spun off names: sons of bank presidents, sons of the owners of brokerage houses, sons of the richest families in America. Kitty listened and nodded. She had sent him to college for this, not for modern Eastern European history.

She crossed the room, measuring her steps along the flowered carpet, thinking. She turned. "Just tell me one thing. If you hadn't been so busy lining up votes, if you'd taken that exam yourself—do you think you could have passed it? Be honest with me now."

Jay gave a quick, unhesitating nod. "Willi was using my lecture notes. And a few of my ideas."

"And do you think you can win this election?"

"I'm popular, Mom. The fellows *like* me." There was no cringing, no apology in his voice now. He had his dad's eager white gash of a smile. "I know I can win."

"You're that certain, are you?"

His voice made a fist. "I've never been more certain of anything in my life."

"Good. Have you had your dinner?"

Kitty ordered lobster thermidor and fresh asparagus, raspberries with whipped cream and a bottle of chilled Moët and Chandon. They ate and they talked and they laughed, and all the tears and tension vanished. When the champagne was finished, Jay suggested ordering another bottle. The ormolu clock on the mantelpiece chimed nine and nine-thirty and ten, and they talked and laughed and got giddy, not like mother and son but like old friends.

The clock chimed eleven. Suddenly Jay was quiet. Kitty asked what the matter was.

"They're not going to throw me out," he said, "are they?"

"They're not going to throw you out," Kitty said, and her voice was stern.

Jay's eyes came up from the bubbles of his glass. He rose, bumping into the table with its lace cloth and cut crystal. Champagne spilled. He bent down and kissed Kitty on the forehead.

"You're an angel, Mom. Do you know that?"

Kitty found herself laughing like a girl, almost embarrassed. "You're the angel," she said. "My own little angel. Don't you worry now. Everything's going to be all right."

"Goodnight, Mom," Jay said. "And thank you."

Jay took the elevator to the lobby and went straight to the bar. Beneath the relief, a champagne-dulled fear still throbbed in him. He showed the bartender his driver's license to prove he was of age and ordered a double scotch and then another.

The fear was quieter now. He took a taxi back to Harvard Square.

He thought of going back to the club or to his room in Eliot House, but it was only midnight. The bars were open for an hour still and he felt good now. He decided to celebrate. He'd go to Clancy's and have another scotch and pick up a town girl.

By 11:30 the next morning the dean of undergraduates still had not phoned. Kitty's feet were so sore from pacing the hotel room that she kicked off her shoes. Her mouth had the foul taste of chain-smoked Camels and her mind kept careening uselessly between panic and anger.

At 11:31 the telephone jangled and she seized the receiver. "Your son, Mrs. Stokes," a man said, and she told him to send her son up. She lit her fourteenth cigarette and got into her shoes and wondered what Jay could want, what new disaster had struck. She heard a knock.

When she pulled the door open it was not Jay who stood there, but Bart. He wore a baggy tweed jacket with leather elbow patches. There were sickly crescents under his eyes that betrayed hours of night study. She tried to hide her surprise.

"Bart—how nice to see you." She kissed him quickly and then she was moving away, back to the cigarettes on the coffee table, to the suitcase still open on the baggage stand.

"Jay said you were in town." Bart's voice, even as a knife edge, stopped her. "He said you had dinner together."

"I had to come up on business," Kitty said. "It was quite sudden." She felt awkward lying. Her hands dove into make-work, needlessly readjusting folds of clothing in the suitcase.

"I wish you and I could have had dinner," Bart said.

She glanced up at him. His brown eyes were huge and heavy, like a dog's. "Next time, darling. I'll phone ahead and we'll plan a nice long weekend, just you and me and Jay."

He did not answer but just stood there. His silence seemed to reproach her. She fumbled for words, for something to fill in the empty space between them.

"I'll be glad when this war is over and you can get nylons again."

"They say it can't go on much longer," Bart said. "Hitler's running out of raw materials."

"Is that what your professors are teaching you?" she said brightly.

The phone rang again. She tried to hold back a little and not run to it. A voice announced the dean of undergraduates. "Put him through," Kitty said, cradling the receiver tight to her ear so that Bart could not overhear.

Another voice came on the line. "Mrs. Stokes, I'll be right up."

The phone went dead and she realized the dean was there in the hotel, on his way to the room. *Damn,* she thought, *Bart would have to pop up now, of all times!*

Bart was still explaining World War II. She didn't hear him. She was listening for the sound of the elevator. It came. She crossed the room swiftly, anticipating the knock, and opened the door. The dean stood stiffly in the hallway, his face as pale as his camel's hair topcoat. She tried to read him for some clue to Jay's fate. She did not think the dean would be quite so pale if he had had his way.

"The regents have voted," he said. "They accept your offer."

Relief seeped into the joints of her arms and legs. "And the other part—have the regents agreed to that too?"

"The charges against your son and Mr. Strauss have been dropped."

She remembered that Bart was standing in the room behind her. She stood aside. "Mr. Sloane, won't you come in? Do you know my other son, Bart?"

"There's never been any need for us to meet," Mr. Sloane said. He did not come in.

Bart stretched a hand forward. "How do you do, sir?"

Without stepping through the doorway, the dean gave Bart's hand a quick snap of a shake. "Please forgive me," the dean said. "I have other business to attend to. Good day, Mrs. Stokes."

Kitty watched him hurry back toward the elevator. *He's a poor loser,* she thought. She shut the door. For one instant, leaning against it, she felt weak.

"What was that about charges?" Bart said.

"The university made a stupid mistake." Kitty swooped about the room, gathering up her suitcase and her mink. "And I'm about to miss my train."

"What has Jay done this time?"

Kitty wheeled on Bart. "Jay has done nothing, nothing at all—and you have no right to eavesdrop on my conversations! Do you understand?"

"Yes—I'm afraid I do."

She stared at him, and anger gave way to mystification. She could not understand Bart. He had let his expensive clothes become shabby and there was a hint of stooped posture to his twenty-year-old body. Yet there was an odd strength to his standing there and she sensed in him a danger to Jay.

"Oh Bart, I didn't mean to sound angry," she said quickly. "I've had a very trying two days." She dumped the suitcase and the mink on a chair. She went to him and hugged him. She could feel the hesitant touch of his hands on her back. "People running universities are as bad as people running governments. They can't do anything right. I didn't mean to shout. Do you forgive me?"

"There's nothing to forgive."

Bart had a strange, hurt look. She remembered it from his childhood, from his hospital bed in Maine. She could no more fathom it now than she could then, but she knew it meant surrender and she knew she had neutralized any hostility toward Jay, at least for a while longer.

"We'll have dinner next time," she promised, reckless with relief. "Just you and I."

"I'd like that," he said. "I'd like that very much."

He carried her suitcase downstairs for her. Next time never came

## *Chapter 13*

TUESDAY OF THE FOLLOWING week Kitty sat in her study reviewing the proposed budget for the Clinic's next fiscal year. It was three-fifteen on a gray afternoon. She had drunk four cups of coffee since lunch. Camel stubs overflowed the Steuben ashtray on her desk, and the right side of her forehead ached. She turned irritably at the sound of a knock. Vicky Jennings stood in the doorway.

"What is it?" Kitty said.

"Your mother-in-law's nurse."

Kitty sighed. Since his retirement, John Stokes Sr. had entered a sort of second childhood, with the result that his wife's nurse spent more time looking after the old man than after her own charge. There were times when Kitty regretted having John Stokes Sr. as a neighbor.

With her mechanical pencil she made a checkmark in the border of the budget at the point where she had stopped. She took the elevator down to the drawing room. One glance at the nurse's haggard face told her that the problem was not just another of John Stokes, Senior's runnings-away or public urinatings.

"Yes, Miss Carlin?"

"I couldn't wake Mrs. Stokes up after her nap. There wasn't any pulse, so I called the doctor, and . . ." The nurse was clenching back tears.

*Oh God*, Kitty thought. "Is she—?"

The nurse nodded.

Kitty sank onto the edge of the sofa. "Where's Mr. Stokes?"

"He's playing billiards at his club, ma'am."

Kitty remembered that Tuesday was John Stokes, Sr.'s billiard afternoon. The Foundation had hired a companion-bodyguard for him and had managed to get the man a membership in the Racquet and Tennis so they could play together.

"Has he been told?" Kitty asked.

The nurse shook her head. "No, ma'am—I don't know if he'd understand."

John Stokes Sr. understood. Kitty told him in the back seat of the limousine. His eyes flexed as though they were trying to squeeze out tears.

"It's my fault," he said. "She was twenty years dying, but I killed her."

Kitty quickly pressed the button that raised the partition between them and the servants. "You did nothing of the sort, Father. Would you like a little brandy? I'm sure the doctor wouldn't mind. You've had a terrible shock."

John Stokes Sr. raised a hand in feeble refusal, but Kitty opened the bar and poured him a half shot of Rémy Martin. He took a long time staring at it.

"Do you suppose God's angry at me?"

"You're being a child, Father."

"If I were God, I'd be angry at me. Melissa's with God now and she's probably telling him terrible things about me. I'll bet God hates me now."

"No one hates you, Father."

"I'd like to talk to a minister."

"I think that would be a mistake today. You can talk to a minister tomorrow."

"A Methodist, Kitty—not an Episcopalian. And I want him to handle the funeral."

"Of course, Father—whatever you wish."

She got him home and handed him over to Nurse Carlin. Then she rang Johnny, who broke down and cried on the phone. "It's better this way, Johnny," she said. "It's truly better."

In her heart she was not certain that anything was better at all. It was just the way things were. It occurred to her that one day she would be dead, that people would be phoning one another to say it was truly better this way. The sad, unutterable loneliness of things overwhelmed her, and when Vicky Jennings came into the room she hugged her tight just to cling to something living.

"I didn't love her," Kitty said, and surprised herself by letting tears spill down her face. "It wouldn't be so awful if only I'd loved her."

"I know, I know," Vicky said, hugging back.

Feeling a little more in control of herself now but still needing to hold Vicky's hand, Kitty sank onto the sofa. "I can't even move," she said.

"Don't," Vicky said. She made a personal phone call to the director of the Hartford-New Haven railroad, arranging two priority seats on the Boston-New York train for Jay and Bart. After that, she telegraphed the boys to come home for their grandmother's funeral.

Bart arrived the next day. His eyes were red and he was wearing a black suit that looked brand-new and rumpled at the same time. Kitty could not imagine how he had managed it.

His brother was not with him.

Kitty rang Jay's dormitory eight times without locating him. She tried his club and even the dean's office, both without success. Twenty-four hours before the funeral a Western Union boy brought a telegram to the house. It was addressed to Kitty and she opened it on the front steps, in the freezing wind.

HAVE WON ELECTION TO CLUB PRESIDENCY STOP AM CELE-BRATING LOVE JAY

Something tapped Jay on the shoulder. He turned irritably. The gray face of Charley, the steward, bobbed up in the dimness. "Telephone call for you, sir."

"I'm not here. I'm not anywhere. You don't know where I am."

"But sir—"

"You heard me."

The face floated away and the girl slipped her hand back into Jay's and their bodies slid back into the rhythm of the music.

The university did not permit women in the clubs, but Charley, the steward, had recruited a half-dozen town girls at twenty dollars a head. Charley had put up blackout curtains on the windows and things had become pretty relaxed by two in the morning. There was a stack of Glenn Miller records on the changer, slow murmuring numbers like "Moonlight Serenade" and "Solitude." The lights were down as low as they'd go, which was close to total darkness.

The club members had been drinking and stuffing themselves for over five hours and taking turns dancing with the girls. But Jay, as president-elect, didn't have to take turns, and he'd had his girl for a half hour now. She was tall and her hair was dark blond. In that light he couldn't be sure how natural it was and in that light he didn't care. He didn't know her name. The room was too dark and he was too far gone on gin and champagne to know if he liked her looks, but he liked the way she moved—slow and independent of the music, almost independent of his lead, tight like a suction cup.

Body heat pooled in the tiny pockets of space between them.

"You know what I wish you'd do?" she said. She had the Cambridge twang, but not as bad as some of the local girls.

"What's that?"

"Guess." Her thigh left the rhythm of the dance and ground slowly against his. Her skirt was low and pleated and Jay's knees caught in it as though in a tide. There had been toasts all night, hail to Jay Stokes, President-elect. Jay had drunk every damned one of them, and his head was miles above his feet. Luckily his feet knew how to dance without him: they'd had the steps drilled into them since dancing school.

"I can't guess," he said.

"Kiss me," she said. "I've been waiting all night. Ever since you walked in."

He could feel her nipples pressing against his shirt. He became more and more certain that beneath the flimsy sweater she was naked from the waist up. The record ended. The needle made a hissing sound in the center groove. Old Charley rushed over to the Victrola and turned the records over. The smooth harmony of the Andrews Sisters singing "Apple Blossom Time" floated through the darkened room.

"Hot in here," the girl murmured, and she undid another button of the sweater, baring a lopsided triangle of throat and shoulder. Her skin was soft and gleaming, beaded with tiny drops of sweat. He sensed that her perfume was meant to be lilac, but it was a wartime substitute, more disturbing than convincing, like saccharine or margarine.

"What's your name?" he asked.

"Mary O'Reilly."

They began dancing again. Someone stumbled and a champagne bucket went over and there was a ribbon of foam across the rug. Feet that danced in that corner made soft slurping sounds.

"Mary's a pretty name," Jay said. In fact, he thought it was an overused name, cheap, like the girl, but at least it wasn't ugly, like O'Reilly.

"What's your name?" she asked.

"Jay."

"Jay's not a name. It's a letter."

"It's short for John." He had a hard-on and there was no way for her not to know it and he didn't think it bothered her in the least.

"John what?"

"John Stokes."

Her eyes gave off a yellowish sparkle in the dark, like a cat's. Girls' eyes always sparkled that way when they learned he was a Stokes. "Then you're the one they're giving this party for?"

"Correction." He smiled. "I'm the one *I'm* giving this party for."

She glanced over to the side of the Great Hall, where a celebration banquet had been laid out on the refreshment table: bourbon and gin and hard-to-get scotch; imported champagne in silver ice buckets; two Virginia hams and a turkey bought on the black market, demolished to near-carcasses. There was probably more decent meat going to waste here, Jay suspected, than her family's ration coupons had allowed her in four years.

The girl nestled tighter against him. She whispered so low and close that her breath tickled his ear. "You know what we could do?"

"What's that, Mary?"

"We could go somewhere. I'm supposed to be with that Higginson jerk but I like you better. Much better."

Jay felt very much the victor that night. He had won the election and the club was his and so was everything in it. The elk's horns and the polished Victorian sofas and the silver mugs were his. The rolled-back silk rug was his, and even Mary

O'Reilly was his if he wanted her. He thought about that and he decided he wanted her very much. She was someone else's date and she would cap the victory for him.

It was fun winning, Jay decided. He'd like to spend his life doing it.

"Okay," he said. "Where do we go?"

She pulled away from him. The movement was teasing and promising at the same time. It was as though they were already making love and she didn't want him to climax just yet. He could tell he was going to like Mary O'Reilly.

"What's the rush?" She moistened her lips with her tongue and her lipstick took on the dark glisten of fresh blood. "I could use another drink."

"Anything you want, honey. Anything at all." He had her, like a popsicle in his hand. His tongue curled. He was going to lick that popsicle clean, and when he was done he was going to toss the stick in the nearest trash bin.

They walked hand in hand to the refreshment table. Great glops of stain dotted the white linen cloth as though a dozen butchers had dried their hands on it. Jay poured Mary O'Reilly a highball glass of champagne.

"What's the matter," she said, "aren't you havin' none?"

"I'd better slow down," Jay said. The room had taken on the slow, familiar spin of a carrousel warming up.

"Come on, keep me company. You're a gentleman, aren't you?"

Mary O'Reilly filled another glass and held it out to him. He could see the aureoles of her nipples through the cheap stretched fabric of her sweater. Her smile was a challenge, an invitation. An artery in his groin began drumming. He accepted the glass and tossed down a mouthful. He almost gagged. It was gin, not champagne.

"Jesus, Mary, you got the wrong bottle."

She squinted at labels and shrugged. "No sense wastin' it. Down the hatch, okay?"

Their eyes met and held, and the gin went down Jay's hatch. It was the equivalent of three stiff drinks, and Mary O'Reilly was holding out another.

Until three minutes before Melissa Stokes's funeral, Kitty kept trying to reach Jay by telephone. She had no luck. His room in Eliot House did not answer. The club steward had no idea where he might be. The dean's office was unable to help. Even as she slipped into the front pew of Christ Church on Park Avenue, a Stokes Petroleum employee was continuing the telephone hunt from the Broad Street office.

Kitty sat stiff-backed and restless between Johnny and his father. She kept glancing past Johnny and Bart in their black suits and narrow black neckties, to the empty space where her eldest son should have been.

Bits of the service reached her ears. The minister read from Ecclesiastes and Saint Luke, the usual empty words, and the choir sang "Lead, Kindly Light," Melissa Stokes's favorite hymn. The hope kept drumming in Kitty's head that even at this moment Jay was waiting for them back at the house. He simply had to be. *Dear God,* she prayed, *let nothing have happened to him.*

After the service, Kitty readjusted her veil over her face. Armed guards escorted the family out of the church and battered a path through thronged gawkers and newspaper photographers. There were pickets with incredible signs accusing the Stokeses of being war profiteers, and when John Stokes Sr. hobbled down the steps on his two canes a jeering hiss went up. Kitty felt a twinge of pity for the old murderer, but he didn't even glance up, too shut in on his grief and guilt to understand that the insults and catcalls were aimed at him.

At the door of the limousine Kitty felt Johnny's arm stiffen and for a moment she thought he was going to turn and shout at a young woman waving a sign that called the Stokeses imperialist bloodsuckers. "Let it be, Johnny," she soothed. "There's no point answering those idiots."

"It's not fair," Johnny said. "Can't they see Father's old and sick and half senile?"

"Of course they see it. That's what gives them courage."

The limousine took the family back to the house. A wreath of black velvet had been fixed to the door and someone had thrown raw egg at it. "Fix that before the guests get here," Kitty told the maid.

Soon bank presidents and railroad executives and all the millionaires Stokes Petroleum had built and bilked were milling through the ground floor, and Jay still was not there. Kitty circulated, accepting condolences and hand-wringings. Wives said to her, "Isn't it a shame," but she heard them saying to one another, "Isn't it a mercy."

John Stokes Sr. shuffled through the crowd with his canes, nodding. Kitty did not think he understood why all these people were in his son's house, drinking and talking in whispers and trying to seem on the verge of tears. A great many were strangers to him, now that he was retired.

The butler approached apologetically. "A caller, ma'am. I've asked her to wait in the study."

"I can't see callers," Kitty said.

"Ma'am," the butler insisted quietly, "she says her name is Mary Stokes."

Something in the butler's cold squint told Kitty she had better see the woman. She crossed the hallway. Flickering light fell through the open study door onto the long Persian rug. Logs were blazing in the fireplace. Gold titles on leather bindings threw out sparks of reflected glitter.

Kitty came into the room and shut the door. A strange girl stood with her back to the fireplace.

"That fire sure feels good," the stranger said. "Froze my seat off on the bus. Couldn't get a train ticket, had to take a damn bus. We were stuck two hours in New Haven, d'you believe it?"

"You wished to see me?" Kitty said.

"If you're Mrs. John Stokes Jr.," the girl said.

"I am," Kitty said.

The fire backlit the girl and the lighting in the room was dim. Kitty could make out an unkempt fluff of brown hair, a cheap powdered prettiness, an animal hint of youth beneath the shapeless coat.

"And you're Miss Mary Stokes?" she said.

"Mrs.," the girl said. "Mrs. Jay Stokes."

Any possible reply drained from Kitty's lips. In the girl's accent she recognized Boston, not good Boston at all, but the Boston of shanties and docks and shipyards and round-the-clock radio rosaries.

"I married your son the day before yesterday."

An incandescent particle of recognition flashed between them. Kitty watched the girl through shrewd, measuring eyes.

"I don't believe you," Kitty said.

Her eyes had adjusted now. She could see that the girl was wearing a plaid wool coat with a fur collar. The wool could have been the blanket from a Scollay Square flophouse. The collar looked like three dyed rat pelts.

"I got proof." The girl snapped open her purse. It was plastic, dyed and textured to an unconvincing alligator. A threat oozed out of it, acrid and unmistakable as the scent of dime-store perfume that suddenly screamed through the room. The girl held the purse close, and Kitty realized she was nearsighted and too vain to wear glasses.

After an instant's fumbling the girl extracted a long envelope and held it up by the corner. Something within the purse had shattered; a liquid had spilled and an edge of the envelope was freshly moist. Imitation lilac blotted the air.

Kitty took the envelope and lifted the unsealed flap. She drew out a document. Her eyes scanned the Gothic bold lettering. The thing was a marriage license, and it was as genuine as Jay's looping signature. Fury lumped in Kitty's throat, and for a moment there was nothing she could say to this creature who had stolen her son. Instinct told her to rip, claw, destroy. Cunning told her to hold back.

"Won't do you any good to rip it up," the girl said. "The justice of the peace has got a copy and I made three photostats."

"All right." Kitty's voice was low and sheathed in tightly controlled anger. She waved the license as though it were nothing more than a fan to stir the drowsy, fire-warmed air. "Assuming this scrap of paper is genuine, why isn't my son with you?"

For an instant the girl's face opened. The veil of cunning lifted and something close to panic spilled out. The voice was a small tight knot. "'Cause he ran away."

*Good*, Kitty thought. *Good for Jay*. "Ran away where?"

The girl's shoulders shrugged helplessly beneath the wool coat. Kitty wondered what sort of dress she could be wearing that she was so ashamed to take the coat off in a perfectly warm room. A slit of cotton hem showed, uneven and pink.

"I don't know."

Kitty sensed the girl was going to cry. But she did not let her guard down. There must be a lot of Irish girls in a town like Cambridge who get rich Harvard boys drunk and married them and came crying and play-acting to their families. She gloved her voice in softness.

"Would you like some brandy, Mary? You look a little tired."

"Thanks."

Kitty went to the sideboard. There was only Johnny's Courvoisier. She placed a snifter in the girl's shaking hand. "Sit down," Kitty said. "You've had a long ride."

The girl sat on the edge of the leather armchair. Brass studs sparkled behind her head like shop-window Christmas tree lights. She cupped the glass in both hands and took a long swallow. Kitty noted a gag reflex in the lightly acne'd line of her throat.

"When did you last see my son?" Kitty said gently.

"The morning after we were . . . married. When he woke up in the hotel, he didn't remember too much—where we were or who I was. I told him we were married and he didn't believe me. He'd been drinkin'. So I showed him the license."

"How much had you two been drinking?" Kitty was wondering if drunken marriage contracts were valid.

"A lot and then some. Maybe he was still drunk. He sure must've had a hangover. I mean, *I* sure did. He went crazy when he saw that license. He was out of that room like a shot. Left me to pay the bill. And I haven't seen him since."

"Where did he go?"

"He was sayin' crazy things—like he'd disgraced his family and there was no place for him to go except the Army."

"The *Army?*" Kitty cried.

The girl sniffled. "The Army. That's what he said. I think he meant it too."

A cold ball of dread was spinning in Kitty's stomach. Her little boy in training camp? Little Jay on some bullet-ripped Philippine beach? *Not possible,* she told herself. But a dark whisper in the pit of her mind said *Suppose—just suppose.*

She felt that someone had hurled the pieces of a jigsaw puzzle in her face. Hurriedly, she tried to fumble them together. Somehow, with liquor, with sex, this shanty Lorelei had duped her son into marriage. When he awoke to the horror of his situation, little Jay had seen no way out and had fled to the Army. The poor brave boy found it easier to face death than disgrace. His dad's bravery, that; and his dad's foolishness.

Kitty's blood raged at the thought of Tyrone Duncannon's son having to interrupt his studies, throw away his club presidency, toss aside everything it had taken all these years to win. No: she would not permit it.

"Excuse me just one moment, Mary. Help yourself to another brandy."

Kitty left the room. She locked the study doors behind her and pocketed the key. She wedged through the mourners and found Johnny talking to the vice president of the Corn Exchange Bank. She signaled. "Could I talk to you for a moment, Johnny?"

They went into the pantry. Kitty closed both doors so the servants wouldn't overhear. "Jay has enlisted in the Army."

The expression bled from Johnny's face.

"I don't know the details," she sighed, and she reached into some fertile depth of her mind and found enough of them to tide her over. "Apparently he was depressed over his grandmother and got drunk—I don't know exactly. He enlisted two days ago in Boston."

Johnny's eyes were white saucers of alarm. "Have you talked to him?"

"I've talked to a friend of his." This was not the time, Kitty decided, to tell Johnny the entire gruesome truth. He had enough to deal with. "She's in the study; I'm trying to calm her down. My hands are full, Johnny—first your mother and now this. Do you suppose you could go upstairs and get on the phone and speak to General Wetmore? He does owe us a favor, after all."

"You're right," Johnny said. "The General would know how to take care of this." His eyes had a crumpled, slightly scared look, as though things had started moving too fast for him since this war began.

Kitty waited until the elevator door had closed behind Johnny. She hurried into the living room. The air was thick now with liquor fumes and smoke. Servants with canapés pried their way between the mourners. Voices were still pitched at the level of condolence, but talk was of Hitler and tax shelters.

She located Justin Lasting in the crook of the Steinway grand, talking with the wife of a director of the Erie-Lackawanna. She apologized and said she must talk to him privately. The director's wife nodded compassionately.

Justin Lasting had aged. He was a widower now and walked with a slight limp these days. He gave Kitty an odd look when she unlocked the study door, but he was an employee and he didn't ask questions.

Mary Stokes was sitting in the armchair. She was staring

at the log fire. Her crimson church-window fingernails were drumming on the armrest. She looked tired and wary and Kitty suspected she'd had more than just another brandy.

"Justin, this is Mary. Mary has married Jay."

It was part of Justin Lasting's job never to be surprised at anything. He didn't look surprised now. "Have you now, Mary," he said. "Well, I think we should have a little talk about that."

He stood before the girl. He folded his hands behind him. His belly looked rich and well-fed in its pin-striped gray flannel vest with a gold watch chain stretched across it like an incised twenty-four-carat scar. He looked up at the ceiling and down at the floor. The girl's gaze followed his, as though he had her eyes on a string. Abruptly, he looked her in the face.

"I take it this marriage has been consummated?"

"Been what?" the girl said.

"Have you and Jay Stokes had sexual intercourse?"

The girl frowned at the technical phrase. "Sure," she said.

"How old are you, Mary?"

"What difference does it make?"

"You're under twenty-one, obviously."

The girl drew herself up full height. Her head almost reached to the top of the brass-studded backrest. "You assume wrong, mister. I was twenty-one last May." Her lips formed a tiny arc of triumphant smile.

"You must be aware that Jay Stokes is under twenty-one."

"So what?"

"He's a minor, Mary, and you're not."

"Minors can get married."

*She's done this before,* Kitty realized. *She's done it before and she still does it badly.*

"*Females* over eighteen can get married," Justin Lasting said, gentle and explanatory as a schoolmaster. "But under Massachusetts law, males cannot without their parents' permission. It's rape."

A chuckle bubbled up from the girl's throat. "You gotta be kiddin'."

"You got him drunk, Mary. We'll be able to find witnesses to that. Waiters, cab drivers, the justice of the peace. It's amazing what people can remember when a reward is offered. You took him to a hotel. The desk clerk can attest to that. So will your signatures in the register. You took that drunk boy to a sleazy hotel bed and you raped him. Do you know the penalty for rape, Mary?"

"Nobody raped nobody." The girl stood and gathered her coat around her. She had the pitiful look of a child dressed in her mother's clothes. "We was married fair and square."

"I'm just telling you where you stand legally, before you get yourself into further trouble."

Anger stabbed out from the girl's eyes. "Jay's the one who's in trouble, 'cause I ain't lettin' go."

"You haven't anything to hold on to, Mary. You forced John Stokes the Third into an illegal marriage, you raped him, and he left you. Even if the law allowed him to marry, which it does not, do you think any court would believe he wanted to marry *you?*"

"You bet he wanted to, and then some."

"I said *marry,* Mary. The thing they do in church."

"You want me to go to the newspapers?"

"Tell us what *you* want, Mary," Kitty said pleasantly, neutrally. "That's the important thing."

The girl wheeled on Kitty, her face set in a shriek. "Five thousand dollars, that's what I want. Gimme five stinkin' thousand and you can have the spoiled brat back."

It was not so much hatred that lashed through Kitty as revulsion, the same coolly destructive instinct she would have felt toward any crawling reptile she discovered in her bed. "Two thousand," Kitty spat back.

The girl's jaw dropped as though a tendon had snapped at the side of her face. Justin Lasting arched a questioning eyebrow. Kitty knew what he was thinking: the girl had named her price, it was cheap, let her have it, get her signature on the necessary papers, let her go.

But Kitty knew something else. The girl was a shark—perhaps a baby shark, but a shark nonetheless. Whether they gave her five thousand or five million, blood once tasted would bring her back. She had to be beaten down and beaten down mercilessly. She had to leave this house so bruised and battered that she'd sooner take her chances under a locomotive than ever again try to hold up the Stokeses.

The girl took a deep breath. Her coat slipped open. Above the waist she was wearing a tight machine-knit red jersey with dark stains. Nothing else. No wonder she'd frozen in New

Haven. "I told you my price and it's five thousand."

"Mary," Kitty said, and merely to pronounce the name made her mouth feel like the inside of a garbage can. "You're not worth it." Hadn't the ignorant floozy called Jay a spoiled brat?

"All right, I'm goin' to the papers." The girl whipped her coat shut and took one striding step toward the door.

"And tell them what, Mary?" The stiletto point of Kitty's voice stopped her in her tracks. "That you gave my boy a blow job? Have you read the laws of the Commonwealth of Massachusetts? There's a word for what you did to Jay, and doing it to a minor is worse, and I can dump you in the women's pen for it."

The girl's face was a blanched oval of shock.

"Justin," Kitty said. "Call the police."

The girl's eyes skittered from Kitty to Justin Lasting. Her hands jerked out, placating, trembling. "Hold it a minute. Four thousand?"

Kitty saw that police were a touchy point with Mary. She tossed Justin Lasting a nod and he went to the phone and dialed "O".

"Okay, okay," the girl said. "Two thousand. But would you throw in a bus ticket back to Boston?"

"You'll get a hotel room for the night," Kitty said, "and tomorrow you'll sign the papers Mr. Lasting brings you. You'll surrender the original of that marriage license, and if I ever catch you near my boy again—"

The girl's palms were upraised, flags of surrender jittering in a wind. "Okay, okay—just make it cash, will you?"

"Make it cash, Justin, and get her out of here."

"Come along, my dear," Justin Lasting said. He held the door for Mrs. John Stokes III, like a gentleman, and Kitty poured herself a double Courvoisier.

The crisis demanded Kitty's attention 100 percent. Luckily, she had Vicky Jennings, who over the years had become as indispensable to her as the fingers of her right hand. For two days the housekeeping details of Kitty's life were Vicky's job. She moved the appointments and the dinners that could be moved and cheerfully stood in for Kitty at those that could not. She became, in effect, Kitty's life-support.

Naturally, since it was her job to help hide it, she had to be told the truth. She did not ask questions. She radiated no shock, no judgment. She simply helped, and she simply saved Kitty's life.

There was so much to do and do quickly that Kitty was in terror of omitting some tiny yet crucial detail. A man had to be sent to Mattapan to bribe the justice of the peace. Airtight papers had to be drawn, signed by the girl, witnessed; they had to be locked away in a Chase Bank vault where, Kitty hoped, they would never again be exposed to the light of day.

Kitty had to personally instill in the girl such a cauterizing fear of the consequences that she would not so much as whisper to the press; the girl had then to be sneaked back to Boston and an *in camera* annulment had to be procured from a suspicious judge with a hunger for fifty thousand dollars.

Somehow, within forty-eight hours, Kitty managed it all.

Friday evening, as she returned from a Clinic board meeting that had run two hours overtime, a maid informed her that Master Jay had come home. Kitty rushed into the living room, her Persian lamb coat dangling from one arm.

The butler had lit a fire. The huge room was crackling with warmth, almost cozily. Johnny stood by the fireplace, his familiar stirrup cup of quinine and bitters in one hand. He was talking to a general whom Kitty did not recognize. Johnny introduced them. She saw that Justin Lasting was there. But she did not see Jay.

At first she thought someone had played a very cruel joke.

And then a figure rose from the chair nearest the fireplace. It turned and came toward her with the slow, limping shuffle of a wounded ghost. It wore a buck private's cloth cap and new-looking olive drabs, and at that distance, halfway across the room, it took Kitty an instant to recognize Jay, poor little Jay. Her heart stopped in her. His face was creased as an old man's, the cheeks shadowy hollows. *Good God,* she wondered, *what does the Army do to them in training camp?*

Kitty cried his name and ran to him. He stared at her one silent moment with eyes that had the blind sparkle of two holes punched in a jack-o'-lantern. He fell into her arms and she felt a weight of fatigue and bafflement and pain that she could scarcely hold up.

She covered Jay with kisses and walked him, like a nurse, to the sofa. She sat him down and sat beside him and held his hands pressed tight in hers. He began crying soft hiccups of sobs.

"Mom, I've done it this time."

"Don't worry, darling," she soothed, smoothing down his hair and his collar and the sleeves of his horrible wool jacket.

"I've disgraced you."

"It's been taken care of, everything's all right, please don't worry."

He raised his gaze, blue and wounded, to hers. "Am I still your son, Mom?"

"Of course you're still my son." She pressed him against her. "We'll get you out of these awful clothes and burn them and run you a good hot bath with Epsom salts. Johnny, let's have a bottle of the good champagne."

Johnny hesitated. "Of course," he said after a moment. "Whatever you say, Kitty."

This was a holiday. Tyrone Duncannon's son was safe and he was home. Kitty's heart was singing.

"Oh Mom," Jay whimpered, his voice muffled against her navy-blue dress. "I don't deserve you."

When Bart got back to the house that evening he heard Glenn Miller records in the living room. He could not imagine who was playing jazz two days after his grandmother's burial, and as he handed the butler his overcoat he asked what was going on.

"Your brother's home, sir."

Bart stared toward the open doorway at the end of the hall. He heard his mother's laughter and the clinking of glasses. "I'm going to my room," he said.

Three minutes later Kitty knocked on Bart's door and found him sitting on his bed. He had gotten out his childhood stamp collection and the leather album was open on his knees.

"What's wrong with you?" Kitty said.

Her son did not look up and she sat next to him. He pulled away.

"Come downstairs, Bart. Please. Jay's home. He's dying to see you."

"It's not right," Bart said. His voice was tight and pitched oddly high. "Grandma's no sooner buried than you're playing music and laughing."

Kitty wondered at the boyhood squabble between her sons that had persisted like poison ivy down the years. "We're celebrating. Jay's safe and we're glad. Aren't you glad too, Bart?"

"He didn't even come to the funeral and you're playing jazz for him."

Kitty drew back. Anger stiffened her voice. "Your brother didn't know about the funeral. He volunteered to fight for his country."

"Volunteered for two days?" A fitful scorn flickered in Bart's eyes. "How brave of him. How very brave."

Kitty rose. She could not bear to sit on the same bed with this child of the Stokeses. Words shot out of her. "Yes, it was brave of him! Brave and decent and manly, not like..." She stopped before she said things that could not be taken back.

"Not like me? Why don't you come out and say it?"

She stared at Bart, this stranger with his glasses and pale skin and childish jealousies. "I've tried and I've tried," she said helplessly, "but I'll never understand you."

His eyes met hers unwaveringly. "No," he said, "I doubt you ever will."

# Chapter 14

1945 CHANGED EVERYTHING. It even changed Kitty a little. She turned forty and discovered her first gray hairs. She plucked them out. FDR died in the arms of a woman who was neither his wife nor his mistress. It was hushed up, and the mistress took the rap. Truman inherited a terrifying new toy called the atom bomb. That couldn't be hushed up.

In April Kitty and Johnny flew to Mexico City for dinner with Nelson Rockefeller. At that time Nelson was temporary Assistant Secretary of State, and he'd chosen to serve dinner in the Emperor Maximilian's old suite in Chapultepec Castle. Among the generals at dinner was the Argentinian vice president Juan Perón. Nelson kept arguing that Argentina must declare war on Germany.

"Time is running out," he said. "The armistice will be signed in two weeks at the most."

Kitty was sitting on Nelson's right. She could tell he was making a great many people angry, and not just the Argentinians. "Nelson," she said, "did I ever tell you I once met your Aunt Edith?"

Nelson's spoon stopped so suddenly that a raspberry fell to the tablecloth.

"She was dancing with a prizefighter," Kitty said, "and very well, too."

After dinner Perón's mistress, Eva Duarte, followed Kitty into the bathroom that had been the Empress Carlotta's. "Rockefeller is serious or drunk?" she said.

There had been a good deal of Moët and Chandon with the dessert raspberries. "Maybe both," Kitty said.

The petite dyed blonde eyed her shrewdly. "You and your husband agree with him?"

"We came to dinner, didn't we?" Kitty said. Since Argentina could buy the Venezuelan oil on which it depended only through a Stokes or a Rockefeller subsidiary, it was obvious why Nelson had invited Kitty and Johnny.

"Germany is already dead," Eva Duarte said. "Even an animal does not urinate on a corpse. Can I borrow your lipstick?"

"Certainly," Kitty said. The lipstick was in a gold case from Cartier.

"*Bonito*," Eva Duarte said; pouting in front of a gilt-framed eighteenth-century mirror, she redrew her mouth. "Rockefeller leaves Argentina no honorable choice."

"Of course Argentina has an honorable choice," Kitty said. "You can buy your oil from the Stokeses instead of the Rockefellers. We'll give you a lower price and longer credit terms."

And thus, in the last week of the European war, Argentina became an ally of the United States and a customer of Stokes Petroleum. After that, it was simply a matter of three months and two atomic bombs, and the second war in Kitty's memory that America had waged to make the world safe for democracy ended and half of Europe and Asia were safe for Joseph Stalin, as she had suspected all along they would be.

American boys started coming home. Teen-age girls wore ugly white socks and swooned over Frank Sinatra, and the pregnancy rate shot up. The first nylons came back on the market and women lined up at department stores to get them. Radio stations still played "Sentimental Journey" and "Don't Fence Me In," but there was a new type of jazz in New York and Chicago called bebop.

Johnny developed arthritis in his right knee and talked about "slowing down." The next moment he was flying off to South America to snap up as much oil land as the Venezuelan senate would sell him. He traveled a great deal, and if he didn't seem especially happy, at least he kept himself busy.

Kitty gave two million to Harvard Law and Harvard Law accepted Jay. Bart enrolled in Harvard Business School and Kitty didn't need to give them a cent. Her foundation contributed untaxed hundreds of thousands to Democratic election campaigns, and Truman's attorney general gave Stokes Petroleum the German patents, seized during the war along with prints of *The Cabinet of Dr. Caligari,* for processing coal into gasoline. The company buried the process and oil stayed on top.

Truman pushed the British out of the Mideast and Stokes Petroleum threw its weight behind the local mobsters and got thirty-year leases on half the Arab peninsula. Kitty became a closet Zionist and siphoned over one hundred twelve million into the creation of a Jewish homeland. She foresaw that in ten years or twenty, when the Arabs reneged, America—and Stokes Petroleum—would need a moral pretext to invade the area and a friendly country to do it from. Besides, she'd seen the Auschwitz photographs and they reminded her of what John Stokes Sr. had done to the strikers in 1922.

Company subsidiaries plunked down oil rigs in the Caribbean and the Indian Ocean and the South China Sea. Stokes prospectors delving for oil bombed thousands of square miles of seabed off East Africa and Greenland and achieved an astonishing 42 percent success rate. The sun never set on the wells and refineries and filling stations controlled by Stokes Petroleum's shadow corporations. They employed more people than the population of Norway and Sweden combined and they showed pre-tax revenues equal to the United States defense budget.

Tyrone Duncannon's son had come of age, and Tyrone Duncannon's bride had built him an empire bigger than Hitler's and better hidden than the Pope's.

Bart was trying to poke a cufflink through his French cuff when the telephone rang. He answered in breathless annoyance and his mother said, "Good gracious, is that you, Bart?"

"It's me. How are you, Mom?"

"Frantic, as usual." A tiny laugh, perfect and charming and ever so slightly self-deprecating, traveled up the lines from the townhouse in Manhattan to the room in the student dorm on the south bank of the Charles River.

But Bart knew his mother better than that. She was not frantic now and she never had been, and he doubted whether any shock or catastrophe would ever puncture that calm in which she seemed to have been born sheathed. "Anything I can do to help?" he said, knowing there must be or she wouldn't have phoned.

"As a matter of fact there is, if you'd be an angel." When she wanted things she still used words like *angel*. The evidence of the years washed away, and some childish part of him kept hoping she really meant them.

"Of course, Mom. Anything at all."

"It's Jay."

The old fatigue came into Bart and he slumped into a canvas sling chair.

"I haven't been able to reach him. Tonight's your dad's birthday, and Jay's card hasn't arrived and your dad's terribly disappointed."

"Maybe Jay didn't send a card."

"Of course he sent a card, it just hasn't got here. Yours was lovely, by the way."

"What do you want me to do?"

"If you possibly can—and if it's a nuisance, please say so—could you be a darling and locate your brother and ask him to phone? Johnny's feeling old and he's gotten terribly sensitive about birthdays."

"I have a date tonight, but I'll look for Jay."

"Bart, you're a dear. Who's the girl?"

He thought she did a nice job of sounding interested. "No one you'd know, Mom."

"Is it serious? That's silly of me, you couldn't *not* be serious about anything."

"It could become serious," Bart said. "I'll let you know."

In fact, on Bart's side at least, it had already become serious. Vinnie had Kitty's green eyes and reddish hair and teasing distance, and he supposed that was why he felt such a stabbing ache for her. He'd taken her to three concerts with Koussevitzky conducting, and he'd managed to get tickets for the Boston tryout of Maxwell Anderson's *Joan of Lorraine,* and Vinnie had let him kiss her exactly one and one half times.

"Darling, that's wonderful. Johnny sends love. Don't forget about Jay, now." The phone made a kissing sound and the connection broke.

Bart stared at the dead receiver a moment and then he glanced at his watch and saw he had very little time. He dialed Jay's room at the law school dorm and got no answer. He dialed Jay's club and asked for his brother. The steward wanted to know who was calling.

"It's his brother—Bart Stokes." Bart had never met the steward, but he had spoken to him so often, tracking down Jay, that he had formed a mental image of a bent old retainer attached to the rasp of a voice.

"His mother was just calling," the steward said. "I couldn't very well tell her he was at Mrs. Freemont's, but I'm sure it's all right to tell you, sir."

Bart had never heard of Mrs. Freemont. "Do you have the number?"

The steward gave him the number and address. Bart tried ringing but kept getting a busy signal. The address was Commonwealth Avenue, not far from Beacon Street where he was picking up his date. He decided to save time and deliver the message in person.

The streetlights were starting to come on when Bart climbed the stone steps and lifted the brass doorknocker of Mrs. Freemont's house. The door was opened by a girl with long, dark hair. Her eyes moved carefully up and down Bart.

"Help you?" She stood in such a way that, small as she was, he could not see past her into the house. She didn't look old enough to be a Mrs., but she was wearing a pretty pink dress, not a servant's uniform, and there was something proprietary in the way she stood and tilted her head up at him.

"Mrs. Freemont?" Bart said.

Her eyes narrowed and for a moment he thought he had offended her. But she smiled and said, "Oh no, I'm Beth. Did you want to see Mrs. Freemont?"

Bart explained that he was looking for his brother.

"You better come in." The girl stood aside, leaving just enough room for him to squeeze past her into the house. He was faintly embarrassed at having to press against her. The hall was dimly lit and he made out an odd sort of luxury: wallpaper of red velvet roses, turn-of-the-century carved wood furniture, an unlit crystal chandelier monumental as a woman's hoopskirt. The air was heavy and sweet and his ear detected wisps of laughter from up the stairs.

"He may be a while yet," the girl said. "Can I get you anything? A beer? Something stronger?"

"No, thanks."

The girl studied him a moment. Her eyes were large and brown. There was amusement in them but he could not be sure if there was mockery as well. He felt his face warm.

"I'll go tell him." The girl scurried up the stairs, her legs flashing tan beneath a whirl of skirt.

Bart waited. He sensed it was stupid of him to be standing there in Mrs. Freemont's hallway, but he hadn't the least idea why. The girl came back down the stairs carrying a small silver tray with a martini glass.

"I brought you a manhattan," she said. "Your brother will be along."

The way she watched him reminded him of a nurse in a hospital. He didn't want to hurt her feelings, so he took the drink and sipped. It was very sweet, very strong, and he tried to make a face as though he liked it.

"You don't come here very much, do you?" the girl said.

It seemed an odd question. "I've never been here before."

The girl gave him a curious, appraising glance. "It's a nice house—clean and friendly. Everything's aboveboard. You'll never get your pocket picked. You ought to come here sometime. We're better than Johnson's."

Bart nodded, trying to look as though he understood what she was talking about.

"Don't tell me you've decided to take the plunge, Bart." There was a thumping step on the stairs. Jay stood there buttoning his shirt, grinning boozily.

Bart took a step backward.

"Hell, it's only Beth. She won't eat you." Jay burst out laughing.

Bart sensed the girl recoil from an obscenity he had only dimly grasped. "Mom phoned," he said.

Jay began looping his tie under his collar. "Oh?"

"Your forgot to send Dad a birthday card. She wants you to phone him tonight."

"Is it his birthday again? I swear he has two a year."

"Will you please do it now? Before you have any more to drink?"

"You don't have to boss me," Jay said. "I'll do it when I feel like it."

"Don't hurt her, Jay."

"Christ, you two are a team. Take him upstairs, Beth. See if you can wean him from his mother."

Jay tossed a ten-dollar bill into the air. It circled down the stairwell and landed at the girl's feet. Except for the trembling hand that held the tray, she did not move.

Understanding crashed in on Bart. Mrs. Freemont's was a whorehouse. Jay had been upstairs with a whore, and this girl with large brown eyes who had been nice to him was a whore too. Jay saw his look and broke out into ugly, cruel laughter.

"No, thanks," Bart stammered. "I—I've got a date."

The color drained from the girl's face as though she'd been slapped. Bart knew he handled it wrong and made a fool of himself. He stumbled from the house to his car and sat fighting back tears of humiliation.

He was ten minutes late arriving at Vinnie Pierpont's. The girl who he supposed did the cleaning let him in. He felt safe in the Pierpont house, glad to be in somebody's home.

"Miss Pierpont, please," he said.

The girl wore a low skirt and high wool socks, but there was a glint of steel at her right knee and he could see she wore a leg brace. Limping slightly, she showed him to the living room.

Bart sat on the edge of the sofa with his fingers pressed together between his knees. He thought of Jay and the girl at Mrs. Freemont's and his heart dropped eight stories inside him. He blotted the thought out.

Vinnie Pierpont's father came into the living room. He was wearing an old cardigan with elbow patches, and a lit pipe dangled comfortably from the corner of his mouth.

"Nice to see you, Bart," he said.

Bart jumped to his feet. "Nice to see you, sir."

Vinnie's father padded in his slippers to the secretary where the family kept their liquor. "I'm going to fix myself a manhattan. Care for one?"

"No, thanks, sir. I've already had one."

Vinnie's father gave him a quick glance. "What do you think of the stock market, Bart? Have you been noticing IBM?" Vinnie's father was in charge of trusts and investments for a State Street bank and he was always asking what Bart thought about the market.

"I think we're in the beginning of a boom, sir. IBM strikes me as having excellent prospects."

"I've got a tip for you." Vinnie's father mixed his manhattan in a glass and stirred it with a long, flat-tongued spoon. "Louisiana Coastal. Keep it under your hat. It's going to go sky-high."

"Thank you, sir. I'll remember that."

"Father's been telling everyone about Louisiana Coastal." Vinnie Pierpont stood in the arched doorway. She was wearing a green dress and Bart noticed it was that new look that came way down below the knees. She had let her hair hang to her shoulders and it was a soft, glowing red.

"I haven't told anyone but your Uncle Clyde," Vinnie's father said.

She gave Bart a little kiss on the cheek and slid her arm through his. She had a lovely sort of evening smell.

"Where are you kids going for dinner?" Vinnie's father asked.

"I've made reservations at Locke-Ober's, sir," Bart said. He did not enjoy expensive restaurants but he had a feeling Vinnie did and he wanted to make her happy.

"Oysters Rockefeller," Vinnie's father said. "Locke-Ober's has terrific oysters Rockefeller."

"Oh, Father," Vinnie said, "you don't need to tell Bart about oysters!"

At dinner, Bart couldn't help thinking of the Pierponts and their unpretentious home. He liked their cozy overstuffed sofas that seemed to date from long ago, so unlike the constantly changing furniture in his mother's living room. The Pierponts were the sort of people who would be loyal to their sofas and chairs. Bart stared at Vinnie Pierpont across the flickering candle in its hurricane glass, and he found himself liking her family very much and wishing they could be his.

"It's nice of your parents to give that girl a job," Bart said. "She must be awfully clumsy around the house."

Vinnie Pierpont's green eyes glinted and her lips parted and her small narrow-tipped teeth cut short an intake of breath. "Who in the world are you talking about?"

"That girl with the limp who answers the door."

Vinnie Pierpont's throat pushed up a soft bubbling laugh. "Oh, you meant Toni—Antonia. She's my older sister."

Bart averted his eyes to his plate and pushed a chunk of flounder with the tip of his fork. He felt it was an evening of spilled glasses and car doors slammed on ladies' dresses. "I'm sorry."

Vinnie Pierpont didn't seem in the least offended. "It's a perfectly natural mistake. I suppose she does slouch around the house like a servant sometimes."

Bart felt the blood rushing to his face, as though Vinnie Pierpont's sister was there at the table with them and he had insulted her all over again. "I'm sorry I was so rude to her."

"You couldn't be rude if you wanted to. I don't think you know how."

"Oh yes, I can. I'm awfully rude sometimes. I don't notice things and I hurt people's feelings."

"You certainly have never hurt mine." Vinnie Pierpont's smile had a magical power of forgiveness, like an Episcopalian priest's sacramental gesture. Bart thought what fine people the Pierponts were, how comfortable he felt with them.

"I hope I never hurt you, Vinnie." He placed his hand on hers and squeezed gently.

After a moment of silence her hand slid away and busied itself with a butter knife. He watched her tiny teeth break off snaps of the breadstick. She chewed like a delicate little animal.

"Why does your sister limp?" Bart asked.

"She has a bad hip and she has to wear a brace."

Bart felt an overwhelming empathy for the poor girl. "I suppose she can't swim or play tennis or do anything like that."

"She swims," Vinnie Pierpont said. "It's part of her therapy. She's had the brace since she was a child—ever since I can remember. She's used to it. She hates it when people feel sorry for her."

"I'm not sorry for her. I'm just sorry I treated her like a servant. I asked her if 'Miss Pierpont' was home."

"What's wrong with that?"

"She's Miss Pierpont too."

"You have a funny way of seeing things, Bart. It's really quite sweet." Vinnie Pierpont blotted her lips on the linen napkin with the restaurant's monogram. "We'd better order coffee or we're going to be late for that concert."

They sat in the eighth row of the orchestra. There hadn't been time to check Vinnie Pierpont's beige coat and she placed it over her knees. Bart debated during the Sibelius whether or not to press his leg against hers. The coat seemed to make it all right, and during the third movement he allowed his knee to brush against her thigh.

Through the layers of woolen cloth he could feel her not pulling away. He wondered whether he dared press harder or whether she'd notice and feel insulted or annoyed. She wasn't like Jay's girls and he was glad she wasn't. But sometimes he felt a terrible need to touch her and be touched back.

After the concert he drove Vinnie Pierpont back to Beacon Hill. She kept humming a tune from the Sibelius. She had a light, clear voice and Bart thought how nice it would be to have a house where Vinnie Pierpont was humming all the time.

He switched off the motor and walked around the car to open the door for her. She angled her cheek to his kiss but without thinking he gripped her hard and pressed his lips against hers. She seemed too surprised to pull away. Quick as a thief, his hand grazed her waist and darted up to the side of her breast. He felt the straps and buttons of a bra and at first thought they were her.

"Bart!" she cried. Her face went rigid and she yanked away.

He felt helpless as a schoolboy caught cheating. "I'm sorry, Vinnie."

Gradually the stern line of her mouth eased. She adjusted her coat collar. "Goodness," she said. "Goodness gracious." She glanced at dark windows along the street.

"I said I'm sorry, Vinnie."

"I know." She took his hand and held it. "We have to watch it, Bart. You know that. We don't want to get carried away."

"Of course not," Bart said. "I didn't mean—"

She pressed a finger against his lips. "Will you phone me tomorrow?"

He was glad she still wanted him to phone. "Of course I'll phone you. I'll phone you anytime you want, Vinnie."

"Tomorrow, around five?"

"Thank you, Vinnie. Thank you very much."

Vinnie Pierpont wondered why Bart Stokes had to drive a two-year-old Mercury when he had all that money. She waved goodby to him from the steps and threw him a kiss, and then she bolted the door and paused a moment catching her breath. She reached under her dress to adjust the bra catch that he had mangled and she thought, *Oh no, my sweet stolid solid gold Bart, you're not getting a feel of these tits till we're engaged.*

She had everything planned.

Her coming-out was set for spring. She would pressure her father into hiring the Copley Plaza ballroom and Meyer Davis and his orchestra. Bart would be her escort. They would go steady until her nineteenth birthday, and then her father would announce the engagement. There would be snickering that the Stokeses weren't Boston and they weren't even New York, really, and everyone knew about that mother. But jealous snickering didn't bother Vinnie Pierpont.

She heard the squeak of her sister's brace, high and nagging as a starved mouse. Antonia Pierpont stood gazing down from the stairway, her face a dark question mark.

Vinnie's hand was still fishing for the bra catch. "What are you staring at, Toni?"

"Mother and Father got tired waiting up," Antonia said. "They've gone to bed."

Vinnie hung up her coat in the closet. It was a decent coat but it wasn't mink. She was tired of decent coats and decent food and no servants. She was tired of her sister watching her with those flat, dead eyes.

"It was a long concert." Vinnie swept up the stairs and her sister barely stepped aside for her. "By the way, Toni, you ought to do something about the way you dress. Bart Stokes said you look like a servant."

"Thank you for telling me," Antonia said. There was ice in her voice.

"I'm only telling you for your own good. There's no reason for you to look such a fright all the time. No wonder people are put off by you."

"Are you put off by me, Vinnie?"

"Why on earth should I be put off by my own sister?"

"I don't know, but you keep hurting me, and I wonder if it's because you're scared of me."

"What a stupid, horrible thing to say." Vinnie Pierpont stomped to her bedroom and slammed the door behind her.

Toni Pierpont stood alone in the hallway, watching to see if the light would click on beneath her parents' door. It didn't.

After a moment she went to her bedroom. She took off the steel brace and placed it in its corner. Hopping, she got into bed. She had not prayed for years, but tonight she prayed.

*Please, dear God, don't let me hate Vinnie. Don't let me
hate anyone.*

She wanted to cry. She wanted a pillow drenched in repentance. But she had never been able to cry at will. She had
trained herself far too long not to cry at all.

There was a child in Toni Pierpont who had never run or
played tag or ridden a horse; who had never danced; who had
never openly wept. "Be brave, Toni, you're a Pierpont after
all," Mother had said when the little girl wasn't able to join
the class outing to the Minute Man monument in Concord.
Long afterward, when the little girl had grown into a young
woman, the same voice had explained why she was not to be
given a coming-out party: "We're not that rich, darling. And
besides, it's not as though you could dance."

There were other memories, stabs of pain and boredom that
never went away—afternoons in the heated pool at Massachusetts General Hospital; floating with human tadpoles who
had bent legs or withered legs or no legs; obeying the suntanned
amazon who made her stretch and contract: "Reach, Toni—
reach! That's a good girl!"

Those were the Wednesdays of Toni Pierpont's childhood.
Those were the Wednesdays of her future.

Once, twelve years old, she had sat on her bed and seen
that her own leg was good, not bent or withered. She had
unlocked it from its steel prison and taken three halting steps
and three surer steps and finally, one hand clenching the banister, she had walked all the way down the stairs. Her mother,
instead of being pleased, had frowned and said with all sorts
of patience, "If you don't wear it your hip will be ground to
bone meal in fifteen years."

Toni had shouted, "I'd rather walk for fifteen years than
stumble for a lifetime!"

That had been the only time Mother had ever struck her
across the face.

And now, seven years later, seven years spent locked in a
brace, Toni Pierpont lay behind her locked bedroom door and
clenched her eyes shut, and instead of sleeping she saw her
little sister climbing trees and riding rented horses. She saw
Vinnie surrounded with playmates while she had none. She
saw young men whisking Vinnie out on dates, the embarrassment tucked under their faces when they had to make small

talk with the lame sister. She saw Vinnie's sterling silver junior mixed-doubles tennis trophy, and she remembered the press of bodies as she'd sat with her parents in the Chestnut Hill Country Club bleachers.

Vinnie's limbs had been a golden blur against the white of her tennis suit. She'd returned shot after shot in killing volleys, and the pride in Mother and Father's eyes had grown till it gleamed like coated pearls. Vinnie had come running off the court clutching her sterling silver cup. People had shouted and clapped, and Mother and Father had kissed and hugged her, and so had Toni.

Vinnie had smelled of clean sweat and suntan oil and victory, and Father had said, "This cup will look dandy over the fireplace." Ever since, the silver cup had occupied the place of honor in the living room. Antonia had poured her envy into her pillow. She had begged God to give her some way of making her parents as proud of her as they were of Vinnie.

One day when the cleaning woman had had to stay home with the flu, it occurred to Toni to tidy the house. Mother came home from her bridge luncheon and saw the living room vacuumed and the dining table polished. The look that came into her eyes was not the pride that Toni had hoped for; it was something else, pleased but calculating.

"Why, Toni," Mother said, "you did a wonderful job."

After that the cleaning woman came less and less often, and Mother let Toni do more and more of the cleaning. At Christmas there was a brush attachment for the vacuum cleaner in Toni's stocking.

"It does venetian blinds," Mother explained.

Once Toni had overheard her parents arguing through the heating vent. "But she *likes* to do the cleaning," Mother said. "It makes her feel useful. It's her way of contributing."

"It doesn't look right," Father said.

"We might as well face the fact, she's never going to look right no matter what we do. And besides, after all the money we've poured into that leg of hers, she's saving us twelve dollars a week. I suppose you *want* to go back to domestic vermouth and chuck steak?"

"I just think it might look a little more democratic if you gave Vinnie a chore or two. She could make up her own bed, couldn't she?"

Toni Pierpont pulled the pillow over her ears, blotting out

the shrieks of memory. Gradually, mercifully, there was silence. Consoling dreams began to trickle through her head.

She saw herself in a white gown at her own coming-out party. Dozens of young men vied for the chance to dance with her. She waltzed with the handsomest, richest young man of all and her feet were sure and swift and unencumbered. Her partner breathed a proposal of marriage in her ear. She laughed and accepted and suddenly, at the side of the ballroom, she saw Vinnie weeping in a chair, poor clubfooted Vinnie caught in a monstrous steel trap of a shoe.

Toni sat up in bed and switched on the light. An idea ticked in her like a hidden clock. Slowly she slid her legs out from under the sheet and looked at them. They seemed perfectly good legs: one a little less rounded at the calf than the other, but still strong enough to bend and stretch. And dance.

*Why not?* she asked herself. *Why does it have to be a dream?*

She stood and braced herself on the back of a chair and limped toward the mirror. She shook her hair back from her eyes, stood straight, coaxed her lips into a smile.

She could almost imagine herself pretty.

*I will dance,* she decided. *I will dance at Vinnie's coming-out.*

# Chapter 15

NATURALLY, it had to be secret.

Toni lied to Mother and said the physiotherapist wanted Mondays as well as Wednesdays. She closed her account at Bay State Savings. With four hundred and twelve dollars in her purse, she presented herself at the Arthur Murray School of Dance.

The registrar, a chubby woman with dyed black hair, looked with distrust at the brace. "But you're handicapped!"

"My money isn't," Toni said.

"Our guarantee won't apply. And we certainly can't take responsibility if you hurt yourself."

"I won't hurt myself." Toni paid for twenty-four private lessons in advance so as to get the discount rate.

"That—*thing,*" her instructor stammered. He had slicked-back hair and an Italian name and he didn't seem to know the English word for "brace." "How can I teach you to dance in that thing?"

Toni sat on a wood-slat chair and unhitched the thing. She stood. At first her leg tingled almost painfully, and then, as she stepped toward the instructor, life began throbbing into it. The instructor put a record on the phonograph. Toni recognized it, an instrumental arrangement of "So in Love" from Cole Porter's new hit musical, *Kiss Me, Kate*.

The instructor took her in his arms at a two-foot distance. His eyes were wary. "If I hurt you, Miss Pierpont, you tell me?"

"You won't hurt me," she told him.

The second Wednesday afternoon in March, Toni cut physiotherapy and went instead to Horowitz's department store on Washington Street. She said she wished to speak with Mr. Horowitz personally, that she had been a classmate of his daughter's at Miss Potter's Day School. She was told to take the elevator to the tenth floor.

"Something about my daughter?" Mr. Horowitz said. He was a short man with curly, graying hair. He was extremely tan for the time of year and the stripes on his suit were rather broad. "Is something the matter?"

Toni knew she was taking a risk. Mr. Horowitz was, in every way, a stranger. He was not of her age or sex or religion. She sensed that these were important differences. She tried to hide her nervousness by sitting absolutely straight in her chair and looking him absolutely straight in the eye.

"You may have heard Becky mention my sister Vinnie," she said. "They used to have several classes together."

Mr. Horowitz held a pencil poised to tap the desktop. His eyebrows formed a rippling knot of impatience.

"My sister Vinnie will be having her coming-out this May. It will be a large coming-out. My father will probably rent the Copley Plaza ballroom."

All sorts of pain began piling up in Mr. Horowitz's face. "And how does this—coming-out concern my daughter?"

For an instant Toni envied Becky Horowitz, who had a father who cared. "I want a gown for my sister's coming-out. I want the finest gown in your store."

"Gowns," Mr. Horowitz said quietly, "are on the fifth floor."

"I want a discount."

Mr. Horowitz's eyebrows shot up almost to his hairline. His fists pressed against the desk in a movement that lifted him from his chair. "Miss Pierpont, you have your nerve! Tell me one good reason I should give you or your sister anything! My Becky was in that school from third grade till college, and do you know how many birthday parties she gave and how many she was never asked back to? For three years now Becky's heard those girls twittering about their debuts, and not one, not even her so-called friends, have invited her to a single coming-out party!"

"Neither have they invited me, Mr. Horowitz, and I'm not even Jewish." Toni drew up her skirt. She lifted her leg slowly so that the brace drew itself out almost full length, like a waking steel snake.

Mr. Horowitz stared one gawking moment. "Becky's talked about you," he said. "I didn't remember the name, but I . . ."

"You remembered the brace. Everybody does."

"Becky says you've been nice to her."

"And Becky's been nice to me."

"All right," Mr. Horowitz said. "Have the salesman phone me. I'll give you thirty percent off. Not on the originals, though. I can't give you anything on the originals. We don't make money on those."

For a moment Toni was silent. Thirty percent was not enough. Besides, she wanted a Paris original, something better than her parents could possibly afford for Vinnie. She knew Horowitz's had a handful of Diors, Chanels, eight-hundred-dollar gowns as good as anything at Bergdorf's. No one bought them: Horowitz's customers didn't have that kind of money. The gowns were purely for show windows and prestige.

"Mr. Horowitz, if I get Becky invited to my sister's coming-out, will you lend me one of your originals?"

"Miss Pierpont, if you can get my daughter invited to your sister's coming-out, I'll *give* you one of the originals."

Invitations had to be ordered in early spring. Mother toyed with the idea of having them printed in that new raised-ink process that looked like engraving but cost a hundred dollars less. Vinnie said printing would make her a laughingstock: the boys at Harvard felt the backs of invitations; engraved had ridges, printed were smooth, and no one worthwhile ever accepted the smooth.

"If we're spending twenty-five hundred on a party," Father said, "it seems kind of silly to skimp a hundred on the invitations."

Toni had never heard Father mention the cost of the party before. It was very nearly half what she calculated his annual salary to be, and he didn't seem in the least bothered by the expense. Once, when the physiotherapy bills had come to two hundred dollars in a single year, Mother had said, "Because of Toni we can't afford a dishwasher." Now they were going to spend a hundred eighty dollars on invitations for Vinnie, and no one even mentioned a dishwasher.

Two huge cardboard cartons arrived from the engraver five weeks later. Mother did not want to hire a social secretary to address envelopes, and Vinnie said she would be a laughing-stock if she did it herself. Toni had won two penmanship prizes at Miss Potter's, so Mother asked her to be a dear. For over a week, every evening after dinner, Toni sat with the family in the living room and addressed Vinnie's invitations.

"Why aren't Bart Stokes's parents on the guest list?" she asked.

Secret glances flew between Vinnie and Mother. "We don't know Mr. and Mrs. Stokes," Mother said.

Toni did not smile, but she was satisfied. There obviously had not yet been any proposal. "I want to invite Becky Horowitz to the party," she said.

"Horowitz?" Mother said.

"I never had a party of my own. You could at least let me invite a friend to Vinnie's."

"I won't have Becky Horowitz," Vinnie said.

"Who *is* this Horowitz person?" Mother said.

"She went to school with us," Toni said, "and she's my very best friend."

"She has no poise," Vinnie said, "and her father runs that store on Washington Street."

"*That* Horowitz," Mother said. She had bought rugs for upstairs at Horowitz's sales and winter coats and underwear from Horowitz's bargain-basement clear-outs. Her face wore a thoughtful look. "Well, if this girl is such a good friend of Toni's . . ."

"I'll be an absolute laughingstock," Vinnie said. "No one ever invites Becky Horowitz anywhere!"

Father folded his *Evening Transcript* and tamped fresh to-bacco into his pipe. The room smelled like Virginia in the rain. "Toni has a right to ask a friend," he said.

Vinnie slammed her book shut. "Why must you all gang up on me?"

"No one's ganging up on you, darling," Mother said.

Vinnie sprang to her feet red-faced. "If Becky Horowitz comes we might as well invite the milkman!"

"I don't see any connection," Father said, "between Becky Horowitz and the milkman. Now, either you'll be a good sport about this or you can go to your room."

"You've just ruined my party!" Vinnie cried. She dashed from the room. There was a rush of feet up the stairs and a moment later a door slammed.

Mother set down her crewel work. "I'd better go talk to her."

Father smiled and lit his pipe. "Women," he said.

Toni took one of the heavy, cream-colored inner envelopes and inked across its face, in tight swirling strokes, *Miss Horowitz.*

The month before the coming-out, Mother bought dance records and Vinnie practiced the foxtrot barefoot with her father on the living-room rug. When Father was at work Mother showed her how the rhumba was done. When the girls were alone Vinnie danced by herself, waltzing up and down stairs, swaying with imagined partners, and her lips curved in a foretaste of triumph.

Vinnie did not do her share of the kitchen chores that month. "She's got to practice her steps," Mother said. Every evening Toni cleared the dinner table and washed the dishes, and over the sound of running water she could hear dance music blare from the old Victrola in the living room.

The week before the coming-out, Vinnie preempted every mirror in the house. With her green eyes trapped adoringly in their own gaze, she plaited her red hair this way and that, held the coming-out gown to her breast, fistfuls of Mother's necklaces to her throat, testing one arrangement of silk and jewel against another.

Sometimes Mother offered a suggestion. "Emerald's too old for you, darling. The setting's too fussy. Perhaps your grandmother's ruby." Out from the locked strongbox in the closet would come hand-me-down riches from the days before the Crash, sacred relics Toni had never been allowed to touch. Vinnie would plunge her hands into the box, and a brooch or tiara would wink.

"That was your great-aunt Eleanor's," Mother said.

Four hands fussed and Vinnie approached the mirror, drew back, flirted this way and that with her reflection. And all the while hatred gathered in Toni's throat in a tough, burning lump.

The day of the coming-out, Vinnie napped and Mother glided from room to room, smiling. Toni wondered if it had been like this before the Crash: servants and caterers and fresh flowers and tables of rented linen and crystal in the dining room and study; the crisp odor of pastry shells and spice in the kitchen; a refrigerator stuffed with trays of canapés, moist beneath their cellophane and bright as all the flowers of an English formal garden.

Toni answered the phone and took deliveries and made herself useful. "We're going to put the coats in your room, dear," Mother said, so she cleared the knickknacks off her bureau and put away the dolls that Vinnie found so embarrassing. Father came home at three-thirty, just to be around in case he was needed, and put on his slippers. At four o'clock Toni said she was not feeling well.

A shadow flicked across Mother's face. "You're not going to get sick on us now, are you, dear?"

Toni explained that her hip was hurting and she ought to get to the hospital for physiotherapy. Mother had a troubled look.

"Don't worry, Mother, I've vacuumed upstairs." In fact, Toni had vacuumed the entire upstairs and even the attic stairway, just in case a Harvard boy opened a door by accident. Mother always worried about someone's opening a door by accident.

Toni asked if it would be all right if she skipped dinner.

Mother thought a moment. "We could move Freddy Haversham to the main table, I suppose."

"Maybe I'll go to a movie after therapy," Toni said. "I'd prefer to stay out of the way tonight. This hip is just killing me."

Mother's face made a quick, involuntary movement, and Toni could see she was relieved. "I'm sorry you're not feeling well, but you'd better do whatever you think is best for your hip."

Toni clumped down Beacon Hill and waited for the trolley. She arrived at Elizabeth Arden's exactly on time for her four-thirty appointment. She had a manicure and a facial. She gave the hair stylist a photograph she'd saved from the March *Harper's Bazaar* and said she wanted to look exactly like that.

She consulted with the makeup man. He said the line of her lip needed to be corrected and her eyelashes had to be thickened at the outside with tiny threads of mink; her nose could use narrowing with two dabs of shadow and her cheekbones could be made slightly higher with correctly applied blush. He showed her exactly how to do it and watched while she made the attempt herself. After three tries she had it.

Counting tips, she spent forty-eight dollars at Elizabeth Arden's.

She wandered in the courtyard of the Isabella Stuart Gardner museum till closing, and then she went to the RKO on Washington Street and sat through *The Treasure of the Sierra Madre*. Her heart was pounding and she kept glancing at her watch. By ten o'clock she had seen Humphrey Bogart die twice. She took a taxi home.

The house was deserted: no family, no rented servants, only the wreckage left by forty guests. Toni picked her way through tables with bright spills and their place cards and flowers askew. She found a last bottle of unopened champagne in the refrigerator, opened it, rinsed a rented champagne glass and went upstairs. Someone had left a Brooks Brothers raincoat on her bed.

She took off her clothes and slid her leg out of the brace. She stretched it, massaged it, stood on it. She walked to her parents' bathroom, slowly, equalizing her steps. She ran a steaming hot bath and filled it with Mother's most expensive oils and bubbles and salts. She arranged pillows and cushions on her parents' bed and sat sipping iced champagne. The bathroom door was open a crack, and a hot breeze filtered into the bedroom moist and smelling of fresh-cut gardenia and lilac.

Toni took her champagne into the tub. She had a long, dreaming soak. She dried herself on a huge towel with Mother's monogram and powdered her body in Mother's scented French talc. She perfumed her throat and behind her ears with tiny squirts from Mother's Chanel. It was forbidden perfume, an impossibility during the war years and even now a luxury.

Her mother's voice played through her memory. *Never ever touch my Chanel!* She fondled the square cut-glass bottle with its gold-meshed atomizer. She applied a light mist of the perfume to her armpits and groin. Especially the groin.

The dress was hidden on the top shelf of her bedroom closet. She stood on a chair and took down the blue-and-white striped Horowitz Department Store box. She lifted the dress from its nest of tissue wrapping, stepped into it, zipped and fastened it. She twirled in front of her dresser mirror and she twirled in front of the hallway mirror and in front of Mother's mirror. The skirt spun out like a huge white rose opening its petals.

After she had toasted herself with two more glasses of champagne she telephoned for a taxi. At twenty minutes before midnight she checked her coat and stepped through the glass doors into her sister's party.

The Copley Plaza ballroom was a storm of laughter and shrieks. Waving arms and chattering smiles sailed through drifting pockets of light. The twelve-piece orchestra that Father had hired was whipping up a samba and the beat tingled up from the floor and into Toni's legs like tiny electric shocks.

She stood on tiptoe to peer over bobbing heads and bare shoulders. She saw her parents' table and pried her way toward it through whirls of debutantes and college boys and rushing waiters.

"Hello, Mother. Hello, Father." Toni bent to give and receive kisses. As she straightened up and saw her mother's face, a white moon of disbelief, she knew her gown and hairdo were a success.

"Why, Toni," Father said, "you look like a million dollars. Glad you're feeling better."

"What in the world have you done to yourself?" Mother said.

"Took a bath and had a nap." Toni sat and picked up a long-stemmed glass. "Who belongs to this?"

"That's Vinnie's champagne," Mother said. "Have you put some kind of makeup on your eyes?"

"That orchestra's fabulous." Toni took a long bubbling sip of her sister's champagne. "Vinnie must be having the time of her life."

"There's something on your eyelids," Mother said, "something blue."

"It's called eye shadow, Mother."

"You're much too young. It makes you look like an old woman. Go take it off."

Bart Stokes and Vinnie came back to the table, flushed and

staggering, like explorers who'd hacked their way through a tropical jungle. Vinnie threw herself into a chair and said she'd never danced so hard in her life.

"You just rest awhile, darling." Mother snapped her purse open and leaned forward with a paper hankie to wipe the moisture from Vinnie's forehead. "Toni drank your champagne, but there must be a waiter around somewhere."

Vinnie's head snapped around and there was an instant of unguarded shock in her eyes. "Why, Toni—no one told me you'd be here."

"I just couldn't stay away," Toni said.

Bart Stokes was staring at her too. His white bow tie had almost come undone and there was sweat running down the creases of his smile. "We've met but we've never been introduced. I'm Ba—Bart Stokes."

"I remember you, Bart," Toni said, and she remembered he'd taken her for a servant.

"Did you change your hair?" he said. "You changed something. You look terrific."

"Thank you, Bart. I just felt I ought to fix myself up a bit for my little sister's coming-out."

"You did a terrific job. I wouldn't have recognized you."

"And you look very dapper in your tails."

"I rented them. They don't really fit."

"They look perfect to me."

"You don't think the shoulders are a little broad? I feel I'm wearing football padding."

"Not at all. That's the style nowadays. Say, Bart, do you by any chance rhumba?"

He hesitated, embarrassed, and she knew he was wondering about her brace. "Well, I could give it a try," he said. "Would you excuse us, Vinnie?"

Vinnie's jaw dropped an inch and she looked like a ventriloquist's dummy gulping for some sort of protest.

Toni led Bart out onto the dance floor. He was an awkward dancer and she kept wishing the orchestra would settle down into a foxtrot. "I'm afraid I don't do this very well," he said.

"You have a good strong step," Toni said.

"You follow very nicely. It's so easy to dance with you. Do you dance much?"

Toni was aware of classmates from Miss Potter's staring at her. They looked surprised and betrayed, as though she'd broken an unwritten rule that had declared her a wallflower in perpetuity. She felt a glow in her blood. "Vinnie's the one who gets asked to dance all the time. No one ever notices me." She could see her mother's scowl, tracking them like radar, caught in a border of light at the edge of the floor. "I'm glad you noticed me, Bart. I was beginning to feel like the little match girl."

"You're certainly no little match girl," Bart said. For a while they didn't talk and his feet kept subdividing the beat into nervous little shuffles. "You say Vinnie gets a lot of invitations?"

Toni smiled sympathetically. "You're very fond of her, aren't you?"

"I'm afraid I've grown more than fond of her."

"You're not comfortable with it, are you?"

"You're a very perceptive person, Toni. I've never felt quite this way before and I'm scared stiff."

"Why?"

"I don't know what the hell she feels about me."

"Well, she's been going out with you six months. That's much longer than usual for Vinnie."

He was silent a moment. "Does Vinnie ever—I know I shouldn't ask, but does she ever talk about me?"

"Vinnie doesn't take me into her confidence. She doesn't like me."

"I can't imagine anyone's not liking you."

"Vinnie doesn't."

Bart looked baffled, and then he grinned as though he'd caught on to a joke. "You certainly say what's on your mind, Toni. You're very different from your sister, do you know that?"

"Thank you, Bart. That's the nicest compliment you could pay me."

By the time Bart took Toni back to the table Vinnie had torn the petals from two white roses and ripped them into tiny specks. Bart asked Vinnie to dance, and Toni was left alone with her mother.

"Whose dress is that?" Mother peered at her through tiny slits of rage. "Where did you get it?"

"It's mine, Mother. It comes from Horowitz's dress salon. Do you like it?"

"How did you pay for it?"

"By getting Becky Horowitz an invitation."

The arch of Mother's eyebrows became a dark wedge.

"Don't look so surprised, Mother. I was being thrifty. After all, Vinnie's party is costing a fortune, and my leg has cost us a fortune, and there just isn't money for a foolish ball gown. I thought you'd be proud of me."

"Not when you make an idiot of yourself cavorting like that on the dance floor."

"I'm sorry. Did I embarrass you?"

"What do you think? People were noticing."

"What were they noticing, Mother?"

"Be realistic, Toni. You can't expect to throw yourself into a rhumba with ten pounds of steel strapped to your leg."

Toni's lips shaped a slow smile. "But Mother—I'm not wearing the brace."

Mother was speechless a moment, and then her hand shot under the table and groped along Toni's knee. "Why, you little idiot! You go home this minute and get back into your brace before you lame yourself for *life!*"

Toni shook her head. She loved the feel of her hair swaying. "I don't care if I'm in a wheelchair from tomorrow to the day I die. I've dragged that lump of steel around for fifteen years, and tonight I'm *dancing.*"

"Oh no, you're not," Mother warned in a spitting whisper. "This is your sister's party, and you're not going to disgrace her!"

"I've had six months' dancing lessons," Toni said softly. "I've had my hair done especially for tonight. I'm wearing the best gown in this room. I'm beautiful, Mother, and I'm a damned good dancer, and I may outshine Vinnie, but I certainly won't disgrace her."

Mother's face puffed up like a red balloon, and suddenly it collapsed on itself. "Why are you doing this?"

"Because I want men to admire me and I want to live just once before I'm dead."

Mother squinted at Toni as though a lid had been yanked off a well and she were peering down at unsuspected snakes and slime. "Are you that jealous of your sister?"

"Why shouldn't I be jealous? You've given her this party and you've never given me anything except a hereditary limp."

The orchestra launched into a raucous medley from *Oklahoma!*

Mother sat taller in her chair. A tendon of bra-strap peeked out from her gown. "I forbid you to do any more dancing. You've damaged your health enough for one evening. And I forbid you to go near Bart Stokes again. He's your sister's fiancé, and you leave him alone."

"Fiancé?" Toni twirled the stem of her glass. "Has she finally wormed a proposal out of him?"

For an instant Mother's rage was like a bell jar clamped down around them, blotting out music and laughter and ringing glasses. Her hand jerked up and swiped toward Toni's face, and then Toni's unflinching gaze stopped it dead. Party sounds floated back into the vacuum. The hand crawled back to Mother's lap, ashamed, defeated. "You vicious—little—cripple!"

"Not a cripple yet, Mother, but if you want me vicious I can try."

Toni got up and pried her way through the guests to the little table where Becky Horowitz was sitting alone. "Why, Becky," she said, "what's happened to your date?"

For one instant Becky's face was nakedly unhappy, and then a smiling mask dropped into place. "Phil went to get drinks."

"That bar's a mob scene. He'll be ten minutes at least." Toni took Becky's hand. "Do you know Bart Stokes? You've absolutely hypnotized him. He thinks you're the prettiest thing here."

"Oh, Toni," Becky said, and Toni couldn't help thinking that the girl was pretty, but it was a sorrowful sort of prettiness that didn't fit with blond laughter and popping corks. "You have such an imagination."

"He's asked me to introduce you," Toni said, "and he's very shy, so you have to be nice to him."

"Now you're making *me* shy."

"Then the two of you will get along beautifully." Toni pulled Becky back to the family table. Father and Bart and Vinnie had returned, and Vinnie threw Toni and Becky a quick scowl of unwelcome. "Mother, Father," Toni said brightly, "you must have met my friend Becky in the receiving line."

"Of course," Mother said stiffly.

"We're one seat short," Father said. He begged an empty chair from the next table and wedged it into the circle. "I think we can all squeeze in, can't we?"

Toni nudged Becky into the empty seat beside Bart. They

traded how-do-you-do's, and Mother said, "Well, Becky, you must tell us about yourself. How are you liking Miss Potter's?"

"Honestly, Mother," Toni said. "Vinnie doesn't want to hear school talk tonight of all nights! Bart, why don't you show Becky how beautifully you lindy?"

Bart looked startled. "Why, I—of course. Would you care to dance, Miss Horowitz?"

"Well, I'd—yes, I would," Becky said. She excused herself and Bart took her out to the dance floor. The orchestra ripped into a deafening chorus of "Zip-a-dee-doo-dah."

"You did that on purpose!" Vinnie cried.

"What in the world are you talking about?" Toni said.

"You threw that Horowitz girl at Vinnie's date," Mother said.

"Honestly," Toni said. "I was just being polite to a guest."

"Now, Toni," Father said, "you did it just to tease your sister, and I wish you'd stop."

"What's the matter with you people?" Toni said. "Are you scared he'll elope with someone else before Vinnie can rope him?"

Vinnie pounded a fist on the table. Champagne glasses jumped. "I hate you!"

"Now, now," Father said. "Let's keep it down to a dull roar."

Vinnie's nose had blotched red and choked-back tears sputtered in her throat. "She's made me a laughingstock! Look at them—jitterbugging—Bart Stokes and the rag merchant's daughter!"

Toni twirled a swizzle stick in her champagne and Mother delved into her purse and pressed a fresh piece of tissue paper into Vinnie's hand. "There, there," Mother said. "Don't cry. Whatever you do, *don't cry*."

"Toni's going to behave herself," Father said. "Aren't you, Toni?"

"Toni's going to go home," Mother said, eyes commanding.

Toni smiled her good-little-girl smile. She rose. The champagne had done more than give her two feet and a tongue. It had made her wild and rebellious and alive. She didn't care if this turned out to be the last night of her life: she was going to grab every second of it. "All right—I'll go home. And I'll ask Bart Stokes to escort me."

"Toni," Mother said, "if you dare—"

A man stepped between them. "Mrs. Pierpont—Mr. Pierpont?" He thrust out a hand. The action threw him off balance, and he almost didn't recover. "Jay Stokes—Bart's brother."

Mother slapped a smile over her face. She rose halfway from her chair. "Why, yes—how do you do?"

"Sorry to miss dinner," Jay Stokes said. He stood smirking his apology. "Hope I didn't throw your table off."

Father pushed up from his chair. "Didn't louse us up in the least. Won't you have a seat?"

Jay Stokes didn't seem to have heard. His eyes narrowed on Toni and he took a lurching step. "And you must be *Miss* Pierpont." He grinned and the air was full of gin vapors. "Don't think we've met."

"No, Jay," Toni said. "We haven't."

"Thanks for the dinner that I missed and thanks for this party and thanks for the booze and my apologies for being so goddamned drunk."

Toni smiled. "We wouldn't put out liquor if we didn't expect the guests to enjoy it."

Jay Stokes lobbed a gesture out toward the dance floor. "How about it?"

Toni glanced at the table. Her family seemed frozen in a still photograph. "Love to."

Jay Stokes led her out among the dancers and took her immediately in a close grip. "Did you dye your hair for the big night?" he asked.

"What makes you think that?" Toni said.

"Bart said your hair was red, but it looks brunette to me."

Toni realized he had mistaken her for Vinnie. "Do you believe everything your brother says?"

"He says you like concerts."

"I loathe them."

"He says you're stingy with goodnight kisses."

Toni gave Jay a kiss on the mouth. He jabbed his tongue into hers. It tasted of tobacco and gin but she did not withdraw. Out of the corner of her eye she could see Vinnie watching from the table.

"I hope that's not goodnight," Jay said.

"No, Jay. That's hello. Goodnight comes later."

Jay Stokes clearly did not give a damn about the music. Everyone else on the floor was hopping, but he ground his hips very slowly against hers. Toni smiled. She enjoyed being outrageous and she enjoyed the thought that tomorrow she and not Vinnie would be the talk of Harvard and M.I.T.

"What the hell do you see in Bart?" Jay asked.

"Money."

He burst out laughing. "Are you really serious about that jerk?"

"Why shouldn't I be?"

"He wouldn't know what to do with you. The only woman he ever saw naked was his mother, the day he was born."

"And you would know what to do with me?"

He pressed against her. He had an erection. His hand dropped down to her thigh. His tongue was very near her ear. "I could think of a few things," he whispered.

Toni could not help loving the moment. In a room full of prissy debutantes, here she was slouched against a drunk's hard-on; and he was not just any common college drunk, he was a millionaire drunk, and he wanted her, he wanted the little cripple that no one had ever looked at till tonight.

"Jay," she said, "I'm a lady. You have to telephone and bring flowers and meet my parents and sit and chat. And then we can fuck."

For an instant he seemed genuinely tongue-tied: not with shock, but with admiration. "Lady, you got yourself a date. How do I reach you?"

"We're in the book."

"Which book?"

"Both. We're the Beacon Hill Pierponts. And I'm not Vinnie—I'm Antonia, the cripple. You can call me Toni."

She turned, leaving him drop-jawed, and went back to the table. Mother was sitting alone and fuming.

"This is the most important night of your sister's life and she's in the ladies' room sick to her stomach!"

"It's her own fault," Toni said. "She swills champagne like a dehydrated pig."

"You're to blame and you know it! You've behaved revoltingly. Now, you just get your coat, young lady, and *scram!*"

Toni saw Bart approaching. "And who'll entertain the guest of honor while Vinnie's pulling herself together?" She downed someone's abandoned half-glass of champagne. Recklessness was bubbling through her.

"Don't you dare! Toni, I absolutely forbid you!"

Toni rose and took Bart's arm.

"Won't you sit, Bart?" Mother patted a seat. "Vinnie will be right back."

Toni danced in place, brushing her hips against Bart. "Honestly, Mother, you know how long it takes Vinnie to do anything in a bathroom, let alone be sick to her stomach. And in the meantime, all this heavenly music is going to waste."

Bart's brow wrinkled. "I'm sorry about Vinnie. Is there anything I can do?"

"Not a thing in the world," Toni said. "Let's dance."

"Just a moment," Mother said. "Toni's leg can't take this much activity."

"Now, Mother, you're a dear to worry, but my leg's fine and dandy." Toni pulled Bart back into the dance.

"Are you sure about that leg?" Bart said.

"Mother's an old hen," Toni said. "Always nervous, always pestering. If you ask me, that's why Vinnie's sick. Well, *we* don't have to be nervous, do we?" She nestled against him. "You're not paying for the party and I'm not trying to get married."

The orchestra was playing "People Will Say We're in Love," and Bart seemed too startled to answer. Toni experimented, doing things Jay had done. She could feel Bart's embarrassment, his pulling back, but she kept pressing and gradually she was aware of a peculiar flat hardness between his legs. At first she thought he must be grotesquely misshapen and then she realized he was wearing a jockstrap. Initially she was stunned and then she wanted to laugh: he was a boy, scared of his reaction to women; no wonder Vinnie had been able to lead him around by the nose!

"Toni, I'm sorry." Bart's face was as red as a glass of Father's port wine.

"Sorry?" Toni slid herself tighter against him. "Don't you know it's flattering to a girl?"

There were beads of sweat on Bart's face and his voice was pinched. "You're not like your sister, not at all."

"And you're not the least like that brother of yours. He's a playboy and you're serious. That's very attractive to women. Do you know how attractive you are to women?"

Bart blinked. "Well, I . . ."

"You don't know it, do you? Well, you are. And I'll tell

you something else. I'm very attracted to you. And I know you're attracted to me. And you know something, Bart? I'm proud that you're attracted to me."

His arms tightened around her. "Oh, Toni, you're so different from her! You're just great!"

# Chapter 16

TUESDAY, JUST BEFORE NOON, Bart telephoned Kitty from Grand Central Station and said if she didn't mind he'd like to bring a friend home to meet her. Kitty was in the middle of preparing a speech for the League of Women Voters and she was four days behind on her correspondence.

"Is it important?"

"It's important to me, Mom."

Bart had never in his life brought a friend home, and Kitty couldn't help wondering what this could all be about. "Well, why don't you bring your friend around one—we'll have lunch. It's chicken salad, I'm afraid."

"Chicken salad sounds terrific."

They arrived exactly on time. Kitty had never seen her son so proud or smiling. The girl's name was Antonia, Toni for short. Her skin was dark with the translucence of pearl. Her hair was deep chestnut and it had definitely been to the beauty parlor. Kitty's blood smelled danger. "I'm so glad you could come," she told the girl. "I don't often get to meet Bart's friends."

"Bart has said so many wonderful things about you and your house and your work." The girl's eyelids dipped when she spoke. The voice was low and throaty and the accent was Boston, the unfaceable definitely right sort of Boston.

"Has he?" Kitty led the way to the dining room. There was something wrong. Wasn't the girl's name supposed to be Lavinia? "He's kept you a complete mystery, Toni."

The girl was built delicately and slightly. There was a suggestion of soft rounded hips beneath her ridiculous Scotch plaid skirt. Kitty could not fit the girl into her image of Bart's type. She'd have expected him to turn up someone more intellectual, brilliant in a retiring sort of way: a wallflower like himself. This girl seemed more like someone Jay might date once or twice.

"Toni won't be a mystery much longer," Bart said. "We're going to get married."

There was a terrible moment of silence and Kitty tried to control the racing of her thoughts. She couldn't imagine Bart wanting to marry a stranger in a plaid skirt, but she could imagine a stranger wanting to marry Bart's money. That at least made sense. She slid a smile into place. "This calls for a celebration. Toni, do you enjoy champagne?"

"I adore it."

That made sense, too. Kitty reached a foot for the button beneath the carpet. "Marie, is there any of the 'forty-three Mumm's still on ice?"

Kitty phoned and phoned, but Johnny was not at his office the entire afternoon. Her head felt as though it were going to explode. It wasn't till six that evening that Johnny's limousine drew up to the front door. She headed him off in the hallway and whisked him into the study.

"What's the matter?" Johnny said. "You look like hell."

"Sit down, Johnny. This is as bad as Venezuelan Shell and you're not going to like it."

"I'm sitting."

"Bart wants to get married."

"So?"

Kitty yanked open the desk drawer and thrust a manila folder at him. It held two dozen pages of a Dun and Bradstreet financial snoop job. "Amory Pierpont of Boston—the father of your daughter-in-law unless we do something about it right now."

Johnny slipped his spectacles over his nose and stared at

the pages. "Jesus Christ," Johnny said. "The poor guy would do better playing the horses."

"They're paupers. He's on commission for an eighth-rate bank and they can barely meet their mortgage."

"Come on, Kitty. You were a pauper and it didn't stop us."

"I don't trust her."

"Aren't you overdoing this? Bart's been seeing Lavinia Pierpont for months, and the only thing that surprises me is that *you're* surprised."

"It's not Lavinia he wants to marry. *Now* he wants her sister Antonia. She's two years older and she's got some kind of disease and the family has spent a fortune trying to cure her."

Johnny went to the highboy and, forsaking his quinine and bitters, poured himself a gin on ice.

"Look at the facts, Johnny. Bart will inherit a fortune. Neither of these Pierpont girls has a cent. For nine months Bart has been mooning about Lavinia Lavinia Lavinia, and suddenly this Antonia beats her out in the home stretch. He's known her five days and he wants to marry her. It makes no sense at all."

Johnny sipped gin. "I knew I wanted to marry you in thirty seconds."

"It's not the same, Johnny."

"It's exactly the same. Love's not supposed to make sense."

"If it *is* love. But I'm positive she's tricked him."

The ghost of an old wound flickered in Johnny's eyes. "You can't know that."

"They're up in the conservatory. Go look at her and decide for yourself."

Johnny took the elevator to the top floor. He was going to meet the girl his son had chosen, and suddenly he ached. The past was alive in him again, bleeding. He wondered if love was the same for everyone, a shadow tiptoeing away before you'd barely had a chance to kiss.

He went to the glass door. He could see them on the bench behind the azaleas. The girl was dressed in a plaid skirt and even in half profile she possessed the impossible beauty of the very young. The glass door was misted on the inside and they were blurred and perfectly still, like figures in an old family snapshot. They were holding hands, not even aware that he was there.

Johnny watched them a long moment. He saw his own youth

and he yearned for its sweet boundless ignorance. When he rapped and opened the door, Bart rose from the bench.

"Dad, I'd like you to meet Toni Pierpont."

She was dark and, from two feet away, flawless. Her eyes did not seem quite so shy as the hand she held out. There was a small ruby ring on her finger, and Johnny wondered if Bart had given it to her.

"How do you do," Johnny said, and the girl murmured how glad she was to meet him.

"I love your greenhouse," she said. "It's spring all year round here."

"I understand you're from Boston," Johnny said. "Boston's a lovely town."

"But New York has the opera—I adore the opera, don't you, Mr. Stokes?"

"Why Toni," Bart said, "you never mentioned opera. I'd have bought tickets."

"I'm sure we can get tickets for Toni," Johnny said. "You two are thinking of marriage, is that right?"

The girl glanced at Bart.

"I didn't expect Toni to say yes." Bart put an arm around the girl's shoulder and pulled her against him. "Isn't she lovely, Dad? I feel so goddamned lucky."

"Oh, Bart," the girl said, almost chidingly, and now she glanced at Johnny.

The glance bothered him and for a moment he couldn't put his finger on the reason. And then it came to him. She glanced at people as though she were looking in a mirror. She was checking her appearance by their reaction.

"You two will be staying to dinner, won't you?" Johnny said.

"Damned right we're staying to dinner," Bart said.

"Good. Your mother and I can get to know Toni a little better."

"You're going to love her, Dad."

Johnny did not love the girl. His first instinct was not even to like her. She struck him as undeniably pretty and pert and 100 percent phony. He prayed God he was being fair. "It's a serious step," he said. "We'd better all give it some thought."

"Come on, Dad. You're going to scare Toni to death with talk like that!"

* * *

But Toni wasn't the least bit scared at dinner.

A fifth place had been set at the long table, and a slender woman with gray-blond hair joined them. At first, from the way the others treated her, Toni took the woman for a member of the family, some kind of in-law or unmarried aunt. Her name was Jennings and the others called her Vicky. She dressed with immaculate plainness and, though she said very little, she listened alertly, her blue eyes sharp and darting.

Conversation was boring, and Mr. and Mrs. Stokes were as boring as their son. Toni amused herself trying to imagine the naked hate on her family's faces when she came home married to twenty million dollars.

Bart's mother kept calling for more wine, but Toni noticed that she and the Jennings woman drank very little. After dessert, pears poached in red wine, Mrs. Stokes excused herself from the table.

"Perhaps we'd better take care of those letters, Vicky," she said, and Toni realized the woman must be some kind of secretary. Mrs. Stokes bent down and kissed Toni on the cheek. "You've made me very happy, Toni dear," she said.


Kitty took Vicky to the upstairs sitting room. Vicky had seen the evidence, had spent an entire dinner observing and judging it. Kitty needed the verdict of a trusted friend, needed to know if it echoed her own alarm.

"How does the girl strike you?" she said.

Vicky regarded her quietly. "I only saw her for forty-five minutes."

"Your first impressions are usually reliable," Kitty said.

Vicky clasped her hands in her lap and smiled a smile strangely lacking in malice. "She's not shy and she doesn't hesitate. She thinks Puccini wrote *Traviata* and she says so."

"Then you agree she's stupid."

"Not stupid, Kitty. She's learning. I suspect she's a fast learner. You asked about opera and she had to improvise. Next time you see her she'll have done her homework."

"Anyone can do homework," Kitty said. "Do you think she's a match for Bart? Do you think she can do anything for him?"

"Does Bart need anything done for him?"

Kitty rolled a Camel restlessly in her fingers. "Marriage is an opportunity," she said. "I want Bart to make the most of it." What Kitty meant and what she wanted Vicky to say was that Antonia Pierpont was a waste of an opportunity, that she did nothing for the social advancement of Bart or his family.

"Bart's trying to find himself," Vicky said. "He's at that age where he thinks he can find himself in someone else."

"He won't find anything in her," Kitty said.

"He'll have to learn that himself," Vicky said.

Kitty walked to the table and snatched up the cigarette lighter. It took her three angry thumb-flips to wrench flame from it. "I don't want him making a mistake."

"Perhaps *you're* making the mistake, Kitty. You hardly know the girl and yet you've already made up your mind about her."

"Have I?"

Vicky nodded. "Oh yes, indeed you have. I was watching your eyes at dinner. You have enough of her in you to know exactly what she's after."

"And you think she has enough of me in her to get it," Kitty said. The idea stung, which proved there was more truth in it than she cared to admit. She pressed her teeth slowly down on her lip. "I don't like her and I don't want him marrying her. I'm going to put a stop to it—tonight, if possible."

"I think you're wrong, Kitty. If you openly block her you're blocking him too. That makes them allies. A lot of children have married for no better reason than to thumb their noses at their parents. Why don't you let them get to know one another? I bet they'll change their minds."

Kitty shook her head sharply. "That's too risky."

"Not as risky as opposing them."

Kitty gazed at her friend and adviser and a thought that had once or twice crossed her mind occurred to her again. Vicky Jennings had no private life that Kitty had ever detected. In view of this limitation or quirk or whatever it was, Vicky's judgments often struck Kitty as prodigies of intuition. But tonight Vicky's intuition did not agree with Kitty's, and Kitty wondered if this was perhaps the proof of inexperience.

This time, Kitty realized, she would have to act without advice. "Can you keep the girl occupied a half hour or so?" she said.

"I'll be glad to. But do be careful."

Vicky rose and rustled out of the room and Kitty called for a bottle of Courvoisier and three snifters and a small pot of iced tea. She poured an inch of cognac into two snifters and an inch of tea into the third. She sent for Johnny and Bart. She handed them each a cognac. She lifted her snifter of tea.

"To us," she proposed. "To happiness." She gulped back her tea in a swift flip of the head. Bart took his cognac in a single swallow.

Kitty commenced.

She praised Antonia Pierpont, praised her beauty, her breeding, her brains, praised the perfection of the match and the marital harmony that would inevitably blossom from it. Several times Johnny cleared his throat and seemed on the verge of hawking up a protest, but she silenced him with a flick of the eyes. After eight minutes of praise Bart's face was flushed and grinning and she judged that the brandy had sufficiently diffused itself through his bloodstream.

"What do you say to a June wedding?" she suggested. "Do you suppose Toni's parents would agree?"

"June?" Johnny said. His eyes were orbs barely holding back shock.

"Now, Johnny," Kitty said, "I'm asking Bart, not you."

"June would be wonderful," Bart said.

"Late-ish June," Kitty said. "That would give you time to graduate."

Bart's head came around slowly, like a dog sniffing something dead in the wall.

"You do intend to graduate business school," Kitty said, "don't you?"

"But, Mom, that's two years."

"Of course it's two years; and then you'll marry Toni. Your dad and I will send you on a honeymoon around the world and you'll come back to your own business."

"I do think your mother has a point," Johnny said. "After all, you hardly know the girl. And we don't know her at all."

"Know her!" Kitty cried. "Anyone can see she's perfectly adorable. Johnny, this is an occasion. Bart's glass is empty."

Afterward, Bart took Toni in a taxi to the little park south of Sutton Place. It was dark and they stood hand-in-hand at the railing and she sensed an uneasiness creeping between them. Across the East River a sign was blinking the words PEARL-

WICK HAMPERS. A barge making its way upstream hooted and left a valley of silence.

"Toni . . ."

"What?"

"You know how very much I love you, don't you?"

She nuzzled automatically against his shoulder. "Of course I do."

After a while, in exactly the same tone, he said, "Toni—do you trust me?"

There was something childish about his questioning, but he was always childish and for a moment she could not tell why this evening it bothered her. "Is there any reason I shouldn't trust you?"

"Do you trust our love?"

"What are you getting at?" She looked at him. In the moonlight his face was white as a flag of surrender. "Something's happened. Tell me what's happened."

He stared a long while at the blinking sign. "Mom and Dad and I had a talk. A long talk. A very good talk. They're very loving people, Toni. They think you're wonderful."

Very dimly she began to see that his words were cloaking something. "Then what's the matter?"

He was smiling very hard, very steadily. "Mom and Dad feel if we got to know one another better—if we were engaged awhile, a year or so—"

The words went into her like a knife. The doctor had said that without the brace her hip might hold out ten, fifteen years. No more. Bart was asking for a tenth of her life, throwing it away like a college weekend.

"A year!" Toni cried. "She made you agree to a year?"

"Toni—be reasonable." He tried to take her in his arms but she stepped aside. "I can't hurt them. I just *can't.*"

The idea came to Toni that she might not be able to count on Bart Stokes, that Vinnie and Mother and Father might have the last laugh after all. She could not bear that; she would sooner die.

"And me," she said. "Doesn't it matter if you hurt *me?*"

"I'd never hurt you."

"Then marry me now. You're an adult. I'm over eighteen. We don't need anyone's permission."

His eyes did not leave her. He sank onto a bench. "What difference can it make, Toni? Please be reasonable. We'll be together—we'll see one another—nothing will change."

"Everything will change. If she can get a year out of you she can get ten. And ten years is just about all the time I've got."

He peered at her. "Toni—do you have some kind of disease?"

She stiffened, not caring if anger edged into her voice now. "What if I do? Make up your mind, Bart—marry me now, or forget it."

His eyes clenched shut and he was pounding his head with his fist. "Don't do this to me! Oh, Toni, why can't you just *trust* me?"

"Bart, *I can't afford to wait.*"

His gaze was like an open wound dripping down her skirt.

"All right, then." She flung her wool coat over her shoulder. "Your mother can keep you!"

The milk train got her to Boston at 3:38 A.M. She slammed into a phone booth in South Station. Information gave her the number. It rang twenty-eight times and her fingernails were digging bloody crescents into her palms.

A bad-tempered voice finally said hello and her mouth shaped a honey-drop purr. "Jay, is that you?"

"Who's this?"

"We danced at my sister's coming-out, remember?" There was a moment in which he obviously did not remember and she said, "You thought I was Vinnie."

"Oh, yeah." The voice was different now: warm and false and more awake. "How've you been, Joanie?"

*Toni,* she wanted to scream: *Toni Pierpont and I'm just as good as you or your brother or stinking Irish mother!*

"I've been thinking about that raincheck," she said.

"Oh yeah? What raincheck was that?"

"You promised me a fuck."

For forty-eight hours Jay Stokes lay in a hollow just below the surface of consciousness. His head was a gin-soaked jumble and sharp little fragments of memory kept jabbing through the fog. He was aware of damp rags on his forehead, hands changing sheets underneath him, someone moving and fussing around him.

He tried to open his eyes. The light scorched and he fell back into dull, moaning pain.

"Oh yes, my sweet, you'll be all right, you'll be fine."

Very slowly his ear tagged the voice. Toni. Not Mary O'Reilly. Antonia Pierpont this time. Broad arrogant vowels and *r*'s in the wrong places. *Roar meat*. They'd laughed about *roar meat*. Where had that been? His mind traced a thread back to the waterfront, a restaurant upstairs with sawdust on the floor, blowsy waitresses, steak too rare.

Gradually the last two days came into focus. He remembered the hotel bar and his hand on Antonia's blouse, not that it mattered whose blouse he rumpled, but Toni was supposed to be Bart's girl and Bart needed showing, and that made it fun.

"I've found a darling house on Brattle Street." Toni was sitting on the bed and her hip pressed his thigh through the covers. "Five bedrooms, can you believe it, and all they want is three hundred a month. What do you think, yes or no? I really don't think we're going to find anything better."

He remembered other yeses, yes to another drink, and to another and another, yes to a taxi ride, yes to the old fart who asked if he took this woman, and the snickering thought in the back of his head *I'm taking this woman and when I've taken enough I'm dumping her*.

"Five bedrooms sounds darling," Jay said, mimicking the slightly irritating mannerism of her voice, "and what darling place is this we're in now?"

"The Tremont. We've got a suite but we won't need to stay. The house is furnished and we can move in as soon as you sign the check. How's your head?"

"My head's absolutely lousy."

"Naughty boy." She bent down and her lips were cool on his forehead. "You rest up now. I'm going to look at dishwashers."

He heard the soft thud of a door pulled shut and he raised himself to a sitting position. He saw himself in the mirror, an unshaved mass of bath towel and bloat and blistered lips.

"Good God," he muttered. His eye prowled the dimness, seeking the way out.

Escape was Mother, as it had always been, and Mother was the telephone and the telephone had to be somewhere. He stumbled over the baggage stand and an unfamiliar suitcase spilled eight Boston *Transcripts*. Now who the hell, he wondered, would put eight Boston *Transcripts* into a cheap cardboard suitcase?

It came to him, flickeringly, that Antonia Pierpont had put

eight Boston *Transcripts* into an eight-dollar suitcase from Filene's and she'd done it sometime before they'd registered at the hotel.

He found a phone jack behind the sofa. The cord led him to a closet. The phone was buried beneath two pillows. He propped himself on the pillows and placed a collect call and for ten minutes his skin crawled ice caterpillars.

"Mom, that you?"

"Jay—what in the world, have you got some kind of cold?"

"Sick—very sick." He tried to think himself sicker than he actually felt. He needed blind, maximum sympathy. "Throwing-up sick."

"What did you eat?"

"Don't know."

"Where are you?"

"Don't know. Don't know anything. Never seen this room before."

"Well, is it a hospital? Jay, I don't like the way you're sounding at all. Who's with you? Is there a doctor with you? Jay, are you there?"

"Toni," he said. "Toni Pierpont's with me."

A shocked intake of breath whooshed through the phone. When his mother finally spoke, her words came like slow separate strokes of a scalpel. "Antonia Pierpont? She's in that room with you now?"

"Mom, Mom, Mom—get me out of this."

"I can't get you out till I know exactly what you're in."

"Think I'm married."

A silence came screaming from the receiver. He did not know if his mother was still there, and a sudden terror rose gagging in him.

*"You've—married—that—woman?"*

"Couldn't help it. Tricked me."

"Haven't you got one particle of brain in your head?"

"Don't shout, Mom. Please don't shout." Jay began crying softly, mouthpiece cupped to his sobs. "Can't stand it when you shout. Help me. Please."

After a silence she spoke again, her voice in a totally different key. "Now listen to me very carefully, Jay. Leave that phone off the hook. Do you understand me? Don't hang up. I'll have this call traced, but it will take a good twenty minutes. I can't do a thing till I know where you are. I'm going away now but don't, for God's sake, hang up and don't leave that room."

"Mom—I love you."

"We'll talk about that later."

It took thirty-five minutes to trace the call, and then in white fury Kitty phoned Justin Lasting and explained the unspeakable folly that Jay had been duped into. "Get to Boston as quickly as you can and get Jay away from that woman."

"Now, Kitty." The voice was bland and medicinal, like emulsion of cod liver oil. "If they're legally married it may be a little difficult."

"I don't *want* them married! *Jay* doesn't want them married! He was on the phone to me in *tears!* I give you one hundred twenty thousand dollars a year, and you could at least be a friend the one time in my life that I need you!"

"Now, Kitty. I'm going to do whatever can be done and then I'll get back to you. And don't you go rushing up there. You'll only make things worse and then we'll never be able to spring Jay. These Pierponts may be paupers, but they're not fools, and we're certainly not dealing with a half-witted Scollay Square tart."

Kitty sat with a dead phone cradled in her lap. She saw her every hope, her every prayer, overturned. She saw the pure water of her dreams spilling down the dry dead gullies of this wretched earth and vanishing into mud. She saw Tyrone Duncannon's son broken, buried.

Slowly, she lifted the receiver again and dialed. She told Johnny's secretary to break into the conference. "He's married her," she said dully.

"Who?" Johnny said.

"Jay. He's married Toni Pierpont."

"I'll be right there," Johnny said.

The family lawyers scheduled the meeting for Thursday at twelve-thirty.

The chauffeur had trouble finding the gabled house on Brattle Street, and Kitty and Johnny arrived twenty minutes late. Antonia and Jay and Mr. and Mrs. Amory Pierpont were waiting for them in the sunken living room. The house smelled as though the previous tenant had owned dogs.

Jay kissed his mother and shook his father's hand and dropped into a wing chair. He looked blank and helpless and limp, as though an avalanche had severed him from his body. There was an embarrassed silence and Mr. Pierpont cracked his knuckles.

"Johnny," Kitty said, "why don't you give the Pierponts the gist of our proposal?"

Mr. and Mrs. Pierpont nodded as though that were a good idea. Johnny opened his briefcase. He took out folders and spread them on the coffee table. Mrs. Pierpont perched forward on her chair, and her glance met Kitty's for one instant of undisguised calculation. Johnny snapped a pair of spectacles over his nose.

"We suggest, first of all," Johnny said, "that the marriage between your daughter and our son be annulled."

"Aren't there technical problems?" Mr. Pierpont asked quietly.

"Not if Antonia and Jay execute the proper affadavits."

Mr. Pierpont examined the document that Johnny handed him. "But wouldn't this constitute a lie?" Mr. Pierpont said. "If the marriage has already been consummated—"

Kitty saw that Mrs. Pierpont was watching her husband, telling him wordlessly to shut up. Mrs. Pierpont had sense.

"That would depend," Johnny said.

Mr. Pierpont flipped pages. They were beautifully typed, with red line margins, fastened at the corner with a yellow ribbon. Kitty had sat up two nights with the family lawyers hacking out every comma and *wherefore* and she understood the look on Amory Pierpont's face. "But if Toni signed this," he said, "and it became a matter of public record—"

"Let me look." Mrs. Pierpont snatched the papers from her husband. She held them at a trembling arm's length and her squint narrowed. "Would it have to go into the public record? I mean, can't records be sealed by judicial order?"

"Absolutely," Johnny said. "We intend to handle all this with the absolute minimum of public fuss. Or any sort of fuss, for that matter."

"It seems to me," Mr. Pierpont said, "we're going to an awful lot of fuss with this annulment; and we're darkening Toni's name in the bargain. Annulling the marriage isn't at all the same thing as annulling her... condition. Mr. Stokes, if you had a daughter of your own, I'm sure you'd understand my reservations."

Mrs. Pierpont was watching her husband again. Her teeth bit down slowly over her lower lip.

"Absolutely," Johnny nodded. "I understand your reservations completely."

"But try to understand *our* position," Kitty said. "Jay's having terrible problems in law school, and this is altogether the wrong time for a marriage."

Mr. Pierpont was thoughtful a moment. "If all you're worried about is Jay's graduating from law school, couldn't the kids sign a legal separation? I mean, wouldn't it be simpler and more—straightforward?"

"A separation would be an entanglement," Kitty said. "We'd rather Jay had as few entanglements as possible till he gets his degree."

"I don't think you've grasped the entire gist of our proposal," Johnny said.

"Amory," Mrs. Pierpont said, "let Mr. Stokes outline the entire gist before you start shooting it down."

"I'm not shooting anything down," Mr. Pierpont said. He glanced at his daughter. She was slouched in a corner of the sofa, swinging her legs idly. "I just feel someone has to look out for Toni."

"I'm sure the Stokeses understand we want to look out for Toni," Mrs. Pierpont said.

"After the annulment," Johnny said, "we'll deposit twenty thousand per annum in Antonia's bank account until Jay graduates. After graduation, the children will be free to marry."

Mrs. Pierpont crossed her arms. She stared at the ceiling. Her thoughts seemed to be somewhere else for a moment. "Well, Amory?" she said. "How does that strike you?"

"It's generous, of course," Mr. Pierpont said.

Kitty couldn't help thinking he looked very much the small-time investment banker. She could imagine the turned shirt collar and the cuffs beginning to fray beneath his neatly pressed flannel jacket. His cordovan shoes had a lovely deep shine, which meant he had not had a new pair for six or seven years. He looked shrewd enough to hold out for more money, but at the same time he was an old Bostonian and he might have some chivalric notion of salvaging the family's reputation.

"All the same," Mr. Pierpont said, "it seems an awful lot of fuss. I'd like to know what the kids think. After all, it's their marriage we're kicking around."

Kitty's eyes went to her son. "Jay, what do you think?"

"Whatever you and Dad say, Mom. It's okay by me."

Kitty's eyes moved to Toni. The girl rose from the sofa, smoothly, like a cat uncoiling. She went to Jay and sat on the arm of the chair. She poked a finger in his hair and made swirls like a child drawing in sand. Jay did not move.

"First of all," Toni said, "Jay has flunked law school. The marriage is being announced in the evening papers and they've already gone to press. I was a virgin till I married and I have a notarized statement from a doctor proving it. I love Jay and he loves me and I'm not letting him go. And I don't think twenty thousand a year is enough."

Kitty drew in a long breath. "Johnny," she said, "perhaps we could step into the dining room with Mr. and Mrs. Pierpont."

The four parents went into the dining room. Johnny shut the glass doors and Kitty explained to Mr. and Mrs. Pierpont how easily and swiftly the Stokes empire would pulverize them if they didn't bring their daughter around.

The Pierponts understood.

They took their daughter into the kitchen. They shut the door and, to be sure they couldn't be overheard, Mrs. Pierpont opened the cold water faucet. The sink was a jumble of unwashed dishes and floating scraps of scrambled egg, and she dried her hand on a damp dishtowel. She then turned and slapped her daughter across the face.

"For God's sake," Mr. Pierpont said, "can't we be reasonable about this?" His eyes flitted from one woman to the other like moths in helpless search for a safe place to alight. "Toni," he said, "if you're doing this for money, you're making the most tragic mistake of your life."

"How would you know anything about money?" she said. "You've never had a cent. All you've got is a Beacon Hill mortgage. It may be enough for the two of you to be pedigreed beggars the rest of your lives. It's not enough for me."

"Is that what you think of us?" Mother said.

"Mother, two years ago the Social Register raised its subscription price. You had to tell the milkman to stop delivering heavy cream."

"In this life," Father said, "you can't have everything."

"Why not?" Toni shot back. "Jay Stokes does."

"He has a bad reputation," Father said. "Drinks too much.

Uncle Clyde says he threw up at a *Lampoon* dinner at the Atheneum."

"And everyone knows he runs around," Mother said. "Don't think he'll change for you."

Toni wondered how much the Stokeses had offered her parents: a hundred thousand? a million? third assistant directorship of one of their foundations?

Father said Jay hung out at disorderly houses, and Mother said Toni could be jeopardizing her health.

"Mother, we passed our syphilis tests."

Mother winced, and Father said, "He's a playboy. Believe me, I know the type. I've handled trusts for them. He'll disgrace you. You'll be utterly miserable."

"We're only thinking of *you*," Mother said.

"The way you've always thought of me?" Toni said.

Mother actually looked shocked and a little hurt, and it seemed to Toni not completely an act. "Do you actually think," Mother said, "there's ever been a day we haven't put your happiness first and foremost?"

Toni thought of all the days and nights of her life and she couldn't bring herself to answer.

"All right," Father said. "I might as well be frank about this. The Stokeses have made it clear that unless this marriage is dissolved—well, the going will get pretty rough for us. They have the power to yank our top five trusts. The bank will retire me rather than let that happen."

"Do you have any idea how large your father's pension is?" Mother said. "We'll be ruined—worse than ruined!"

Toni looked at her mother and father, jibbering like trapped mice. After all the years of being made to feel a burden and a freak, of being treated worse than a servant, she found she had only one word to say.

"Good."

The wedding was announced the next day in the Boston *Herald*, in the column next to a story continued from page one. It was the photograph of Toni that yanked Bart's eye.

He was standing on the traffic island in the middle of Harvard Square and it was as though a pistol had been fired two inches from his ear. Trucks and buses and cars shot past, horns hooting and bells clanging. A frightened pigeon sliced up into the air with the snap of a fan jerked open.

He lost his balance and stumbled forward off the curb.
Brakes hissed and drivers shouted. He plunged through traffic
to the sidewalk and the paper slid from his hands. He needed
silence. He needed to curl up at the bottom of a cool, dark
sea.

He found a bar and took a stool. He ordered bourbon—
Jay's drink because today was Jay's day. It seemed all the days
of his life had been Jay's. He gulped his bourbon and looked
around him.

The bar had Miss Rhinegold posters, and the bartender used
a false-bottomed shot glass and joked in a Boston Irish brogue.

Bart pounded a fist against his temple. The photograph of
Toni, the caption—Mrs. John Stokes III—kept smashing at
him. She was gone. He could not believe it, but she was gone.
He didn't want to think. He wanted to be swept along by
currents beyond his control. He saw the dark lovely face of
the girl they had taken from him. He heard his brother's blond
laughter, his mother begging him to wait.

Gradually a cold whisper of an idea came to him. He watered
it with bourbon after bourbon and, like a miraculous beanstalk,
it grew till it was a deafening cry in his blood.

He began to walk. The Cambridge street pitched and ca-
reened but it could not deflect him. He headed for the MTA
subway entrance. A sour wind blew up the stairway. In the
rear car of the train, between two empty seats, he nursed his
cargo of dead love and dead trust. The train hurtled through
tunnels and across bridges, carrying him where the cry said he
must go.

Struggling up the stairs, he fell only once. His mind was
numb but his feet kept going. The air was gray, with dampness
slipping down. He came to the house and lifted the brass knocker.

A woman let him in. She had a huge bosom and she minced
and twittered and never stopped talking. At the end of the
hallway a girl crossed through a cone of Tiffany-stained light,
carrying a tray of drinks.

"Her," Bart said.

The twittering woman caught herself in mid-syllable. *"Her?"*

"She's the one I want."

"Well . . ." The woman's eyes went crafty. "Beth has duties,
you know. I'm really not sure I can spare her."

In Bart's memory, a ten-dollar bill fluttered down a stairwell. "Fifteen dollars," he said.

"Try to keep it to half an hour, will you, dear?" The woman took his money and snapped her fingers. "Beth. You have a caller."

The girl led him up to the third floor. Rooms had been divided into cubicles with flimsy wood doors. She snapped a latch behind them. There was a bed with sheets and no blankets. She folded her arms and watched him. She had dark hair but she was not beautiful in the way of Toni. Bart was not sure if she was beautiful at all.

"You don't remember me?" he said, obscurely hurt that she didn't.

"You sure you got the right girl? I'm usually in the kitchen."

A consoling night filled the cubicle. Sounds wandered in and out, dim and tiny and nibbling. "I'm sure."

The girl sighed and tugged at a zipper on her dress.

"Don't." Bart emptied his pockets onto the bed. There was a rain of keys, coins, ten-dollar bills that he had drawn from the bank for two weeks' expenses. "Take it," he said.

The girl stared. Her lips made a quick counting movement. Her eyes came up at him, dark and disbelieving and wary. "What do I have to do?"

"Marry me."

She darted a hand toward the door. "You're drunk."

"There won't be any sex. You don't have to even kiss me. Just marry me for two days."

"Let go of me."

He saw that he had seized her wrist. He released her. "I'll give you two hundred dollars. A hundred a day."

Her eyes went again to the money. "I don't get it. Why?"

"I just want my family to meet my wife."

# *Chapter 17*

KITTY AND JOHNNY had planned an elaborate formal dinner for John Stokes, Senior's ninetieth birthday, and there was no way not to go through with it. She wanted to put a bullet through Antonia Pierpont's head or, failing that, her own, and instead she had to contend with cooks and seating plans and florists.

As usual, Vicky Jennings was a godsend, suggesting and listening and disentangling the confusion of Kitty's thoughts as easily as she straightened out the dessert order from Rumpelmayer's. Last year the rage had been individual baked Alaska, known at Stokeses' dinners as *omelettes norvégiennes*. This year it was to be dessert crepes stuffed with imported preserves made by the Trappist monks. When Kitty discovered the day of the party that the caterer had sent ordinary marmalade she lashed out at an aspic mold, shattering it and scattering madrilene all over cook's clean kitchen.

Vicky sat Kitty down in the pantry and bolted both swinging doors shut. "Now, you're not going to destroy your party because of eight jars of apricot honey preserves," Vicky said. "And you're not going to destroy it because of Antonia Pierpont either."

Kitty looked at Vicky and saw calm and reason and knew Vicky was right and almost began crying.

"You just have to keep going forward one step at a time," Vicky said. "When there's nothing intelligent to be done, don't do anything. You'll only make a mess. There's aspic on your skirt."

"Don't take that I-told-you-so tone."

"I'm not taking any tone. But you're going to have a rotten party if you don't pull yourself together."

"How can I? How could anyone?" Kitty made fists, but there was nothing to strike them against. "How could he have married her?"

Vicky sighed and touched her shoulder gently. "Kitty, it's done."

"It's my fault." Kitty blotted the stinging of her eyes against her wrists. "You warned me and I ignored you. You know it's my fault."

"I don't know anything of the sort. Now stop blaming yourself. You didn't cause it. People cause their own lives."

"I should have known what she was up to. I should have protected Jay."

"You can't protect people from their own mistakes, Kitty. Only they can do that, and they have to make mistakes before they learn."

"But he's my *son*."

"Does his marriage change that? You'll deal with it, Kitty—but don't deal with it today when you have forty-two guests coming to dinner."

Kitty realized Vicky was right: the world could not stop turning simply because Jay had gotten himself into a tragic impasse. A little of the helpless rage lifted from her, like static dissipating into cool air. "I'm dead wrong and you're dead right, Vicky—and I resent you for it."

"Then say something nasty. You'll feel better."

"I don't think you're wise at all. You're just practical, damn you."

Vicky smiled and kissed her. "Have a bash."

The party that night was a grand, white-tie occasion. Bank presidents, senators, senior partners and glittering wives filled the dining room.

As a surprise, because John Stokes loved her recording of

the "Shadow Song" from Meyerbeer's *Dinorah,* Kitty had invited Lily Pons, the Metropolitan Opera coloratura, and her husband, André Kostelanetz, the conductor. The Kostelanetzes had asked if they might invite their house guests, the Duke and Duchess of Windsor. Kitty had heard rumors about the royal couple. "I hear they charge money to appear at parties," she'd said. Lily Pons had sworn that, in the first place, the Windsors never charged; and in the second place, they would never charge Kitty.

And so, as John Stokes Sr. rose to deliver his mid-dinner remarks, the former king of England was sitting at the table discussing bridge hands with Mrs. August Belmont. John Stokes Sr. tapped a butter knife against a wineglass, and a hush sliced the chatter.

"Your royal highnesses, honored guests, ladies and gentlemen—I'm sure you've all heard the old saying 'Money isn't everything.'"

A silence teetering on embarrassment rippled through the room.

"Well, I'd like to share with you something I've discovered about this whole process called life. The older I get and the richer I get, the more I realize . . ."

He let a very long moment pass.

"Age isn't everything either."

There was an instant's pained silence, and then the Duchess of Windsor cried, "How perfectly charming."

The duke said, "Wonderful, wonderful," and the other guests began clapping and laughing as they would have for a child. Whispers ran round the table: *perfectly amazing . . . and at his age, too . . .*

John Stokes Sr. was an American institution and he had endured.

Two champagnes, a Rhône, and three *premier cru* Rothschild burgundies were served. Through open glass doors a string quartet spun out Franz Schubert and Rodgers and Hammerstein. The wife of the English ambassador wore spider mums entwined in her hair. New York State's senior senator was explaining the British impressionists to her. Johnny was laughing and Kitty had put on a new blue Givenchy gown, and she suspected that John Stokes Sr., slumped back into the chair of honor, had turned down his hearing aid.

During squab, the butler bent to Kitty's left ear and whispered, "It's Mr. Bart, ma'am, with a young lady."

Kitty could see it was Mr. Bart with a young someone. They were quite visible in the doorway, Bart in one of his shoddy brown suits, a woman in a black raincoat with green shoes that looked plastic. Kitty smiled an apology to the director of Corning Glass and excused herself as though it were nothing more than the kitchen reporting a fallen *soufflé aux framboises*.

Before anyone else could notice the newcomers, she advanced—arms open and a smile fixed to her face—and swept Bart and the stranger beyond the dining-room sightlines.

"Brought you something, Mom," Bart said.

Kitty smelled liquor and deviltry, and because deviltry was not at all like Bart, her defenses went on red alert.

"Mom, meet Beth. Beth, meet Mom."

The girl was slender and dark. Her eyes touched Kitty with a fixed, almost kindly curiosity. Kitty let nothing show whatsoever.

"How do you do, Beth. Won't you both come into the drawing room?"

Kitty had the butler bring Johnny. When he saw the girl and saw Bart's condition, Johnny's face contracted the tiniest degree, like a fist tensed inside a pocket.

"What's got into you, Son?" Johnny said. "What the dickens do you think you're doing? I'd say you're drunk."

"I'm drunk and I'm celebrating," Bart said. "When I learned I wasn't good enough for the girl you wanted Jay to have, I found another girl. Mom, Dad—Dad, Mom—meet the newest Mrs. Stokes. Give her a nice warm welcome into the clan."

The girl's chin came up one fraction of a degree. Her hands were pressed together and they seemed to tremble. The room was perfectly still. Time congealed.

The dark of Johnny's face stirred. "You've got it all wrong, Son. We had nothing to do with Jay's marriage."

"We'd have done anything we could to prevent it," Kitty said. "We're heartbroken over it—as heartbroken as you."

"Then cheer up," Bart said. "I've brought you a present to take your mind off your troubles. A whore."

The girl did not move. Color brushed her cheeks.

"For God's sake, Bart," Kitty said. "Where are your manners?"

"It's all right, Mrs. Stokes," the girl said. Her voice was a low whisper. "I do work in a whorehouse, and maybe that makes me a whore."

Johnny's eyes heaped disbelief on the girl.

"You've killed off everything I ever wanted or loved," Bart said. "Now I don't care. I don't give a damn anymore. I'm past it."

"Don't raise your voice to your mother," Johnny said.

"Someone has to raise his voice to her. You've never had the guts."

"I said don't shout," Johnny said. "I meant it."

"Worried about the guests hearing? Worried they'll learn about the Stokes women? Let me tell you about the Stokes women, Dad. One's a whore and one's a tramp and one's a calculating bitch."

Johnny slapped Bart.

"Save your strength, Johnny," Kitty said. "He's hell-bent on being childish and disgraceful."

Bart grinned. Skeletal hollows slashed his cheeks. "That's right. Hell-bent. I'm going to spend my life disgracing you. I'll disgrace you both so badly you'll never be able to cover up like you did for Jay."

Impatience came sighing from Kitty. Bart and his mischief were just an exasperating footnote to her misery. She turned to the girl. "And are you drunk too?"

"I don't drink."

"Then we can talk sensibly. How much do you want?"

"How much what do I want?"

The milk-white innocence was too much. Kitty brought her fist down on the mantelpiece and a Sèvres shepherdess jumped. "Don't play-act for me. You came here for money and we both know it."

"I don't deny it," the girl said.

"How much, then?"

"Two hundred dollars."

"Two—?" Kitty's face darkened. "What kind of joke are you two playing? Bart, this is your grandfather's ninetieth birthday, and for you to pick this of all nights for a sophomoric prank—"

"It's not a prank," the girl said. "Two hundred dollars was what we agreed on."

Kitty's eyes darted from face to face. "Johnny, give her a

hundred now and a hundred when she signs the papers."

Johnny opened his crepe-thin Mark Cross wallet and drew out a new hundred-dollar bill. The girl did not take it. The bill fluttered to the silk carpet like a circling leaf.

"Your son's already paid me," she said.

Kitty wheeled on the boy. "I never imagined you had such contempt for us—or for yourself."

Judgment smoldered in the girl's eyes, but it was not a judgment on Bart or his contempt. "Your son has my address," she said. "Just mail me the papers. With a return envelope." Her raincoat whispered as she crossed the room.

"One moment, young woman," Johnny said.

She didn't stop. It was as though Johnny had said nothing at all.

"Young woman, I told you to wait a moment."

She half-turned in the doorway. Her eyes were dark and alive and unblinking. "Mr. Stokes—Mrs. Stokes—I've been rented, not bought. I've done my job. I'm not staying married to your son and I'm not staying in this house or listening to any of you one minute longer."

She was gone.

Bart gazed in the direction of the empty door and then he moved toward it.

"And where do you think you're going?" Johnny said.

"I'm going after her."

"What's all the ruckus?" John Stokes Sr. stood in the doorway, very old and very still, his eyes moving from Kitty to Johnny to Bart.

"There's been a little problem, Father," Kitty said. "Nothing to concern yourself with."

He came forward into the room, like a shrewd animal sniffing out a scent. "Just how little is this problem that my own grandson can't come in and wish me happy birthday?"

"Happy birthday, Grandpa," Bart said. "I'm married."

"Bart," Kitty said sharply, "this is hardly the time or place."

John Stokes, Senior's step faltered. "Married?" His eyes were eager and light. He clapped Bart on the back. "Then what's all the fuss? Bring the newlyweds into the dining room and let's toast them!"

Johnny exhaled a deep-drawn sigh. "You wouldn't want to toast this bride, Father."

"Why not? She got three noses?"

"She's a whore," Bart said.

Kitty spun on him. "Bart, for God's sake!"

John Stokes Sr. had the look of a rabbit caught suddenly in a trap. "This is a joke, isn't it? Why are you joking with me?" He took an unsteady backward step. The armchair caught him and he sank into the deep green velvet cushion like a stone dropping to the ocean floor.

"Bart's drunk," Kitty said. "Don't mind him."

"We don't know anything about the girl," Johnny said.

"Except that she's a whore," Bart said.

John Stokes Sr. was staring in utter panic, and Bart realized that he had actually frightened the old man. For the first time in his life he was aware that he was a little taller than his father and a great deal taller than his mother. He suddenly felt very sober, very strong, very much himself.

"And do you know something, Grandpa? Stokes money couldn't buy that poor dumb whore. Banks and universities and South American republics cave in at the touch of a Stokes pinkie—and that girl told Mr. and Mrs. John Stokes Jr. to bug off. I like that. I like that very much. I'm going after her."

Johnny moved to block the door. "Stop while you're ahead, Son. You're drunk and you don't know what you're doing. You've had a close scrape, but if we can believe that girl— and I tend to think we can—she's willing to let you go."

"Don't any of you realize a miracle just happened?" Bart said. But he saw they realized nothing. "I've been waiting for that miracle my whole life." He pushed his father aside.

"If you go after her," Johnny said in an absolutely even voice, "you'll never have one cent from this family again."

Bart met Johnny's eyes. He saw something weaken and shrink in his father. The tails and starched shirt suddenly had nothing to cling to. "That would be the most loving kindness any of you has ever done me."

"Bart!" Kitty screamed. "You're in no condition to leave this house! I forbid it!"

Bart turned from his parents' twisted faces. It was as though the walls with their clutter of antiques and paintings and Chinese porcelain had fallen away like the painted flats of a stage set.

A door slammed behind him and his parents' house was gone. There was only the boundlessness of the unwalled, unseen horizon and the easy whisper of traffic.

Bart Stokes was free. He broke into a run.

* * *

Kitty put a hand on Johnny's shoulder, holding him back. "No, Johnny. You'll only argue. Tomorrow he won't even remember. The lawyers can handle it. We'd better get back to our guests."

In the corner of the room, a sound was coming out of John Stokes Sr. like air from a busted, flapping balloon. He lifted a water glass from the table and tried to bring it to his lips. His hands seemed to fight one another and water spilled down his chin.

"Father!" Kitty cried.

Before Kitty or Johnny could reach him the old man jerked forward. His face came slapping down sideways onto the arm of the chair.

Kitty rushed to him and felt along the almost fleshless wrist. She could not tell if there was a faint beating in it, or if the beating was her own blood. After a moment of searching she began to sense that John Stokes Sr. was no longer in the room with them.

Gently, she shook the old man. His eyes did not open and his head seemed to be held to his shoulders by strands of rag.

"Johnny," she said.

Johnny's face was white and stricken.

"Call Dr. Bergman."

Bart looked west and east. The rain had stopped. The stunted city trees shook off their last drops of water. His eyes plucked Beth from the dark, a gliding shadow against the gates that guarded his mother's new foundation.

He called and moved quickly in her direction. She did not seem to have heard. Her head was half bent and her feet were soundless and they did not hesitate till the corner of Fifth Avenue.

A double-decker bus came to a stop. She looked around. He waved and shouted but he could not tell if she saw him. She stood back to let people off the bus and then the doors swallowed her.

Bart felt a violent surge of power in his lungs and legs. He raced now, sprinting the last distance. He reached the bus just as it began to move. He grabbed at the door's rubber lips and they clamped down on his hands.

At first he was running and then he was being dragged, and then the gaping mouth of a truck came screaming down on him.

Dr. Bergman apologized for being delayed. "There was some kind of traffic accident just down the block."

"Thank God you're here," Kitty said, closing the study door. She and Johnny had laid John Stokes Sr. on the couch, a pillow beneath his head and another beneath his feet. Johnny had managed to get the jacket off him and had loosened the white tie and boiled shirt.

Quietly, quickly, Dr. Bergman examined the old man. Instruments flashed out of his monogrammed leather bag and vanished back into it. The doctor's mouth became a taut, lipless line.

Kitty hovered over him, not so close as to get in his way. She could see the old man's pupils were totally different sizes, one a pinprick and the other so huge it blacked out the iris.

"He's had a stroke," the doctor said.

Kitty stepped back.

Dr. Bergman got to his feet. "May I use this phone?"

"Of course," Kitty said. "How severe?"

"We'll just have to see." Grimly, the doctor called for an ambulance, and Kitty could tell from his voice that the stroke was far worse than severe.

"Bart did this!" Johnny cried. "Bart and his goddamned whore!"

"Now, Johnny," Kitty said sharply. "Have yourself some brandy and just try to keep calm."

She went to the dining room. She explained that all the excitement had tired the guest of honor. Ten minutes later the ambulance arrived, without siren, and quietly took John Stokes Sr. away.

On the second day the wound stopped draining and on the third the sweats vanished. On the fourth day, just after midnight, Bart's temperature fell below 100. By sunrise it had fallen to normal, and Beth opened the window just a crack.

A sour breeze herded sounds of the city down the alley. She could hear Bart breathing gently and easily and she knew he would be well. She went about the bare little room tidying. She neatened the sofa she had slept on. From a florist on the corner she bought twelve cents' worth of daffodils. She put them in a milk bottle and placed them by the bed so they would be the first things he saw when he opened his eyes.

She pulled a chair to the bedside. From time to time she placed her book face down on her lap and just stared at his face, beginning to burn again with the warm sun of health. A little after ten o'clock his eyes flickered open.

"You almost killed yourself," she said.

His gaze moved slowly toward her. He did not know where he was, but he had the impression that it was late and everyone had gone except the one girl who sat in shadow just beyond the pale light that sieved through the window. "Is this a hospital?" he asked.

"Rooming house."

His eyes remained on hers. He stared as though she were not quite real. "How did I get here?"

"I brought you in a taxi. The landlady thought you were drunk. You were talking to yourself."

"What was I saying?"

"Things . . ." Beth turned a page of her book. "She didn't want to take us. But I paid in advance."

Bart inched his hand toward his head. It did not seem to remember the way. His fingers felt a mass of gauze. "What's the bandage for?"

"You split your scalp. Thirteen stitches. There was so much bleeding they couldn't use anesthetic." Her eyes winced with remembered pain and then she was up and bustling, lifting his head and fluffing his pillow. "Do you have a headache?"

"I don't think so."

Her hand lay a moment on his forehead.

"I feel kind of light," he said.

"You haven't eaten anything but broth. That's why you're light-headed. If you get double vision or your mouth drops you're supposed to go back to the hospital."

Bart's eyes took in her hair and eyes and lips, the white throat curving down from the little chin, the thin shoulders and small, resolute breasts. He sighed deeply and then he smiled. "No, I don't have double vision. There's only one of you. What are you reading?"

"The Bible."

"Why?"

"I like some of the stories." She laid her book down. "Do you suppose you can eat something solid?"

"Anything. I'm starved."

"I'm not supposed to bring food in, but there's a delicatessen on the corner. I could sneak up some spaghetti and meatballs."

"Beth," he said. "Thank you."

All that day and night, whenever he opened his eyes, she was sitting in the chair with her book. In the morning she brought him a newspaper and more spaghetti. "I'll phone your family," she said. "You'll be more comfortable there till you recover."

"I'm recovering just fine."

"You'll have clean sheets and real meals. You won't have to eat spaghetti and meatballs twice a day."

"I never want to see those people again in my life."

She watched him a moment. "Your color's better. You won't be needing me around much longer."

"Don't go." He reached a hand for her.

"Come on now. You've had me four days more than you paid for. If I phone Mrs. Freemont with another excuse she'll sack me for sure, and then where will I be?"

"You don't have to work for that woman. You're married now."

Beth's hand wrenched free from his. "We made a deal. I kept my end and then some. You just make sure you keep yours."

"I want you, Beth. With you I'm strong."

"You don't want me." Her voice hardened. "All you want's a red flag to wave in your family's face. Well, I don't want to live off you, and I sure don't want to live off them."

"We can get jobs. No one has to live off anyone."

"I already have a job."

"That kind of work isn't any good."

"It pays okay." A flush of anger showed through in her face. "I'm doing all right. Putting aside a little. One day I can be my own boss."

"You're your own boss now."

"Not married I'm not. Having a husband's like—it's being a child." Her voice shook, like a fist remembering hate. "Belonging to someone else. Having to obey. I don't ever want that to happen again in my life."

"You have to obey Mrs. Freemont, don't you?"

"I can quit anytime I want."

"And can't you quit marriage anytime you want?"

"No. You can't." She shook her head and her voice crawled back into itself. "I wish I'd never gotten into this. It's not worth two hundred."

Bart slid one leg out of bed and then the other. He got up too quickly and had to hold on to the chair to fend off dizziness. "Try it one week more. What's the harm?" He laid a hand on her shoulder and kneaded the tensed flesh till it began to yield. "One week more. If it doesn't work, go back to Mrs. Freemont."

Beth stared at him. His eyes were soft and they sent uneasiness sweeping through her. She pushed him away and went to the window. Her fingers picked at the curtain hem. Little boys were playing stickball down in the alley.

"Why do you want *me?*" she pleaded. "Why don't you get yourself a rich, beautiful girl? Someone that can stand up to those folks of yours?"

*"You* stood up to them."

"I couldn't do it for long."

"Maybe you don't know yourself. Maybe I see something in you that you don't. And maybe someday you'll find something in me that I don't even know is there."

His words stroked something in her. It stirred and sent out tiny warning signals. "What the hell do you see in me?" she cried. "What do you *want* from me?"

"An ally."

"Ally—you make it sound like World War Two."

"Isn't it?"

She turned. His watching face seemed fresh-scrubbed and child-like and frighteningly innocent. There was a private place in Beth where she hid all her hurt. When anyone came near the place she concealed it with silence or a soft laugh or a smile. They usually passed by, never suspecting the secret door in her. But now this stranger stood before her, seeing the layers of her. She felt he knew her as he knew his own reflection.

"Don't you need someone on your side?" he said.

"Maybe." She had not realized until that moment how very tired she was, how much she needed someone on her side. "Maybe I do, just in case."

* * *

John Stokes Sr. did not regain consciousness. Doctors managed to keep him going on catheters and IVs. Kitty and Johnny went to the clinic daily to visit him. He looked like a breathing corpse. The doctors said he was gaining strength, but Kitty never saw any change in his condition.

"It's Bart's fault," Johnny kept saying. "Bart's and that woman's."

It seemed to Kitty that a man of John Stokes, Senior's age would have had his stroke sooner or later, with or without Bart's incomprehensible conduct. But when she tried gently to disagree with Johnny, he became almost violent. She accepted that Bart was not a subject for discussion; and when she hired a private detective to locate their son, she did not tell Johnny.

The detective's few leads led nowhere. The fact was that Bart and Beth had broken completely with the Stokes world. They no longer used the family name. With part of the money left in Bart's checking account they paid the deposit on a walk-up in a Lower East Side tenement. Bart was good with figures: he found a job in a bank. Beth was fast with her fingers and she found a job in a loft-factory stitching silk flowers to hats.

Between them, they had enough.

Bart did not have to learn happiness. Given the chance, he moved toward it instinctively, like a plant reaching for the sun. He was overeducated for the job of teller; the work demanded minute attention and it was dull; but for the first time in his life he had to earn his own living and was loved. He developed a sense of accomplishment out of all proportion to the amount he earned or was loved.

Beth had to learn happiness. She had built a wall around herself thick enough and high enough to fend off the world. She knew the world's dreams and despairs and she had survived them. She had become comfortable behind her wall, like a plant that had learned to grow in the dark.

For a time she was frightened of Bart. She tried to keep a distance between them. But he did not beat her or desert her or do any of the things she had come to expect of men. He was there for meals. He was there when she awoke at night. He was there.

Gradually her wall came down. A warm wind swept over her and the sunlight bewildered her. She tried not to trust the warmth or the sunlight but bit by bit she failed, till one day she could not quite remember what it had been like behind the wall or why she had ever lived there at all.

In the third month of her pregnancy Beth finally went to the public health clinic in her neighborhood. It made her uneasy that the hospital had a saint's name and the nurse who took down her information wore a nun's wimple. At first, as though holding an animal tight on a leash, she was able to control the uneasiness.

She waited almost two hours in a room full of pregnant women till finally a doctor called her into his office. A young nun helped her undress and the doctor poked and prodded and tapped her. By then the fright was tugging and gnawing at her and she wasn't sure she could keep her grip on it.

The doctor put a stethoscope, cold as a cube of ice, to her skin. "Sit still. Don't jerk. Breathe in. Breathe out. Hold your breath."

He told her to lie down on the examining table and to place her feet in the stirrups. She obeyed. Rubber-gloved fingers probed and jabbed at her.

The doctor's thin face twisted with righteousness. "When did you have the abortion?"

The fright within Beth tore loose and swept over her like a black tide. She screamed. The doctor struck her across the face.

"Eleven months ago," she whispered.

"Then it's a piss-poor job. Did you do it yourself?"

She felt tiny and helpless and she knew the doctor wanted her to feel despicable too. "A doctor did it."

"What's his name?"

"I can't tell you that."

"In your position, young woman, I'd be a little more co-operative. The fetus may be infected. Assuming you don't miscarry, the delivery will rip you open like a side of beef. You run a damned good chance of killing yourself if you don't get competent attention. So tell me the man's name."

"Are you saying you won't care for me if I don't?"

"If you expect care from me, you can start by showing a little concern for the unborn."

Anger gave her momentary courage. "My past is none of your business."

"You can't take that tone with me. You're a criminal and a charity case."

She disentangled her feet from the stirrups and sat up. "Then at least I won't be *your* charity case."

"What do you think you're doing?"

"Dressing. I'm going to find a doctor, not a prosecutor."

She dressed. No one helped her. She left the hospital. No one stopped her. She went to Washington Square and sat on a bench. Slowly the fear receded far enough to allow her to think.

She saw that if she wanted the baby she would have to pay a private doctor, one who didn't bully his patients or make deals with the police.

She went home and put on a clean dress and a hat and white gloves. She found a doctor that afternoon. His office was in a brownstone on Ninth Street, just off Fifth Avenue. She paid ten dollars cash just for an examination.

"There are complicating factors." The doctor's voice was gentle and reassuring. "Nothing to worry about. We'll get you through."

"How much?" she asked.


"Four hundred dollars," Beth said.

Bart's eyes flinched. Four hundred was practically two months of his salary, three of hers. It was eight months' rent on their one-room walk-up. "Maybe we should look for another clinic," he said.

"I can't go to a public clinic."

They were sitting at the little secondhand table with its checkered oilcloth. It was Wednesday, meat night. She had put daffodils on the table. She had spent a little extra to get lean corned beef, and she'd tried to make it delicious with potato and cabbage and horseradish.

"I wish I didn't have to tell you this," she said. But she saw it was no good burying the truth. "A year ago I was in trouble. A man helped me. A good man."

She could not bear to watch the understanding dawn in Bart's face. Her eyes fled from his, circling the apartment with its patchy plaster and cracked linoleum and five-and-dime curtains they'd bought to make it homey. It seemed insubstantial, a magic-lantern slide lit by one frail candle. A single word could blow it all out.

"The public doctors will want his name and they'll give it to the police. I can't do that, Bart. I couldn't live with it." She raised her eyes to his. He was silent and she could not read him and the old wind of fear swept through her. "Is there anything you want to know? Anything you want to . . . change?"

Bart's jaw and throat worked as though choking back a cry. He got up and paced and the color washed out of his face.

Beth cleared the table and stacked the crockery in the sink. She ran the water and fussed with the dishcloth. After a moment that had been an eternity she felt his hand on her cheek.

"I'll get the money." His face was his own again and she knew she was safe. "Don't you worry about anything."

Thursday afternoon, just before the shade was pulled down over the bank's front window, Bart dusted his jacket and straightened his tie and knocked on his boss's door. "Mr. Downey, could I have a word?"

"What is it?"

The voice did not smile or invite, but Bart stepped into the office anyway. Mr. Downey's plump fingers prowled the pages of an open ledger and Bart shortened the speech he'd rehearsed.

"Mr. Downey sir, I've worked for you almost eleven months now."

Floyd James Downey Jr., director of the Eighth Street branch of First Manhattan National Bank, sighed. He swung back in his swivel chair.

"In all that time, sir, I haven't had a single complaint about my work."

"I've got a complaint." Mr. Downey drew a gold watch he'd inherited from his grandfather out of his vest pocket. There was engraving inside the lid. "It's five twenty-five and you're not in your cage."

"Thursday is slow, sir. The other teller said he could take over for a minute."

"If it's a raise you've come about, you can discuss that with me during your lunch hour." Mr. Downey bent back to his ledger. "After you've been with us two years."

"I'm not asking for a raise, sir. I need a loan."

Mr. Downey looked up. "What for?"

"A personal matter, sir."

A barrier went up in Mr. Downey's eyes and Bart saw he had made a mistake.

"Medical, sir."

Mr. Downey's lips pressed together, grim and narrow as the slash mark of a razor, and Bart saw he had made the mistake bigger. "How much?"

"Four hundred dollars, sir."

"What kind of collateral are you offering?"

"The best, sir. Myself. I figure if you take eight dollars a week off my salary I can pay it back with interest in a year and six weeks."

"You're asking me to secure a loan on the probability of your continued employment here?"

A flush crawled up Bart's collar. He wondered if it was this way for stockbrokers laying their schemes before the banks where his father was major depositor. He wondered if it had been this way for workers begging credit from his grandfather's stores. "I'm a good risk, sir. I know my work. My accounts are always wrapped up first and I've never been more than twelve cents off at the end of a day. And, naturally, I'd expect to pay higher interest."

"Any banker who agreed to such an arrangement would be undeserving of his depositors' trust. A loan has to be secured by something tangible. Stocks. Bonds. Jewelry. Real estate. An automobile."

It had never occurred to Bart that an honest man's word was not his collateral. Till that moment he had believed the things he'd been taught. Now he grew up. "If I had stocks or bonds or an automobile I wouldn't need four hundred dollars."

"Banking is banking, young man. Not charity. Now get back to your cage."

# Chapter 18

KITTY'S DETECTIVE TURNED up a marked dollar bill that Bart's savings bank had mistakenly given him when he closed his account. He—or someone—had spent it at S. Klein's department store on Union Square, seven weeks later. Tracking down that one dollar had cost Kitty over five thousand and the better part of a year. She still did not know if Bart was healthy or sick, divorced or still married to his prostitute, when he would break again like a storm into her family's life. The uncertainty clouded her waking days like an unresolved note in a musical composition.

In the meantime, she had to do the necessary for Jay. She set up a trust so that Harvard Law students could spend summers clerking for Supreme Court justices. Harvard Law took Jay back and graduated him eighth from the bottom of his class. Kitty fought for that eighth, because Harvard Law had wanted to put Jay at the rock bottom, and she couldn't very well ask Gilbert and Comstock to take on rock-bottom anything, not even a Stokes.

The firm of Gilbert and Comstock handled wills, trusts, shelters, and two New York State charitable foundations for the family. If any of the Stokeses had had to pay a penny in personal income tax, Gilbert and Comstock would have handled that penny as well and charged $375 an hour to do it.

The firm occupied floors 18 through 23 of a building with Art Deco friezes two doors down from Trinity Church, not far from the summit of that gentle incline called Wall Street. There were twenty-nine full partners and fifty-two associates, and after Kitty summoned Mr. Comstock to lunch at the Colony Club, there was Jay too.

Mr. Comstock felt that wills might agree with a young man of Jay's abilities. Jay was put in charge of Park Avenue widows who had nothing better to do with their old age than Philharmonic fund-raising and codicils. That sort of thing was the make-work of the legal profession, and Kitty sensed a grave restlessness in her son.

At dinners and Sunday lunches, when she made the unavoidable gesture of including Antonia, Jay had a tendency to drop out of conversation and stare at the crystal. Kitty wondered about him that spring and summer. She wondered about his well-being and about the bear-trap of a marriage he had caught himself in.

It was just after 6 P.M. and the month was September, and Kitty was still wondering about her son when Mr. Gilbert phoned. He said one of Jay's clients had died. Kitty was sorry to hear it. Mr. Gilbert sounded sorry too.

It seemed that Jay had drawn the will so that the estate descended *per sterpes*. Mr. Gilbert explained that the little Latin phrase reinherited a grandson whom the lady had detested and previously disinherited. The heirs were suing. The question was not so much Jay's law or even his Latin as it was twelve million dollars, a great deal of money to that sort of people. Mr. Gilbert honestly wondered if there was not some arena other than Gilbert and Comstock where Jay might better realize his far-ranging potential.

At five after six, in the gathering September dusk, Kitty admitted to herself that law was all wrong for Jay, had been all wrong all along. It was a coffin walling in his spirit.

On the other hand, she hadn't the faintest idea what he should do instead.

"Jay, darling, may I ask you a terribly personal question?"
"J. W. Harper."
They were sitting at a sunny corner table in the Cafe Cham-

bord, and Kitty could see the sun was going to do very little good. "What did you say?"

"J. W. Harper That's a terribly personal answer." Jay's tongue seemed to dig in the floor of his mouth for words. "I've been drinking J. W. Harper on the rocks. Four of them. Boom-boom-boom-boom. Next question."

"This is not a cross-examination," Kitty said, "and we didn't ask Justin here to discuss boom-boom."

Justin Lasting acknowledged mention of his name with the most serene of nods. Since he had been spoken of and not to, he did not seem to feel the need to reply or help Kitty out in any way. He had consumed a *tranche de terrine de canard à l'orange* and half a Pouilly Fumard Montrachet, and Kitty hoped it would not prove a waste of forty-three dollars to have invited him.

The Cafe Chambord was at that time the most expensive restaurant in New York. A three-egg omelette cost nine dollars, and an omelette with Beluga caviar cost twenty-nine. Kitty had selected the restaurant not for its preposterous cuisine or its diamond-clawed habitués, but out of a dim hope that its prices would solemnize the occasion. It was rather like dropping a hundred-dollar bill into the collection plate: for ten minutes she needed God on her side.

"I'd like to know if you've had any thoughts about your life," she said

"My *life?*" Jay looked astonished. "No, no thoughts in particular. What did you have in mind?"

"Are you satisfied with the way it's going? Not just the Gilbert and Comstock business, but your whole life. Are you pleased?"

"I don't think much about that. Should I?"

It was a tragedy, Kitty thought: dissipation gave Jay the complexion of a suntanned poet. If only his face would blotch or sag, maybe women would stop looking at him and he'd slow down. Kitty sighed. He was too damned handsome and that dimple was murder.

"Isn't there something you'd like to do," she said, "I mean really *do?*"

"I'd like to see the Himalayas."

"You can do that anytime. Isn't there something you'd like to achieve?"

"If you mean would I like to make the Olympic ski team,

yes I'd love to—but I'm a little old to start training."

Kitty smothered an impulse to yank his sarcasm from him like a bandage from a wound. He was hurt, dangerously hurt, his bravado said as much, and she knew she must probe cautiously. "I mean seriously, Jay. Is law enough for you? Is New York enough? Is marriage enough? Don't you ever dream of something more?"

"Everybody dreams."

"All right—what do you dream of?"

For a moment Jay did not speak, and when he did his voice had changed. "Being good at something. Being the best at one thing in this world."

Hope sprang up in Kitty. "What thing?"

"If I knew that, you wouldn't be criticizing me, would you?"

"Darling, I'm not criticizing. I'm asking."

Jay laid two hands firmly on the table. "Mom, your face is a dead giveaway. You may think you're asking, but you're telling me my life is no damned good. You're criticizing my job, you're criticizing my wife; for all I know, you're criticizing the way my tie is knotted."

"Your tie's beautifully knotted. I'm just trying to think who could have picked it out. Did Toni?"

*"And* you're criticizing my drinking."

"I haven't mentioned your drinking."

Jay smiled the most sorrowful smile Kitty had ever seen. "That's your way of criticizing, Mom. Silence. Eyes averted. Tolerance. Oh, the blast furnace of your tolerance. You've put us all through it."

She supposed in his position she would have felt a little defensive too. "I'm sorry, Jay. Do you feel I'm prying? Are you angry with me?"

"Of course you're prying and of course I'm angry. I love you, Mom, and I wouldn't want you any different, so pry away. I'm an open clam. And I'd like some J. W. Harper on the rocks if that waiter ever condescends to ask."

Kitty's mind hesitated between two trapezes. She could not decide whether Jay needed job counseling—she'd heard of institutes that ran five-hundred-dollar aptitude tests; or whether he needed psychotherapy—maybe it was all in his head, or in his childhood. She opted for Jay's way: booze. *In vino veritas*, and what she was stalking that afternoon was some fast, solid *veritas*.

She raised a hand and snapped two fingers and Jay got his J. W. Harper on the rocks. She let him have three swallows before plunging onward. "Darling—in all your life—has there ever been one special thing you've really and truly loved doing? Something you might make a career of? You see, I have a terrible feeling you don't truly love the law, and it seems such a waste to devote yourself to something you don't love."

"You mean the law doesn't love me."

"I mean you could easily free yourself. You're not married to it."

"There you go on Toni again."

"I'm talking about you and you only, and I'm asking what you intend to make of yourself while you still have youth and options."

There was a tiny chanticleer on the tip of Jay's red plastic swizzle stick and he was absently crushing its miniature head between his fingers. "Well, I've always enjoyed playing the piano."

"You hated playing the piano. Be serious, please, Jay. My head's splitting."

"We've ruled out sports and mountain climbing, and I suppose a safari's out of the question."

"Darling, I've brought Justin along to give us his very valuable advice, and you're making a joke out of this."

"But, Mom, the awful truth is I'm telling the truth. The things I'd love to do are cotton-picking dumb. If I weren't a Stokes and if you didn't have this notion that Stokeses have to amount to God, I'd be a beach bum having the time of my life."

"Do you have any idea how deeply that hurts me?"

"Yes, Mom, I do, and do you think it doesn't hurt me?" Veins made a pulsing road map of Jay's forehead. "How the hell can I give you an answer in five seconds when I haven't been able to come up with one in twenty-six years? Do you think I don't know I'm going nowhere? Do you think I like it? I don't need you and Justin putting on your Greek tragic masks to know I'm a washout."

"Oh, Jay. Oh, Jay." Kitty's hand made a mitten around Jay's. "That isn't so and it isn't at all what I meant."

"Your mother raised an interesting point a moment ago." Justin Lasting's smile managed a sort of unfaltering benevolence. "Has there ever been one thing in your life, one moment that—shines?"

Jay tipped his chair back on its hind legs. "That takes some thinking." He stared at the ceiling. He stared at his shrimp fork. His eyes were sad. They seemed to trace a horizon beyond the restaurant walls. "Well, aside from the obvious excesses and indecencies, I suppose the happiest event in my life was the club election."

"Why?" Justin Lasting asked.

"Because I won. Because for one instant it was as though I'd done something terrific that no one else on earth could do, and the whole world loved me for it."

For a long moment neither Kitty nor Justin Lasting spoke. It was as though a deep gong had been struck and they were each waiting for its last reverberation to die away.

"The word you're looking for," Justin said, "is *politics.*"

Half of Jay's mouth smiled and the other half didn't seem to find it worth bothering. "Thanks, but I'll leave the politics to Harry S Truman."

"No, Jay," Kitty said urgently, realizing this was a possible opening to the future. "Think about it. Justin has a point. You won that election and you loved winning it."

Justin Lasting placed both elbows on the table. He stared into Jay's eyes. "Politics *is* winning," he said.

Jay jabbed his roosterless swizzle stick at an ice cube. "I couldn't win dogcatcher in Peoria."

"Why must you disparage yourself?" Kitty said. "You're your own worst enemy. You could easily win election to—" She thought an instant. "Well, Abraham Lincoln didn't start at the top, did he?"

"I'm not Abraham Lincoln."

"But *you* can start at the top," Justin Lasting said. "Or damned near it."

"This is crazy," Jay said.

"See, you're doing it again," Kitty said. "It isn't crazy at all. Do you think you have to be superhuman to go into politics?" When she reflected, it made hereditary sense: he'd inherited political drive from his father, from Tyrone Duncannon. All he needed was encouragement. "Justin, tell Jay what it takes to go into politics."

"Good hard work, good hard management, good hard cash."

"You could work hard, Jay," Kitty said. "If it were something you really loved."

"Dogcatcher."

"Stop using that word. Justin Lasting would not waste our time or his own proposing that you run for anything less than—" Kitty directed her glance at Justin Lasting, who was brushing the shrapnel of a hard roll from the tablecloth. "What did you have in mind, Justin?"

"There's a state senate slot coming up in Massachusetts. Saltonstall's retiring. They're looking for someone young—unknown—able."

"Who would Jay be running against?"

Justin Lasting described the man: he had the machine behind him but he was sixty-nine, had a bad voting record, and was under suspicion for hanky-panky with state highway funds. "You could blow him down with half a million dollars."

"The problem is," Jay said, "I've got a wife and she hates Boston and she'll never agree to go back there—so why don't we talk about badminton?"

"Antonia will go along with whatever you decide," Kitty said.


"I hate Boston."

"Now, Toni," Kitty said, "Boston has a wonderful symphony and splendid universities. And after all, you *are* society there."

"I'm society *here*. Anyway, I hate the symphony and I hate Harvard."

"But don't you see, if you helped Jay as state senator, in a term or two he could run for governor. You'd be the governor's wife—the very young wife of a very important governor."

Toni tugged at the sleeve of her blue Schiaparelli dress. She lifted the lid of a Steuben glass box and lit a cigarette.

"And it wouldn't have to stop there," Kitty said. "It could go higher—much, much higher. Do consider it, darling. It would give your lives direction."

Toni uncoiled herself from her deep square chair. She paced to the window and she paced to the Steinway and her silk dress made a swishing sound, like a racehorse flicking its tail. She had done the Sutton Place living room in glass and chrome and deep cream shag. Kitty couldn't help thinking she'd done it that way because it showed off her dark hair and olive skin and the color of any dress she happened to wear. The room was a canvas and Toni was a splotch of vividness splashed across it, like one of those modern paintings that people always said grew on you.

"You mean it would be good for Jay," Toni said. "You're not thinking of me. You never think of me at all. It's always, 'This will be good for Jay' and 'Wouldn't that help Jay's career?' Jay doesn't have a career. He doesn't do anything in that office but talk to you on the phone two hours a day. All the partners are laughing at it."

"What I'm trying to tell you is you could help Jay start a real career and it could go very, very far for you both."

"All my friends are here in New York. It's taken me eight months to decorate this apartment. And now you want me to throw everything away so that your little boy can play politics. Jay doesn't even *like* politics."

"You're quite mistaken, Toni. Jay has a deep interest in his country and he wants to make something of himself. I should think you'd want to back him up."

"Massachusetts is not Jay's country. It's a backwater and I don't want to live there."

Kitty saw that she was arguing with a child—a child with lacquered hair and glossy nails and diamond starburst brooches from Cartier's, but a very stubborn child nonetheless. "You drink too much," Kitty said.

Toni's head came around slowly.

"You both drink too much," Kitty said. "I want you to stop drinking and I want you to have a baby. A baby will give you something to do besides getting drunk in the Polo Room and the Stork Club."

Toni seemed to consider a great many replies, few of them pleasant, and finally she said, "I don't know how I feel about a baby. It's too soon for all that."

"And eventually it will be too late."

A genuine red seemed to flare beneath Toni's lightly applied rouge. "I'm twenty years old and I'm not about to sell my apartment and give up my friends and go raise babies in Boston. You're not going to turn me into a Back Bay squaw."

"If you have a son, Toni, I'll give you one million dollars."

Toni raised her chin to blow a ripple of smoke into the air. "A trust, I suppose? Interest for me and principal for the child?"

"A million dollars free and clear."

Toni's forefinger stroked the arched white line of her throat. "Well, I might do some thinking about that."

"In addition . ." Kitty paused to stub out her Camel. She was trying to cut down: her lung man had said no more than a pack a day. She couldn't believe that her daughter-in-law didn't know the difference between a cloisonné fruit bowl and an ashtray, but there was only the bowl on the coffee table, with a thin film of gray powder in the hollow, like the ashes of a very small dead person. "In addition, I can put you in touch with an excellent hip man."

"My hip is my business." Toni's voice was suddenly not childish or whining at all. It was cold and definite as a nutcracker coming down on a macadamia.

"You know, darling," Kitty said pleasantly, "Jay's grandmother was an invalid. It's not very nice to have to spend your life in a wheel chair, and I gather you're going to have to do just that in five years or so if you don't see a very good specialist. It's the hip joint, isn't it? You're wearing it down by not using a brace?"

"It's my hip," Toni said, "and my life."

"But Dr. Hugh Philby is the very best hip man in the country—some say in the world."

Toni smiled. She was staring at one of her oils, a square within a square, the difference between the colors of the two squares so faint you had to squint to see it at all. There was a man in Greenwich Village doing a lot of the squares within squares these days, and Kitty had gathered they were going for several thousand dollars apiece and climbing. It wasn't that she begrudged Toni the money; it wasn't that at all.

It was just that there were certain of Toni's smiles that she detested.

"Dr. Hugh Philby is already caring for me," Toni said. She turned to see Kitty's reaction.

"I know, darling. But if you do as I say, he'll keep on caring for you."

That spring, as Jay was planning his campaign, the North Koreans invaded the Republic of South Korea. Since Jay was entering the race late and battling for every headline he could get, Justin Lasting mapped out a back-breaking six-week blitzkrieg of a campaign. Close to thirty researchers, accountants and detectives mined every available ounce of innuendo and bona fide dirt on Jay's opponent. A Pulitzer-Prize-winning Broadway playwright refined the material, larded it with promises that would have made FDR blush, and shaped it into speeches that not only packed in the voters but brought them screaming to their feet with applause.

Although Kitty had reservations about the strategy, she could not deny its effectiveness. By mid-August, Jay was not only the most recognizable candidate within his district, he was getting favorable mentions in the Boston papers—and not all of them were paid for. He spent fourteen hours and more a day, speaking in every town, hamlet, train station and bus depot in the East Berkshires. He shook hands, kissed babies, flattered housewives by eating their pies. Justin Lasting dressed him in workshirts and neatly pressed dungarees. He absolutely forbade suits, vests, and neckties, just as he absolutely banned Kitty and Johnny from the campaign.

"Jay's not running as a Stokes," Justin Lasting said. "He's a man of the people who just happens to be a millionaire."

Toni was reshaped into a woman of the people who just happened to be a millionaire's wife. Justin Lasting chose her dresses, her hairstyle, her few pieces of jewelry. She hated them all, and she hated the things he made her say to interviewers—but most of all she hated the car: he insisted not only that she and Jay ride in a beat-up Mercury, but that Jay drive it himself—showing the voters that even if he were not exactly a self-made man, he was a self-reliant one.

Toni and Jay had a great many arguments in that Mercury. In the final week of the campaign, as they passed a chipped signpost that said EAST OTIS, POP. 620, she felt her life go pitch-black, as though someone had switched off the light at the end of a corridor.

"Jay," she said, "I can't take it."

He looked at her. "What can't you take?"

On either side of the road hayfields stretched away like tattered straw rugs thrown over dirt floors. "This place," she said. "This campaign."

"Is it just coincidence, Toni? I finally find something in life that interests me, and suddenly you can't take it."

"I'm glad for you, Jay, and I don't mind helping. But please—just for tonight—can't we stay in a decent hotel with decent plumbing? I'm sick of canned orange juice and weak coffee and water pipes that fart rust."

"If they had a Ritz in Berkshire County," he said impatiently, "we'd be staying there. But this happens not to be Ritz country."

"They have a Ritz in Boston."

"That's a four-hour drive."

"It's twenty minutes by plane."

"We don't have a plane."

"It's not as though we were poor, Jay!"

"Toni—the people in this county don't drink espresso with milk for breakfast. They don't drive their Mercedes to the music shed at Tanglewood. They drink canned orange juice and their plumbing shits and for the time being we're one of them—*got it?*"

She saw that he didn't understand, that he didn't even want to understand. At eight o'clock that evening, when they were the last people in the dining room in the run-down country inn where Justin Lasting had booked them for the night, Toni threw her napkin into her dinner plate.

"I'm sick of hotel restaurants where they fry your broiled filet of sole!"

Jay sighed. "I'm sorry if life isn't easy enough for you, Toni, but you're just going to have to learn to cope."

"Don't you dare condescend!"

"Then don't make me."

He was being a selfish pig, refusing to listen to anyone else's side of things, and she told him so and then, without waiting for coffee, stormed from the table. As she passed the front desk the clerk called to her. "Letter for you, Mrs. Stokes."

She glanced at it in the elevator. It had been mailed to her and Jay at the Sutton Place apartment in New York. There was no return address and the handwriting was far too beautiful to be that of anyone she knew personally. Someone had scrawled at the bottom *forward to HQ*. The paper was heavy ecru, and the name *Tiffany* embossed under the flap drew her attention momentarily from her anger.

There was a second, ungummed envelope within the first. A half tissue fluttered to the elevator floor as she drew out the engraved invitation.

*Mr. and Mrs. Amory Fenimore Pierpont III / request the honour of your presence / at the marriage of their daughter / Lavinia / to / Doctor Karl Joris Engulesco / on Friday the*

*eleventh of June / one thousand nine hundred and fifty / at*
*twelve o'clock / Saint Joseph's Church / Boston / and afterward*
*at / the Atheneum*

The invitation hit Toni like a totally unexpected slap. Her
first reaction was surprise, but once she was back in the hotel
room a series of little stings began to sink in.

The wedding and the reception were by now six weeks past.
Not a single member of her family had thought to tell her that
her sister was to be married. She had no idea who Dr. Karl
Joris Engulesco was or what he was a doctor of. She'd had no
idea that her father had scraped together the money or the votes
to join the Boston Atheneum. Finally, peering closely at the
postmark, she saw that the invitation had been mailed three
days after the event.

The slight, she was convinced, was intentional. She was
mentally adding up the cost of Tiffany invitations and Saint
Joseph's Church and the Boston Atheneum when Jay burst into
the hotel room.

"Do you realize what you just did in front of those waiters?"
he shouted.

She sat up on the bed. "Vinnie got married," she said. "He
sounds Rumanian. Father joined the Atheneum just to give her
a reception."

"I'm talking about those waiters, and don't try to change
the subject."

She couldn't remember exactly why she and Jay had argued.
The details were jumbled with images of Vinnie's reception:
an eight-foot smoked Scottish salmon, and a three-tier cake,
and Mother and Father greeting guests at the top of the marble
staircase. The images came at her sharp and cutting as razor
strokes, and when they faded Jay was still shouting about the
waiters.

"You seem to care more about waiters' feelings than your
wife's," she said. "Or is it just that they vote in this state and
I don't?"

"Yes they *do* vote and I *am* courting votes and it's about
time you grasped that fact and watched your drinking!"

"What's wrong with my drinking?"

"Two highballs and five glasses of wine."

"*I wasn't drunk!*"

"You sure did a good job of fooling that dining room!"

"Who saw? You, me, two stupid Portuguese waiters who you said yourself don't know the difference between medium-rare and charred—two fucking votes!"

"And if you ever cost me two fucking votes again—" He stared at her, veins rigid in his throat, and then he spun and slammed the door behind him.

The hotel room was suddenly as tiny and stifling as a coffin. Toni pushed to her feet and stumbled to the window. As she opened it a mosquito bit her on the arm. She slapped, and the slap hurt more than the bite. She stood trying to hug the pain out.

She gazed down at her breasts. The pressure of her arms made them look fat. *It's not fair*, she thought: *Jay drinks eight martinis with lunch and doesn't gain an ounce. If I so much as look at a glass of sherry I can't get into my bra.*

She walked to the bathroom mirror. Plumpness stared back at her: round face and jiggling boobs and too many dimples.

*This campaign is wrecking me. Another month like this and they'll have to strip the fat off me with a buzz saw. I've got to get back to the city, back to the health spa and the masseur . . .*

She wondered if she'd ever be able to get into her Chanels again. Her eye fell on Vinnie's wedding invitation, half-crumpled on the bedside table. A sudden determination seized her. She ripped the invitation into pieces small enough to flush down the toilet. She dressed quickly and went down the fire stairs and left the hotel through the back door. She hurried past a shuttered cafeteria and a dark five-and-ten and crossed the town square with its empty bandstand and came to a blinking neon sign and a door spilling light and laughter and music.

She drew a deep breath and went in.

There was a smell of beer and peanuts. There were men in undershirts and men with checkered shirts rolled up to their biceps, huddled like football teams around tables of half-empty mugs. Heads turned and eyes stared at her. Voices dipped and for a moment the loudest sound was a woman on the jukebox crooning, "See the pyramids along the Nile."

Toni knew she didn't belong there. So what.

She went to an opening at the bar and it opened a little wider for her. The bartender had cropped red hair and no sideburns. She ordered a martini. He gave her a tumbler of gin with a very large unpitted olive. She sipped around the olive and gradually a comforting numbness began seeping through her.

She didn't keep count of the martinis. She didn't keep track of the time. Several of the men began returning her smile and a few came close enough to jostle her when they reached for a refill. And then a voice very close to her ear said, "Good evening, my dear. Enjoying yourself?"

She turned. A gray-headed man, overweight and pin-striped in a suit that cloaked the slight stoop of age, came abruptly into focus. She recognized Justin Lasting.

"Do I look as though I'm enjoying myself?" she said.

"You look as though you've had a long, tiring day and ought to be in bed getting ready for another long, tiring day."

"I'm tired of long, tiring days."

"You're not helping Jay any getting drunk in public."

"I've been helping Jay twenty-four hours a day for six weeks. I've earned a night off."

"In politics, my dear, there's no such thing as a night off. In recognition of that fact I've ordered a bottle of Bombay gin and it's in a bucket of ice right by your bed. Now, wouldn't that be cozier than all these farmers and factory workers?"

"Stop treating me like some kind of two-year-old. What the hell do you people take me for?"

"I take you for an adult who happens to be Jay Stokes's wife, and it's time you started acting it." His fingers closed on her elbow, tight as a steel trap. "Do you understand the word *act*, my dear? It's what performers do to earn their pay. Now come along—that glass is empty."

Election Day morning a New York policeman came to the house and asked to speak to Kitty. He radiated menace as tangible as the holster at his hip. Kitty had known guns before, but she had never been in the same living room with one.

He handed her a wallet. "Would you have a look at this, please?"

She opened it. The leather was inexpensive, the stitching beginning to come apart. She leafed through plastic-sheathed photos of a young woman she didn't know but who was still oddly familiar, a pale thing with dark hair who wore a two-piece bathing suit in one snapshot and a frilly-collared dress in another.

And then she came to a snapshot of a woman on horseback just outside the stable at John Stokes, Senior's place in Maine. With a shock that leaped the twelve-year gap she recognized herself. For a moment she forgot the policeman waiting at her elbow. She remembered Bart and his little Kodak. She thought how quickly, how stealthily time slipped past.

"It looks like my younger son's," she said cautiously, not knowing whether to feel relieved or alarmed that some trace of him had turned up.

"We arrested a thief this morning. This wallet was in his possession."

Kitty's mind struggled to make some kind of connection. "I take it this thief must have robbed my son?"

The policeman did not seem to take it that way at all.

"Mrs. Stokes, why don't you come down to the station house? Quietly—nothing official. You'd better have a look at the suspect."

She caught a warning glint of disaster: Bart mixed up with the police on Jay's election day.

"We can go in my car," the officer said.

Kitty sat grim and tight-lipped, letting the city blur past the window of the unmarked police car. The officer held the jail-house door for her. Kitty's nostrils winced at the stench of disinfectant. The officer waved to the policeman at the front desk, then led Kitty up two flights of peeling stairs. They passed a barred cage that held three women dressed like prostitutes.

The officer led Kitty to a cramped dark room. "Do you smoke?" he asked.

"Sometimes."

"Don't. It's a one-way mirror—he'll see the match."

Kitty stared through the mirror. The man on the bench was in no condition to see a match or anything else. He was sound asleep. It was surprising how little difference the year and the beard and mustache made.

"It's my son," Kitty said, carefully mastering any emotion in her voice. "Bart Stokes."

The officer did not seem in the least surprised. "Let's go to my office, Mrs. Stokes."

He shut the door behind them and motioned her to a chair.

"You knew your son took a job at a bank under a false name?"

She saw no reason not to be, within limits, honest. "I've

known nothing at all about him for almost a year. How much
is he accused of stealing?"

"Four hundred dollars."

Anger shot through her. *He would do this,* she thought. *He
would endanger Jay's career for four hundred contemptible
dollars.* The officer handed her a sheet of slick paper smelling
faintly of duplicating fluid. It appeared to be the complaint.

Kitty saw with relief that Bart had been booked under his
false name. She also saw his address, near the Bowery, and
the name and address of the bank officer pressing charges.
"May I keep this?" she asked.

The officer nodded. "We'll hold him till you get it straightened out, Mrs. Stokes. Take your time and don't worry. He
won't be talking to anyone. And neither will I."

Kitty gazed at the officer. He did not have the face of a
Good Samaritan. He would have to be paid off—handsomely.
"I realize you've gone out of your way. I appreciate your
kindness, officer."

"Sloane," he said. "Sergeant Bill Sloane."

"I'll be in touch with you, Sergeant Sloane. Very soon."


Kitty realized that if she was to head off scandal she needed
to know why Bart had committed theft and what else he had
mixed himself up in. At the same time she could not risk
approaching him directly. Even if he was not publicly recognizable, she was. Instead she took a taxi to Broome Street, the
address on the complaint.

She climbed three tenement flights and knocked on the door
of the rear apartment. The girl who let her in did not in the
least resemble the snapshot in Bart's wallet.

"Mrs. Christiansen?" Kitty said pleasantly.

The girl shook her head. "Beth's in the hospital. I'm the
neighbor. She asked me to water the plants."

The room was dark, the one window giving onto an airshaft.
Kitty's eye took in the little scars of fresh carpentry and paint.
The immaculate housekeeping only emphasized every crack in
the linoleum, every leaking water stain in the wall. She saw
that Bart and Beth Christiansen had no money, none at all.

"Is Mrs. Christiansen sick?" Kitty asked.

"Oh no, ma'am." The girl smiled, shaking her head. "She
had a baby."

*So that's it,* Kitty thought—*a four-hundred-dollar baby.* "Could you tell me which hospital she's in?"

Kitty found the girl who called herself Beth Christiansen sitting up in a bed in the corner of the maternity ward. The girl's face was strained with the effort of hiding her surprise. "How did you trace us?" she said.

It occurred to Kitty that Beth did not know her husband was in jail. "I hired a detective," she said. It was not exactly a lie.

Instantly the girl's face was watchful. Kitty had expected that. But there was serenity in the face too, and Kitty had not expected that. She realized the girl did not know of the theft either. Something warned her to be gentle.

"Wouldn't you hire a detective if your son vanished?" she said.

"Bart hasn't vanished," Beth said.

Kitty inventoried the girl, forcing herself to be as objective as she would have been counting bonds in a safe-deposit box. There was anger and there was pain in the face, which Kitty expected in an enemy, but there was kindness too and Kitty was not certain how to cope with it. "He's left home, given up his education, changed his name, never contacted us— wouldn't you call that vanishing?"

Beth's hands fidgeted, hiding in a Kleenex. Kitty saw that one of the nails was badly chipped.

"He's afraid," Beth said.

"Afraid of what?"

"Of things starting up again."

"What things? Starting up how?"

"Will you be angry if I tell the truth?"

Kitty threw a precautionary glance behind her. The young mother in the next bed was sleeping. "I want the truth," Kitty said. "That's why I came."

"Bart wasn't happy with his family. He wasn't happy being a Stokes."

"No," Kitty admitted. "He wasn't."

"He's happy now," Beth said. "He's working like the devil and he's dead tired half the time, but he's proving himself— proving he can hold a job and pay his rent and feed himself and make it on his own. Oh, if you could see where we live I know it wouldn't seem he has anything. But he does."

Kitty had heard the clichés about innocent whores and she

had laughed at them. Yet she sensed an innocence in this girl and, more disturbingly, she sensed the power beneath that innocence. She realized she had committed a grave tactical error: she had walked into a contest with no assurance of winning it.

"He has a great deal," Kitty said. "He has you."

Beth glanced down at her torn fingernail. "And I have him. You probably think I'm getting the better end of the bargain— me being who I am and him who he is. And it's true."

The facts were plain to Kitty. Bart and his wife were starving. Starvation had turned him into a petty felon. He was a mine buried in a very important canal, and unless that mine were defused Jay might never get through to the ocean. Reconciliation was essential.

"I haven't come to judge," Kitty said. "I haven't the right. I've come to make peace."

"But no one's at war."

"Bart's at war. He's at war with his father and me and everything he thinks we represent."

"No," the girl said. "He's at peace for the first time in his life. And if you'll excuse my saying so, it would be kinder and wiser to leave him alone—for a while, at least, till he finds his way."

It had been many years since anyone had flatly contradicted Kitty. She was careful to glove her voice in kindness. "But in the meantime, isn't there some way we could help?"

"With all due respect, Mrs. Stokes, you could help by staying out of it."

Kitty bit her lip. "Bart wouldn't have to know."

"I want Bart to make up with his family," the girl said. "I want it as badly as you do. But you can't push it. Something like that has to happen on its own. If he knew about detectives and you coming to see me on the sly—he might not see things your way."

Kitty sat stung and rebuffed, but—dimly—she understood why her son loved this girl. The child did not know how to lie. "Are you going to tell Bart we've spoken?"

"No."

With that guarantee, Kitty could not resist one last attempt at negotiation. "And how is your baby?" she asked.

The girl smiled. "He's beautiful. Seven and a half pounds. He's sleeping now. We haven't thought what to name him."

"Isn't there something we could do for the child?"

The girl shook her head. "Not yet."

"Bart's grandfather is old," Kitty said. "He's not well. He's dying in fact. He asks for Bart." It was almost the truth. If the old man ever regained consciousness, if he ever regained the power to think and to speak, he would ask for Bart—Kitty was sure of it.

"Bart will come back to you," the girl said, "one of these days."

Kitty bent over the bed and kissed her. The kiss was not a lie. "You're very kind, Beth. And you're good for him. Bring him home to us soon."

It was the best that could be done.

Kitty spent the rest of the day with lawyers. A great deal had to be accomplished swiftly and without leaving breadcrumb trails to Stokes Industries. Bart's bank had to be bribed into dropping charges. The police had to be rewarded. Kitty's role had to be kept secret and Johnny had to be kept in impregnable ignorance of the entire affair.

It was an intricate, expensive, nerve-consuming process. Vicky Jennings, quiet and resourceful, helped as always. Kitty could never have managed without her. By the time they returned home, the Massachusetts polls had closed and the election returns were in. By the narrowest margin in the history of the county, Jay Stokes had won election to the state legislature.

# *Chapter 19*

JOHN STOKES SR. never knew of his grandson's victory. Seven weeks after Jay took office, the old man's heart stopped. Resuscitation failed. He was pronounced dead at 5:30 A.M. The news was made public at noon.

Within twenty-four hours obituaries appeared in over eighty-two languages and countries. All were clipped and forwarded to Sixty-second Street by the family's press-cutting services. The Stokes home and office switchboards were clogged with calls. Eighteen extra lines had to be run into the Broad Street office alone. In the next four business days Stokes Industries secretaries filed over eighteen thousand notes of condolence.

Johnny took his father's death badly. He hid in silence, in leather chairs with the drapes drawn. For forty-eight hours Kitty forced herself to let him be, to let him handle it his own way. And then she said, "Johnny, enough is enough."

The sound of her voice drew his gaze up out of the shadow. His face was strangely childlike.

"You've got to pull yourself out of this." She could feel the unyielding rigidity of the muscles in his neck, braced against some violent movement within him.

"They killed him," he said softly.

"Who, Johnny?"

"Bart and his whore—they did this."

*Can he believe what he's saying?* she wondered. "Johnny," she soothed. "He was old. He had a full, wonderful life. No one killed him."

Johnny's father was buried at the family estate in Maine, in the little plot of consecrated land where Melissa Barton Stokes had been laid to rest before him. Even though the service was specifically limited to family and immediate friends and associates, hundreds of limousines filled the driveway and as many millionaires crowded the lawn.

The dark suit that Johnny wore to the burial was only six months old, but it was already too large for him. He'd lost a great deal of weight and it worried Kitty. He was gazing across the grave toward the driveway when a dented gray Volkswagen pulled to a stop among the Rolls-Royces. Johnny froze. His face was pained and tight, and at first Kitty could not grasp the meaning of his half-exhaled sigh.

And then a man in a shabby suit stepped out of the Volkswagen and came around to open the passenger door. It was Bart, and the woman who got out was his wife Beth.

A red flush was creeping up Johnny's neck and his jaw was shaking. "How dare he bring that woman here?"

"Johnny, please," Kitty said. She took his hand and gripped it tight, as though she were pulling a drowning man onto a raft. Finally, mercifully, the Episcopal minister began reading from the Book of Common Prayer. When he came to the words "In my Father's house are many mansions," she saw in her mind the houses in New York and Maine and Bartonville and she imagined John Stokes, Senior's first mansion, a rooming house in Cleveland where an eighteen-year-old had pored over his pasteboard-covered account books till each cent balanced. She thought of rooms in five-hundred-thousand-dollar houses with twelve-foot French windows and teakwood filing cabinets and telephones that were already disconnected. It was strange to reflect that in a dozen tiny ways she was going to miss her father-in-law.

By the time the sun came out, a deep hush had settled over the mourners. They were thinking perhaps not of John Stokes Sr., but of their own deaths that would one day come. They were thinking of last things, and for the moment, at least, death had conquered dollars.

Light began seeping out of the forest, across the lawns and gardens. The birds sounded cheerful and out of place. A child of the universe had died, but the universe still lived. A breeze brought a sweet smell of lilies from the coffin. Kitty shifted. Finally the minister cast a sprinkle of water and the first handful of dirt, and John Stokes Sr. was laid back into the earth that had made him rich.

Kitty could feel hundreds of eyes upon her and Johnny, inspecting for cracks in their grief. She could sense anger digging its claws into Johnny. He was peering over the mourners, looking for Bart, not even bothering to cover up. She kept a tight squeeze on his hand, trying to will calm into him, and braced herself to receive condolences for them both.

The mourners filed past, their voices a low jumble of sympathy. Some of them Kitty remembered and some she could not place. There were faces she knew from weddings and board meetings, faces she knew only from other funerals. There was Antonia, theatrically tossing a white rose into an open grave and kissing Kitty and Johnny on both cheeks. Her hair was dark and lovely and it looked as though it had taken three specialists all morning. And there was Jay, with bloodshot eyes and spearmint masking the liquor on his breath.

*Of course he's had a drink,* Kitty thought, *he's heartbroken over his grandfather.*

And long afterward there was Bart, his face dark and brooding and quiet, like a house with the shades pulled down. His wife was directly behind him, and Kitty's heart thumped like a fist against her ribs. She could not tell how Johnny was going to react, but she recognized that the moment was dangerous because it was public.

"Remember, Johnny," she whispered. "He's your son."

"He's not my son," Johnny said through gritted teeth. "Not so long as he's married to that woman."

Instinct warned Kitty to move quickly.

"Bart, dearest." She pressed her younger son against her and drew him to one cheek and then the other. His shoulders felt thin and his jacket felt too flimsy for the cool day. A veil of hurt seemed stretched across his eyes.

"Hello, Mom, hello, Dad," he said quietly.

Johnny drew himself up. The muscles of his jaw showed taut and motionless.

Kitty did not trust the sudden silence. It was like the last muffled tick of an anarchist's bomb. "Thank you for coming," she said, as much for Johnny as for herself. "Thank you both." She hugged the girl quickly.

It was Johnny's turn now. He stared at the girl's outstretched hand. His eyes went cold and blank. Kitty realized it wasn't working. This should have been a reconciliation and it wasn't coming off.

The moment stretched like a dangerously fraying thread. Others were noticing. Whispers rippled out.

The girl bowed her head, acknowledging the snub. She edged past Johnny.

Bart's eyes sparked with anger. He turned to the mourner behind him—a small, stooped man in a dark overcoat—and nodded. "Serve the papers," Bart said.

The man darted out of line and slapped an envelope into Johnny's hand. There was a puzzled crease in Johnny's brow, and then his eyes went huge and white.

"What is it?" Kitty cried. "What's the matter?"

He thrust the document at her and she saw that it was a court subpoena. Kitty could not speak. Amazement left her without words.

Before she could react, the next man in line was clasping her hand and the subpoena in it. "Lyndon Johnson, ma'am," he said. "Your father-in-law did a lot of business in my state. I met you three years ago, under happier circumstances."

She tried to place the tall, dark-haired man with the Texas accent. "Senator Johnson," she said.

He smiled broadly. "That's right, ma'am. Please call me Lyndon. My deepest condolences to you and your husband."

"Johnny," Kitty said, "Senator Johnson came all the way from Washington to—"

She turned, but Johnny was not there. He had shoved aside condolences and was wrenching an opening through the crowd. He caught Bart at the door of his Volkswagen and spun him around.

"That was a filthy thing to do," Johnny said.

His son looked him icily in the eye. "You brought it on yourself. You could have shaken my wife's hand. She's as good as any crook or killer in the place."

Johnny struck his son across the cheek. Blood gushed from Bart's nose but he didn't blink.

"I'm not afraid, Dad. I used to be scared stiff of all of you, but that's finished. Grandpa left me that money and I don't intend to wait while you play games with it. My lawyers will be talking to you."

Reporters caught the scent of trouble and came rushing. Kitty had had her doubts about admitting those reporters. By the time she had pushed her way to the scene of the fight, Johnny had smashed two cameras and Justin Lasting was passing out hundred-dollar bills.

The subpoena turned out to be a show-cause order of unbelievable malice. Bart's lawyers challenged the bona fides of the estate executors. They demanded immediate probate of the will, and independent audit, and the posting of an escrow bond to protect Bart's inheritance.

Johnny fought the order, but the District Court upheld Bart. Johnny's lawyers urged him, for the sake of appearances—and of the estate—not to appeal; and Kitty begged him, for God's sake, to listen to the lawyers.

Johnny yielded, but Kitty knew there was now a poisonous growth planted in his heart that nothing would ever uproot.

For Bart, the inheritance had frightening overtones. He knew what money could buy, but he also knew what it cost. He knew the rich, and they were exiles from the land of the living and the loving. He did not want to turn into one of them.

Two nights and a day he spent arguing with Beth and with himself. He had proved his point and he was tempted to renounce the inheritance. She listened and nodded, and from time to time in a gentle voice she answered.

"It's not the money you hate," she said. "It's what the money does. Most men are twisted by it. But there's another way. You can change things. You have the money to fight money."

*The money to fight money,* Bart thought. The more he thought of it the more the rightness of it struck him. But how was he to do it?

Bart's mind groped and stumbled and kept groping. He turned the one room of the third-story walk-up into a library. For weeks he studied financial pages and journals of finance and company reports. He had a banker's cunning and he memorized every cranny and hole of his inheritance and every cranny and hole of the market.

One morning at four o'clock, as he drank black coffee and

squinted at stock listings, the baby cried in its crib. He went to feed it, and a switch clicked in his mind. He glimpsed the way. It was tricky and risky. It was full of hairpin turns, but he saw it as clearly as a mountain trail in the dawn.

He went to the president of the trust company that was acting as executor of his grandfather's estate.

"Yes, young man?"

"I want to pledge my inheritance as security for a loan."

The president of the trust company nodded. He did not approve, but he had a half century's experience in handling rich boys in a rush. "How large a loan?"

"The entire inheritance."

The president of the trust company did not believe it. Such things were not done. He got up from his chair and took a deep breath. He explained to this rash young man in the ill-fitting suit that the very idea was impossible, quite impossible.

"The money belongs to me," Bart Stokes said politely.

The older man stared at him in astonishment. "It would be a complete abrogation of our fiduciary responsibility were I to accede to such a request."

"I'm not requesting," Bart said. "I'm instructing you."

The president of the trust company summoned one of the vice presidents, and the vice president summoned three assistant vice presidents. The directors of the trust company reasoned with Bart and argued with him, and one of them even raised his voice and said this was the most damned foolish thing he'd ever heard of.

Bart did not budge.

One hour and forty-two minutes later he was striding down Wall Street with a banker's draft for one hundred fifty million dollars tucked in his breast pocket. He personally delivered his order to a brokerage house that handled eighteen of the Stokes trusts' portfolios.

"I'm interested in International Computers," he said.

"A fine company, sir. Well-run. A lot of people think the stock's overpriced at three hundred a share, but if I may say so, there's splendid opportunity for growth and it strikes me as a fair price, very fair in view of performance."

"I want to buy on margin."

"Naturally, sir."

"The maximum margin."

The broker glanced up nervously, as though afraid the Stokes heir wanted more margin than the government permitted. "You do realize that the SEC limits us to fifty percent?"

"I realize that. We'll go halves."

"You were thinking of how many shares, sir?"

"I was thinking of two hundred million dollars' worth."

The broker gulped.

Bart gave the man a check for one hundred million and very precise instructions: the orders were to be farmed out to other brokerage houses. The stock was to be bought in street name accounts, so that no one would know one man was behind the transaction. Buy and sell orders were to be carefully orchestrated so that the price of the stock would reflect as little suspicious activity as possible.

"Yes, sir; of course, sir." The broker was sweating, but his face was eager and shiny and red as a McIntosh apple. He would get an enormous commission. "We're specialists at this sort of thing, sir. Just leave it to us."

Six months later, Bart Stokes controlled two hundred million dollars' worth of the common stock of International Computer, just under seven hundred thousand shares. During that time whispers had raced through Wall Street that a takeover was in the works, and speculators had driven the price up twenty-five dollars. The morning after Easter, Bart strolled into his broker's office.

"I want to sell one million shares of International Computer," he said.

The broker pulled at his collar. His face was embarrassed. "But, sir, begging your pardon, sir, you don't *own* one million shares."

"I want to sell one million shares in three months' time. And I want two hundred ninety-eight dollars per share."

The broker swallowed. "But there's no need to take such a loss. The stock is selling at 327 now, and it's bound to go to—"

Bart cut the broker short. "I'm selling at 298. I want the contracts by the end of the month."

"You won't have any trouble finding buyers, sir." There was a deep vertical line down the center of the broker's forehead. "You may have a great deal of trouble finding the stock."

"Just get me the buyers."

Eight days later the broker telephoned. "You have your buyers, sir."

"They're committed? No way they can get out?"

"No way they'd want to get out, sir. At that price I could have sold a million more shares."

"Let's start at a hundred thousand."

"Sir?"

"Dump a hundred thousand shares of International Computer."

"But, sir—"

"Dump them. Ten thousand a day."

For three days the market absorbed the shares. The price rose and steadied at 340. The fourth day it dropped back to 320. There were rumors that the smart money was bailing out. The price sagged to 313. There were rumors that the company was in trouble. The stock skidded to 290.

The broker phoned. His voice was unmoored, like a balloon tugging loose. "You're committing suicide, sir."

"And you're getting a whopping commission. Keep dumping."

When the stock crashed to 160 the broker phoned again. He was screaming. "At 150 we're below your margin, sir."

"Then you'll just have to dump everything, won't you?"

The stock was hurtling downward now, a bobsled out of control. At 150 the brokerage house ordered all the subbrokers to dump. Panic hit the market. Institutions and foundations dumped. Trust funds and mutual funds dumped. Widows in Wichita and speculators in Spokane dumped. International Computer hit a sixty-year low of forty-nine dollars per share.

Bart stepped in with the remainder of his inheritance, $50 million cash. He sopped up one million shares of International Computer. Eighteen days later, when the purchase orders came due, he sold the stock at the price that his buyers had agreed on: 298 per share.

In less than nine months, he had almost doubled his inheritance.

He returned to his broker. The man eyed him with a mixture of wariness and greed.

"I'd like to put that money into bank stock," Bart said.

"All of it, sir?"

"All of it. Quietly. Through different brokers."

"Which banks, sir?"

"Manhattan National."

"Just Manhattan National?"

"Just Manhattan National."

"On margin?"

"On margin."

Word leaked out that John Stokes's grandson took the second oldest bank in New York for the same sort of fools as International Computer. The directors, with assets of $600 billion under their control, fought back. They bought up their own stock, manipulating the price skyward. While this made it much more expensive for Bart Stokes to pull the same sort of shark tactics he had with International Computer, it also increased the value of his holdings 12 percent in fourteen days. When he walked into the boardroom of Manhattan National, he controlled stock in the bank worth more than $700 million.

There were handshakes and good mornings. The president of the bank offered Bart a seat at the conference table. A secretary set a cup of coffee before him. Bart sipped. Silence stretched like a rubber band about to snap.

"Mr. Stokes," the president said, "I'm going to be very blunt about this."

"Please," Bart said, smiling. He was still wearing his shabby suit. "Let's both be blunt."

"There's no way you're going to engineer a panic in Manhattan National stock."

"I don't want to engineer a panic."

"What do you want, then?"

"A position."

"With us?"

"With you."

The president of Manhattan National stared at the smiling young man in the ill-fitting suit and ill-advised broad-striped necktie. His hands made a guillotine gesture. "Impossible."

Bart gazed a long moment at the smooth veined face with its three chins spilling like an orgy of frogs' bellies. "It's too bad you've shifted so much of your assets into your own stock. You're at the limit now. When I dump my shares, you're going to take quite a loss. The government will have to step in. You'll lose your top corporate accounts. And I doubt you'll be getting many more trusts."

The president's lips pressed together till they were as gray as the rest of his face. "Which position did you have in mind?"

"I'd like to work near the top, sir. How about—*your* position?"

Thursday afternoon the director of the Eighth Street branch of Manhattan National presented himself at the bank's main office on Wall Street. "The president asked to see me."

"Mr. Downey?" The receptionist smiled. "He's expecting you."

Mr. Downey flicked a spot of lint from his gray flannel jacket. He straightened his Racquet Club tie. He squared his shoulders and strode through the door. He had a billiard date at five-thirty and he hoped this would be short. On the other hand, if it were a question of a raise or promotion, to hell with billiards.

Mr. Downey took three steps across the beige carpet, then stopped short. The new president of Manhattan National was a young man, perhaps some twenty years younger than Mr. Downey, and there was something disturbingly familiar about his face. "You wished to see me, sir?"

The new president did not rise. He did not invite Mr. Downey to sit. He swung back in his swivel chair. He drew a gold watch from his pocket and spent a long time popping the lid open and shut.

Mr. Downey felt a flush of annoyance creeping up from his collar.

Finally the president's eyes met his coldly. "Floyd James Downey Jr.?"

"Yes, sir."

"Do you remember me?"

"Remember you?" Something in Mr. Downey hesitated.

"It was a little over a year ago. You refused me a loan."

Mr. Downey tried to smile. "A loan, sir?"

"Four hundred dollars."

In his twenty-seven years with Manhattan National, Floyd James Downey Jr. had refused many men loans: he liked to joke that the only bums he trusted were the ones who asked for a million dollars.

"I used to work for you, Mr. Downey."

Mr. Downey forced himself to smile, but a disturbing memory was itching at the back of his head.

"You had me put in jail," the president said.

"Your collateral—" Mr. Downey stammered. "Your collateral didn't seem exactly—adequate."

"You lack judgment, Downey."

"Judgment, sir?" Floyd James Downey Jr. could feel the universe giving way at his sphincter.

"You're a poor judge of men, and that means you're a poor judge of risk—which makes you a poor banker."

"I was only trying to do my job, sir."

"Why don't you try somewhere else, Downey?"

"Sir?"

"You're fired."


"How refreshing to meet a woman who knows how to get to the point," Howard Bergman said. He stared at Kitty and his eyes glinted as if at some secret joke. "You go straight to the problem. Maybe you should have been a surgeon."

The problem, as usual, had been money. It took more to fund the Clinic than to run a dozen summer homes in Newport. It had occurred to Kitty to set up tax shelters and shell companies in publicly sold Clinic stock. Apparently no one had ever thought of rigging the market and playing tax loopholes for charity.

*It's not done,* the accountants had said.

*It hasn't been done yet but it's going to be done now,* Kitty had said for over two hours.

The accountants had gone, pummeled and finally acquiescent, and now Howard Bergman held her in the cool admiring measure of his gaze. They were alone with six empty coffee cups in a penthouse suite in the Pierre and she could feel the tension of his mind locked in calculation.

"Think we've earned a drink?" he said. "There's some good scotch in the bar."

"I think we've earned a meal. Aren't you hungry after all that? *My* treat."

"You rush too much, Kitty."

He poured her a drink that was exactly the size and strength she would have poured herself. She had an unnerving feeling that he knew her much too well, knew not just the skeletons in her closet but the skeleton in her flesh. There were only love seats in the suite, so they sat on a love seat and sipped.

She knew without looking that his arm was resting behind her back. She had an awareness of the possibilities of the moment, of all the space in her life waiting to be filled, that was so swift and enveloping she almost wanted to let go, like a child hurtling down a slide.

After a moment he pulled her head against him.

She stiffened and pulled away and almost immediately felt like a fool, and a sad one at that. *He wants me, I want him,* she thought. *Why can't I do it?*

She went to the window. The blue had bled from the sky like the color from an old dress. Shadows of trees stretched across Fifth Avenue. People on the open-deck buses had turned up their collars. It was getting cold and late.

"Why not, Kitty?" Howard said. "It's what you want too."

She could think of nothing to say that didn't sound like a three-cent Episcopal Church pamphlet for teen-agers. Her argument was with herself, not with him. When she turned around, Howard's arm was still stretched across the love seat. Nothing had changed in the room, but in some way everything had changed.

"Don't forget you're human, Kitty, or one of these days you might just run amok."

"Little Catholic girls don't run amok." She'd meant the remark to sound funny but firm, but somehow it came out sounding a bit regretful.

"Little Jewish boys don't believe that," he said.

"I'm sorry, Howard. I'm not very hungry after all."

"No dinner?" he said.

"Raincheck."

She left quickly. As she was stepping out of the elevator into the lobby, two tiny and startlingly well-dressed people came in from the street. She recognized the Duke and Duchess of Windsor. They looked in bad tempers and Kitty did not feel up to chitchat anyway. She ducked out the side door before they could see her.

Riding home in the limousine, she fished in her purse for the Tiffany keychain that Johnny had given her on their nineteenth anniversary. It occurred to her that she had a great many keys in her life and not a single door that interested her.

Jay's child was born that winter. Kitty and Johnny canceled all appointments for half a day and dashed up to Boston in the family's private two-prop airplane. The baby weighed eight pounds three ounces. His eyes were the pale delicate blue of robin's eggs and they dwelt brightly on Kitty when she took him in her arms.

"What are you calling him?" Johnny asked.

The hospital room smelled of dozens of bouquets banked on the dresser. Antonia was a madonna of shadowed coolness in her pillowed bed. "John Stokes," she said.

"The Fourth," Jay said proudly.

"Hell of a name for a little kid," Johnny said.

Kitty gazed down at the child. *Not John Stokes, the Fourth,* she thought: *Tyrone Duncannon, the Third. That's who you are.* "What about nicknaming him Jason?" she said.

"Why Jason?" Toni said.

"For Jay's son."

Johnny nodded. "Jason. That's better. I like that. Wish someone had called *me* Jason when I was a kid."

There was laughter and Jay and Toni were both talking at once, like excited parents, and Johnny was asking questions at the same time, like an excited grandpa. Kitty let the voices wash over her. She cradled the baby and rocked it, feeling the beat of its tiny, determined drum of a heart.

Twenty minutes loped by like painted horses on a merry-go-round, and then Jay lifted the child from Kitty's arms. "Better let Toni and Jason rest," he said. He carried the baby like an armful of eggshells back to the bed. For an instant he and Toni and Jason looked like the posed photograph of a very happy family.

Perhaps, Kitty reflected, the child would mark the healing of the marriage. She'd seen miraculous healings before. Why not Toni and Jay? She kissed Toni on the forehead.

"He's a beautiful child," she said. "Get your rest, my darling. Having the baby is the easy part. Now the work starts."

"I'll do my best, Mother."

Kitty went with the men into the hall and then said she'd forgotten something, she'd only be a minute.

"Woman talk?" Jay said, smiling and handsome.

"Mother talk," Kitty said. "I'll meet you downstairs."

Kitty came back into the hospital room. She closed the door behind her. Toni was reaching across the baby for a cigarette. She struck a match and two pinpricks of reflected fire dotted her eyes.

"What are you doing with that cigarette?" Kitty cried.

"Smoking. Does it bother you?"

"It most certainly does. You have an infant in your arms and you're blowing cancer in its face."

A white line appeared around Toni's mouth. She flicked the dead match at a bedside bowl of roses. "The doctor didn't say anything about not smoking."

"You could show a little maternal sense."

Toni's lips tensed like a bow about to shoot an arrow. There was an instant's stillness. She sighed a cloud of white smoke and twisted to grind the cigarette out in a dish of barely touched apricot compote. The baby's hand, smooth and tiny and unreal in its miniature perfection, trailed blindly after her.

Kitty was uneasily aware of Toni's milk-swollen breasts, the nipples pushing like hard little thumbs against the half-closed gown. For the time being little Jason needed those breasts. She fought to keep an edge of anger from creeping into her voice. "I didn't mean to seem rude. I was only thinking of the child."

Toni was silent, watching Kitty, measuring her.

Kitty snapped open her purse. She took out the check—one million dollars, drawn and certified on the household account at Manufacturer's Hanover Trust. She handed it over. "For services rendered," she said. "Payment in full."

Toni stared at the check. An odd, faraway smile came over her face. With two swift rips she tore the check into halves, the halves into quarters. She let them flutter to the floor.

"Surprised, Mother? Don't be. It's not that I don't want your money. I just want more of it."

It took Kitty a moment to recover the power of speech. "We had a verbal agreement," she said.

Toni nodded. "That I would produce a son. I've kept that agreement. But now you've changed the terms. You expect me to be not just a breeding mare but a draft mule too. That costs more."

Kitty's head exploded in a rush of blood and anger. "Then you'll sign a legally binding contract."

"Binding me to what?"

"To Jay. You'll agree to a code of behavior. You'll renounce all rights to the child. All rights to seek divorce. All rights to Jay's property."

Toni lit another cigarette. "That will be three million, tax-free. Four, if you expect me to give up smoking."

* * *

By the time she returned home, Kitty's joy had shriveled in her like a dead leaf. "You seem tired," Vicky Jennings said.

"Not tired," Kitty said, "just exhausted."

"Why?"

"I don't know. Perhaps because I'm a grandmother now. I feel old."

Vicky looked at her with concern. "But Kitty, you've been a grandmother for years now—ever since Bart's first child."

Kitty flushed as she would have at a Freudian slip of the tongue. "What I meant was, I'm a grandmother again."

What she meant was, she was a grandmother for the first time.

Three months after Jason's birth and six weeks after signing the marital agreement, Toni faced her hip specialist in his wood-paneled consulting room. "The hip has been giving me no trouble," she said brightly, "none at all."

The doctor nodded. He felt sorry for this woman who couldn't face a bad prognosis without decking herself in ten thousand dollars' worth of Cartier amulets.

"It feels as good as the other hip," she said. "Even better. Why, I've actually been able to dance a little." She caught herself. "Nothing strenuous—just a little fox-trot the other night."

"And you've been playing tennis?" the doctor asked.

"I have no backhand at the net," she admitted, "but that's me—not my hip. Do you play tennis, Doctor?"

"I told you not to play tennis."

"Did you? I thought you said nothing strenuous."

"I did say nothing strenuous. Those were my exact words."

"You can't blame me for wanting to keep my weight down, can you? The pregnancy added eighteen pounds—and I still haven't shed them all."

"Antonia," the doctor said in a voice that absolutely refused to respond to her cheerfulness, "weight is not your problem. Now, I can understand if you want to shave a few pounds from your tummy, but there are safe ways to do that. You can do sit-ups or side-bends. If you want me to recommend a physical therapist, I'd be glad to."

She caught the kindness in his voice and on his face: it was a totally unprovoked kindness and it struck her with the viciousness of a slap. "A therapist? But, Doctor, I'm not paralyzed."

"We have to think of the future."

She did not know if he meant *future* in the sense of the preventable or of the inevitable. She was not certain she wanted to know.

"Why don't I map out a little therapeutic program for you? They've excellent facilities at Mass General—and I believe they hold group classes Wednesday afternoons."

"Of course," Toni said. "You're absolutely right, Doctor."

But as she stepped into the sunlight and bustle of Commonwealth Avenue, she was thinking not of the future but of last weekend on Fisher's Island, where at Mimsy Cavanaugh's dinner she'd heard about a new hip man, not totally loved by the AMA, who was performing miracles with Plexiglas hip joints and neuraxon tissue from chickens.

It was time, she decided, to change doctors.

In the normal course of events Kitty saw very little of Howard Bergman's wife. Occasionally they ran into one another at receptions and opening nights, and once at Winthrop Rockefeller's she saw Phoebe talking to Henri Matisse and Senator Jacob Javits and boring them both.

It seemed to Kitty that there were some women who genuinely aroused men's admiration, while there were others, like Phoebe Bergman, who aroused only their politeness. She wondered if Howard Bergman loved his wife. She tried dispassionately to see it, and then it occurred to her that she was not being dispassionate at all, she was disliking the woman.

Later at the same party, when she went to find an empty bathroom, she opened a door and met Phoebe Bergman's bloodshot eyes in the mirror. "Excuse me," she apologized.

A man's arm shot out and closed the door in her face. Kitty turned back to the hallway and bumped into Howard Bergman and realized he had seen the arm too. Words refused to come out of her throat.

"Kitty," he said, "I know. I know you know. I'd rather not discuss it."

She kept her gaze steady and fought back a sudden enveloping sadness.

\* \* \*

Phoebe Bergman died in a car crash in Southhampton that Christmas Eve. If a Venezuelan polo player had not died in the car with her, Kitty would have thought it was suicide. The Stokes public relations people did as good a job hushing it up as could be managed under the circumstances. Howard Bergman took a week off after the funeral, but otherwise did not interrupt his practice.

Kitty dreaded her semiannual physical, not knowing exactly how to face him. She kept thinking about the last time they'd been alone, and the events and nonevents of that afternoon stirred uncomfortably in her memory.

Howard took her blood and listened to her heart and lungs and hammered her reflexes. There was none of the usual banter. His face was weary and squinted up. There were more tiny lines around his eyes than she remembered.

*He's older,* she thought. *We're both older.*

She kept waiting for him to look at her. Her face was ready and friendly but he wouldn't look at her, and finally, impulsively, she took his arm. "Howard—cut it out."

"You're in good health, Kitty."

"But I don't think *you* are."

He pulled back, and she felt rejection so physical that she had to bite down on an unthinking protest.

"I'll have the results next week," he said.

"I'm your friend, Howard. You know that."

"I know, and thank you. It's just that healing is a long process and I do it best alone."

She had a sudden sense of him, an exhibit in a museum of suffering marked DO NOT TOUCH. "Will you phone one of these days?"

He nodded. "Sooner than that."

But of course he didn't.

# Chapter 20

NEW YEAR'S CAME and went. Jay took office and was appointed to the State Roads Committee. He and Toni moved into a fourteen-room brick-and-pillar federal house in Brookline, just fifteen minutes by car from downtown Boston. Little Jason said his first word—"Ga." At least Toni claimed it was a word.

The British tested an A-bomb, the United States tested an H-bomb, and Antonia wrecked the dining-room furniture in a fight that had begun, oddly enough, over Jay's burning a piece of raisin toast. That spring their marriage, which had been crumbling in private from almost the very beginning, began crumbling in public—if State Attorney General Potter Wentworth's living room could be considered public.

The Attorney General's receptions were occasions for Boston Brahmins to get together with machine politicians and Harvard-educated Italo-Irish power brokers. The women were political wives—haggard, heavy-drinking, and almost always over forty; and the liquor was never any good. Jay made it policy to come late and cut his appearance short.

When he and Toni arrived at the April reception, two dozen white-haired people were still milling on the second story of the Beacon Hill townhouse, sipping sherry, talking loudly.

"Let's make this fast, Jay," Toni said.

They had been arguing in a mild sort of way—he forgot whether it had been about his drinking or Jason's nanny's drinking—but he was in no rush to get back to the dispute, and the party offered a temporary sanctuary. Toni let herself be cornered by an M.I.T. economist, and Jay pried his way to an unattended cloth-covered table that served as the bar. There were silver bowls of potato chips and crystal decanters of sherry that he suspected was not imported. He found a bottle of Old Retainer blended whiskey that someone had hidden on a shelf behind the Thackeray. He was a little high from the three scotches he'd had at home, and he wanted to stay that way.

He poured himself a generous double.

Turning, he bumped into a blond girl who was reaching across the bar for the sherry. She had wide-set green eyes with mysterious sleepy lids and she did not look at all like the Attorney General's sort of people.

Jay smiled and said, "Hey, are you sure you're at the right party?"

"I'm at the right place. I'm not sure it's a party." She was pretty and young, and the condescension in her voice exactly matched the condescension in the glance she threw about the room.

"Funny—you don't look Republican to me."

"I'm not. I'm a Spartacist. That's a rebellious offshoot of Socialist Workers."

Jay could not read the girl. He couldn't tell if she was joking. He couldn't tell if she even knew who he was. There was a teasing hint of availability in the way she held herself and he couldn't tell if it was intentional or not. "I'm not up on the Socialist Workers," he said. "Sorry."

"We're a revisionist Trotskyite splinter faction—which couldn't interest you less, could it?"

"Wrong. It fascinates me."

"Then you're easily fascinated."

"Especially when I find blond anarchists prowling Beacon Hill powwows."

"Trotskyites are not anarchists. That's a Stalinist lie."

She delivered the line with the finality of an exit cue, then turned and moved away. Jay sensed he had in some way offended her, but he followed her anyway. They wound up in the back of the room where the crowd was beginning to thin out.

"But you're here for some reason," he said.

"Don't worry. I'm not planting bombs."

"That's a shame. A bomb might pick up the party."

"Until I'm independently wealthy I can't afford to blow up my employers."

"Which of these corpses employ you?"

"Only the well-paying ones."

"What the hell do you do for them?"

"Position papers."

"Are you any good at it?"

"I'm the best." She gazed coolly into his eyes. "I do yours."

"Any I'd be apt to remember?"

"Oh, the tough ones and the tricky ones and the two-places-at-once kind."

"My positions sound interesting."

She shrugged and it irked him. She was acting as though she were doing him some kind of favor humoring the only man under sixty in the entire room. "You want to condemn three miles along Route Five to expand the highway. You also want to lease the land at a dollar a year to a shopping center contractor." The arched eyebrows made it clear she was light-years above such contemptible conniving.

"That sounds kind of double-jointed," Jay said.

"I guess politicians have to be," she said.

"Sounds dirty too." Jay's gaze pinned her.

She didn't blink. "In this society politicians have to be that too."

"Think I stand a chance?"

She gave him a glance so direct and unteasing that it amounted to the biggest tease of all. "You stand a chance with me, Mr. Stokes. Trotskyites still have to build a united front in America."

"Not a bad policy, Miss—"

She put a cigarette in her mouth. Jay lit it.

"Trueblood," she said. "That's really my name, it's American Indian. I get the blond hair from my mother. First name, Lucy Anne. That's two names, but in my case it counts as one. My coconspirators call me Bloody Lou."

"May I call you Bloody Lou too?"

"You can call me anything anytime, Mr. Stokes."

She gave him her number but he lost the matchbook it was

scrawled in and didn't phone. They met by accident four weeks later in the Parker House bar. Jay was waiting for a staff assistant, and Lucy Anne didn't say who she was waiting for. He offered her a drink, she accepted, and they got into a long discussion of flying saucers.

He ordered another round and, when his assistant still hadn't shown up, still another. "I'm going to fire that assistant," he said, and then he looked at Lucy Anne with her long sweep of blond hair and said, "On second thought, maybe he deserves a raise."

They were roaring with laughter at something or other when suddenly she asked him his zodiacal sign.

"Capricorn. Why?" In fact, he hadn't the faintest idea of his sign, but he sensed she'd take him for an imbecile if he admitted it.

Her green eyes rested thoughtfully on him. "I don't think it's going to work."

"What's not?"

"You and me."

He looked at her in amazement and stifled an impulse to guffaw. "You believe in astrology?"

"A person has to believe in something," she said quietly.

Which struck him as an admission that she took the stars more seriously than she did Leon Trotsky.

"Come on, Bloody Lou." He put twenty dollars down on the table. "There's only one way to find out whether you and I are going to work or not."

He took her upstairs to the staff suite. He made love to her, phoned room service for more drinks, made love to her again. Sex hadn't felt so good since his college days. He wondered if it was time for him to give up affairs and take a mistress.

"Can I see you again?" he asked.

She nodded. "Next Tuesday."

After that, they saw one another at least twice a week. It wasn't just sex: they went to museums, drove to the beach, threw frisbees and played tennis. He knew he was taking chances being seen with her in public, but the weather was beautiful that summer, the Common was in bloom, his home life with Toni was not in bloom, and he knew he'd never be so young again.

And then one Tuesday in August Bloody Lou failed to show up for a date. He phoned her. There was no answer. He had more to drink, and by the time he got home to Toni's party he was drunk. He had the impression he ruined that evening for a great many people.

He didn't see or hear from Bloody Lou for almost three months. It was at another of Potter Wentworth's soirees that he ran into her again. He was not so drunk that he couldn't recognize her.

"Hiya, fella," he said.

"Hiya." Her eyes had developed into deep green wounds. "You've been away."

"That was a mistake," she said. "I'm back."

He drained his drink, refilled it, took her by the hand and led her to a room that he didn't think anyone was using.

Toni extricated herself from the Attorney General's grip and his chitchat and went looking for Jay and/or her coat. She wedged her way through the guests into the hallway and opened the study door. Jay and a strange girl were fumbling half-naked on the couch.

Toni's heart gave a sickening wrench. She'd suspected her husband screwed other women, but she'd never caught him at it before.

"Okay, Jay, time's up." She lit a cigarette and stood exhaling hot smoke. She took in the panic of Jay's eyes and realized he didn't even know where he was. "Get your pants on, get rid of her, and get me out of here before I murder you both."

Jay scrambled off the sofa. He knew he was looped and he knew he ought to care. Black figures rippled and twisted in the doorway. He slid into his trousers, rocking on his bare feet. He had one sharp, cold thought: *I've fucked it.*

Toni pushed him through a storm of voices and light. Night air washed over him in a chilling wave.

"Toni, I'm sorry."

"You disgust me." She unlocked the passenger door and stuffed him into the Buick. She walked around the front of the car and slid behind the wheel.

"Look," he said, "I was drunk and I didn't know what I was doing."

"I'll tell you what you were doing. You were disgracing yourself. You were also disgracing the Attorney General, who happens to be supporting your so-called political career. And last but not least you were disgracing me, the little woman who happens to be married to you, or did that little fact slip your mind in the heat of the moment?"

"I said I'm sorry."

"You're worse than sorry, Jay. You're a washout. As a man, as a senator, as a husband."

An ache welled up through his lungs. He saw with the sidelong clarity of alcohol that she was right, and he saw that if she didn't stop being right he was going to hate her for it. "You don't have to be vicious," he said.

"Tonight I have a right."

"You always have a reason, don't you."

"You always give me one." She adjusted a little plastic cushion behind the small of her back, then started the motor.

"Toni, how the hell did this happen? How did we turn into this?"

"Because you drink too much and you're a goddamned mess and you screw around too much and you never touch me, that's how we turned into this." She sat twisting her wedding ring, waiting for the light to turn green.

"Did it ever occur to you that if things were different between us, maybe I wouldn't need to?"

"Need to!" The light turned. She threw the car into gear. It lurched forward. "So it's my fault you can't keep your fly zipped at a party! Well, let me tell you, Jay Stokes, I happen to be one hell of a beautiful woman and a goddamned good lay and you're goddamned lucky I'm willing to be seen with you in public after that display!"

"You're doing me a favor, hey?"

"You know it—and it's time you started doing me a few. Like being sober now and then in public. Or being a husband now and then in private."

"You don't ask small favors, do you?"

"Look, you dumb bastard—if it wasn't for me, Potter Wentworth would have axed you the minute he saw your bare ass on that couch."

"So you saved my career, did you?"

"You know it."

"Then you can have my career, you're so good at running it. And you can have Potter Wentworth too, you're so good at stroking the old fart." He reached across her and snapped off the ignition. The car slid to a stop behind a gasoline truck. Somebody honked in back of them. "I'm getting out here."

She stared at him, jaw trembling. "You're really plastered this time, aren't you?"

"And facing up to you, and don't you hate it."

"If you get out of this car—"

"Look, bitch, you can't threaten me. I'm sick of you. I'm sick of your nagging. I'm sick of paying your bills. I'm sick of trying to put space between us in that goddamned double bed. I don't love you anymore, I don't want you anymore, I'm not scared of you anymore. So why don't you just go have yourself a good four-car collision."

He threw the car door open. Commonwealth Avenue shimmered in the drizzle. He put a foot down, testing the reality of the asphalt.

"I'm warning you, Jay, if you get out of this car, you and I are through!"

"Toni, you just made yourself a deal. So long, sweetheart."

During his 1951 visit to New York City, Albert Schweitzer approached Kitty to discuss setting up a liver cancer clinic at his hospital in Gabon. Kitty had virtually said yes and they were just finishing up their tea when the butler announced Mrs. Stokes.

Toni was wearing a mauve silk dress, and it was clear from the perfection of the design and fit that she had too little to do with her time and too many charge accounts to do it with. "Am I barging in?" she said. "Sorry. Tiffany's said it would take three weeks at least to engrave the at-home cards, so I thought I'd stop by and tell you the news in person."

"Dr. Schweitzer, this is my daughter-in-law," Kitty said coolly.

The old man rose stiffly and bent over Toni's hand. He apologized and said he had to be going. Kitty saw her guest to the front door. When she came back to the study, Toni was lighting a pink cigarette from a Stork Club matchbook.

"That was rude of you, Toni. You interrupted us. Now, what at-home cards are you talking about?"

"I'm moving back to New York."

"You can't."

"Certainly I can. We've kept the apartment at Sutton Place. All it needs is a little dusting."

"I have your agreement in writing, and I warn you—I'll enforce it. You'll stay in Boston with your husband."

"I'd love to, Mother, but he's left me—vanished. No goodby, no forwarding address. I'm all alone, and quite frankly I prefer to be all alone in New York."

A winged telepathy brushed Kitty: there was more than exaggeration here—there was a particle of truth, a dangerous particle. "When did this happen?"

"When I caught him with another woman four days ago."

Kitty sank back into her chair. "Then it's only a spat. You'll both simmer down. Jay will be home in a day or two."

"I wouldn't be so sure of that. It's not all that easy to come back from where Jay's gone."

Kitty's glance poked up sharply. "Then you *do* know where he is."

"Not exactly. He phoned and said he'd joined the Army—but who knows where *they've* sent him?"

Kitty gulped down panic and fought to keep her eyes cold and steady and unbelieving. "The Army? That's impossible."

Toni sighed. "Jay is obviously tired of playing senator and wants to play soldier."

"But we're at war!"

"If Jay didn't know that, I'm sure he's found out by now."

Kitty had the office check. It was true; worse than true. Jay had joined the armed forces as a buck private.

Kitty's thoughts were gnarled and tangled. She couldn't see her way out. All her certainties came unmoored and rattled in her like seeds in a maraca.

For forty-eight hours she and Johnny made phone calls, and the minute they placed the receivers back in the cradles the phones were jangling with inquiries from the press about Jay's enlisting. They gave the press not a particle of information, and Washington gave them not much more than two particles of confusion. Realizing they could achieve nothing long-distance, they went personally to the Pentagon.

Kitty did not shout, but her eyes were blazing and there was no requesting left in her voice. Sweat ran down the soft lines of two-star and three-star generals' faces. "You do realize, Mr. and Mrs. Stokes," they said, "in times of national emergency—"

"Johnny," Kitty cut in, "this is getting us nowhere."

The Secretary of Defense was a Princeton classmate and clubmate of Johnny's and there was no way he could refuse them three minutes. "How are you, Kitty, Johnny?" he said, coming out from behind a desk as large as a Ping-Pong table. "By God, it's good to see you. Now, what's all this fuss?"

They explained

He waved them silent. "Ixnay. I'm not going to touch it."

"If there's a question of money," Johnny said, "if a contribution—"

"You don't seem to understand. You mean to say you don't know?" The Secretary of Defense had a shave that made his dense beard follicles look like the shine on a very pale Granny Smith apple, and his eyes flicked out the gray menace of razor blades.

"Know what?" Johnny said.

"Your boy bought his way into the Army. He paid five thousand dollars. He wanted active duty, he wanted it immediately, and he didn't want his family meddling. We have the clerk who took the money. Not that the bribe's the issue."

Shock and anger pulsed in Kitty. "What is the issue, then?"

"If we sprang Jay now, it would look like favoritism. We have enough trouble getting the public to accept the draft. We don't need class war on top of the Korean War. I'm sorry— but this time I'm afraid no can do."

A secretary showed them out. A door shut and Kitty stood alone with Johnny in an empty anteroom, her hopes bleached out like film yanked from a camera.

Kitty and Johnny pulled all the strings they could to keep Jay's unit from being sent to Korea. The strings failed and the unit went abroad. Through the Stokes army of informers and press clippers and government liaison men they kept track, dreading each messenger, each envelope, each ringing phone that might bring word of some harm to Jay.

Seven weeks later Kitty was aware of voices at the front door. She recognized Johnny, home from work much too early. She darted into the hallway.

Johnny's face was white as bled veal. "General Wetmore phoned," he said.

His words hit her like a whipcrack. General Wetmore was the war, and the war was Jay. Her mind went skidding through possibilities, all horrible. "What's happened to Jay?"

"I'm going to have a martini—I think you'd better have one too." Johnny went into the study. She watched him fuss with ice cubes and the sterling silver jigger he'd won in the Racquet Club squash finals.

A sudden, bursting certainty swelled in her veins. "I'd rather hear it straight out, Johnny. Has Jay been killed?"

Johnny poured two drinks and gave her one. He emptied half of his in a head-back, walloping gulp. "The North Koreans took him prisoner last night."

For an instant the wind choked off in Kitty's throat. She managed to whisper, "But he's—alive?"

"Pray God," Johnny said. "We'll know the minute General Wetmore has word."

Kitty covered her face three seconds too late. Tears spilled through her fingers. "Hold me, Johnny. Please, just hold me."

For Kitty and Johnny the months that followed were an acid bath of frustration. They couldn't get through to the North Koreans. They could barely get through to their own government. They bombarded the Army for some clue as to Jay's whereabouts, some hope of his being alive. They donated hugely to the Red Cross, the so-called International Red Cross, which turned out to have no international clout whatsoever.

They pressured the State Department and they pestered Johnny's old billiard-playing chum Dean Acheson, who was Secretary of State. He was willing to play billiards anywhere, anytime, it seemed, but he wouldn't lift a finger for Jay. They reminded Trygve Lie, the Secretary General of the United Nations, of favors that the Stokes Fund of Alabama had done that institution. "I'm sorry," he said in his dour, maddening Norwegian accent. "If I took sides in these conflicts my usefulness would be compromised."

It simply did not seem possible that in the second half of the twentieth century, in a world of sane men and sane money, Communists and capitalists could be living on one planet pretending that they were at opposite ends of the firmament. There had to be a phone call or a letter or a dollar that could somehow sneak across the gap.

Yet even with money, every inquiry, every effort took time, and Kitty felt the panic of Jay trapped, perhaps dying, of time running out.

She followed up every lead, no matter how minuscule the hope. She haunted the U.N. missions. She felt out the Russians and was rebuffed by a man in a nylon shirt. She felt out the

Rumanians, who needed oil technology, and the Yugoslavians, who were said to be independent of Stalin now. There was a hint that a member of the Nigerian trade delegation could get through to an Albanian who knew some highly placed North Koreans. But in the end it was always the same: the waiting, the begging, and finally, going home and pulling the blinds and lying down in the embering ashes of dead hope. Kitty came to hate the governments and the agencies and the embassies, the stupid cunning of the faces, the replies that promised everything and delivered nothing.

And Antonia, naturally, made matters a hundred times worse.

Kitty's service sent a shower of gossip column clippings: Toni Stokes at this nightclub or that Broadway opening, on the arm of this tycoon or that actor. Fifth Avenue stores sent unpaid bills. Georges Kaplan threatened to sue over a twelve-thousand-dollar white mink.

That mink appeared on the front page of every afternoon tabloid in the city when Toni went to the Stork Club with a party that included Josephine Baker, the black singer who had scandalized Paris by dancing in a skirt and bra of bananas. The club owner, Sherman Billingsley, had refused to let the party in. FBI director J. Edgar Hoover, who apparently kept a corner table in the club, interposed himself. According to Walter Winchell's column, which spelled things out with asterisks, Hoover said he didn't go to nigger clubs and niggers could damned well stay away from his. Miss Baker had blown marijuana in his face and called him an overweight, overpaid faggot with elevator lifts in his shoes.

Hoover's bodyguards had done the rest.

If it had been only a question of extravagance and publicity, Kitty might have tolerated it. But the Sunday after the Stork Club incident, Jason's nanny—a Jamaican called Essie—came to see Kitty and said that Toni was entertaining men at the apartment.

"What do you mean, 'entertaining'?" Kitty said.

There was not a flicker of hesitation or deceit in the old woman's eyes. "They stay over, ma'am."

At that, the murderess in Kitty awoke. Ten minutes later, unannounced, she was standing in Toni's living room. "I understand you've been bringing men home," she said.

Antonia picked up her cigarette from the low teakwood table. "That's hardly worth an auto-da-fé, Mother."

Kitty had expected denial, and for an instant she was thrown off her strategy. "You are married to my son."

"In name only."

"You will not drag that name through public mud."

Antonia rose and her feet snipped off a little circle around the Turkish carpet. "You and your public this, public that. All you think about is Jay and his brilliant career. It so happens I have a life too, and I intend to live it while I can."

Kitty gazed at her daughter-in-law. The girl dressed like a French king's slut. Her neckline revealed too much breast and too many diamonds much too early in the day. "Not on Jay's money you won't."

"And just what do you think I am—some kind of bought slave?"

"More a hired servant—and a damned poor one, considering you can't even do your job."

"Maybe I don't want the job."

The sentence died in a sigh, trailing clouds of implication.

"Well, Toni—just what *do* you want?"

Toni turned and her eyes took hold of Kitty in a way they never had before. "Would it surprise you to know I've been thinking of divorce?"

"You signed a contract."

"I know."

"You realize what you'd be giving up?"

"I know that too."

Kitty smelled bluff. "What grounds?"

"That would be up to the lawyers. Desertion, maybe."

"The fact that Jay has the courage and patriotism to volunteer for military service is not desertion."

"Would you rather I sue for adultery?"

All the years of Jay's marriage, Kitty had thought she knew this creature, knew the rock-bottom of its malice. Now a fog of doubt began drifting in on her, hazing her certainties. "Jay would counter-sue."

"How?"

"By proxy."

"By you, in other words?"

"There's no way you'd get the child—or child support—or alimony."

"And if you did that, Jay can kiss politics goodby. So stop trying to run my life, Mother. I can handle it myself, thanks."

Kitty stared at this thing called a daughter-in-law and marveled at the intricacy with which stupidity and cunning had intertwined themselves in her. "Can you really handle your life, Toni? Can you handle anything? Can you handle money, or drinking, or men—or your own agreements?"

"That's a chance you're just going to have to take—if you ever expect to get Jay into the state house."

Antonia, of course, had a point. The governorship had figured in Kitty's thoughts, though the idea of running Jay for the office had not been hers but Justin Lasting's. He'd told her never to lose sight of the bright side: Jay's captivity, painful as it was at the moment, would in the long run translate into an avalanche of gubernatorial votes. He had even stopped by the house to show Kitty a press kit he was toying with: *Jay Stokes, the unforgotten hero*.

There were photographs of Jay rowing with the Harvard junior varsity eight, and of Jay in his graduation robes, and a recent one of Jay looking very young in his buck private's uniform. Kitty looked over the layout and began to cry.

Justin Lasting put his hands on her shoulders. "What's the matter, Kitty kiddo?"

He still called her "Kitty kiddo," and that made her want to cry even more. She waved a blind hand toward the photographs. "We don't even know if he's dead or alive!"

Justin Lasting sat down on the sofa beside her and took her hand in his. "Don't you ever lose faith, Kitty—you of all people."

She choked back a sniffle. "Sometimes I think I'm down to my last ounce of faith."

"You just hang on to that ounce."

She saw that the age lines in his face had become deep and indelible. His hands shook and his jaw had developed a tremor. She had never mentioned retirement and he had never brought the question up. She hoped he never would. "But the North Koreans won't talk to us, they won't even admit they have him. We can't get through to them, Justin. Nothing's worked."

Justin Lasting pulled thoughtfully at a jowl. "Maybe it's time you consulted your expert."

"You're my expert, Justin."

"Hell, not me—I don't know beans. I'm talking about your

German kid at Harvard—that professor of East European studies."

"You mean Jay's friend, Willi Strauss?" The idea stirred in her like a little breeze.

Justin Lasting nodded. "Wasn't he exchange professor last year at Warsaw University? You picked up the tab. You pick up all his tabs. He knows the Communists, Kitty. That's his job. And he owes you."

Kitty phoned Willi Strauss that afternoon. Twelve days later, he returned her call. "I'm just back from Budapest and leaving for Lima tomorrow. I could squeeze in a meeting at three-thirty tomorrow, but it would have to be here in Cambridge."

It was not exactly the way Kitty would have expected an employee to talk to her, but then, Willi Strauss was not exactly an employee.

"I realize how valuable your time is," she said. "Tomorrow at three-thirty will be fine."

# Chapter 21

WILLI STRAUSS KEPT Kitty waiting barely three minutes after she announced herself to his secretary. The man who came striding out to greet her was tall, with close-cropped steel-blond hair. He seemed to have grown in height and breadth and assurance from the young undergraduate she had met eight years ago. In his handshake and in the line of his shoulders she discerned the strength of a man who played squash an hour a day every day of his life.

"Won't you come in, Mrs. Stokes?"

She walked into his office and stood there, frightened. He'd saved Jay twice before, once as a stranger and once as a friend; and now she was going to ask him the impossible, to save Jay again.

He smiled. "It's been a long time."

"It has, hasn't it."

"Brandy?" he offered. "Smoke?"

"No, thank you," Kitty said. She sat.

Willi Strauss's walls held a neat clutter of mementos spelling out his travels and contacts. There were discreet photographs of Willi Strauss and heads of state, a granite Vietnamese Buddha on the mantel above the fireplace, a papal cross framed on a dark velvet backing. There was a Chinese screen made of exquisite handpainted silk panels. She wondered where he'd gotten it. Such things rarely came on the market since the fall of China, and when they did they cost far more than a professor's salary, even the Stokes professor of modern Eastern European history.

"That's a lovely screen," she said.

"Thank you."

"Mainland China, isn't it?"

"Of course."

"How did you get it?"

He steepled his fingers together. "I never name my sources. But you didn't come to Cambridge to discuss sixteenth-century screens."

"No, Dr. Strauss. I came to discuss sources."

"I don't discuss them."

"You have access to the Communists, Dr. Strauss—and they have my son."

"The North Koreans have your son, Mrs. Stokes—not the Chinese."

"North Korea is a wholly-owned subsidiary of China. Even the *Wall Street Journal* knows that."

"Ah, but who owns the Chinese?"

"I've been to the Russians. They're determined not to negotiate."

Willi Strauss tamped tobacco into a pipe and took his time lighting it. "How can you expect them to negotiate? Your government is dumping thirty thousand tons of TNT a day on their newest client."

"I'm willing to negotiate privately. I'll go to the back room of the lowest dive in the lowest Marxist republic on earth and sign agreements binding the Stokes corporations."

"That could be construed as trading with the enemy."

"Mr. Dulles is waging war against the Soviet Union—I am not."

"You're still an American citizen—like me."

"The Stokes corporations of Liechtenstein and Switzerland are not American citizens, and they command assets of over three hundred billion."

His eye appraised her. "And what do these corporations have to offer the Soviets?"

"Oil and computer technology, state-of-the art industrial diamond drill bits."

"I'm not certain you quite understand the Soviets."

"I understand they're a holding corporation with half of Asia in their portfolio and my son is rotting over there."

"Mrs. Stokes, for the Russians to hand your son back to you would be the same as the United States' admitting it owned Latin America and administered the Brazilian police. You have to approach this tactfully. In my opinion, you should deal through one of the Russian subsidiaries—an inconspicuous subsidiary at that." He exhaled a long, generous cloud of smoke. "For example, the United States is on reasonable terms with Poland. Now, suppose you asked Poland to help."

"But *can* Poland help?"

His eyes crinkled. "It might just turn out that Poland has some surprising inks to North Korea. Russia would cancel out of the arrangement. The Russians prefer to work that way."

"Can you bring it off?" she asked.

His eyebrows and shoulders shrugged simultaneously. "Mrs. Stokes, I'm an immigrant Jewish professor at a liberal university. There's a man in Washington called Joseph McCarthy. I have to be careful."

She tried to gauge this man. The face was like a tribal mask of intelligence and it told her, personally, very little about Willi Strauss. He was handsome, and she sensed that handsomeness was the last thing in the world that mattered to him. His forehead was narrow and high, the nose straight and long and so un-Semitic it surprised her he'd ever been a candidate for Hitler's ovens. "Dr. Strauss," she said, "don't you feel you owe my family *anything?*"

Willi Strauss sighed. "I once had a mother, a father, two sisters and a brother. The Nazis gassed them. You gave me a scholarship and a visa. As a result I'm here and I'm alive. I owe you everything."

"Then, in the name of God or honor or whatever you believe in—help me save my son!"

His eyes met hers and did not flinch. "You're not going to prod me with slogans, Mrs. Stokes."

"Then your answer is no?"

His eyes were the blue of an overcast North Sea. They took hold of what they saw, and what they saw was Kitty Stokes in need. "No, Mrs. Stokes. My answer is yes. We'll do it, but

*my* way—my contacts, my methods, and—after we succeed—
my price."

Nine days later, armed with visas and vouchers and dip-
lomatic passports, Kitty and Willi Strauss settled down into
first-class seats on the New York–Vienna Pan Am flight. As
the plane climbed into the night, Kitty felt cold. She asked the
stewardess to bring back her mink.

Willi Strauss kept sucking at an unlit pipe, checking proofs
of an article for *Foreign Affairs*. Kitty envied his concentration.
She tried to sleep. Halfway across the Atlantic they met the
dawn, a disappointing gray smudge. Sleep never came.

They arrived in Vienna at three in the afternoon and already
the sun was gone. It was dark when they deplaned at Warsaw
and handed their passports to a soldier with a semiautomatic
rifle strapped to his shoulder. The night was drizzling, and the
Poles who drove them to their hotel had sullen, heavy faces.

Again, Kitty couldn't sleep.

In the morning she put on three thousand dollars' worth of
jewels. The drizzle had become snow. There were no taxis and
Kitty and Willi Strauss walked to the ministry. Stingingly cold
snowflakes pushed their way past her fur collar.

Most of the city was yellow cinderblock. It looked decayed
and rebuilt at the same time, like a mouth half-worked over
by a cheap dentist. People and traffic were as sparse as the
skeletal trees gripping the edges of the sidewalk. There were
armed soldiers patrolling in pairs, and a few civilians hurrying
like refugees in old black-and-white newsreels.

The minister was waiting for them in his office. He greeted
them in English. He had eyes and posture of granite and Kitty
knew he was no common civilian poured into a general's uniform but a seasoned and very bored murderer.

Willi Strauss outlined the sorts of exchanges that might be
worked out between Stokes Industries and the People's Republic of Poland. The minister puffed slowly, noncommittally
on his Cuban cigar.

"Naturally," Willi Strauss said, "the policy of the American
Government in no way reflects Mrs. Stokes's personal feelings
toward the liberation struggle in Southeast Asia."

"In no way," Kitty said.

The minister's rimless spectacles glinted at her like the eyes
of a troll lying in wait under a bridge. "The liberation of South-

east Asia," he said, 'is a mere change of costume for a people long since become insignificant."

"I'm still willing to help with the costumes," Kitty said.

"I'll have to make inquiries," the minister said. "Come back tomorrow."

Kitty and Willi Strauss waited at the ministry all the next morning. Shortly before noon the minister's secretary came down the stairs on clattering heels.

"The minister regrets it is impossible." In the secretary's face there was not a wrinkle of compassion. "He can do nothing."

Kitty did not react. A skin of disbelief sheathed her. Willi Strauss guided her back into the street. "You have to understand," he said. "That's the way these people do things."

Her last restraint gave way. Tears froze on her cheeks. Willi Strauss hugged her gently. She pulled away and walked ahead of him, not wanting sympathy or phony reassurances, forcing herself to accept that this time the sun just wasn't going to rise.

When they reached the hotel, word had come for them to be at the airport in forty-five minutes.

Two soldiers hustled them onto a transport plane that had been shabbily refitted to take passengers. They were the only two aboard. Kitty sank into a seat whose upholstery had been patched up with electrician's tape. She stared out the window at the night that passed for Polish afternoon; Willi Strauss opened his briefcase and continued rewriting his *Foreign Affairs* proofs. A young soldier passed a tray of what seemed to be lend-lease Spam sandwiches and lukewarm Nescafé.

The plane stopped at Moscow to refuel and take on five other passengers, and it stopped at Ulan Bator to refuel and let the five others off. Early in the morning of the third straight day of flight, the plane landed at Aoji-Dong, North Korea.

Kitty had expected the Orient to be different from the world she knew, but dawn smelled the same here. The mountains stood out faintly from the same darkness, a little more olive than the olive-drab sky. A man who said his name was Dr. Tim Kom helped them into a jeep marked MADE IN OSHKOSH USA. He asked if they were tired. Kitty let Willi Strauss do the answering.

The road was muddy and pitted with broken tank treads. There were dead cattle in the ditches. The trees had branches like charred bone. Snow lay in patches on straw roofs and on sagging tents in the fields. A truck came rattling by. It was loaded with wounded men, bandaged legs dangling out over the tailgates.

They drove fifteen minutes. The North Korean driver slammed the jeep to a buttock-murdering stop. As Willi Strauss helped Kitty out, something shot up over the mountain into the sky. It was like an exploding red spider with a million wriggling legs.

"My God," Kitty said, "is the war this far north?"

"Not officially," Dr. Tim Kom said pleasantly.

A soldier led them through a barbed chicken wire enclosure. Quonsets had been strung together like a labyrinth of mole burrows. Kitty had to stoop. There were voices and the steel curved walls gave Korean a nattering sound.

The conference room had been hung with astonishingly fake oriental lacquers and pictures, the sort sold to tourists at World Fairs. The chief negotiator was tall and thin and unbelievably old, with a horribly bent arm that looked as though it had been caught in one of Stalin's purges.

He introduced the generals and their interpreters, and Kitty realized she was not going to be given a chance to sleep or change or even to go to the bathroom. Shriveled walnut faces gazed upon her. She gathered that one of the generals had come down from Peking and another was attached to the Soviet trade mission.

An old woman served cups of scorching, tasteless water that apparently passed for tea. The generals began discussing the need to upgrade oil refinement capability in the North Korean peninsula.

Kitty cut in: "Where's my son?"

Walnut faces became rigid and black eyes gazed stolidly. The interpreter spoke. "Negotiate first, son later."

"You've got it backwards," Kitty said. "Son first, negotiate later."

Kitty followed the North Korean guard. Their feet sent rifle-shot echoes volleying through the half-lit corridor. They passed cells with bunks and slop pails. They passed shadows that stirred, but it was too dark to see their sex or race or even if they were human. The stink of rot and feces was not human, and Kitty shuddered and fought the nausea that pushed up against her lungs.

The guard stopped her at the end of the corridor.

A thin gray shape of something anthropoid was lumped on a straw mattress. The door gave a squeak and light spilled in. The figure looked up, squinting. Kitty stared at the gaunt, underweight, unshaved thing, and then she reached to steady herself on the barred door.

"My God—*Jay!*"

Jay stumbled to his feet. It was as though they'd taken her son's body and drained him out of it. He stood framed uncertainly in the darkness of the cell, his face a crater of shock and bafflement.

"Mom?"

She rushed to him. She couldn't help it. She blanketed him in hugs and kisses. "Oh Jay, Jay, I never thought I'd see you again!"

She pressed him to her. His shoulders made alarmingly thin ridges through the flimsy Korean shirt. A sour smell rose out of him, like bedsheets left too long in a damp hamper, and his skin had the dry crinkling feel of old newspaper.

"Jesus Christ," he said. "They weren't lying—it really is you!" He backed off unsteadily, staring as though he still couldn't believe she was there. She supposed she must look strange in her neat little Fifth Avenue suit and her pillbox hat. She'd dressed like that on purpose. She wanted him to know there was still a world and pride and life going on out there.

"How did you get here?" he said, and amazement showed in his face.

"They're not giving us much time, Jay. The general said ten minutes."

He kept staring at her with that happy drunken look. *Let him be happy,* she thought. *Let him be drunken.*

"Mom," he said, "I swear you're getting younger every day."

That he should try to be charming in this pigpen made her want to cry.

"How are you, Mom?"

"Wonderful!"

"And Dad?"

"Sends his love." She sniffled and held Jay at arm's length, tallying up the wreck they'd made of him. *There ought to be some sort of international law,* she thought: *what the hell do we pay the U.N. for?*

He forced a grin. "You think the Army's made a man out of me?"

"You've lost weight. Aren't they feeding you?"

"Same old Mom. They feed me tea and rice and sometimes, for variety, a little rice and tea."

"I'll see if something else can't be worked out." She peered around the cell. It was loathsome and dank, something a rat wouldn't sleep in—ten times worse than any company shack in Bartonville.

"These are the luxury quarters," he said. "I started out in a cesspool with eleven other prisoners."

She shook her head, not believing people could put human beings in such places. "What do you do all day?"

"Nothing. I sit."

"It must be horrible to sit and do nothing. It must be torture."

"It was at first. But then I learned how to think. You know, I'd never done any real thinking in my life until they put me here. And I've realized—I couldn't begin to tell you the things I've realized."

His eyes were much too big for his face. They looked like holes punched by a maniac in a guttering jack-o'-lantern, and they terrified her.

"What kind of things have you realized, Jay? Tell me. I'd like to hear."

He sat and for a moment he was silent. When he spoke his voice was darker, his words measured. "All my life I've hated myself and all my life I've been hurting myself. I screwed up prep school and I screwed up college and I screwed up politics. I screwed up my marriage and I screwed up everyone I ever loved." He looked up at her. "Especially you, Mom."

"Jay," Kitty cried, "oh my poor, poor Jay! Have they been torturing you or drugging you?"

"Mom, this isn't torture or drugs. This is me."

"It's not you, it's not you at all! It's some awful thing they've done to you!"

He did not answer and he did not move but she could see an answer move in him, the tendons in his neck and forearms standing out like wires. "You've been through hell, Jay; and I'm proud of you and your family's proud of you and so's the whole state of Massachusetts."

Jay looked somberly at her, flexing the lines of his forehead.

"I don't want to be a senator, Mom. I don't want to be a husband or father. God help me, I don't even want to be your son. I don't want anything except to be left to myself."

The words ripped from her. "Like *this?*"

"Why not? I'm a coward." He turned away from her. "I didn't have the guts to kill myself, so I enlisted and hoped the Koreans would do it for me. Looks like I screwed that up too."

"Jay, it's not true and you don't mean it."

"I couldn't cope, Mom. I was in over my head and I always will be. Some people can cope and others shouldn't try." He sank back onto the bunk and Kitty could see his eyes, huge and shining against the black wall.

"No, Jay," she said. "This isn't you. This is not my son."

"Look at me, Mom. The real, unshaven, self-pitying me. Can't you see me for what I am? Can't you recognize a bum and a loser?"

"I recognize the man you can be. I recognize my son. You didn't give up when you were a little boy and you're not going to give up now. I'm going to get you out of here. You have my solemn promise."

"What's the point? What do I have to go back to? A wife I can't stand and a job I can't do? I'd rather be dead."

"No you wouldn't. You have a son."

"He'll be better off without me."

"You have a hundred thousand constituents who've proved they believe in you."

"A hundred thousand poor fools who'd sell their votes for a dime."

"Listen to me, Jay Stokes. You've had far more calamity in the last year than most humans know in a lifetime. And you've borne it—and borne it bravely. You're dazed and you're exhausted, but it's not the end. You'll be on your feet again."

"What if I don't *want* to be on my feet? What if I just want to lie down and curl up and sleep forever?"

She looked at her son and saw suicide in his eyes. A knot of fear began to tighten in her stomach. "Jay—for God's sake—you've worked so hard, come so far—you're not going to give up now!"

He sat still and impassive and his voice came in a soft whisper that chilled her. "Mom, I'm sorry. Sometimes I feel there's just nothing left inside me."

"But there is, Jay. There *is*. And we're going to work to-gether—you and I. We're going to get you out of here. We're going to clear up your marriage and your work and we're going to turn your life around."

Jay stared at the slit in the wall, out at the world of mist and drizzle. "Why do you care, Mom? Why do you care for *me?*"

"How could I *not* care?"

He reached a hand for her. "Am I still your son, Mom? Still?"

"Always."

Negotiations resumed the next morning. Everyone agreed that since an American company could not trade with the enemy, an intermediary corporation would have to be set up in a neutral country. Unfortunately, one of the generals refused to consider Morocco and another refused to consider Madagascar. There were blazes of argument that went untranslated. Kitty tried to smile, but the voices nagged at her ears like insects and she felt a hot impulse to slap them down.

Suddenly her Irish mouth got away from her and took charge on its own. "What in the world difference does it make where we locate the company? It can be Mongolia, for all I care— or Monaco!"

Evidently two of the generals found her outburst amusing. They exchanged nods and clucks. The chief negotiator banged the table with the palm of his hand. Quiet was restored. He gazed at Kitty with creaky dignity.

"We shall be friends," he said sternly, and Kitty could hear the sound of threat in his voice.

"We're discussing dollars and drill bits," Willi Strauss cut in, "not political orthodoxies." He drew an analogy to the religious civil wars in Bohemia in the fifteenth century. The analogy went on too long and Kitty could see the generals turn restless under the harangue.

"In short, gentlemen," Willi Strauss said, "the shit has hit the fan."

A puzzled squint came into the interpreter's eyes. Kitty suspected him of an appalling literal-mindedness. The conference was suddenly an explosion of shouts and table thumps. Kitty did not understand the eight different dialects, but she recognized invective when she heard it.

She whacked the table with the flat of her hand. "Will you idiots *shut up?*" she shouted.

Silence slammed down.

She slapped a smile over her rage and took a lunge at reconciliation. She began to talk in the only way that mattered: as a mother and a businesswoman. She offered thirty million dollars in drawing rights on the Liechtenstein corporation, carte blanche on Stokes Industries' patents and technology. She demanded her son.

Willi Strauss stared at her aghast. She didn't give a damn if he thought it was a giveaway.

In twenty minutes she and the generals were old friends. In two hours the deal was settled, and Jay was—*en principe,* as the French say—free.

They let her see Jay once more. She explained that he would be released in the very first exchange of prisoners. "Stay well till then, Jay. Please just stay well."

He kissed her and promised, but when she walked out of the prison and stared up at the sky, she saw his haunted face hovering in the air in front of her, and she knew the problem was not what the North Koreans were doing to Jay but what he was doing to himself.

She had Willi Strauss tack a protocol onto the agreement: Jay was to have a cellmate, a chess set, books, fresh fruit, meat, and letters through the Red Cross. "They won't like it," Willi Strauss said. "He'll be living better than they do."

Nevertheless, after five hours of further negotiating, Jay's captors agreed; Kitty and Willi Strauss celebrated their victory by ordering champagne at dinner on the Bombay-Tehran flight. It was their first semi-decent meal in six days of brown rice and flaked porgy.

"Now tell me about Jay's political apparatus," Willi Strauss said.

"Most people would say he has none left," Kitty said.

"Most people are idiots."

The Air India stewardess brought Napoleon brandy and two snifters. The snifters were glass and Kitty wondered how they survived on an East Asian route.

"How large a staff did he have in the last campaign?" Willi Strauss asked.

"About two hundred full-time employees."

"Can he up that to two thousand?"

"He could up it to twenty thousand. Why do you ask?"

Willi Strauss's gaze fixed Kitty. "I've given you what you asked," he said. "You agreed to pay whatever price I asked in return."

Warning memories stirred in the back of Kitty's head, childhood fairy tales of princesses bargaining with devils in disguise. "Within reason," she said.

"I and I alone shall direct Jay's career."

Kitty let a long, throat-scalding swallow of brandy trickle into her throat. *This man has the habit of mastery,* she realized; *and if I'm not careful he'll be the master of Kitty Stokes.* "That depends," she said. "What did you have in mind for him?"

"A great deal."

"Be specific."

"Mrs. Stokes, I'm not interested in directing the fortunes of state senators—although we shall make your son state senator again. I'm not even especially interested in state governors, although he'll be governor too."

Kitty looked at this man whose mind wasted not a movement. *He's like me,* she thought: *nothing deflects him.* "What does interest you, Dr. Strauss?"

"To be perfectly candid, the problem is not that you are too ambitious for your son, but not nearly ambitious enough."

"I'm doing my human utmost."

"But now there are two of us to do our human utmost. The next decade will be crucial. We must map our strategy, build our forces, lay our groundwork. Jay and his team must be in form when the moment comes to attack."

"To attack what?"

"What do you think, Mrs. Stokes? There is only one office in the world that matters."

He obviously didn't mean Pope, she reflected, and he couldn't mean Premier of Russia. "You actually think—do you really think that one day Jay can be . . . ?" She couldn't bring herself to say the words.

"I don't think it, Mrs. Stokes—I know it. I've known it for many years."

Their eyes met, and in that instant she knew it too. "There's a problem," she said. "His marriage."

"Did we or did we not agree that I was to manage Jay's career?"

"I'm not talking about politics—I'm talking about his life.

The marriage is miserable and they both want a divorce."

Willi Strauss shook his head. "In your son's position, marriage is politics. No President of the United States has ever been divorced. The answer is no—no divorce for Jay Stokes ever."

# *Chapter 22*

WHILE KITTY WAS in North Korea a letter came to Johnny at the Broad Street office. It was handwritten on paper torn from a loose-leaf binder and it was signed *Hedda Hagstrom*. A lot of people with names he had never heard of wanted to see Johnny these days, but this particular name kept tugging at his memory.

And then he remembered the housekeeper from years ago in Bartonville. He sent a reply. He barely recognized the stooped old woman who came to his office. He offered her a chair, trying to be cordial.

"I remember you when you were a boy, sir," she said. "You've certainly grown up."

"Have you been well, Miss Hagstrom?"

"Not very well, sir."

"I'm sorry to hear that. Are you still doing housework?"

"No one would hire me, sir. Who'd trust a seventy-seven-year-old woman, sacked with no reference?"

It did not jibe with his memory that she'd been let go without a reference. His guard went up. "How have you been getting by?"

"Oh, this and that. I've been a waitress in restaurants and I've made beds in hotels—nothing as fine as when I was with the Stokeses. I'm on relief at the moment."

"I'm sorry."

"It keeps me alive. I've lost weight and my gums have shrunk and I need new teeth and relief won't pay for those, but I'm alive."

He wondered why she didn't come right out and ask for money. "Why didn't you tell us you needed help?" he said.

"What would have been the point, sir? You know how Mrs. Stokes hates me." She lifted her eyes and her gaze slid into his like a cold blade. "I don't mean your mother, sir. She had a heart that was all love and we were best of friends. But your Kitty, sir—she hates me."

"I'm sure that's not so."

Miss Hagstrom's eyebrows flattened and her words came tumbling out with the rhythm of rehearsed speech. "She's a clever one, sir. She can hide her feelings and a lot else too. But she never hid a thing from me, and begging your pardon, that's why she hates me."

"You're quite mistaken."

"Your Kitty could fool the Virgin Mary, sir."

It occurred to Johnny that Miss Hagstrom was crazy.

"She wasn't in that house three minutes," the old woman said, "before she had your mother wrapped around her finger. She was going to work on your father too. Any fool could see it was only a matter of time till she got around to you, sir. I was on to her from the start—which is why she had me fired. You knew it was her that had me fired, didn't you?"

Johnny's eyes snapped up at her. She was crazy and a liar to boot. "That's not true. You have no right to say that."

Miss Hagstrom did not flinch. A tiny smile lifted the corner of her mouth. "You remember I used to get hunches? Like that chauffeur that was siphoning gas out of your dad's Hispano Suiza? Or that Norwegian girl that was stealing spoons?"

"No, I can't say I remember."

"Well, I'm a good judge of servants—having been one myself for so much of my life. I had a hunch about that Kitty— from the very beginning."

A surge of impatience began building in Johnny.

"Wasn't just the way she forced herself into the house— went behind my back, she did, gave your mother some sob

story about how her family was gunned down in that graveyard."

Johnny was certain now that she was after money. He couldn't
for the life of him fathom why she bothered with lies, particularly lies that could only turn him against her. And suddenly
he understood: the pathetic old crone was not simply crazy,
but stark raving mindless. He felt an overwhelming sadness
for her.

"And it wasn't just the way she set her sights on you, sir,
because, begging your pardon, she didn't make much of a secret
about that. What really got me to thinking was that doctor
friend of hers—if you can call the likes of him a doctor."

"Dr. Bergman is a fine physician."

"Begging your pardon, sir, but those two cooked up some
kind of deal."

Johnny flicked a warning glance up at her. But if she saw,
it did not deter her.

"Remember how she took sick all of a sudden and he said
she needed to go to the mountains?"

"Of course I remember. She had tuberculosis."

"My cousin Emma died of tuberculosis, sir, and I can tell
you, when you got TB you don't gain weight—you lose."

"It was a mild case."

"I'll say. Four months in the mountains and she was cured."

"People have been known to recover. Particularly from mild
cases."

"And if it was that mild, how come no one could go visit
her? How come the letters had to go through that doctor fellow?
Not that I read them, sir, but I couldn't help seeing the postmarks and the addresses."

Johnny's impatience was spilling over into anger now. "Miss
Hagstrom, my wife had been through a harrowing experience.
She had a diseased childhood and when she was carrying her
first child her health was precarious. It was her doctor's judgment that she had to be given absolute rest. And it's mine that
this is absolutely none of your business. Now, if you'll excuse
me—"

"That baby she brought home didn't look so precarious to
me. Supposed to be two weeks old—looked more like three
months."

"Miss Hagstrom, you're making a very unwarranted judgment about my wife and myself. And I resent it. Now I'm

sorry, but I have a busy schedule today, and—"

Miss Hagstrom sat forward eagerly in the armchair. Her voice became a hot, rushing whisper. "Not about you, sir. About her and that doctor friend and someone else."

Johnny suddenly saw her meaning. He knew if he valued anything in his life he should dodge it, thrust it aside. But an old hesitation from out of the past gripped him. He let her go on.

"Because after she sacked me, I checked into some things. I checked that Bergman fellow and I checked that clinic in Aspen. It took me some time, I can tell you, but I checked. You might be interested to know, the time she was supposed to be having that baby, there was no Stokes in any clinic in Aspen."

"We didn't want publicity. She entered the clinic under an assumed name."

"And the birth certificate was under an assumed name?"

"Naturally not."

"Then who signed it?"

"I'd assume Dr. Bergman did."

"And do you know the kind of work he did in Youngstown?"

"Poor people, I believe."

"Union men and their families. Doesn't it seem funny he'd take time off from all his poor people to go out to Colorado and sign a rich woman's baby's birth certificate?"

It did seem funny. It had seemed funny even then. But Johnny had loved her. He'd been frightened of losing her. He said now the same thing he had said long ago. "Dr. Howard Bergman is my wife's doctor. She has implicit trust in him and so do I."

"And do you know who else's doctor he was?"

"How should I know that? And why should I care?"

"The night of the Bartonville riot—the nine people that died in that graveyard—Dr. Howard Bergman signed the death certificates." Miss Hagstrom snapped open her two-quart purse. She placed a clutch of photographic enlargements on Johnny's desk. They were held together with a paperclip. "These are copies," she said. "The originals are on file in Wilster County courthouse."

Idly, Johnny's finger nudged the paperclip. It left a ghostly mark of rust. "Dr. Bergman had strong labor sympathies," he said.

"And your wife gave him a clinic—why?"

"He's a fine man and a fine doctor and for eighteen years he kept her and that whole town from dying of typhoid. Why shouldn't she want to help his work?"

"This may be part of the reason why she was so helpful, sir." Miss Hagstrom added another document to the pile.

Johnny stared at the faded lines of tiny, skilled penmanship. They seemed to come from another century. "I don't understand what this is."

"It's a page of the parish register from the Roman Catholic church in Bartonville. They tore the church down, sir, and the original register is with the archdiocese. It took me from the day I was fired till last week to track down that page and get a copy. I didn't want to come to you till I had something definite. You see the date, sir?"

Johnny looked again. He saw the year and the month and the day of the Bartonville massacre.

"If you look halfway down the page, sir, you'll see there was a wedding that day."

Johnny looked halfway down the page. It took a moment to decipher the names. One of them of course he knew. The other he did not.

In that moment the mystery of the past fell away and understanding gripped him. He rose trembling to his feet.

"What do you want, Miss Hagstrom? Money?"

He seized his checkbook and scrawled a check and thrust it at her. "Here's your down payment."

Miss Hagstrom's hand did not even move toward the check. Her eyes met his serenely. "I don't want you thinking I'm a common blackmailer, sir."

"I don't think that at all, Miss Hagstrom. You must hate my wife with a hatred that's far from common."

"I just don't like to see anyone getting away with anything, sir." Miss Hagstrom took the check, folded it crisply without looking at it, and tucked it into her purse.

Johnny turned away. His voice was choked. "Miss Hagstrom, I happen to love my wife."

Miss Hagstrom made a dusting motion as though flicking crumbs from her skirt. She rose to her feet. She seemed taller than when she'd come in. "I'm sorry sir, but I couldn't go to my grave with an easy conscience if I'd kept this to myself."

"Easy conscience or not, Miss Hagstrom, you'll keep it to yourself now."

* * *

Kitty's plane touched down four and a half maddening hours late at Idlewild Airport. A traffic accident had closed all but one lane of the midtown tunnel, and by the time the limousine got her home to Sixty-second Street it was after three o'clock in the morning.

She was not surprised that Johnny and the servants had given up waiting and gone to bed. She went to Johnny's room. The bedside light was still burning. Johnny had fallen asleep in his silk bathrobe without turning the covers down. She bent over him and kissed his forehead.

"Johnny," she said softly. "Wake up, darling."

His eyes flicked open. For a moment he stared at her, blinking as though she were a stranger. And then he said, "Hello, Kitty. What time is it?"

She glanced at the bedside clock and the cup beside it. "Three-thirty. You went to sleep without finishing your cocoa. It's all scummy."

"I never finish my cocoa," he said. "Half a cup's all it takes to knock me out." He heaved himself up onto his elbows into an almost sitting position. "You're looking rested, Kitty. Was it a good trip?"

She was startled he could even ask. "Didn't you get my cable from London?"

"It came yesterday," he said, and there was a little less vagueness in his voice now. "Jay's all right, then?"

"He's lost weight and he's depressed, but they've promised to treat him better. They've got him in striped pajamas that look like mattress ticking. At least he hasn't got lice or any of those intestinal bugs."

"That's a blessing."

"He sends his love to you, Johnny. He misses you terribly."

She would have expected Johnny to be beside himself with happiness. Instead, he was odd and faraway with a peculiar deadness in his voice. "Jay's quite a boy," was all he said.

"I think all this hell he's gone through will wind up making him stronger." She sat down on the edge of the bed and Johnny moved his leg to make room for her. "Johnny, we're going to have to talk to a lawyer. Someone from the international division, someone reliable."

"That can wait till tomorrow, can't it?"

She supposed he was tired. She forgave him. She pressed his hand in hers and went on excitedly. "I had to bargain with the North Koreans. They want drill bits and industrial diamonds and we have to work something out through a Portuguese company in Goa."

"We don't need to work it out tonight, do we?"

"We have to work it out in a day or two and I want you to have a chance to sleep on it. Technically we're trading with the enemy, except on paper we're trading with a neutral and it's the neutral that's trading with the enemy, except we control the neutral, so there you are."

Johnny's hand withdrew. He looked at her questioningly. "And are they going to release Jay?"

"We have to wait for the State Department to arrange an exchange of prisoners. The North Koreans will set Jay free with the very first batch."

"Once they get their drill bits and diamonds."

Sarcasm was very unlike Johnny. She sharpened her senses, trying to feel out what it was that had shifted in him. "I had to offer them something, Johnny. It's not as though I were handing over blueprints for an atom bomb."

"No, it's not like that."

"A few drill bits and diamonds aren't going to alter the course of history. Besides, everyone says the war's going to wind down. Willi Strauss says it hasn't got a chance of lasting another year."

"Willi Strauss seems to have a fondness for predictions."

"I'm doing the right thing, aren't I, Johnny?" It had never occurred to her that he could possibly question her actions, but for some reason it occurred to her now. "You can't abandon a son just because some people in Washington are scared of Communists."

"I don't know if it's right," Johnny said, "but what choice is there?"

Kitty sighed, relieved that he saw it her way. "The lawyer has to be reliable, Johnny. And fast. The fastest we've got. This whole thing has to go through in forty-eight hours."

He was silent a moment. And then he stared at her. It was a fond stare but an odd one, as though she were a photograph in an old family album, more remembered than real.

"It means everything to you, doesn't it?" Johnny said.

She nodded. "It's as though God took him and then gave him back."

"I guess that's God's prerogative."

She had never known her husband to mention God in that tone of voice. "You look funny, Johnny. Is there some reason you're staring at me like that?"

"I'm glad for you, that's all. You've worked all your life for Jay. It would have been dreadful if you'd lost him over there in Korea. It would have been the most dreadful thing in the world for you."

But Johnny didn't look at all glad to her. He looked something else, something she couldn't put a name to. It was as though he'd been working much too long at the office. She saw a pile of papers on the bedspread next to him. She peered at them.

"Johnny, what are these?"

"I was having another look at my will."

"Why in the world? You're well, aren't you?"

"I felt the will should be up-to-date—just in case you had bad news about Jay."

She shuddered at the very idea. "I wish you'd keep that thing in the office. It's bad luck to have it at home."

"I'll take it down tomorrow."

"Thank you, darling." She knew she was being silly and superstitious, and she was grateful to him for indulging her. She kissed him again on the forehead. "And goodnight."

His voice stopped her at the door. "Kitty—I'm truly glad."

She turned, smiling, glad she had Johnny to come home to. "You said that already, darling. I know."

"I'm glad we've had these years. I'm glad I've known someone like you. I've never been sure what I wanted in life, but you've always had purpose enough for the two of us. In a way, that's kept me going."

She frowned, trying to fathom the oddness of him. "I'm not sure I understand you, Johnny. That's an awfully strange thing to say."

"I'm saying thank you—for all the years."

"But Johnny, we've still got a lot of years ahead."

"Thank you anyway."

She shook her head. "You are odd, Johnny—but I don't

suppose I'd love you if you weren't. Sleep tight."

"You too."

At breakfast Johnny knocked her life down.

"If it's all the same to you, Kitty," he said, "I'd like to stay in Maine."

"Stay?" She laid her butterknife back on the plate, half a butterball still clinging to it. "What do you mean, stay?"

For a moment he was silent, as though trying to find exactly the right words. "I've had a hectic life and I'd like the rest of it to be peaceful."

A wall of astonishment went up in Kitty. "You don't want to spend the rest of your life in Maine, surely."

He didn't answer. She saw it was exactly what he did want, and she saw he had thought it out carefully.

"What about work?" she said. "What about the company?"

His shoulders rose and fell like a sigh. "I'm practically retired anyway. Don't worry, I wouldn't expect you to come with me."

There was a still and empty space between them. It was as though a kaleidoscope had shifted a bare fraction of a degree and a totally unsuspected pattern leaped out of bits and pieces that had always been there.

"I just don't have your energy, Kitty. And I don't want to tie you down."

There was an undertone of defeat to what Johnny was saying and the way he was saying it. It disturbed Kitty. She felt death had moved one step nearer.

"It sounds as though you're talking divorce."

Johnny shook his head. "You know me better than that, Kitty."

"I don't know if I know you at all." Her teeth bit down on her lip. "Do you want it to be a legal separation?"

"Not necessarily," he said. "That will depend."

"On what?"

"Whether or not you object to Vicky Jennings' coming with me."

Kitty felt no shock, only a numb hole where shock and jealousy should have been. She sat silent, staring into her coffee, trying to slow the rush of her thoughts. She had believed in her bond with Johnny, believed that they were equals and friends and, if not lovers, at least loving. Now, without warning, the bond had snapped. She had her children, she had her possessions, but she no longer had Johnny.

"Do you love her?" she said. "Is that the reason?"

"No, Kitty. I love you."

Her mind clutched for some sort of understanding. "But you and Vicky—want to live together?"

"I'm comfortable with her."

She could feel terrors as old as her first breath waiting to pounce on her defenselessness: fear of the dark, fear of dying, fear of being alone. "And you're not comfortable with me?"

His mouth shaped a half-smile and his eyes held hers a moment. "I'll always be comfortable with what we've had."

She looked at him. His gaze was gentle with the peace of a burden laid down, and she knew that whatever they had had was finished. *Marriages fall apart all the time*, she thought. *I'm strong. I'll get through this*.

But there was a suffocating weight in her breast and it did not pass. When Vicky came to Kitty's workroom that morning at ten, as she had every morning of their working lives, Kitty just stared at her, realizing she had overlooked some hidden signpost in this woman.

"I feel I ought to shoot you or break something or get drunk."

"Then maybe you should." There was none of the cringing of the caught-out husband-stealer in Vicky Jennings. She faced Kitty neatly and firmly, with no shame in her eyes.

"I guess my pride's hurt more than anything," Kitty said. "I knew Johnny must have someone, but I never dreamed it could be you. You seemed such a perennial virgin."

"Don't hate me, Kitty. I tried so hard not to deceive you."

"You didn't deceive me. I deceived myself. I thought you were my friends—both of you."

"We are. And I hope we always will be."

"'Always' is a pretty long chunk of time. When are you and Johnny leaving?"

"As soon as my work here is finished. How long will you be needing me?"

"You've spoiled me, Vicky. There won't be a day of my life I don't need you." Kitty sighed. "All right, business as usual. We have eight dozen calls to make to Washington."

\* \* \*

Johnny placed no obstacle in the way of the North Korean ransom, and Kitty placed none in the way of his move. It was a simple exchange.

Within two weeks Jay's freedom was an accomplished fact, awaiting only a break in the political climate. Willi Strauss suggested it might be effective to have Jay awarded a Medal of Honor while he was still officially missing in action.

Kitty pulled strings. In a sad little Rose Garden ceremony, President Dwight D. Eisenhower handed medals to parents of six boys killed in action and to Kitty and Johnny. Early that spring, when the political break still had not come, Johnny and Vicky relocated to the house in Maine.

At first Kitty panicked at the thought of being without Johnny, not knowing what was happening and, worse, not knowing what was going to happen. For the first time in her life she glimpsed the terrifying temptation of despair.

She built barricades.

She scheduled meetings, hired architects for a new wing on the children's pavilion, gave five trunks of clothing to Good Will, discovered that opera—which had always seemed so safe and boring—was very upsetting and gave away all her tickets. She looked up old and ex-friends, gave to every charity that asked, decided to watch her drinking very carefully. She hid a book of Kahlil Gibran under the Kleenex in her bedside table, swallowed her fear of the subjunctive and hired a French tutor guaranteed to be ruthless. She actually went to a lecture series sponsored by one of her foundations.

Stuffing her days with activity, she stamped out all leisure, all thought. When sleep proved elusive she started taking the collected works of Emile Zola to bed. Zola consoled, suggesting things could be very much worse. He also suggested there was not nearly enough sex in her life. Of course she'd known that a long time.

She adjusted to her changed status, perhaps because there was nothing to adjust to, not even so much as a snicker at a board meeting about her grass widowhood. It seemed that whatever the Stokeses chose to do was acceptable in the eyes of the world.

* * *

Vicky Jennings reported to Kitty faithfully by letter every week. In an age when most communications went by telephone or telegraph or inter-office memo, Kitty got very little personal mail. She enjoyed Vicky's gossipy handwritten notes. She came to look forward to them.

It pleased her to hear that Johnny was buying books on gardening and experimenting with hybrid roses. She was glad he'd gotten out his oil paints and pastels and taken up art again. She remembered that he had had talent, once.

And yet she still could not understand his motives, and not understanding worried her. One weekend evening in Maine as she and Vicky sat on the terrace—just the two of them with after-dinner drinks, staring out at the moonlit ocean that seemed as sleek and restlessly muscled as a shark's skin—she asked, "Why is Johnny doing this? Why is he here?"

Vicky's face was dark, strained with the effort of framing her reply. She was almost half a lifetime older than the girl Kitty had hired. She was an equal now. There was no bossing her or cross-examining her. She studied Kitty gravely and her fingers drew a restless musical note from the rim of her glass.

"He's never told me," she said. "I've never asked."

"He doesn't confide in you?" Kitty asked, amazed.

An undefinable look crossed Vicky's face. "Some things," she said, "but not that."

Kitty had an ear for people. She could tell when they were lying, just as she knew by rapping if a wall were hollow. She knew Vicky was not lying. Whatever she was not telling she honestly did not know. Kitty stared at this softly groomed woman with neat gray hair. She supposed Johnny loved the gray hair. Otherwise Vicky could have had it dyed.

"Is it my fault?" Kitty whispered. "Please—don't try to spare my feelings. I have to know."

Vicky gazed out at the sky above the Atlantic, where the Big Dipper seemed to have lost part of its handle. "He loves you, Kitty. At night he says *your* name, not mine."

Kitty felt the darkness around her. The air shivered. "If Johnny ever needs me," she said, "if there's ever anything I can do, any way I can help, you'll let me know, won't you?"

Johnny himself, she knew, would never tell her if he needed her; and the truth, perhaps, was that he never would again.

Vicky's gaze met Kitty's. "Of course I'll tell you." There was no triumph in the voice, merely kindness unmarred by pity.

"Thank you, Vicky," Kitty said. "Thank you for loving him."

In the fall Kitty went to Howard Bergman for her physical. She had the appointment after Eleanor Roosevelt and exchanged hellos with the former First Lady.

"What's wrong with Eleanor?" she asked Howard.

"Just a checkup," he said.

He hammered Kitty's reflexes and tapped and poked and squinted. It seemed to her he had recovered from the shock of his widowing and was his old methodical self again.

She sat waiting for what he would say. "Well, Howard—am I alive?" She drew her examination smock a little tighter around her. He hadn't even noticed her tan.

He sat looking across the table at her. "Are you drinking more coffee than usual?"

"Gallons."

"Why?"

"To keep me going. It's better than drugs, isn't it?"

"Are you depressed over something?"

"I'm trying not to be."

"What's the matter, Kitty?"

"Johnny's leaving me. That's the wrong tense. He's left. I'm alone, Howard, and I hate it. There's no one I can talk to. I didn't talk to Johnny much, God knows, but what a difference a few grunts at the breakfast table make. I haven't got anyone now." It was hard to believe she was saying or feeling these things. The tightness in her throat seemed to belong to someone else. "I'm frightened."

Howard watched her sympathetically. "Frightened of what, Kitty?"

"That things are going to stay this way from now on."

"Nothing ever stays the same. Count on it."

He touched her hand and suddenly there was no fear in her, no worry of seeming an idiot or a child. Tears spilled out of her and he held her in a tight clasp that needed no words.

A long time afterward he was still staring at her and she saw concern in his handsome, middle-aged face. "How long is it since you've had yourself a real cry?"

"Not so very long," she lied.

"You ought to indulge yourself a little more often. It's healthy for you. Now if you're all cried out, let's go have dinner. I'll call the Côte Basque."

"Howard, I can't."

"I'm sorry, Kitty—you can and you will. It's about time you lavished a modicum of creature comfort on yourself—or allowed me to."

His hand was still holding hers, and it told her everything she had tried to deny for five years.

"What about your other patients?"

"I didn't schedule any after you, Kitty."

She realized this was to be it, then—their first date, the widower and the de facto divorcee. Under any other circumstances seduction would have been in order, but there was nothing left to seduce—they had known one another too long and too well. By unspoken consent, they settled instead for a sumptuous dinner.

They gorged themselves on *quenelles de brochette* and *steak au poivre*. They downed a bottle of Pouilly Fumé and two of Château Margaux. They spoke very little but smiled a great deal, like playmates. From time to time, when Howard's gaze rose to meet hers, her breath seemed to break into sharp little pieces in the back of her throat.

It was dark by the time they came out onto Fifty-fifth Street. A Checker cab was letting off a fare in front of the St. Regis and they grabbed it. They sank into the leather seat, happy and a little bloated.

"Where to?" the driver asked.

They looked at one another and began laughing. "We should have planned this a little better," Howard said.

"It wouldn't be any fun if we had," Kitty said. "I've got an idea. The Stokes Fund keeps a suite at the Carlyle. There's no one in it tonight."

Madison Avenue slid smoothly past the cab windows. Howard pulled her against him. Their mouths came together and stayed locked till she had to turn away for air.

"Shouldn't we wait till we've checked in?" she murmured.

"We've done enough waiting," he said.

They must have been drunk. They kissed in the elevator, and the elevator man pretended not to see. Kitty used her key to let them into the suite.

She had no sooner closed the door behind them than Howard was sliding the dress from her shoulders. The hooks of her bra gave him no trouble at all. He held her at arm's length, staring at her free-hanging breasts with just the same look in his eyes Tyrone Duncannon had once had.

"You're tan," he said approvingly.

She was glad she was tan, and when she unbuttoned his shirt and pressed against him she was glad he exercised.

He led her into the bedroom. "Which bed?" he said.

"I always sleep on the right."

"So do I."

"Then it's going to be crowded."

"Good."

She abandoned herself to the smooth shuddering contentment of skin against skin. *It's so easy,* she thought, *like jumping into the water and swimming,* and she wondered what had taken her so long.

"That's why they call it foreplay," she said. "It's a game, isn't it?"

"And we both win," he said.

His mouth was on her breast and then went down slowly to where his hand had stroked her into preparedness. There was no talking after that, only winning.

Kitty would have thought she was a little too old and too set in her ways to learn comfort, but it was surprising how easily she adjusted to having a lover. She lived in limbo that year, guilty at not feeling more guilt, relieved at the relief she felt from the simply biological joy of being touched by another human being, glad that Howard was there during the months of helplessly waiting for Jay to come home.

She remembered very little of the beginning of the affair, except that the least pressure of Howard's fingertips could turn her into a mindless bundle. They made love often and sometimes ridiculously, like young people, in stopped elevators and empty offices and Cadillacs parked in country roads. They were together in their desire as she could remember being together with few people.

Life and the world suddenly took on the aspect of opportunity. She enjoyed things. *Parsifal* at the Met was beautiful when you had a knee to press yours against.

"Darling," she said, "shouldn't I change doctors?"

Howard's eyebrow rose in a now familiar half-arch. "Why?"

"Now that you're my you-know. Isn't that like family? Don't medical ethics forbid you to treat me?"

"The whole point of a you-know is that it's not family."

"But when I come to you for an examination it seems so . . ."

"So what?"

"Pornographic."

"Well, Kitty, that's why I never schedule patients after you."

It surprised her that happiness could be so uncomplicated.

By winter of 1954 what had begun as a naive and simple Red scare had developed into a witch-burning anti-Communist panic. Edward R. Murrow, one of the directors of the CBS Television network, invited Kitty to his screening room and showed her seven hours of the Army-McCarthy hearings.

He had chain-smoked four packs of cigarettes by the time the lights came up. "Kitty," he said, "will you back me up if I blow the whistle on Senator McCarthy?"

"What kind of backing do you need, Ed?"

"I'm going to edit this footage down to an hour show—use the senator's own words and actions to hang him."

"He has a lot of admirers—and they'll want your scalp."

"I don't care about his admirers. Will Stokes Industries withdraw its advertising from CBS?"

Kitty thought about that. The senator was a demagogue and a disaster for the country. The tide would very soon have to turn against him, and for the sake of Jay's political career Stokes Industries might as well be riding the incoming waves. "You're not planning any exposés of the oil industry, are you, Ed?" she joked.

"Not for a millennium or two."

Murrow's shows were seen by more viewers than any other television news program. By supporting him now when he needed help, she could win favorable, possibly glowing coverage for Jay in the years ahead. That there would be years ahead she had to take on faith.

"Okay, Ed. Stokes Industries will do better than that. We'll sponsor this show, and if any advertisers boycott the network because of it, we'll buy up their space. Good enough?"

Edward R. Murrow broke into a grin. "Good enough, ma'am."

That evening Kitty phoned Joe Kennedy in Hyannisport.

"There's a lot of your boy Bobby in the Army-McCarthy footage," she said.

Joe Kennedy chuckled. "He's looking good, isn't he?"

"He looks like shit, Joe. You have no business letting him work for that madman, at least not on camera." She told Joe Kennedy what CBS was planning. "Use your clout, Joe. Have them edit away from Bobby and onto Roy Cohn—unless you want Bobby remembered for all time as an s.o.b."

The Murrow show on McCarthy aired in March, and it signaled the return of a degree of rationality to American politics. U.S. negotiators could begin to deal with North Koreans without being labeled Communist agents, and in July a cease-fire was finally negotiated.

Forty-eight hours later, Kitty stood alongside a runway at Idlewild International Airport. The day was blazing sun. She shaded her eyes as she squinted up at the stratosphere for some sign of the military transport bearing her boy home.

Willi Strauss was with her. Howard Bergman had offered to come, but for appearance's sake she had decided against it. Johnny had had to stay in Maine—for health reasons, he'd said. She did not understand his absence, but she accepted it.

It wasn't till twenty-three minutes after ten, over an hour behind schedule, that a great shrieking bullet of a military transport dipped down from the sky, flicking a shadow across the asphalt. Kitty's heart stopped. The ground crew shoved the movable stairway to the plane. After an endless moment the door cranked open. Military and State Department nonentities began trickling down the stairs.

A sudden, annihilating doubt gripped her: *he's not on board—something's gone wrong!*

And then came two four-star generals and the American ambassador to Free China and, behind them, almost as though leaning on them, a bent, shrunken figure that paused at the top of the stairway. It drew itself up to an instant's full height. The sun caught the gold glint of a medal pinned to the jacket. A hand came up in salute, quick and exact as a straight-edged razor snapped open. There was a moment's immobility, a pained smile . . .

*Jay!* Kitty realized. *Here! home! alive!* A stab of pride and gladness choked off her breath.

Jay's hand fell. Gripping the rail, he began his slow, limping descent of the stairway. Several steps behind, a Red Cross nurse followed, and her distance emphasized the courage of his walking without crutch or human support.

Memories swelled within Kitty, blotting out the image on the runway. She saw the infant and the boy and the young man, glowing with hope and health and promise: and now this torn, tortured scarecrow, bearing the honor of his nation.

He had covered almost half the distance between them. Kitty ran forward, shouting Jay's name, and he fell the last stumbling step into her arms.

"Jay! Oh my dearest Jay!"

"Hiya, Mom."

"Can you stand?"

"Depends how long."

Kitty thought how noble he was, lean and brave as an ancient martyr. "Only a little longer," she said.

Willi Strauss took Jay's other arm. "Can you make it as far as that building?" he said.

"You remember your old friend Willi Strauss, don't you?" Kitty said. But she saw from the blank look on Jay's face that it was hard for him to remember, and she realized how much the year's captivity had drained him.

"Sure," he said after a hesitation that was just an instant too long. "How are you, fella? Good to see you."

Kitty and Willi got Jay into an isolated room in the customs shed.

"Jay," Willi said, "before you go out to meet the press, there are a few things—"

"Can't it wait, Willi? I'm bushed. I need a drink and a shave and a long, long nap."

Willi pulled a narrow steel flask from his breast pocket and handed it to Jay.

"Thanks, fella." Jay plugged the flask to his lips.

"It's not an interview," Willi said. "You don't have to answer questions. They just want to photograph you."

"I look like the wolf man," Jay said.

"That beard is perfect for the homecoming hero."

"So I'm a hero?"

Willi nodded. "Page one."

"Bullshit."

"Jay," Kitty said, "the way you face those men could affect

the rest of your political career. I know it's not the first thing you want to think about, but be sensible—please."

"All I want to do for the rest of my political career is sleep."

She couldn't fathom his listlessness. It frightened her. He was alive and home and free, and yet he was a robot. It was as though he had brought his prison cell with him. "Jay," she said, "aren't you glad to be back? Aren't you glad about anything?"

He wiped his mouth with the back of his hand and waved a reek of brandy. "Mom, I am unbelievably, unspeakably happy. I've never been so happy in my life. I'm so goddamned happy I could even kiss Toni."

"I'm glad you feel that way," Willi Strauss said, "because that's one of the matters we have to discuss."

Wariness flicked in Jay's eyes.

"Do you suppose," Willi Strauss said, "there's any way you and Toni could manage to get along? For a little while at least?"

"Sure we could get along—twenty thousand miles apart."

"Isn't there any possibility for compromise?"

"I don't mean to sound cruel. Toni's had a tough life. She's had that hip and that family and she's had me, and I understand why she's the way she is. But one of the great things about being in a little box in Korea was that Toni was on the other side of the earth."

"Willi doesn't mean you two should get back together," Kitty said. "Not like before."

"What *does* he mean, Mom?"

"Well, there is Jason to think of—and appearances do count."

"Come on, divorce isn't a scandal these days."

"But it seems such a waste," Willi Strauss said. "After all, Toni's very popular with the press and the public."

"Let the press and the public marry her."

"And she's calmed down enormously," Kitty said. "She's truly grown during this—ordeal."

"Don't you think you might be able to arrange some sort of—well, some sort of facade with her," Willi Strauss said, "if the details were carefully worked out?" What Willi Strauss did not say was that Toni was no more anxious for a facade than Jay, but the Clinic had put her new hip specialist on salary and she had very little choice if she wished to keep walking.

"What would the point be?" Jay said.

"Your political career," Willi Strauss said.

"Hey, fella, I haven't got a career, remember? I got drunk and walked out on it."

"From some people's point of view," Kitty said, "what you did was very brave."

"Not showing up to vote on my own bill, you call that brave?"

"Putting your life in jeopardy for your country, when as an elected official you're exempt from the draft—I call that brave," Willi Strauss said. "And so do a hundred thousand men and women who happen to be your constituents."

"I don't have constituents—not after a year's hooky."

"There's a huge reservoir of goodwill for you in Massachusetts," Willi Strauss said. "As far as those men and women are concerned, you didn't desert them—you served them in a higher and far braver way by putting your life on the line for them."

"Hey, fella," Jay said, "excuse my asking, but what business is it of yours anyway?"

"Willi's on the team now," Kitty said.

"Team?"

"Your team. Willi says you'd be a fool not to run for governor. I know it's much too early to be discussing all this and it's the last thing in the world you want to talk about on your first day home—but we ought to bear it in mind as an option."

Jay's eyes went from one of them to the other. "You two are funny—you call yourselves realists and you're dreamers."

"It doesn't have to be a dream," Willi Strauss said. "You have the inside track."

Kitty pinned Jay's medal over the flap of his breast pocket.

"What's that?" he said.

"You won it," she said.

"The hell I did."

She straightened his jacket so the photographers would be sure to see he'd come home a lieutenant. "Couldn't you act glad to see Toni—just a little?" Kitty said. "She really is fond of you, even if it's not the sort of fondness that makes a marriage work. She does want to help you, Jay, and she'll do anything she can for your career. Be nice to her—please?"

Jay shrugged. His smile broke through. "I take it back, Mom. You're a realist through and through. You've got me campaigning already."

"I'm only thinking of your future."

"Well, I suppose it's thanks to you I have a future to think about."

Willi Strauss opened a door. "Toni's waiting, Jay. In there. Be good to her."

Jay sighed. "I'll try—for the photographers' sake."

"Toni first," Willi said. "Then the press."

Jay went through alone into a large undecorated steel tub of a room. There was a Pan Am poster of the Plaza Toros in Madrid, and there was Toni coming hesitantly to meet him, expensive and fragile as a single cut orchid.

"Hello, Jay."

"Hello, Toni."

She stopped a distance away, like a once disobedient but now repentant dog afraid of being struck. She peered up at him from under a broad-brimmed gray felt hat. The hat made her look all sorts of things he knew she wasn't, like old-fashioned and very young and very shy, and he suspected she'd spent the better part of an hour picking it out of her collection.

"Where's Jason?" he said.

"Waiting outside. We're supposed to have a minute alone, just you and I—to get reacquainted."

"Is that what you want, Toni?"

"If it's what *you* want."

"How's Jason?"

"Jason's fine. He wants to see you."

"I want to see him."

There was a trembling in Toni's stare. "You've lost weight. That's quite a haircut they gave you."

"At least they left the roots in."

She didn't seem to know how to take the remark. She smiled with a tentativeness that was almost painful. "Jay, we won't be able to talk later. I just wanted to say ... I'm sorry we argued."

"Which argument, Toni? Which of the hundreds?"

"All of them. I just wanted you to know I'm sorry."

To his amazement, he felt an indefinable pity for this creature whose eyes were dark wounds bleeding in shadow. "I'm sorry too," he said.

She began crying. He sensed the crying was real.

"Why so happy to see me?" he said.

She took a step toward him and he put his arms around her. "I'm so scared," she said.

"What of?"

"Of your mother and Willi Strauss and what they're planning for us. Jay, I'm so scared of being chained together and hating each other and everything starting all over again."

"Does it have to start all over again?"

"It will," she said. "I know myself. And I know you, a little." She gripped him. "Jay, you can divorce me." She was pleading with a desperation and earnestness he had never before seen in her. "You can have Jason. You can have whatever you want. You can start over again. You'll still have your career and we won't have to spend our lives hating each other. We can make up our minds now and walk out of this room free. Jay, say it. Say you'll divorce me. Say it now, while we're still friends."

Jay peered at Toni and her broad-brimmed hat and an aching indecision rose in him. What she said was true and perhaps she even meant it as a kindness and not a tactic. Yet coming from Toni, truth and kindness carried an undertone of contradiction. He turned her words over in his mind, searching for some telltale fingerprint of motive.

"You've met someone, haven't you?" he said.

Bewilderment flashed through her face.

"You want to marry someone else and you want to dump me and Jason and make a million while you're at it."

Her eyes were fierce and roaring. "I hate you!" she spat.

"That's never been a secret."

Her voice was suddenly murderous. "Goddamn you, Jay Stokes! You had your chance—don't ever say I didn't give you your chance!"

# *Chapter 23*

THE NATION WAS hungry for heroes, and Jay Stokes was the right hero with the right organization behind him. Willi Strauss concentrated his political strategy on image and media management. It was for the sake of image that Jay went back to boots and jeans and workshirts. It was for the sake of image, too, that Toni was put in the hands of a psychotherapist who could be counted on to prescribe tranquilizing drugs of the requisite strength.

The incumbent from Jay's old district was dislodged by the offer of the directorship of a Stokes foundation in Honolulu, and Jay was again elected state senator from Berkshire County.

Though the legislative budget allowed Jay a staff of eight, that was not nearly enough for Willi Strauss's plans. A privately payrolled staff of thirty-two was assembled. It included two graduating *Law Review* editors from Harvard and the playwright who had written Jay's speeches six years earlier.

Willi Strauss taught Jay the two essentials any politician must know: how to use money to get the work done one couldn't do oneself—this was usually called "delegating authority," though in fact it was a delegation of labor; and, just as important, how to avoid negative publicity.

Again, money was the key. Media space was bought up—not simply during election campaigns, but year round, in the name of the lesser-known Stokes subsidiaries and of companies doing business with them. The space was usually devoted to harmless public interest ads, but it was available at a moment's notice whenever circumstances required the planting of an item favorable to Jay Stokes. Just as importantly, it was permanently unavailable to the opposition.

The system worked beautifully in getting Jay reelected to the state senate, and when it came time to run him for the governorship, Willi Strauss was able to orchestrate an almost 70 percent media blackout of the rival candidate.

On an impulse, Kitty went to Cole Porter in his suite at the Waldorf Towers. She asked if he would consider writing a campaign song for Jay, as Irving Berlin had done for Ike in the last election.

She'd not seen Cole since the horseback-riding accident at Piping Rock Country Club that had taken his leg. He was impeccably dressed and groomed, still the same gallant man who'd sent her roses thirty-five years ago.

"I'm sorry, Kitty." He smiled sadly. "I'm writing a musical for television, and I'm in deep, deep trouble with my producer."

"Well, it was only a thought," she said regretfully.

"Come on back when he's running for President and I'll be glad to oblige."

Even without benefit of a Cole Porter jingle, Jay won the election. His victory was hardly stunning—a mere two-point lead on his opponent—but a win was a win.

In January he moved into the governor's mansion. He spent his first day in office, with the aid of his eight-man state-paid staff, hanging his French Impressionists.

On their first anniversary Howard Bergman had given Kitty a pair of diamond earrings from Harry Winston. On their second he gave her a two-foot doll from F.A.O. Schwartz with green agate eyes and a porcelain face and red hair the color hers had been as a child. The doll had a dress of real silk and lace and shoes of real satin.

When Kitty opened the box and saw what he'd given her, she burst unaccountably into tears. The only doll she'd ever owned had been a little rag thing.

"How did you know?" she said.

He smiled. "Doesn't every little girl want one?"

She loved Howard Bergman.

New England springs are always seasons of cold and rain, but that spring—when it finally came—was one of the harshest in living memory. On the coast of Maine, the skin-peeling five-foot snows of March gave way to the bone-soaking wind-lashed rains of April. The Atlantic broke over the seawall that John Stokes Sr. had built thirty-two years earlier and came flooding across the lower lawns of the estate.

Johnny Stokes put on his boots and raincoat and went to check the burlap wrapping on his rose bushes. He came back with a running nose and sneezes. Two days later he had come down with a cough and a low-grade fever.

He had always had a slight smoker's cough, but the sound of this one was different. It seemed to come from the depth of him and Vicky Jennings did not like it. Through the bath that joined their bedrooms she could hear the spasms and hawking that ripped at him. The fifth night they went on for almost an hour. She wrapped herself in a bathrobe and went to him.

"Johnny, you've had this cough for a week now," she said. "Tomorrow we're calling the doctor."

His eyes were sunken and sleepless. The hollows in his face were shadowed. She touched a hand to his forehead. Something cold and damp throbbed beneath the drum-tight skin.

"I'm going to get you a hot-water bottle," she said.

"I'm all right," he protested. The words seemed to fight their way up through layers of phlegm.

"You don't look all right."

"The cough keeps me awake," he said. "If I could sleep, I'd be fine."

Vicky fixed Johnny a hot-water bottle and a mixture of honey and whiskey that had been her mother's remedy for coughing. She slipped into bed with him. They snuggled with the hot-water bottle between them.

He managed to sleep four hours without coughing.

The next morning he drove into the village to see the local doctor. When he came home in the early afternoon he was turned in on himself and preoccupied. Vicky asked about the doctor and the examination. He answered in grunts. He spent the rest of the day in an easy chair, watching the light of the fireplace sift across the study walls.

Vicky tried to interest him in a cup of tea. He shook his head. When she reached to touch him he moved away from her hand—not cruelly, but gently, as though for her sake he had quarantined himself.

He telephoned long-distance that evening and two days later he had a visitor from New York—not the doctor that Vicky had expected but a lawyer. They spent the better part of the day locked in the study, and twice Vicky heard Johnny's shouts rise above the lawyer's. Five hours later they emerged. The lawyer, white-faced, did not stay to dinner.

"Is there a problem?" Vicky asked Johnny.

"Just some papers," he said. "This new breed of lawyers think they're too good for paperwork."

Vicky was not convinced. His eyes avoided hers and sweat gleamed in the lines of his face. She was certain something was the matter.

He coughed less after that. Vicky found a bottle of cough syrup in the medicine cabinet. The local doctor had prescribed it and according to the label it contained codeine. In her next letter to Kitty, Vicky mentioned as casually as possible the cough and the lawyer. In her reply Kitty did not pick up on either, so the matter rested there.

It was none of Vicky's business. She was not Johnny Stokes's wife, and though she loved him, she was not a paid nag.

Still she could not help wondering why a man would see a lawyer about a cough.

With the coming of the sixties, society loosened up a little. The governor of a large northeastern state divorced his wife of twenty-five years to marry a younger woman; the younger woman divorced her husband to marry the governor; and the governor put the husband on his private staff. In another era it might have been called mate-swapping for money, but now it was called sophisticated, a sign of the way things were.

No one remembered when Ingrid Bergman had been anything but a saint, and Elizabeth Taylor stole Debbie Reynolds' husband and still won an Academy Award. The man in the White House had mistresses and people knew it, and what was more, they enjoyed knowing it.

In the summer of Jay's fifth year as governor of Massachusetts, Kitty and Howard traveled openly together to Europe. They visited Somerset Maugham at his Côte d'Azur villa. Pi-

casso and Cocteau came to lunch, speaking only French, and
Winston Churchill sketched an astonishingly bad portrait of
them and gave it to Kitty.

Kitty and Howard flew on to Marshal Tito's private island
in the Adriatic. She dislocated a knee on the rocky beach and
had to cut short the vacation and fly home.

Howard advised her to conduct business from a chaise longue
in her bedroom till she mended. When Willi Strauss came
calling three days later, she could tell it was not a simple
welcome-home or get-well visit: there were new lines in his
face.

"You love Jay, don't you?" he said.

She dropped a smile over her amazement. "What in the
world kind of question is that?"

"How far would you go to help him?"

"Willi, tell me straight out: what's wrong?"

Willi snapped open his briefcase. He placed documents in
Kitty's hand. The accounts and amounts differed from sheet
to sheet, but there was a dismal sameness to the deficits at the
bottom of each column.

Willi sat silently, letting Kitty soak in the facts. She grasped
that Jay's government was broke, flat scandalously cleaned-
out broke. The books were so crooked and out-of-whack that
no accounting shell games could save the situation.

"It can't be hidden through another election," Willi said.

"Well—what's the solution?"

His fingertips played against one another as though he were
doodling on a mirror. "Massachusetts will establish public corporations for housing, hospitals, libraries, airports, highways.
Their budgets will be met by special bond issues."

Kitty's mind jumped ahead. "And the money you raise by
selling these bonds will be siphoned off to pay interest on these
debts?"

"It's standard accounting," Willi said, "and it's relatively
legal under the Massachusetts constitution."

"But, Willi, public bond issues have to be voted by the
taxpayers."

Something predatory unmasked itself in Willi's face. "The
taxpayers won't get a chance. The bonds will be floated by
Rockland County, not the state."

Kitty sat up in surprise. "But Rockland County has no
money."

Willi nodded. "The proposition authorizing the bonds will

also authorize an increase in welfare payments. The voters will pass it. They're all on welfare and it will be money in their pockets."

"And how is this county of paupers going to back its bonds?"

"With the county's moral pledge," Willi said. "In fact, we're calling the Rockland County bonds Moral Obligation Notes."

"And when the county defaults?" Kitty said.

"The state is obligated by law to pick up the tab."

It was a clever scheme and an ugly one, but Kitty did not bother pronouncing a value judgment. Morals were not her field. Jay was.

"These bonds reflect on Jay's political reputation," she said. "And they'll be worthless at maturity."

"Maturity is thirty years away," Willi said. "By then Jay will have long been in and out of the White House."

"I understand how you've structured it, Willi. But even if you can stick Massachusetts with debt service in perpetuity, somebody still has to buy the bonds *now*. And there aren't that many fools born in a thousand years."

He was silent, but it was not a confused or baffled or apologetic silence. There was utter tranquility in him.

"How in the world do you expect to raise the money in time?" Kitty proceded.

His eyes fixed on her, tiny and tight as coiled springs. *"You're* going to get the money, Kitty."

She realized her mouth was hanging open. "You know, Willi, I used to think you were sly. But now I don't think so at all."

"Oh, I'm sly," he said. "I'm very sly."

"Not if you expect me to throw a quarter of Stokes Industries into a liquidation sale to post bail for the Commonwealth of Massachusetts."

There was caginess in his eyes and she caught the wink of something rapid and catlike. "Kitty, you haven't reviewed your assets."

She flung down the documents, exasperated. "What do you expect me to do, sell off Sumatra and take a 90 percent loss to salvage your preposterous Rockland County bubble?"

"You don't have to sell anything, Kitty. You don't have to buy anything."

"Then what in the world are you suggesting?"

"Your son."

For a moment she didn't grasp what he was saying.

"The other son, Kitty. The banker. Bart. Ask him to underwrite the bonds."

Her mind instantly flicked the idea aside. "Bart hates Jay."

"He doesn't hate *you*. Go to him, Kitty. Go as a mother. Give him your hand in love and reconciliation."

Kitty stared out the window at drizzle and early evening. An ache twisted in her. "Just to sell bonds?" she said. "What if he says no? What if he won't even see me?"

Willi's hand was on her shoulder. "Bart's your flesh and blood. Kitty, that's the greatest *in* of all."

As always, Willi was right.

Bart took Kitty's phone call personally. "Of course, Mother," he said, though he used to call her "Mom." "Come down to the office and let's talk."

She got her dislocated knee and her crutches into the limousine and she went down to Wall Street.

He was waiting just at the door of the inner office. Mother and son stared at one another across a gap of nine feet and eighteen years and she could not tell what he was thinking. After a long moment Bart held out a hand and Kitty kissed him.

"Hello, Bart."

"Hello, Mother."

It was a cold, sunny exchange of greetings, correct as a winter's day. Bart was very straight in the shoulders as he led her into the office. He closed the door. Soft polarized window light played over desktop Brancusis and late-period Cézannes. Kitty and Bart were alone. She was relieved when he sat in the chair facing her, not at his desk.

"Mother," he said, "why are you here?"

A great many things had changed. He dressed well. He was handsome now. She sensed he had lost a little of his fear of her, and of the world too.

"Don't you think it's about time?" she said.

But he wasn't about to let her wriggle free so easily. "Why, after all the years' silence, do you suddenly pop up?"

She swallowed. Her hesitation was novel to him—and pleasing. "How's Beth?" she said. For an instant the non sequitur seemed to hover in the air.

"Do you give a damn?"

His tone shook her. "I wouldn't ask if I didn't."

"Beth's fine. She'll be happy to know we met today. She thinks family rifts are unhealthy."

"I agree with Beth," Kitty said.

"How's Father?" he asked.

"Didn't you used to call him 'Dad'?"

"How is he?"

"He's slowing down. He lives in Maine now."

"I'd heard," Bart said, and Kitty wondered what exactly he'd heard.

"He's well," she said. "He gardens. He paints. He's developed a collector's passion for Toby mugs. Do you remember, they used to sell them at Abercrombie's? They're a rarity now—the authentic ones. He's had special shelves put into his dressing room to hold them. He misses you."

Bart ached. All the lies of the past nibbled at him like a tide lapping at a beach. He felt eroded and old. "He misses me, does he? Tell him I'm in the phone book. My secretary is very good at taking messages."

"I wish you wouldn't sound that way," Kitty said. "It's not like you."

"I'm not much like me anymore, Mother."

Kitty sat staring at him, rebuffed. Her mind combed the rushing years. There'd been so many once, and now they seemed almost used up. Bart was no longer the boy who had been her son. He had children. She had grandchildren that she'd never even seen or held.

"You've put on weight," she said. "It suits you."

"*You* haven't," he said. "That suits you too."

"I count calories, drink skim milk, that sort of nonsense."

"You didn't drag your broken leg down here to compare diets."

"You're not making this easy for me, are you?"

"No."

"You have three children?" she said.

"At last count. And you?"

It took an instant for the sting to register. "Bart, can't you see I'm trying?"

"You shouldn't have to try," he said.

"Sometimes things aren't the way they should be. Bart, it's not my fault alone. Your father still hasn't accepted realities."

"At least he's made up his mind about me," Bart said, "unlike you."

"That's not so—that's not fair. Don't attack me, Bart. Not when I'm trying so hard. Can't we please be friends again?"

Bart stared at this stranger, as lovely and smooth and neat as her tailored salmon silk, and his eyes stung with blinked-back salt. He'd accepted her absence, learned to live with the secret pain of it, and now she was destroying the one certainty she'd ever given him—distance. A toy-smashing, cat-strangling rage pushed up from his stomach and gripped him by the lungs.

"What good is 'friends'?" He leaped up. "You're my mother! If you can't love me, then be angry at me—shout at me, curse me, strike me—at least show that you have a parent's feeling, even if it's only hate! Give me *something*, Mother—give me some part of yourself that *cares!*"

She shrank back from his windmilling arms and flying spittle. Her mind clutched for some way to charm him out of this. "Of course I care, how can you think I don't?"

"Because we've shared this earth for thirty-eight years, and not once in all that time have you given me the slightest sign that you even regard me as your offspring. No matter how I've hurt you or failed you, I'm just as much your son as Jay is. And I always will be, whether you accept it or not."

"You've never hurt me," she said quietly. "You've never failed me."

"Then no matter what the hell it is you hold in your heart against me—"

"There's nothing I hold against you."

He shouted her down. "My son and my daughter are just as much your flesh and blood as Jay's son, yet you've shut them out. Why? Because you don't like my wife's pedigree?"

He had not intended to shout at her. He saw confusion, wild and uncontrolled, shining in her eyes. He saw her fingers dig into her chair as though it had suddenly taken a roller-coaster lurch forward. "That's not it, Bart, that's not it at all!"

"What if you or one of my children should die before you've even met? It would be as though you'd never had that grandchild! It would be extinguishing part of yourself—and for what, pride? Your grandchildren are you—just as much as I'm you—and one day we may be all that's left of you. So I suggest you stop regarding my wife as scum and me as Jay's afterbirth!"

And then Kitty did something Bart was defenseless against because he had never known or imagined her to do such a thing. She screamed at him, a long shrill yowl that was not even her voice but the screech of an animal trapped against a wall.

"Will you shut up?" she cried. "Will you just shut the hell up?"

Bart stared at her. Tears came so gradually that they did not spill but pooled in the corners of his eyes, making her image waver.

There was an instant of frozen immobility and she hobbled to him. "Bart, I'm sorry, I didn't mean—"

He looked up at her with marveling eyes. "Do you realize that's the first time you've ever lost your temper with me?"

She held back, trying to understand, failing utterly. But when he smiled she smiled, alert to his every shift, making herself a mirror because instinct whispered to her that it was the only way to win him over. "Is it?" she said. "I suppose maybe it is."

He began laughing and Kitty paced her laughter to his.

"When we were boys," he said, "you used to lose your temper at Jay all the time and never at me."

"But you were an angel—of course I never was angry at you."

"You don't know how I used to pray you'd be furious at me—just once—spank me, just once."

"I never needed to spank you."

"I broke that tulip vase the Danish ambassador gave you just so you'd spank me. And you never did."

"*You* broke the vase?" She put appropriate amazement into her voice even though she couldn't for the life of her remember the vase. Right now it was the most important vase in the world. Jay's bonds depended on it.

Bart nodded. "And Jay got the spanking."

"I had to spank Jay all the time," she said. "He was a devil." She sensed that a poisonous abscess had been lanced, a crisis passed.

There was a silent moment of recovery, and Bart asked, "How is he?"

"Your brother's doing wonderfully," she said.

"I've read the papers, Mother. I mean how *is* the old son-of-a-gun? Tell me some of the things that don't make the New York *Times*."

She told him some of the things that hadn't made the New York *Times*—innocent little funny things. Bart smiled and nodded, and gradually the conversation settled into a lurching question-and-answer rhythm. They were like two hopeless amateurs learning to bat a tennis ball back and forth across the net.

Beneath the chatter, Kitty tried to take the temperature of his feelings. The jealousy of his brother seemed to be safely past, something they could ignore. She inchwormed her way toward the Massachusetts Moral Obligation Bonds.

"Mob," Bart said.

"What?" There was panic in her eyes, and she reminded him of an aerialist who had missed her trapeze.

"Moral Obligation Bonds," he said. "The initials spell 'mob.'"

He was smiling, and she folded her hands and smiled back. "I've been nagging Jay to throw some business your way," she said.

He froze, not at first believing he'd heard it. In those two seconds all of the bad years came washing back like spilled coffee. He understood what she was after. He wasn't surprised. He'd known since childhood that there was only one son in her heart, and that son was his brother. He'd known she judged the rest of humankind according as they could help or hinder Jay Stokes. He'd known it all his life except for one moment of brief shining ignorance in this room, and now the old knowledge was back, cutting like a fine-tempered knife that had never lost its edge.

*I'm her child too,* he thought. *How can she not love her own child? How can she show it like that?*

He watched her and saw she did not know what she had killed. She did not know that till that moment he had loved her better than anyone in the world. He did not speak because he was not sure he could keep from coming apart.

"After all, we are a family," she said brightly, "and why shouldn't you get the commission?"

Bart leaned forward. Kitty sensed he was on the verge of turning cooperative and she warned herself not to rush things. This was the most delicate part of the maneuver.

"I'll need to know a little more about these bonds," Bart said.

Kitty explained. Bart listened. It was obvious to him she had rehearsed her speech down to the smallest hesitation, and he understood the scheme long before she'd finished.

"Let's see if I've got this right, Mother. Thanks to anomalies in the Massachusetts constitution, these bonds are perfectly legal. They're also perfectly fraudulent."

Kitty flinched. Bart had something she wanted and it gave him control. It seemed he was stretching the taste of control like a boy teasing a wad of bubble gum. He was frightening her for the sheer Halloween fun of it.

"They're loaded dice," he said, "and they're loaded against the buyer. At maturity they won't be worth a dime. A second issue will have to be floated to meet interest on the first, and a third to meet interest on the second, and so on until the SEC steps in."

She kept her voice neutral, uninflammatory. "They'll make money," she said softly.

"For the government that issues them," he answered.

"And the broker that sells them," she said.

"And the speculators that puff them," he shot back.

"All right, they'll make money for speculators," she cried. "So what? You're a banker, not a virgin."

"I'm a damned good banker, Mother, and as far as I can see, Jay's bonds will make money for everyone but the residents of Massachusetts. They'll be left with a billion-dollar tab and a tax collector's gun at their heads."

The smell of his righteousness made the anger rise in Kitty, but she fought to hold it down. "Massachusetts is not your bank's concern, Bart."

For a moment he was silent, almost sullenly silent. He was a house with the shutters closed and she couldn't see a thing move inside him. Finally he steepled his fingers together and gazed at her.

"I have one question about this ingenious bond issue," he said. "If I involve the bank, will Father invite Beth and me to Maine?"

Kitty couldn't believe she'd heard it. She couldn't believe he wanted nothing more than that.

"I'd like Beth to see the house where I grew up," he said softly. "I'd like her to meet you and Father again."

She wanted to laugh. She had pulled it off after all. She felt giddy as a stripped helium balloon. Promises spilled out of her. "Of course Beth can come—and the children too. Come to Maine. Come to Sixty-Second Street. She can meet me anytime she likes. As for your father, all that will take is a phone call."

She went to him and kissed him.

"You understand the bank's involvement can't be public," he said. "We'll set up a syndicate of regional banks. They'll buy the bonds with laundered funds. There'll be no link to me."

It struck her that he was setting it up like a foolproof crime. Of course it wasn't a crime at all, but there was no harm in being foolproof and there was no harm in keeping the Stokes name out of it either.

"That's even better," she said. She held him at arm's length, staring happily. "We're friends now, aren't we, Bart? Let's never be anything else."

Kitty moved quickly. She had Bart and Beth to Sixty-second Street, to a dinner of reconciliation and cold tarragon lobster. It went much more easily than she would ever have hoped possible.

Beth had changed. She dressed beautifully. She used the right forks. She demonstrated a forthright intelligence that kept conversation lively. And it was obvious from her eyes that she worshiped her husband.

*Why,* Kitty wondered, *couldn't Jay have found a woman like that?*

Kitty flew to Maine the next day in the small family jet. She found Johnny down by his rose bushes, pleased and not at all surprised to see her. They chatted and strolled. His hair was almost white, and he walked nowadays with the deliberate step of age. He had developed an annoying little cough that kept interrupting conversation.

She worked around to the subject of Bart. "After all, he is your son too," she said. "It would be a shame to let this grudge drag on another dozen years. Who knows if any of us will even be around then?"

It was a fine Maine day. The air was sweet with fresh-mown grass and somewhere in a maple two orioles were polishing a duet.

Kitty and Johnny came to the summer house and sat down on the round bench. Johnny smiled, but his eyes were serious in their nest of crinkles. "Do you want me to see him again, Kitty? Do you really want that?"

"I want you to see them both," she said. "Please Johnny. I want it more than anything else in the whole world. After all, we are a family. Shouldn't we start acting like one? While we still have time?"

The sound of surf rose and fell in the distance like the breath of a sleeping giant.

"You've never taken his side before," Johnny said.

"And I've been wrong, Johnny—very wrong."

Beth came into the bedroom just as Bart was hanging up the telephone. He sat with the phone in his lap gazing out the window. She could tell by the quality of his silence that something had just changed the shape of his life—and of hers too.

"That was my father," he said. "That was Dad."

She tried to hide her surprise. "What did he want?"

"He wants to see us," Bart said. When he turned toward her there was something new in his eyes. They did not look like Bart Stokes's eyes at all, but like a little boy's on the brink of tears.

She sat on a chair facing him and pulled a careful neutrality around herself. "Both of us?" she said.

She kept her gaze fixed on him but he did not look directly at her. A moment passed and she could see the muscles of his throat working.

"Dad wants to make up," Bart said.

"He said that?" she pressed. "Those were his words?"

"He says it's time. He wants to set things straight for once and all."

Bart took her hand. She could feel the fever of happiness in him and she did not trust it.

"And do you want to make up with him, Bart? Do you want to set things straight?"

"I do. Oh God, I do."

She could see he was trying to blink back tears. They came anyway, bright glistening smears in the tiny lines of his face. *Why can't I be happy with him,* she wondered. *He's wanted this for so long and now at last it's happening.* But a warning screeched inside her.

"It seems sudden," she said, "doesn't it?"

"Twelve years isn't sudden," said Bart.

"When does he want to see us?"

"Next weekend."

She was silent, gathering strength. "Bart," she said, "are you sure?"

He nodded. She wasn't sure the nod told the whole story. She looked at his joy and she feared for him. She pressed his hand to her cheek.

"Then I want it too, my darling."

On Saturday morning Bart and Beth flew to Bangor. They rented a car at the airport and drove to the old estate. Bart got out of the car and stood in the driveway gazing at the old house. To Beth's eyes the ivy on the brick walls needed pruning and had obviously needed it for several years. The lawn was scrubby and brown. It was not at all the green palace he had described from his childhood memories.

As he lifted the brass doorknocker her heart was beating so hard that it pained her. There were two cannon thuds and silence closing over them. He gripped Beth's hand. From inside she could hear a jumble of footsteps and voices. She felt him brace for hectic hugs and hellos.

But when the door opened there was only a middle-aged woman called Vicky Jennings. "Welcome home, Bart," she said.

Beth saw stress and worry and a smile that did not disguise a thing.

"It's good to have you back." Vicky Jennings brushed a quick kiss onto Bart's cheek. He introduced Beth. Vicky greeted her with the same quick cordiality. She herded them toward the living room.

Bart stopped short at the sight of the old man in the armchair. The living-room shades were half-drawn. In the dim light Bart's father had the look of a hospital patient who had been permitted to put on clothes and sit up to receive visitors. His tweed jacket did not appear old or even worn, but it was oddly large for him.

Bart's legs tensed beneath the press of his flannels. "Hello, Dad," he said.

Johnny rose from his chair. He stretched out his hand with the painful ceremonial dignity of an ambassador. "Hello, Son."

The old man seemed sad and resigned, as though life had become too long for him. Bart couldn't understand it. John

Stokes Jr. had everything in the world and he chose to sit alone in a dark room watching TV with the sound turned down.

Bart half-turned to include Beth. He swallowed to moisten the dryness in his throat. "You've met my wife," he said.

"Once," Johnny said.

*Twice,* Bart thought.

"How do you do, young woman?" Johnny said.

"How do you do, sir," she answered.

Father and daughter-in-law did not so much shake hands as graze fingertips, and then John Stokes Jr. and Bart and Beth sat in the living room of the old country house and tried to find something painless to talk about.

Bart heard no love in his father's voice, none of the promised reconciliation. He could not fathom the look on his father's face or the desolate silence beneath his chatter. There was sadness in it and hurt and anger; there was nothing that Bart had hoped for, but there were a hundred things he had feared.

"You must wonder why I asked you here," Johnny said. His hands fidgeted in his lap. "The fact is, it's time to put my life in order. I've debated how to do this. It seems to me indirection would be crueler than directness. So I'm going to attack the matter head-on."

The room seemed suddenly small and cramped. Bart had a disturbing impression that there was less light, less oxygen than a moment ago.

"You knew I didn't approve of your marriage. I still don't."

Bart blinked. Disbelief caught him in the chest like the kick of a horse. "I thought you might have changed your mind."

"I haven't," the old man said.

Bart jumped to his feet. "Then why in God's name did you invite us here?"

"To ask you one last favor. Now, please, please just hear me out."

*How could I have not known,* Bart wondered. *How could I have been fool enough not to know till this moment that it was just another trick?*

"If you and this young woman do as I ask," the old man said, including Beth in a long, appraising glance, "I'll cut Jay out of my will."

Bart could not believe he was hearing it.

"The two of you may divide his share as you see fit. And I'm prepared to put that in ironclad writing. My request is this:

I want you to divorce. Naturally, I'll pay the expenses."

In that instant Bart saw his father with the clarity of day, a crazy old man tottering toward sunset. It was Beth who broke the silence.

"Please, may I say something, Mr. Stokes?" There was gentleness in her voice and not a shadow of anger. "You don't need to answer. Just listen to me a minute and try to understand, and then I promise I'll never bother you again. I know you don't respect me. You can't. But I know something else too. You and I respect the same thing—the truth. If it weren't for the truth, you and I could have been friends. Maybe we could even have been father and daughter. But the truth had to be faced and it had to be spoken, and so we'll never be father and daughter. That's a high price, but we paid it—and we have our truth. Now there's another truth to be faced and spoken. I'm talking about your grandchildren, Mr. Stokes. Even if you could divorce me out of the family, they'd still be your flesh and blood—and mine. We would always be linked. No court can change that."

Johnny stared at the woman. There was something natural and unfussy about her, and it showed in the face that was pale and quiet and utterly without makeup or guile. He sensed in her a layer of truthfulness, hidden and unbreakable. He had a disturbing conviction that he had known her before, long ago. He remembered another girl, one who had been, briefly, good-natured and giving. He remembered a faraway season of happiness that had never returned.

"Bart can have other children," he said.

"But *you* can't, Mr. Stokes."

Johnny bit back anger and for an instant his pulled-tight mouth gave him a lipless look. He mastered himself and gathered all the gentleness left in him into one last appeal. "Release my son while there's still time. Free him to marry another woman."

Bart cut in. "What other woman do you have in mind?"

The old man drew himself up stiffly. "A decent woman. A woman your grandmother could have been proud of."

"Did it ever occur to you I might not want your idea of freedom or decency?"

"You will, someday." Johnny had set the course of this meeting and he did not deviate from it. With surgical precision, he explained the division of Jay's inheritance. He explained the benefits for Bart and Beth, the trust funds, the tax exemptions, the income in perpetuity.

For Bart it was as though his father had reached out and struck him. For a moment he was stunned. He was aware of a vein pumping furiously in his throat and a salt taste flooding his mouth. "Your financial concern is all very touching," he said, his voice tight, "but it comes a little late in the day to carry much weight."

"I'm only asking you to learn from my mistake," Johnny said.

"What mistake?" Bart shouted. "Your wife? Your mistress?" He whirled on the old man. "Your life?"

The stillness in the room took on the heaviness of a coffin lid. There was a violent wrench in Johnny's left arm, as though a synapse somewhere inside him had shorted.

"That's a cruel and unjust thing to say," the old man said in a barely audible voice.

"And your judging me isn't cruel or unjust? How dare you presume to judge me, let alone buy me? I wouldn't trade Beth for ten million of your fortunes!"

Johnny did not answer.

Bart stared at the old man huddled before him in baggy tweed, collar and necktie drooping like a noose on a skeleton. Gradually Bart's rage passed and left only a feeling of utter finality. It was a feeling of unaccustomed peace because there was no hope whatsoever left in it. He realized he had come to the end of this path: there was no need to go through these brambles ever again.

"Come on, Beth," he said. "We're going home."

# Chapter 24

FOR MOST OF his short life, Jason Stokes was a quiet boy—so quiet, in fact, that it was not till his eleventh birthday that Kitty glimpsed the true depth of him.

Toni had organized a celebration. It was to have been a family affair, but Jay at the last moment had had to stay in Boston to steer a tax abatement bill through committee. Toni had bulked out the guest list with some neighbors and their children. A Boston caterer had set up a tent and buffet on the beach at West Yarmouth where Toni and Jay were renting a summer house.

The children were playing on the beach, but Kitty noticed that Jason did not mix with them. He sat in the tent listening to the grown-ups, not talking. The breeze ruffled his red-blond hair. His fingers drummed a pattern on his knees over and over, never changing. Something seemed to shut him off from the world. In his silence Kitty sensed intelligence and burgeoning dreams.

The air was turning chilly and the sky was darkening when the boy asked, "Can I go swimming now, Mom?"

"Not so soon after all that ice cream," Toni said. "You'll get cramps. You'd better wait an hour."

There was a moment of smoldering blue-eyed silence and then the boy got up and left the tent. His stride was long and straight and he set out along the Cape Cod shore away from the other children.

"Something's bothering him," Kitty said. "Is it that his father's not here?"

"Jason's used to that," Toni said. "His father's never been home for any of his birthdays."

Kitty assumed that the remark was an exaggeration. As a matter of course she never replied to any of Toni's *in absentia* carping at Jay, but simply refused to let it irritate her. She lowered the backrest of her deck chair and closed her eyes and rested. She could hear waves and birds in the sky and not far from the tent the laughing of children. She was troubled that her grandson was not among them.

Five seconds later it happened. A boy's voice cried out for help. Kitty's eyes snapped open. Toni was staring out of the tent, face white with terror. A premonition stabbed at Kitty.

"Jason!" she cried.

The two women ran quickly up the beach. The wind had risen and the waves had turned ugly and crashing. Low clouds were sweeping in darkly. The sea was dotted with whitecaps. A cold lump formed in Kitty's gut.

The ocean was black now, hurling itself at the beach with low moaning rushes. The earth shook with the explosion of ten-foot waves. Kitty squinted into the wind. A dozen yards from shore two heads and necks barely extended from the trough between two swells.

She could make out two boys. One was dark and wiry, arms flailing crazily. The other was blond and tan, wearing the same striped sports shirt Jason had worn. They were struggling not only against the surf but against each other. For a moment the blond boy prevailed, fighting the pull of the current and the thrashing of his companion. The strokes of his arms carried them both forward in perfect timing with the waves.

But now the sea sucked him back. The wave behind the boys flew apart, somersaulting them backward. It closed over them, burying them, and came crashing forward. The ocean spun the two figures around and around again, jumbling them like tossed bits of a jigsaw puzzle.

And then the blond boy staggered up the beach, dragging

the dark boy with him. Out of reach of the sea, he laid the boy down on the sand. He peeled off his own shirt and bunched it into a pillow beneath the dark boy's head. A woman rushed forward, shouting. Another straddled the dark boy and began artificial respiration. There were cries for a doctor, an ambulance.

The blond boy moved through the circle of onlookers. His arms and shoulders were a crisscross of cuts and scratches. One of his eyes was bruised and puffy.

Toni held out her arms. "Jason!" she shrieked.

His teeth made a white nervous gash across his face. "I'm sorry, Mom," he said. "I had to go in. He was drowning."

Toni wrapped him in a fleecy towel and began patting fiercely. Whatever the boy was thinking was hidden behind the silent mask of his young face. He stood there swaddled and shivering and he reminded Kitty strangely of something, someone. Water beaded his face and goose bumps stood out on his arms.

And then Kitty saw it.

He had his grandfather's hay-colored hair and his eyes were glowing green embers. Certainty rose in her like a radio signal on a stormy night. *He's a hero*, she realized. *He's Tyrone Duncannon all over again*.

Bart Stokes met his nephew only once in his life. The boy was an adolescent by then and it shocked Bart to realize how swiftly the years had passed. They had been comfortable years, years of growth. With the birth of a baby girl his family numbered four. So far as he could tell, they were a happy family.

He had managed his bank aggressively and imaginatively. With branches and affiliates in forty-eight states and thirty-one foreign countries, it was ranked by *Fortune* magazine the sixth largest in the world and still growing. His wealth had increased to many times the fortune he had inherited. It was only his lack of flamboyance and the ingenuity of lawyers and accountants that kept him from being rumored a billionaire.

He owned a Fifth Avenue apartment in New York City and a country home with 142 acres in Brewster, New York. He owned a ski lodge in Aspen, Colorado. He employed twenty-three full-time servants, including gardeners, to maintain his three homes. His children went to private schools. He belonged to four clubs but rarely went to them. He gave generously and unobtrusively to charity. He made it bank policy to extend credit to the working poor. This was not at all the same thing as charity but was popularly felt to be.

The press treated him favorably; of course the press barons borrowed from his banks to finance their expansion. Governors and senators came to him for advice and for money. Harvard gave him an honorary doctorate of law. So far as the general public knew anything at all about him, they liked him. They considered him a successful man and a good one.

Bart Stokes considered himself neither, for he did not think in such categories. He knew he was not evil and, for him, that was enough. Except for his wife he had few real friends.

Jason Stokes could have been a second friend.

The opportunity came one night in June. The watchman at Bart's country estate saw something bunched up on the ground outside the gatehouse. He shined his flashlight on what he took to be a discarded mailbag. It moved. He saw it was a young boy, unconscious and filthy. He crouched to examine the youth. There was a dollar and seventeen cents in the hip pocket but no identification.

The watchman telephoned the main house. It was eleven-forty Saturday night. By midnight the boy was stretched on a guestroom bed.

Bart Stokes sat watching the young stranger's face. The doctor came at twelve-thirty, wearing blue jeans over his pajamas. He examined the boy silently, poking and tapping and stethoscoping. He rolled back the eyelids and for a long time shined a penlight into the unresponding pupils.

"This kid is drunk," the doctor said. There was an edge of impatience to the diagnosis.

"Then it's not serious?" Bart questioned.

"That depends whether you consider fourteen-year-old drunks serious or not. It shouldn't take more than twenty-four hours for him to come around. He'll have a headache. Give him some aspirin and fruit juice. If he can hold food down, feed him."

Beth Stokes stood in the doorway, knotting the belt of her bathrobe. "Wouldn't the boy be better off in a hospital?" she said. "He's a complete stranger to us."

"There's no reason he can't sleep it off here," Bart said.

The doctor glanced from one of them to the other. "That's for you to decide. There's nothing else I can do, so goodnight."

He was gone, and Beth Stokes stared at her husband, unable

to decide whether she was irritated or enraged or just plain curious about the workings of his mind. After more than a decade of marriage he still had ways of baffling her.

She did not argue. "Don't stay up too long," she said.

She left him standing by the bed. He was still there when the boy awoke the next day.

"You're Jason Stokes," Bart said.

The boy nodded. There was pain in his face and it was more than just the pain of a hangover. Bart brought aspirin and fruit juice and food. He watched as the boy ate hungrily and then tried to stand.

Jason Stokes was tall and thin and handled his body awkwardly.

"Don't push yourself," Bart said. "Don't get up before you feel ready."

The boy lay down again.

"Jason," Bart said with absolutely no judgment in his voice, "why were you drinking?"

The discussion that followed was long and personal and basically one-sided. Bart listened quietly, sharing the boy's pain, and very slowly, like an animal moving one paw at a time, Jason inched toward the truth. Bart had known next to nothing of Jason and his childhood, but as he listened icy blasts of memory gusted through him. It was as though his own life were repeating itself. He recognized the same mother who had never cared and the same father who was never there and the same loneliness that throbbed like a toothache in the soul.

The empathy in Bart grew till he could no longer tell if he was hearing the boy or reliving the nausea of his own past. He placed his hand on Jason's. "I'm sorry," he said. "I'm so goddamned sorry."

And then Jason said something that oddly touched Bart. His voice was barely audible and his face was soft in the dying window light. He said, "I want to come live with you."

Bart found it difficult to speak. He understood why Jason did not want to live at home and he understood what was being offered—a chance to adopt a son and in the same stroke to leave his brother childless; a chance to balance and close that long unpaid, long overdue account.

But he couldn't help wondering if the boy was really all that innocent. He wondered how much Jason knew of the old hatred and hurts between Bart and Jay Stokes; he wondered if this might not be some cunning attempt to inflame the old wound all over again.

"Do you know what I think is wrong between you and your dad, Jason? I think he's hurt you and you're determined to hurt him worse. I felt that way about someone once. It ate me up. Don't let it eat you up, Jason. You have too much life ahead of you."

The boy got to his feet. He spoke with an icy rage that chilled Bart. "You don't see him for what he is. None of you do."

"Fathers are always larger than life to their children. You see him as much more than he is. You need a little distance, Jason."

"Look what he's done to that state," Jason cried.

Bart could not believe the boy was so worked up over his father's politics or bookkeeping. It went deeper. "I understand your idealism," Bart said softly. "You're young and you're just discovering what it is to believe. And I understand your outrage. You want the world to be perfect."

"That's not it, Uncle Bart."

It was odd to think that this was the only person in the whole world to whom he was Uncle Bart.

"I just thought there was some difference between a banker and a thief."

The conversation had taken an unexpected swerve and Bart could only stare in bafflement at the boy.

"I know a little about the banking system," Jason said. "We studied the Federal Reserve in American history."

"It sounds like you go to a good school," Bart said.

"I did a term paper on the Rockland County bonds."

Suddenly Bart glimpsed what might be tearing at the boy. "Did you," he said neutrally.

"They're not worth a penny."

"The market doesn't seem to agree with you."

"The market never got a chance to agree or disagree. Those bonds are backed by zilch and they were foisted on the public."

"That's a pretty reckless conclusion coming from a pretty young man. Is that what you said in your term paper?"

"No, but it's what I'm saying to you. You're involved, aren't you? You pulled the strings. Why? What made you do it?"

It astonished Bart that a boy so young could feel a rage so

violent, so political. He'd thought that violence and politics
came a little later in a young man's life. "Tell me, Jason—
what did you get on that term paper?"

"I got an A-minus."

"And did you find any evidence linking me to those bonds?"

"Of course not. You don't work that way."

"And did you find anything illegal in the bonds themselves?"

"You draw a pretty wavy line between illegal and crooked.
Tell me this, Uncle Bart: who pays when the whole scheme
goes bust?"

Bart took the measure of the boy's anger. It was almost at
critical mass. All it needed was a focus. He realized that with
one word he could turn this child into a bomb and explode it
in Jay Stokes's face.

But a voice in him resisted. *I have no right to take another
man's child. A man's child is his posterity, his only survival.*

Bart Stokes was not a cruel man, but he feigned cruelty at
that instant. "Look, Jason. In many ways your father is im-
pulsive and badly advised, and he may not be everyone's idea
of a governor. But why don't we leave that to a majority vote
of the electorate and not the hotheaded opinion of one Groton
freshman?"

The ploy was crude but effective—too effective. John Stokes
III took off Bart's pajamas and put on his own dirty clothes
and left Bart's house. Bart never saw him or communicated
with him again.

It occurred to Bart to contact his brother and express concern
about the boy, but then he thought better of the idea. He suspected Jay would take it as meddling and it would only fuel
whatever was already wrong between father and son.

From time to time, as the years went by, an image of the
boy flashed into Bart's mind. He would feel a sadness he had
not known since his own childhood.

It was many years before Toni suspected the dark side of
her only child.

Jason had always been a quiet boy and he seemed to have
trouble making friends. Two or three times when he was growing up he tried to run away from home, and once he vanished
from boarding school for four days before showing up drunk,
refusing to say where he'd been. If the school had expelled

him Toni would have worried. But he was a good student, in fact a brilliant one, and they only put him on probation for a term.

It wasn't until Jason's sophomore year at Harvard when he vanished from campus that she became alarmed. Newspapers and television were full of student protests and drugs and teen-age anarchists. Jay hired a detective firm who specialized in tracking down runaway children of the super-rich—and in keeping them out of the news.

The state police searched and the FBI searched and the private detective searched, and no one turned up so much as a hair of Jason Stokes. Toni began having dreams that her son was dead. She woke up screaming. Jay made her change psy-chiatrists and go to a man who prescribed injections of Valium.

The shots were no more help than the police.

One evening that summer a government investigator came to the house. What he said about Jason was worse than anything Toni had imagined even in nightmares. She listened quietly, not moving, but a lump of protest formed in her throat and began suffocating her.

She could not, would not believe her son was involved in drug-running or pornographic films.

The light caught the investigator's glasses. They became flashing circles with no eyes behind them. The man said Jason had shot a storekeeper during a robbery.

Toni could no longer keep silent. "You don't know my son." In her mind she could see the six-year-old face, the blond curls, the deep-set green eyes and thoughtfully pouting lower lip.

"Let me tell you about your son," the man said. "He's a rat like ten thousand other penthouse radicals and charge-card ter-rorists. They blow their heads with acid and they blow their veins with speed and smack and they blow themselves up with homemade bombs and they don't care who they take with them. They're evil and they're sick and they hate you, lady—yeah, you. If you want my advice, get down on your knees and pray God Almighty to keep two million miles between you and that kid."

"How dare you " Toni said.

"I dare, lady, I dare. My son got mixed up with kids like yours—and he's dead because of them."

After the investigator had gone there was a silence in Jay that Toni had never heard before. It was metal cutting into bone. It was a fish trying to cough up a hook and it terrified her.

"Don't believe that man," she said. "None of it's true."

Jay's eyelids flicked down wearily. "There are witnesses," he said.

"I'm a witness too!" Toni cried. "I know my son!"

Jay sighed, and it was as though he were accusing her of responsibility, of raising Jason wrong.

The search went on. Jay's public relations men were able to keep Jason out of the news and off the FBI's most-wanted circulars, but that was all they were able to do. Months passed with no word.

Toni took to searching the newspapers herself, especially the smudgy counterculture weeklies for sale in Harvard Square. She was certain that in some line of print in some personal ad from a post office box in some Canadian city or other she would find a hidden clue leading to her son.

Oddly enough, it was the magazine section of the Sunday New York *Times* that pointed her in a new direction. In an article on New England desserts she found a mention of Harvard professor Dr. Karl Engulesco, hero and host to young activists, whose New England-born and bred wife Lavinia was famous for her hasty pudding.

An accompanying photograph showed a typical Engulesco open-house spread. There were home-baked cakes and breads, a steaming bowl of the cornmeal and molasses pudding and a sterling silver trophy cup filled with dates that had been rolled in coconut shavings. Toni had seen a cup like that only once in her life: her sister had won it in the Chestnut Hill Country Club junior mixed tennis doubles.

She read the article with great care and learned that Mrs. Engulesco was a Boston Pierpont and that the pudding was a family tradition. The Engulescos were listed in the directory. She phoned.

The voice that answered was her sister Vinnie's.

"I saw your pudding in the New York *Times*," Toni said.

"I've been seeing you in the Boston *Globe* for years," Vinnie laughed, her voice sounding not a day older than Toni remembered and not in the least angry. "Come on over and see the house and meet Karl."

Toni was nervous when she saw the house on Brattle Street where the Engulescos lived. It was the same house that she and Jay had rented as newlyweds. She stood knocking at the door a good five minutes and was beginning to think she'd heard Vinnie wrong when she'd said noon, and then a dented gray Volkswagen wheeled into the drive and Vinnie sprang out, lifting off a fur cap and spilling gray curls.

"What have you done to yourself?" Vinnie cried. "You look like a million dollars."

She unlocked the door and threw it open. The house still smelled of dogs. Vinnie poured sherry and flung up a wall of chatter. She was the same Vinnie with the addition of eighteen years and thirty pounds. She had a double chin now and a huge bosom that was almost grandmotherly. She seized Toni's hand on the sofa. "What do you think of Erwin Piscator's death?" she cried.

"Piscator?" Toni said.

"And De Gaulle starting a second term, can you believe it, another seven years of *that?*"

"I don't know much about De Gaulle," Toni said.

"Of course not." Vinnie refilled their glasses. "You're interested in local politics. Karl has to take a more international view of things." She went on to describe her husband's work with international committees on human rights.

It still wasn't clear to Toni what Dr. Engulesco actually taught. It seemed to her that Vinnie was bantering the way she would with another faculty wife that she saw every afternoon of her life. "Vinnie I need your help," she said. "I know it's strange to ask a favor after eighteen years, but—"

Vinnie waved a chubby wrist and a green bead bracelet tinkled. "Eighteen years? I don't believe it, but I suppose you're right. Who has time to keep track? Goodness, you haven't aged more than ten years, Toni. I probably look like the older sister now. And your leg seems—cured?"

"You look wonderful," Toni said.

"Oh, I'm not doing so badly for a mother of three healthy kids. Of course I don't go to the beauty parlor anymore—I give the money to Amnesty International. Are you interested, by the way? We're always looking for sponsors."

Vinnie's voice scampered on, playful and cutting as a violin bow, and Toni couldn't help sensing she was being intentionally put off. Vinnie's monologue centered on her husband, his Harvard lectures that were overattended, his speaking tours that were sell-outs, his books that were being brought out in paperback, so great was the demand, his standing in the academic community, his phenomenal popularity with the young rebels of the radical left.

"Sometimes it's almost embarrassing," Vinnie said. "He's such a star everyone wants to go to bed with him—even some of the *men!* Well, I'm sure you have the same problem. Karl saw Jay the other day at the Atheneum. He said Jay looked really quite handsome still."

Words poured from her, and they did not even slow when a door slammed and Toni saw a tall, thin man advancing toward them down the hallway.

"There you are, Karl," Vinnie said. "We were just talking about you. Come meet my big sister Toni."

Dr. Karl Engulesco had a widow's peak of thick black hair that made the sides of his head look bone-white and bone-bald. He took Toni's hand and bent over it. She thought she heard his heels click.

"Toni phoned after eighteen years," Vinnie said. "Isn't that sweet?"

"I dine with your husband sometimes," Dr. Engulesco said.

Toni stared at the half-familiar face, the cheeks blue with beard shadow, and realized she'd seen photographs of him in the radical newspapers she'd bought at Harvard Square.

"My son Jason went to your lectures," she blurted. It was a lie and a long shot, but she had a feeling Dr. Engulesco was connected in circles that touched the circles where Jason had vanished.

"So do eighteen hundred other undergrads," Vinnie said.

"Darling," Dr. Engulesco said, "have you seen my *Lampoon* tie? I won't be coming home before the dinner."

"I sent it to the cleaner. Isn't it in the plastic bag with your tux? Go look."

He was gone and Vinnie took Toni by the hand again.

"Have you had lunch? Let's go look in the fridge for some munchies."

Munchies turned out to be carrot sticks and leftover yogurt dip on a breadboard on the kitchen table.

"I'd like to ask Karl about my son Jason," Toni said.

"He wouldn't remember him," Vinnie said through a full mouth. "He has section men to handle the students."

"Jason has vanished into some sort of underground," Toni said. "I think it's the same people you cook hasty pudding for."

A frown crossed Vinnie's forehead. She looked at her sister with mild interest and then bit into another carrot stick.

"I'd like to find him," Toni said.

There was an instant's foaming silence before Vinnie said, "Karl's contacts in the underground are protected by freedom of the press, you know."

"I just want to find my son and I think Karl could help."

Vinnie shook her head energetically. "Your son wouldn't be in the underground—not *Karl's* underground."

"How can you be so sure?" Toni said.

"Because he's your son, yours and Jay's."

"I'd still like to ask your husband."

"That's not very smart of you, Toni."

"I'm not interested in being smart. I want to find him. If Karl can't help he may know someone who can."

"You seem to think my husband is some sort of Hollywood agent of the left, that you can just walk in here and talk out a deal."

"If I can I'd like to."

"Karl's not some state senator that you and Jay can co-opt with a flick of a thousand-dollar bill."

"He happens to be my brother-in-law," Toni said. "I'm asking him to help a member of his own family."

Vinnie's eyes became huge. She sprang up from the table. "As if family ever meant a damned thing to you. Do you know who's paying for Mother and Father's second mortgage? Karl and I are—and on a professor's salary!"

"I never knew Mother and Father had a second mortgage."

"Well, now you know, and if family is so important to you, why don't you do something about it? And *then* maybe Karl will talk to you about your son."

Toni's parents didn't seem in the least astonished when she broke her silence of almost twenty years and phoned. "Come see us," they said with a pleasantness that was not like them at all.

She was surprised how much courage it took to return to the house on West Cedar Street on Beacon Hill. Everything was older. There were still the slip-covered sofas and faded rugs and the smell of pipe tobacco, but the ceilings seemed lower and the rooms darker than she remembered, and there was a large Zenith color TV where the piano should have been.

Father shouted hello from the sofa. He had gone totally bald and his leg was in a cast and he was watching the daytime soap operas.

Mother's hair was white. She walked with a cane now and her old Lowestoft teacups showed cracks where she'd stuck the handles back on with epoxy.

"You seem well," Toni said.

"We get by," Father said.

"We don't get by," Mother said. "No one gets by with prices what they are today. How's your leg, Toni? I see you're still walking without your brace."

"My leg's fine," Toni said. "You're right, prices are terrible."

"And at our age," Father said.

"Everything gets worse when you're old," Mother said. "They keep raising prices, but no one raises your father's pension."

"I'm glad Father has a pension," Toni said.

"It's not nearly enough," Mother said. "There are already two mortgages on the house. I don't know how we'll raise any more cash to meet bills."

"We may have to sell," Father said.

Mother leaned stiffly forward and poured more hot water into the tea leaves.

"I'll pay your mortgages," Toni said.

Mother's stirring hand slowed. "That's very sweet of you, Toni."

"Damned sweet of you," Father said.

"Of course we can never pay you back," Mother said.

"Why should you?" Toni said. "I've taken a lot from you in my life, you can take a little from me."

"Would you like some almond cake?" Mother said. "It used to be your favorite."

"Where did you ever get the idea I liked almond cake?" Toni said.

"Of course you did," Mother said. It occurred to Toni that they shared very different pasts. "You're sure you don't want the last piece?"

"I'm sure, Mother."

Mother stared, not critically but curiously. "Are you dieting? You look well. I wish you'd speak to Vinnie—she's lost all pride in her appearance."

"Vinnie's a goddamned mess," Father said. "Her husband's a Communist and someone should pick up that living room of theirs."

Mother sniffed but added no criticism. Toni realized that her parents didn't love Vinnie anymore. It occurred to her that they didn't love anyone anymore, not even one another.

"How's Jay?" Mother asked.

"Jay's fine," Toni said.

"And your son?"

"Jason's fine too."

"Still at Harvard? We heard he was at Harvard. Not taking any of Karl's courses, I hope."

"Jason's taking a year off."

Father began talking about his own Harvard days and the year he had taken off to go West. He'd changed a great many of his stories, and Toni realized he was making things up. She wondered if he'd always made things up.

She couldn't sit still for more than an hour of the television and Mother and Father interrupting one another. She made up an appointment and kissed them goodby.

She went down Beacon Hill on foot, thinking that when she had seen her parents with an eight-year-old's eyes they'd been ogres, and now they were slightly ridiculous old dwarfs. She didn't see how she could have hated them, how she could have bothered.

*What have I spent my life doing?* she wondered.

She went home and got drunk. The following week she assumed her parents' mortgages, and the week after that Vinnie's husband gave her five minutes on the phone and said he'd do his best about Jason.

Dr. Karl Engulesco's best came to exactly nothing. Weeks and months passed with no word of the boy, and the last tiny rubber band holding Toni together seemed to snap. She stopped caring. She began putting on weight again. She started drinking in public again. She met a leading man from the company of a Broadway-bound musical and a Boston *Globe* photographer snapped them coming out of the Copley Plaza bar.

Jay exploded, screaming that she was trying to ruin him. The harangue became too much for her.

"Lay off me, Jay. I didn't kill anyone. I didn't burn down an orphanage."

"The only thing you burned down was the last timber of

this marriage, which is understandable, considering it's unfit for human habitation!"

There was a boozy righteous whine in his voice and she realized this wasn't going to blow over as easily as she'd hoped.

"What is not understandable or forgivable," he cried, "is flaunting your assignations in front of the media!"

"It was a cocktail, not an assignation. I didn't even finish the goddamned daiquiri."

"You have the IQ of a nit. We're paying a fortune to keep Jason out of the papers, wherever he is and whatever the hell he's doing, and we don't need *you* making headlines!"

"Then why don't you pay another fortune and maybe they won't write about me either?"

He struck her across the cheek. It was a wild, back-of-the-hand blow. It spun her around and almost knocked her down. She shook the stars out of her head and spat on him.

"Go to hell, Jay."

She was sick of him, sick of her whole shouting-match of a life. She got into the Mercedes and drove. The country place in the Berkshires was three hours away on the turnpike. There were forty-one hundred acres of foothill with brooks and valleys and deer and trout and electric fences. It was deserted this time of year, a place where a person could feel alone, and that was what she wanted.

She arrived in the early evening. She fixed herself a stiff drink and went to the bedroom and gulped two sleeping pills. From the window she could see the sun dropping behind the forest. Evening was seeping across the lawns and untended gardens. Peacefulness gradually engulfed her. She crawled between the bedsheets and sank into drugged unconsciousness.

Something awakened her in the middle of the night.

She looked at the phosphorescent traveling clock and saw that it was a little after three. The darkness in the room seemed alien, alive. She took a deep swallow of air and was aware of a knotting fear sealing off her breath.

She sat bolt upright. A man was standing at the foot of her bed, watching her.

She snapped on the light.

He was bearded and scruffy. His hair was long and matted. But she recognized the eyes. Her tongue struggled to shake off the drugs.

"Jason . . . ?"

He stared at her. "Why are you here?" There was a deadness in his voice, and in a flash she knew he was not only high on something but armed.

Her fingers drew up white-knuckled fistfuls of bedclothes around her neck. She couldn't believe she was frightened that her own son might rape her, but she was. The possibility was there, tangible, paralyzing. She tried to make her tongue work.

"No reason," she whispered. "I had to get away. That's all."

He moved closer. His body was tense, as though awaiting some signal to spring on her. *My own son,* she thought, *my own son.* She tried to remember the Lord's prayer and her mind couldn't get past *who art in heaven . . .*

"You shouldn't have come," he said. "That was a mistake."

"I'll go," she stammered through blanketing panic. "I'll go now."

He looked at her steadily. His hand came out of his pocket, dangerously sinewed but empty, thank God, empty. She realized how tall and broad and lethally strong he had grown. The pouting child's mouth had become a razor-thin line of determination.

"Get going," he commanded, "before the others come back."

Even in her fear, there was still a residue of mother in her. "What others? Jason, what are you involved in?"

"There isn't time to explain."

"Can't we at least talk?"

"We could have. We can't anymore. Get going."

Toni reached Boston an hour after dawn. She agonized whether or not to tell Jay that she had seen their son. She skirted around the subject and Jay cut her short.

"We're paying detectives and public relations people to take care of that."

"You don't love him," she said. "You don't love anyone."

"Drop it, Toni. You don't know beans, and besides there's nothing you can do about it."

She didn't drop it. In small ways she tried to help without exactly betraying Jason. She suggested to the private detectives that they might want to check out the house in the Berkshires.

Tolerantly, they checked it out. They said there had been vandals, but they turned up no sign of Jason.

\* \* \*

The 1968 elections were approaching, and from what Toni could see, her missing son was no longer the only front-burner issue for Jay Stokes. She was there when Willi Strauss said the dogfight for the Republican nomination was going to be the dirtiest in half a century, but there was no question the Stokes machine could maneuver the party into choosing Jay.

Thoughtfully, Jay set down his scotch and water. "You mean I'm somehow going to parlay seventeen months in a North Korean doghouse and ten years in the governor's mansion into an electoral landslide?"

"You're going to parlay them into eight years in the White House," Willi Strauss said, and Toni realized they were discussing the presidency of the United States.

It somehow seemed unreal and unimportant and much too much work. Toni went along passively with the campaign, not protesting but not really helping either. She had the impression the doctor was putting something new into her shots, and it seemed easier to go along than to object.

Jay had an uphill job from the beginning. His being a direct descendant of John Stokes I was a huge debit in the bank of liberal opinion, while his social legislation on behalf of the people of Massachusetts was, in Kitty's opinion, fanatically misrepresented by the conservative press. Luckily the Stokes billions, siphoned through third-party checks from the Broad Street office, spoke louder and longer than all Jay's adversaries.

Months before the presidential campaign officially began, Willi Strauss assembled a team of forty-seven top political minds in a suite at the Boston Ritz. They wrote a dummy platform, a contingency platform, and a rebuttal platform; and they blocked a forty-million-dollar general strategy.

Willi had negotiated a deal to give Nelson Rockefeller the vice presidency, and this caused terrific disagreement. Jay pointed out that Rockefeller was a documented backstabber and was known to want the top slot for himself.

"I'm aware of that," Willi Strauss said. "But think of it as a nonaggression pact. It gives us time." He remarked privately to Kitty that the decisive factor in the battle for the nomination was not going to be who stood where on what, but megabucks and the candidate's ability to sense shifts in public desire and to alter image accordingly.

For nine grueling months Willi sensed and Jay shifted and Stokes Industries paid the bills. Jay scored a consistently respectable third in all the primaries except New Hampshire and Alabama. By the time of the Republican convention in Miami, four hundred and eighteen delegates were pledged for Jay Stokes. Another two hundred eighty-four had indicated a willingness to switch to his side on the second ballot.

All this, of course, cost money, and the campaign was well over its original forty-million-dollar limit. But they were dollars well spent. Newspapers and magazines and TV commentators said Jay Stokes was coming up fast. And no one, but no one, mentioned a massacre that had taken place in 1922 in the little Catholic graveyard in Bartonville.

It was a new world, a world that did not remember.

Kitty held her breath. Three days before the convention it seemed it might just happen: Jay was within snatching distance of an upset victory.

But the evening before the convention, it all changed.

*Grass Roots,* a radical student newspaper, had announced a counterconvention to be held at 6 P.M. in the park at Seventy-second Street and Biscayne Boulevard. It was obviously to be a "Legalize Marijuana" rally, but it promised to be a comic break in the boredom of politics, and 6 P.M. was a dead spot in the evening news. Television was there.

Kitty was in the hotel suite with Jay and his team, watching.

A crowd of people stood milling under the palm trees on Seventy-second Street, lit by a sun just beginning to set. From the tops of sound trucks the cameras of three networks gazed down at tourists and hippies and old retired folk, gazed along avenues of shops and eateries and neon signs to the pink-tipped wedding-cake skyline of Miami Beach's hotel row.

For a while nothing happened and the cameras snatched closeups: an old Jewish woman eating a knish from a paperbag, a Cuban changing the batteries in his transistor radio, a mongrel urinating on a poster of a beaming Nelson Rockefeller.

And then a young man in ragged blue jeans hopped up onto a park bench. The shuffling and pushing stopped. The crowd fell silent. The cameras zoomed in for tight shots.

"Brothers—sisters—" the young man shouted, "wake up!"

In the hotel suite Willi Strauss hushed the others and said, "Someone turn that thing up."

Someone turned the television up. The blond-bearded teenager was screaming and waving like a mad Viking, haranguing the crowd. Somehow the TV audio picked his voice out of the blanketing jets and traffic.

"If you're against war you're against the war in Vietnam! If you're against the war in Vietnam you're against capitalism, because capitalism *is* the war in Vietnam! And if you're against capitalism you're against John Stokes because he *is* capitalism and he *is* the war!"

"Hophead Marxist," Jay said, sloshing scotch into a glass.

One of the advisers said, "Diners Club anarchist," and there was laughter.

"For Christ's sake, Jay," Willi Strauss said, "shut up and listen. That's your son."

# Chapter 25

"HOW LONG WILL you flush your blood and your dollars down the bottomless toilet of imperialism?"

The figure on the TV screen needed a haircut and a shave and a bath. He was wearing a filthy shirt and a bead necklace. Something glinted in one ear, and Kitty wondered, *Good God, has he pierced his ear?* All the same, part of her could not help thinking how splendid he looked, how handsome and brave, how like Tyrone Duncannon—though the things he was shouting were not handsome at all.

"If you allow your so-called representatives to nominate this murderer, this thief—then you are installing war as the permanent, undeclared policy of this nation: war abroad, war at home, one war incivisible with poverty and death for all except the millionaires."

The boy took a wallet from his hip pocket and from the wallet he took a card. He waved it slowly through the air, like a magician preparing his audience for amazement. He flicked a flame from a cigarette lighter and held it to the edge of the card. After a moment he raised a fistful of fire over his head.

"I have broken the so-called law," he cried. "I have burned my draft card and declared my allegiance to the people! If I am different from any other American, if I can stand here untouched simply because my name is John Stokes the Fourth—then I am proof that America is a lie!"

That was the signal. Policemen came piercing through the crowd like bullet-propelled antipersonnel darts. Gun butts and nightsticks swung and smashed. Hatred spurted from leathery mouths, red screams spilled from ripped faces.

The first blow struck Jason from the side. Half his face was instant purple mush. He fell forward off the bench and the police were upon him like a horde of crazed maggots.

Unblinking, all-seeing, all-recording, the black unafraid eyes of the TV cameras looked on. The police smashed and they kicked till they had emptied the park and made a pulp of Jay Stokes's son—and his political chances.

Jay set down his glass. The room was shocked into silence. "I'll kill him," Jay whispered. "I swear I'll murder that hippie bastard."

And suddenly he was not whispering or sitting, but standing and shouting a babble of bottle-smashing, arm-waving filth.

"Jay," Kitty said, "for God's sake."

"He's fucked me!" Jay kicked the TV. A technicolor spark seared the screen, and only a fast-leaping aide kept the set from crashing to the floor. "That self-righteous prick has fucked me!"

Willi Strauss wrapped a soothing arm around Jay's shoulder. "We're going to have to rework your speech, Jay. We'll put in a statement. Freedom of speech. Bill of Rights. Though you don't agree with a word your son said, you defend to the death his right and the right of every American to et cetera, et cetera."

Kitty wasn't certain. She watched Jay sink dizzily down onto the sofa. "Are you sure that's wise, Willi?"

"Look around you," Willi Strauss said. "What's happening in America? We're a nation in agony. The war has turned father against son, son against father. There isn't a parent in the U.S. who doesn't know exactly what Jay went through today, who doesn't feel for him. Let's mobilize that sympathy and *use* it."

Kitty wanted to believe him, but it felt dangerously late for dreams. "How, Willi? How?"

Jay sat red-eyed and brooding; his fingers trembled against the rim of his highball glass. Conventioneer shouts and call-girl giggles drifted up through the floor from the suite below.

"What could be more stirring," Willi Strauss said, "than if

Jason publicly recanted—publicly made up with Jay? It would be a kind of national healing. Money couldn't buy that kind of press."

Kitty didn't like the sound of that word *recant*. It sounded like Joan of Arc in the clutches of the Inquisition. It sounded like Stalin's brainwashed toadies perjuring themselves at the Moscow trials. It sounded like a gun held at the head of a confused, doped adolescent.

"What would make Jason recant?" Kitty said.

"Sometimes a simple, direct appeal can be most persuasive," Willi Strauss said.

Jay drained his highball to the ice cubes. He had the face of a hundred-year-old man. The months of campaigning had left him grooved and gray. Kitty could see his bone-weariness. He'd drunk too much, worried too much, eaten too little, skipped too much sleep. She could see the anger and the failure in him, and worst of all she could see the gathering shadow of giving up.

"It can't be done." There was a curious metallic flatness to Jay's voice. "The boy hates me. The hatred goes back too far, too deep."

Willi Strauss sat forward in his chair. "Which is why *I* have to talk to him, Jay—not you. Don't you go anywhere near him."

Jay's eyes went quickly to his mother, questioning. She felt herself like a feather floating down through space, choosing which side of a delicately balanced scale to land on.

"Willi's right," she said. "Let him handle Jason. And Jay, you get some sleep."

Willi Strauss went to the Federal Detention Center during lunch hour the next day. He had thought about the meeting beforehand and he felt sure he could handle it in half an hour.

A guard took him to Jason Stokes's cell and swung the door open. On the cot against the wall the boy lay very still. Willi Strauss approached softly and looked down at him. The boy's hippie-length hair formed a pool of cornsilk on the pillow and his face was stained with bruises. He didn't look even twenty years old.

Willi Strauss stood gazing at the boy, and a sudden tiredness came down on him. He would go home early today, he decided.

He raised a hand to an ache in his temple. His shadow fell across the cot.

The boy seemed to feel its weight. His head turned and his eyes opened. He raised himself quickly to a sitting position.

Willi Strauss placed a hand gently against the boy's shoulder. "Don't tire yourself," he said. "I won't stay long."

"Stay as long as you like. We're on government property."

Willi Strauss ignored the sarcasm. He sat on the edge of the cot and fixed the boy with his eyes. "Your father wants to help you," he said. "He wants to get you out of this mess."

"I'm not in a mess. Dad's in a mess. The country's in a mess. I'm in the clear."

The boy's voice made Willi Strauss realize this wasn't going to be as easy as he'd hoped. "You take things too seriously, Jason. You don't understand that politics is nonsense. The men who practice it are fools. I'm a fool. Your father's a fool. Yesterday, when you burned that draft card, you became a fool. We're all fools, so stop turning it into martyrdom."

"Bullshit."

Willi Strauss did not skip a beat, but simply changed direction. "This may surprise you, Jason, but your father's proud of you. He's proud of the stand you've taken."

"Double bullshit."

This time Willi Strauss did not change direction. "He knows why you did it. He knows you love your country. But don't you see there was no need for that card-burning charade? We're in the real world now, Jason. You're not pitching a pup tent in the woods. There's a real war on. Magic tricks won't solve anything."

The boy listened quietly, not moving. He seemed thinner than Willi Strauss remembered and certainly less clean. "Mr. Strauss," the boy said, "do you honestly think this country could survive my father's presidency?"

"Don't you trust the voters, Jason?"

"He'll bleed this country the way he bled Massachusetts."

Willi Strauss sighed. You could give teen-agers every advantage of breeding and education and position, yet if you waved a cause in front of them, shouted "Vive la people!" they'd stampede to become communists, anarchists, fascists, anything at all you told them to be. *Too bad,* Willi Strauss thought, *I didn't reach him before his professor did.*

"Now just listen to me, Jason. Listen to me a minute and try to understand. I don't fool myself. I'm your father's man and I admit it. But you *are* fooling yourself. The truth is, you don't give a damn about Massachusetts. You don't give a damn about taxes or welfare rolls or armaments. The plain and simple truth is, you hate your father."

"Jesus Freudian Christ—I can handle my problems with my father."

"You wouldn't be here if you could, Jason. You'll do anything to destroy him, even if it means destroying yourself. And the irony, the tragedy, is, that man loves you—and you don't even know it. He wants your love. He desperately wants it. He knows he'll have to work for it, work hard to make up for all the years he's neglected you—but can't you let him try? Give him a second chance to be a father, Jason."

The boy stared at Willi Strauss. "How do I give him a second chance?"

"You reregister for the draft."

Jason did not answer. His face was blank. The air was very close in the cell. The smell of disinfectant pressed in like fog.

Quickly, Willi Strauss sketched in the details. Up to a half million dollars of tax-free money would be siphoned into any organizations or to any individuals of Jason's choosing; or even to Jason himself. Charges stemming from the draft-card burning would, of course, be dropped.

After a puzzling silence, the boy finally spoke. "What kind of a hold does he have on you, Mr. Strauss? You're not stupid. Why do you help him? Is money that important to you?"

"Your father has been a good friend to me practically all my life," Willi Strauss said. "In some ways he's been my only friend. I owe him everything. And frankly, I think you owe him a little."

The boy put out a thundering silence.

"I'm not here to lecture you, Jason, or to argue with you. We agree on too many things. We both love this country. And we both love your father."

"I hate him," the boy said.

"That kind of hate is just love turned around. I know, Jason. I went through it with my own father. Every son does. And if you let that hatred steer you, someday you'll be sorry."

"I'll never be sorry. I did what had to be done. And if it's not enough, I'll do more."

Willi Strauss saw it was time to change direction. "I don't

think you quite grasp your situation. As of today, you're a criminal. You're also liable for the draft. If you don't cooperate, you will be drafted and you will probably see active duty and you stand a very good chance of being killed."

"Dad owns the Selective Service and he owns the Army and the Viet Cong too, is that the way it is?"

"In effect," Willi Strauss said.

He could see anger leap up in the boy, blind and violent and shouting down walls.

"You can tell that bastard to go to hell!" the boy screamed. "This is my country too, and he's not going to make me or anyone else vanish with a wave of his wallet!"

Willi Strauss moved to the barred window and remained standing there. His brain did nothing of its own volition but seemed merely to gaze on what had been brought before it. "You need a rest. You really do, Jason. The young have remarkable powers of recuperation. Take a rest and you'll snap back in no time."

"You're still ladling bullshit, Mr. Strauss. I'm going to fight him. And I'm not going to stop till I've won."

Willi Strauss remembered a time and a world when young men had believed such things—and done them. Those men were dead now.

Willi Strauss had survived.

"As you get older, Jason, you'll find that where there's no hope of victory, there's no point to the fight."

"Then I hope I never get older."

*With that attitude,* Willi Strauss reflected, *you might just get your wish.* He did not have a lifetime to spend in collegiate debate. He signaled the guard to unlock the cell. "Is there someplace we can talk?" he whispered.

They went together into the parking lot outside the detention center—the tall crewcut man with the leathery scowl, and Willi Strauss with the eight-hundred-dollar pigskin attaché case that Jay Stokes had given him for Christmas.

"Cigarette?" Willi Strauss offered.

"All right," the man accepted as though he were doing Willi Strauss a favor; and he was.

Willi Strauss lit them both from the silver pocket lighter that had been the gift of Nikita Khrushchev, the recently deposed Soviet Premier. He explained what he needed and what he was willing to pay for it.

The man's eyes narrowed. He watched Willi Strauss's mouth,

but he listened with his nose, sniffing for two things: the risk and the money.

By the time Willi Strauss had finished describing his proposal, the sky had turned dark with thick hurrying clouds. A salt wind was blowing up from the Gulf. The man shifted his feet.

"How soon can you do it?" Willi Strauss said.

"How soon can you pay me?"

"I can give you half right now."

"Go to the men's room. Third stall from the left. Put the money in the toilet-paper dispenser."

When Willi Strauss returned from the men's room he shook the man's hand and thanked him and stepped into the back seat of the black Lincoln Continental limousine that had brought him to the detention center. He instructed the driver to take him three miles along the coast highway and to wait at the side of the road.

The door rammed open. Light crashed into the cell, silhouetting the rigid bulk of a man holding a gun.

Jason Stokes raised his eyes and took the guard in with a swift glance.

The guard stood there. His teeth were a startling white and the hard leathered skin of his face and bare forearms glowed as if it had been buffed with saddle wax. He was silent. He stood staring at John Stokes IV, the rich kid turned rebel cowering there in the dark.

The boy studied the play of expression on the guard's face and a sudden premonition shot into his mind.

The guard stepped into the cell. He slammed the door behind him.

Denial surged through the boy and then terror. He backed into the corner of the cell and then up onto the corner of the bed.

The guard took three steps forward. A slow smile seeped across his face. With a suddenness that allowed no reaction time, the guard jammed the gun butt up into the boy's groin.

The boy let out a low moan and doubled at the waist. The breath came out of him in a sharp sighing rush. The guard struck with the butt again.

This time there was vomit.

Hands swift now, fingers spread, the guard clutched the boy

by the throat. The boy thrashed his head. His eyes widened. He sucked in his breath, and when no breath could get past the squeezing fingers he gulped for air.

The guard's hands tightened. The boy's dread-struck eyes drank in the truth of this moment.

In forty seconds Jason Stokes was unconscious. In another thirty it was finished. The guard made a noose of the bedsheet and strung the body to the barred window.

The sun was beginning its descent toward the Gulf of Mexico. Shadows lengthened across the Florida peninsula. The day was drowsing toward late afternoon.

A black Lincoln Continental limousine idled beside the thruway. The motor was running to keep the air conditioning on, and the windows were up to keep the cool air in. In the back seat, cigarette smoke pulsed from Willi Strauss's mouth. He had gone through an entire pack.

Pink tailfeathers of day were fluttering at the western horizon when the car telephone finally rang. Willi Strauss grabbed the receiver. He pressed it to his ear tightly enough so no sound would leak to the driver.

He listened and nodded and answered in grunts and monosyllables. When the guard at the Federal Detention Center had rung off, Willi Strauss dialed the land operator and asked to be connected to Jay's hotel.

"How did it go?" Jay said.

Willi Strauss laid the groundwork. "I'm worried. The boy's irrational—depressed—I think it's a mistake for him to be alone. He could easily harm himself."

Because she happened to be near the phone, it was Kitty who took the call that came from the Federal Detention Center that evening. At first she did not attempt to move or even to think. She remembered there had been gladioluses in the hospital the day Jason was born. She remembered one Christmas when he had annoyed her blowing a toy trumpet.

A tiredness overcame her. *God, let me sleep*, she thought. It was as though she had gone through her whole life without sleeping, and her body, rebelling at last, refused to put out another ounce of strength.

She dared not give in to the fatigue. She went ashen-faced to tell Jay. He looked up from his position paper on Alaskan seabed materials. He saw her rigid and pale and silent.

"What's the matter, Mom?" he said. "You look like hell."

She could think of no other way to say it. "Jason hanged himself in his cell."

Jay's face blanked out like a television with the cord yanked. His head dropped into his hands, and when he looked up again it was as though he was standing at the outer edge of life staring at the space beyond.

"Jason," he whispered. "Poor goddamned little Jason." He began sobbing helplessly. "I should have gone to him!"

Kitty placed her hands gently on his shoulders. She knew that Jason's mother had to be told. "Where's Toni?"

"In the bedroom."

They went together. Toni listened and then her face twisted. She fought her mouth with her bunched fists and then she gave in and threw her head back and howled.

Jay rushed to her. She buried herself against his chest. Her eyes squeezed shut and tears poured down her cheeks. It took twenty minutes to bring her under control, and when Jay finally pried her fists open her nails had gouged flesh from her palms.

Willi Strauss came back to the hotel late that evening. Kitty and Jay and Toni sat huddled on the sofa and listened to him. At that moment, for the only time in their lives, the three of them were a family.

Very carefully, very coolly, Willi Strauss explained exactly what had happened and how. He blamed it on prison conditions. He ground a half-smoked cigarette in the ashtray so violently that the filtered stub broke off. "This isn't the first suicide they've had in that place."

None of the Stokeses spoke. The room was silence and breath going in and out and one single thought screaming in three different heads.

"I've made arrangements," Willi Strauss said. "The funeral's in Boston, the day after tomorrow."

Kitty stared at him. Two tiny vertical lines stood out between her eyebrows. "That's very fast, Willi," she said.

"There's no point dragging this out," Willi Strauss said.

"Doesn't the law require an autopsy?" Kitty said.

"We can get around that," Willi Strauss said. "Unless Jay wants to insist."

"No," Jay said dully. "I don't insist."

"Good," Willi Strauss said. "You're sparing yourself and the country a lot of needless suffering."

Toni drew herself up straight. She had lost weight during the campaign. The months had dug craters around her eyes. "What if *I* insist?" she said.

Willi Strauss said, "I wouldn't—" but then he looked at Toni and something in her eyes made him break off. "Naturally, Toni, I understand your feelings. But we ought to consider this in the context of the total picture."

"And what's that?" Toni said, directing her gaze straight at him.

"This is a tragedy, a terrible tragedy, and there's going to be sympathy," Willi Strauss said. "Jay has a damned good chance now of capturing the nomination."

Toni rose from the sofa. She crossed to Willi Strauss's chair and stood staring down at him. Her eyes were lidded and her mouth was tiny and tight, as though preparing to spit. She slapped Willi Strauss across the face.

"Now, Toni," Willi Strauss said, cool and understanding, but he said no more, because she slapped him a second time, cutting off words, and a third, drawing a spit-cocoon of blood from the corner of his lips, and again and again, until Kitty and Jay had to pull her off him and phone for Jay's private physician to come immediately and jab her in the arm with a massive dose of intramuscular sedative. A bellboy helped the doctor carry her unconscious to bed.

The book-lined room was dark except for the light of the murmuring television set. Bart Stokes sat stiffly in an armchair. His eyes were fixed on the images that flicked across the screen, images of a boy who had been too gentle and too easily wounded and who now was gone.

It shocked Bart Stokes to be still alive while a boy who might have been one of his own sons was dead. It shocked him, too, that the networks had gotten hold of home movies and snapshots from summer camp, letters to parents and even a diary, that all the residue of a human life had been boiled down in less than twenty-four hours to an unpaid political announcement for Jay Stokes's candidacy.

Bart peered down at his trembling hands. His mind was icy

with thoughts that made him shiver. Sickness overwhelmed him, a sickness he had borne all his life but whose strength he had not truly known till now.

"How dare they use his death," he said.

From across the room his wife looked up at him. "Bart, are you all right?"

For Bart Stokes the moment of struggle was endless, and when he finally rose from his chair he wasn't sure whether he or the sickness had won. "No," he said, "I'm not all right. I have to do something."

He left the room. A resolve beat in his blood. *That boy will have justice,* he decided. *He will have it now and from this day forward.*

When he lifted the telephone receiver Bart's hand was steady and his heart was no longer a battlefield. He calculated a moment, then jabbed a seven-digit number.

With one call he arranged the immediate, 100 percent collapse of his brother Jay's Moral Obligation Bonds.

# *Chapter 26*

JASON'S FUNERAL INVOLVED logistical details, like invitations and seating, and painful ones, like the interstate shipping of the body. Willi Strauss and his staff handled them all with incredible speed and smoothness, and two days after the death of John Stokes IV, Kitty and Jay and Toni sat in the front-right pew of Saint James's Church, Boston, hearing the minister say, "I am the resurrection and the life," and wishing, wishing it could only be so.

Toni collapsed almost immediately after the service and had to be taken to a private suite at Massachusetts General. Even though the doctors sedated her to unconsciousness, Jay said he wanted to stay with her.

Willi Strauss put a hand on Jay's shoulder. "Jay," he said, "there is nothing of value on this earth that's not paid for with human blood. You've paid. You've paid horribly. Don't let that payment go for naught. Take what you've paid for—if not for your own sake, then for your son's. Go back to Miami and take the nomination."

Kitty was silent. She saw that this was the greatest and the most tragic opportunity of Jay's life. He would never again

417

know such pain or possess such power. She nodded. "Willi's right, Jay," she said.

Jay's eyes went from his mother to his adviser and back to Kitty. She could almost hear the thoughts in him, slicing against one another like swords.

"How soon can the jet be ready?" he said.

"Forty minutes," Willi Strauss answered.

Naturally, in these changed circumstances, Willi Strauss expected offers from the opposition. Naturally, they came.

Only one was worth his while. A vice president of the National Bahamas Export Bank had phoned during his absence and left a message asking Willi to meet him for breakfast at the International House of Pancakes in downtown Miami.

"You realize we can engineer a panic in Massachusetts Moral Obligation Bonds," the vice president said. He handled the laundering of funds for Jay Stokes's chief opponent and his bank was a known cat's paw for Bart Stokes's. He took his orders from Manhattan and Zurich and, if only as proxy, he wielded enormous power over the economy.

Willi Strauss's mind went into overdrive and raced through a most probable scenario. "I realize you've already engineered a panic in them," he said. He also realized that he was no longer riding a winning horse. Somehow, the fix was on. The how did not matter, but the fix did.

Willi Strauss glanced at the vice president's pineapple pancakes, wondered how people could eat, let alone digest, such things, and told the waitress he would have coffee.

"What will it take," the vice president asked, "to induce Jay Stokes to withdraw his candidacy?"

"With the sort of publicity he's been getting, it will take a hell of a lot more than a failed bond issue." In fact, Willi Strauss knew, it would take nothing more; but the habit of negotiating died hard.

"How much more?"

Willi Strauss told him how much more.

The vice president coughed into his napkin. "We can't promise you a cabinet position, not at this stage. We have to maintain our options."

Willi Strauss shrugged and spread his hands. "In that case you've come to the wrong Judas."

Willi Strauss rose. He was halfway to the door when the vice president called to him.

"Mr. Strauss, just a moment, please."

Over two thousand delegates crammed into the convention hall that night. It seemed to Kitty that all the hope and horror of the campaign had been crammed in there too. Though the hall was air conditioned, the glaring TV lights and massed bodies had driven the temperature to a suffocation point.

The chairman called the convention to order seven minutes behind schedule. The speeches began. There were introductions to the introductions. It seemed to Kitty that every underling in the nation who had ever raised a dime for the party was given a two-minute ego trip at the mike.

It was after eleven and the proceedings were an hour behind schedule by the time Jay's turn came to speak. As the chairman called his name, Kitty could feel a hot wind of sympathy sweep across the room.

Jay walked tall and straight out onto the podium. He took the center microphone and laid his three-page speech unobtrusively on the lectern. It had been bashed out in relays, under Willi Strauss's supervision, by three brilliant boys from the Harvard *Crimson,* and there had not been time for Jay to memorize it or to feed it to the teleprompter.

Applause ripped through the crowd. The delegates did not give Jay a chance. They sprang to their feet, a dozen of them, then two dozen, than a dozen dozen. A roar built till it burst into the open and filled the hall. Two thousand men and women stood screaming and shouting and clapping. Many were weeping at the same time.

Jay raised his hands for silence. He had to keep them raised. The applause was like a wild thing that had burst its cage. It took twenty-three minutes to quiet the delegates and get them back into their seats.

"My fellow Americans," Jay began, his voice choked and tight, "as we look at our nation we see cities enveloped in smoke and flame. We hear sirens in the night. We see Americans dying on distant battlefields abroad. At home, we see disenchantment and violence. We see division between blacks and whites, between the poor and the affluent, between young and old, and yes, between parents and children."

He paused, and the hall held its breath. When he spoke

again there were tears on his cheeks and a cracking in his voice.

"*I say to you*—if we are not to commit suicide as a nation— we must end the division. *The hour has come for reconciliation.*"

The delegates were on their feet again. This time they stood on chairs. Some had placards. They cheered so loudly Jay had to shout. Even with the mike volume boosted to the top he was inaudible.

It seemed to Kitty that the delegates were shaking the universe by the roots, that this was the dawn of what historians would one day call the Age of Jay Stokes.

Jay raised his hands again. There was no silencing the will and the love of the people. Finally, eloquently, he let his hands drop. He stood at the microphone, silent tears streaming down his face. He gazed out at the tumult, thinking his own still thoughts of triumph and the loss that had brought it.

Kitty's heart broke for him and sang for him. Her eyes misted. God had taken, and the taking had been terrible. But He had given too and the giving had been wondrous. For at that point Kitty knew that Tyrone Duncannon's son would be the next President of the United States.

Afterward, Willi Strauss was waiting in a limousine to take Kitty and Jay to the hotel where the Senate Minority Leader was staying. Kitty suspected he was going to tell Jay the nomination was his. When she saw the Secretary of State and the president of the Ford Foundation in the suite, she was sure.

They introduced a short, neatly dressed man from the Securities and Exchange Commission. He had a pencil mustache and a problem pronouncing the letter *r*. Kitty did not see exactly how he fitted in, but she supposed he was someone's personal friend.

She didn't want to be in the way of business, and after one ginger ale she tried to excuse herself.

Willi Strauss said, "Kitty, you'd better stay," and she realized he knew a little bit more about this impromptu meeting than she did.

The Senate Minority Leader said there was some terrible news. "I'm sorry, Jay, I know what you've been through, but it can't wait. It has to be discussed tonight."

Jay poured himself a double scotch on the rocks and waited for the bad news.

The man from the SEC cleared his throat. He spoke in a rambling way about the Rockland County Moral Obligation Bonds. The politicians' faces were blank as a calm sea, and to Kitty that signaled shipwreck ahead. She knew instantly that this was not going to be the barbecue, drunken and giddy and red-white-and-blue, that she had hoped.

The SEC man said, almost apologetically, that the bonds had failed.

Jay sprang up from his chair. "That's not possible. The bonds were up when the market closed yesterday."

"You have five major buyers, Jay," the Senate Minority Leader said. "They dumped this afternoon."

"But the National Bank of New York—"

"Gave the first sell order."

It was Willi Strauss who finally, gravely, spoke. "If Jay keeps to his present course and seeks nomination—"

*"If!"* Kitty cried. A sudden and chilling premonition gripped her. "What are you talking about, Willi? There's no *if* involved!"

"There's a very great if." Willi Strauss's voice was firm, his manner solemn but confident. The long, exhausting day had not even put a rumple in it. "Jay's enemies are prepared to mount a campaign of harassment and character assassination against him the likes of which I've never seen in my entire career. They're pursuing a scorched-earth policy. Every tree in the forest will fall. The whole matter is at the precipice now."

It seemed to Kitty that even for a Harvard professor those were a great many metaphors.

Jay broke the silence. "What the hell are you talking about, Willi?"

"There's a move to lay the failure of the Moral Obligation Bonds personally on you. After all, you are governor now and you were then."

"That's ridiculous," Jay said. "Half the states in the union are bankrupt. No one blames the governors. The country's bankrupt. No one's blaming the President."

"There's tremendous pressure for an SEC investigation." Willi Strauss glanced at the man from SEC and confirmation came with a quiet nod.

"We've survived a dozen of those," Jay said.

"Not during a campaign," Willi Strauss reminded him.

Kitty was listening to two sounds. She heard what Willi Strauss was saying, but beneath it she heard what he was not saying. It was the second, inaudible sound that held her attention, like a deep organ note vibrating through a cathedral floor. "What are you telling us, Willi? How can all this possibly affect Jay's campaign?"

"There's much more to it," Willi Strauss said. "The fix is on the FBI to testify that Jason was involved with some pretty unsavory goings-on."

"Testify?" Jay said. "There's no trial. There's no hearing. Will you stop beating around the bush, Willi, and tell us what the hell you know?"

"There'll be a high-level leak to the national press," Willi Strauss said.

"What can they leak?" Kitty said.

There was a barely perceptible shift to the set of Willi Strauss's facial muscles. Kitty sensed that he was ashamed.

"You don't want to know," he said.

"I most certainly do," said Jay.

Willi Strauss sighed. "Their tactics imply the deepest corruption and perversion of the criminal justice system since the Civil War. I'm afraid we've come to the era of total political control."

Kitty was impatient now and more than a little terrified. "Willi, you've mentioned those bonds and not a single other shred of hard-core fact."

"Perhaps these will be hard-core enough for you." Willi Strauss laid an envelope on the glass-topped coffee table.

Kitty looked and winced. She felt as though a horse had kicked her in the stomach. The photographs were fuzzy and the color was wildly off. She did not recognize either of the young women, but one of the young men could have passed for Jason. With computer enhancement—and Kitty didn't doubt Jay's enemies had computers—he could probably pass for an identical twin. Perhaps, by some irony too ghastly to think about, the young man actually *was* Jason.

Jay reached for the photographs.

"You don't want to look at them," Kitty said.

But Jay looked at them, each one in turn, like cards in a hand of bridge. The corner of his mouth went limp. His face began to twist and pull. He blotted his eye quickly with the back of his hand.

"Is that all they've got?" Kitty said.

"Isn't it enough?" Willi Strauss said.

"But what does—" She groped for a word. "What does fornication have to do with politics?"

"Nothing," Willi Strauss said. "And everything."

"They won't dare use it," she said. "The boy's hardly in his grave."

Willi Strauss lit his pipe. Kitty noticed that the hand holding the match trembled. He took almost thirty seconds breathing flame into the Virginia tobacco. His eyes narrowed and they did not look straight at her.

"There's more," he said.

Kitty had known there was more. She had seen the flash of manila and she knew there was still a folder in the pigskin attaché case. Willi Strauss bent down and handed it to her now, and as Kitty leafed through the pages she felt she was wading slow-motion through a nightmare.

Somehow, Jay's enemies had uncovered the North Korean deal.

Kitty laid the documents on the table and with the tip of her finger steered them toward Jay.

Jay's lips moved silently as he skimmed. He shook his head. "How the hell did these surface?"

The Senate Minority Leader's eyes had the dull metallic gleam of gun barrels trained on Jay. "The bonds have failed," he said. "Your son posed for porno. And your family made a deal with the Commies."

"I don't believe this," Jay said.

"You better believe it, Jay," the Senate Minority Leader said, "and you better believe it's going to cost you the nomination."

Understanding took a moment to sink in, and when it did Jay almost gagged on it. A stillness fell on the room. Jay swept bottles and glasses and documents from the table and sent them smashing to the floor. The others remained silent. After all, if a man had lost not only his son but the nomination as well, you had to allow him a little craziness.

"Jay," Kitty pleaded.

He flung her aside and stumbled from the room.

"Let him go," Willi Strauss said. "Let him get it out of his system."

Kitty sat with her heart pounding. She could not believe it

had happened so quickly, that it was all over for Jay, that he had come this far for nothing.

"Kitty," Willi Strauss said, "we'd better have a talk—just the two of us."

There was still a residue of blind hope left in Kitty. She reasoned that Willi Strauss had fumbled Jay into this mess, and he of all people ought to know how to get Jay out again.

They had the talk in Kitty's hotel room. Just the two of them.

"Damn it, Kitty," Willi Strauss said. "Politically speaking, Jay's a young man. He just doesn't have the type of organization that the opposition does."

This was news to Kitty, but she let Willi Strauss go on.

"If Jay runs in four or eight years he's a shoo-in. If he tries to run now they'll shoot him down and he'll never get up again."

Kitty didn't understand it all yet, but she understood one thing: she had put her trust and her dollars in Willi Strauss and she was now paying the price for that act. The plain truth was that Willi Strauss not only ran Jay's organization, he *was* Jay's organization. He was the contacts, the records, the strategy. If, for whatever reason, he didn't want Jay to snatch the nomination tomorrow night, Jay would not snatch it.

The matter was that simple, that black and white.

"And what do we do for the next four years?" she asked coldly, bitterly. "Or the next eight?"

Willi Strauss looked up from his pipe. He had been tapping it against the ashtray, staring at the red glow in the bowl. He smiled affably. "We use the time to infiltrate the opposition."

"Who do we send in to infiltrate?"

"Me."

Kitty stared at him. A rotten taste flooded the back of her mouth. In her mind the last piece of a jigsaw puzzle slipped into place. She saw how cunningly Willi Strauss had used the Stokeses, how totally he had betrayed them. "Get out," she said.

"Kitty, I understand if you're upset, but I honestly—"

*"Get out!"*

After one glance at the look in her eyes, Willi Strauss did just that.

\* \* \*

For the next twelve hours, as Kitty moved from bedroom to sitting room lighting and stubbing out Chesterfields, Jay raged through the bars and after-hours clubs of Miami. When a whore brought him staggering back to the suite at the Fontainebleau, Kitty was terrified—not at his torn clothes or blackened face but at his eyes.

A bomb had gone off in them, and nothing that she recognized was left standing.

"Jay, it's not the end," she said. "Not unless you let it be."

Jay stared at her and burst out laughing and pitched face-first onto the floor.

The new President was inaugurated that January. Willi Strauss, to no one's surprise—certainly not Kitty's—was named Secretary of State.

Jay and Toni moved out of politics and back to the New York co-op in Sutton Place. Kitty heard reports that they were fighting and not always in private. The family's public relations team kept it out of the papers, as for half a century they had every Stokes scandal.

The Stokes public relations team were the best in the business, and they were paid a considerable sum to remain so. Consequently, Kitty was outraged when a paperback called *Cover-up* appeared that spring in bookstores across the nation. It had been issued by a major reprint publisher and it purported to tell the whole truth about Barton Stokes.

What was more, Kitty could see at one leafing, it did exactly that—ruthlessly and horribly.

She stormed into the Sixth Avenue office and confronted the public relations men in a fury.

"How in God's name did this happen?" She waved the book in their faces.

"We're just as baffled as you, Mrs. Stokes." To hear them explain it, the book had materialized out of nowhere, like an assassin's bullet.

It struck Kitty that the publisher was spending a fortune in ads, far more than any book could reasonably be expected to earn back. A dreadful doubt pulled at her. She went to Jay with a copy of *Cover-up*. "Have you seen this?"

"I've glanced at it," Jay said.

"Who's responsible for it?"

Jay shrugged and pulled at an ear. It pained Kitty to see the weight his face had put on. He was obviously drinking much too much. "The name's right there on the cover," he said, "Arthur M. Someone-or-other."

Kitty swung the book like a blade bisecting space. "Arthur M. Someone-or-other did not have the money to do this or the research or the motive. Somebody's behind him."

It took two heaves for Jay to get himself out of the easy chair. He paced a moment, then whirled. "Mom, what difference does it make? Every damned word in that book is true. Bart *did* marry a girl from a whorehouse. He *did* embezzle from a bank. He *did* fire the man who uncovered it. He *did* manipulate stock. There's not a lie in that pamphlet."

"Oh Jay," she sighed. "Oh Jay . . ." She covered her eyes.

"What are you being so dramatic about?"

*"You did this!"*

He was staring at her coolly. Not a breath of denial came from him. "And what if I did?"

"After all the years, all the effort . . ." She wanted to sob.

"Come off it, Mom, it's only a pamphlet."

"It's a low, vicious hatchet job. It's beneath contempt. *How could you?*" She took three steps toward him and she could see a flutter of fear in his eyes.

"I was angry. Hasn't anyone ever made you so angry you wanted to tear him apart?"

"People have made me angry—but no one's ever made me stupid." She flung the book halfway across the room. It thudded against the brass fire screen, so cheaply bound the title page fell out. Weariness gripped her. "What did you hope to accomplish?"

"I don't know. Get even for Bart's dumping those bonds, I suppose." Jay crossed to the bar and poured himself what appeared to be a triple scotch straight up.

She watched him swallow half of it. Anger writhed in her stomach. "You call it getting even? You've made a filthy, ugly fool of yourself in front of the whole world—you've shown you're a rotten, vicious loser."

Jay tossed a contemptuous glance toward the fireplace and the ripped book that lay there. "The world won't know who paid for that book."

"Bart will know!" Kitty was shouting now. "What if he retaliates? What if he publishes a pamphlet just as sleazy as that? What if he tells about your cheating at Harvard? Your first marriage? Your World War Two record? The truth about your Korean War decoration?"

"Mom, calm down. It doesn't matter. Don't you see, I'm finished. I've been finished since Miami. You can't do anything more to a man who's already finished."

"I thought *he* was a child—but you're an infant! When he struck to hurt you, at least he hurt *you,* not himself. But when you struck to hurt him, you *destroyed* yourself!"

"Mom, I'm deeply and truly sorry. I didn't realize you'd take it this way."

"You don't understand, do you." She spoke softly now, her voice barely a whisper. "You still don't realize what you've done."

"I realize I've made you unhappy and I'm sorry."

She stared at him. She could not see how Tyrone Duncannon's son could knowingly blot out all career, all future, all hope. She could not see how he could willfully sink himself in suicide.

"You've broken my heart, Jay. At long, long last—you've done it."

For a moment he said nothing. And then he took a long swallow of scotch. "Come on, Mom. It may have been dumb of me, but it's not the end of the world."

"It could very easily be the end of everything we've ever worked for."

There was scotch dribbling down his chin. He didn't bother to wipe it away. "Listen to me," he said, his voice flat and cold and not the voice of Jay Stokes at all. "I've paid my debts. I've spent over half my life in a shitty marriage. I've lost my son, my only child. I'm an alcoholic. And why? Because I was chasing some half-assed dream of yours all my life—not *my* dream, *yours!* I don't owe anyone anything—least of all you!"

He poured himself another glass of scotch. He stood facing her, his eyes nailing her, and swallowed half the drink in a gulp. His whole chin was glistening now. Something juvenile and vicious glinted in his eyes.

"You've ridden me my whole life," he said. "Well, you can just get the hell off. I'm not going to be your goddamned broomstick any longer."

Kitty sucked in her breath. The silence in the room expanded and contracted like a giant laboring heart. "If your father could see you . . ."

He wheeled on her, slopping scotch on the rug. "You never gave a fart about the old fool—why should I?"

"How dare you?" She sprang to her feet. The blood was hissing in her ears. "If you knew what your father had done— if you knew what he suffered and what hopes he had for you—"

"I know exactly what my father's done and I should have done it long ago. He told you to fuck off!"

Kitty stood paralyzed. She didn't believe she was hearing this. She didn't believe Tyrone Duncannon's son could say such things.

"As far as I'm concerned," Jay screamed, the veins rigid in his temples and throat, "you can *both* fuck off!"

She crossed the room and knocked the glass out of his hand.

He gulped and stared at her and seemed to come down a little from his craziness. "Get out of my life, Mom," he said in a voice that was absolutely, frighteningly sober.

"You don't mean that," she said.

"I mean it. I'm not even asking for three wishes. Just one. Get out."

"It's not you talking. It's the liquor."

His eyes came up at her. "Liquor's the only way I have the guts to tell you the truth. So listen. I'm through living life by someone else's cockamamie blueprint. From now on I'm going to do what I want. And if I want to drink and screw and fight with Toni in public or publish the truth about my shit-eating brother, I damned well will!"

The words tore a piece out of her. She could not answer. She could not believe the coldness of his eyes. A murderer's gaze would have had more love in it.

"Goodby, Mom," he said.

Her breath was rough in her throat. Something burning inched up her face. *He doesn't mean it,* she told herself. *He'll be sober tomorrow or the day after. He'll phone and say he's sorry.*

She turned quickly. Without waiting for the maid, without blinking or stumbling, she took her sable from the hall closet and let herself out of the apartment.

* * *

Toni had heard.

She had stood in the bedroom hallway and listened through the closed door to two adults going at one another like savage children. And a strange thing happened. The little spark of bravery left in her burned a tiny opening through the barricade that had walled it in.

She went to Jay. The living room was broodingly quiet, blanketed in air conditioning and drawn blinds. "Jay," she said, "did you mean what you said to her? Did you really mean it?"

She watched Jay pour himself a scotch. It looked like a fresh bottle of Chivas.

"Of course I meant it," he slurred.

"Then you'll forget her? You'll forget all those schemes of hers and the whole damned family?"

"That's just what I'm on the verge of accomplishing."

"How much have you drunk?"

"Get off my back."

She fought to keep her courage from breaking into pieces. "How much, Jay?"

"Three doubles."

Toni dropped an ice cube into a tumbler. She poured herself a double and downed it. Forcing her mind away from the liquor and onto the pheasant etched into the glass, she poured a second double and downed it and a third and downed it too.

Jay was watching her, impressed.

"We're even," she said. "Ready for a refill?"

"Sure. Why not."

He gave her his glass. She poured another round and handed him his drink.

"Jay, I want to get laid."

His eyes fixed her with bleary uncaring. "So go get laid."

"I don't want to go anywhere. I want to get laid in my own house by my own husband, right here, right now."

Jay looked at her. He arched an eyebrow. "You mean that? Right here?"

She unzipped her dress. "It's a good rug. Let's get it filthy."

It was a good rug. They got it filthy.

And something old came back into their lives that was very new to them.

Toni and Jay Stokes discovered they were tired of fighting,

that there were other ways of being together. Cautiously, step by step, they disarmed.

They began going to the same museum openings, to the same dinners and concerts. They took up tennis again and played mixed doubles. For the hell of it, they perfected a little system of signaling at bridge.

They experimented. They had dry evenings when they ate at home and neither of them drank. They lost weight. Toni cut back on the Valium shots. Friends remarked that they were looking better. They slept better too, and no longer jerked away when they accidentally touched in the double bed. They made an effort to make love on a more regular basis. Much of the time it worked, and after a while it wasn't such an effort at all.

After six months of no squabbles, friends considered them positively dull. They bought a lovely old mansion in the Hamptons with forty acres and worked at making it their home.

Gradually, the memory of their dead son lost its power to poison their lives. They stopped blaming one another. They stopped blaming themselves. They no longer worried about their successes and their failures, about elections or dessert soufflés for twenty. They were no longer in a contest with the universe, and the world no longer drove them apart.

If they had played their cards right, it could have been the beginning of happily ever after.

# *Chapter 27*

FOR SIX MONTHS Kitty lived in growing terror that Jay would never speak to her again. And then, out of the blue, he phoned and invited her to lunch at the Harvard Club.

He apologized for the argument. He said he had cut down on his drinking and his women. She could see the difference in his appearance. His youth and strength and confidence seemed to have flowed back. Hope returned to Kitty. She began to think that perhaps by the time of the next election, or the one after that, Jay might be ready for another try at the top.

Her one fear was that Bart would retaliate for the pamphlet, that the retaliation would be so total and crushing that Jay would never get to his feet again. She held her breath. For almost nine months the retaliation did not come. Bart's office did not even comment on the pamphlet.

But one weekend in Maine Kitty picked up the local newspaper. She flinched. Beth Stokes was scheduled on a national talk show that evening. Among the topics discussed would be the charges raised in *Cover-up*.

Kitty knew that Johnny preferred "Movie of the Week" to talk shows, and he had virtually forbidden Beth's name to be mentioned in the house. But there was only one television set working.

"Johnny," she said, "I've got to see this."

To her surprise, he wanted to watch it with her. They sat in Johnny's bedroom, Kitty on the sofa, Johnny in the easy chair with a tumbler of his favorite bourbon and water. The interviewer's name was Deborah Thomas. She had artful blond hair and was said to be a shark who went straight for the underbelly.

"Then you did work in a whorehouse? You don't deny that?"

Beth Stokes's poise under attack was remarkable. The soft smiling line of her mouth did not waver. She wore a high-necked maroon silk blouse and no jewelry that Kitty could see. Her hair was natural, beginning to gray. It was the interviewer who looked like the whore, and a low-cut one at that.

"I don't deny it at all," Beth said. "I made beds and I mixed drinks. College boys drank manhattans and a lot of sweet things in those days."

"Did you ever—you know—sell your body?"

"You may find this hard to believe, Deborah, but I never once did. And I'm not hedging or playing with words. I never slept with a single man while I was under that roof."

"Were you a virgin?"

"No, at the time I entered the whorehouse I hadn't been a virgin for some time."

"How old were you at the time?"

"Sixteen."

"Why did you work in such a place?"

"In those days, if you were under seventeen, you couldn't legally get a job without your parents' permission. I didn't have my parents' permission. I'd run away from home in Haverhill, Massachusetts. I had no qualifications, and Deborah, I mean *none*. The only job I could find, the only job where no one asked questions, where I could get room and board and a semblance of security, was in that whorehouse."

"Were you mistreated? Did your employer abuse you?"

"Legally, my employer was in violation of child labor laws. But Deborah, you have to bear in mind that the law *is* blind, and in my case—I came from a very difficult home—I was better off in that whorehouse than in Haverhill. The law of course would have returned me to my parents, and that was what I dreaded."

"You had a tragic childhood, then?"

"A hard one. My parents beat me."

"Were you an only child?"

"I was the only child that lived."

"Then you must have some strong feelings about child abuse."

Beth nodded. "Children are the last defenseless minority in this country. They have few rights, fewer advocates—and they are the worst exploited minority because the exploitation is too often invisible."

"Do you think the state should intervene?"

"I think parents should be loving."

"And I'm sure our viewers couldn't agree more." The shot changed to another angle, and the interviewer shifted smoothly in her chair. "For those of you who are tuning in late, my guest Elizabeth Stokes and I are discussing the book *Cover-up, The Story of Barton Stokes,* which has appeared on newsstands nationwide and aroused so much controversy. Now Beth, the author of this book alleges that your husband worked for a bank in New York City under an assumed name, that he embezzled money . . ."

Kitty knew the entire story. She had lived it. She was impressed that Beth answered point by point, never once raising her voice, never leaving a sentence dangling or a smear unanswered. Yes, she admitted, Bart Stokes had stolen. Yes, it had been covered up.

"And why did your husband need the four hundred dollars?"

"For me. I was pregnant, and the pregnancy was what doctors used to call 'difficult.'"

"But even in 1946, couldn't you have gone to a public hospital? Couldn't you have applied for public funds?"

"Not legally, Deborah. We were needy at the time, we were without funds, but it was by choice. Bart was, after all, a Stokes. We had no right to take public money."

"Now, the author of *Cover-up* gives a slightly different explanation. He says you *did* go to a public hospital, you *did* attempt to be treated under a publicly funded program, but—"

"But I'd had an abortion," Beth cut in. "The hospital refused to treat me unless I gave them the name of the doctor who'd performed the operation, so that they could turn him over to the police. I couldn't do that."

Kitty drew in a deep breath. This part of the story was new. She looked at the wing chair to see how Johnny was taking it.

He had huddled into shadow. His fingers gripped at the armrests. His silence was bunched up, tight, like a scream about to rip loose.

She made a move to turn off the set. Johnny's voice came out roughly, like sandpaper on glass.

*"Leave it on."*

Kitty left it on. The interviewer was facing the camera now.

"Abortion is fairly common nowadays," she said, "but I should remind our viewers that in 1946 it was hardly a routine procedure. Society was against it, the law was against it, and medicine was against it." She turned again to Beth. "What made you, Elizabeth Stokes, flout the moral code of the time?"

"I had no choice. I was sixteen, I was alone, I was pregnant."

"As a woman who later gave birth to three healthy children, you have no regrets when you look back?"

"None at all."

"But didn't you consider the alternatives? Having the child, putting it up for adoption?"

"Not for a moment. It wouldn't have been fair to the adoptive parents or to the child."

"Why not?"

"Deborah, my mother and father are both dead, and I'm going to tell you the reason. I'd been raped. What happened to me happens to thousands of girls every year. I know by saying this on television I'm going to offend those of your viewers who'd rather bury disagreeable facts than face them— but maybe I can give courage and hope to some child or young girl who's in the position I was in then. You see, the man who raped me was my father."

A glass smashed to the marble hearth. Kitty whirled at the sound.

A groaning was coming out of Johnny. A spasm ripped his body and flung him forward against the table and onto the floor.

"Johnny!"

Kitty leaped up and crouched quickly beside him. A cocoon of spittle was pushing out of his mouth. She rolled back his cuff, clutched for a pulse. It was there, hammering. She turned up an eyelid. His pupil was gazing into the top of his skull.

"Johnny—my God!"

She stumbled to her feet and ran screaming for Vicky Jennings.

\* \* \*

They rushed Johnny to the hospital at Bangor. The emergency room was shrill with bells and beeps and voices and fluorescent light. There were patients on stretchers and patients in wheelchairs, some half-naked and bandaged, some still dressed and bleeding through their clothes. They all seemed to be dying, anesthetized by their own pain.

Two interns moved a dead man and put Johnny on a table. He had not regained consciousness. They drew a curtain around him and said they were sorry, but Kitty and Vicky would have to wait outside.

The two women read all the magazines in the waiting room. The world felt far away. It was almost three o'clock in the morning when a doctor stepped briskly into the corridor. He introduced himself and said tests had revealed alcohol in the patient's bloodstream. He asked about Johnny's drinking habits.

It had been years since Kitty had known anything firsthand about her husband's drinking. She appealed to Vicky with a sideways glance.

"He drinks a little now and then," Vicky said.

If the doctor was surprised that it was the secretary and not the wife who answered, he did not show it. "How much?" he asked.

"Mr. Stokes would know that better than I," Vicky said.

*Does she mean Johnny drinks alone?* Kitty wondered.

"We have asked him," the doctor said. "But in these cases the patient is apt to lie." The doctor's face was a dark, worried squint. He had an Arabic name and an East Indian accent, and Kitty deduced he was Pakistani. She wondered if he understood her English. She was certain she was not understanding his.

"Why should my husband lie?" Kitty said.

"Many people are ashamed of alcoholism," the doctor said.

"My husband is not an alcoholic."

The doctor did not acknowledge her. Even more astonishingly, he asked if Mr. Stokes had any history of epilepsy.

"Of course not," Kitty said, surprised at her own vehemence.

"Tonight he suffered an epileptic seizure."

"What's that got to do with alcohol?"

"Epilepsy does not suddenly appear in late middle age—

unless there are aggravating circumstances. Such as drink."

Kitty was not about to let Johnny be called a closet lush. "Isn't there another explanation, Doctor? Couldn't a shock have brought it on? Because I can assure you, Johnny did have a shock tonight."

"You do not understand the etiology of the disease. Mr. Stokes has been drinking alcohol sufficiently long and in sufficient quantity that it has begun to interfere with the electrical activity of his brain."

Kitty could not buy it. "Are you saying he's alcoholic, or are you saying he's epileptic?"

The doctor had bright, mousy eyes and his fingers kept picking at a thin little mustache. "Mrs. Stokes, he is both."

Kitty flatly refused to accept that. "I'll want a second opinion," she said.

"Of course."

Kitty signed Johnny out of the hospital on a stretcher. She and Vicky flew with him to New York in the family jet. An ambulance was waiting to rush him to the Clinic. Kitty held his hand while the siren screamed. The doctors had given him phenobarbital to raise the seizure threshold and he slept all the way.

That afternoon Kitty sat down with Howard Bergman to hear the second opinion. "How long has he been coughing like that?" he asked.

Kitty shifted uneasily in the chair. Something in Howard's eyes seemed to accuse her of negligence. "He's always had a smoker's cough," she said.

"Our X-rays show the hospital in Bangor slipped up."

"I *knew* it!" Kitty said.

Howard studied her a moment. "Brace yourself, Kitty. Johnny has cancer."

Nothing moved in the room. A jolt of denial went through her. The tick of the grandfather clock seemed to come very late and the rest of the diagnosis seemed to reach her from a great distance. She was able to grasp that tumors had formed in both Johnny's lungs. Malignant cells had entered the bloodstream. They had metastasized to the brain and triggered the seizure.

"I'm sorry, Kitty," Howard said. He looked at her with a compassion that spanned the decades of their lives together.

"The disease is too far advanced for surgery. We'll do whatever else we can."

She waited in a chair in Johnny's hospital room. He lay muffled and silent in his bed. Several times he seemed near waking and then slid back into unconsciousness.

Finally he opened his eyes. No one had shaved him and he looked lost and scared and unkempt like a homeless old dog.

Kitty told him where he was. She told him Howard Bergman's diagnosis. He smiled the strangest smile she had ever seen, and for the first time in her life she glimpsed the effort that went into his gallantry. She wanted desperately to offer him some prop to endurance.

"You're going to pull through this, Johnny."

"That so?"

There was an odd mischievousness to the question that she couldn't fathom. "We have the top specialists in the field," she said. "For once they're going to earn their pay."

"God bless you, Kitty. I wish I were a fighter like you."

"You are, Johnny. You *are.*"

Kitty and Vicky divided their vigils. Vicky took nights. Kitty came and sat by Johnny's bed every afternoon.

Sometimes they talked, and sometimes Johnny just stretched out his hand and Kitty held it tight. "Tell Bart I'd like to see him," Johnny said. "I'd like to see his wife too—and the kids."

Under other circumstances Kitty would have been pleased that Johnny wanted to see his relatives. But now all she could think was that he was very like a man making his peace with the world before dying.

She relayed his wish.

Bart visited the Clinic with Beth and the children. Johnny at last met his grandchildren. They had grown into young adults, well behaved in the presence of illness. Johnny told Kitty he liked them. "Better late than never," he said.

Jay visited too. Sometimes he brought Toni, and always he brought a bottle and got drunk, right there at Johnny's bedside. And Johnny never protested.

There were other visitors, friends and employees and life-time servants. The list had to be kept small because Johnny tired easily.

One day when Kitty and Vicky were both there, the President of the United States dropped in to visit. Naturally, since taking office he had become a personal friend; but Kitty couldn't help thinking of him, for all his soft accent and gentle manners, as the man who had taken the nomination from Jay. He was wearing striped silk pajamas and he had a deck of cards in his hand. He said he was in the Clinic for a routine checkup and felt like gambling.

"How's your poker, ladies?" he asked.

"Kitty's the best," Johnny said.

The President arched a bushy gray eyebrow at her. "We'll see about that."

The President shuffled the cards. Johnny cut. The President dealt; during the game he flirted with Vicky, and Kitty reflected that he must be the one man in the country who didn't know she was Johnny's mistress. He charmed Johnny's private nurse into bringing them a coffeepot of pure alcohol and a lemon. They all got high on ethyl martinis with a twist.

It was an evening of laughing and not caring about the country or cancer. Kitty and Vicky both had amazing runs of luck, capped by a full house and two straights. They cleaned the men out of their pocket money—eighteen hundred dollars—and went home rich and glowing.

Yet Kitty could see that something was clearly wrong. Over the weeks, Johnny lost weight horribly. His talk more and more often rambled. For all the miracles of Stokes-funded cancer research, Kitty could no longer be certain he was going to pull through.

One Thursday after visiting hours she stood in the Clinic corridor alone in a soft swirl of nurses and interns. She began to face doubts. She had spent four hours at Johnny's bedside, silent hours mostly, and there was a queer hollowness inside her, as though her heart had caved in. It was all she could do to steel herself in practicality and walk to the elevator.

"Mrs. Stokes?" A young man blocked her way. Smiling, he held out a hand. "Dr. Rossi," he said. "Dr. Desmond Rossi. I work here."

"Of course," Kitty said, though there was no *of course* in her mind at all—only a vague intuition that she knew his type. She took his hand with an annoyed awareness that this was the wrong time and place for smiles and introductions.

"We have to talk," he said.

"If you phone my secretary I'm sure you can make an appointment."

There was something hungry in his eyes, and her tone of voice did not drive it away. "We have to talk now—about your husband."

The word did it. She gave him her attention. "What about my husband?"

"I'm concerned about his treatment. In fact I'm alarmed. And I think you ought to be alarmed too. If you'd care to come to my office, it's just down the hallway."

*Alarmed?* she wondered. *What's alarming about Johnny's treatment?* She followed down the corridor and into another wing. The young doctor's step did not betray alarm; far from it. He closed the door softly behind them. She saw at a glance he had the office of a sixty-three-thousand-dollar-a-year man.

"Won't you have a chair, Mrs. Stokes?"

She sensed more youth in the doctor than he wished to reveal and suspected his mustache was a cover-up. She sat on a graceful wood chair bearing the Harvard *veritas* insignia.

The doctor parked a slender buttock on the corner of his desk, a position that raised him above Kitty. He was dressed in a dark three-piece suit appropriate to his salary. He swung a briefcase onto his lap. It was polished steerhide. His shoes, she saw, were polished steerhide too. The steers matched.

The doctor's eyes were not those of a steer but of a smaller, cleverer, less edible animal. He clicked open the snaps of the briefcase. The lid rose with hydraulic smoothness and she saw the Gucci trademark.

"Perhaps you'd care to glance at the treatment authorized for Mr. Stokes." The doctor leaned forward to hand her two sets of Xeroxes. They appeared to have been quickly, perhaps furtively, copied. One consisted of duplicates of the daily sheets from the patient's chart. The handwriting was Dr. Howard Bergman's.

The other, and messier, set was copies of computer printout. The accordion-fold paper had obviously not been tailored to Xerox machines. Kitty's eyes skimmed grains of aspirin and endless cc's of Demerol. There were nightly doses of barbiturate, increasing, and noontime wallops of methamphetamine.

The handwritten records were apparently medicine pre-

scribed; the computerized, medicine delivered. At a glance the
two records appeared to be identical. Kitty handed back the
documents.

An emptiness waited to be filled.

Clearly the young doctor thought he had some kind of hold
on her. His ambition showed raw and red, like steak dripping
from a butcher's grinder. Kitty felt old with the knowledge of
other people's ambition.

"My husband is in pain," she said quietly. "I see nothing
abnormal in these prescriptions. Obviously you do."

"Very abnormal," the doctor said.

Kitty wondered what sort of ignoramus this young man took
her for. Was he trying to frighten her with a narcotics charge?
The tactic did not fit with the salary.

"Obviously," she said, "the Demerol is for pain. The barbiturate is to control the seizure threshold. The amphetamine
counteracts the sedative side effects. I have implicit trust in
Dr. Bergman."

"Mrs. Stokes, you understand that what I'm telling you must
be confidential. Your husband is being treated for pain. He is
not being treated in any way for cancer. He's not getting chemotherapy. He's not getting radiology. He's being allowed to
die."

Denial ballooned in the pit of her stomach. "I don't believe
you."

"Mrs. Stokes, have you ever known anyone undergoing
chemotherapy or radiation treatment?"

"Yes, I have."

"And what happened to their hair?"

"They lost it."

"Mrs. Stokes: your husband still has his hair."

Kitty sat rigid on the *veritas* chair, her fingers locking on
themselves. A fog of plausibility began to close in on her.
There was the fact of Johnny's weight loss and wretched appearance and rambling speech, the overnight descent toward
skeletal senility. "But how—?" she stammered. "How could
Dr. Bergman overlook—?"

"It couldn't be oversight," Dr. Desmond Rossi cut in.

"But how could Dr. Bergman *knowingly*—?"

"I suggest you ask him yourself, and as soon as possible."

\* \* \*

Kitty realized that there was absolutely no time for hesitation. She told her office to locate Howard Bergman. It turned out he was at a small dinner party at a Beekman Place townhouse.

Kitty did not phone ahead. She presented herself at the front door and told the stuttering hostess that she must speak with Dr. Bergman immediately and privately.

Howard Bergman, dinner napkin still in hand, met her in a small drawing room on the second floor.

"Johnny's not getting treatment for cancer. Why not?" she demanded.

Howard Bergman had the look on his face of a man honestly in pain. He went to the window and stood gazing down at the evening dark of the garden and the black flowing velvet of the East River beyond it. His voice was pale and pained and tight. "Johnny doesn't want treatment."

Kitty frowned, trying to grasp his meaning. "That's not possible."

"Kitty, he's refused it."

"Refused?" Kitty's mind whirled. "How could he refuse? *Why* would he refuse?"

"All I know is that his lawyers served us a restraining order."

For an instant there were no words in her, only disbelief whooshing from a slack jaw.

"There's not a damned thing we can do, Kitty. He went to court years ago and got the order."

Anger leaped up in Kitty. "No court can order you to let a man die."

"This court can, Kitty, because this man wants to die."

"You have no right to—"

"It's *Johnny's* right," Howard cut in.

Kitty stood for a moment, rage choking off her breath. "How long have you known?" she finally managed to whisper.

"Since he checked into the Clinic."

*"And you didn't tell me?"*

"He's my patient, Kitty. He wanted it kept confidential."

On the other side of the closed door, a universe away, voices laughed.

"I want to see this court order," Kitty said.

* * *

It turned into a night of crosstown dashes in the limousine and phone calls rousing lawyers and district-court judges from bed. The lawyers and judges agreed that there was no shaking the court order, certainly not at this hour.

In desperation Kitty phoned Justin Lasting. He was now in his eighties, but age had not robbed him of one spark of intelligence or slyness. Kitty explained the situation. Justin Lasting tightened the sash of his bathrobe. He did not seem in the least shocked. It occurred to her that she had never seen him shocked in all the years she'd known him.

"What if I take him out of state," she said, "beyond New York jurisdiction?"

He shook his head "The order rests on Johnny's right to die. The deposition invoking that right was taken when presumably Johnny was of sound mind and sounder body than at present. There's not a state in the union that won't honor it."

"I'll take him to Mexico," Kitty said. "Catholics won't let him die."

"His attorneys would block you. They'd have state troopers at the airport to stop you. Obviously they've been prepared for this a good long time. They're armed."

Kitty held her head in her hands and for the first time in her life understood the full irrational force of the law. "What can I do?" she sobbed.

"Go to him, Kitty Talk to him. Reason with him. Make him change his mind. He loves you, Kitty. You can do it. You *have* to do it."

Kitty returned to the Clinic before breakfast. The shade was up in Johnny's room and there was an odd gentle glow like sunlight that had found its way to the bottom of a well.

In the bed against the wall Johnny lay very still. Kitty approached softly and looked down at him. His face was a colorless membrane stretched over his skull, and yet it was masked in a secret smile. He looked old and young at the same time, like a hundred-year-old newborn infant.

"I know what you've done, Johnny," she said. "I know about the deposition and the court order."

His eyes opened.

"Johnny, I'm begging you. Set them aside. I have a legal stenographer and a district judge waiting. The hospital can begin treating you immediately."

"No," he said. "I won't have treatment." His voice was unbending and it terrified her. Instinct warned her not to waste time arguing or pleading.

"All right, Johnny, I'll fight you. I have lawyers too."

His eyes gripped her and his voice was tough in a way she had never heard before. "I'm going to do it my way, Kitty. Someday you'll understand."

"I won't let you die," she said.

"It's not *your* choice. This time *I* have the high card."

She couldn't be sure if it was Demerol or Johnny talking. What did he mean? What card?

He pointed to the drawer of the bedside table. "Open it."

She obeyed. There was no card in the drawer—only a key with the number of a safe-deposit box cut into it.

"Chase Manhattan Bank," he said. "Rockefeller Center. Take the elevator to vault level."

She remained motionless by the bed, listening and scared. This voice that knew what it wanted was not the voice of Johnny Stokes at all.

"My lawyers have the sealed originals of the documents in the box. If you fight me, they'll be sent to every newspaper in the country. If you let me die, the originals will be given to you unopened. Don't fight me, Kitty. For Jay's sake, don't fight me."


Kitty went to the bank and signed the register. A guard let her take a metal box from the vault into a private cubicle. She locked the door. She opened the box.

There were two manila envelopes. She paused. A dull warning pain flicked through her. She drew a careful breath and opened the heavier envelope. It held nine pieces of paper.

They were photocopies of government forms, slick and almost damp to the touch. At first she thought they were drivers' licenses and she wondered, *Why would Johnny have these?*

And then she saw the names.

Ronald O'Rourke. Seth MacLagger. *Ronnie and Seth*, she thought, and the past was whispering through her like a breeze trickling through a crack in the window.

Joseph Costello. Thomas Carmody. Richard Lannigan. *Joey and Tommy and Richie*. Their faces and voices filled her mind and she could smell them and she was thinking of people and places she hadn't seen in half a century—her dad and Father

Jack and fat Edie Costello; the old company store with its burlap sacks of grain that you could never keep the mice out of; the shack with the dirt floor that she had called home; the taste of canned beans that made your stomach tighten like a fist.

She struggled to get something straight in her head. These couldn't be drivers' licenses. Joey Costello had never had a penny to own a car. No one in Bartonville had. And besides, Joey had died in the shooting and so had Richie and Tommy and Ronnie . . .

*Death certificates* she realized . . . signed by Dr. Howard Bergman. The Bartonville Nine.

And the name on the sixth was Tyrone Duncannon.

Now the past was screaming through her like wind through an open tunnel. She ripped open the second envelope. Her heart hammered in her throat. There was a ringing in her ears.

A piece of paper tumbled out.

It took her a moment to make sense of what she held. The photostat showed jagged edges where a page had been ripped from its binding. The neat, tiny penmanship had faded like dried blood. Kitty squinted. It was like trying to read the scars of long-healed wounds.

She made out that it was an entry in a parish register. A marriage. She saw Tyrone Duncannon's name and she saw her maiden name and she saw the date.

A cry broke from the hollow inside her. Understanding came, stumbling and shot with pain.

Johnny knew!

But *how* had he known?

How long had he known?

She put her head down on the table and sobbed. She was alone and she could not bear it. In a soundproof, thiefproof cubicle two stories below the richest street in the world, shadows and silence and wealth enclosed her. All the betrayals of her life blanketed her.

"I did the right thing!" she cried. "I did! I did!"

There was no answer, no confirmation, no denial. And something in her wondered, *Have I ever done a single right thing in my life?*

She was old. Her strength was gone and with it her certainty. She had no answers left.

She took the envelopes home. Though they were only copies, she burned the contents to ashes in her bedroom fireplace.

\* \* \*

The end was not long in coming.

A little after three the next morning an urgent voice on the telephone told Kitty she had better get back to the Clinic quickly. Jay and Toni and Vicky Jennings were there. Bart was there too, sitting stiffly on the far side of the room, and Beth was with him.

But it was Kitty that Johnny had asked to see.

A young nurse hurried her through Johnny's door. The lights in his room were very low and his eyes were two dull gleams in the shadow.

"Sorry I'm a little vague today," he said, and Kitty realized he thought it was still daylight. "They're giving me that Demerol around the clock now. Makes me drift. Strangest things come into my head. Know what I thought of the other day?"

"What was that, Johnny?" Kitty drew a chair close.

The bed had been cranked so he could sit halfway up with the help of three pillows. The nurse must have just given him a needle. He spoke disjointedly. She sensed the waves of unconsciousness pressing closer and closer together in him.

If he was at all afraid, his eyes did not show it. For his sake she tried to smile and be brave. He smiled back at her.

"Remember that first time I took you to dinner—that old speakeasy with all the mirrors in it? Remember I kept pouring wine in your glass to get you drunk?"

"Yes, Johnny." She nodded her head. "I remember."

"Everywhere I looked there was a reflection of you. I never saw anything so pretty. I couldn't believe you were interested in a dunce like me."

"You were never a dunce, Johnny."

"I was a dunce, and if it hadn't been for you I would have stayed one. You made me, Kitty. You made my life. You could have had anyone. You were so bright and alive and young. You looked so pretty and you chose me. Thank you, Kitty. It's been all right, hasn't it?"

Suddenly she was not sure what he meant. Suddenly she was not sure she could keep smiling.

"You and me," he said. "We've been all right, haven't we?" His eyes searched hers and she realized this was the most important question he had ever asked her.

"Johnny," she blurted. "I'm sorry."

There was no change in Johnny's expression. Nothing moved in his face. Nothing shifted in his eyes. "You don't really regret anything, do you, Kitty?"

She gazed at him and her lips trembled. She thought of a thousand old hopes and promises, all failed, all broken, trips they had never taken, time they had never spent together, kisses they had never kissed, evenings she had meant to telephone him in Maine and had let something else come up instead. She thought how quickly the changeable present becomes the unchangeable past, how quickly *now* slips into *forever*. She remembered strange things, smells especially—the old books in his study, those oil paints he used to doodle with . . .

But she could not remember the last time they'd made love. She could not remember their last embrace. She could not remember when she had last said, *I love you, Johnny.*

She could not remember why she had chosen to love a dead man instead of this living one; and now he, too, was going from her.

Her eyes turned on him, hot and running tears.

"You don't regret anything do you?" he said again.

It seemed to her, at that moment, she regretted all the choices of her life. But she knew what he wanted to hear.

"No, Johnny, not a thing."

He nodded, relieved. "What the hell did you see in me?" He reached for her hand. "Do you still see it?"

She stared at her husband. It suddenly seemed she had always seen him without knowing it. "Johnny, you're my only friend—the only friend I've ever had."

"Don't miss me too much, Kitty. You've put up with me for a hell of a long time. I must have bored you sick sometimes."

"That's not true, Johnny. That's never been true."

"I'm not bright like you," he said. "Oh, I understand a few things. But you understand everything. Except maybe Bart. Don't forget to look after him a little too. He may not show it, but he needs mothering just as much as his brother."

Kitty was afraid. Her heart thudded against her ribs and the image in front of her eyes trembled. A battle was raging between her mind and heart. She wanted him to go peacefully, but she craved absolution.

"Johnny," she whispered, "I opened the safe-deposit box. I saw the papers. Please—*please forgive me.*"

He raised a finger, silencing her.

They stared at one another, two people on the brink of aloneness together now for the last time and yet, in an odd way, together for the first time in their lives. It was as though they were seeing one another from a completely new perspective.

"How strange life has been!" he said. "How strange it is! Even now!" After a long, silent moment he squeezed her hand. "You won't forget Bart, will you Kitty? Promise?"

She squeezed back. "I promise I won't, Johnny."

"Thank you for sitting here with me. Thank you for everything."

"I love sitting with you, Johnny."

He sighed. "My eyes weigh a ton. It's that Demerol. They're giving me so much. I feel dozy all the time."

"You doze, Johnny. I'll be here."

"You'll be here when I wake up?"

"Right here beside you."

He smiled and closed his eyes.

Kitty stayed right there, squeezing his hand. Gradually he stopped squeezing back. He never woke up again.

# Chapter 28

KITTY SPOKE TO Bart before the funeral, while the promise was still alive in her. They sat in the study on Sixty-second Street, and he listened with the courteous, distant manner of a Joint Chief of Staff at a briefing.

Finally he said, "Why?"

"Because your father wanted us to make up. Let's forget the past. Let's forget the bonds. Can't we just be friends?"

Bart's smooth porcelain gaze fixed on her. "Mother, I'll admit I wanted your love. I fought for your love. But after Jay had his turn at the teat there was never any left over for me—and there never will be."

She drew back. "You've been angry at me all these years, and now when I'm old and alone you finally have the courage to hurt me."

He shook his head and there was sadness in his eyes. "I'm not angry, Mother. I'm not even sorry anymore. Father's free at last. And when I look at Jay, I see how lucky I was. I escaped."

She could feel the old imagined betrayals still smarting in him. "I've always suspected you hated your brother. Till this moment, I never suspected how much you hated me."

"I don't hate anyone, Mother. I'm past that."

She didn't believe him. She didn't believe he'd ever be past it. "I'm sorry for you, Bart. I'm sorry for anyone who stores up such bitterness in his heart."

"Don't start worrying about me at this late date. I'll get by. I always have, haven't I?" He kissed her with a gentleness that caught her totally unprepared. "Take care of yourself—and of Jay."

The funeral was family and close friends only—three hundred and fifty-two of them. Kitty followed the coffin into the warm April sunlight and watched the workmen lay Johnny next to his mother and father, beside the plot that would one day be hers.

Vicky Jennings stood silently beside her. Kitty was aware of the onlookers watching the curious pair they made, the wife and the mistress locked in mourning. She didn't care about onlookers. She took Vicky's hand and held it through the final prayers. She could feel the shaking of silent sobs.

Afterward they rode back in the limousine together. They cried in one another's arms. They cried because of Johnny, but they cried too because they had been young together, because they had been friends and enemies together, because they were still together and nothing else seemed to be together at all.

They didn't speak till the end of the ride.

"He doesn't seem gone," Kitty said. "I can't believe it's happened."

"I won't believe it," Vicky said. "Not today. Tomorrow I'll make myself believe it a little, and a little bit more the day after that, and maybe in a month I'll believe it."

How like Vicky to have a plan, Kitty thought. *Why don't I have a plan?* she wondered. "What are you going to do now?" she asked.

Vicky sighed and pulled at the fingers of her black gloves. "I don't know. I'll close up the house I suppose." Johnny had left it to her; the little graveyard went to one of the family trusts.

"Will you sell it?" Kitty asked.

"Do you want it?" Vicky said.

"Not without Johnny," Kitty said.

"Neither do I."

"Someone will want it," Kitty said, though she couldn't

imagine who would want a coal-heated thirty-room mansion nowadays. "If I can help, Vicky, in any way..."

Vicky kissed her quickly.

"I've never helped you at all, Vicky, and you've helped me all my life."

"Have I? I'm glad."

"I want to help you now. What do you need? What can I do?"

"Just write to me now and then, Kitty. Promise not to forget me—please."

An era was ending for Kitty, and it was not ending gently. She was losing piece after piece of her world to eternity.

Over the next three years Howard Bergman, the last person on earth she could really talk to, had three strokes and two heart attacks. He told her that though they were minor, they were adding up and he expected to die quite suddenly and quite soon.

She hugged him quickly. "Don't say that, Howard."

"What's wrong with saying the truth?"

"It's not the truth. It's only a possibility, and don't say it."

At their last meeting he told her there was something he'd always wondered. "Who was Jay's father? I never believed it was Johnny."

She stared into her scotch and then she told him the whole story. It all seemed far away and long past, like something that had happened once upon a time to someone else.

He listened gravely and then he nodded. "Well, Kitty, you would have made a much better Jew than me."

"Why do you say that?"

"You've worked out one of the most elaborate contracts with the Almighty that I've ever heard of."

"What's elaborate about a simple promise?"

"Sticking to it is elaborate. The universe has gone through holocausts and light years and you're still in that graveyard shaking your fist."

"Do you think I was wrong?"

"Not wrong, just blind. But determination is always blind, isn't it? How else can it succeed?"

She sighed. "But I haven't succeeded."

"You will, Kitty," he said. "Just keep your eyes shut and keep shaking that fist."

"You're laughing at me."

"Only because you're adorable."

"Children are adorable," she said. "Old bags like me aren't."

"You're adorable, Kitty." He kissed her lightly on the forehead. "Take my word for it."

They slept in their separate houses that night, as they often did, and Howard Bergman died in his sleep. It was Dr. Desmond Rossi of the Clinic who phoned Kitty and broke the news to her.

She felt grief, but it wasn't the suffocating numbness she'd felt over Johnny. It was a very different feeling now, like waiting for room in a crowded elevator. Even if you were momentarily separated from your companions, everyone rode sooner or later to that other floor. Howard Bergman had gotten in first, that was all.

In accordance with his wishes, there was no service, no eulogy or prayer at the crematorium. An organist played Bach's *Komm, süsse Tod,* and Howard Bergman's coffin, laden with white flowers, was committed to the flame.

Kitty retired to her townhouse for three days until she had exhausted the need to weep over things that were gone. She knew no tears could call back the past, and she fixed her mind more resolutely than ever on the time remaining to her, on the here and now, and prayed that with all its confusion and opportunity it would offer one last chance to realize the dream of her life.

In many respects, times were good.

Stokes Industries were making an escalating percentage of Arab oil price increases and they were thriving as never before. There was a threat from Mexican oil, since Mexico had enough to fuel the U.S. for eighty years and was next door. Stokes lobbyists kept Mexican oil out of the newspapers and out of the country, and the nation went on believing that its lifeline lay to the Stokes footholds in the Mideast.

By the mid-seventies, profits of Stokes Industries were stratospheric—and they, of course, were only the profits that showed on paper.

Yet the profits were useless.

Though half the House of Representatives and two thirds of the Senate were millionaires and no one but a multimillionaire could afford to run for President, the kingmakers and caucuses refused time and time again to consider a Jay Stokes candidacy, let alone a trial balloon. Jay's money and his alone, it appeared, was tainted; the world of power had closed ranks against him.

But Kitty could not believe, would not accept, that it was all over. She encouraged Jay to speak out on public issues, to create and fund and chair committees on the arts and the sciences and on the choices confronting America. Whatever could keep him in the public awareness was done and publicized.

At the same time she made an effort to swallow the past and her pride and keep channels to her other son open and, on the surface at least, friendly. In certain inevitable respects Bart was becoming a minor political power in his own right: he served as president of a commission to investigate the demonetization of gold; he acted as minister without portfolio to negotiate Chinese reparations for American property seized in the revolution; the government implemented what newspapers called "the Stokes Plan" for funding industrialization in China and the Third World; and just when Kitty thought Bart might be turning into the Republicrat's top China man, he took over assistant directorship of the General Accounting Office.

Kitty tried to have Bart and Beth to dinner at least once a month. But there were years when they were in Washington or out of the country and she saw them only three or four times. She memorized their children's birthdays and interests and made sure they got good, appropriate presents. She did everything she could, short of putting him on the payroll, to make Bart one of her army of the best and most influential minds in America, an army standing and ready, awaiting the call that would summon them into battle for Jay.

Kitty had known that the call must come sooner or later, but she had never imagined that it would come from Dr. Desmond Rossi so many years after Johnny and Howard's deaths.

"I have information that concerns your son Jay," Dr. Rossi said. "It can't be discussed on the phone."

Kitty felt no more friendliness toward Dr. Rossi than toward the angel of death, but he was head of the Clinic now and his information had, in the past, been solid.

"Come to the house at three," she said.

When the butler showed Dr. Rossi into the study, Kitty was sitting at her desk going over Sumatra accounts.

"Have you been following the Kentucky grand jury rigging scandal?" the doctor asked. He was older. His face was lined and unevenly colored, like a baseball glove that had been broken in too quickly. "It's clear that the Vice President is implicated. He'll be sacked before the campaign. The President will have to choose a new running mate."

Kitty gazed at Dr. Rossi's eyes, ice-bright as always.

"The next Vice President," he said, "will become President of the United States."

"That happens very rarely," Kitty said.

"But in this case it's a certainty."

Kitty did not move or speak or react in any way.

"Are you aware," Dr. Rossi said, "that the President checked into the Clinic for exploratory surgery last September? The press called it a long Labor Day weekend at Camp David."

Kitty was aware of this. After all, she owned the Clinic. She owned a great deal of American cancer research, and if the breakthrough ever came, the chances were that Stokes Industries would own the drug patents as well.

"The tumors were nonmalignant," Kitty said.

The doctor nodded. "And the nonmalignancy has returned."

Kitty's eyes drilled into the thin slant of Dr. Rossi's. It took her a moment to fully grasp his meaning. "How do you come by this information?" she asked.

He drew himself up. "Two weekends ago the President signed into the Clinic for his annual checkup. He used the same false name as always. It happened to be similar to one of my patients'—a spleen cancer, charity case. The President was given a clean bill of health. My man died."

"Of spleen cancer?" Kitty said.

"Of spleen cancer with a surprising last-minute complication. According to the X-rays, he developed cancer throughout his right lung and the bottom third of his left—overnight."

Kitty began to make out the broad outline of Dr. Rossi's intent. She could begin to see where he was leading her.

"In other words," he said, "because of the similarity in names, my patient's lung X-rays were switched with the President's. My patient kept his spleen, but he got the President's lungs and the President got my patient's."

Kitty hesitated on the threshold of belief. It seemed too easy. "But if that's true, then the President . . ."

"Is dying, Mrs. Stokes. And no one knows it. Not his

doctors, not his aides, not his family, not even the President himself. No one but you and me."

"You can't be sure of that," she said evenly.

"But I can be. You see, I've checked. My patient's lung X-rays are in the President's file. Naturally, they're nontumorous."

Kitty felt the blood moving into her face and knew if she wasn't careful she would redden. "But the Clinic does autopsies on charity cases. Someone would realize there'd been a switch."

"Mrs. Stokes," the doctor said quietly, "I performed the autopsy myself."

Even before their eyes met and locked, she understood and she saw him see her understand.

"I altered the autopsy report," he said.

A queasiness pushed up against Kitty's lungs. She couldn't answer. She saw what he was offering Jay, saw that it was worth any price, any at all. She moved her head slowly up and down. The gesture did not commit her.

"I'd give the President six months to a year after inauguration," the doctor said, "add or shave a month. There won't be any clinically unmistakable signs until—oh, I'd say summer after inauguration at the earliest."

"But if treatment now could add years or months to the President's life . . ."

"It can't." There was a smile on the doctor's lips and she realized he did not know it was there. Eagerness had unmoored him. He knew what this information was worth to her, and he knew what her gratitude would be worth to him. "He's too far gone for surgery. And as you know, chemotherapy is not a cure. It's a crude holding operation. It kills cells, healthy and diseased alike. In fact, it's often a race to see which will kill the patient first, the cancer or the therapy. The President, I can assure you, will be dead of one or the other within fourteen months."

She saw the structure Dr. Desmond Rossi had built, but an inner voice warned her not to slide her foot in yet. She would have liked to think the voice was conscience. "But, Doctor, don't medical ethics require you to tell him?"

He had the untroubled gaze of the new generation who were gradually taking over the helms of the world. "An argument could be made that the longer the President goes without knowing, the longer he can function normally—and the longer the nation benefits. Of course," the doctor added, "that's the ethical argument—not the medical."

Kitty stared past Dr. Desmond Rossi, past this present moment toward the future that was tapping secretly on the windowpane, begging to be let in.

Time had slowed her down like an old cat and she knew it. Decisions could not be jumped to. They had to be pondered and weighed and approached step by laborious step.

For over a week, with all the force of her heart and mind, she debated the best course for Jay. After all, he and Toni were happy. They served on museum and hospital boards. They took cruises together. They sponsored cotillions and horse shows and charities. It was years since gossip or any of the columns had linked them with drinking or fighting or infidelities. Occasionally a magazine or Sunday supplement would praise Jay's growing collection of German Expressionist painters or Toni's work with retarded children. They were held up in the media as a handsome, productive couple. The Archbishop of Canterbury was not afraid to be photographed lunching with them at Piping Rock.

But was that really happiness, Kitty wondered. Was it the sort of happiness that truly mattered, or was it just two people holding hands in a peaceful garden waiting for the sun to set?

For seven days Kitty paced and pondered and tried to shake her head free of doubts and what-ifs. For seven days she could not make her thoughts cohere. She vacillated between hope at what could be attained and horror at what had to be done to reach it.

Her conscience dangled and ached like a half-amputated limb till finally, on the eighth morning, she said to hell with it and lopped it off and picked up the phone and called Willi Strauss.

They met in the whispering twilight of Willi Strauss's Fifth Avenue club. He moved toward her across the member's lounge with the awesome confidence of a warship going into battle—an old ship, a new battle.

"Hello, Kitty. This is a pleasure. A real pleasure."

"Hello, Willi."

He gripped her hand and she placed a kiss on his cheek. To her surprise, she felt a twinge of nostalgia; after all, Willi Strauss had played his part in the Stokes saga, like a faithful dog in a family photograph. *Only this old dog,* she reminded herself, *still has teeth.*

"Drink?" he offered.

"Why not."

They sat in a corner by the fireplace. It was not satisfactory. There were too many people slowing down to look at them or interrupting with hellos, too many waiters asking with grave courtesy to take their order. Willi was limelight and everyone seemed to want a little of the glow. *Even me,* Kitty thought: *especially me.*

She tried to chat. "You're holding up well, Willi."

His face crinkled pleasantly. "I try."

The trying showed. The blue of his eyes was grayer than she remembered, the smile more frequent and a little thinner-lipped. He sat a little less tall in his chair than she recalled, and his dark suit seemed tailored to hide his middle. His hair had gone thin on top, and there were more silky white streaks than blond.

"And how's the President holding up?" she asked.

"Thank God for modern science." Willi Strauss shook his head. "He's taking pills to sleep and pills to stay awake and pills to go to the bathroom and pills not to go. He's drinking too much and he's smoking too much and until that cough clears up, I'm not letting him near a press conference."

Kitty dropped a mask of not-caring over her expression. "Is his health really that bad? I mean, he sounds a mess."

Willi Strauss shrugged and searched for a cashew in the bowl of mixed nuts. "What can I say? He passed his checkup—at your Clinic, by the way."

Kitty leaned forward a little and lowered her voice. "Willi, what will he do about the Vice President?"

Willi Strauss found his nut and bit into it. "Let things cool down and ax him."

"Won't that be awfully near the campaign?"

"Not *near,* Kitty. *During.*"

"Who will he run instead?"

"If I knew that, the President wouldn't have a cough."

A moment ticked by before Kitty spoke. "I've been thinking, Willi. I've been thinking about this very carefully. Jay could run for Vice President. I think he'd be an asset; don't you?"

Willi Strauss jiggled the ice in his vodka. He didn't answer. Kitty's senses were suddenly on fire like a hunter's. Her nose strained to sniff out the smell of this vacuum. Her ears pricked to pierce through to the sound beneath his silence.

At that instant. with flawlessly wrong timing, a waiter told them their table was ready.

Kitty swallowed her exasperation and followed Willi upstairs to the dining room. They sat down to an undistinguished meal redeemed by vintage wine and a salad of absolutely perfect avocados vinaigrette. They made conversation and it drifted and groaned like a ship coming out of drydock. When she could no longer bear the utter mindless et cetera of Willi's small talk she again brought up Jay and the vice presidency.

"Keep your boy out of that slot, Kitty. It's janitorial and it's a dead end. Make him president of one of your foundations. Give him a museum. Set up a big gun research committee and have him chair it."

"I've tried, believe me. But Jay's not interested in museums or committees. He wants the real thing, Willi. Those days as governor were the happiest of his life. He's more smitten with politics than you."

Willi Strauss fetched up a smile. "Now, Kitty, you could hardly call me smitten with anything. I'm very careful about that."

She looked at the hovering wineglass and Willi Strauss's middle-aged face behind it. The face seemed scarred with victories and it aroused an unexpected, unnerving pity in her. "You've made yourself into a legend, Willi. You've done it as carefully as any President. Through all the years of obscurity and humiliation you've been building. And you know damned well it wasn't Jay you were building. It was you, Willi Strauss, maker of politicians. And the master builder has outlived his own building. You've survived, Willi. And survival is what makes legends. And that's why you're sitting at the President's right hand. And that's why, after he goes, you'll be sitting at the next President's right hand. And who knows, maybe the next one's too."

He was staring at her. "You dislike me, don't you?"

She laughed a little too automatically. He saluted her with his glass.

"I'm comfortable with people who dislike me," he said. "There's no legend to maintain."

"You're wrong, Willi. I'm very fond of you."

Willi Strauss pushed his hair back from his forehead and

let out a dry rasp of a laugh. Kitty found the laugh reassuring.
It proved they could approach dangerous ground and still be
friends.

"You're not fond of me at all, Kitty. I betrayed your son.
I jumped to the winning team. I'm not apologizing, by the
way."

"I'm not asking for your apology, Willi. I'm asking for your
help."

He bit into a celery stalk that he had hoarded through the
dessert course on his bread plate. "Kitty, I owe you nothing."

"It's not a question of owing. And you wouldn't just be
helping Jay. You'd be helping the President. You'd be heading
off a scandal. What would it cost you?"

Willi Strauss ran his tongue back and forth across his teeth.
"It would cost me nothing. It would cost Jay what little chance
he has left."

"Jay has nothing left unless you give him this opportunity,"
she said. "History is passing him by and he's not even a footnote."

"The Stokeses will be a great deal more than a footnote in
the history of this century."

"That's posterity. Jay needs something now. And you can
get it for him."

Willi Strauss leaned forward, elbows on the table. "And
precisely what could Jay contribute to the ticket?"

Relief flowed back into Kitty's lungs. She felt like a drowning swimmer who had finally flailed her way near enough to
the shore to touch bottom.

"Money, Willi. Money."

From that moment on, Kitty felt supple and strong and swift
in the certainty of her intention. She telephoned Jay in the
Hamptons and went out by helicopter. The house and grounds
were immaculate in the thousand tiny and perfect ways that
only money can accomplish.

Jay was sunning in a deck chair and Toni sat at the edge of
the pool, her legs dangling lazy and long and brown in the
water. Kitty was struck by the matched normality of their appearance, testimony to the skill of God only knew how many
doctors. She couldn't for the life of her see or even remember
which hip had caused all the trouble.

As she came across the lawn she heard Toni saying, "I

didn't call her an alcoholic. I said she *dresses* like one."

Kitty kissed them both and pulled up a deck chair and joined the conversation. She spent that afternoon trying to gauge the status of her son's marriage.

Jay and Toni seemed happy that day, as they had in recent years, but less than ever did it strike Kitty as first-rate happiness. It seemed like a wound that had been beautifully bandaged but left uncleaned. Though their drinking was now private instead of public, there was still a little too much of it. There were too many new Chagalls on the walls and too many pointless beautiful people at dinner, and all the cheerfulness was carried on in shouts.

It was not really happiness, Kitty decided. It was not even real fun.

She caught restlessness in Jay's eyes after dinner. It told her everything she needed to know. He was not happy with his life. He was ready for a change.

She brought matters into the open the next day when they were alone at the pool. "Jay, let me ask you something." She looked him straight in the eye. "Do you have any ambition left?"

He tossed her a frowning glance. "Now, what the hell is that supposed to mean?"

"You used to have ambition and I want to know if it will ever come back."

Jay hoisted himself out of the pool and flung himself dripping onto a deck chair. He closed his eyes against the noon sun. "Mom, I am blissfully, overwhelmingly glad to be leading my life. I am arguing with nobody on earth, least of all myself. I'm even managing to get along with my wife. At long last you could call me satisfied."

"And don't you ever think of the future?"

"There comes a time in life when the future loses its importance."

"That's not so," she said. "There's always a future."

"Not for me, Mom. There used to be, but thank God there isn't anymore."

"But there *is*, Jay. For you especially." She added, "Especially now."

Jay stared at her and there was genuine curiosity in his eyes. It pained her to see how this premature retirement of his was slowing him down. He was like a man living his life with all the windows shut. A sort of mustiness was beginning to collect around him. He had the beginnings of a pronounced paunch.

"Would you care to clarify that point?" he said.

"You haven't been beaten, Jay. You were never beaten. And it's criminal for you to coop yourself up licking your wounds like a broken-backed dog. You belong in public life."

His gaze flinched down to his hands and then toward the terrace, as though he hoped an interruption would come bounding out the door. "I *am* in public life," he said, "in my way."

"Collecting paintings and dusting sculpture is not public life. You can do far better than that."

He shrugged and there was a soft, humorous look in his eyes. With a shock she realized he was tolerating her. "Mom, I love art. I'm lucky I found out in time to do something about it."

"Art is for artists and old men. You'll have plenty of time for it later."

"Did you come to lecture me on the evils of the ivory tower?"

"Not exactly."

"Then stop beating around the bush."

Kitty knew he was right. Best to say it and get it over with before Toni came out with her drinks and chatter. "Jay, what I'm about to tell you you're not to repeat to a soul, not ever." Now it was Kitty who glanced toward the terrace. "The President is not a well man. He's not going to live through another term."

"I'm sorry to hear that," said Jay. "He's a good, harmless President."

"We're all sorry to hear it. That's not the point."

He watched her and there was a sort of compassion in his watching. It struck her that something was askew. The compassion should have been flowing in the other direction. "Then what *is* the point, Mom?"

"He's determined to run for reelection anyway, and he's going to win and he's going to need a new Vice President."

Jay's eyes narrowed and his voice was cautious now. "Go on."

"The President will be dead within a year and the Vice President will have the White House."

Jay looked away. The muscles in his jaw clenched. She could see him chewing on a thought like a piece of tough steak. Then he sprang to his feet. She felt distance and fog rushing in between them. His voice was edged in misunderstanding. "I don't know why I listen to you. After all these years I ought to know better. You didn't come to talk. You didn't even come to persuade. You came to bulldoze, and if I don't let you bulldoze me you're going to twist me like a licorice stick and get what you want anyway."

She touched a calming hand to his arm. "It's not what *I* want, Jay. It's what *you* want. It's what you've spent your life trying to get, and at long last it's within reach."

He pulled away with an abruptness that was almost savage. "Every time in my life I've ever reached for something I've gotten my hand slapped back."

"Not this time, Jay. *This is a sure thing.*"

The silence dropped to a deeper, more dangerous groove. "Mom, why don't you take your sure thing and bury it and kick dust over it?"

She wheeled on him. "Do you think the vice presidency's beneath you, is that the trouble?"

They were staring venom at one another. And then suddenly he burst out laughing and staggered so painfully to his deck chair that she thought he'd ruptured his appendix.

"You can call me many things, Mom, but a snob isn't one of them. I kissed public ass to be governor of Massachusetts. I kissed Republican ass chasing the presidential nomination, and that's as dirty as ass comes. But history was unimpressed with my ass-kissing and history has dealt me out. Amen."

"There's still history to be written," Kitty said quietly.

"I'm already in the books, Mom. I'm the son of robber barons and the father of a flag-burning radical. In an honest election I'd probably get three Vegetarian-Libertarian votes. I'm not presidential timber. I'm not even vice presidential timber. I'm coffin timber."

He was his own worst enemy, and she was furious at him. But she fought to keep her voice down and her temper leashed. "You don't have to be timber, goddammit. This time it's not structured that way!"

He sighed and the day seemed to ripple over the lawn like a shadow. "Mom, you're my mother and I love you, but I wish to God you'd just face facts *once.*"

"I *am* facing facts!" she cried. "It's you who have your eyes shut!"

He shook his head sadly. "You don't understand, Mom.

There's nothing left inside me. I want to curl up and sleep."

"You'll get your strength back," she said. "Give yourself time."

"Dear old Mom," he said. "You've never lost faith in your little boy, have you?"

"I'll always have faith in you—till the day I die."

"Don't say that. I can't imagine your not being here." He reached for his glass. She knew it was straight scotch. It went down him much too easily.

"Jay, don't drink so much. That stuff's terrible for your health."

"I've wasted my life. I might as well waste my health."

She moved beside him. "You haven't wasted your life."

"I've never accomplished a damned thing."

"That's not true, Jay."

He gazed at her, blinking against the sun. "It was all your doing. You've given me everything, Mom. Maybe you should have given me less. Maybe then I'd have amounted to something." He drained the glass and sat up. "It's a perfect day for sailing."

He slapped the chair and sprang to his feet.

"You can sail anytime," Kitty said. "But you'll never have this chance again."

His eyes half-closed and his entire face and body seemed suddenly drawn down. His voice was thick and crusted. "Do you think I don't want it? Do you think I haven't wanted it for twenty years?"

*Thank God,* she thought: *thank you, God!* "Then grab it."

"I'm so sore from grabbing. I'm so maimed and ripped and crippled from it, and now when I've barely patched myself together you come and rip the bandages off and tell me to try, try again."

She stared at his eyes and saw the fever still there, turned down like a pilot light ready to ignite. She knew there was still strength in him, but it was strength chained and caged and afraid.

"I'm not young anymore, Mom. I'm tired."

She stared unblinking at her son. She understood the problem. Greatness was an exaggeration—not just of the good in a man, but of everything. There was great courage in Jay Stokes, but it was matched by great doubt. Greatness confused him because he did not understand its contradictions. He had to be held and soothed and pointed like a champion thorough-bred at the start of a race.

"You *are* strong, Jay. You'll always be strong." She glanced again toward the terrace. "Isn't there anyone around here to bring us a drink?"

He seemed surprised. "Isn't it a little early in the day for you?"

"You deserve a drink," she said. "And so do I."

Jay told Toni his decision as they were dining alone that evening.

She dropped her fork back into the stuffed avocado. *"Why?"* she cried.

"Because it's my last chance."

"You don't want it—oh please, Jay, don't say you want it!"

His silence said he wanted it.

She stared at him across the flickering dinner candles, trying to grasp the dimensions of this madness. "Your mother's behind this."

"That's not so, Toni. It's my own decision."

"She kneads you like sourdough—even now."

"Let's leave my mother out of this."

"You're *old*, Jay—and you're still not grown up! When finally we've got a little something in life of our own, you're ready to throw it all away to go chasing another one of her pipe dreams. Oh, Jay, haven't you learned *anything* in all these years?"

"You're wrong, Toni. In a very few months you'll see just how wrong."

But in the months that followed it seemed to Toni she was far from wrong.

The house in the Hamptons and the Sutton Place co-op were suddenly offices, full of strangers thirty years younger than Jay, noisy with teletypes and extra phones and TVs turned to all three network newscasts at once. Jay himself floated on a cloud of doctor-administered pep shots and—since he'd sworn off liquor—white wine, cordoned off from any sort of reality by a mob of gray-suited, grinning advisers and tacticians, the cream of last year's graduate schools, hand-skimmed by Willi Strauss.

The polls said the President was doing well, which everyone on Jay's staff took to mean Jay was doing well. Toni was given a secretary whose only job it was to communicate with Jay's secretary, and the only time she saw her husband was when he was asleep or when they both were smiling for photographers in Wichita or Denver or San Diego.

Toni began drinking again—partly out of boredom, partly out of anger, but mostly out of something deeper, an intuition she didn't wish to confront that the homestretch of her life was bringing her right back to zero. The campaign committee provided doctors, and since the doctors provided bags of pills for everything from hangover to depression to fatigue, she figured what the hell and threw herself into hangover and depression and fatigue and let one lousy day spill over into another.

By the end of the campaign she had developed a round-the-clock headache and a recurrence of the old limp in her right leg. She decided it was time to see her own doctor, a reliable man who wasn't on Jay's committee's payroll.

"You've been putting far too much strain on that hip joint," the doctor said. "I'm surprised you're not in pain."

"Of course I'm not in pain." It wasn't exactly a lie: Toni hadn't been in pain since she'd discovered Valium.

"We're going to have to operate," the doctor said.

She brightened. "Another implant?"

"We can't do another implant. There's nothing left to attach."

She frowned, not wanting to believe she was hearing him right. "Then why operate?"

"If we don't get that pin out it could sever a nerve."

Toni's next question was soft, barely audible even to herself, not because she was afraid of the truth—not deeply afraid—but because she just wanted to let the truth sleep a little longer. "But can I walk without the pin?"

"With or without the pin, you shouldn't be walking."

She felt the thumping suffocation in her breast that was the first whisper of panic. "What's left for me, then?"

"We'll just have to see."

At that instant Toni felt the overwhelming need for physical reassurance: she wished someone, anyone, would just reach out and touch her.

But Jay was out conquering the world again, too busy to

hear her even if she screamed from her deathbed; and there was a desk between her and the doctor, marking the chasm between the sick and the healthy, between the dying and the living, between Toni Pierpont Stokes and all the rest of humanity.

She gathered together her last breadcrumbs of courage. "How long—do I have?"

"You have the rest of your life."

"How long does the hip have?"

"Before the stress snaps the bone? That depends when you go disco'ing next."

"I don't dance that much."

"You shouldn't dance at all. You should cultivate non-physical ways of relaxing."

"Like sitting at the opera? Sitting at a bridge table? Sitting in a wheelchair?" *I'll kill myself first,* she thought.

"I didn't say 'wheelchair,'" the doctor said. "I said we'd see."

"Am I allowed to walk out of this office?"

"You're allowed to walk out of this office. We'll schedule the operation in ten days or so."

"Thank you, Doctor. Thank you for being so direct." She gathered her purse and rose to leave. As her hand touched the doorknob the doctor's voice stopped her.

"By the way, Mrs. Stokes—congratulations."

She turned, not understanding.

"The election," he said. "I hear it's going to be a clean sweep."

And it was.

And Toni didn't give a crap.

Just to show how little of a crap she gave about anything, she spent the night of Jay's victory in a Washington, D.C., disco.

# Chapter 29

THE MUSIC BURST like World War III in Toni's ears. Everyone at the bar was shouting. In the mirror behind the bottles there were detonations of ultraviolet strobe, and ghosts of dancers radiated a pulsing half-life white.

The bartender extended a tiny plastic envelope of cocaine across the bar. The disco lights streamed ribbons of color across his naked chest. From a three-foot distance he looked unreal, like a man who had airbrushed himself into a boy.

"On the house, Toni," he said. His face was molded around a very stoned smirk.

Toni glanced down at her empty lap. "Hell- I haven't got my purse."

The fat man on the stool beside hers held out a tightly rolled hundred-dollar bill. He had hungry, deep-buried eyes. She'd been aware of him tracking her in the mirror, pretending to read labels on bottles on the bar.

Thanking him, Toni emptied a powdered spill of coke on the bar. She put one end of the bill to her nostril and passed the other end in a vacuum-cleaning motion back and forth over the powder until there was none left.

"If you'd allow me," the fat man said, "could I offer you another? On me?"

His gaze hammered her in an odd way. For a moment she couldn't tell what in the world he expected in return. No one gave out free coke and she could tell he was gay, so he obviously wasn't after her bod. Then she realized he recognized her and this was his way of nailing a celebrity. She handed him back his money.

"Can I take a raincheck?" she said. "I'd better catch that purse before it's across the state line."

She stood a moment at the bar, centering herself, adjusting to the environment. Swirling fists of disco music beat the ceiling. The dancers were splashing waves of billboard colors. Actors from a touring company at Kennedy Center, government underlings, street kids, hairdressers moved sweet and silken and synchronized, glowing with the grime and sweat of dancing.

The floor sprawled in two dangerous levels. Toni maneuvered carefully into the human overspill. She sought out her image in the mirrored wall. Squinting, she detached herself for one blinding instant from the crush of bodies: a woman in white disco pants with tits that gave a car-hop lift to her floppily tied Calvin Klein blouse. In this light the face still had youth, but it was youth with a Cinderella deadline.

She moved quickly.

A hand touched hers and a thin Latin, whose facelift had put him back in his thirties, stood there. His eyes were reproachful and his body curved sullenly in ass-hugging black silk. His gold necklace pendant was a popper holder, and it seemed familiar from a time and place more distant than eternity.

She recognized the purse slung over his shoulder because it was hers, winking sequins and all.

*My purse,* she reasoned. *My partner.*

The coke was speeding through her now, icing her nostrils, lifting the top of her skull. Time and space etched themselves in neon. The Latin was clicking imaginary castanets, luring her into the dance. She felt a magnificent confusion between her body and his. She felt her own movements flowing into the universe and rebounding back into her with added energy like waves off a swimming-pool wall.

She let herself splash down into the sea of naked shrugging

shoulders. She was floating and the floating was sublime until something pulled her eyes to the right. She saw Willi Strauss emerge from the white wall of dancing flesh.

He bore straight down on her, like the residue of a time capsule in his three-piece suit. She tried not to giggle and the trying detonated a loud, high-pitched laugh.

Willi Strauss's smile clicked on and off like a light on a marquee. "You have no business being here, Toni. You should be with Jay."

She looked at Willi Strauss and felt an insult tugging at her lips. In the midst of all this life he seemed dark and dead, like Dracula stalking the discos, and that suddenly struck her as unexpectedly, fantastically, utterly marvelous coming from a Secretary of State.

"I'm always with Jay," she said. "I'm always with my husband, even when he's off in some bayou a million miles away dredging up votes."

Willi Strauss shouted over the music, driving his words at her one at a time like carefully hammered nails. "Toni, they've conceded. Jay won the election. Your husband is Vice President of the United States."

Amazement struck her in a slow blue arc—amazement not that Jay had won, but at how little it mattered. Light nudged her like a splash of silver dollars. The light was more to the flashbulb than the strobe end of the spectrum, and Toni was suddenly aware of photographers.

Someone asked, "What do you think of your husband's victory, Mrs. Stokes?" and a reporter's great hungry smile screamed in the strobe-slashed darkness.

She raised her arms above her head and brought her hands together and slowly arched like a gypsy dancer, pushing her bosom out against her blouse. "Jay's going to be the greatest Vice President we've ever had!" she shouted. "He's going to fight for human rights and he's not going to let any American ever be poor or bored again!"

Willi Strauss laid a hand on her bare shoulder. "Come to the victory celebration, Toni. The limo's waiting."

"You're not taking me from my friends, Willi. No one's ever going to take me from my friends again."

Her partner's tiny hips kept shifting, never losing touch with the music. He held out a fresh popper. She took it and crushed it quickly to her nose. Suddenly the room came at her in waves.

A razor flash of pain, unbelievably intense, shot through her hip. Smaller flashes pulsed after it, diminishing like dissonant echoes.

The world blinked on and off and she was aware of Willi Strauss's mouth ovaled in indignation. "These are not your friends, Toni. Your friends are at the Statler Hilton ballroom."

Shadows fused and separated, always in time to the pounding music. Her leg seemed to be dragging behind her, a numb deadweight. She sensed that something important had happened to her, something she had always known would happen one day, but she couldn't remember what.

The dancers around them slowed and some froze, pausing to stare at the two celebrities locked in defiance. There was a bubble of syncopation and Toni and Willi Strauss occupied the dead center of a fleeting silence.

"Politics bore me. I never want to see those people again," she said.

Willi Strauss's eyes hurled fury at her. "Don't you give a damn about Jay?"

She mimed *no* with a flutter of her hands.

A waiter who obviously doubled as a bouncer caught a whiff of trouble and backed up threateningly, but Willi Strauss did not budge.

"Come with me, Toni."

"Let go of me, Willi."

"Don't make a scene."

"Then stop pawing me." She flung his arm off, and when it would not stay flung she screamed to the floor full of her new friends, "Will someone get this creep off my back?"

She was aware of the shattered phosphorescence of Willi Strauss's eyes, a flurry of arms and protests blanketed by a glacier of music sweeping down, and then she was kissing and hugging all sorts of cuddly men with tape recorders and flashbulbs, and the next thing she knew she was flat on her ass on the floor with no idea how she'd gotten there and no intention at all of ever getting up again.

Someone asked why she was here instead of with the Vice President-elect. She thought a minute.

"I'm here because I've survived. I want to show the world that it's possible to survive. So please tell them Antonia Pierpont Stokes has survived. Tell the world. And please tell Boston too."

* * *

"Maybe it's just as well," Willi Strauss sighed. "She's drunk—or something."

"Knowing Toni," Jay said, "she's drunk *and* something." The evening of his triumph had taken on an old, familiar, bitter taste. He realized that these last years, the good days of his marriage, had been only a sham, Toni's way of contriving the ultimate letdown.

"Then it's all to the good," Willi Strauss said. "We don't need people knowing."

"People know already," Jay said. "Nothing stays secret nowadays."

"Raise your chin, Mr. Stokes."

Jay raised his chin and the makeup artist fluffed a powderpuff over his throat. She had dark dancing eyes and creamy post-adolescent skin, and it struck Jay that she was awfully young to have made it into a union. As she repenciled his eyebrows her breasts kept pressing against his barber's smock. *Maybe not that young,* Jay thought.

"Smile."

Jay smiled.

"A real smile, Mr. Stokes. Come on. You've got lots to smile about tonight."

Jay thought about all he had to smile about tonight and he made what he hoped would pass for a real smile.

The girl worked at his upper lip with a tiny mink brush that made him want to sneeze. "You've got nice teeth. Are they caps?"

"They're mine."

"Then you want to really smile so people can see they're yours."

"Can I stop smiling?"

"You can do any little thing you want, Mr. Stokes." She probed him with a long look. "So long as you don't touch those eyebrows. Will that be all?" There was a wink in her voice.

Jay had met plenty of flirty teen-aged girls on the campaign. Most of them made no secret they were out to lay a politician. "Young lady," he said, "you tell me if that will be all. You're the expert."

"You look great to me, Mr. Stokes." She handed him the mirror.

Beneath her handiwork he could dimly make out himself, variations on an old, old theme. "It's all there," he sighed. "I'm everything the press kit says I am."

She whisked the smock off him and packed up the mirror and the cosmetics. "Mr. Stokes, it's been a pleasure working with a winner."

He didn't know what to say except, "Thank you."

"I'd kiss you except it'd spoil the makeup."

He made a victory sign. "Raincheck?"

"Raincheck." She grinned and slapped her makeup case shut and vanished from the makeshift cubicle.

"All set?" Willi Strauss said. "It's almost time."

Like a fight manager taking his champ into the ring, he led Jay out into the banquet hall, through cigarette smoke and shadows and shifting lights. There were whistles and applause and groping, congratulating hands.

A disturbing sense of emptiness nagged at Jay. There seemed to be nothing inside him, not a single thought or feeling, not even the acceptance speech he'd spent two days memorizing. "She should have been here, at least out of friendship," he said. "Or don't we even have friendship to show for our three miserable decades?"

"You're exaggerating this," Willi Strauss said. "It's not as though she were the First Lady."

"It's still a goddamned embarrassment. She's making an idiot out of me."

High above the powerful carbon-arc lamps twilight floated in pale indoor pools. The ballroom was a confusion of countdowns and last-minute scrambles. Warning lights flashed and two-ton cameras dollied to the ready, and underlings scattered like protesters about to be gunned down in front of the Winter Palace.

"Cool down, *amigo*. And good luck." Willi Strauss patted Jay's arm.

And then Jay was alone.

"Mr. Stokes, this way please." A middle-echelon executive of one of the networks guided Jay across a tangle of cables to the rear of the grandstand. The President was glancing over the notes of his acceptance speech. His wife placed a very neat, very official kiss on Jay's cheek.

"All aboard?" the President said.

Jay nodded.

The President's eyes narrowed around their German-made gaspermeable contact lenses. "But your wife—where's Toni?"

"Indisposed," Jay said grimly. "She sends her regrets."

For an instant the President's carefully composed face was lined with confusion. "She *can't* send regrets!"

Jay turned to an aide. "Would you get my mother, please?"

It took over a minute to locate her, and the President kept glancing at his watch. A smile was fixed precariously to Kitty's lips as she stepped behind the grandstand.

"You're pinch-hitting for Toni, Mom." Jay hugged her.

She stood there white-faced, stuttering *buts* and *I-can'ts*. The President took her hand and said with obvious relief, "Welcome aboard, Kitty," and it was settled. They filed up onto the grandstand and faced the ten-minute ovation.

Kitty never let go of Jay's hand.

She stood at the climax of her life, the goal of every breath and effort. Nothing could mar this moment, not the screaming crowd or the heat or the circus of noise, not even Toni's absence.

A young girl called Kitty Kellogg had made a promise over half a century ago, and now an old woman had kept it.

That was all that mattered.

When the last clap had been clapped, the last straw boater tossed into the air, when the ovation was squeezed dry, the President made his speech. It was a long, hot river of promises and it was constantly interrupted by screams and applause so predictable they might have been poured out of a tape recorder.

And then it was Jay's turn.

"Good luck," Kitty whispered, and he realized she truly meant it: with a mother's never-ending gift for panic, she believed something could still go wrong.

He squeezed her hand and took the mike and stood facing the teleprompter and the crowd beyond. The red light signaled that the center camera was live.

"Fellow Americans," he began.

The director had told him to look into the camera eye as though it were a person, but Jay found himself staring beyond the camera into the real eyes of a real person. She was standing between two men but she didn't seem to be with either of them. She was staring straight at Jay, like two thousand others in the room. She had high cheekbones and deeply tanned skin and blond hair that fell to her waist. She was wearing designer jeans that gave her hips the curving unreal symmetry of a violin.

He recognized his makeup girl.

The speech spooled out of him automatically, reliably, like a piano piece which, once memorized in childhood, the fingers never forget. *I'm going to fuck that girl,* he realized. *I'm going to finish this hogwash speech and cut short the handshakes and then I'm going to fuck her.*

Suddenly he felt good. He could feel his sinews and his cock strong and ready, his intention flexed and sure inside him. He was back into *now*. The whole damned yesterday of Toni, the whole damned tomorrow of politicians, couldn't touch him.

"And with God's help, we will achieve that dream—and more. God bless you all." He had come, somehow, to the end. Applause exploded.

The President pumped his hand and clapped him on the shoulder. The President's wife hugged him. His mother hugged and clung to him, her eyes bright as a child's. Tears were streaming down her face and he could feel a trembling in her embrace.

Over her shoulder he saw that the girl was still there, still watching, waiting for him like a blank check made out to the order of Jay Stokes.

He kissed his mother goodnight. She held to him for a long time. There was something awed and faraway in her eyes, and he wondered if she had drunk a little too much at dinner or if it was just age catching up with her. He was glad she had a chauffeur.

"Take care, Mom," he said. "I'll talk to you tomorrow."

"Phone me in New York. I'm going home tonight."

"How come?"

"I'll only be in the way down here. And I prefer to wake up in my own bed. The older I get the more I need the familiar."

"You've earned it, Mom. I'll phone in the morning."

"First thing?"

He found her eagerness oddly touching, curiously young. He looked at this woman he had known all his life and yet in a way never known. Time was taking nibbles from her face, but there was still beauty in the eyes, a sky-blue hopefulness that had never dimmed. In her way she was unchanging, and in his way he loved her for it.

This evening, he realized, was as much her triumph as his; perhaps more hers. Of the two of them, she had worked far harder and hoped far longer.

"First thing," he promised.

He walked her to the door and handed her to an aide. He watched her go, her step steady and firm. She turned, as he had known she would, and waved. He waved back.

It was their last farewell.

Jay hurried back through an eight-yard gauntlet of obligatory handshakes, grinning and nodding and yessing and thanking. The girl was still waiting when he broke into the clear. She accepted his arm around her shoulder and fell smiling right into step with him.

"Which door?" he said.

She pointed. "That one. There are no newsmen."

She knew her way around. There were no newsmen, and there was a taxi waiting across the street. They whistled and waved and ran through the drizzle. She got into the cab first and slid halfway across the back seat and no further. Their thighs pressed together as the cab pulled into traffic.

"Naval Observatory," Jay told the driver.

"Why?" the girl said.

"Do you like to fly?"

"I *am* flying." She took a neatly rolled joint from her purse and offered him a drag.

"I mean really fly, kiddo." He inhaled deeply and held the smoke to a count of ten and stared at her.

In the light of traffic flicking by she seemed unbelievably young and smoother than whipped egg yolk. She carried her sexiness with an off-handedness that was almost endearing, as though in her heart of hearts she was not a makeup artist at all but a serious young thing bucking for a Ph.D. in Proust or top swan in a ballet.

"They've got a heliport out at the Observatory," he said. "I used to fly a copter in the war." She looked at him and he added, "Korean War."

"I know," she said.

"I've got a place way up north on Long Island."

"I know that too."

"Would you like to see it?"

"Tonight?"

"Shouldn't be more than forty minutes by copter."

"And where's the little wife?"

"Does it matter?"

"Does it matter to you?"

His mind raked back over an inventory of waste. "It hasn't mattered for twenty years."

"I'd love to see your place on Long Island."

It tends to be foggy at four in the morning of an autumn day in the lower Delaware River Valley, and the fog can seem impenetrable when low-lying clouds black out the first tentative stabs of dawn, as they did the morning after Election Day. At ground level, even with fog lights, visibility was scarcely twenty feet when Elling Mills, a fifty-two-year-old chicken farmer, turned his pickup truck off State Highway 46 onto a dirt road eight miles north of the little town of Carneys Point, New Jersey.

He and his wife Rhoda were startled by a screeching that seemed to come from the darkness almost directly overhead. Lifting his eyes from the road, Mills saw with amazement what seemed to be an airborne searchlight careening from side to side no more than a hundred feet above the ground.

The light swerved into a sudden dip and vanished. A half second later came an ear-shattering, metallic crash. A reddish pulsating glow appeared in Mills's rearview mirror. He slammed the truck to a screeching halt and leaped out into the damp, still-night air.

Stumbling and clawing across rock abutments, he tracked the red glow to its source: a signal light atop a helicopter that had crumpled like a ruptured bellows against a deserted silo. The propeller had stopped, but Mills could hear a low, intermittent throbbing sound, as though a five-kilowatt generator were giving up the ghost.

He edged closer to the wreck. Smoke was steaming out of the cracks around the doors and at ten feet he could feel an almost comfortable warmth, like that of a campfire. "Anyone in there?" he yelled.

He got no reply.

Something was giving off a hissing sound and black gobbets of oil were dribbling down the side of the craft, but he could see no flame. He wrenched the canopy partway open. A ripple of heat seared past, followed by a billowing rush of smoke that left him momentarily blinded and coughing.

The craft had U. S. Navy markings, and reason told Mills there had to be a Navy pilot in a Navy helicopter. He thought he saw something curled against the control panel, thrown there by the force of the crash. It was too dark to be sure. He ran back to the pickup and had Rhoda hand him the flashlight.

Playing the beam across the thinning smoke in the copter, he made out what seemed to be a human form crushed into the far corner. Holding the light closer, Mills made out a heavyset, gray-haired man, head slumped to the side. In the tiny glow of green coming from a light on the panel, blood was visible trickling from the man's mouth.

"Jesus!" Mills muttered. Perhaps it was a case of death mimicking life—the mouth yanked open in surprise, seemingly about to scream—but some indefinable instinct told Mills that the man might possibly, miraculously, still be alive.

Two wires had been ripped from the panel, and just above them was what looked like an *on-off* switch. Though he realized he was taking a chance with his life, Elling Mills reached through the window. Heat singed the hairs on his wrist. The switch was jammed, and it took not the flick Mills had expected but an upward punch to force it to the *off* position.

The low throbbing sound died. Mills shouted over his shoulder for his wife to call for help on the CB radio: "There's a man in here—he's hurt! I'm going in after him!"

The door was so crushed out of shape Mills couldn't slide it far enough to get through. He had to crawl to the other side of the copter and enter through the other door. There was still enough smoke in the cabin to make his eyes tear, and the leather seats were scalding to the touch of his bare hands, but he managed to crawl in far enough to take hold of one of the man's arms.

It was only then that Mills began to appreciate the near-impossibility of the task he'd taken on: the seat was bolted to the floor, and a gnarled elastic-strap ran around the man's waist and torso, binding him to the chair. Mills called again to his wife, this time for a knife.

Rhoda Mills came running. She held a flashlight and Elling slashed and cut at the safety belt. It took him almost two minutes to cut the man free and drag him headfirst through the door.

Grunting and panting, terrified the copter might explode, Rhoda helped lower the deadweight down to the ground and carry it a safe distance.

The crab grass was damp with dew, as wet as if there'd been a spring shower. She spread her wool coat to make a bed of sorts for the injured, perhaps dead, man.

Rhoda and Elling Mills had never seen a face like the one they gazed down at that early morning. The eyes were sightless pools of blood; the nose had splayed flat to the side, like something out of a Picasso portrait, and a deep cut across both upper and lower lips gave the impression of a second mouth running at right angles to the real one. Down to the hip, the right side of the torso was a shapeless pulp of blood and flesh, cloth and bone that seemed to have been put high-speed through a food processor.

Most shocking of all to churchgoing Methodists like Elling and Rhoda Mills, the belt and fly of the man's trousers had somehow come undone, exposing his penis and a horrifying bite-like wound on the underside of the glans. In an unthinking, reflexive act of modesty, Elling Mills tucked the penis back into the trousers and zippered the fly. He was stunned to feel a faint pulse in the femoral artery.

"Rhoda!" he gasped. "His heart's pumping!"

Rhoda Mills placed her ear against the injured man's chest. She could hear breathing. It was not easy or strong or even regular breathing, but at least it was breath, and Rhoda Mills cradled his head in her lap, a little higher than the rest of him so he wouldn't choke on his own blood. She kept him cradled like that until the state police arrived.

The junior officer went straight to the helicopter and the lieutenant searched the injured man's pockets. He found a gold key chain with over a dozen keys and a gold-monogrammed hand-tooled Florentine leather wallet. He flipped through the money—Rhoda saw a ladder of credit cards spill out—and he flipped through the identification, which Rhoda couldn't read upside down, and he said "Jesus Christ!" and hurried back to the car.

He was talking on the radio when the junior officer yelled, "There's another one in here!"

Rhoda twisted her head, careful not to let the injured man slide from her lap, and she saw her husband and the state trooper lowering a second body from the helicopter.

Even in the fog Rhoda could see that it was a woman, naked to the waist. Rhoda could see too that the woman was dead, because her head was dangling by half a neck.

The phone call awakened Willi Strauss in his home in Chevy Chase at 5:12 A.M.

Though the man stuttered and the connection kept phasing in and out, Willi Strauss grasped the situation immediately. A helicopter had crashed; a strange girl who had worked for the campaign was dead in questionable circumstances; and Jay Stokes, dying, had become a grave liability to the administration and to the United States—and to Willi Strauss.

His mind played among alternatives. He saw only one solution. Carefully, he wrote down the man's name and rank. "Tell no one," he said.

A bubble of astonishment came over the line.

"Keep an absolute blackout on this," Willi Strauss said, "till I arrive."

"But we've got to get him to the hospital."

"You'll do nothing. I want no radio communications, no telephone calls, no publicity whatsoever. When I say blackout I mean just that. I'll straighten this mess out myself."

"But sir, the man's dying!"

"I fully grasp the gravity of the situation. I take full responsibility." Willi Strauss broke the connection and dialed the home number of Howard Huffmeyer, a physician who could be trusted. "Howie, can you meet me in twenty minutes? Something has come up. It's sticky and I need your help."

For two hours in that damp hayfield Rhoda Mills cradled the dying man's head. Her legs were aching from trying to hold still as a pillow. She was freezing from the surrender of her coat. Blood had soaked through her skirt and she was near crying. "Elling, where the hell is that ambulance?"

"The troopers said they radioed."

"That was two hours ago. Go use our radio."

The lieutenant blocked Elling Mills's way. "There's no need for that, sir. Help is coming."

The sun was well over the treetops and Rhoda Mills couldn't even feel a whisper of breath in the injured man when an unmarked station wagon pulled off the road. The lieutenant bent down to the driver's window and carried on a conversation with someone Rhoda couldn't see, and then he crossed the field and told her she could go now.

"We'll take charge," he said.

Rhoda's voice was a long-drawn-out arc of fury. "Like you took charge for the last two hours? This man's going to *die* because of you and your taking charge!"

The lieutenant touched his gun and Rhoda Mills got the message. She eased the injured man's head down onto the grass. She couldn't help thinking that if she could just peel back the blood and the wreckage she'd recognize the face.

Rhoda and Elling Mills climbed into the cab of their pickup. "I don't like it one bit," she said.

"None of our business, honey. We did our damnedest."

In the rearview mirror Rhoda Mills squinted at the jiggling image of the unmarked station wagon and the men in dark coats crossing the field. "And they didn't do a damned thing—just stood there, almost like they *wanted* him to die."


A cool wind rippled the hayfield. The sun had turned the dew to vapor that was colored like the rainbow in a fountain's spray. Dr. Howard Huffmeyer surveyed the damage. Quickly and efficiently, he dictated to an assistant.

"Deep lacerations right side of face, neck, chest. Nasal cartilage splintered. Sinus cavity crushed. Jawbone severed. Evidence of throat trauma. Cerebral concussion. Probable cause of death, massive cerebral hemorrhage."

Willi Strauss took the notepad from the assistant. He carefully removed the page of writing and tucked it into his wallet. "That won't do, Howie," he said. "We're going to have to think of something a little less dramatic."

Dr. Howard Huffmeyer gazed dumbfounded at the Secretary of State.

"Why don't we talk about it on the ride back?" Willi Strauss suggested.

The state troopers wrapped the body and placed it on a stretcher. An unmarked police station wagon carried Willi Strauss and Dr. Huffmeyer and the dead man to the private airport at Daretown, New Jersey.


Willi Strauss had unofficially advised two Presidents of the United States, and now, at six-thirty in the morning in a White House bedroom, he was arguing officially with a third.

"You can't just pop a man into a top political slot like that,"
he said.

The President put a friendly hand on Willi Strauss's shoulder. "Aren't you forgetting your history, Willi? Seems to me
Winthrop and Nelson Rockefeller never held an elected office
in their lives until they stepped into those governorships."

"Arkansas and New York are not the entire United States
of America."

"You're going to tell me Earl Warren had never been elected
anything when he ran for V.P. in forty-eight?"

There were deep lines of fatigue around the President's eyes,
as though sleeplessness had begun stealing the flesh from his
face. He was obviously a very tired man. Willi Strauss did not
shout.

"At least it was up to the voters, Mr. President—and Earl
Warren lost, remember?"

The President padded in his slippers to the bookcase. He
took down a recent *Information, Please* almanac that had been
bound in leather. He thumbed through an index. "Well, Henry
Wallace didn't lose. All he did was edit farmers' magazines
till F.D.R. made him Secretary of Agriculture and moved him
over to V.P. in forty-one."

Willi Strauss sighed. "Granted, it was a rubber stamp. But
at least there was the formality of an election."

"What the hell's so sacred about formality? Bobby Kennedy
didn't have anything but a second-rate law school diploma when
Jack made him Attorney General. That's a hell of a lot more
important position than V.P., and his brother just handed it to
him! No one screamed about that—not even you, Willi."

"It was a cabinet position and Jack was within his rights.
The vice presidency is an elected position."

"To my way of thinking it's no position at all—hell, Cool-
idge and Truman began their administrations without one."

Willi Strauss was not opposed to the President's choice. In
fact, he was in favor of it. He argued partly to hide his own
aims and partly out of conviction that an adviser's agreement
must always carry a price tag.

"The public might accept no Vice President, but mark my
words, Mr. President, they will never accept an appointed
V.P."

The President paced to the window. "Bullshit. The Constitution provides for one." He stared down at the south lawn a moment, and then with a sudden broad smile he turned back to Willi Strauss. "Look at Jerry Ford—that ignoramus was Vice President *and* President and he was never elected to either position! Ford's our precedent!"

Willi Strauss let a silence pass. "Gerald Ford at least had political experience," he said.

"So does my man." The President leafed excitedly through his almanac till he found exactly what he was looking for. "He has as much experience as old Charley Dawes!"

"Who the hell," Willi Strauss said, "is old Charley Dawes?"

The President thrust the book at him. "Read all about him, Willi. He was Vice President in twenty-five and a damned good one."

Forty-five minutes later, a blaring ambulance with four motorcycle police escorts was transporting the body of Jay Stokes up Third Avenue in Manhattan to the private wing of the Howard Bergman Clinic.

At eight-fifteen that morning, the Clinic's press secretary announced to the media of a stunned nation that John Stokes III, affectionately known to millions by his boyhood nickname of "Jay," had succumbed peacefully in his sleep to the bursting of a cerebral aneurysm.

*He died at the high point of a career of public service as distinguished as it was dedicated,* the secretary's statement ran. *He suffered no pain.*

Kitty awoke with a disturbing sense of something missing. The bedroom blinds were slatted with sunlight, yet the house was still. It should have been a morning of noise and phones and congratulations, but she had heard the phone ring only once, dimly, in her half-sleep. She did not know it had been Bart telling the servants to kill the phone bell and hold off all visitors till he got to the house.

She wondered why Jay did not ring as he had promised. She debated whether or not to call him, but decided not to be a nuisance.

She had her breakfast and shut herself in her office. She got down to work as usual. Her days had thinned out, like trees at the edge of the forest. Being able now to see to the end of them, she played favorites with none, not even today. It was a day like any of the others remaining to her, and she made use of it.

It was a little after nine and she was going over her annual speech for the League of Women Voters when she heard voices. The butler rapped softly on the half-opened door. There was an indefinable hint of disaster in his bearing. He announced Bart, and Bart came into the room stiffly, not smiling.

"Good morning, Mother," he said. He held out his hand.

The butler came back with a coffee tray. Kitty had not asked for coffee. Bart had, she realized. She tried to pierce the oddness of his face and voice. There was something off, something subtly wrong in every intonation, in the very way he moved.

When the butler had poured coffee and gone, Bart said, "Maybe you'd better sit down." His face was white and stretched, like his voice.

A sickening premonition gripped Kitty. "What's happened?" She fought to control her voice. "What's happened to Jay?"

"There's been an accident."

She saw Bart swallow. She braced for the worst and it came.

"Jay rented a helicopter last night."

She heard the words but she couldn't make sense of them. "A helicopter? Why?"

"Mother, he was piloting the copter himself. It crashed."

She stared at Bart in disbelief. What he was saying seemed to come from a dream, from some glacially distant infinity.

"Jay is dead."

Kitty stiffened. Nausea almost took her. Her mouth twisted and her eyes blinked, stinging. The room darkened and rippled. She could not see Bart. She could not see anything at all. A ringing in her ears deafened her. She fought to control the shaking that was pushing up through her, and then she gave in to it and buried her face in her hands.

Bart watched.

A dull tiredness came over him. He could hear her grief and see it, and her grieving was as full of Jay as her life had always been. He could not grieve with her. She had labored all her days for a worthless cheat and finally she had been cheated.

He had fantasied this moment of justice. In a way he had

foreseen it, rocked himself to sleep with it all the nights of his life. And now that it was here there was no satisfaction in it. He saw his mother, a weeping old lady with no friends, no home, no family, no son.

"Oh God," she sobbed. "Oh my God."

Bart had never before heard such a wounded cry from his mother, from any human being. He knew, if ever they were to heal the thing that was wrong between them, now was the time and the move must be his.

"Mother, I'm sorry," he said. *"And I love you."*

She looked up at him, and there was something new and tiny and frightened in her eyes. The sobs stopped. "Help me," she said. "Help me to the couch."

He guided her across the room. She dropped onto the cushioned daybed. He watched her stare at the coffee on the table, watched her struggle to wrap herself in the soft foam of habit.

"Thank you," she said chokingly. "Thank you for being the one to tell me."

She fumbled the cup to her lips. He could tell it had no taste for her, and suddenly her pain rose up in his chest and filled him as though it were his own.

"Is there anything I can do?" he said, and at that moment he meant it. At a single word the barriers were ready to fall. If she would just say *hold me* or *stay with me*, the past would have no more power to stand between them.

She stared at him, her face sagging. Slowly she held out her two empty hands. The silence trembled with her whisper.

*"Forgive me."*

The President of the United States telephoned late that afternoon. Kitty took the call in her bedroom.

"Kitty," the President said, "please accept my condolences."

"Thank you."

"Your son Jay was a fine man, one of the ablest leaders this country has produced. His loss has been a terrible blow both to this nation and to me personally. If there's anything I or my administration can do—"

Kitty shivered and drew her sweater more tightly around the pain and emptiness within her. "Thank you," she whispered.

"You've given two fine men to the service of this nation. The thanks are mine."

At the word *two* he attention flickered.

"Under the Constitution," the President said, "under these circumstances, it is my duty to appoint a Vice President. My cabinet is in full agreement with my choice. Frankly, I can think of none finer. I hope it will be some small consolation to you to know that you will still have a boy in the highest ranks of government. I am appointing your son Bart."

# *Chapter 30*

IN THE PARKED LIMOUSINE, a boy with a tooth-marked ballpoint pen waited for Kitty Stokes to answer his question. She felt absurdly nervous, as nervous as the seventeen-year-old girl who had lied to her father and run to keep a tryst with her lover so astonishingly long ago. *Part of me is still seventeen,* she realized. *Part of me is still thirty and still fifty and still every age I ever was.*

"The promise was this," she said. "I vowed I would conquer the world for my son."

*And I did,* she thought. *The wrong world, the wrong son.*

The boy wrote with grave care. "Did you succeed," he asked, "or did you fail?"

"I failed," she said. "Reaching for the one goal I ever set myself, I failed. The human beings I loved most, I failed. In every venture, every hope, every promise—I failed."

And why did something in her whisper, *Thank God I failed?* For it came to her that the failure did not feel like defeat, but like the surrender of stepping through a doorway into the sun.

The boy wrote slowly, saving the dots over the *i*'s till last, and then his gaze came up at her. He was smiling as though he with his few years understood what she with so many still

485

did not grasp. And in that smile, as suddenly as if a curtain had been lifted, Kitty saw something beyond time, beyond the little bounds of her life: She saw the admiration of youth and the compassion of age. She saw her father and her husbands and her sons and her grandchildren. She saw every person and thing she had ever loved in this world, but the seeing was purged of striving and possessing, and the thing she saw was for one moment serene and free and changeless.

Then the boy spoke, and the curtain fell. "And finally, Mrs. Stokes, what has been the most important day of your life?"

Before she could answer there was a knocking on the limousine window. She glanced up. Bart and Beth and their children and grandson stood grinning and waving on the sidewalk. She leaned forward to throw open the door.

"Bart wants to ride with you," Beth said.

"Can I, Great-grandma?" the little child begged. He was blond and eager and six years old, with all the world and all the future ahead of him.

Kitty stretched to kiss the others, then patted the space beside her. "There's plenty of room—come sit next to me."

Bart Stokes III scrambled into the car and sat next to his great-grandmother.

Bart waved again from the sidewalk. "Meet you back at the house, Mom," he called.

Kitty was glad a house with people was waiting for her, even if it was just for today.

"Mrs. Stokes," a voice said.

She gave a little start. She had forgotten that the boy from the school newspaper was still there.

"You were going to tell me the most important day of your life."

"The most important?" Kitty's mind sifted the days of the past, and not one of them mattered. Her eyes went from the boy who was her great-grandson to the boy who was not, and it was as though the universe had at last let her glimpse the smile on its face.

Now she saw. She saw all the old threads broken and the tiny new thread begun, so late—so late. But at last, dimly, she saw the design almost completed, and she saw that all her choosing and struggling, her winning and wanting and losing, had been only a part of it, and not the greater part at all.

"Today," she said. "Today is the most important day of my life."

She took her great-grandson's hand and squeezed and felt his fingers answer. A new thought came to her.

"Or maybe—tomorrow."

# Biographical Note

*Edward Stewart* was educated at Phillips Exeter and at Harvard, where he was an editor of the *Lampoon*. After college, he studied musical composition in Paris and at the Ecoles d'Art Americaines in Fontainebleau. He worked as a composer and arranger before turning to screenwriting and fiction. In addition to short stories and reportage, he has published eight novels, including *Orpheus on Top*, *Ballerina*, and *They've Shot the President's Daughter!* His works have been translated into eleven foreign languages. Mr. Stewart lives in his hometown, New York City.

# Bestsellers you've been hearing about—and want to read